THE ROAD OF BONES

THE ASHEN
BOOK 1

DEMI WINTERS

ISBN 978-1-7389960-1-8 (print)

978-1-7389960-0-1 (ebook)

978-1-7389960-2-5 (hardcover)

Developmental Editing: Chersti Nieveen at Writer Therapy

Copy Editing: A.E. Mann Editing Services

Proofreading: Grey Moth Editing

Cover Art: Rony Bermudez

Chapter Headings & Section Break Art: Letters by Lila

Map: Eternal Geekery

Sensitivity Readers: Ruthie Bowles and Gianna Marie

Translations & pronunciation: Saxica Ltd.

For those who've had to put one foot in front of the other, even when it was really hard.

AUTHOR'S NOTE

The Road of Bones takes place in a dark fantasy world and is intended for mature (18+) readers. Some scenes may make certain readers uncomfortable. A full list of content warnings is available at:

https://demiwinters.com/trigger-warnings/

or by scanning the code below:

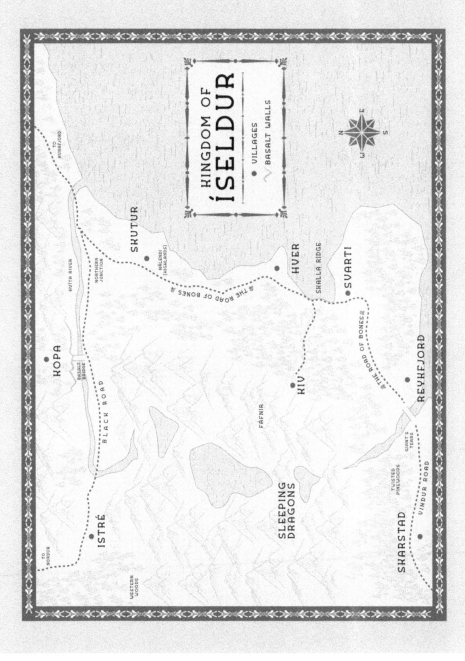

PRONUNCIATION GUIDE

Author's note- Many of the words and names in this book are derived from Old Norse and/or Icelandic; ð and þ characters have been converted to 'th' and æ to 'ae' for readability

- **Bjáni-** byan-ee
- **Dúlla-** doo-la
- **Eystri-** ay-stri
- **Flíta-** flee-ta
- **Hevrít-** hev-reet
- **Hjarta-** h-yar-ta
- **Hver-** kveh-r
- **Hvíta-** kvee-ta
- **Íseldur-** ees-eld-oor
- **Klaernar-** klite-nar
- **Kunta-** koo-nta
- **Lébrynja-** lyeh-bryn-ya
- **Myrkur-** mihr-koor
- **Nordur-** nor-door
- **Reykfjord-** rake-fyoord
- **Róa-** r-oh-a
- **Signe-** sig-nuh

- **Skjöld**- shk-ul-d
- **Skógungar**- shk-oon-gar
- **Slátrari**- sl-ow-trar-ee
- **Stjarna**- stya-tna
- **Sudur**- soo-door
- **Urka**- oor-ka
- **Vestir**- vest-eer

GLOSSARY

- **Berskium-** powder mined near Reykfjord; taken by the Klaernar to maintain their large stature and strength
- **Bjáni-** fool; an insult
- **Brennsa-** fire whiskey
- **Dúlla-** 'doll'- term of endearment amongst women
- **Eisa Volsik-** former princess of Íseldur; was murdered by King Ivar —her body impaled upon a pillar in the pits of Askaborg Castle.
- **Eystri-** the eastern-most territory of Íseldur
- **Flíta-** pheonix-like butterflies whose wings light up when they fly. In their old age, they burst into flames, a caterpillar emerging from the ashes.
- **Galdra-** magic-wielding person; also called Ashen; outlawed by King Ivar
- **Hábrók-** god of battle, honor, luck and weather; one of the old gods of Íseldur
- **Hevrít-** an Íseldurian long-bladed dagger
- **Hindrium-** specialized metal that inhibits magical abilities of the Galdra
- **Hóra-** whore
- **Illmarr-** scaled vampire of the sea; can be lured by eel blood and felled by rowan arrows

- **Íseldur-** kingdom of Ice and Fire; the island nation where this book takes place
- **Ivar Ironheart-** the new king of Íseldur who seized the crown from King Kjartan Volsik seventeen years ago
- **Kjartan Volsik-** former king of Íseldur; murdered by King Ivar using the blood-eagle method in the pits of Askaborg Castle.
- **Klaernar-** King Ivar's specialized soldiers. Also known as the King's Claws
- **Kopa-** large stone city in the northern parts of Eystri territory
- **Kunta-** cunt; an insult
- **Lébrynja-** specialized, lightweight armor made of tiny leather-like scales. Worn by the Bloodaxe Crew.
- **Malla-** goddess of love, war and death; name of one of the moons; one of the old gods of Íseldur
- **Marra-** goddess of knowledge, healing and peace; name of one of the moons; one of the old gods of Íseldur
- **Myrkur-** god of chaos and darkness; one of the old gods of Íseldur
- **Nordur-** the northern-most territory of Íseldur
- **Norvaland-** isle northeast of Íseldur; was overthrown by Ivar's father Harald, who now sits on the throne.
- **Róa-** a hot beverage served in Íseldur, made from the bark of the róabush
- **Saga Volsik-** former princess of Íseldur; was seized by King Ivar and raised as his ward; is betrothed to his son Prince Bjorn
- **Skarpling-** a small, mouse-sized creature with quills on its back.
- **Skjöld-** a dried leaf taken to treat headaches
- **Skógungar-** a forest walker; a peaceful tree-like creature who lives in the Western Woods
- **Slátrari-** 'the butcher'; a murderer who burns people from the inside out
- **Svalla Volsik-** former queen of Íseldur; was murdered by King Ivar —her body impaled upon a pillar in the pits of Askaborg Castle.
- **Stjarna-** 'mother of stars'; Sunnvald's wife; goddess of weaving, fertility, guidance; one of the old gods of Íseldur
- **Sudur-** the southern-most territory of Íseldur; houses the capital city
- **Sunnavík-** capital city of Íseldur where Askaborg Castle is found

- **Sunnvald-** the Sun God—king of the old gods of Íseldur; god of fire and might
- **Thrall-** enslaved person; in the kingdom of Íseldur they are most often brought in from Norvaland and marked on their inner wrist.
- **Urka-** a large nation to the east of Íseldur; where the line of Urkan Kings, including Ivar Ironheart, originated
- **Ursir-** the Bear God worshipped by King Ivar and fellow Urkans; belief imposed upon Íseldurians
- **Vampire deer-** carnivorous deer who hunt mammals and drain their blood
- **Vestir-** the western-most territory of Íseldur; houses the Western Woods
- **Wolfspider-** large spider covered in shaggy gray fur
- **Zagadka-** mysterious island nation to the south of Íseldur

PART I
Flames

"Fear not death, for the hour of your doom is set and none may escape it."

-Völsunga Saga

ONE

SKARSTAD

Silla Nordvig believed in the little signs the old gods left for mortals—red skies to foretell surprise, the flíta to usher in change, and the black hawk as a herald of death. Above all else, she knew that bad fortune came in threes, so it should not have come as a surprise when those wretched bells started ringing. She jumped in fright all the same.

Washing the bread dough from her hands, Silla dried them on the coarse material of her homespun skirts. *Ashes*, she thought. This week was truly taking a toll on her.

It had all started to unravel when Olaf the Red had requested tenancy payment a week ahead of schedule, stretching their threadbare budget beyond its limits. Next, Silla had burned her thumb while pulling barley cakes from the embers, dropping the full batch into the cookfire. Grains were growing more and more costly—after three long winters in a row, crops were stunted, and the harvest would be grim. Silla had earned herself a stern verbal lashing for her mistake.

And now, the third instance of ill fortune this week—those foulsome bells.

Silla smoothed the floral embroidery along the belt of her blue apron dress, the same worn by all of Jarl Gunnell's domestic hands, and made her way outdoors. The jangle of iron keys signaled the arrival of Bera, Jarl Gunnell's wife and head of the household. Silla quickly found her place in line, fingers threading tightly together as Bera counted them.

"Twelve. All right on your way, you lot," she ushered them in a gentle voice. "Let us hope this is swift. For all involved."

A light breeze caressed Silla's face and pulled a few chestnut coils from her tightly-woven braid as she stepped along the path. For a gray day, it was pleasantly warm, the sun obscured by clouds. A wasp buzzed at her face, and she swatted it away. Birds twittered from the gardens of the homestead. It was almost peaceful for a moment. Until the following toll of the bell, long and so loud, it set Silla's teeth on edge.

She matched her steps to the others, keeping her eyes on the blue skirts of the girl ahead of her. They walked in a single line, making their way down the rutted lane. Silla didn't have to look to know Jarl Gunnell and his men—warriors, stablemen, and field workers alike—would be following behind. The jarl was one of the few members of nobility who did not use enslaved thralls brought over from Norvaland, but if he had, they would join as well. The bells were nothing if not the great equalizer, demanding the presence of every Íseldurian over ten winters of age, regardless of class.

Silla glanced toward the stables but could not see her father. He'd be there somewhere, amongst the fieldworkers in his dirt-stained gray tunic. He'd be wiping grime from his face, worrying about her, about *them*, deciding they'd lingered too long in Skarstad. It would be time for a fresh start. Another one.

They walked along the packed dirt road and through a gate in the stockade walls of the village, past timber homes topped with thatched roofs. While orderly woodpiles were stacked neatly before the homes, the cabbage yards overflowed with kitchen herbs and vegetables. Skarstad itself was small and unremarkable, interchangeable with most towns in Sudur lands. Silla should know; she'd lived in so many of them. Neatly laid out and encircled by tall defensive walls, it held two main thoroughfares which intersected in a central, tree-lined courtyard. The mead hall was neatly maintained, the stoops well swept, the square stained with blood.

The bells grew louder as they approached the square, each clang more menacing than the last. The sounds vibrated through Silla's bones, ratcheting her insides tighter and tighter with each step closer. Men and women, merchants and farmers alike joined them until a throng crowded the road. At last, they rounded the corner into the central courtyard. Silla shuffled toward the towering Klaernar warrior standing by a wagon piled with jagged black rocks; he passed one out to each who entered the courtyard. Silla kept her eyes low as she waited, knowing what she'd see if she lifted her gaze. Muffled voices floated through the square, pleading. Begging.

It is in vain, she thought with distaste.

The oppressive presence of the Klaernar warrior looming before her stifled the air. Occasionally called the Claws of the King, the Klaernar were all physically imposing, and Silla kept her gaze trained on the warrior's boots. They were worn, smudged with dirt, a sight she found oddly comforting—proof he was, in fact, human. If she lifted her eyes, Silla knew she'd see he wore a shirt of black chain mail, punctuated by screaming bear shoulder plates in shining silver. Knew that she'd see three claw marks tattooed along the man's right cheek.

She'd heard rumors the second sons of Íseldur were not just physically changed once they took the claw, but mentally as well. Something happened when they went through the Ritual and pledged themselves to King Ivar and his Bear God, Ursir. No matter how diminutive their stature before the Ritual, they returned transformed—tall and built like mountains, their newly-inked faces etched in permanent scowls. It was said they carried Ursir's blessing in their veins, which only deepened Silla's unease.

As the King's Claw placed a chunk of raw obsidian in her palm, Silla's hand dipped under its weight. She stared at the flat, glossy surface. How could something be so beautiful and yet so ugly all at once?

The resounding chimes startled her from her thoughts, so loud they were near deafening in the square. Silla lurched forward, eyes darting in search of the blues of Jarl Gunnel's help. Somehow, she had lost them. Silla lifted her eyes, just for a heartbeat, to try to get her bearings.

It was a mistake; she'd known it to be but couldn't stop herself. Three sets of v-shaped columns stretched up from the circular dais in the center of the square, a runic altar stone centrally positioned. Each condemned was secured to a set of wooden pillars, arms stretched wide between them, feet secured together at the base. Iron bridles muzzled their faces and smothered their voices. A pity the contraptions didn't shield their eyes; those unfortunate souls saw it all—the crowd, the rocks, the imminence of death. Anticipation was an equal part of the punishment, Silla supposed.

She stood on shaky legs, her gaze locking with the woman in the middle. Her eyes were wild with fear, the whites flashing. Heart dropping like a stone, Silla realized she was not a woman at all but a girl in her early teens. The girl's face swam, her brown eyes dissolving to Mother's vibrant green, urging her to look away—

No.

With a shaky exhale, Silla forced her gaze to the ground. Now was no time for those memories to surface.

"Next!" boomed the Klaernar, snapping her out of her thoughts.

Eyes searching, Silla finally caught sight of the blues and browns to her right and made her way quickly toward the group.

The little blonde girl was with them, small and out of place amongst Jarl Gunnell's help. Her unkempt blonde hair was plastered to her neck, her face smeared with dirt. Haunting blue eyes, which tilted up at the outer corners, gazed at Silla as the girl fidgeted with the hem of her torn and rumpled night-dress. "You should pay better attention," came the girl's young voice.

Silla had tried to guess the girl's age, and her best estimate sat at five or six winters. "And you should mind your manners," she said absently.

"What did you say, Katrin?" asked Bera, her voice stern.

Silla's gaze shot to Bera's steely face. "I—it was not you to whom I spoke," she muttered.

"Who then? Who were you speaking to?"

Her eyes flicked back to where the girl had stood moments before—now nothing but empty space. *You've said enough,* thought Silla, pressing her lips together. *Gather your wits, Silla Margrét.*

"So hard to find good help," muttered Bera. "Lazy or touched in the head."

Silla inhaled deeply as she looked away. Spotting a familiar blond head threaded with gray, her eyes locked onto her father's. He seemed to sag when he saw her, as though he'd been holding his breath. Beside him stood the kindly stablehand who'd provided them with furs and a few kitchen provisions when Silla and her father had first arrived in Skarstad—Tolvik, if memory served her. With a grim smile upon his face, Tolvik's silver head dipped, and Silla returned the gesture.

The clouds parted, sunbeams streaming down from the sky, catching sparkling minerals in the flagstones of the street and warming Silla's back.

Mercifully, the bells stopped. Several minutes passed, and the crowd grew larger, filling the square and spilling out into side streets. Hushed conversation and restless energy descended into the courtyard; the tension was so thick, you could cleave it with an axe.

At last, the speaker of the god entered the courtyard. Ursir's Gothi was a tall man, his pale, bald skull glinting in the sun-filled square. He wore flowing brown robes clasped around his shoulders, the hem embroidered with shining golden runes. Two tall Klaernar warriors flanked the Gothi, bear pelts wrapped around their shoulders indicating their rank as kapteins at the very least. Like all of the King's Claws, they wore their beards long and woven into twin braids; handaxes, swords, and daggers were strapped at their hips.

One of the kapteins procured a piece of parchment and began to read, his voice rising loud and clear through the courtyard. "By order of King Ivar Iron-heart, of the great line of Urkan Sea Kings, son of King Harald of Norvaland, and great sovereign of the Kingdom of Íseldur, we have brought Agnes Svrak, Lisbet Kir, and Ragna Skuli before us in our sacred duty to pass judgment. They stand accused of the willful use of magic." The kaptein looked into the crowd. "What say you, the people of Skarstad, of these women who so flagrantly disregard the rules of our kingdom? These women who do not believe in our laws?"

"Guilty!" chanted the crowd. It was an empty ritual, these trials. Never did anyone call out for the condemned to be freed.

With judgment passed, the Gothi stepped to the first of the condemned, drawing a sacred dagger and golden bowl from the folds of his robes. The woman pulled against her bindings to no avail, her muffled pleas growing more desperate as the man sliced into the vein of her inner elbow, collecting a stream of blood in the gilded bowl.

"As are all of the Galdra, they are sentenced to death by stoning," boomed the kaptein. "But first, a Letting will pay penance to the King of Gods."

Ravens cawed ominously from the top of the bell tower as the crowd waited in silence, and the rock grew unbearably heavy in Silla's hand. After a long minute, the bowl had filled, and the Gothi dipped his fingers in the blood before dragging them in a series of lines and circles along the woman's forehead —the runic symbol barring her entry to Ursir's Sacred Forest in the afterlife. The bald-headed man moved to the altar stone, chanting in Urkan as he poured the remainder over the runic inscriptions.

As the Gothi moved to the next condemned, Silla's gaze was drawn to the puddle of crimson on the dais, blood falling in a slow drizzle from the first woman's elbow. How many times would this happen? How many men and women would die before the Bear God's appetite for blood was satisfied— before Ivar Ironheart's hatred of the Galdra was quelled?

The muffled pleas of the condemned grew more desperate, more urgent, and Silla realized that the Gothi had fulfilled his role and had turned to the crowd.

"Now you will prove your loyalty to Ursir, to King Ivar Ironheart, with their blood!" The crowd cheered, though some looked simply resigned to the gory task at hand.

The first stone was cast, thudding through the silence of the square. Silla's vision twinned for a brief moment, her mother's screams ringing in her skull. Gritting her teeth, she struggled to rein in the memories. She could not fall apart, not here, not now.

More stones were thrown. A squelch preceded a muffled cry. Silla kept her eyes downcast and gripped her rock tightly as the cries of the villagers and the screams of the women wove together, a jarring melody that made her skin crawl. Edging toward the dais with the rest of Jarl Gunnell's help, she saw Bera cast her stone from the corner of her eye. But Silla was frozen in place, staring.

Anger sparked inside her like a firestone struck. *Wrong. This is all wrong.*

"Throw it," said the little blonde girl. "Your skin is too smooth for the whipping post."

Silla sucked in a deep breath, pulled her arm back, and launched the rock toward the dais. She did not look to see if it hit its target.

On and on it went, an unending torrent of blood and fury. The ravens screamed overhead; blood pooling on the dais long after the women's screams had faded; long after their battered heads hung limp. The Klaernar roamed through the crowd in search of uncast stones, while the aftertaste of violence hung heavy in the air.

The kaptein's voice rang out. "Let this serve as a warning to those drawn to the temptation of magic. Ursir will set you a fate you cannot escape. You will pay in blood." With that, the spectacle had ended, and the crowd turned to leave. Silla's nerves jangled, her feet heavy as iron.

Think hearthfire thoughts, she imagined her mother saying. *The kind of thoughts that warm you through.*

Baby seals. Sneezing. The scent of books.

A cry rose up, disrupting her thoughts. Silla's eyes darted up with the rest of the crowd, to the sky where a shape crawled slowly across the sun. The light was swallowed, leaving them in ghostly twilight.

"The sun is stolen!" cried a woman, and Silla realized at last—it was an eclipse.

"Sunnvald is angered!" came a man's ragged voice...a familiar voice. "He shows His disapproval for the slaughter!"

Heart thudding, Silla's gaze flew to the Klaernar kapteins, observing a quick succession of hand gestures. Three Klaernar rooted the culprit from the crowd, over where she'd last seen her father. Panic rose within her as the kapteins dragged the man to the dais, and she looked at his face.

It was Tolvik.

Silla exhaled in relief, then chastised herself. It was not her father, no, but Tolvik was a good and kind man. Bile rose in her throat, and she could not look away as the tallest of the Klaernar cut the binds of one of the condemned free. Her corpse landed with a loud thud, limbs protruding at unnatural angles. With ruthless efficiency, the kaptein began to secure Tolvik's wrists to the pillars.

But the old man seemed only to be spurred on. "The old gods will not stand for this! They punish us already with the long winters!"

"Silence!" bellowed the kaptein, his palm cracking across Tolvik's face.

Tolvik blinked, then his eyes flashed with determination. "They will cleanse the lands with fire! It has been done before! It will happen again!"

Silla's stomach clenched tight as the second kaptein stepped to Tolvik, wrenching his mouth open. A blade flashed through the air, Tolvik's screams reaching a shrill crescendo before dampening to choked sobs. The kaptein turned to the crowd, something landing with a wet thud. Tolvik's agonized face came into view, blood leaking from his mouth, and nausea clawed up Silla's throat. His tongue. They'd cut out his tongue.

"Has anyone else pagan thoughts they'd care to voice?" bellowed the kaptein. The crowd grew silent, and the shadow moved from the sun, casting the square into a luminescent golden hue—wrong, all wrong, for the somber mood hanging over the courtyard.

"There is one true God," shouted the Gothi, slicing into Tolvik's vein. Blood drizzled from his elbow into the golden bowl. "The King of Gods. The *Warrior* God."

Deathly silence filled the square as the Gothi drew the runic symbol on Tolvik's forehead, as he poured the blood over the altar stone. A kaptein passed the Gothi a gauntlet, and he pulled it on, steel claws glinting from the knuckles.

"He is the God of Tooth and Claw. And His name is Ursir!"

Look away, Silla urged herself, but she could not. Not even as Tolvik's tunic was lifted and the claws raked across the soft flesh of his belly. Not even as the older man's entrails spilled out like pink, twisting eels. Tolvik screamed with agony Silla felt in her bones, in her very soul.

He was still alive when the crowd flowed from the square.

Still alive when the ravens swooped down from above.

Still alive when they began to feast on him.

Silla tried to block all of this from her mind, focusing with all of her strength on the blue skirts of the girl in front of her—tracing the roughspun threads, counting the scattered holes where sparks from the cookfire had landed. Dazed, Silla followed these skirts down the trodden dirt road, through the stockade walls, and up toward Jarl Gunnell's homestead. It was miraculous that her feet were moving, as numbness had taken over, her mind frozen.

She was not sure how far she'd walked when a dull sound droned in her ears, a small yellow and black creature entering her vision. Another wasp? Silla blinked as it buzzed right at her face, landing on her nose.

"What—" she started, swatting it away.

"Old fool," muttered Bera, distracting Silla from the insect.

Her thoughts returned to the square. What had come over Tolvik? He'd been clever and kind. To speak of the old gods, to invoke the name of Sunnvald in the presence of the Klaernar, was to ask for death. Silla's father had made it clear enough to her that while it was their duty to honor their ancestral gods, it must be done behind closed doors. And so long as King Ivar sat on the throne, that was how it must be.

Had Tolvik forgotten himself?

Her mind circled back to the eclipse. There was no doubt now; there was no clearer indication that it was time for them to leave. If history had taught her anything, it was that the eclipse was a harbinger of darkness—bad things inevitably followed.

They passed the outbuildings and reached the door to the longhouse, pausing to wait for Bera to slide a key into the iron padlock. Silla felt as though the single hour had lasted an entire week. Muscles aching as if she'd walked all day, she was a husk of herself.

"Well now," said Bera, as they entered the longhouse. "Who's ready for a hot cup of róa?"

TWO

Silla leaned against the heavy ashwood walls of the stables, glancing toward the fields of stunted barley and rye in search of her father's tall silhouette. Although the seventh chime had sounded, the late summer sunset meant the homestead was still well-lit.

After the eventful morning, a peace had settled, and the air was silent save for the gentle whicker of horses and hushed conversation from within the stables. Despite this, Silla was sick over what happened to Tolvik earlier in the day. Perhaps she was a coward, but she could not bring herself to go into the stables to see the faces of those who knew him well. She simply wished to see her father, hear his calming voice, and reassure herself that he was all right.

Silla pulled the leather tie from her hair, then unthreaded the braid which ran down her spine. Curls sprang loose around her shoulders, and she worked her fingers to massage the ache from her scalp.

The heavy doors to the stables thudded shut, and Silla jumped with a loud gasp.

"I did not mean to frighten you." A dark figure had emerged, changing course and moving toward her. Silla squinted, trying to make out his face. As the figure moved out of the shadows with a slow ambling gait, she recognized him as the farrier. Scratching his beard, the man smiled at her. "You're Hafnar's daughter, are you not? Katrin?"

Silla stared blankly for the span of a heartbeat, before remembering Hafnar was the name by which Matthias currently went. "Gods' ashes," blurted Silla. "I'm twitchy as a squirrel today. Yes to both questions." Her eyes locked onto his—dark and kind with creases from smiling. "And you're Kiljan, correct?"

He nodded, extending a hand. "Well met."

Silla slid her palm into his, eyes darting down. His tanned hands were large and well-muscled; she supposed one's hands must grow strong in his line of work. Kiljan leaned on the wall beside her, the faint scent of horses and coal dust meeting her nostrils. "You work the cookfires?"

"Yes. I've been assigned breads, which I don't mind in the least. Did you know there are *nine* different types of bread? With loaves and flatbreads and panbreads, how could you ever be bored?" Noticing the blank look on Kiljan's face, she paused. *You're babbling again,* she chastised herself. *Ask him about himself.* "And you work with the horses?"

He nodded.

Silla smiled. "That must be nice. I love horses. I hope to have my own one day."

"They do make for good company."

She leaned closer. "Between us, I prefer horses more than some people. Several of them, really."

"I'd have to agree with you, Katrin." Kiljan chuckled softly. "How does Skarstad suit you?"

"Oh, it's lovely," she replied, then frowned. "Though, this week has not been quite as lovely. How fare the stablehands after what happened to Tolvik?"

Kiljan looked at the ground. "Mood is somber."

She hugged herself. "I can imagine. Did you know him well?"

"Worked with him for five...six turns of winter now? I cannot believe it."

She frowned. "How awful—"

"It's time to leave."

Silla's head snapped up at the familiar voice, her gaze locking onto eyes of icy blue. While he moved like a young man, her father was beginning to show his age, through streaks of gray in his blond hair and beard, and the lines etched into his pale forehead. She took in the rest of him—dirt-stained gray tunic layered with a leather jerkin, hevrít, handaxe, and daggers sheathed in his belt.

Never unarmed, this father of mine, she thought wryly. As a child, she'd found herself wondering if he slept with his hevrít and had pulled back the blanket to find out—only to have him grasp her wrist and twist it roughly. As sleep had dissolved from his eyes, he'd apologized profusely, warning her never

THE ROAD OF BONES

to startle a sleeping man. He'd then shown her the long blade he indeed kept beneath his pillow; his favored bone-hilted hevrít.

The tension inside Silla slid away, and she launched herself forward, hugging her father tightly. His heavy arms wrapped around her, and for just a moment, the foulness of the week seemed to melt away. She drew back, and her father pulled on her elbow, steering her down the lane toward their home on the outskirts of town. Silla glanced back at Kiljan, whose mouth opened, then closed.

"Until tomorrow, Kiljan," her father said, his voice gruffer than usual.

Silla frowned. It had been abrupt and perhaps a bit rude of a departure. "Well met, Kiljan!" she called feebly over her shoulder with a small wave.

Silla blew a wayward coil of hair away from her face. After twenty turns of winter, she had never kissed another. It had been so long since she'd had a true friend. She loved her father. She was safe and loved in return. Things could be worse. But they could also be better.

She craved something. She craved *more*. Friendship. To fall in love. To live. How could she do this while always looking over her shoulder, while she and her father floated through life like wraiths in the darkness? They lived the life of survival, doing what they must to earn enough sólas to survive, never staying more than three months in one place. Silla had always found work by the cook-fires, and her father usually obtained labor on a farmstead. She admired the way he melded into each new job and each new town seamlessly—he reminded her of the frost foxes, whose fur shifted colors to blend in with their surroundings.

But lately, there had been a troubling weariness to him, and Silla's unease had grown. Long days working in the fields took a toll on him, as did the constant travel. They couldn't keep on like this forever. What they really needed was safety. Somewhere they could rest their tired feet and stay for longer than three months.

"Silla, did you hear me?"

She frowned. "I'm afraid I was dreaming on my feet once again."

"Save the dreams for your sleep tonight, Moonflower," he teased. "I said it is time we leave Skarstad."

Silla sighed as they turned to walk along Vindur Road, back toward the outbuilding on Olaf's steading which they currently called home.

She'd figured they were leaving, but now that he'd spoken the words, anticipation and nervousness mingled together. Of course, there was the fresh start,

11

the promise of something new. But there was also the danger of the road, the empty stomachs, blisters and exhaustion.

She stared at the packed earth road as they stepped along it. "Where shall our wanderings take us next?"

"Kopa."

Her gaze snapped to him, and she laughed. "Very funny, Father."

"It is no jest. I've received a long-awaited message by falcon inviting us to Kopa."

She studied his serious face while her stomach twisted. "Kopa? Father, that is...a month's travel at the very least, is it not?"

She chewed on her lip. Surely he was joking. Perhaps the sun had muddled his mind. But when she looked into his eyes, she found them bright and clear.

"Why not Reykfjord? I believe it is four days walk. Bera has said they make the best spiced mead in the kingdom. We could find work with the mead makers and live our finest lives."

But her father was stubborn on the matter. "Kopa would be an adventure."

Silla snorted. Adventure. She'd had enough of that in the last ten years. "Really, Father. If you wish for adventure, we could simply wander into the Twisted Pinewoods. That would be sure to satisfy your cravings for danger. We could hunt for blood-thirsty forest creatures, like the vampire deer or the grim-wolves." She was silent for a moment. "Of all the places in Íseldur, why Kopa?"

Silla was not even sure where to place it on a map. All she knew was that it was north. *Far* north, though not quite as far as the lands of Nordur, which, as she recalled, lay so far north they experienced a single hour of daylight in the cold winter months. No force in this world could draw her there.

He turned to her, his eyes grave. "I've had word, Silla. There are shield-homes for those in need. A safe refuge where we could catch our breaths."

Silla reeled. A shield-house. Could this truly be real?

She approached the topic cautiously. "Assuming we decided to go to Kopa —and Father, please notice I've used the word 'assuming'—we'd have to do it in several stages. Our sólas would run out far before we reached it. Those roads... they are arduous to travel, are they not?"

"Very," he replied, a wistful look in his eye. "I traveled there myself as a young man. We rode all the way from Kopa to Sunnavík. It took us a full month and a half...but Silla, it was more beautiful than you could imagine. Long have I felt the call of the north, and this message settles it. Fortune takes us to Kopa. To safety." There was a vibrancy in his voice that was catching.

Silla's hand went mindlessly to the vial hanging on a leather cord around her neck, caressing the smooth metal. This talk of messages from the north had come from nowhere. What was he doing sending falcons—and whom was he sending them to?

"Well," she said slowly, breathing in pine and juniper as the woods climbed up on either side of the road, "if your heart is set on Kopa, then let us make our way first to Reykfjord. We will discuss it while we walk."

"I'll sway you, Moonflower," said her father affectionately, wrapping a brawny arm around her waist and squeezing her tight. Half a head taller than her, he laid his cheek on her hair. "We must leave at first light. Did you collect your wages?"

She nodded, patting the leather purse secured to her belt, sólas and a few kressens clinking together within.

"Good."

As they made their way along the road, Silla wondered who she would be this time? She'd already been Thordis, Ingunn, Gudrunn, and now Katrin. Perhaps she'd be Atta in this new place. Yes. Atta had a pleasing sound to it.

The clouds dispersed, sunlight catching on damp pine needles and bracken blanketing the forest floor. A bird called from somewhere high above, and Silla craned her neck to see it. Squinting, she could just make it out—long black wings, curved yellow beak, and a streak of white across its feather tails.

Black hawk, she realized with horror. As she laid a hand on her father's forearm, Silla's senses sharpened to an alarming point. Twigs cracked discordantly, raising the fine hairs on her arms. The screech of a nearby owl made her jump in fright.

"Silla?" her father asked, but it was too late.

Figures emerged like wolves from the shadows, black-clad and lithe with biting steel blades. Before Silla and her father could react, they were surrounded.

Silla's heart stumbled as she assessed the situation: six men fortified by shirts of black mail, armed with greataxes and swords. Their beards were twisted into twin braids in the fashion favored by King Ivar and his fellow Urkans.

Her first thought was Klaernar. Had her time run out? Had the whispers of the haunted girl finally reached their ears? The tales of the girl who sees the unseen? She'd been careful in Skarstad, but addressing the little blonde girl in the town square had been a foolish slipup.

But these men did not have the screaming bear shoulder plates, nor the tattoo markings on their faces.

"What is it you want?" demanded her father. "We have only a few coins, but they are yours."

The tallest of the men stepped forward, hair an unkempt brown and eyes black as night. "We do not want your coins." His eyes narrowed, lips curving into a malicious smile. "You know why we're here, *Tómas.*"

Silla's brows knit together at the unfamiliar name. Then the knot in her stomach loosened—they had mistaken her and her father for someone else. But as her eyes darted to her father, ice slid down her spine.

His face corpse white, he swayed on his feet. "You are mistaken; I'm Hafnar, not Tómas. And this is my daughter, Katrin."

The man laughed, cold and mirthless. He strolled around them, stroking his beard. "Do you think me a fool? We've searched many long years for you, Tómas, and today, your fortune has ended. There is no escape."

Silla's pulse pounded in her ears. Mistake. Clearly, this was a mistake. But why did her father look as though he'd seen a ghost?

Reminding herself of the dagger sheathed at her ankle, Silla gathered her courage. "He is *not* Tómas. You have the wrong man."

"Tómas, Tómas, Tómas," tutted the leader. "You disappoint me. Have you told her nothing?" He chuckled and turned his black gaze on Silla. "Forget your loyalty to this man. He is not even your kin—you share no blood."

Silla's gaze bounced from the stranger back to her father. His eyes met hers, and she saw it—confirmation, regret, and, most chillingly, fear.

The man nodded and two warriors surged forward, seizing her roughly. Her father roared, lunging at them, but more men advanced. A crack echoed in the roadway as a man struck him with the back of his hand, other warriors restraining his arms behind his back

"No!" Silla thrashed against the warriors who held her, trying to reach her father, but their grip was ironclad.

The leader brought his face to hers, so near she smelled his sour breath. She squeezed her eyes shut, trying to recoil, but someone behind her pressed her forward. "She has the scar," he murmured, his gloved finger tracing the tiny crescent-shaped mark beside her left eye. "It's her."

The man released her, and Silla blinked, sucking in desperate breaths to calm her racing heart. What in the eternal fires was going on?

Staring at Silla, there was a cruel smile upon the leader's lips. "Queen Signe has been searching for you, girl."

She blinked.

"You'll take her over my cold corpse," spat her father.

"It can be done, Tómas. Your death is long overdue," replied the black-eyed man, turning to him.

But her father had already wrenched free from his captors, unsheathed his hevrít, and rolled on the ground. He slashed his blade upward with smooth and fluid movement, as if he'd done it a thousand times before. The leader escaped the hissing blade by a hair's breadth, and with quick, spry movement, her father was on his feet, hevrít swinging toward a new adversary's neck. The warrior twisted, narrowly dodging the blade.

Silla watched the man who had raised her in complete disbelief. His movements were agile, powerful, practiced. As he swung his hevrít in an aggressive flurry and easily evaded his opponents, she could not reconcile this man with the one she knew, the gentle giant who worked the fields and brought her heart-shaped rocks.

The woods exploded with shouts and frenzied motion. Her arm was released as one of her captors lunged at her father. Silla scrambled to action, shoving her foot down hard upon the boot of her remaining captor and wrenching free from his grip. Crouching down, she gripped the dagger sheathed at her ankle and tugged—to no avail. With a grunt of frustration, she yanked again on the stubborn handle, but it would not budge.

On the edge of her vision, her father battled four men, hair flying, hevrít singing through the air quicker than she could track. A sickening squelch captured her attention, a man falling to the ground. Quicker than lightning, her father grabbed the fallen man's axe, slashing it down upon a new opponent with such strength it sheared through the warrior's shirt of mail. The man crumbled with a keening wail, and her father was already pulling the blade free from the broken rivets, kicking back a third man who lunged at him.

Through the panic, the turmoil, the pounding in her ears, Silla heard the memory of her father's words.

Promise me, Moonflower. If we are attacked, you will run. Do not try to fight. Do not let them take you.

Silla looked to the shadows of the pinewoods, then sprang from her crouch toward the trees.

She made it two steps.

An arm came from nowhere, wrapping around her throat and squeezing tightly. Momentum kept her feet going, swinging them off the ground as the arm yanked her back against a hard chest.

"Where are you running to?" rasped a voice—the leader. Frost spread through Silla's veins. "Worry not. The queen will not kill you. Not right away, that is."

Silla's eyes bulged as she gasped for breath, her hands clawing desperately at the arm around her throat and the face behind her. Nails sinking into skin, she pulled. The man cursed, but his arm only tightened around her throat, a second arm encircling her waist, pinning her hands. She kicked, flailed, an animal desperate for freedom, but nothing loosened his hold.

The sounds of battle faded. Time ceased to have meaning. Her entire world honed in on the pain in her neck, the frantic need for air. Shooting stars danced before her, the edges of her vision darkening, closing in on her.

She was falling.

Her vision bloomed red.

And then, darkness surrounded her.

———

THE SMELL OF EARTH. A coppery taste in her mouth. A great weight upon her. Ragged, gasping sounds.

Awareness returned to her, sudden as a summer storm. They were *her* sounds. She sucked in desperate, wheezing breaths as lights popped in her vision. Her neck and face were red hot and throbbing.

Silla assessed her situation. She lay in a ditch, trapped beneath something heavy. Turning her head, her stomach lurched—black eyes, open and lifeless. She wriggled, her father's handaxe coming into view—buried in the man's skull. Silla held herself very still then. Had the others not seen her? Did they believe her dead? But the clash of swords, the grunts and shouts had faded. Now there was only unearthly stillness.

Silence so loud it hurt her ears.

"Father," she croaked. A frenzied burst of energy forced her limbs into movement. She squirmed until she freed herself from the man's weight.

Getting to her feet, Silla took in the scene on Vindur Road.

Death. Everywhere.

It was a nightmare, a horrid nightmare from which she could not awaken. Corpses were strewn across the road, ravens feasting upon them, the low buzz of carrion flies vibrating the air. She stepped over a severed hand, sending the birds into an angry retreat—walked past a man with a hevrít buried halfway through his neck. A wet, choking noise caught her attention, and Silla scrambled to the middle of the carnage, where a familiar figure lay motionless.

Rusted red oozed from at least four wounds in her father's torso. Bodies surrounded him, one sprawled across his legs, impaled on a sword so thoroughly it protruded from his back.

Relief surged through her as her father's chest rose and fell, blood seeping from his wounds with each breath. "Father!" she cried, trying to heave the man from him, but the body wouldn't budge.

Silla fell to her knees beside her father, placing a hand on his cheek. This man did not look like her father at all. His face was smeared with gore, his hair matted and red. Her peaceful, gentle giant of a father. How had this happened? Tears spilled over, leaving wet tracks down her cheeks.

"Father!" she whispered.

Her father's eyelids fluttered open.

"Silla," he rattled. His voice was wrong—all wrong.

"Father," Silla sobbed. "Father. You're alive! You will be all right. I will find a healer and bring her to you."

"Moonflower," said her father. "No. My fate is set."

A sob built in Silla's throat. "No, Father, you must not—"

Her father lifted a crimson-stained finger to her lips, and she forced herself to hush.

"My hevrít," he rasped, and her gaze bounced from corpse to corpse until she found it, the polished bone hilt severing the man's neck. It took several attempts to tug it free, making a sickening wet sound as it came loose, but she swallowed back the bile rising in her throat and rushed back to her father. The salt of her tears pricked her tongue as she clasped his hands around the ivory hilt —a weapon to protect him as he traveled the afterlife and settled amongst the stars.

"You must know," he whispered. "I loved you like my own kin."

Shock rippled through Silla at his confession. He coughed, hot blood splattering across her cheek.

"Mattress," her father's eyes fluttered as he took a ragged breath. "Bed...go to Kopa." He labored with another breath. "Do not let the queen take you. You're...survivor." A wet rattle escaped him, shivering across her skin and clawing down her spine. Silla watched in horror as the life faded from his eyes.

"No!" She pulled his head into her lap, smoothing the hair from his face. A quiet sob broke in her chest as she held the only person she had in this world. Tears dripped onto his blood-marred face, clearing paths as they rolled across it.

A twig cracked, Silla's gaze leaping to the woods. Probably an animal or a mischievous forest spirit, but she couldn't take any chances. And while she wished to hold and mourn her father, to give him a proper burial, there was urgency.

You must run.

A primitive part of her mind took hold. Silla pulled the coins from her father's pockets, then rose.

And then, she ran.

THREE

As the door of the outbuilding slammed against the wall, Silla's legs collapsed beneath her, and she fell to the packed earth floor. The energy surging through her blood had faded, her senses now muffled as though she were underwater.

The hut on the edge of Olaf the Red's property was small, formerly used to house field thralls, until fresh quarters had been built for them. A single room, it had a central rectangular hearth above which an iron cookpot hung. The rest of the room was sparse; on one side, a trunk and straw mattresses were heaped with furs and a few woolen blankets, on the other, a trestle table was flanked by benches, shelves housing food supplies overhead. The top shelf served as their makeshift altar. Low burnt candles sat before bread heels and two cups of mead —one for the gods, one for the spirits. Silla looked around the room with despair. It was drafty and sparse, but it was theirs...*had been* theirs for a few short months.

With prodding fingers, she assessed her face and neck. Sharp pain beneath her eye and along the swollen flesh of her throat suggested she'd have substantial bruising to deal with. She allowed herself a few minutes to gather her thoughts, to allow what happened to sink into her bones. She knew her father had died— she'd seen his chest rise and fall that final time, had watched the life leave his eyes. Despite this, she listened for him. Any moment now, she'd hear the thud of his boots on the landing. He'd wrap her in his arms, and all would be set right.

Tears flooded her eyes, spilling down her cheeks, and she frantically swiped them away. *You must leave this place*, she reminded herself, but her thoughts were so hazy she could scarcely think.

"You could not unsheathe your dagger," said the girl from the corner of the room, snapping Silla from her thoughts. She cast an irritated look at the girl, then glanced at her trembling hands in the dim light of the hut. To her great dismay, they were smeared with her father's blood.

The queen will not kill you. Not right away, that is. The warrior's words rang in her skull and Silla squeezed her eyes shut.

"Why does the queen wish you dead, Silla?" asked the little blonde girl.

The very thought made Silla's chest tighten. "Stop," she growled. "I must focus. I need to move quickly."

Moving to a bucket of water near the hearth, Silla scrubbed the blood from her hands, then her face. She patted her cheeks dry with a nearby scrap of linen, then stared at it numbly. She'd dried their bowls from the daymeal with that linen earlier this morning, and there it still lay.

Everything in their rustic hut was the same, just as they'd left it that morning. Her father's blue tunic lay sprawled across his bed, his wolfskin gloves draped from the table to dry, the heart-shaped rock he'd brought her from the field sat beside Silla's bed. How could these details remain unchanged when everything else in her life had been brought to such ruin?

She bunched the linen up and flung it, but there was no time for anger.

"The mattress," said the girl, pointing to the beds.

Silla chewed on her lip. "Something...hidden under the mattress?"

"I love a riddle," exclaimed the girl, clapping her hands together.

Moving toward the beds, curiosity nipped at Silla. She pulled the furs from her father's bed and set them aside. Her fingers moved beneath the straw mattress, searching for something out of sorts along the pallet beneath, but finding nothing. After searching beneath her own to no avail, Silla began to wonder if the words had simply been the ramblings of a dying man.

"What about *inside* the mattress?" asked the little blonde girl, scratching her elbow.

Yanking at the dagger sheathed in her boot, Silla grew irritated as the blade pulled free with ease. "Foulsome thing," she muttered, glaring at it.

She ran the blade along the edge of her father's mattress, then reached her hand into the straw bedding within. Almost immediately, her hand closed around something, and she pulled out a rough-spun bag.

Silla crossed the room and dumped the contents onto the table. Sólas and kressens bounced out, and as she tilted the bag up, she spotted something lodged in the bottom—parchment folded into a small square. Unfolding it carefully, she read the words aloud:

> Tómas,
>
> My sincerest apologies for such a late reply. The Mossarokk message post has long been abandoned, and patrol riders stumbled by chance across your letters—thankfully allies of ours. Eystri lands have many refuges for those in need. Come to Kopa before winter's turn, and we will get you and your daughter situated in a shield-house.
>
> Ask for Skeggagrim at the house with the blue shutters, beside the Dragon's Lair Inn, Kopa, Eystri.
>
> Best of luck on your journey.
>
> Your friend.

"Skeggagrim?" asked the blonde girl, clutching the edge of the table beside Silla's elbow. "It has the sound of a character in a skald's tale. A troll, perhaps."

Silla flipped the parchment over in search of more information, but it was blank. As much as she loathed the idea of traveling such a long distance, the prospect of safety was alluring. More than alluring...it was the thing she most desperately longed for in life, written in ink.

"I suppose I'm going to Kopa."

"*We're* going to Kopa?" exclaimed the girl. "An adventure, how fun!"

Kopa would be an adventure, her father had said earlier. Tears began to gather once more, and Silla forced her body to move.

Folding the parchment back up, she placed it into the bag with the coins from the table and those in her purse. She tucked the bag down her linen underdress, fingers prodding for the pocket she'd sewn on the inside next to her hip. After traveling the roads of Sudur long enough, Silla knew that one always kept valuables secured and hidden.

Moving back to her father's bed, Silla's fingers wrapped around the scratchy woolen material of his tunic, and she couldn't resist. Bringing it to her nose, Silla breathed in his scent before crushing it to her chest. This tunic held the last remnants of him. It was foolish, she had limited space, but she stuffed the tunic into her hemp sack anyway.

Pulling the heart-shaped rock from beside her own bed, her fingers ran over the smooth surface. Into the bag it went. From the trunk beside her bed, Silla pulled underdresses and a thick woolen apron dress, an antler-carved comb, and her red cloak. Her fingers smoothed along the fur-trimmed hood. Red was not a color in which to disappear, but it was thick and quilted, and where she was going, she'd need warmth.

Silla moved to the cook shelves, grabbing a skin for water and wrapping up blackened bread in a scrap of linen. She plunged apples and carrots, hard cheese, and smoked elk into the sack. Staring at the offerings at their makeshift altar, Silla paused. *What a lot of good these did*, she thought to herself, then frowned.

The gods do not work as we expect them to, Moonflower, her father would tell her.

With a heavy breath, she whisked the bread crusts onto the floor, and moved the candles to the food supplies shelf—erasing any evidence that they worshiped the old gods.

Silla grabbed the small wooden box that sat next to a stack of weathered bowls. Pulling it down, she flipped the lid up and looked inside. Her eyes settled upon the green leaves, gnarled and piled upon each other. Lifting the vial from where it rested against her collarbones, she removed the stopper and pressed as many leaves as she could fit inside, then added the box to her sack.

"You could have one right now," suggested the girl. Longing slithered through Silla's veins.

"Soon," she whispered, surveying the room. The outbuilding was still and quiet, dim light from the fading day pouring through the opened doorway.

A loud crack sounded from outside. Silla dropped the sack, diving under a bench and pulling a sheepskin down to shade her from view. An apple wobbled across the floor, her heart beating like a war drum.

She counted her breaths as she waited.

One. Two. Three. Four. Five.

Nothing. The building was silent. It was nothing. Silla forced breath into her body, then pushed herself from under the bench.

She wondered about the animals on Vindur Road, the grimwolves, whose howls she'd heard during the last full moons, and the bears, who left the tree bark scratched up along the road. Worse yet, the creatures said to haunt the woods, the stuff of nightmares. The vampire deer who hunted in packs, draining victims of blood. The wolfspiders and others whose names she didn't care to learn.

"You need a weapon," said the girl with a scowl, her thin arms crossed over her dirty nightdress.

Silla glanced down at her ankle, where the dagger was sheathed once more.

"Useless, loathsome thing," muttered Silla bitterly. How meaningless it was to carry a dagger when she could not unsheathe it in her hour of need. It was an illusion of protection, a false sense of security. Slinging the sack over her shoulder, she took a last look around the building. Despair and grief were beginning to scratch at her throat, but she swallowed them back.

Walking through the open doorway, Silla's eyes darted right to left, then down the packed dirt trail that led to Vindur Road.

The sky had darkened but the clouds had cleared and the setting sun cast golden light upon the path before her. Silla veered left, rounding to the back of the hut where her father kept the tools supplied by Olaf. She ran her fingers along the iron tongs, the axe, the hacksaw. They fell upon the hammer, feeling the smooth curve of the wood, measuring its weight. Not too heavy, but enough weight to do damage.

"Perfect," encouraged the girl. "Best to get walking."

Rounding to the front of the structure, Silla took one last breath on the hut's steps, on this threshold between the comfort and familiarity of her old life and the dangerous unknown of the new. Then, she stepped away from it. She walked down the glowing pathway and onto Vindur Road, hurrying away from Skarstad, away from her father, and away from her shattered life.

FOUR

THE TWISTED PINEWOODS

S illa walked with speed and purpose through the woods. Fear pushed her grief aside, and she focused everything she had on putting as many miles between herself and those dead warriors as she could. For long hours, she pressed herself hard, the hammer gripped in one hand and the strap of her shouldered bag clutched in the other.

The woods were eerie enough during the daytime, but they were a different world at night, a land of shadows and shapes constantly shifting on the edges of her vision. Silla kept a keen eye on the road, determined not to let the mischievous forest spirits have their way. Her mother had told tales of malevolent spirits shifting the trails and reforming the woods until folk grew hopelessly lost. But these tales had also told of kind spirits who, when treated with respect, would grant favors and blessings to the humans who traveled within their lands.

In the dark of night, it was unnaturally quiet, almost as if the forest were holding its breath. Still, Silla pressed on between the gnarled trunks of the Twisted Pinewoods. This section of the forest had garnered its nickname due to a distortion in the pine trunks, warped and misshapen into menacing forms. Was this the doing of troublesome spirits? Silla could not say, but it had a decidedly chilling effect which kept her feet hurrying.

In the back of her mind, she knew it was not safe for a woman to travel alone on this road. Not only was it dangerous, but Ursir's teachings dictated that women must be chaperoned by their husband, brother, or father after darkness.

"You have none of those," said the girl, swinging a stick at a clump of bracken.

Silla huffed. "We must be quick," she said. The road had laws unto itself, rife with thieves, warbands who controlled passage through various sections, and other dangerous, desperate men. Her only hope was her stealth, to remain undetected. "Best to keep in the woods; we'll travel by night, sleep by day," she murmured.

"Are we nearly there?" whined the girl.

Silla snorted. "Give or take four nights."

Four long nights, and she'd reach Reykfjord. Then she could breathe, re-evaluate, and decide what to do next. It felt monumental, impossible when considered as a whole. Grief began to creep into the widening cracks in her spirit, and Silla forced her attention to her steps as she put one foot in front of the other. It was all she could do.

Silla had never enjoyed the dark, and she was grateful when the sister moons rose shortly after sunset—Malla, big and bold and bright, and Marra, small but calm and unwavering. Under the milky glow, fans of white lichen unfurled, exposing their frilled edges to the moonlight, while clusters of snowcap mushrooms released luminescent spores, like tiny stars glinting in the midnight forest. Silla had seen this before—this was not her first time walking in the woods after dark—but the beauty of it made her feel just a little less alone.

On the road, Silla was powerless to stop the flow of revelations from seeping into her mind.

I loved you like my own kin.

Her father's words rang in her ears, each time, her chest tightening and grief clawing forth with more vigor. Grief, but also anger—how could he have kept such a thing from her?

If Matthias is not my blood father, then who is? she wondered. *How did he come to have me? Did he steal me? Are my blood parents alive and searching for me?*

"It seems unlikely," said Silla aloud. She could not imagine it—her gentle father stealing a child. It had been the two of them against the world, but now she bitterly searched for new meaning in the life they'd lived on the run together.

Queen Signe has been searching for you, girl.

The other words she could not shake. The queen wanted her—had been searching for her. But she had to have the wrong person. This had to be a misunderstanding.

She has the scar. It's her.

Her fingers traced the tiny, crescent-shaped scar at the corner of her left eye. Bumped her eye on a table corner, she'd always been told. Had that been a lie, along with Matthias's name? Along with the fact they shared no blood?

"I've heard Queen Signe is like a queen from a skald's tale," mused the girl.

Silla considered what she knew of Queen Signe. She knew the queen had formerly been a princess of Norvaland, that she had the white-gold hair that was so coveted in that kingdom. Silla knew that of her seven siblings, Signe alone was saved by the Urkans upon their invasion, prized for her beauty and taken to be Ivar's bride.

Perhaps the queen could influence her husband, but to Silla's knowledge, Signe was not involved in running the kingdom. The Klaernar, land management, laws, and rule, was all King Ivar and the jarls who served him. But the warriors on the road had clearly stated the *queen* wanted Silla, not the king.

So what did she want with Silla?

"To kill you," replied the girl. "Though not right away."

"You are not reassuring in the least," whispered Silla.

A flap of wings overhead shattered the stillness of the woods. Instinctively, Silla sprang deeper into the forest, darting between the twisted stems, then diving behind a bushy juniper. She held her body taut, the hammer poised as she examined Vindur Road.

One. Two. Three. Four. Five.

Nothing.

It was always nothing. But one of these times, it might be something. A grimwolf or a bear or a vampire deer or worse, a man. After several strained minutes, she eased herself from behind the scraggly bush and continued alongside the road, keeping to the shadowy forest.

The moons were low in the sky when she finally relented to sleep. Silla walked deeper into the woods for a half-mile, marking the trees with a shallow scratch of her knife so that the trickster spirits could not trap her in the depths. She found the broad trunk of a rowan tree, the ground beneath it carpeted in moss, and set down her bag. Snapping a dead and brittle branch from the tree's base, Silla dragged it along the ground until she formed a circle around the tree and where she'd sleep.

"Sunnvald, protect me," she murmured. "Malla, grant me courage. Marra, bless me with wisdom. Stjarna, light my path." Her faith wavering, the words felt empty. If the gods were real, how could they have let this happen?

Silla stepped into the circle, moaning with relief as she sank onto soft moss. Resting her back against the trunk, Silla pulled out the heart-shaped rock, smoothing her fingers over it. It felt strangely comforting to hold it, this thing that her father had given her. She felt disoriented, confused. How could her father be gone when just hours before, they'd awoken as they did each morning? How could he be gone when his tunic still held his scent?

A crack from above her had Silla leaping to her feet, grasping wildly for the hammer. She stared into inky blackness above her. There was a hint of motion, then a swoop of wings and an owl came into view. The hammer was poised to attack as she stared into black eyes set against a ghostly white face.

Laughter burst from Silla, high and brittle, as the hilarity of the situation dawned on her. "Gather your wits, Silla Margrét," she told herself.

"Madder than a berserker," giggled the girl.

With a shake of her head, Silla sank back down. "What does an owl foretell?" she mused, nibbling on some bread and an apple.

"Sleep," yawned the little blonde girl, curling up beside her. "An owl foretells sleep."

Silla left her apple core and the toughest part of the bread as an offering to the spirits. They hadn't hindered her progress thus far, and she hoped to keep in their good graces. But even as she closed her sack, her stomach felt hollow. She had to ration wisely if she wanted to survive the trip to Reykfjord. And beyond that, if she was to make it to Kopa, she'd need to be clever. She did not need to count the coins in her pocket to know it wasn't enough for passage north.

Stashing the food into her bag, she pulled out her red cloak and spread it out like a blanket. Silla stared at the dark canopy above. Something about the earthen, mossy smell, the sturdy tree behind her, triggered a memory from within. Another cold night spent on the forest floor, another night backed against a tree.

"I know you're cold, Moonflower. Take my socks, put them on your hands. They're clean, don't worry. Tomorrow, we'll be in Holt, and we'll be warming our toes by the fire, sipping hot cups of róa."

Silla wiped tears from her cheeks and pulled the woolen socks onto her hands and over the sleeves of her dress. It helped a bit. She wriggled deeper beneath her cloak. Sadness had dogged her steps all day. Her feet ached. And she was so tired that her eyelids throbbed.

"Remember, we're survivors, Silla. We can do hard things. We do what we must to stay alive. We'll be safe in Holt."

"But why did we have to leave Geirborg, Father? I liked it there."

Her father ran a hand through his blond hair. It was more and more unkempt, now that her mother was not around to trim it. Silla noticed streaks of gray had begun to appear; his face was more weathered than it had been months earlier.

"Because, Moonflower. If people realize you see things that aren't there, the Klaernar will come calling."

His breath clouded the air. The cold was so penetrative in the forest; it was impossible to shake off once it sank into your bones.

"But I don't know how to do magic. I am not Galdra. She's simply a spirit friend."

"I know, Silla, I know, and it's not fair. But it won't matter to them."

"I miss Mama." Gods how she missed her. Silla had been twelve years old—had lost her mother two years before. The stability she'd known all her life had vanished in an instant. Gone was her home in Hildar, her tree swing, her chickens.

Her father let out a long breath. "I miss her too, Moonflower. Aye, but I do."

He sank to the ground beside her, pulled her next to him, and spread a woolen blanket over them. After a moment, his warmth settled over her.

Silla closed her eyes. She had her father. She was safe. They'd get through this together. It was the two of them against the world.

She breathed deeply, her worry dissolving as she exhaled.

Silla's eyes stung from the memory. Her head pounded with the force of hammer strikes. Her body ached everywhere. Finally, she let her walls down.

Fear had pressed her grief aside all day, but now she allowed it in. It flowed into her like a tide of despair, inundating her so wholly she thought she might drown. Tears streamed down her face, and her body wrenched with each sob. She thought of her father, of what he'd revealed, of how he'd left her.

He'd left her.

It was selfish, but she cursed him. Cursed him for leaving her alone in this world with nothing but unanswered questions and a monumental task. Kopa. Safety awaited her in Kopa...but how was she to get there?

"I won't leave you," whispered the little girl, tucking her messy hair behind her ears. "I'll stay by your side."

Silla blinked at the girl, grateful for her presence, real or not.

Pain lashed through her skull. Flinching, Silla closed her eyes and weathered it like a battering storm. She'd spent her life fearing these headaches—spent her life avoiding them at all costs. But right now, the pain was so exquisite, so consuming and needy, it pushed her grief aside. There was something comforting about this pain—it was a pain she could control, could wipe away with a single, gnarled skjöld leaf.

She should have taken her dose of skjöld when she'd set out from her home, but her thoughts had been slow and cumbersome in the haze of grief. Her body reminded her, as it always did. Vision darkening, it felt as though knives plunged into her skull.

"Take the skjöld, Silla," urged the girl. "You'll feel better."

As her vision swirled back, Silla gasped in a lungful of air. Her fingers wrapped around the vial hanging from her neck. She removed the stopper and plucked a twisted green leaf with trembling fingers. Tea was clearly not an option in the depths of the Twisted Pinewoods, so Silla tucked the leaf right into her cheek. It was earthy and bitter, and she chewed it as much as she could before swallowing it down with a grimace.

Silla stared at the vial. One leaf per day had been her ration for the past ten years. But tonight was different. Everything had changed. She hesitated, then pulled a second leaf and placed it in her mouth. She didn't want to think anymore, didn't want to feel. She wanted to kill her feelings, the way the warriors on the road had killed her father.

Two leaves should do the trick.

Silla put the lid back on the vial and tucked it beneath her collar. She stared into darkness. Warmth bloomed in her stomach, spiraling up her spine then back down again, shimmering out to the tips of each of her fingers and toes. Bursts of light popped in her vision, vivid whorls of pink, blue, and yellow, and Silla's chest relaxed, her breaths deepening.

She'd slipped out of her skin, the burden on her shoulders left behind, and for the moment, Silla just *was*.

FIVE

Something was following Silla.

Two hours earlier, she'd bent her foot sideways on a root, sending searing pain up her ankle. Lowering herself to the ground, she'd leaned against the twisted trunk of a pine and loosened her boot. Much to her relief, after freeing her foot from its confines, she found it aching but not badly injured.

"Perhaps the spirits found your offering lacking," mused the little blonde girl.

With a sigh, Silla had persisted. But the going had been slow through the edge of the woods. Fog twined around gnarled trunks, obscuring the uneven ground. The sky was veiled by heavy clouds, the white lichen and snowcap mushrooms dormant in the absence of moonlight. Instead, the forest was layered with shadows upon shadows. Tripping had been inevitable.

"My feet ache," the girl had complained over and over, and Silla had to agree —everything throbbed.

"Pain means we're alive," said Silla softly, though it did little to encourage her.

As she massaged her ankle, Silla's veins shivered, carrying the distinct feeling that she was being watched. But when she peered into the woods, she could not distinguish anything in the shades of gray and black.

"Something follows us," said the little blonde girl, casting a look over her shoulder.

"I feel it as well," murmured Silla.

Once she started walking for the night, Silla tried not to stop. Stopping was when grief swamped her. When her mind replayed those life-altering moments on the road—the clash of metal as swords and daggers met, the crushing panic as her neck was squeezed, the scent of earth and iron as she blinked back to consciousness, a dead warrior's body pinning her down. And those words which had shattered her life so completely. *He is not even your kin.*

It was easier to keep walking, to keep pushing forward. And so, she carried on.

The feeling of being watched clung to her for hours. The woods hummed with energy, the hairs on her arms standing on edge. With muscles which seemed unable to unclench, her pace had quickened, feet moving over the uneven ground with reckless urgency. But Silla couldn't keep on like this, not with days still separating her from Reykfjord.

The blackness of night had faded to the darkest of grays, the ground ever so slightly easier to see. And then she heard it—the clatter of hooves and men's voices, jarringly loud in the silence of the woods.

Her heart slammed into her ribs, and Silla flattened herself to the ground with a curse. Why had she chosen red of all the cloaks in the market? A nice neutral color like gray or evergreen would have better suited her situation. But the red had been so bright and festive and had made her smile...

She was at least twenty paces from the riders, and with darkness clinging to the trees, Silla prayed she would not be seen.

Shadowy men rode by with a wagon bumping behind them. Wisps of their conversation reached her ears.

"Half a day's ride from Reykfjord," came one voice.

"'Twill be a brief visit," said another, "if the Bloodaxe Crew awaits us. I've an offer they won't be able to resist."

The clatter of hooves obscured the rest of the conversation, and soon the woods drifted back into silence.

"We must rest," said the girl with a yawn. "And I must relieve myself."

Silla was overcome with exhaustion. She'd walked for at least ten hours, and her body screamed for rest. Still, she pulled herself up and pressed deeper into the forest, scoring the trees as she went. By the time she found a secluded stand of birch to make camp, the sky had lightened a few more shades of gray.

A creature of ritual, Silla made her circle, spoke words to the old gods, and settled onto the soft forest floor. She smoothed her hand over the heart-shaped rock, seeking comfort. It felt as though the trees had grown eyes. Unease spilled through her, pooling in her stomach. The rational side of her mind told her she needed rest, needed food and water, that she could not continue at this pace. The irrational side told her some creature was waiting for her to fall asleep before it tore into her with fangs and claws.

Alone, she thought. She was all alone.

Silla was acutely aware of this fact. Not just in the woods, but in the world. If something happened to her, who would help her? If she died, who would mourn her? Who would know she'd ever walked this world?

"I'm here," said the girl, settling down beside her.

"You're not real," whispered Silla. She missed her father with every beat of her heart, with every breath which filled her lungs.

A hot tear rolled down her cheek.

She flinched at the flutter of wings overhead. Silla gazed into dark, eerie eyes set against a bone-white face, and the tension in her body loosened.

"Feathers," she whispered to the owl. "You frightened me. Do you not have some poor mouse to stalk?" The owl blinked, then settled deeper onto the branch, gazing down upon them.

"That owl is looking at me strangely," complained the girl. "Make it stop."

"Was it you following us tonight?" whispered Silla. "Have the spirits sent you to guide us? If so, might I ask you to fly *ahead* of us tomorrow, so it does not feel like some beast stalks us."

"Or you could hoot," suggested the little girl. "It is far too quiet in these woods."

Silla sorted through her provisions while nibbling on bread. With reluctance, she divided her best apple, placing half of it beyond her protective circle with some of her precious cheese, hoping the spirits would appreciate this offering. As she ate the other half of the apple, she stared at the pair of skjöld leaves in her palm. After a long moment of deliberation, she tucked both leaves into her cheek, glancing up at the owl.

Perhaps Silla was imagining it, but she sensed disapproval in the harsh glare of the creature's dark eyes. The owl blinked, its eyes fluttering shut.

"Good night, Feathers," she whispered. Curling onto her side, Silla stared at the heart-shaped rock, thinking of her father's blue eyes and reassuring presence. She imagined that, like the owl, he watched over her. Without her father beside her, Silla felt empty...incomplete. Who was she without him? Tears stung her eyes as she waited for bliss and warmth to seep through her, displacing the grief. No more feeling. She couldn't bear it.

Silla gripped her hammer as the leaves took hold, pleasure finally skating through her veins, lights glowing before her eyes like the luminescent snowcap spores under moonlight.

The heart-shaped rock was the last thing she saw before drifting into a broken sleep.

———

SILLA AWOKE TO A BRITTLE CRACK.

Her tongue was stuck to the roof of her mouth, arm twitching as though urging her to move. Eyes fluttering open to daylight, her blood held the remnants of that second skjöld leaf, though the bliss in her veins was now a dull trickle. "Too early," mumbled Silla, throwing an elbow over her eyes. "Too bright." She tried in vain to burrow back into into sleepy forgetfulness.

"Aye, lads, what have we here?"

Shock jolted through her, memory surging in its wake. There were voices. There should *not* be voices.

Silla sat up, her vision warping, then settling. Gripping the hammer, she stared into cold brown eyes. Mind sluggish, she blinked to clear sleep and skjöld from it, collecting what information she could. Daytime. Gray skies. Men— four of them. Looking at her.

Silla cursed herself for taking the second leaf. How utterly reckless of her when she needed her wits about her. Her skull pulsated with the echoes of the skjöld; she needed water. Needed far more sleep. Needed another leaf.

One of the men stepped forward, and Silla could only stare back. The man's hard life was evident in the deep lines and scars carved into his ruddy face, a wild look to his wiry beard and long hair. Behind him stood three more men, each with a spear and wooden shield clutched in hand.

"Perhaps they're good men," said the little girl, squinting at them. "Perhaps the spirits have sent them to help you."

Silla glanced at the place where she'd left her offering—no trace of it left. But as her gaze returned to the men before her and she took in the hardness in their eyes, her hopes that these men would provide aid faded. Shields clutched in hand were painted with a faded sigil—a wreath of thorny brambles with swords crossed behind. A chill settled in her bones. These men belonged to the Battle Thorns warband which prowled these parts.

The man scrubbed a hand through his scraggly black beard. "Seems we've a problem. You've not paid for passage through these woods." His eyes were impassive, but they held a frightening coldness. "Now, what's to be done about it, woman?"

Silla could not seem to shape words.

"Here's some advice for you. Next time you trespass on Battle Thorns land, make *some* attempt to cover your tracks." The men behind the leader chuckled. "Some of us like the challenge of a chase."

The leader's gaze fell down her neck, then lower. He ran his tongue across his upper teeth. "How is it you're all alone? Where is your chaperone?" His eyes were back on hers, and they held a look she couldn't quite understand. But the crawling sensation beneath her skin told her it was nothing she wanted to know.

"There's her bag, chief." A bald-headed, heavily muscled warrior gestured to her rucksack. The arms crossed over his chest were as large as tree trunks.

Silla gripped her bag—her entire life. She was as good as dead without it.

The chief's dark eyes shifted to her hand, then flicked back to her face. "I advise you not to anger me, woman. Give it to me."

Her grip only tightened.

The warrior reached for her bag, and Silla didn't think—she just swung. It happened in slow motion. The hammer arced down, landing square in the middle of the chief's hand. She heard the unmistakable crunch of shattering bones. The man's stoic face twisted in agony, and he let out an animalistic howl, yanking his hand back.

Pain screamed from her cheek, her vision exploding with bursts of light. Everything seemed slurred and slowed. It took her a moment to realize she'd been backhanded, the hammer pried from her, that she'd been jerked to her feet.

"You've set your fate now, woman," growled the chief, clutching his hand. His bored expression was now distorted with fury, and Silla blinked rapidly, trying to clear her mind.

The bald warrior twisted her arms behind her and yanked her tight to his chest. "Shouldn't've done that." A horrid combination of rotten cheese and stale fire whiskey snaked up her nostrils.

Silla's heart raced and her vision swam as the warband crowded around her bag. She gulped down frantic breaths, needing to regain some semblance of control. They tossed her spare garments to the ground and began distributing her food amongst them. When at last they reached the bottom, they threw the sack to the ground, turning on her. The roughspun bag filled with coins was heavy against her hip, and Silla hoped with all her might they would not discover it.

The leader stalked slowly toward her. "No coins? We know you'd not be on the road without sólas." His eyes were black, a predator honed in on his prey. "Now, where might you be hiding them?" His eyes raked down to her feet and crawled back up. "We shall relish in searching them out."

"Let me free," said Silla in a hoarse voice, an idea sluggishly forming. "My father is there, beyond the copse. If I scream, he'll come running and bury his axe in your skull."

The men scanned the woods, but they were not convinced, and she knew— she'd waited too long for this ruse to work. Curse the leaves and curse her poor judgment and curse her horrid luck.

"Go on, then," said the chief, holding her gaze in challenge.

"He has much battle fame," she lied. "But he'll make it slow and leave you for last. I give you this one chance. Go now, or become food for the crows."

"You have a bold tongue," said the chief with a low chuckle. He was close to her now, and with his uninjured hand, brushed a strand of hair from Silla's face. "I like that. We'll find your sólas, then collect extra tribute." His dirt-stained fingers trailed down her face, along the curve of her neck and tracing the sensitive skin of her collarbone.

His hand strayed lower, reaching to unfasten her overdress. Panic rising, Silla's eyes snapped shut. Had she truly escaped the attack on Vindur Road, left everything she knew behind for *this*? A scream built in her throat, despite the fact there was no father to rescue her, despite the fact she was a half-mile from the road, in the depths of the woods. No one could hear her.

But Silla choked on that scream as she was knocked sideways, her head bouncing on a mat of soft moss. She blinked. The must of wet fur mingled with the mineral scent of blood.

Her heart pounded once, then twice. A bone-shaking growl erupted in the woods, causing a knot of birds to cloud the sky.

Silla turned her head slowly to the left, afraid of what she'd see.

A grimwolf. The largest she'd ever seen.

Is this real? she wondered. Lights popped in her vision, energy thrashing through her veins. Despite this, her head felt remarkably clear.

The grimwolf was the size of a small horse, with paws as large as plates.

Standing over the prone form of the bald warrior, its three-inch-long claws pierced his chest. A high-pitched bleating sound echoed through the clearing, and Silla realized with horror that it came from the man. He writhed with desperation, but she knew it was to no avail. She could feel it in her heart. Could taste it in the air.

The grimwolf lowered its head and ripped out the man's throat in a single, brutal motion.

The warriors behind her screamed, branches whipping as they frantically retreated into the woods, abandoning her in the clearing with the beast.

The grimwolf lifted its head, tangled gore spilling from its maw. Drawing its lips back, the bloody mangle fell to the ground, revealing glinting pointed teeth. It took a step toward Silla, and she fought to control her breath. This creature was pure power, the king of these woods. It could end her with barely a thought, could snap her bones and tear her throat as quickly as it had the man on the ground beneath it.

Silla froze in place, fear or instinct telling her to remain still. The grimwolf's bright yellow eyes studied her as if it was deciding where to tear into her first—belly? Throat? The soft parts of her thighs? It lifted its nose, a breath huffing the air, and Silla held so still she did not dare breathe. The beast's eyes honed in on something behind her.

Crouching low to the ground, the grimwolf launched. A flash of silver fur was all she saw as it sailed straight over her in a powerful, fluid motion. It landed silently in the moss, loosing a snarl as it pressed into the greater forest.

Silla found herself alone yet again with death. Had the wolf been sent by the spirits, or had it been acting of its own accord? She couldn't allow herself the time to dwell on it.

"I've never seen anything like it," said the little blonde girl, crouching down to inspect the man's mangled throat.

The terror in his unseeing eyes was plain to see, blood gushing around the torn muscles and tendons of his butchered neck. The girl picked up a stick, poking at a dangling shred of flesh, and Silla pressed the back of her hand to her mouth to quell her rising nausea. Forcing herself to turn, she wrestled with her bag, shoving the rock, Matthias's tunic, and her strewn garments inside. Her hand closed around the familiar comfort of the hammer.

Then Silla whirled and ran as fast as her feet could manage. The woods were a blur of green foliage and ghostly twisted stems. Even as a branch whipped across her face, she didn't stop. Silla leaped over rocks and roots and gnarled plants, stepping over fallen trees and dried creek beds. She ran from the muffled screams and snarls behind her. She ran toward nothing, toward more of the same ashy-gray sky, the same trees, and same moss. Fueled by blind fear, she ran until her legs crumpled, and she folded her body over a fallen log covered in lichen.

And then, she laughed.

It was not her usual laugh, melodic and carefree. This laugh was wild and hoarse, cutting through the forest's silence like a freshly sharpened hevrít. Silla rolled over and leaned against the log.

"You're going mad," said the girl wryly, arms crossed over her torn night-dress as she leaned against a birch tree.

Was Silla far enough from the grimwolf? Would it be satisfied with the four men it would surely have killed by now and leave her be? She assessed herself. Her run through the forest seemed to have cleared the skjöld from her blood. Her cheek stung slightly, but she was unhurt. She had her bag, her coins.

"They've taken your food, your reserves of skjöld leaves, and your water-skin," said the girl, peeking into the bag.

Silla put a hand to the bridge of her nose and squeezed. "It will be difficult," she said breathlessly. "Nearly impossible." Tears burned her eyes. "Hearthfire thoughts," she told herself, blinking rapidly. "Lightning. Sweet rolls. Clean stockings."

She took a deep breath.

Held it in.

Released it slowly.

Difficult, but *not* impossible. She had the skjöld leaves in the vial strung around her neck. There were streams to drink from, and perhaps she could find something to eat in the woods. Her mother had taught her of herbs and plant lore. It was still *quite* possible.

As Silla turned, assessing the woods and the cloud-obscured sky, a sinking sensation settled into her stomach. The trees all looked the same, and she'd run without marking her path.

"The spirits have tricked you," the little girl said, looking up at her with those unnerving blue eyes. "And now you are lost."

"Think," Silla told herself, turning around in the woods. "Think, think, think."

It all looked the same. The same moss-covered boulders and clawed brambles and blanched birch stems. The sky was thick with clouds—it was sometime in the early afternoon. Impossible to discern the sun's position.

She'd run a great distance from the grimwolf; at least twenty minutes. If she picked the wrong direction, if she walked the wrong way, Silla was in danger of losing the road entirely, of becoming swallowed into the vast wildness of the Twisted Pinewoods.

To the north lay the Sleeping Dragons, the desolate and dangerous range of dormant volcanoes. To the east lay Reykfjord, but also the Giant's Tears, a deep gorge with a wild, impassible river and several cascading waterfalls. West would take her back to Skarstad. It was south Silla needed to get back to Vindur Road so she could cross the bridge over the gorge and slip through the stockade walls of Reykfjord.

Once in Reykfjord, Silla could fade into the obscurity of the city, blend in with the other nameless faces and regroup. But at the moment, the plan was laughably out of grasp. She was alone in the Twisted Pinewoods without food or drink and had completely lost her bearings. She wouldn't say the word the girl had uttered. Wouldn't give voice to the panic which was now creeping up on her.

"What would Father do?" she asked herself.

"He'd never have gotten into this mess," said the little girl, with hands on her hips.

"Oh, gods." Tears threatened, but Silla pushed them back. "Silla Margrét, you can do this. You're a survivor. You can be clever when you need to be, can't you? You will figure this out. Think. Think."

Silla stared at the sky, wishing it was dark and clear. The old tales told that the stars were the ancestors immortalized in light, guided by the brightest of them all—the Mother Star—sitting in the north. If Silla could find the Mother Star, she could regain her bearings...

"Unfortunate about the clouds," the girl sighed.

Motion in the sky caught Silla's eye—birds; a group of them flying in wedge formation. As she blinked at the dark forms flapping so high above her, the name graylag geese came from somewhere in the echoes of her mother's voice.

They live in the north, returning south close to midsummer.

Her heart skipped. The geese were flying to her right.

Hiking her bag over her shoulder, Silla marched in the direction the birds had flown. It was the best chance she had.

She reached Vindur Road nearly an hour later, her weary bones groaning with relief. She hadn't dared to take her eyes from the direction the birds had flown, afraid she'd lose her bearings once more. When at last the trees opened up to the barren gash of Vindur Road, she'd finally allowed her eyes to squeeze shut.

Silla sank on the edge of the road, folding herself over bent knees. She wasn't used to this: the surging energy in her blood, the fear, the unease. The cycle of terror and relief endlessly depleting.

She had forgotten what safe felt like, wondered how she'd ever taken it for granted, how she'd taken her father for granted. How she'd lamented when the market hadn't had the arctic thyme she'd sought or when her mistress had been sharp with her. It all seemed so inconsequential now, so trivial. What she would do to go back to that, to trade her new reality for those annoyances.

"I cannot do this all the way to Kopa," she whispered. "I must find another way."

The girl hugged her knees beside Silla in silent agreement. Rising to weary feet, Silla walked twenty paces into the woods. "Another night in the woods might be the end of us. We won't stop walking until we reach Reykfjord."

SIX

REYKFJORD

Skraeda Holf had been watching her prey for the better part of an hour. Seated on the opposite end of the long table, she kept her gaze trained on the fire flickering in a nearby hearth, watching the warrior from the corner of her eye. The mead hall in Reykfjord had grown busy as the hour progressed, gaps on the benches filling as patrons took their seats and drank horn after horn of ale.

Where are your companions, warrior? Skraeda wondered, sipping from her clay cup. The honeyed taste of mead spread across her tongue, helping to soothe her growing impatience. A month she'd watched the warrior and his friends, a month she'd planned for today. Hindrium cuffs sat heavy in her pocket, and with the twitch of her hand, men positioned at each corner of the mead hall would descend upon the warrior and his friends.

Turning her head slightly, Skraeda gazed at the man between the copper braids spilling over her shoulder. He was large, the sealskin cloak wrapped around him only adding to his bulk. Black hair knotted at his crown, the man leaned on the long table, glowering into his cup of ale. Outwardly, he was a fearsome warrior. But she could sense a ribbon of angst undulating constantly from the man's aura.

"What have you to be nervous about, warrior?" Skraeda asked softly. She strummed through his emotions like the strings of a harp, tugging gently, so gently, upon the thread of his angst. Even from a distance she could see sweat dotting his brow. The warrior cast a look over his shoulder, hand tugging at his black beard. *Someone grows worried*, thought Skraeda, a slow smile creeping across her lips.

She would have drawn him in already if it wasn't for those same three men he met weekly, each spooling similar threads of quivering angst. Even without her Solacer intuition, Skraeda would have known the men hid something. The others in the mead hall shared the kind of camaraderie which comes from many drunken nights spent together. But those four warriors were the black sheep of the family, keeping only to themselves.

Because you hide your true nature, she thought. The Galdra had an emotional signature—angst mixed with fear and a touch of excitement. But the true test was when a Klaernar warrior walked past—fear looping brighter, revulsion weaving in. *Where are your friends? When shall they join us?*

Glancing at the door of the mead hall, Skraeda's irritation drove higher, her gift growing muted. She delved her hand into her pocket, thumb stroking along the smooth strands of Ilka's braid. The knots in Skraeda's chest loosened slightly.

Patience, sister, she imagined Ilka whispering in her ear. *The rabbit comes easily to the clever wolf who waits.* Ilka had been the twin with the patience. Skraeda on the other hand, was the one with ambition, with daring. The one who fearlessly took what she wanted.

And when she'd laid eyes upon the four warriors that first time, Skraeda had decided her sister was right. If she set her trap just right and remained patient, four fat rabbits would come directly to her. And then, perhaps she could finally leave Reykfjord and return to the comforts of Sunnavík. The very idea was like sunshine warming her insides.

For three months now, she'd been in Reykfjord, with its reek of fish and salt-tinged gales. It was fish and fish and more fish here. And when it was not fresh fish, it was whale steaks or smoked herring or dried cod. She'd eaten so much fish, Skraeda could smell it on her skin. She yearned for lamb and rabbit and roasted boar served with juniper sauce—anything other than wretched fish.

Iron hinges creaked as the door to the mead hall was pushed open, four Klaernar striding in.

Skraeda cursed under her breath as she sensed a fiery burst of fear from the Galdra warrior she watched, twining with repulsion. Her suspicions were confirmed—the man was Galdra indeed—but the miserable Klaernar would ensure his friends did not join him. And if Skraeda couldn't bring in all four, she'd need to arrange for the men she'd hired to return another day. That was, of course, if the Klaernar didn't frighten the group of warriors off permanently.

The boots of the King's Claws thudded against the wooden flooring of the mead hall as they rounded the long table and started toward the man.

"Gods' sacred ashes," Skraeda seethed under her breath. The Klaernar were going to ruin all of her work.

The warrior's fear was now a bright rope flailing wildly. Skraeda drew it into her mind's grasp, drawing from the heart of her galdur and adding her soothing touch. Loosening his grip on the cup, the warrior let out a long exhale.

Her brows furrowed as the King's Claws walked past the man, without so much of a look in his direction. The leading Klaernar's gaze fell onto her, and suddenly Skraeda felt like the prey.

Fighting the old urge to flee, she forced herself to meet the man's cold, dark eyes. Her skin prickled at the dimness of his emotions. The Klaernar were all like that—cold and unfeeling compared to the regular population. She suspected it was not by accident but by design—the berskium powder, which they took during the Rite and monthly doses afterward, not only enhanced their physical strength, but it altered a part of their minds. Their emotions seemed dulled during the regular day, but Skraeda had noted this changed during episodes of battle and violence—their anger and excitement enhanced, fear and empathy smothered.

"Skraeda Clever Tongue," said the leading King's Claw, approaching.

And with that, all eyes in the mead hall fell upon her, and her cover was ruined.

Skraeda ran a hand down her face with a heavy exhale, then turned her glare upon the Klaernar. "You've just ruined a month's work."

Behind the Klaernar, the black-haired warrior stood and made his way to the door. Skraeda slammed her cup down upon the table, sloshing mead over the sides. Not only had he frightened off her mark, but he'd spoken the name she'd garnered from the Klaernar loud enough for all in the mead hall to hear. She could never return here again.

Undeterred, the leading Klaernar produced a rolled parchment from his cloak, handing it to Skraeda. "You've a new assignment. Correspondence has come from Her Highness."

Skraeda snatched the scroll from the man, tearing open the seal stamped with a wasp sigil, and greedily read the words within.

Skraeda,

A target has slipped us. We search for a woman of twenty winters with curly brown hair, a small scar at the corner of her eye. She may be traveling through Reykfjord. Meet Kommandor Thord's men on the bridge and look for anything unusual. She must be brought in at all costs. More information to come.

I know you won't let me down.

Yours,
Signe

Frustration bubbled in Skraeda's blood. A change...after all these weeks of planning, all of her hard work was scrapped, just like that.

And yet, the queen's curved letters gave her pause.

Brought in at all costs.

More information to come.

This was new. There was something here, something out of the ordinary. And Her Highness called upon Skraeda. There was opportunity to be had. Besides the fact that she would not let her queen down—the consequences of failure were too dire.

Draining the rest of her mead, Skraeda stood.

"Take me to Thord."

SEVEN

THE TWISTED PINEWOODS

O n and on Silla walked, each hour like a blade twisting deeper inside her. Her blisters stung, her ankle throbbed, even her hair seemed to ache for the love of the gods. But still she walked, stepping over the soft, uneven ground. One foot in front of the other over and over, with the singular goal of getting to Reykfjord.

Hours passed, her energy flagging, her mood growing somber. Silla's mouth was so dry it felt grainy. She needed to find water—and soon.

"Rallying cry, Silla," she told herself quietly. "On the bright side, you did not get eaten by a giant wolf." At the thought of the grimwolf, Silla cast a look over her shoulder—no flash of silver fur, no gleam of yellow eyes. No movement. The woods were still and silent. "You are *going* to do this. You'll make it to Reykfjord and bathe yourself clean, then wrap up in a blanket and eat sweet rolls before the fire."

"I'm hungry," moaned the girl from beside her.

Silla's own stomach complained loudly, but she ignored it. "Then try not to think of food," she suggested.

"Now that's all I'll think of!"

Silla was silent.

"Imagine if we had sweet rolls—freshly baked in Jarl Gunnell's clay oven and smeared with butter," said the girl, clasping her hands together as she walked alongside Silla.

"Oh please, no," moaned Silla.

"Or some hard cheese."

Silla ran a hand down her face. "What is the point of you? To torment me?"

"I'm simply saying what we're both thinking."

"What about chicken, roasted on a spit," said Silla. "Basted with butter and stuffed with leeks and herbs."

"*Oh*," moaned the little girl. "I might actually die for that."

They played this torturous game for longer than Silla cared to admit. When at last she saw the glint of a stream, she ran, dropped to her knees, and scooped cool water between her palms. She drank desperately at first and continued until the sharp edges of hunger were dulled. After splashing her face, Silla pulled off her stockings and dipped her feet into the water. She sighed as the burn of her blisters was dampened. But slowly, the urgency came back, the feeling that she'd stayed too long.

She still wore her blue apron dress with Jarl Gunnell's flower sigil, so Silla quickly pulled it off and changed into clean clothing—a fresh linen underdress and heavier wool apron dress layered over it.

"Perhaps you should braid your hair, Silla," suggested the little blonde girl, dipping her toes into the stream.

"Good idea," replied Silla, using her fingers to pull the tangles from it. She needed to make herself as inconspicuous as possible. After securing her braids with leather ties, she pulled on fresh stockings, wincing as she squeezed her feet back into her boots. Pulling on her cloak, she hoisted her bag over her shoulder, clutched the hammer, and continued.

The darkest hour of the night had passed, and the sky was fading to gray.

Before long, there were riders on the road—travelers on horseback, farmers hauling wagons. Silla eyed the carts enviously. Surely with so much traffic, she must be near Reykfjord. She decided to chance the road, praying she could blend in amongst the others traveling along it.

It was a clear morning, and the sun was soon warming her face as she dragged herself along the road, wincing with each step. She was bone-weary, an exhaustion she'd never felt before. She stumbled over the smallest of rocks. Hunger ravaged her. Each step was a tremendous effort. But she was near; she could feel it.

The clatter of hooves and squeak of wheels raised the hairs on her neck, but Silla kept her eyes on the road, stepping one foot in front of the other.

"Hello!" called a woman's voice, and its sound calmed Silla's rattling nerves.

She whirled to face a woman sitting astride a brown mare, a weathered wagon jostling behind them.

"Well met," replied Silla, shielding her eyes from the sun as she looked up at the woman. She wore a plain linen dress, her shoulders wrapped in a weathered cloak lined with fur. "Do you know how far it is to Reykfjord?"

The woman slowed the horse, squinting down. "It is several hours' walk yet." Her voice was gentle, but her words wrought havoc—*several hours*. Silla tried not to sag in response to the news.

"We'll have to rest," said the girl. "We cannot do *hours*."

The woman studied Silla silently, and she wondered how ragged she looked with the forest clinging to her, not to mention the bruising on her neck and eye. "You're welcome to ride on my wagon," the woman said at last.

Silla was silent a moment, studying her face. Stern brown eyes, a small mole on her forehead, her hair secured beneath a swath of white linen. The woman had an honest look to her, but doubt lingered in Silla's mind.

"You should not be alone on this road." The woman glanced over her shoulder. "There are warbands and creatures. And a murderer has been hunting along these parts."

Silla blinked quickly as this news settled. "Ashes! A murderer? Truly?"

"Yes. The Slátrari, they are calling him. Bodies found tied to posts or pillars or trees in the Reykfjord area, burnt from the inside out. They say he burns his victims alive. It is not safe. I am Vigdis. My nephew Dalli rides in the back as a chaperone. We are headed to the wharf to deliver our wares. You are welcome to ride with us."

News of the murderer made her decision easy. Silla nodded at Vigdis. "My thanks," she said, then rounded the back of the wagon, stacked high with crates of eggs and squawking chickens.

"Chickens," the girl said with excitement, and Silla smiled. A good omen from the gods, at long last.

She accepted a hand up from Dalli, who, as it turned out, was a scraggly boy of sixteen or so, a knit cap pulled over his brow. He smiled at Silla, his gaze drifting to the hammer clutched in her hand. She quickly jammed it under her leg and smiled weakly back.

Silla shielded her eyes from the sun, squinting at Dalli, then studying the crates surrounding her. Her eyes fell upon small speckled eggs nestled in a wooden box beside her. "What are these?" she asked Dalli.

"Winterwing eggs," he replied.

THE ROAD OF BONES

Winterwing eggs were a delicacy so rare Silla had never cooked with them. "They must be very valuable," she said absently.

Dalli eyed her with suspicion, and she decided it best if she kept her mouth shut. Using her sack as a pillow, Silla reclined against the crates.

The wagon rumbled along the road, bouncing over ruts and potholes, the wheels groaning and squeaking. Sunlight covered her like a warm blanket, and Silla's eyelids grew heavy...so heavy. With the first semblance of safety in nearly twenty-four hours, her eyes fell shut, and sleep pulled her under.

———

"WHAT IS YOUR BUSINESS?"

Something sharp and forceful in the voice yanked Silla from sleep. The wagon had stopped, the sun crawling higher in the sky now. Silla glanced at Dalli, who smiled shyly. As she looked out the back of the wagon, she realized they were on a timbered bridge, what must be the Giant's Tears thundering beneath them. Were they at the entrance to Reykfjord?

"Heading to the wharf," replied Vigdis from atop her horse.

"Klaernar," whispered Dalli, the corner of his lip curled. "They've barricaded the bridge and are searching for something."

Silla's heart dropped into her stomach. "For what?" she whispered back. Craning her neck, she could not see over the stacks of crates.

"I do not know."

"Who do you carry?" came the gruff voice.

"My niece and nephew," replied Vigdis, and Silla could have kissed her.

"You haven't come across a woman, have you?" It was a woman's voice now, giving Silla pause. "Traveling alone. Has seen twenty winters. Curly hair, small scar in the corner of her eye."

Silla's chest tightened. She kept her face neutral, but, inside, she was trying to corral her tumultuous thoughts.

"We're on a bridge," said the girl, perched atop the tallest stack of crates, a hand shielding her eyes from the sun. "You cannot run. There is no escape."

Silla knew her words to be true. This was it. She'd either be captured, or she'd be granted her freedom. Everything hinged on this moment.

Her curly hair was braided, but the bruising, the scar, they were readily visible. Pulling up the hood of her cloak, Silla's eyes flitted to her mud-caked boots, and she impulsively reached down, then smeared it on her face, ensuring that the scar at the corner of her eye and the bruise on her cheek were both covered.

"No, we have not seen a woman," came Vigdis' voice, impatient. "I've seen no one. We must get to the wharf before the merchant ship departs. Have we leave to enter the city?"

"We shall check the wagon, then you'll have your leave," came the unidentified woman's voice. Footfalls thudded softly on the timber panels of the bridge. One step. Two. Three.

"Calm yourself or they'll hear the beating of your heart," urged the girl.

Forcing in a long, deep breath, Silla's hand squeezed the vial that hung around her neck tightly. *Sunnvald, protect me,* she thought. *Malla, grant me courage.*

A woman warrior with bright red hair appeared at the back of the wagon— eyes burning like the blue core of a flame, she had pale, freckled skin, and her hair was braided back in neat rows along the sides of her skull. The woman's shirt of mail caught the sunlight, forcing Silla to squint.

A Klaernar joined the woman, and Silla stared at the three clawed tattoos stretching across his cheek as the realization struck her—the queen had now involved the King's Claws in her search for Silla.

"I do not like this woman," muttered the girl from her perch up high.

The woman warrior's severe eyes scoured the wagon, passing over Dalli and settling on Silla.

"Your niece, you said?" she called up to Vigdis, her eyes scrutinizing Silla with an intensity that made goosebumps race up her arms. She kept her gaze impassive, her hands folded in her lap.

"She looks at you too closely," said the girl.

Fool, Silla thought. *Halfwit, you're caught. You should not have accepted a ride.* After all her struggles, she would be captured. Everything she'd been through would be for naught.

"Yes," Silla heard Vigdis say from up front. "My niece, Una. My nephew, Dalli."

The red-haired warrior looked at Silla for a heartbeat longer. Her lip curled. "Filthy," she muttered under her breath.

As the woman warrior and her Klaernar companion turned to walk to the front of the wagon, Silla closed her eyes, letting out a shaky exhale. A moment later, the wagon rolled to motion. They passed four Klaernar leaning against a bridge guardrail, the woman warrior standing apart. Silla watched as the towering forms dwindled, then faded into the distance.

And then, she smiled.

Dalli's voice caused her smile to falter. "Are you Galdra?"

"No," said Silla, but she saw no hardness in his eyes. His aunt had lied to the Klaernar, and he himself had not given her up. The kindness from these strangers was so touching, tears sprang to her eyes.

"If you are not Galdra, then why do they hunt for you?" He watched her with apprehension and perhaps, a hint of admiration.

If only I understood it, Dalli, Silla thought, letting out a long breath.

Instead, she said, "I was in the wrong place at the wrong time. They believe I am someone I'm not. You and your aunt have just saved my life."

They passed between tall timber walls edged with moss and lichen. Silla held her breath as she gazed up at the sheer size of them.

Reykfjord. She squeezed her eyes shut, half-delirious, half-disbelieving. It had been a hope on the wind—a dream.

She had made it.

"I knew you would, Silla," grinned the little girl, revealing a missing bottom tooth.

They wove along a wide avenue crowded with people, carts, and livestock. After the eerie quiet of the woods, the chaos of the city was a beautiful melody to Silla's ears. The rumble of conversation, the trill of vendors, children crying, a man haggling with a shopkeeper; they all competed for her attention. They were the sounds of a city, the sounds of anonymity. Of temporary freedom. Silla was wide awake and alive in her skin.

A smile cracked across her face, and she devoured the city's sights.

The cart ambled past rows of timber-sided homes topped with turfed roofs, but as they progressed deeper into the city, stone structures began to appear. She inhaled the rich scent of spiced róa and baked sweet rolls as they passed a bakehouse; stale mead and ale as they passed a mead hall; iron and leather as they passed a forge.

Silla was taken aback by the sheer size of Reykfjord; she'd known it was a city, but it had been years since she'd been anywhere this large. Whereas Skarstad had been well-ordered and monotone, Reykfjord was quite the opposite. Ancient crumbling stonework was juxtaposed with newer wooden structures, sometimes directly adjacent to one another. Narrow lanes twisted off the main road in a discordant collection of rutted paths. Everywhere she looked were signs that this city was a constantly shifting, living thing.

The cart rumbled past a boarded-up stone structure, and something caught Silla's eye—an ornately carved Sun Cross peeking out from behind cracked panels. Shielding her eyes, Silla looked up, up, and took in the impossibly tall spire which once would have been crowned with Sunnvald's starburst.

After many long minutes, they descended a snaking roadway down toward the quay. Salt air and the pungent smell of fish stung her nostrils, and a new scene developed before her eyes. Dozens of sleek wooden vessels were anchored at a labyrinth of docks, dragons and snarling wolves and the occasional mermaid carved into the prows. As they neared the bustling wharf, a forest of masts sprouted before her eyes, framed by black stone cliffs. Taking in the charcoal hue of the fjords, Silla didn't doubt how the city had gotten the name Reyk-fjord—*the smoky fjord*.

The area bustled with merchants and vendors, crates and sacks and livestock being loaded and unloaded from ships in a dizzying swirl of motion.

"What about a ship?" asked the girl, looking toward the docks.

What about a ship? mused Silla. Could a ship take her north to Kopa? It would certainly be quicker than traveling by road.

"Perhaps not," the girl said a moment later, as Silla spotted people clustered around black-clad figures at the dock entries—Klaernar searching crates and boxes and inspecting individuals.

Panic began to squeeze her chest. There were a dozen or more of them down here. She needed to get away from this wharf.

The wagon rolled to a stop, and Silla jumped off. She paused as Vigdis climbed down from her horse.

"My thanks," breathed Silla, looking into the woman's earnest brown eyes. "Thank you for your protection—for what you did on the bridge. I know the penalty for harboring a fugitive is death. Your risk is not lightly taken."

The woman picked up Silla's hands, holding them gently between her own. She was silent a moment before speaking. "I did so as I wish someone might have helped my sister, Dalli's mother, when they came for her."

Silla's heart felt cracked open. "Una?"

The woman nodded.

"I will think of her tonight," said Silla. "I will hold her name in my heart. I will think of you, of Dalli. You are good people. I would soon be dead if not for your actions. My thanks."

Vigdis nodded. "What will you do?" she asked, glancing over her shoulder to where the Klaernar stood. "I fear Reykfjord will not be safe for you. The Klaernar are thick in the streets."

Silla chewed her lip. For so many days, her goal had been Reykfjord, but now that she'd arrived, she saw that it was true. Reykfjord would not be safe for her, she could not linger for long. "North," she said absently. "I must go north."

Get to Kopa, she thought. *Find Skeggagrim. Disappear from this world.*

"Then you must travel the Road of Bones," said Vigdis, something passing behind her eyes. "'Tis a dangerous road. Would be best for you to find some companions."

Silla nodded.

"May fortune favor you," said Vigdis, turning back to her wagon.

"You must move away from this place," said the little girl, hugging herself. "The air doesn't feel right here."

Silla tugged her hood farther down and tucked the hammer into her bag. Then, she edged toward the road snaking back up to Reykfjord.

Once above, Silla slipped down narrow side streets, weaving through the throngs of people. Heartened by her progress, Silla felt something she hadn't in days. Hope. She'd survived four nights alone in the woods and had slipped past the Klaernar. She might just be able to do this. The excitement of Reykfjord could not smother her burning hunger, nor calm her trembling hands. She needed to find food, a place to rest. As the narrow lane snaked around a bend, Silla glanced up. Her heart skipped.

Before her stood a charcoal building with yellow shutters thrown wide; above a door hung a white wooden sign, swinging gently on its metal rod. The words *The Owl's Hollow Inn* were scrawled with a curving flourish. And below these words, a hand-painted barn owl with eerily familiar eyes beckoned her forward.

"Well met, Feathers." Silla smiled, then crossed the road.

EIGHT

REYKFJORD

Leaning through a haze of pipe smoke, Jonas Svik clasped the other man's forearm just below the elbow. As second in command of the Bloodaxe Crew, he'd learned early on the importance of a firm and confident handshake in this line of work. Any sign of weakness, a flinch, a tremble, and that contract could slip into the night like a hóra with a palm full of coins.

The man's brown eyes were bracketed with fine lines but perceptive as ever. Eye contact was just as crucial as the firmness of the handshake, especially to a man like Magnus Hansson, who took the Urkan traditions seriously. As King Ivar's Chief Hirdman, Magnus's battle glory and reputation preceded him wherever he went. Not just his cunning and strategic mind, but the other side of him, the side which had earned him the name Heart Eater. It was said he was so skilled with a knife, he could split a man's chest wide while his heart still beat. Some believed Magnus gained strength and power from consuming his enemy's heart while it was still warm and quivering.

Jonas couldn't say he bought into the Urkan rituals—the belief that Ursir's blessing could be paid for in blood. But he could say for certain that Magnus was a man you did not want to cross.

Magnus released Jonas's arm, and the two men took their seats across the table from one another. Jonas settled beside the headman of the Bloodaxe Crew, Reynir Bjarg, whose towering form was folded into his chair, an ankle resting on his knee. Guttering torchlight played along Rey's brown cheekbones, and he regarded Magnus with dark eyes set into his trademark impassive look.

Some might think Rey unexpected as the leader of the infamous Bloodaxe Crew; with his immaculately trimmed black beard, and his lébrynja armor always flawlessly oiled, he was far more clean-cut than most warriors. Jonas knew better than to think this man anything but fierce—lethal on the battlefield and terrifying once angered, Rey could throw a look so cutting he'd earned the name Axe Eyes.

"Bjarg, Svik. My thanks for meeting under unusual circumstances," said Magnus as he lifted a carved pipe to his lips. Inhaling, he paused a moment before blowing smoke across the heavy, scarred table.

The smoke seemed to glow in the dim light of the room. The sweet and earthy scent reached Jonas's nostrils, and his stomach curled. It was not entirely unpleasant, but the uninvited vision of his pipe-smoking father was called to memory.

"It's no short distance to travel from Sunnavík to Reykfjord, Magnus," said Rey. His chair groaned beneath his bulk as he leaned forward, steepling his fingers together. "I'll admit, it has stirred intrigue amongst the Crew."

When they'd gotten word that Magnus Hansson would be arriving in Reykfjord and had requested an audience with them, the Bloodaxe Crew had vibrated with curiosity, wagering on what it could be this time. What would draw the Heart Eater to leave the comforts of the capital of Íseldur? So long as it wasn't like the last job they'd done for the king, Jonas was happy.

It had been three months since that job, retrieving Jarl Hati's runaway daughter. It had taken the Crew a few weeks to find her, holed up with a farmhand at an inn near Svaldrin. They'd quickly dealt with the boy and had hauled the wretched woman back to Sunnavík. The trip had been a nightmare, the woman whining and pleading how she loved the farmhand, that she wanted free of her father. His temples had throbbed for the entire week-long journey. Jonas still remembered the relief at handing her back to her father. Sweet, glorious silence.

"Yes. Well, I've many embers to stamp out on this trip," muttered Magnus, drawing Jonas from his thoughts. "I gather you've heard of the damnable situation at the berskium mines?"

Rey pressed his fingers together once more. "I've heard rumors. It is grim?"

"Two foremen dead, the main shaft destroyed. The year's cache of berskium set to ruin. We'll need to arrange import from Norvaland or another Urkan colony." Magnus drew in a deep breath from his pipe, blowing it out slowly. "The king will not be pleased at this news. And do not start me on this...Slátrari character."

"Slátrari?" asked Jonas. "The butcher?"

Magnus tilted his head back and stared at the ceiling for a moment. "A murderer prowling this region." A vein pulsed in Magnus's pale temple. "Burns his victims from the inside. 'Tis unnatural. Between us, we believe he must be Galdra.

"But back to our dealings. Ivar Ironheart has a job that requires your skills." Magnus paused, staring at the roof. "There have been troubling affairs in the north. In Istré, a pile of shite near the border of Vestur and Nordur lands. It began with the vanishings of livestock. A sheep here, a cow there. Unconcerning, save for the blood flecking the animals left behind. Unfortunately, it was not long after that farmers began to disappear as well. There is evidence of violence and struggle. Blood spattered across walls, rooms torn to shreds. Claw marks across the floor as if they'd been dragged."

Rey and Jonas shared a look. This was gearing up to be far more interesting than a runaway jarl's daughter.

"We've had message by falcon from Istré, yet still we do not understand these happenings. The locals claim it is a thick, white mist." Magnus pinched the bridge of his nose.

"Mist?" repeated Rey.

Magnus sighed. "Oh, but there's more. They say the mist has the sound of a beating heart."

Jonas's brows dipped down.

Magnus continued. "The farmers claim that this mist pulses with a strange rhythm, like the beating of a heart. That it starts low and grows louder and louder. And then, it simply stops, leaving blood and missing people in its wake."

"But surely it must be a creature," said Jonas.

"No living person has seen a creature," said Magnus. "But I agree, it must be so. Have you heard of such a thing?"

"No." Rey pursed his lips, and silence stretched through the room.

"Could it be grimwolves?" interjected Jonas. "The claw marks..."

"Skógungar have impressive claws," mused Rey. "The forest walkers," he added, for Magnus's benefit. "But they're a peaceful lot unless provoked. Could the locals have angered them somehow? Ventured into their groves, cut down a sacred hjarta tree?"

Magnus shrugged. "I cannot say."

Rey shifted in his chair. "This mist is puzzling indeed. A heartbeat—it has the sound of something ancient."

Taking another puff of his pipe, Magnus blew it out and continued. "We sent a battalion of Klaernar from Kopa to assist a few weeks past." His voice trailed off, the corners of his lips dipping down. "An incident has occurred. The Klaernar's bodies were discovered in Istré's town square. They were...secured to Ursir's pillars by strange-looking vines. They'd been stabbed through the heart, though by something wider and rounder than a sword or dagger. And all around the bodies, a symbol was written in blood, over and over. A Sun Cross." Magnus's jaw flexed. "King Ivar has grown furious and has placed urgency on this task."

"Is it not the rebels?" asked Rey, scratching his black beard. "They seem the type to taunt King Ivar with the Volsik sigil."

Magnus shook his head. "Impossible to say for certain, but our watchers suggest the rebels were not near at the time."

Rey was silent a moment, staring at the roof. "It seems two different hands are at play," he murmured.

"Entirely different victims," added Jonas. "Are we certain they're the same attackers?"

Magnus sucked on his pipe, blowing a stream of smoke out slowly. "No. We cannot know. It is possible. The information we have is unreliable. You know the northmen...sundrunk in the summer and cabinmad in the winter. Their superstitions make it difficult to discern fact from fiction."

Jonas understood why Magnus had sought them out. Rey and his Bloodaxe Crew had established a reputation for dispatching particularly stubborn creatures.

Half a year earlier, they'd been sent out by Magnus to deal with a pack of blood-thirsty illmarr, the scaly vampires of the sea who'd been terrorizing the fishermen south of the capital. It had taken the Bloodaxe Crew weeks of research and planning before they discovered arrows fashioned from rowan wood were efficient at piercing their scales and they could lure the illmarr from the waters with buckets of eel blood. After that, it had been a simple task of picking them off one by one.

The mysterious pulsing mist, the missing livestock and farmers, the murdered Klaernar...now *this* felt like a challenge. Something different.

"You want us to discover what has stolen the farmers and killed the Klaernar," mused Rey, his fingers drumming on the curved arms of his chair, "and dispatch them."

"Yes. And we need this problem solved quickly so that seeds of discord do not spread. Do not disclose the nature of this job to anyone—locals or otherwise—particularly about the Klaernar and the Sun Cross. The Gothi in Istré has cleaned up the mess and has ordered a Letting to earn back Ursir's favor. And you must keep the details of this job secret, by sword if necessary."

Rey pressed his fingers together. If Jonas knew anything about the Bloodaxe Crew's headman, he knew Rey was running figures through his head. The fact that Magnus had traveled so far to see them meant that he specifically sought them out for this job. The fact that there were so many unknowns about their target, the secrecy, the risks and long journey...this one would pay big.

"It can be done," said Rey, his gaze unflinching, "but it is a long journey, and a job of great risk. Istré is a month's travel from here; we'll need provisions—"

"If you accept this job, Bjarg, you must leave tomorrow," said Magnus, leaning forward on the table. The air in the room seemed to crackle with intensity, but neither Rey nor Jonas looked away. "We've brought rhodium blades up with us from the treasury in Sunnavík. Let me know where your supply wagon is stored, and I'll arrange for them to be offloaded."

"Rhodium blades could prove helpful," murmured Rey.

Rhodium, the rare metal which was nearly unbreakable and particularly lethal to the type of creatures lurking in the Western Woods. Magnus was taking no chances.

"If you have need of extra warriors, Bjarg, you may contact the Klaernar garrison in Kopa. Kommandor Valf is under orders to provide men and whatever assistance you should require."

Jonas raised his eyebrows, his eagerness only growing. He knew Rey was already dreaming about ordering those kuntas around. He thanked the gods Rey had obtained special permission from Magnus to exclude his younger brother Ilías from recruitment to their ranks; as a second son, by law, he should have been conscripted at eighteen.

Rey paused. "First light tomorrow. That shall be a trial to accomplish. It *could* be done..."

"Pay is ten thousand sólas, with two thousand paid upon acceptance of the job." Magnus reached into the bag beside his chair, retrieved a linen sack, and dropped it onto the table surface with a heavy thud. Coins clinked together, echoing loudly in the room.

Jonas's heart might have stopped. His fingers gripped the arms of his chair. That was more coin than the Bloodaxe Crew had *ever* been paid. That kind of money... it was life-altering. His thoughts swirled, but Rey's low voice grounded him. "Jonas? Have you any concerns?"

Jonas shook his head. All he could think of were the sólas in that bag. Any other concerns had vacated him the second the coins hit the desk.

"Well then, Magnus," said Rey, extending his hand, "it is settled." Magnus grasped his arm below the elbow and nodded his head.

"It is settled."

———

"WELL, AXE EYES?" asked Ilías as Rey and Jonas approached the end of the long table occupied by the Bloodaxe Crew. Ilías made a space on the bench beside him, Jonas nodding at his younger brother as he took a seat. The mead hall was a beast, alive and roaring.

The last rays of sunlight streamed through the open windows onto rows of worn trestle tables lined with wooden benches; smoke from hearthfires and the scent of charred meat filled the air. Jonas guessed the eighth chime would sound soon, as it appeared the residents of Reykfjord had turned out in full force to drink their nightly fill; horns of ale, cups of mead and brennsa were passed out; warriors, merchants, and craftsmen sitting shoulder to shoulder, sharing tales and games of dice.

Jonas braced his hands on the table, looking around at Ilías, Sigrún, Hekla, and Gunnar. "Foulsome job. You'll all despise it."

"Truly?" asked Gunnar, his dark eyes narrowed, wide mouth pulled into a grimace. The golden light washed across him, glinting off the dark brown bridge of his nose and his thick black locs.

Jonas started ticking off fingers. "Mysterious vanishings, permission to order around the Klaernar, pays ten thousand sólas...awful, truly just—"

Sigrún inhaled sharply from across the table, the surprise plain in her penetrative brown eyes. Her long blonde braids were flipped to the left side of her head, exposing the glossy burn scars which climbed up her neck and along the right side of her skull. As surprise melted into excitement, a smile curved her lips, and Jonas matched it with his own.

"No," said Ilías, knocking Jonas on the shoulder. "If you're lying..."

Rey waved two fingers at the barkeep. "We shall raise a cup to this one."

What is the job? Sigrún signed in a rapid sequence of hand gestures. After five years spent traveling with her, interpreting was second nature to Jonas and the rest of the Bloodaxe Crew.

Rey leaned an elbow on the table. "Istré has a problem. We're to solve it."

"Where in the arse end of Íseldur is Istré?" asked Ilías, a little too loudly. Jonas could tell his younger brother had indulged in several horns of ale while awaiting their return.

Rey leveled Ilías with a look making whatever else he was about to say dry up in his mouth. "Hold your cursed tongue, Ilías, or I'll tie a line to your horse and drag you to Istré."

Ilías frowned. "Please. I'm as impenetrable as a shield wall."

Rey scowled. "Right. That is why you shared Gunnar's aversion to spiders with the whole of Svaldrin's mead hall."

"Think they can just crawl into your furs and make themselves at home," muttered Gunnar.

"Or when you placed herring in Hekla's bedding but couldn't keep silent long enough for her to find it...."

"You can still expect retribution for that," grumbled Hekla, tapping her metal fingers on the table.

"Or when you told Kraki every slanderous thought we'd ever shared in confidence—"

"All right, Axe Eyes, you're as subtle as a war hammer. You've made your point." Ilías cast a look at the roof, placing a hand over his heart. "I swear by the Almighty Bear God, by Malla's tits and Hábrók's hairy toes, I shall not speak a word of this."

Rey rolled his eyes, then leaned forward, beckoning the Crew closer. "Magnus has advised—this job must be kept silent, by any means necessary."

He relayed the details of the job in a low voice. "The rhodium blades shall be loaded into our supply wagon tonight, and we leave tomorrow at first light," he finished. "Our food kit should be adequate, but we'll replenish provisions in Svarti."

"Might I offer my assistance in sorting the wagon, Axe Eyes?" asked Ilías. Jonas fought back a smile. Always teasing, this brother of his.

"No hand touches the wagon but mine," snapped Rey, predictably.

"First light," mused Hekla, her amber eyes flitting to Jonas. "Certain you can manage, Wolf?"

Jonas straightened, smoothing a palm down the front of his favorite tunic—a fine-spun garment in blue which brought out his eyes. "Whatever do you mean, Hekla?"

Hekla smirked. "You know. Rósanna. Rósalind. I no longer bother to learn the names of your dalliances."

"Nor do I." Jonas's smile deepened. "I simply call her Red—I've learned that picking a distinctive feature is far easier than trying to recall a name."

Hekla shook her head, her lip curled. "Of course you would, Wolf. Don't stay up too late." Mischief flashed in her eyes. "Or *do* stay up. I'll collect wagers on your arrival time tomorrow. My coin will be placed on your tardiness."

"I'll be sure to retire early," said Jonas dryly. "My thanks, Mother."

The verbal equivalent of an elbow to the ribs had the desired effect. Hekla's mouth twisted into a snarl. "Do—not—call—me—that—" In two heartbeats, she had him in a headlock, wrenching him off the bench between the rows of tables. With the push of a button, silver claws protracted from her prosthetic arm and grazed dangerously against his throat. "Must I teach you *another* lesson, Jonas?"

"Did you damage your head, Hekla? I recall it was you learning the last time," said Jonas through clenched teeth. He kicked out low, knocking her off-balance. As Hekla tumbled backward, her hand fisted his tunic, pulling him down with her. Together, they crashed onto the table behind them.

The shattering of a clay cup and honeyed scent of mead indicated a drink had been a casualty of their games. He twisted himself free from Hekla's grip, just in time to see a small figure cloaked in red swishing between the tables, toward the door of the mead hall.

"Hai!" boomed the barkeep, unloading an army of clay cups filled with brennsa onto their table. "You'll frighten my patrons off with your antics! Knock it off or knock out." He jerked his thumb toward the door.

Hekla smoothed her black hair and climbed back onto the bench. "Our sincerest apologies, Leif. You'll soon be rid of us." She turned to the Crew, lifting a cup. "To battle glory and fortune."

The others drank back the liquid and slammed their cups down on the table.

"You'll be leaving?" came a silky voice from behind Jonas. A familiar slender hand curled over his shoulder. He turned, taking in Red's heavily lashed blue eyes and glossy red hair, the lower lip jutting out in a pout.

Blood warming at the sight of her, Jonas covered her hand with his. "Afraid so, Red."

He ignored Hekla's rolling eyes.

"We still have tonight." Jonas watched as Red's eyes darkened, and she brought her other hand to his nape, scratching her nails along his neck. He immediately started making plans for those nails, for those lips. Sliding his hand into her hair, Jonas pulled until her ear was right beside his lips. "Wait for me in the room," he whispered. "Wear the red underdress." Releasing her, he smiled to himself.

As she glided toward the lodgings at the rear of the mead hall, Jonas threw back a cup of whiskey.

I'll take that wager, Sigrún signed, pulling a throaty laugh from Hekla.

NINE

THE ROAD OF BONES

Ten thousand *sólas.*

As he rode along the Road of Bones, Jonas could not stop thinking of it. It was more than they'd ever been paid for a job. Nearly two thousand sólas per member of the Bloodaxe Crew. What that meant for Jonas, for Ilías? It meant they'd soon be able to retake what was rightfully theirs. For five years it had been Jonas's sole focus, the thing which kept him going when he woke up with a frosted beard, or when an illmarr managed to shred through his armor. After this job, he and his brother would be just short of it— a year, perhaps two more, and they'd have sufficient funds.

Jonas pulled the hammered silver talisman from his pocket. Rubbing his thumb along the ridged surface, he allowed himself to imagine it—he and Ilías in their shared longhouse, restored to its former glory. They'd start by replacing the beams. The roof would need fresh thatching, the stonework of the hearth to be re-cast, the outbuildings on the property razed and built from scratch.

As he tried to recall how the longhouse had looked when he was a boy, Jonas's mind could not help but drift to times long gone, and he was helpless as the memory took front and center in his mind:

Sitting at the bench of the long table, Jonas scraped his blade along the wood's edge, mesmerized by the curling ribbon as he shaped the tip of a sword. It wouldn't be long until he had finished this project, until he could teach Ilías the movements he'd studied from sparring warriors at the Spring Assembly.

Nearby, a pot hung over the crackling hearthfire, filling the longhouse with the scent of mutton stew. Across from him sat his mother, spinning wool on a distaff. She hummed as she worked, the sound surrounding him like a warm embrace.

"Beautiful, my little pup," said his mama, nodding at his sword. Pride filled Jonas's chest as he matched her smile with his own. "You'll make a fine swordsman one day."

"Do you think it?" asked Jonas, smoothing a sharp edge on the pommel.

"Oh yes," she murmured. "Just like your grandfather."

Jonas's hand found the talisman hanging around his neck. Family, respect, duty, *his grandfather had told Jonas as he'd handed him the hammered silver disk.* Your father is hopeless, and so it shall be your path to walk, Jonas. Swear it to me, pup. Swear on the talisman that you'll embody these values in all that you do.

I swear it on this talisman, grandfather, *Jonas had said solemnly. It was bare hours later that his grandfather's corpse lay cold on the bed, claimed by the consuming sickness he'd long fought.*

"Tell me tales of his battle glory, Mama," begged Jonas, though he knew them by heart.

"Very well," she said, a smile upon her lips. "He left to make a name for himself, long before I was born. But it is important to remember—"

"Yes, yes," said Jonas, impatient to get to the violent parts. "His heart remained here, on these lands. Our ancestors, his duty to the family, always called to him."

"Smart tongue you have," teased his mother.

A crash from outdoors set the hairs on the back of Jonas's neck on edge. No, he thought. It was too early for his father to have returned to the steading. But the foul curse bellowed from beyond the doors of the longhouse told him otherwise.

"Go," whispered his mother. "Find your brother, go to the elm tree. Do not come back until the sun is beyond the horizon."

Anger flared in Jonas's chest, and he brandished his wooden sword. "I will protect you."

His mother's face had drained of blood, her hands trembling. "No, my little pup. You must not. The last time...I cannot bear for him to turn his fists on you again. Go, I beg of you. Your brother needs you."

Guilt burned inside him as he recalled his shame. The last time he'd tried to intervene, his father had beaten Jonas unconscious. When he'd awoken, his mother had been bedridden for two days. What kind of a man was he, when he couldn't protect his own mother?

But the fear in her eyes forced Jonas to move to the back door. He paused in the doorway, his hand squeezing around the hilt of his carved sword. As the sound of his father bursting through the main door met his ears, Jonas fled.

Gritting his teeth, he tried to clear his mind. It was difficult, as always, to think of the future without the past pushing in. "Family, respect, duty," Jonas whispered soundlessly, forcing his thoughts to the future. Ilías would marry and carry on the Svik name. There would be children and laughter and peace. The forge restored, the lands worked back to prosperity. And Jonas...Jonas would be free. What would it feel like? That was more difficult for him to imagine.

Jonas was silent as the Crew meandered their horses along the Road of Bones, the wagon creaking behind Rey's white mare.

Hekla's voice pulled him from his thoughts. "My surprise to find you on time today, Jonas. Did Red not keep you awake all night after all?"

"A gentleman does not disclose," replied Jonas. In truth, she had kept him up late, though in part because Jonas had first made a trip to his hoard to bury their portion of the funds paid up front. The brothers had sólas stashed in all corners of Íseldur, and soon...soon, they would dig them up and buy back their lands. So it was only after reburying the chest beneath a stump on the outskirts of Reykfjord that Jonas had made his way to Red's quarters, finding her waiting in the dress, just as he'd requested.

"Gentleman?" snorted Hekla. "Then it cannot be you we speak of, Wolf."

Jonas bit down on his back teeth. "And you slept well, Hekla? No strapping young warrior to haul you over his shoulder?" *Or perhaps the reverse*, he wisely decided not to add.

She rolled her shoulders. "Malla's tits. You know I'll not be going back down *that* road." The black lines of her prosthetic arm glinted in the sunlight as if in agreement.

Jonas saw Gunnar shifting on his horse from the corner of his eye and smirked. Those two thought they were so sly.

"'Twas a love affair between Leif's supply of brennsa and I," Hekla continued. "Though Rey was of great assistance."

Rey let out a low sound of acknowledgment but kept his gaze straight ahead. Jonas assessed him, noting the ashen color of his headman's skin, the purple smudges beneath his eyes. Had Rey truly overindulged on brennsa?

How very unlike him to do anything to compromise his perfectly crafted control. Perhaps the sólas had him in a celebratory mood last night as well.

"Rey?" chuckled Jonas, "you're looking well."

Rey just grunted.

"Did not spend the evening arranging the wagon, then?"

"Should've," muttered Rey. "Why are the birds so rutting loud today?"

"Axe Eyes has just realized he's no longer a sprightly eighteen-year-old," chirped Ilías, far too perky for the time of day. In truth, Rey had seen only five winters more than Ilías's twenty-one. But in maturity, it seemed more like decades.

"You looking for *another* reminder that I'm your headman, Ilías No Beard?" growled Rey.

"I believe we settled on Ilías the Cunning," replied Ilías, stroking the wispy blond beard growing along his jaw. It *was* beginning to fill in, but was so fair it was difficult to see.

"Was it not Ilías Horse Breath?" asked Hekla with a cackle.

Ilías Believes Himself Invincible, signed Sigrún, Gunnar translating for her.

"Ilías Never Checks His Flank," Jonas added with a smirk.

He knew his brother would act affronted, but secretly delighted in these exchanges. Ilías's easygoing nature was something Jonas admired deeply and wished he himself had. As the older brother, the one who'd borne the burden of responsibility as long as he could remember, he'd never had a chance to develop such a nature.

"All right," exclaimed Ilías. "Enough. Let us have another Crew meeting and discuss it at the evening meal."

"I gather you didn't get a look at the metal?" Hekla asked Rey, tilting her head toward the wagon.

"No. 'Twas dark. Magnus reported four broadswords, eight daggers, three short swords." Rey winced. "Stableboy was drunk. They'd best all be there."

"What is the plan for this job?" asked Gunnar, sidling between Hekla and Jonas's mounts.

Rey was silent for a moment. "This one shall require additional scouting. We'll survey the locations of the abductions and speak to locals. We must observe this...mist. Determine if it is indeed cloaking creatures. We'll determine numbers, strength, formations, strategy, and then create a plan of attack."

Mist with a heartbeat, signed Sigrún, Ilías repeating it aloud for the whole of the Crew to hear. *Claw marks. Blood. These are feeble details.*

"And the Sun Cross," added Jonas. "The Klaernar corpses."

The more he considered it, the more the Sun Cross and the dead Klaernar did not fit with the other murders. The Sun Cross was the Volsik's sigil and suggested support of their line.

The Urkans were Sea Kings to some and a plague to others. They raided and conquered, mercilessly crushing all who stood in their way. It had been seventeen years since King Ivar had seized the throne of Íseldur, and most in the kingdom had moved on with their lives. Yet Jonas knew there were some who harbored bitter resentment against King Ivar.

It was impossible to forget the brutal affair with the Volsik family seventeen years ago. After usurping the throne, King Ivar had mandated the public's attendance in the pits of Askaborg castle where King Kjartan, Queen Svalla, and their young daughter, Princess Eisa, were strung on pillars. Svalla and Eisa had met quick deaths at the point of Ivar's sword. But Kjartan...he'd suffered a long, painful death. Through the mead halls it had been whispered—Kjartan Volsik's back had been sliced open, ribs splayed wide, and with final nauseating flourish, his lungs had been draped outside of his body, like the gory wings of a bird. A blood eagle, the Urkans called it. But they'd also whispered that, much to King Ivar's chagrin, King Kjartan had faced death with dignity, not a scream slipping from his lips.

Only one of the great Volsik line had survived the sacking of Sunnavík—five year old Princess Saga, raised as Ivar's ward and future bride for his son Bjorn.

Undoubtedly, there were Volsik supporters scattered across the kingdom, and with the Sun Cross painted in blood, it was no wonder King Ivar wanted this dealt with swiftly.

Rey's voice pulled Jonas from his thoughts. "Kraki has the guide on Íseldur's creatures. Loathe as I am to suggest it, that book might hold the key to understanding this mist."

A chorus of groans filled the air.

"How, exactly, do you propose to convince him to hand it over, Axe Eyes?" demanded Hekla.

Rey let out a long exhale. "I was hoping *please* would suffice."

"Not a chance," said Gunnar. "Not after we ousted him. Kraki holds his grudges tighter than his cup of brennsa. We'll need to be cunning to get the information."

"Do your contacts in Svarti have a copy of the book, Rey?" asked Jonas.

Anything to avoid trekking several days off the Road of Bones to see the cranky former leader of the Bloodaxe Crew.

Rey was silent a moment. "I do not believe so. The book was rare to start with, and most copies have been destroyed through the years by the Klaernar. I will ask them, but Kraki has the only surviving copy that I'm aware of."

"Perhaps a distraction," mused Hekla. "One to divert his attention while the other lifts the book."

"Kraki's too clever for that," said Jonas. "The moment he sees us, he'll slam the door in our faces. There must be another way. A way to get him to drop his guard."

"Well," grumbled Rey, "we have a long ride before Skalla Ridge to figure it out."

———

THE BLOODAXE CREW continued down the road for several more hours. As the sun dropped lower in the sky and the shadows began to stretch across the Road of Bones, Sigrún whistled twice from the front of the pack. The Crew pulled off the road, following a goat track through the trees, down a hill, and into a grassy glade sprinkled with tiny white flowers. After dismounting, Sigrún trudged back to smear out the wagon and horse tracks with a branch.

The rest of the Crew settled into the comfort of their nightly routine. Jonas scoured the woods for sticks and branches. Summer meant the sun would be up long into the evening, and he could easily make out Ilías pulling saddles, Hekla and Gunnar brushing down the horses, and Sigrún arriving back and drawing supplies from her saddlesack. He carried an armload of logs from the forest and had them chopped with a few swift swings of the axe, then set to digging out the fire pit.

"Rey, where's the tinderbox?" Jonas asked, searching through the supply bag.

"Picked up a fresh firestone in Reykfjord. Wagon—food kit."

Getting to his feet, Jonas rounded the wagon. He loosened the leather straps which tethered the blanket overtop and, in one fluid motion, yanked it back—

And stared into a pair of widened brown eyes.

TEN

After a night and full day in total darkness, the light was blinding. Silla froze, the hammer clutched to her chest. She couldn't see anything, but she heard him—a man.

The man cursed, then grabbed her collar and hauled her from the wagon, dropping her roughly onto her feet. The unmistakable press of cold steel dug in just below her jaw, and a hand gripped her neck, pinning her against the wagon. As pain flared sharply from her bruised throat, she cried out, the man's grip thankfully loosening.

Silla blinked several times, and her eyes finally adjusted, bringing the man's familiar face into focus. He looked like a prince from a skald's tale, handsome and almost boyish, golden hair and eyes so blue they seemed unreal. But the scar on his cheek and beard added a rugged touch, telling tales of a hard life spent with a blade in hand. As she took in this man, tall, and broad, with the build of a warrior, a flush crept up her neck. Silla opened her mouth to say something but found speech beyond her grasp.

The man's eyes settled on her bruised cheek, then traveled down her neck. His hand moved away from the bruising, rough calluses sliding slowly down the column of her throat, stopping only at the base. As his thumb pressed into the place where her pulse pounded feverishly, Silla flinched.

"You're right to be frightened." The man's gaze continued downward.

"Drop the...hammer?" His lips teased a smile, but his grip on her neck tightened. "Drop it."

Nerves jittering through her, Silla released the hammer, and it fell to the ground with a soft thud. Staring at this man with golden hair and golden skin, her breaths shallowed. All day she'd practiced what she'd say upon her discovery, but now that the moment was here, her mind was utterly blank.

Halfwit! she thought. *Say something.*

The man made a sound of disapproval. "Rey!" he called out. "We've a problem here."

There was a swirl of motion from behind the blond man; soft footsteps, the rustle of clothing, and the familiar slide of metal as swords were unsheathed. Within moments, the group surrounded her, and she squirmed under their scrutiny, a butterfly whose wings were pinned.

"Your red cloak...you were at the mead hall," said the golden man.

Her mouth opened and closed, and then she finally found her voice. Unfortunately, it fell out of her in a jumbled rush. "I-I heard you in the mead hall. Kopa—I must get to Kopa, and my map shows Istré is quite near. It's perfect... you could drop me on your way! I can cook or wash your socks or feed your horses treats. I'm not good at building fires, but I could learn. I'm—"

She locked eyes with the giant of a man she'd followed to the stables, and her voice died in her throat. Peeking from beneath his collar, tattoos swirled, inky black against coppery brown skin. His black hair was shorn short on the sides, and it pushed out from his crown in thick, tight curls that caught the last light of the day, while his beard had been trimmed so neatly it had to have been done this morning. But most striking of all were his eyes—mahogany and so sharp with anger she could feel the scrape of them along her skin. *Ashes*, she thought. Were all these people beautiful? This man's handsomeness, however, was marred by the look of total disgust twisting his face.

Behind him, a rangy blond man with a wispy beard bit down on his fist, his eyes shut in what appeared to be a fit of silent laughter. On his other side stood a woman whose hair was shorn close on the sides, the top braided back. Her skin was a warm golden hue a few shades darker than Silla's own, and her full lips were pressed together as if she too were trying to suppress a smile.

"Search her," ordered the tattooed man. His voice was so deep the tiny hairs on Silla's arms stood on end.

The lanky blond man waved his hand eagerly. "I volunteer!"

"Shut your mouth, Ilías, or I'll do it for you," growled the man. Ashes, but he was tall, a half head taller than all the rest, and Silla surmised he was the leader. He turned to a short woman with delicate features, blonde hair shaved on one side. "Sigrún."

The golden man held her against the wagon while Sigrún stepped forward. As she neared, Silla got a better view. Her eyes traced the shining, striated marks curving up Sigrún's neck and along the base of her skull—burn scars by the looks of them. Her ash blonde hair was braided in a neat row along the edge of the shaved section, with a second, larger braid along her crown. As Sigrún reached for Silla, she noted that the burns scars reached all the way down to her left hand. Sigrún pulled up the sleeve of Silla's dress, examining the underside of her wrist.

"I'm a free woman," Silla murmured, realizing what it was she searched for —the thrall mark, tattooed onto the wrists of the enslaved. The blonde woman slid the sleeve back down, then began to pat Silla down. "I do have a dagger at my ankle."

Silence stretched uncomfortably as Sigrún's hands moved down Silla's torso, over her breasts, and down her stomach, pausing at her hips as she prodded the coin purse in the hidden pocket. Her hands jumped down to Silla's ankle, unsheathing the dagger and passing it to the leader. The man turned it over in his hands, frowning. Sigrún worked her way upward, and Silla's face flushed as the woman's hands moved beneath her skirts.

Finally, Sigrún stepped back, making a quick succession of curious hand gestures to the leader.

"Bag," growled the tattooed giant of a man.

The golden man leaned over Silla's shoulder, peering into the wagon. As his scent filled her nostrils with iron and leather and...well...*man*, Silla's body flushed warm. He pulled out her sack, handing it to the leader.

A protest threatened from the back of her throat, but Silla swallowed it back and watched silently as the leader pulled out her clothing and her father's tunic. Pausing to look at the heart-shaped rock, he threw her an incredulous look before tossing it to the ground with the rest of her things.

The man turned to her, his dark eyes searing into her skin. "No food, no water. No clothing to protect you from the elements. Do you even know what road you're on?"

Silla took in a shaky breath. "Th-the Road of Bones."

"And do you know why it's called the Road of Bones?"

She shook her head.

"It is paved with the bones of travelers who never made it to their destination. It is dangerous. Desolate. And not for the weak."

"I'm not weak," she managed, though her stupid voice wobbled.

They stood in silence for a moment, staring at one another. Then with movement so sudden she hadn't a chance to react in time, the huge man stepped forward and gripped her chin. He lowered himself to her level and stared at her with eyes so intense she yearned to look away. But she didn't. Some instinct told her that she needed to hold his gaze, needed to prove to him that she wasn't weak.

"Tell me why you're where you shouldn't be," he rumbled.

She held his gaze, unflinching. "I need to get to Kopa."

"Tell me why I shouldn't leave you on the side of the road."

She swallowed. "Because I would more than likely die if you did."

He laughed, but the sound was humorless and hollow. "You think the Bloodaxe Crew cares of death? We're already up to our necks in blood, girl."

The Bloodaxe Crew? thought Silla with a shiver. The name stirred a vague memory, something mentioned around the cookfires. A small, but violent crew who could take on anything from outlaws to dark creatures, and left no survivors. *Oh porridge*, she thought. Of all the wagons it could have been, she'd crawled into *theirs*. And in that moment, Silla knew—if she wanted to live, she'd need to be cunning.

The leader's eyes surveyed her cheek, then moved down her throat. As he took in the bruising on her neck, his face soured.

"I can help you," she said, a desperate thought taking root in her mind. "I can help you with that man. Kraki."

The man's eyes met hers with a look so dark it seemed to slice into her skin. "What did you say?"

"I can help you get that book you need."

Her heart pounded louder than a war drum as something shifted behind the man's eyes. "You heard us?"

"Y-yes," Silla managed.

He cast a look at the skies, then grabbed the golden man's dagger, and pressed it tighter to her throat. "Then I'll have no choice but to kill you."

"Wait!" Silla pleaded. Her offer had not been received the way she'd expected, and now her mind scrambled for something—for anything. "Wait, I can help you!"

"We're under orders to keep this job quiet, by blades if we must. But perhaps you're not clever enough to understand what that means."

Desperate words spilled from her. "If there's one talent I have, it's speech. My father always said I've a tongue more golden than an Urkan skald." It was a lie, of course. If anything, Silla's talent lay in speaking before firmly forming thought, as had clearly just occurred. But the words had started, and there was no stopping them now. "If you kill me, you'll have to find another way to convince Kraki. I can help you. Let me distract him for you, or try to draw the information right from him. A plan in case he does not have the book you need."

The giant of a man stared at her as he considered her words. Silla held her lips together to prevent any more words from falling out.

"No," he said, pressing the blade deeper.

"What's the risk to you?" Silla asked, her voice wrenched higher. "Who will I tell out here on this road? Take me to Kraki, and I'll prove my worth. I *will* get you this book."

The leader's eyes roamed her face, settling on the scar beside her left eye. The urge to squirm beneath the weight of his gaze was nearly unbearable, but Silla forced herself to remain still, counting her breaths. One breath. Two. Three.

"Rey," said the golden man. "You cannot be considering this."

The leader's eyes flicked to his companion. "She does seem the type to catch his eye." His gaze drifted to Silla's hair, then back to her face once more. Releasing her chin, the leader stepped back, rubbing his neck. "I will consider your offer. You will live for tonight." Turning, he strode away with long, loping strides. "Bind her!" he barked over his shoulder.

Silla sucked in a breath and held out her hands for the golden man to restrain with a length of rope produced from the wagon.

"Don't get comfortable, Curls," he said with a scowl. The man bound her hands together—tightly, she noted—with a long length dangling free at the end.

"The rope told me as much," she grumbled in reply, staggering after him as he tugged on the free end.

"I cannot believe he's considering it," the man muttered.

They reached the edge of the glade, and he yanked her down, pushing her back against the twisting trunk of a tree. After securing the free length of rope to the tree, the man squatted down, his face less than a foot from hers. His hand delved into his pocket, pulling out a silver disk and rubbing his thumb over it as he watched her.

Silla was unable to look away as the full weight of the warrior's gaze settled on her face. His breath clouded the air between them. "You think you can climb into our wagon and we'll simply give you a free ride?"

"I can help—"

The man clenched the talisman in his fist. "That's not how this world works. You must *earn* your own way."

"I'm a hard worker—"

A line formed between his brows, and he shook his head slowly. "Axe Eyes will come to his senses. He'll never agree to let you live." The warrior stood to his full, impressive height, then ambled off, leaving Silla bound to the tree.

She drew in a long breath, her heart thudding loudly in her chest.

"Rallying cry, Silla," she whispered to herself. "You are still breathing." She could not think of anything else. But in this moment, it was all that mattered.

———

HER HANDS BOUND to the linden tree, Silla maneuvered her body to get a clear view of the Bloodaxe Crew as they set up their camp for the night. The golden warrior had the fire built now, bedrolls were arranged in the long grass of the glade, crates pulled from the wagon and arranged near the flames.

It had been entirely more straightforward than she could have imagined. After much deliberation, Silla had spent two of her precious sólas on a map of Íseldur and had spent the afternoon studying it. The Road of Bones ran due north from Reykfjord in a nearly straight line, passing through the thick forests of Sudur lands, then the barren Hálendi of Eystri lands, ending in a town by the name of Skutur. Then, she'd hook westward on a short stretch labeled the Black Road before crossing the Hvíta River into Kopa. To her surprise, there were numerous volcanoes labeled along the Black Road. Silla had frowned as her finger traced the triangular volcano symbol drawn beside Kopa. Surely it was a misprint.

After studying the map in the quietude of her quarters at the Owl's Hollow Inn, Silla had crept to the mead hall adjacent. She'd eaten a barely-edible bowl of fish stew and nursed a cup of mead. Her fingers had drummed her clay cup as she pondered her next step. And then, the answer had fallen into her lap—or crashed into her from behind.

She'd been beside herself with glee: a wagon heading directly past Kopa, and the men had led her straight to it in the stables behind the Owl's Hollow Inn. Silla should have known it was too easy to be good.

She had not anticipated that she'd climbed into the supply wagon of the notorious Bloodaxe Crew, nor that they worked a job for King Ivar. As she'd listened to them discuss the job they were to accomplish in Istré from under the wagon's cover, unease had settled in her stomach. Silla pulled her lower lip between her teeth as she considered this complication. They worked for the king—she'd never be able to trust them. But that seemed the least of her worries right now.

Revealing that she'd overheard the details of their job had been an unexpected gamble, and now she feared it had sealed a grim fate for her.

For the hundredth time this day, Silla chastised herself for rashly following the leader of this group and the shorter, resplendently-dressed man out to the stable. She should have done more research and waited for a better option—should have lingered and learned what kind of warriors these were.

It was too late now.

Her hands were growing numb, her vision warped—she hadn't eaten or drunk for a full day. The woman with the black braid approached, her face stern but not unfriendly. She dropped into a crouch and peered at Silla.

"What is your name, dúlla?" *Dúlla.* It was a term of endearment Silla's mother had used, and it immediately put her at ease.

"Katrin." The lie dripped from her tongue smoothly. Silla had had so many different names at this point in her life, it was second nature to her.

"I'm Hekla. You know who Ilías is," she gestured to the blond man, talking animatedly at the fire. "You know Sigrún. There's Gunnar, Rey, and Jonas." Silla nodded as Hekla listed off the names, pointing to each individual.

"Where are you from?"

"Skarstad—"

"That's enough, Hekla," ordered the enormous man—Rey. "Not another word until I've decided her fate."

"Giving her water, Axe Eyes," the woman called over her shoulder. "If you intend to kill her, do it honorably. Thirst is a poor death." Hekla muttered something under her breath as she put a waterskin between Silla's bound hands. Unable to get a grip on it, it tumbled to the grass. "Curse the Wolf and his knots," muttered Hekla, working to loosen the strands of rope.

"Oh," moaned Silla as the blood flowed into her fingers. Hekla placed the waterskin back into her hands, and Silla raised it to her lips.

"My thanks," gasped Silla, after she'd nearly drained it empty. With a wordless nod, Hekla took the waterskin and strode back to the group.

Repositioning herself with her back to the tree, Silla watched Sigrún set an iron tripod over the fire. She fitted it with a trammel hook, hanging a blackened pot over the flames, then tossed in several sausages—elk by the looks of them. It wasn't long before a distinctively burnt smell reached Silla's nostrils, her stomach growling all the same.

Jonas and Rey were immersed in an intense discussion—about Silla's offer, she assumed. Her gaze fell to Ilías and Gunnar, huddled over a game of dice. Laughter burst from them; then they grew quiet as they glanced her way. Hekla sat alone, staring blankly into the fire. As Silla's eyes fell to the woman's hand, she realized that it was metal.

Silla watched Sigrún serve up the evening meal in wooden bowls—burnt sausage and plain bread. Gunnar bit into his sausage. He chewed. And chewed. And *chewed*. His swallow was so loud she heard the wet sound of it across the clearing. Nearby, Rey winced as his throat bobbed. It seemed as though he'd given up on chewing and swallowed all the same. A bubble of hope swelled inside Silla. If they gave her a chance, they could eat like royalty.

The summer sun was still up but low in the sky, and a chill had settled in the air. Silla's cloak was still on the ground where Rey had discarded it while rifling through her bag. She'd need something to cover her tonight, or she'd risk freezing.

A dull ache in her temples throbbed. Her body's response was instinctive—her insides braced against the imminence of pain, and her mind careened to the vial hanging around her neck.

Leaves.

Though she thought of them through the day, now that night had settled, now that she'd been discovered, she could relax into their comfort. With great difficulty, Silla worked her bound hands around the vial hanging from her neck. The smooth metal was a reassuring tether to the old and familiar amongst these frightening new surroundings. Flipping the stopper up, she used her teeth to grip one of the leaves and pull it free before replacing the lid.

Silla chewed the bitter leaf.

One more.

Closing her eyes, she fought the impulse to grab another leaf. Now was not the time to dull her wits completely. Leaning against the tree trunk, Silla waited for the skjöld to take effect.

Shick.

Shick.

Shick.

Her lids flew open, her gaze colliding with dark eyes across the fire—Rey's eyes. They watched her as he worked the blade of a hevrít across a whetstone, causing a shiver to crawl down her spine.

Shick.

"This one would be pleasing to the eye if he wasn't so mean," said the little blonde girl in her torn white nightdress, tiny beside Rey's enormous form. The girl traced a finger over Rey's shoulder. "And he's *huge.*"

Silla tried to control her breathing.

Shick.

"This one is funny," the girl continued, squinting over Ilías's shoulder. "I like him. Cheats at dice, though."

Shick.

She moved toward Jonas whose dagger dragged along a small piece of wood, shaping it into something she could not discern. "This one looks like a hero whose tales are recited by the skalds." She sighed, petting the golden warrior's head. The girl leaned down, inhaling. "Oh, you're right, Silla. He smells divine."

Shick.

Silla's face heated, and she closed her eyes. When she opened them, the girl had settled on the ground beside her, folding her scrawny legs up and wrapping her arms around them.

"What is the purpose of you?" asked Silla once more. She kept her voice soft so that it would not carry. "To worsen my troubles? To drive me to madness?"

"How will you convince them?" asked the girl, ignoring her question.

"I've done all I can. My fate rests in their hands. *His* hands."

Shick.

Her eyes flew back to the large man by the fire. Each pass of his blade across the whetstone seemed a quiet threat directed her way.

"What if he decides to kill you?" asked the girl, pushing the matted hair off her face.

"Then I've made a horrible mistake."

A shadow fell across her body and Silla flinched.

"Who do you speak to?"

"No one," breathed Silla, flushing. "Just...myself." She forced a smile to her lips. "A silly habit."

Hekla squatted down, handing Silla her sack and a musty-scented fur.

"So you do not freeze to death," said Hekla in a low voice, a smile teasing her lips.

"My thanks," managed Silla. As she pulled the cloak over herself, layering the fur on top, two strips of smoked elk fell to the ground. Her lips parted, her eyes darting to Hekla—already she was halfway to the fire.

Silla reached for the smoked meat, and for the first time since her discovery in the wagon, she smiled.

ELEVEN

REYKFJORD

Skraeda strode into the longhouse, two dozen tattooed faces turning to watch her at once. Like all Klaernar garrison halls, the Reykfjord branch was sparsely furnished—a great table in the central hall where they took their meals; a hearth where they gathered to drink ale after patrol; smaller rooms at the front of the longhouse used for instructional sessions or, in today's case, interrogations.

Pressing her lips together, Skraeda ignored the stares—in the years she'd worked for the queen, she'd grown used to them. With the exception of Kommandor Thord, the rest of these Klaernar did not know her as Galdra, though it was likely they wondered how she was so adept at drawing admissions. Skraeda had an arrangement with the Klaernar of Reykfjord—she would wrest confessions from those they brought in, and in exchange, she claimed the most interesting amongst them for the queen.

Of course, ample sólas and the threat of a slit throat had ensured that Queen Signe's interest in the Galdra would never reach her husband's ears. What King Ivar would do should he realize his own wife broke his laws, that she had stolen hundreds of Galdra away for her own purposes, Skraeda could not guess.

One of the Klaernar stood, a bear pelt draped around his shoulders—Kommandor Thord. Striding to her, his mouth was a hard line. "Skraeda Clever

Tongue," he greeted her, beckoning her into one of the chambers at the front of the house.

Small and sparsely furnished, it was a room Skraeda had used frequently before. Rush torches mounted on the walls cast light upon the woman sitting on a chair in the middle of the room. The woman's arms were bound behind her back, her pleas muffled by the iron bridle these Klaernar so loved to use.

"Yes," said Skraeda, her eyes settling on the small mole on the woman's forehead. "This is her. I remember her now."

"I'm pleased to hear that," said the Kommandor, finally with the respect in his voice she knew she deserved. "Thanks to your information, it was not a challenge to find her."

After days with no sign of the curly-haired girl, Skraeda had stewed with anger—how could she have slipped through her fingers? The problem had been the fear; the Klaernar inspired so much fear in the population, it had been difficult to sense anyone who stood out.

When she'd pointed that out to Kommandor Thord, he'd simply said, "It is our job. A healthy dose of fear keeps rebellions at bay."

Once, Skraeda too had been among those who feared the Klaernar. Now, she saw them for what they were: witless beasts on the leash of the king, of Magnus Hansson.

After three days on the bridge, they'd called off the search. But it nagged at Skraeda—this unshakeable feeling that she'd missed something. Staring at the rafters above her bed, she'd run through the days in her mind. "Curly hair," she'd murmured. "Curly hair." It could be easily concealed by braiding it back or wearing a hood...

An image flashed in mind—a girl in the back of a wagon, her face smeared with dirt, the hood of her red cloak pulled up over her head. Could that have been her? Had she sensed fear from the girl?

"I sensed fear in her," Skraeda had said, "though the boy beside her—his anger was distractingly loud." Neither of which had been out of the ordinary. But the scar...what of that? "I did not see a scar, but she was so filthy she looked as though she'd bathed with the pigs..." Skraeda had forced an image of the girl into her mind. Red hood. Strange vial tethered around her neck. Chickens— baskets of chickens stacked all around her. And...small, speckled eggs. Winterwing eggs.

"She rode in on a wagon delivering chickens and winterwing eggs to the wharf," Skraeda had told the kommandor after bursting into the garrison hall.

His eyes had flared at that—winterwing eggs were a rare delicacy, and this detail was sure to identify the woman.

But Skraeda's stomach had hollowed out as she'd waited. The girl had slipped right under her nose, and Her Highness would not be pleased. She was to be apprehended at all costs, and Skraeda had failed her. "I will find her," Skraeda had vowed to herself. "I will set things right."

And now here they were, with the woman in custody. The Klaernar had tracked her to a farmstead nearby, returning her to Reykfjord so that Skraeda could question her.

"Where is the boy?" asked Skraeda.

The woman's gaze turned dagger-sharp.

"Boy?" asked the kommandor. "There was no sign of a boy."

Skraeda examined the woman—her homespun wool dress was pitted with small holes, her boots in need of replacement several years past. Despite her shortcomings, the woman held her spine remarkably straight.

"Remove the bridle," said Skraeda, pacing the room to examine the woman from all sides. Wild coils of anger looped from her, twining with smaller threads of fear. Curious that the woman was angrier than she was afraid. Very curious, indeed.

The kommandor loosened the bolt at the back of the bridle and lifted the iron contraption from the woman's head. Skraeda rounded to the front of the woman, sinking into the chair across from her. Red markings curved around the woman's jaw and beneath her nose where the bridle had sat upon her face.

"What is your name?" Skraeda asked.

It was always best to begin with easy questions—to gain a sense of a captive's emotions. As Skraeda expected, the woman clamped her mouth shut, the ribbon of anger burning brighter. But beneath it, Skraeda found the thread of fear, and she jerked it to her roughly.

Satisfaction spread through her as she watched the woman's eyes widen, then flutter. Her head soon fell back as her breathing quickened, whatever memory Skraeda had summoned taking over her consciousness. It was a trick she'd learned over the years of mastering her Solacer skill. She could enhance or dampen emotions, yes, but when she pulled on a thread tightly enough, she'd discovered memories associated with that emotion could be drawn forth as well.

The woman blinked, and when her pupils dilated, Skraeda knew she was back on firm ground with them.

"We can do this the easy way or the hard way," said Skraeda slowly.

"Y-you…" the woman spluttered. Her pulse fluttered at the base of her throat, and Skraeda knew the echoes of her most terrible memory clung to the woman. "You're Galdra!" Her eyes darted to Kommandor Thord. "Why haven't you put her to the pillar?"

Skraeda kept her gaze steady. She enjoyed this part of the interrogation—when the accused realized she was no ally. When they looked to the Klaernar for salvation.

As expected, the kommandor was unmoved. "She has proven herself quite helpful," he murmured from behind Skraeda.

The woman sent Skraeda a glare which could shatter stone. "You are a traitor to your kind," she spat.

Traitor, Ilka's words echoed in her mind. *Traitor. Traitor. Traitor.*

The thread of fear grew slippery in her mind's grasp as anger kindled in Skraeda's veins. She shook her head, forcing in a calming breath.

"I am an opportunist," mused Skraeda, mastering her own emotions. "I do what I must to survive." She leaned forward, bracing her elbows on her knees. "What. Is. Your. Name?"

The woman pressed her lips shut, shaking her head vigorously.

Skraeda smiled, yanking on the thread of fear once more. The woman gasped, letting out a low wail as her head fell back. They always did this…forced her to show them what would happen when they did not provide the answers she needed. And Skraeda would admit that she relished this part of the process.

"No," moaned the woman, her limbs beginning to tremble.

Skraeda wondered what she saw—a loved one's last breath? The violent act of a husband? A terrible accident?

After several long seconds, the woman gasped again, her head jerking up and eyes fluttering open.

"Vigdis," breathed the woman, her pulse racing even faster now.

Skraeda was somewhat disappointed. The woman had confessed so easily. *We are not here to play,* she reminded herself. *We are here to find the girl.*

"Vigdis," repeated Skraeda. "Where is the boy? Your nephew, if I recall."

The thread of fear looped and coiled until it surpassed anger in breadth and brightness. Skraeda allowed her senses to reach out, to thumb gently along it. A reminder.

"You will not find him," said Vigdis, her anger growing once more.

Skraeda smiled. A thrall to her emotions, this woman was. "And what of your *niece*, Vigdis?"

Confusion landed first in the woman's expression, followed soon by understanding.

"Yes," said Skraeda. "You knew we sought that woman, and yet you shielded her." Anger scratched up Skraeda's throat...this woman was the reason she'd been deceived. The reason she'd been shamed in her queen's eyes. "Where is she, Vigdis?" she asked, strumming on the thread of the woman's fear. "The woman who rode in the back of your wagon. She wore a red cloak."

Vigdis's breathing quickened, pulse racing anew. "I do not know," she rasped. "I left her at the wharf and have not seen her since."

Skraeda's own anger flared, and Vigdis's fear slipped through her fingers.

Control yourself, she urged. *Do not let your emotions best you.* After counting to ten, she searched for Vigdis's fear anew.

"What did she tell you?" Skraeda gritted. She grew tired of these games already. The girl needed to be found, needed to be bundled onto a Sunnavík-bound ship before the queen discovered Skraeda's mistake.

Vigdis pulled her lips around her teeth, her eyes lifting to the rafters.

Skraeda tugged on the thread of her fear, not hard enough to bring forth a memory, but just hard enough to remind Vigdis what was at stake.

"I'm not unreasonable, Vigdis," said Skraeda softly. "I will leave your nephew out of this, but only if you tell me everything you know of the girl." She strummed on the woman's fear, watching her pupils dilate, the muscles of her neck strain. "If you do not, Vigdis, I will make things very unpleasant for you. And then, we will find your nephew, and make things very unpleasant for him. Like all Klaernar kommandors, Thord here has been instructed in the art of the blood eagle. Do you think your nephew's heart would give out before his lungs were pried from his chest, or would he live through the whole ordeal?"

"North," spluttered Vigdis. "The girl goes north on the Road of Bones."

"Where," she demanded.

Vigdis shook her head. "She did not say. I swear it to you, on my life..."

Skraeda watched in satisfaction as the woman's brows drew together, a thread of guilt spooling larger. "Oh, Vigdis," cooed Skraeda. "You did what you had to. And now I will grant you the mercy of a quick death." Drawing her hevrít, she slashed it across the woman's throat, looking deep into Vigdis's eyes as they widened then gradually dulled.

The kommandor huffed behind her. "We could have used her for our quota. She could have been put to the pillar."

Skraeda felt the touch of the man's irritation on the air, and her skin prickled. *It is a man's world in which we live, Skraeda,* her queen had told her, in that calming voice of hers. *Let them think us lambs, when truly, we are wolves.*

Lamb, Skraeda was not, and she did not for a second believe the kommandor thought her one.

Wiping her blade clean on the dead woman's skirts, she turned to examine him more closely. Without Vigdis's blaring emotions to drown them out, she could sense the kommandor more easily. Irritation, yes, but also fear, and...oh... a touch of lust. Now that was interesting. But beneath the rippling filaments of Kommandor Thord's emotions was the golden thread—thin and delicate, and the one of most interest to Skraeda.

The urge to draw it to her, to play with this thread, was strong. Long had she pondered the purpose of the golden filament, unique to only the Klaernar. But, duty called, and she needed the Klaernar on her side—needed to appease his pitiful male emotions. And so, she smiled at the kommandor instead.

"This must be kept quiet," said Skraeda. "The queen will send recompense for your time and discretion, Kommandor."

Skraeda made her way to the door.

"Where do you go?" asked Kommandor Thord.

She paused in the doorway. "I go north. I will travel the Road of Bones."

TWELVE

THE ROAD OF BONES

T he little blonde girl was there.

Disheveled hair clung to her sweat-dampened forehead, her upturned blue eyes wide. Silla grasped the girl's cold and clammy hand.

Footsteps sounded in the distance, echoing off the walls, growing louder—they were approaching.

The girl ran her free hand across Silla's cheek. "Look at me," she whispered. "Just breathe. We're not alone. Malla and Marra watch over us." Indeed, light from the sister moons shone through the window, a pillar of milky light stretching across the stone floor. Under the table, the two girls cowered, their little bodies pressed together.

Silla did as instructed. She looked into her eyes, then breathed in deeply through her nose, out through her mouth.

"One. Two. Three. Four. Five."

It almost felt as though it would work for a second.

The footsteps reverberated harshly off the walls now. They would be here soon. There were so many of them. Silla screwed her eyes shut.

They know where we are.

Her grip on the girl's hand tightened. The door burst open, and Silla opened one eye— just a sliver. Just enough to see feet...too many feet. They were surrounded by the sounds of shuffling boots, the scraping of wood against stone as furniture was moved around.

And then it happened—just as it had every time before.

The girl was yanked backward, her hand ripped free from Silla's. A high-pitched scream erupted from her throat.

A sound which would haunt Silla long after she awoke.

"Don't leave me!" the girl cried.

Hands wrapped around Silla's waist, and she was pulled away from the girl. She opened her own mouth.

And screamed.

———

"CURLS," said Jonas, shaking the woman's shoulder as he knelt beside her.

Her dark, arched brows drew together, lips parting as she made to scream once more. Cursing under his breath, Jonas slid his palm over her mouth, giving her a not-so-gentle shake. Still, she did not stir.

He clenched his teeth together, glaring at her. This troublesome woman had been with them for bare hours, and already she was causing problems. If she were to scream once more, she might draw the beasts from the forest. He placed his mouth beside her ear, but grew distracted by the smell of her hair—sweetness mixed with the scent of the forest.

Vampire deer, Jonas reminded himself. *Grimwolves.* If he had to draw his blades in the arse hours of the night, he'd kill her himself. Curse Rey and his indecision. What in the eternal fucking fires had his headman been thinking? The Bloodaxe Crew had a reputation to uphold. They could not afford to hand out free rides...especially not when there were thousands of sólas on the line.

"Katrin!" he whispered, proud of himself for remembering her name.

Finally, the woman's eyes flew open, the whites flashing wildly in the moonlight. Her brows shot up, her mouth widening further.

"Cursed woman, you cannot—" Jonas was interrupted by a hot flash of pain as her nails sank into his hand and sliced across his skin. "Fuck!" he exclaimed, falling back and releasing her.

Katrin flailed, kicking out. She tried to climb to her feet, but the rope securing her to the tree grew taut, causing her to fall onto her stomach. It would have been amusing if her terror wasn't so palpable, if Jonas's hand did not throb with pain. Recoiling, she pushed her spine back into the trunk of the tree.

Jonas scowled at the woman. If she screamed again, if she drew creatures from the woods...it wouldn't happen on his watch.

"Look at me, Katrin," he said in an authoritative voice. "You're all right." Her brown eyes darted to him, then quickly away. Jonas's irritation flared. "Imagine your favorite place in all of Íseldur. Close your eyes if you must." Her eyes closed, and she breathed in sharply through her nose. "Imagine you're in your favorite place. You're safe. Nothing can reach you there."

The woman inhaled, and Jonas was pleased to see the pulse in the hollow of her throat calming.

Where does she go?

His brows drew together as he pushed the intrusive thought aside. Unbidden, Jonas's hand found the hammered silver talisman in his pocket, thumb rubbing across the etched surface. Silently, he watched her breathe. Eventually, the woman's eyes opened, and she tilted her head up to the starry skies above.

"You cannot scream out here," glowered Jonas. "There are grimwolves about. And other things."

"My apologies," said Katrin quietly. "I-I thought you were..." She shook her head. "Nothing. I'm sorry." Her gaze fell to his hand, eyes widening. "I did not mean to scratch you. Are you—"

"Go back to sleep," Jonas muttered, rising to his feet. He turned on his heel and made his way back to the fire to continue his lonely vigil on night watch.

———

THE SUN HAD RISEN but was cloaked by gray clouds as Rey stared at the woman curled beneath the linden tree. Using her sack as a pillow, she'd pulled her crimson cloak around her shoulders and one of the furs from their wagon on top of that. Dark lashes fanned out against pale skin, shining liquid trickling from her parted lips.

She was drooling.

He frowned. What in the eternal fucking fires was this oblivious woman doing out here, in his wagon, in the midst of the biggest damned job they'd ever done? A lost lamb amongst the grimwolves and warbands and murderers who prowled these parts. He should do her a favor and grant her a swift death by the blade of his axe.

That *had* been the plan the night before, but as Rey had moved to draw Jonas's dagger across her throat, something had stopped him. He couldn't be certain what it was—the whisperings of the gods, a stirring in his blood. As his eyes had fallen upon the crescent-shaped scar at the corner of her eye, he'd hesitated.

In his line of work, Rey had learned to make difficult decisions quickly. But that pause...it had changed everything. It was just long enough for the woman's words to penetrate him, for the seeds she'd planted to take root and grow. He had suffered for that pause all night, indecision plaguing him—bring her or kill her. It should not have been a difficult choice, and yet here he was. Still undecided.

When you get soft, people get killed.

The words of Rey's former mentor rang in his ears. While Kraki might be a terrible man, he'd survived as long as he had for a reason. In this country, it was kill or be killed. And if you couldn't trust those who fought and rode and slept beside you, you were as good as dead. Jonas had told him as much the night before. *We cannot afford any complications with this job,* he had said, an eagerness in his voice which Rey had not heard in many long months. Years, perhaps, if he was being honest.

There was truth to Jonas's words, to Kraki's words. Rey knew what must be done. *It is a merciful thing to end her,* he urged himself, reaching for his sword, but something tightened in his chest, and it happened again.

He paused.

Gritting his teeth, anger flared in Rey's gut. Why was he questioning this? This woman had crawled into his wagon, had disrupted his plans, had heard things that were not meant for her ears. She had earned the bite of his blade.

What if she can get the information from Kraki? The thought which had afflicted him all night materialized like fog on a winter sea. Could she be the key to retrieving the information they needed? The gods knew, Kraki would not willingly hand it over to Rey, not after the departure they'd had. And she had a certain look to her, a look he'd seen Kraki lust after time and time again.

Kraki likes them young and...sweet, Rey thought with a curl of his lip. Not something he held in common with the man at all.

Glowering at the sleeping woman, a war raged inside him. He'd already gone over it a thousand times in his mind: kill her today, and stay true to Magnus's rules, or use her to get the information and figure the rest out later.

Keeping her risked their lives—if the Heart Eater were to discover they'd willfully shared the details of this job, he'd demand retribution paid in blood.

But going to Istré without the information they needed was also a considerable risk. Proper preparation for a job was of the utmost importance. They needed that book. And Rey knew he required something...*something* to sway Kraki. It was just possible that this doe-eyed girl with a so-called golden tongue could be the thing they needed.

His decision made, Rey nudged her hip with the toe of his boot and watched her stir awake. She blinked and sat up, looking around, her eyes landing on him. Rey saw it—the moment she recognized him, the moment everything came back to her. Her eyes tightened, and with a quick inhale, she recoiled. His brows snapped together as he scowled at her.

"Tell me your plan," he grumbled.

"Plan?" she repeated, her voice husky with sleep.

He inhaled sharply through his nose, then spoke. "You get us the information we need, we'll take you as far as Kraki. Hver is the nearest town to Skalla Ridge—that's a week's ride."

She gasped, her eyes shining with unshed tears. Rey frowned at the sight. The last thing they needed was a weeping woman traveling with the Bloodaxe Crew. This was a mistake. He should cut her throat and put this mess behind him.

"My thanks!" she exclaimed, springing to her feet and lurching forward. The rope binding her to the tree caught, and she stumbled back.

Rey scowled at her. "Your wits do not impress me thus far," he muttered. She was trying not to smile but was losing the battle. And the more her smile grew, the more his grimace deepened. "This is a terrible idea," he said aloud. "Plan, woman. How will you retrieve this information from him?"

Her smile faltered. "I...well, I must learn all I can of this Kraki, and...study his weaknesses, his vices...and, um, use them against him."

Rey stared blankly at her. Where was this so-called golden tongue of hers? "His weaknesses are pretty girls and brennsa. That enough for you to work with?"

A pink flush crept across her cheeks, and Rey huffed, looking away. A blushing, weeping woman armed with nothing but a hammer—and not even a war hammer, but a gods-forsaken wood crafter's hammer. This would never work. He opened his mouth to say as much, but she beat him to it.

"I won't seduce him." Her words were edged with a surprising layer of conviction, and Rey's gaze slid back to her brown eyes. There was a thin band of gold encircling her pupil, he noted.

"Your virtue more important than your life?" Rey asked, trying not to show his amusement. He wouldn't let Kraki lay a hand on her, but for some reason, he was in no rush to tell her this. Let her squirm a bit. Penance for her transgression.

"Who says my virtue is intact?" she snapped, and his amusement escaped in the form of a scoff. Rey was not nearly so prolific as Jonas, but he could read women well enough.

The woman's eyes narrowed, and she stared at him. Rey blinked—he was unused to strangers holding eye contact for so long. He prided himself on his ability to unnerve others with a single look; he'd earned the name Axe Eyes for a reason, after all. After a moment, the pink in her cheeks deepened to red, and the woman looked away. Satisfaction swelled within him. He'd known he'd read her right—she was a maiden if he'd ever seen one.

"I will get the information without the need for...*that*," muttered the woman.

"As you wish," said Rey.

He stared at her. Her hair was a wild mess of curls, pine needles and bits of moss strewn throughout. Despite this, she looked like she belonged at Ursir's house, or working as a handmaiden for a simpering jarl's wife, not traveling with the Bloodaxe Crew along the Road of Bones.

Mistake, he thought. *She'll be nothing but a distraction when you must be putting your minds together to plan for this job.* Anger flared in his stomach. Anger at this woman for placing the weight of this decision on his shoulders.

But it was done. He'd made his choice, and there was only forward.

"If you're to travel with the Bloodaxe Crew, you'll need to follow the rules, woman."

"Katrin," she said, fire flaring unexpectedly behind her eyes. "You may call me Katrin."

His eyes narrowed. "Here are the rules. One: you do as you're told. I say stay, you stay. I say run, you run. Understand me?"

She nodded.

Rey held up a second finger. "Two: you're honest with us. In our line of work, if you cannot trust the men and women beside you, you're already food for the corpse vultures. No lies. You understand, Katrin?"

Something passed behind the woman's eyes as she nodded. "I can cook for you..."

Irritation flickered inside him. He knew what she was doing, trying to worm her way into the Crew—trying to earn a ride all the way to Kopa. That would never happen. Not on his watch.

He raised a third finger. "Three: you speak of this to no one. If others discover you know of this job, I'll be forced to kill you. If the man who hired us finds out you know of this job, all of our lives are at risk."

Her throat bobbed as she nodded once more.

"We stop for provisions in Svarti. You touch anything in the wagon, you talk too much, you give me any reason to suspect you'll bring danger upon my crew—"

"Let me guess," she said tartly. "You'll kill me."

Rey glowered at her, and the woman's boldness seemed to evaporate. He stepped forward to free her, but she recoiled as far as she could, pressing her back up against the tree.

His stomach twisted. With a deep breath, Rey tried to soften his *axe eyes*. "Would you prefer to eat the daymeal with your hands bound?" he grumbled.

Her lips parted, and the woman hesitated a moment before offering her hands to him. After working the ropes loose, Rey watched her open her small palm, that heart-shaped rock revealed within. Odd one, this woman was. She carried no provisions, her clothing entirely impractical for this road, and yet a rock...that she'd packed?

Rey examined her face once more, his eyes settling on the bruise on her eye, on her neck. His fingers twitched. "We leave in twenty minutes. There's a stream that way if you wish to wash. Eat something. Or don't." Turning on his heel, Rey strode toward the fire.

In his mind, Kraki's words echoed once more.

When you get soft, people get killed.

Rey exhaled heavily. He was going to regret this. He just knew it.

THIRTEEN

Silla blinked as the mountain of a man strode toward the fire. Ashes, but his presence was intimidating. But now that he'd left her alone, a smile spread slowly across her face. He hadn't killed her, and not only that, but she'd earned herself a ride to the town of Hver at the very least. Now a new door had opened. Silla would make herself indispensable. These people would eat like kings, and they'd never be able to let her leave them at Hver. She wiggled with happiness.

No lies. You got it, Katrin? Rey's words repeated in her mind, and her smile faltered.

Well, no, she thought. That would not work for Silla. Secrecy was her cloak of safety; it always had been, and that didn't change simply because an over-grown warrior with frighteningly intense eyes had deemed it so. As the fortunes would have it, Silla had grown adept at lying over the past ten years. She was confident it would not be an issue.

Hands finally freed, Silla gathered her cloak and the heart-shaped rock, fitting them into her bag with the rest of her belongings. The forest clung to her skin, and after a moment of indecision, Silla headed toward the stream.

The morning light caught dew on the grass, glistening like glacial pearls strung on each blade. Perhaps this was a good omen from the gods, a sign that her future was bright. The sound of running water met her ears, a small stream snaking through the field and disappearing into a grove of trees beyond. Dropping to her knees, Silla cupped the cool water and splashed it on her face. So cold that it shocked life back into her sleepy limbs, it felt like a fresh start to this new chapter of her journey.

Sighing with pleasure, she climbed back to her feet, turning to head to the fire. She gasped as she found Jonas standing a few paces away. The golden gleam of his hair drew her attention—sides shorn short, the top was drawn back and knotted at his crown. Though not as tall as Rey, he was still half a head taller than her. Combined with the large arms crossed over his chest and the scowl on his face, he seemed far less of an optimistic omen than the dew had been.

Ashes, she thought. *Why does this man despise me so?*

Silla's face flushed as she remembered waking to him looming over her, his hand clamped over her mouth. Time had slipped, and she'd thought herself back on the road near Skarstad, the warrior choking the life from her while her father fought nearby. She'd scratched him deeply and was embarrassed that he'd witnessed her in that vulnerable moment.

Silla opened her mouth to ask how his hand was, but he beat her to it.

"I do not know how you convinced Axe Eyes," he said in a low voice. "But I will tell you this—we are in the midst of the biggest job we've ever had, and I won't have some mouse coming between me and my sólas."

"Mouse?" she asked. Anger flared in her stomach, and Silla forced in a calming breath. She had to win these people over. Had to earn their trust.

Jonas's gaze dragged from her toes up to the top of her head, so heavy she could feel it on her skin. "Quiet. Compliant. Sneaks into dark corners where she's not welcome."

Silla wanted to burst into laughter. No one had ever deemed her quiet in her life. But this man had clearly already made several assumptions about her.

"Let me reassure you, warrior," she said, holding his gaze. "A mouse is quite adept at staying out of the way. I'm no risk to your precious sólas." She couldn't help the note of contempt in her voice. This man clearly cared for nothing but coin. His jaw flexed as he studied her. Silla felt her face grow hot and forced her feet to move as she pushed past him toward the fire.

Sigrún had fed kindling to the embers, and the blackened pot hung over gently licking flames. The small woman's eyes were a dark brown, her lips a small bow with the hint of a smile as Silla approached. Sigrún's hands moved in gestures Silla did not understand, and Ilías jumped in to interpret. "She asks if you'd like a bowl of porridge?"

"Oh," said Silla, her stomach growling. "That would be lovely."

Sigrún scooped the porridge into a wooden bowl with an audible splat. Silla pressed her lips together as she watched the porridge wobble. Even from where she stood, she could tell it was simultaneously burnt and undercooked.

Silla accepted the bowl from Sigrún with a gracious smile. "My thanks."

The Bloodaxe Crew sat around the fire eating in silence. A beat-up steel kettle was passed between them, each member of the group pouring themselves a steaming cup of spiced róa. Sitting on an empty crate, Silla focused her attention on her porridge, eating it without complaint, even the chewy, burnt bottom crust. Before she could gather the dishes or offer to help with the washing, Sigrún had plucked the bowl from her hands and done it herself.

Silla wandered to Rey's white mare, secured to the wagon. Large brown eyes regarded her from under thick black lashes. "You're a beauty, aren't you?" she murmured. Silla ran a hand down the mare's soft nose, and the horse snorted, nudging her. Her smile spread wide. "You're less surly than your rider. Tell me how to win his favor, girl. I promise I'll save the good carrots for you."

Footfalls crunched in the earth behind her, and Silla needn't look to know it was Rey.

"What's her name?" asked Silla.

"Horse."

Her hand faltered, and she turned on her heel, looking up at him. "You named your horse...Horse?"

The morning light bounced off Rey's midnight-black curls. His thick brows drew together, a line forming between them. "I regret this already." Rey rubbed a hand over his eyes. "Get in the wagon before I change my mind."

Silla avoided his withering glare and made her way around the back of the wagon. Mercifully, they'd left half of the supplies uncovered, and she settled into the pile of furs in the corner, a marked improvement from lying curled on her side in the darkness. But Rey climbed onto the wagon after her, the flatbed rocking back and forth with each step he took, coiling the tension in her body higher and higher.

He loomed over her like a rain cloud covering the sun. The wolfskin pelt draped over his shoulders only broadened him, making him larger and more imposing. Unease pooled in Silla's stomach as Rey retrieved a length of rope from his belt, and began looping it around her hands, securing her to an iron circle embedded in the wagon's wooden siding.

Silla's gaze fell upon his armor—the same, she noted, that all of the Bloodaxe Crew wore—as Rey worked the ropes. Up close, she could see thousands of tiny black leather scales on his armored jacket, highly unlike the heavy shirts of chain mail favored by the King's Claws and other Íseldurian warriors.

Curious, thought Silla, as he straightened.

"I cannot have you plotting to stab me from behind," said Rey. He retreated, jumping off the end of the wagon. "Or touching my things," he mumbled under his breath.

Silla blinked after him. *That man needs to hug a baby or pat a dog,* she thought.

Gazing out the back of the wagon with unfocused eyes, Silla took in the abandoned camp as the cart bounced along the path. The grassy clearing grew smaller, a faint wisp of smoke climbing from the drenched fire.

When at last they reached the somewhat smoother Road of Bones, Silla allowed herself a small smile. They were taking her to Hver. It was a far better outcome than it might have been. It was progress, steps in the right direction. Juniper and pine trees closed in on the road again, obscuring the gloomy skies with spiky sprays of green. After days of desperation, she forced herself to try to relax, but it seemed impossible to accomplish.

It was also impossible to keep memories of her father from springing to mind. Her life had changed so fast it was dizzying, thoughts of her father a twisted mess. He'd died to keep her safe, yet had lied to her all her life. Now she had questions, tormenting and nagging at her, and no one to provide the answers.

The morning unfolded with dreadful monotony. Her eyes went in and out of focus as she drew her thoughts to Kopa, desperate to distract herself from dwelling on her father. Wisps of conversation reached her ears, but the riders kept their distance. The hours droned on endlessly, and Silla reminded herself that though she was motionless, she was getting closer to Kopa. Closer to Skeggagrim. Closer to the shield-house. Closer to safety.

As the cloud-cloaked sun edged toward the horizon, a dull ache built in her temples. Silla's entire body clenched, which only seemed to urge the headache on. Anticipating the pain had been her life as long as she'd known, and she imagined it would be long into the future. Thank the gods above for her skjöld leaves. Knowing she had the remedy tucked against her chest was an immense relief. At this moment, it might be the only thing keeping her together.

She needed a leaf. Needed two. *No,* she told herself. *You need your wits about you.* But her resistance did little to suppress the relentless urges. The leaves could help her forget what had happened in Skarstad, could put her nerves at ease...

But her imminent headache reminded her of that other troubling thing. The Battle Thorns had stolen her reserve of leaves, and she had only what remained in her vial. Silla shuddered at the thought of running out of them. After a bit of struggle with her bound hands, she managed to tuck a single skjöld leaf into her cheek and closed her eyes as the earthy taste filled her mouth.

A sharp whistle from the head of the pack signaled the end of their day; the Bloodaxe Crew pulled well off the Road of Bones, snaking between trees until they came to a stop at an open grassy patch. Silla sighed as the wagon stopped, the break in the ceaseless rumble a joy to her ears. Rey wordlessly freed her from her binds, and Silla clambered from the wagon, watching as the Crew began their nightly routine. Kneeling beside the iron tripod, Sigrún was pulling a pot and other cooking supplies from a crate. Silla took a deep breath and approached.

"Sigrún, I must give my thanks to your crew for your...hospitality. You rode hard today while I had the most splendid nap of my life. Please. Rest, and let me cook."

After a moment of silence, Sigrún subtly inclined her head and wandered off behind the wagon. Silla smiled. At least the women of the Crew seemed kind. Pulling out the cooking supplies, Silla inspected them. A blackened cookpot, a knife, onions, carrots, one tin of dried róa bark, and one of salt.

"*You're* preparing the evening meal?" came a male voice. Silla's gaze met with Ilías', a pair of dead rabbits dangling from his fist.

She smiled at the young warrior. "Yes," she said, casting a cautious look over her shoulder. Rey was nowhere to be seen.

"Thank the gods," he said with a broad smile. "Siggie's aim is impeccable, but her cooking..." He grimaced, then dropped the rabbits to the ground beside Silla, drawing a dagger.

She looked up at him, and she saw it. His profile was undeniably similar to Jonas's, but as he turned to her, his hazel eyes and shade of blond hair set him apart, as did his youthful appearance.

"You are brothers?" she asked.

A line formed between Ilías's drawn brows. "Jonas is my brother. We are kin though, all of us here, blood or not."

Silla's smile deepened. "I like that," she said. "Go. Let me butcher them."

With a nod, Ilías sheathed his dagger and loped off to help Gunnar pound spears into the ground a short distance from the fire—to set up a windbreak, Silla supposed. The wind did seem a touch more frigid this evening.

Years of travel with her father and countless turns of winter spent in kitchens had equipped Silla with ample skill when it came to cooking on the road. She chopped onions and carrots, then set to work skinning and butchering the rabbits.

From the edge of her vision, she saw Jonas digging out a fire pit. *Arse,* she silently cursed him, trying not to look his way. *You can take your cursed sólas and put them where the sun doesn't shine.* But her foolish eyes tracked the flex of his shoulders as he stacked kindling with lichen, the bunch of his breeches around his thighs as he bent low to blow at the flames. Curse him and his hand-someness; it was wasted on a man with a temperament like his.

Thankfully, Ilías and Gunnar finished stretching a woolen blanket out between the spears, and joined Jonas for a game of dice, obscuring him from view. The murmur of voices and rattle of dice merged with the soft crackle of the fire, and the Crew passed a flask around.

Rey joined them, gesturing at Silla. "What is this?"

"She has offered her assistance, Rey," said Gunnar. "It might be nice to try something...different."

"And you're all content to rest your lives in her hands? A stranger?"

Silla watched silently as the others chuckled at Rey. But the big man was not appeased.

"We cannot trust her. She could poison our meal."

"Why would I poison you?" asked Silla. "I need you to get to Kopa."

"Hver," growled Rey. "We are *not* taking you to Kopa."

We shall see about that, Silla thought. But she kept her face straight and nodded at Rey.

"She makes a good point, Axe Eyes," said Ilías, with a swig from his flask. "She needs our help. Why should she poison us?"

Rey scowled but said no more. Perhaps he was also interested in something other than Sigrún's cooking.

For the evening meal, Silla prepared rabbit stew. It was mindless work, a meal she'd prepared a hundred times in her life. Supplementing the scant ingredients in the cooking crate with a glug of brennsa and a few sprigs of arctic thyme she'd spotted on the fringes of camp, it was not long before the scent filled the air, and the Bloodaxe Crew sent curious looks her way.

After serving up the meal and passing out bowls, the group sat around the fire, silent except for slurping and the scrape of spoons. Silla watched in antici-pation, pleased at the enthusiasm with which the warriors ate. Jarl Gunnell and

DEMI WINTERS

his retinue were far more reserved than the Bloodaxe Crew. Unquestionably
eager, they returned for seconds and Rey for thirds.

"Best thing I've eaten in weeks," said Hekla happily. "No offense, Siggie."
The rest of the Bloodaxe Crew nodded their heads, murmuring in agreement.

"The girl worked a miracle," added Gunnar with a grin. "Ilías ate his
vegetables."

"Shut it, Fire Fist," muttered Ilías.

Across the fire, Sigrún gesticulated.

"She says you're welcome to take on the cooking," said Hekla, an amused
smile playing on her lips. "She says she'd far prefer to spend the time
hunting."

Hope bloomed in Silla's chest. Perhaps her cooking would convince them.
Surely warriors of all people *must* place a high priority on the enjoyment of
food? "How do I sign *I'd be happy to?*" she asked, ignoring the glare of the man
they called Axe Eyes.

Sigrún made a slow sequence of hand gestures, which Silla tried her best to
repeat.

Unable to keep the smile from her lips, Silla gathered the bowls, and
Gunnar appeared with a bucket of water that she used to do the washing. As
she placed the last of the wooden bowls back into the crate, Hekla appeared by
her side.

"Have you need to wash? I'm headed to the stream." Hekla nodded her
head toward the edge of the clearing. Eager to make the most of this opening,
Silla pushed to her feet. Grabbing her bag, she followed Hekla across the clearing, then down a sloping hill to a small stream.

Using her left hand, Hekla peeled her strange scaled armor jacket apart
without the need to fiddle with any fastenings or buckles—Silla wondered how,
exactly, it held together so firmly during the day. Shrugging out of it, Hekla
pulled the tunic beneath over her head with one hand, then tugged down her
breeches.

Standing in her undergarments, she twisted off her prosthesis. It released
with a soft click just above the elbow of her right arm, and she laid it down in
the grass. Stepping into the stream, Hekla splashed herself with water, sighing
contentedly as she rubbed the skin beneath the prosthesis, where a small
metallic joint of some sort gleamed in her residual limb.

Pulling off her layered dresses, Silla stepped into the stream to join Hekla.
She'd expected the water to be cold, but not that it would be so frigid it would

steal the breath from her lungs. As she stepped into the shallow stream, a noise of agony escaped her.

Hekla chuckled. "You grow used to it with time."

"I suppose it is rather invigorating," said Silla, rushing to wash herself. Her skin pinked wherever it came in contact with the water.

After a moment, Hekla ran the prosthesis through the stream, rubbing dirt and grime from it, before twisting it back onto the metal piece anchored in her residual limb. Silla had never seen anything like it. It was slender, with gleaming black metallic lines running along the arm and elbow joint to her fingertips. Though it did not move quite like Hekla's flesh arm, it mimicked it remarkably in shape.

"Does the water not damage it?" asked Silla, nodding to the arm.

"Rust-free," said Hekla with pride. She stretched her prosthesis out and tapped a button on the inner wrist, silver claws extending from the knuckles with a soft click. Another tap and they had retracted back in.

"That's amazing," Silla murmured. She lowered herself onto her knees on the stream's edge and scrubbed her hair out in the water. Righting herself, she pulled her comb from her bag and began working it through her tangled hair.

Hekla had dressed and was washing her other garments in the stream. Not wanting to wear the grimy clothing she'd just stepped out of, Silla fished out her other dress—the one from Jarl Gunnell's steading. Having had the opportunity to wash it in Reykfjord, it felt nice to wear something clean.

Joining Hekla by the stream, Silla washed her soiled garments in the frigid waters. Afterward, the two women stood. Hekla's wide amber eyes caught on Silla's bruised neck, the corners of her lips tugging down.

"Are you running from someone, dúlla?" Hekla asked quietly. "A man? Your husband?"

Silla bit her lip, considering her words. But Hekla seemed to take her silence as confirmation.

"Did he do that to you?" she demanded, pointing at Silla's neck.

Silla nodded. Over the years, she'd learned that people saw what they wanted to, and going along with their assumptions was far simpler than crafting her own lies. Still, something about this sat wrong in her stomach.

"Well, curse that evil kunta, Katrin!" hissed Hekla. "I hope you struck the vermin right back. You've done the right thing leaving a foulsome man like that." Hekla lifted her prosthetic arm in the air. "Compliments of my shite of a husband. Former husband," she corrected, a look of glee flashing in her eyes.

Bile rose in Silla's throat. "H-he did that to you?"

"Yes. He was a wretched man with many shortcomings, and he took his frustrations out on me. This was long before my days as a warrior. I was young. I believed...he would change. Thought I could help him. But it was all lies; he never did change. When at last I found the courage to leave, he found me. Got his axe. I tried to fight back, tried to block him, but..."

Silla's mouth fell open.

"Oh, don't worry, dúlla," cackled Hekla. It was a slightly unhinged sound. "My debts to him are repaid in full."

"Did you—is he dead?"

"Oh yes. Very much so."

Silla dressed in silence, absorbing this new information.

Hekla's voice cut through her thoughts. "While I'll admit I'd prefer the use of both my arms, not to have had to learn how to do everything with my left arm, not to have gone through prosthesis after prosthesis before discovering the one that worked for me, I can see now that in some ways, the entire thing was a blessing in disguise."

"What?"

"Oh, yes. After it happened, it struck me: we all must die someday. I squandered too many years on that man...that dishonorable rat. I decided I would do what *I* wanted—to learn how to fight and to travel, to see this kingdom. I want to live free, to live big while my heart still beats." Hekla paused. "And you are also free, dúlla."

"Yes," Silla murmured, her stomach twisting. It felt wrong, this lie. She wished she'd picked another. Hekla seemed a wonderful person, a possible ally, but now she feared she'd ruined it all.

They made their way back to the fire, hanging their wet garments on a line strung between the wagon and a juniper branch. Settling down before the flames, the windbreak was a welcome relief from the brisk air. Silla hauled her hair over a shoulder so the warmth of the fire could help it dry. Clean clothing, freshly bathed, stomach filled, and not on the run. Her blisters and bruises were healing. Hardened warriors surrounded her. For the first time in days, Silla felt content.

But with a few easy words, Rey shattered any peace she'd managed to cultivate.

"Katrin, did you hear of the bodies discovered on the road near Skarstad a few days past?"

Silla's gaze flew to Rey, and she swallowed at what she saw. His eyes held a look of apathy, but something lurked below. Something dangerous.

"Bodies?" asked Gunnar. "How many?"

"Seven."

Sigrún gesticulated, Ilías jumping in to interpret. "You're from Skarstad, are you not, Katrin?"

An uncomfortable silence stretched out around the fire. "I did not hear of it," she lied, praying her words struck true. "That's troubling news."

Rey was unperturbed. "Six bodies clad in black mail—thought to be swords for hire. And one in the gray of Jarl Gunnell. A farmworker, I'm told. Strange," he mused. His words were sharp, his aim impeccable. "Your dress. Is that not the mountain aven embroidered on it? The sigil of Jarl Gunnell?"

Her breaths slowed. Silla looked down at the blue dress she'd donned. At the white flower embellished on the belt. How did he know? Her lips parted a millimeter, and she slammed them shut.

Rey's gaze was unflinching. "Will you tell us what six hired warriors would want with a farmworker, Katrin? Have you any guesses?"

She shook her head slowly.

"Liar," said Rey. A violent storm churned behind his eyes.

Silla swallowed, the eyes of the Bloodaxe Crew upon her.

"Katrin," said Rey. "If you wish to walk out of this glade on your own two feet, you'd best start talking. And you can start with your true name."

FOURTEEN

Silla searched the sky for the Mother Star to ask for guidance, or even the lucky stag constellation to ask for good fortune. But curse the late summer sunsets—it was not yet dark, and there was no escaping this situation. Caught breaking the Bloodaxe Crew's rules, and it hadn't even been a full day. Clearly, the walking mountain was more clever than Silla had realized.

Her eyes met Hekla's and she forced her gaze away. If she was to dig herself out of this hole, she'd need to create a new set of lies, at the cost of this woman's trust. Though she hated it, Silla saw no other option—she could not tell these warriors the truth; they worked for the king and would hand her over for certain.

She took a deep breath. "My name is Silla Nordvig. I thought it best I did not use my true name. I-I was frightened."

Staring into the flames, Silla prepared to spin a tale. "The farmworker on the road near Skarstad...that was my father. Matthias." Over the years, she'd found it best to weave some truths in with the lies. Though, as she considered it, Matthias was not even his true name. Pushing this thought aside, Silla soldiered forward.

"There was a dispute of inheritance by my father's cousin—a troublesome, cruel man who was disowned by his own kin. When his father died and his lands passed on to us, the man became enraged, driving my father and I from it.

This was *our* land, land we rightfully owned, but we were forced...to take work on the jarl's steading so we would not starve. But my father had the documents, had good men to vouch for him at the Midsummer Assembly. It was only a few weeks from now that my father would argue our case, that these lands would surely be restored to us.

"We were on our way home—our temporarily rented quarters just out of Skarstad. The men, they came from the woods and attacked, six against the two of us—an old man and a woman who cannot even draw her dagger. Cowardly men, they were. They killed my father." She buried her face in her hands.

"One man grabbed me by the neck and carried me to the woods. He held me so that I could not breathe. I tried to fight, but..." Silla made the mistake of glancing at Hekla and saw betrayal plain on her face. Wincing, she forced herself to continue. "If my father had not thrown his dagger into the man's back, I would be dead alongside him. I was knocked out. By the time I awoke, it was too late. They were dead—all of them. And I ran."

And now she waited...and prayed to the gods that her story rang true.

The queen will not kill you. Not right away, that is. The memory made her shudder. She could never reveal the truth to these people, these warriors whose allegiance was to the king.

"You're telling me a farmer fought and killed six trained warriors?" Rey's wry voice cut through her hopes.

This man...she needed to be careful here. And Rey had stumbled across the other puzzling detail. Where had Matthias—Tómas—learned to fight like that? It was as if he'd done it his whole life.

"He was a warrior in his day," she said quietly, the only answer which could possibly make sense.

"To whom was he oathsworn?" asked Rey.

Anger stirred in her veins. He was relentless, his questions unending. And she feared each lie she told dug her grave just a little deeper.

"Jarl Braksson," she murmured, thinking of the steading she'd worked at a few years prior.

"Mossfell?" Rey asked, his gaze burning into her. She knew she must hold it, no matter what, she must not flinch or show any sign of deception—her life depended on it.

"Yes. And once he acquired Midfjord, he preferred to keep his summers there." She watched him absorb this information, sifting through it in search of holes. There would be none, if she'd recalled correctly. And for the first time, Silla was grateful to have worked on so many steadings, to have such information at the ready.

The silence in the wake of her words was so loud it hurt her ears. Jonas and Ilías exchanged a weighted look across the fire. Someone needed to say something. Anything. The truth scratched her throat like it was trying to get free.

Rey stood, a muscle in his jaw flexing as he drew his hevrít from its sheath at his hip. He stepped toward her, Silla's pulse leaping. "Why should I let you live? You broke my rules. I cannot trust you. And we cannot have someone we don't trust riding with the Crew." The air shifted with the sharpness of his words.

Silla leapt to her feet, backing away. The firelight danced in his eyes, along his bronzed cheekbone, off the wolfskin cloak wrapped around his shoulders. "Please," she begged. "Please, I'd told you my name before I knew your rules." Her back bumped into the spear rigged as a windbreak.

Rey pressed forward, the long blade of his hevrít glinting malevolently. "Why should I give you another chance? You've proven yourself a liar."

"Because it takes a small man to be ruled by fear, and a large one to show mercy. And anyone can see you are no small man."

Rey's thick brows gathered together, something passing behind his dark eyes. "What did you say?"

Her heart pounded so loudly she could scarcely hear him. "I said—"

"Where did you hear that?" he demanded. "Where did you learn those words?"

Silla's hands were clenched so tight that her nails dug into her palms. "M-my father."

Rey's gaze seemed to settle on her left eye—on her scar—the hevrít dropping limply to his side. Though relief flickered faintly within her, Silla didn't dare move for risk of breaking this spell.

When Rey spoke, it was a low rasp. "Is there a price on your head?"

She took a calming breath. "No."

"They won't come after you?"

"They have what they want. Our land. And no one to contest it."

"So no one will show up here looking for you?"

Silla shook her head slowly, the lies twisting in her stomach.

"Why Kopa? Why not Reykfjord?"

"M-my mother's brother lives in Kopa. I will be safe there. Reykfjord is too near to Skarstad. I fear...I'd always be looking over my shoulder." Her eyes stung. She was exhausted, this conversation drawing the last of her energy reserves.

"Tell me the rules," snapped Rey.

"Do as I'm told," she managed in a quiet voice. "No lies."

"Are you lying to me?"

His cold, dark gaze studied her every breath, her every blink. She shook off the shiver threatening to roll down her spine. "No."

"If you lie to me again, woman, you'll soon find an axe in your skull. There won't be another chance."

Her body sagged. He wasn't going to kill her—tonight.

"I won't lie to you," Silla lied. Gods' sacred ashes, she was lying about lying. How had she gotten to this place? She stared at Rey and wasn't entirely sure where the boldness of her following words came from. "I *will* get to Kopa."

Rey scoffed. "Will you fly there on optimism? Delusion and naivety are a sure way to get killed on this road."

Silent, she held his gaze.

With a shake of his head, Rey pushed past her, then stalked into the darkening woods. Silla stared as his silhouette merged with the shadows, as though they were one and the same.

He'd have killed me, she thought. *He truly would have killed me.* She'd seen it in Rey's eyes—the murderous intent. What had stopped him? Why had he changed his mind? Those words, spoken by her father, repeated in her desperation? *Never mind it all. That man is dangerous,* Silla thought, and she made herself a promise—the next time she feared for her life, she would not hesitate to leave. It just might be that the creatures of the forest were safer than the leader of the Bloodaxe Crew.

Hekla's soft voice shook her from her daze. "There was no husband."

Burning stars. Rey's questioning had been so intense she'd forgotten the rest of the Bloodaxe Crew entirely. She'd forgotten Hekla and how Silla's new story would wound this brave woman who'd been nothing but kind to her. Her chest tightened.

"No," said Silla, sitting back onto her crate near the fire. Her eyes pleaded with Hekla. "I should not have gone along with your assumptions. It was dishonorable of me."

"Hmm," she said, standing. "Such a thing should not be used for stories and schemes." Silla flinched, and Hekla turned, following Rey's retreat into the woods.

Silla was numb as she sat before the fire. A potential friend, her greatest ally thus far, offended beyond measure. And the walking boulder chased her like a wolfhound with the scent of a wounded animal. *But you are breathing,* she thought to herself. She was still breathing. And she would do what she must to keep it that way.

Silence stretched around the fire for several long minutes.

"You've got bigger bollocks than a troll, girl," chuckled Gunnar.

Silla wrinkled her nose. "What?"

Sigrún made hand signals from across the fire.

"Sigrún says *you stared down Axe Eyes like none I've ever seen,*" Jonas said in a lazy voice. Reclined across the fire, his dagger moved over a piece of wood with such dexterity he did not even need to look at it. Her gaze dropped to his hands —so firm and in control, the way they worked the dagger along the piece of wood...

"Thought he'd burst into flames," chirped Ilías, thankfully diverting her attention.

Silla groaned. "He despises me."

Ilías sank beside her, uncapping a flask. "Rey? Don't let him frighten you. He's mostly bluster." He frowned. "Though I did once see him kill a man with a spoon."

Gunnar chuckled. "I forgot about that."

Silla swallowed. "A spoon?"

Ilías did not elaborate. "It is best to be truthful with Axe Eyes. You see how he digs the truth from a person. Faster than it takes to get Fire Fist's mother naked and into the furs."

Gunnar's reply was as sharp as the look he threw at Ilías. "You looking for some broken teeth, No Beard?"

"Don't dwell on it," said Ilías, ignoring Gunnar. "Rey and Hekla—their anger will fade. I would know, being the usual target of their fury."

"She is braver than she looks," said Jonas, watching her. "And less a mouse than she seems." He slid his blade deeper into the wood, bits curling up in its wake. "But you don't belong here, Curls."

An ache panged in Silla's chest at his words. It was nothing new—not belonging—but it hurt all the same.

"Drink some brennsa," said Ilías, passing her the flask. Silla sniffed it, scrunching her nose. "It burns for only a heartbeat or two," he said with a crooked grin.

She brought it to her lips, wincing as the harsh flavors of fire whiskey filled her mouth. It took all of her effort not to spit it right out. Silla coughed as it left a blazing trail across her tongue and down her throat. "Ashes!" she managed, wiping her lips on the back of her hand.

"Ashes?" Ilías repeated with a chuckle, taking back the flask. "You've never tasted brennsa, have you Silla?"

"No," she admitted, looking back to the flames.

"Why not?"

"My father and I kept to ourselves. We did not partake in feasts nor spend time in the mead halls." She felt the touch of Jonas's judgemental gaze on her skin and scowled. Sigrún took the flask from Ilías, tucking it under her arm while she signaled with her hands.

"Sigrún says *fire whiskey is a way of life on the road*," said Gunnar, as Sigrún drank from the flask. "'Tis true. Keeps you warm and helps pass the time. Plus, adding a little fire helps you sleep like a log."

Ilías groaned, Sigrún shaking her head slowly.

"Gunnar, do not infect the girl with your horrid jokes," complained Ilías.

Silla smiled. She could already feel the brennsa uncurling something in her stomach, warming her, slowing her pulse and loosening her up.

"Also," continued Ilías. "If you're to travel with the Bloodaxe Crew, we'll need to work on your cursing."

"What?"

"You'll need to curse, Silla Hammer Hand. It is a basic requirement to ride with the Crew."

A laugh burst from her. "Hammer Hand?"

"We all saw the hammer you carry. A bold choice of weapon, a wood-crafter's hammer is. Only the bravest of warriors would choose such a thing. One deserving of the name Hammer Hand."

She snorted loudly, then clapped a hand over her mouth. "I am rather fierce, aren't I?" she managed. "Though I do not curse."

"You must," said Ilías. "It is good for the health. Releases the tension in your body. Otherwise, the bad feelings gather, with no place to escape."

A smile played on her lips. "Very well." The flask was passed back to Silla, and she took another drink. She managed not to cough this time, though the face she made was most unladylike. "Oh, *barnacles!*" she hissed.

"No, no, no, Hammer Hand. Curse. *Really* curse." Ilías puffed up his chest. "Malla's flaming tits! Cussing arsebadgers! Sheep rutting son of a shit beetle!"

Jonas choked out a laugh, Sigrún snickering softly beside him.

Silla frowned at Ilías, shaking her head. "If one is a son of a beetle, how could they possibly...do that to a sheep? The height difference—it makes no sense, Ilías."

"She has a point, No Beard," chuckled Gunnar.

Ilías waved a hand in the air. "The details do not matter. Only the meaning, which is that they eat sh—"

"I *cannot* say that," interjected Silla before he could finish.

"Why not?"

She merely shook her head. Warmth swam in her stomach, happiness unfolding between her ears. Her emboldened gaze drifted once more to Jonas, wandering up his legs and meandering along his broad warrior's chest. When she reached his face she realized his blue eyes were already on her, his lips curved up at the corners.

Caught, she thought. Shame stinging her cheeks, Silla looked back to the fire. "Fuck," she whispered. The last thing she wanted was this man to think she admired him in any way.

"Louder, Hammer Hand," encouraged Ilías. "Let the gods hear you."

"Fuck!" she said a little louder.

Her lips curved into a small smile as she saw the look of pride on Ilías's face. She liked *some* of these people at least. The ease they had with one another, the camaraderie made her think it would not be so bad to travel with them, so long as she could keep her distance from Axe Eyes and the Wolf.

"I wager we shall have her cursing louder than Fire Fist's mother does in the furs," said Ilías.

Gunnar growled, then launched himself at Ilías. Silla barely managed to leap out of the way in time as the warriors crashed to the ground.

"Won't you stop them?" she asked, gathering her skirts and retreating around the fire. Jonas chuckled softly, while Sigrún merely shrugged. Already, Silla could tell how Gunnar had earned the name Fire Fist; his hands were a blur as they pummeled Ilías.

Silla's brows dipped down. "This is...normal." There was a lone empty crate next to Jonas. Swallowing, Silla lowered herself onto it. Glancing at Jonas, Silla's lips parted. He held a small figurine in his hands, the point of his dagger deepening the grooves of a curving beard and angular armor of the warrior.

"Do you like what you see, Silla?" he murmured, and she snapped her lips shut. Her true name on his lips sounded odd and...pleasing.

"The *figurine* is quite lovely," she managed, then urged herself to offer him some kindness. "You're quite good at that."

"And you're quite good at slithering your way into this Crew," he muttered.

Silla drew in a breath through her nose. "A snake am I now?" she asked. "And here I thought I was a mouse."

"Trouble is what you are," he said, his jarringly-blue eyes lifting to hers. "I'm not fooled."

Her stomach burned, skin prickling. It was becoming clear that traveling with this group would be an exquisite test of her patience and willpower.

"Do not get comfortable," said Jonas, turning back to his carving.

A coarse laugh fell from her lips. "Oh, but being bound to a tree and having my life threatened is such a comfort."

"Some women enjoy the rope."

Silla's mouth fell open. Had he just—did he truly just—she fought the itch to grab the man's dagger and drive it through his hand.

Jonas turned, his gaze raking over her. "I did not think it of you, but I've been wrong in my assumptions in the past."

Silla flew to her feet. Her hands had curled into fists, and she shook them loose. "I think I shall retreat to bed for the night."

Silla moved awkwardly away from the fire, Jonas's low chuckle chasing her into the darkness. Grabbing a fur from the wagon, she picked a spot in the grass to spread out for the night. Curling onto her side, Silla drew up her cloak and the fur, then stared blankly ahead. Would Rey return and drag her from her bed to bind her to a tree?

The little blonde girl settled on her stomach in the grass before her, resting her cheek on her fists. "You must win them over, Silla."

Silla released a long breath. "They make it more difficult than I'd imagined." She'd narrowly avoided Rey's axe tonight, but what would tomorrow bring? The very thought exhausted her.

The girl tucked a messy lock of hair behind her ear. "You can do it. You are a survivor."

Survivor. The word brought tears to her eyes. Silla pulled her father's tunic from the bag, pressing it to her nose. His lingering scent brought her comfort, this last bit of him traveling with her.

"Stay vigilant," the little girl continued. "Win them over, but do not get too close."

Silla nodded. She must win them over without revealing the truth. If the Bloodaxe Crew discovered that the queen hunted Silla, she'd surely be handed over to the crown.

But no matter what, Silla could never let her guard down.

FIFTEEN

"There is only one solution," said Jonas. He pulled the herbal sludge from the bowl, breathing through his mouth as he smeared it along his mother's swollen jaw.

Her glassy eyes stared at the rafters of the longhouse, and he wondered if she was capable of speech in her state. Fingers dipping into the pungent mixture of herbs, he drew more out and smoothed it just below her eye. He'd done a number on her this time, worse than Jonas had seen in months.

"You must divorce him," said Jonas in a low voice, eyes flicking across the room. His father was still passed out, slumped over the table. Even from where he sat, Jonas could smell the reek of urine and ale.

His mother opened her mouth, then closed it. Jonas's eyes narrowed. So she was choosing not to speak.

"If we have neighbors vouch for the nature of your injuries, the Assembly will easily grant you a divorce." Hope inflated in his chest at the thought. A fresh start, the three of them. No more violence. Freed from the shackles of his father's temper, from tip-toeing around him, unsure of which small detail would incense him this time.

It could be laughing at something his father hadn't meant to be funny. It could be his mother had passed his father the bowl of stew with the fewest pieces of mutton. It could be that it was raining, or that he'd lost another ten sólas gambling at the mead hall.

At age ten, Jonas had developed an ear for the pitch of his father's voice. He knew precisely when to make himself small, when to slink into the shadows with Ilías and vanish to the elm tree. He'd learned to endure the sounds of his mother being hurt.

But this plan...it had to work. Their neighbor had found Jonas and Ilías in the elm tree. Had taken one look at the longhouse, then told the boys the word which had filled them with such hope.

"Divorce."

Jonas had clung to this word for weeks, had quietly collected information. He'd learned that if a woman had visible injuries on her body and had honorable people to vouch for her at the Assembly, the Law Speaker would readily grant her a divorce.

His mother's cracked lips parted, the word a bare whisper. "No."

The hope in his chest fizzled out of him, leaving his limbs heavy. "But..."

Her eyes met his—all the brightness which had once shone long having bled out of them. She licked her lips, then spoke in a rusty voice. "He is my husband. I cannot."

Jonas heard the words she did not give voice to.

I love him.

I love him and will not leave.

I love him and will doom you and your brother to this misery.

This was love. It made a person selfish. It enthralled them. Made them walk to their own doom. He looked at his mother, his chest burning with hatred.

Love was nothing but a weapon to be used against you. It was safer to be alone.

Jonas's heart hardened, and he made a silent vow to himself: This will never be you.

―――

JONAS STARTLED AWAKE, nausea coiling in his stomach. After several shallow breaths, he sat up. *Dream*, he told himself. It was naught but a dream. Jonas closed his eyes. Pictured the sturdy trunk of the elm tree, a vibrant spray of branches. He saw the rolling fields of golden wheat; the skies painted with the brushstrokes of the gods—pinks, yellows, blues—as the sun sank below the horizon.

His pulse calmed, and his chest loosened. The dreams were a blessing and a curse; an echo of his past, but a reminder of his future.

Unfamiliar laughter met his ears, and his stomach clenched anew. He'd forgotten for a brief moment that there was another with them for the time being. Sitting, he rubbed the sleep from his eyes.

A gloomy day, the clouds hung low in the sky, a raven calling out from the pinewoods surrounding them. The grass around him was dampened with dew, and Jonas knew it wouldn't be long before it was frost clinging to the blades and the Crew pulled the tents from the wagon.

To his right, Gunnar lay on his stomach, his black locs peeking from beneath a mound of furs. The rest of the bedding had been packed away for the day. Jonas searched for his brother—always the last to rise—before recalling it had been Ilías's night for watch duty.

The scent of cooked food wafted to his nose, and suddenly Jonas was wide awake.

He rolled up his bed, splashed cool water from the stream on his face, and pulled on his lébrynja armor for the day. Smoothing the scales flat across his chest and shoulders, he cast a glance toward the fire. Silla's back shook in silent laughter while Ilías spoke with animation, eyes bright despite a night spent on watch duty.

Jonas felt a swell of affection for his younger brother and a touch of jealousy at his ability to put people at ease. Sure, women flocked to Jonas, but it was all surface level.

Which is what you want, he reminded himself.

Ilías, on the other hand, was a master of befriending others, of charming the stories from them. Even through everything, he hadn't lost that spark. And Jonas hoped he never did.

The clash of metal caught his attention. Rey and Hekla practiced sword-craft on the edge of the glade. He watched Hekla duck low to avoid the arc of Rey's longsword, her unusual left-handed swing a powerful reply. She stumbled, throwing her prosthetic hand down to stabilize her, cursing as the fingers curved up unexpectedly and she fell to the ground. Rey did not relent, and Hekla rolled to escape his advancing blow.

Jonas yawned and sauntered to the fire.

"Morning," he said, his voice thick with sleep.

"Morning, Jonas." Silla pressed a steaming cup of spiced róa into his hands. He stared at it for a long second. She'd eagerly taken over the cooking last night and was up bright and early this morning.

Two meals does not cancel out her trickery, he thought bitterly.

Her eyes met his, her smile just as forced as his own. "Do you like your róa sweetened with honey?" she asked.

"Please," he gritted out.

Her cheeks plumped up, revealing a dimple in her right cheek. "As do I," she said, turning to his brother. "You see, Ilías? You must try it!"

As Silla stirred a spoon of honey into his cup, a scent caught Jonas's attention. It was like porridge, but...nutty.

"What is that smell?" He wandered to the fire, looking into the pot. It appeared as porridge should, not the monstrosity which Sigrún served up each morning. And it smelled...amazing.

"She toasted the porridge," said Ilías from behind him. "*Toasted it.*"

Jonas forced a stony expression to his face, then turned to the curly-haired woman. A red flush crept up her neck, as she handed him a bowl. "It is a basic thing, really. You are too easily impressed, Ilías."

Settling before the fire, Jonas forced his attention to his daymeal. His eyes widened with the first mouthful—he hadn't known porridge could taste like this. It must be, as Ilías put it, the toasting. He considered for a moment what it might be like to eat like this every day on the road. It would make it more bearable. But it would mean pandering to this woman, when the Bloodaxe Crew had more pressing things to worry themselves with.

Rey approached, a sour look on his face as Silla handed him a steaming cup of róa.

"Well met, Rey!" she said brightly. "Have you finished your training? Do you practice each morning?"

Rey scowled. "Do you always speak so much?"

"Yes," the irritating woman chirped. She was remarkably unafraid of Axe Eyes and far less quiet than Jonas had initially assumed. And as his gaze traveled the length of her frumpy dress—buttoned right up to her neck—he wondered what other secrets she might be hiding. *Hábrók's wrinkled bollocks*, he thought, scowling. His dream had muddled his mind.

Silla pressed a bowl into Rey's hands, and it was hard not to notice that it was heaped full of porridge, far larger than any of the other portions. She had already noticed that Rey never stopped eating; the man was permanently hungry.

Rey's scowl deepened. "It is unnatural to be so...joyful at this time of the day."

A laugh bubbled from the back of her throat, but she seemed to realize Rey was serious and made a strange choking sound as she busied herself stirring the porridge. Jonas spent the rest of the daymeal forcing his thoughts to the sólas buried in his caches; to the job in Istré; to his lands. He and Ilías had toiled for five long years to earn it back. Had slept on the cold, hard ground, had spilled blood and paid with their own. When they regained their lands, it would be because they'd *earned* it, not because someone had taken pity on them.

————

THEY SET up camp that night in a clearing in the midst of the pinewoods, the toothy, green needles framing a cloud-covered sky. Sigrún had shot two more rabbits that day, and Silla had cooked them over a spit and served them with the last of the bread. It wasn't her best work, she knew it, but the ingredients she had were so limiting. The Bloodaxe Crew had cleaned their plates, though, and had no complaints amongst them. With mushrooms or additional herbs, Silla could make something that tasted a thousand times better—so good, the Crew would want to keep her with them all the way north.

After washing up, Silla glanced at the Crew. The fire was low and glowing orange; Ilías, Sigrún, and Jonas were huddled together deep in the throes of a game of dice—no sign of Rey, Hekla, or Gunnar.

All evening, she'd managed to keep thoughts of her father from drifting to mind. But now that things were settled for the night, they crept through the bars of her mental cage, filling her with hurt and sorrow.

I loved you like my own kin.

Then why didn't you trust me? she wanted to scream. *Why didn't you tell me the truth?* Silla's fingers skimmed along the vial hanging from her neck, her thoughts shifting in an instant.

Leaves to forget him. Leaves to feel better.

She squeezed her eyes shut, trying to quiet the voice within her. Silla had already taken her allocated skjöld leaf for the night, yet still, her body thirsted for more. Always *one more*. Always *who does it hurt*. Always *you deserve some happiness*. She'd pulled them from the vial, had laid them all out, had counted them once, twice, three times.

Ten.

Ten leaves, ten nights, ten remedies left before she would be powerless as a tide of pain engulfed her. Silla had unfolded her map, had traced her fingers over the dot marked Svarti. If they continued at this pace, they'd reach it before her vial ran empty. She reassured herself over and over, yet still, angst burned in her stomach.

Take one.

"I must move my feet," Silla gritted out, unable to sit with her thoughts and worry any longer. She looked toward the woods. They were silent. Still. And when the Bloodaxe Crew hadn't been watching, she'd slipped some bread crusts into her pocket to leave for the spirits. If she found some edible plants, she could add them to her offering, and perhaps make up for her absence last night.

Picking up an empty storage box from the crate of food provisions, her mind was made up. She'd keep close, and she'd be quick. And with that, Silla slipped into the shadows of the forest.

The woods held a sweet and earthy scent, silent save for the crunch of pine needles beneath Silla's feet as she meandered between stems. After a few minutes, the familiar curl of a wild sorrel leaf set against the bleached stem of a birch caught her attention. Bending low to examine it, she straightened abruptly at the brittle crack of a twig. She turned slowly, letting out a shaky exhale as she recognized the form leaning against a tree.

Jonas.

The last light of the day caught on the bronzed buckles holding his armored jacket together—on the golden swath of hair pulled taut and secured at his crown. Though he said nothing, he watched her with blue eyes so deep and intense, it felt as though he was pulling her into him. Silla opened her mouth, then closed it. "Hello, Jonas," she finally said. "We *must* stop meeting like this." His perplexed look had her pressing her lips tightly together.

His gaze hardened into a scowl. "You should not be alone out here. There are wolves in these woods."

The pull of his eyes intensified, and her skin prickled. "Then I'm grateful for your company, warrior."

His brows dipped lower. "No."

"No?"

"No. I came to bring you back to camp. I have better things to do than to coddle an imprudent girl who wants to pick flowers in a forest filled with monsters."

Silla's hands flexed as she held his gaze. "I'm not a *girl*. I've seen twenty winters." *How old is he?* Silla examined his face. Mid-twenties, perhaps? "And I appreciate your concern, but I do not need coddling."

A smirk curved Jonas's lips as he folded his arms across his chest. "There are things in these woods that would give you nightmares."

"I'm sure they're no match for what I already dream of." The words came out before she could stop herself. Silla's gaze fell to the ground as she was consumed with memories of her nightmare. She hated that he'd seen her in that moment of vulnerability. With a sigh, she shook her head. "Why did you follow me? I thought it would appeal to you for some forest creature to finish me off." Jonas's gaze slid to the tree beside her, his lips thinning.

"You do not wish for that?"

"No."

Surprise washed through her, and Silla found herself abruptly without words.

"Do not take it to mean anything, Curls. It is my foolish conscience and nothing more."

Her brows snapped together, her mind whirling. The overbearing, money-hungry warrior worried for her safety. Had a *conscience*. "Has your conscience seen mushrooms in these woods?"

Jonas cast a look at the skies. "No. My conscience insists you go back to the safety of camp."

"Five minutes." She turned back to the sorrel, bending to pick a handful.

Jonas scoffed. "I cannot decide if you're brave or just a fool."

"Definitely brave," she quipped, tucking the leaves into the storage box. Straightening, she stepped between the trees, studying the ground for mushroom caps.

"I could throw you over my shoulder," growled Jonas, trudging after her.

"And what would you do, then?"

Much to her chagrin, her stomach heated at the thought. Silla decided ignoring him was the best course of action.

A twig snapped violently behind her. "Do not test my patience, Curls."

"Leave me be, Jonas."

"I cannot," he growled.

"Why not?" she demanded, whirling on him. Why did he care? What sort of strange moral code did this man have? Her gaze slid along the scar on his cheekbone. "I...cannot sit there," she muttered, looking away. "I cannot sit with my thoughts. I need to do something. Need to move."

Jonas raked a hand along his hair, tugging on the knot at his crown. With a heavy breath, he said, "Five minutes."

A smile curved the corners of Silla's lips, and she tried not to bounce on her feet. "Your stomach will thank you at the evening meal tomorrow, Jonas, when I have mushrooms and herbs for the stew." *And when the forest spirits don't set fog upon us or open holes in the glades for the horses to trip on,* she did not add.

He grumbled something she couldn't quite hear. They walked in silence, Silla searching in the dim light for any trace of herbs or mushrooms. But the longer they went without sign of edible plants, the more her stomach sank. She'd have to make do with the scant sorrel she'd collected. It was better than nothing.

"Did you truly lose your lands?" asked Jonas, dragging her from her thoughts.

Silla turned and blinked at him. There was something in his expression she couldn't quite place. Slowly, she nodded.

"I am sorry for that." Jonas opened his mouth, then closed it. His eyes hardened. "Still it does not justify your climbing into our wagon."

"Trust me, had I known it was *your* wagon, I'd have stayed far from it," Silla said tartly. "Surely you understand I was desperate. I had no money, feared...my cousin's men would catch me and cut my throat. What would you have me do?"

"I'd expect you to earn your ride, not *steal* it."

"You're quite stubborn," she said, blowing out an exasperated breath. This man's mind was as immovable as a troll who'd seen sunlight.

"I am *determined* because I understand what work is," Jonas returned in a low voice. He prowled toward her, and Silla forced herself to hold her ground. "I have not had things *handed* to me in this world."

Silla could not suppress the laugh which bubbled up. "You think I've had things handed—"

He was closer now, and so much taller than her. Silla's words died on her tongue, her heart pumping energy through her veins. "This job is important. The biggest payout we've ever had. If you ruin it for me—"

Silla's temper flared sharply, powering her limbs. Dropping the storage box, she seized Jonas by the buckles of his armor and forced him back against a tree. Her heart pounded in her ears, body flooding with heat. "Listen, Wolf," she snarled. "I've just watched my father die. Have survived the grimwolves and warbands of the Twisted Pinewoods. I do not need an overgrown, money-greedy warrior to push me around."

Jonas's eyes settled on hers, darkening. "You're not a mouse at all. And you're far from compliant."

Silla's stomach grew light and fluttery at his words, but she hadn't the time to consider them before Jonas's hands shot up. Quicker than she could track, Jonas spun them around, and Silla found her own back pressed into the tree, wrists pinned at her sides. She sucked in a deep breath. Stared into his aggravatingly blue eyes. He was so close she could smell him—iron, leather, and that scent which was all *him*.

Jonas leaned in, his hot breath feathering along her jaw. "I don't care what you think."

For a moment, she could not speak. But she'd had enough of him and wished for him to know it. "Oh, but you do," she whispered, staring hard at the man. "You care what *everyone* thinks, don't you? Because that's all you have— that handsome face of yours. Beneath it, I'm certain there's nothing worth mentioning."

She might have lost her mind—lost all sense of preservation. Silla did not understand why she felt such satisfaction in taunting this warrior—this man who could snap her neck without a second thought. But he'd followed her into the woods. Had told her he did not wish her harm. And each flex of his jaw, each jagged breath against her skin sent a thrill rippling through her blood.

More. She needed more.

Jonas's eyes dipped momentarily to her lips, before meeting her own in a searing gaze. "You should mind your tongue around me."

"Or what?" She licked her lips, her heart thudding in her chest. She could feel the anger—pure and raw—filling the air between them. It should frighten her, but it only livened her, *excited* her.

His blue eyes speared into her. "You *are* trouble, Silla. But there is something you clearly need to be taught." He leaned in, and her eyes fell shut. When he spoke, his voice was low and rough. "Do not play games you cannot win."

Her eyes flew open.

The pressure loosened from her wrists, and Jonas drew back. "Go back to camp. It is not safe in these woods for you." Her foolish body throbbed, aching for his warmth. But Jonas was already stalking off like the wolf he was.

For one dizzying moment, she considered chasing after him. But after several deep breaths of forest air, Silla's senses returned. Retrieving the discarded storage box and pulling out some of the sorrel, she assembled a small altar for the spirits at the base of the tree. Adding the bread crusts with shaking hands, she whispered, "I have no mead, but I hope this will suffice."

And with that, she made her way back to camp, her skin burning with irritation...with anger. But as the flames of the campfire came into view, a thought occurred to her.

Not once in the past twenty minutes had she thought of the leaves...nor of her father.

SIXTEEN

Silla had always been an unapologetically chipper morning person, yet she felt resistance in climbing out from beneath her furs the next day. Already, she'd made a mess of things, and now she'd have to face them —Rey, who doggedly sniffed for her lies; Hekla, whom she'd deeply offended; and Jonas...well, she wasn't sure what to make of their encounter the night prior.

"Rallying cry, Silla," she murmured, weaving her hair into a collection of braids. "It's a new day. A fresh start to make things right."

Another gloomy day, the clouds looked bloated with rain, and her breaths steamed the chilled air. On her way to the fire, Silla passed Rey, working his way through various stances with his longsword. He gripped the hilt with two hands, swinging it around in a powerful curve before rapidly dropping to one knee and raising the blade in a defensive stance. It all happened in two heartbeats or less, movements he'd obviously memorized. Rey's focus was unwavering, and the stern look on his face told her he took it as seriously as the rest of his life.

Sigrún stirred the embers of the fire after a long night on watch duty. As she approached, Sigrún made a gesture with her hands which she now recognized as a greeting, and Silla returned the motion. With a nod, Sigrún wandered toward the stream, and Silla set to work on the daymeal.

After adding kindling to the fire, she set the steel kettle in the flames to boil and toasted the grains for the porridge in the cookpot. It was a relief to bury herself in this mindless work, even for a few hours a day. A tiny bit of normalcy amid the wreckage of her life.

Father would have loved this, Silla thought. Tears stung her eyes as she stirred the grains. "I miss you," she whispered, her chest clenching tight. But such tender thoughts were quickly displaced by anger at her father's betrayal.

Thankfully she hadn't much time to dwell on it, as the Bloodaxe Crew was soon up and keeping her busy. She passed out bowls of porridge and cups of spiced róa, a *good morning* for each person she greeted. Even Hekla, who accepted hers with a silent nod. Even Rey, who merely grunted. And Jonas, whose gaze from across the fire was like a lure hooked in her belly, reeling her in.

Curse that man and his quarrelsome nature. But the night before...had she imagined it, or had something shifted? Thinking of his body pressing her up against the tree stirred something in her veins and made her skin heat. But it didn't matter. Even if Jonas didn't despise her, Silla could not allow him to get close.

After the washing was done and the fire drowned with the dishwater, the Crew mounted their horses. Silla made her way to the shining white mare. Glancing over her shoulder, she withdrew a pilfered carrot from her pocket, holding it for Horse to grab with her front teeth.

"I know, it's small. I promise you'll get better if they allow me to stay," she whispered, stroking Horse's forehead. "Can you help me out with your warrior? Tell me how to earn his trust?"

Horse nudged gently in search of more carrots.

"Tomorrow. I promise it."

Silla stroked down Horse's nose, then climbed on the wagon and settled into her nest of furs. Though he'd left her unbound the night before, Rey secured her hands once more to the loop on the side of the wagon. Under somber skies, they set off down the trail and onto the Road of Bones.

The morning was quiet and spectacularly dull. Silla shifted, trying to get comfortable, and stared, unfocused, out the back of the wagon. She was in the dreamy place between wakefulness and sleep when she saw movement from within the forest. Her spine straightened as she squinted into the woods.

Nothing but stillness.

Probably a deer, she thought, reclining back onto the furs.

A bird trilled, longer and sharper than the others. Something about the sound raised the hairs on her arms. She sat up again.

"Rey?" she called out, but he didn't turn. She was being silly. It was simply a bird or perhaps a playful forest spirit.

But then it happened—so swiftly she barely had time to process it—a rush of warriors from the woods on all sides.

There had to be twenty of them, great axes and shields in hand, hair flying wildly from beneath tarnished helms. The men had a hard look to them, their leather breastplates scuffed and scarred, and on their shield was drawn a black raven with a sword in its beak. Synchronized, the men broke silently off in groups of three or four. This approach was clearly well-planned.

"Rey!" she screamed, but he was already there. His hevrít slashed through her bonds, his strong hands hooking under her arms and hauling her from the furs. She was dropped roughly onto the ground and shoved beneath the wagon.

"Stay there," he barked.

Her pulse beat with the force of a hammer. The rocks of the Road of Bones jutted between her ribs as she worked the rope loose from around her hands, watching three sets of feet approach Rey.

"Iron Ravens control this stretch of the road," growled one of the men. "We must check your wagon. You'll need to procure five hundred sólas for passage."

"*We* do not pay passage," said Rey gruffly. His boots edged a few inches apart. "And you will not touch the wagon. We're under orders to keep the contents confidential."

"Everyone pays passage," came another voice. "Got twenty more in the trees ready to show you the axe."

"Do you know who we are?" asked Rey.

A set of boots stepped forward. "Does not matter. Pay the passage, or we'll withdraw our goodwill."

"We. Do. Not. Pay. Passage," Rey growled. "And let me repeat, since your wits seem dulled: we will defend this wagon by blade. Do you understand that, or must I speak slower?"

The boots edged forward another step. "If you value your life, you will not talk to us like that, warrior," the man spat. "What is in the wagon that is of such value?"

"Spare me your breath," gritted Rey. "You already know."

"Seems to me you've wool in your ears," said the first man. "Show us the wagon, or your bones will join the rest of them on this road."

"Why should I show you when you already know?" asked Rey. "You've waited for us, have you not?"

"Must be something of value," said the first man, edging toward it.

"I would counsel you against that," warned Rey. "Unless you'd like your skull separated from your neck."

Silla heard the soft *shick* of a sword being unsheathed and the crunch of rocks beneath boots as several pairs edged forward. Her pulse took off at a gallop once more. One set of boots lunged toward the back of the wagon. With a low growl, Rey's weight shifted. Silla heard a wet, sucking sound. And then, the warrior grunted and crumbled to the ground.

Widened black eyes stared at her, the man's mouth opening and closing like a fish. He clutched at his neck, blood seeping through his fingers and puddling on the road. A horrid series of desperate gasps sent a shudder through her, and Silla forced her eyes shut until the sounds had extinguished.

"You'll regret that you shite-eating kunta," growled one of the men, and Silla opened her eyes in alarm; several pairs of boots crunched toward them.

"I've been called far worse than that," muttered Rey.

A sharp whistle pierced the air, and chaos descended upon the world.

Screams of fury and the discordant clash of metal shook the air. Rey launched after the other two men, far enough from the wagon that Silla could see him take on both opponents with that ruthless focus she'd seen in his practice sessions. With a brutal slash to one man's neck, an arc of blood spilled through the air, raining across Rey's face and splattering onto the Road of Bones.

"Merciful gods," muttered Silla, revulsion and awe coursing through her. She wanted to look away—but could not. There was a macabre art to what the man did; his sinuous movements delivering death in efficient, if not dramatic, fashion.

Ducking the other man's blow, Rey's blade sank into the back of his opponent's knees. With an animalistic howl, the man crumbled to the ground, his helm tumbling loose. Rey straightened, death incarnate, looming above the warrior, and drove his longsword into the man's skull so thoroughly the crunch of bone echoed off the trees.

Nausea churned in Silla's gut, and she diverted her attention to the rest of the Bloodaxe Crew, who battled a seemingly impossible number of warriors.

Jonas, Ilías, Hekla, and Gunnar fought back-to-back, shields up and swords thrusting through the gaps as the Iron Ravens swarmed upon them. With serpentine speed, Jonas's sword slashed up into the armpit and straight through the neck of one attacker—deeper than Silla thought possible. The man dropped to his knees, crimson bubbling from his lips. With a grunt, Jonas yanked his sword loose, swinging it over-shield and into the throat of the man who had filled the space.

Silla's gaze swept in search of Sigrún, and as a white-fletched arrow pierced the neck of a warrior, she gathered the archer was hidden in the shadows of the woods. Sigrún's arrow felled another warrior charging at Ilías; the man fell to the ground, trampled by his brothers in arms as they surged at the Bloodaxe Crew.

"Arrows!" yelled Rey, and the group crouched low, shields raised overhead, as a volley of arrows rained down upon them. With a curse, Rey charged at the archers, shield raised in one hand, longsword in the other. The archers scattered as Rey's enormous form plowed for them, but they didn't get far. Strike after punishing strike, Rey hacked into them, cutting them down as though they were untrained farmers.

The wall of shields broke, the Bloodaxe Crew rushing free and targeting the Iron Ravens with blade and fury.

Dropping her shield, Hekla became a blaze of claws and dagger, fighting with a series of rapid-fire slashes. Her black braid flying behind her, Hekla's eyes were alight. She looked alive, like she was doing what she was born to do. Ducking, she felled her opponent with a quick left-handed slash behind his knee. Silla glimpsed the glinting silver claws drip crimson before she dragged them across the man's throat.

Four sets of feet crunched quietly on stones as they skirted the wagon. Silla hadn't heard them approach, and neither, apparently, had the Bloodaxe Crew, who had gradually edged away from the wagon as they met a fresh wave of Iron Ravens.

"They're distracted. Unhook the wagon."

No. Panic flared through her. She was unarmed, and the feet were on either side of the wagon now. Horse whinnied, pawing at the ground, but the men were undeterred. They crowded around the buckles, loosening the straps from Rey's white mare.

Silla's eyes darted to the dead man lying at the wagon's rear, to the sword clutched in his lifeless hand. She wriggled on her stomach toward him.

As she reached the back of the wagon, she looked around. With no boots in sight, Silla took a deep breath, then lunged forward. Her cloak caught on a rock, and she tugged at it until it ripped free. Then she extended her shoulder farther,

farther, until her fingers closed around the cool leather hilt, and she pulled it free from the dead warrior's grasp.

Just as relief began to swell in her chest, a heavy boot slammed down on her wrist. A scream tore from her lips, pain knifing up her arm. She tried to wrench free, but her wrist was pinned firmly to the ground.

"Well, well, well," rasped a cold voice. "What have we here?"

A rough, calloused hand hooked under her shoulder, jerking her outward. Rocks dug into the soft flesh of her belly as she was dragged kicking from beneath the wagon. Silla was hauled to her feet and stared into the pale blue eyes of one of the Iron Ravens.

The man's face and armor were smeared with cracked mud. Like with the Battle Thorns warband, she could tell from his eyes that this was a man who'd lived a hard life. There was a hint of desperation which made her blood chill.

"Hello, lovely."

She swung her foot up as hard as she could, right between the man's legs. Howling, he grabbed for a handful of hair, but she was already turning. Silla wrenched herself free, pain flaring from her scalp as a lock tore loose. The knowing feeling inside her took control, steering her as quickly as possible toward the woods.

"Hóra!" she heard behind her, but she didn't pause. She ran, darting between stems, jumping over fallen logs, the trees whipping past her in a flurry of green and brown. Branches lashed Silla's arms, and she hoisted her skirts, cursing them as they hampered her progress. She paused, pressing her back against the scaled trunk of a pine, breaths surging in and out of her.

"Come out, girl," growled a voice from behind her. "We do not bite. Much."

Silla's mind whirled. She knew the farther she got from the Bloodaxe Crew, the more danger she'd be in, but her hiding place was too exposed; the man would soon find her. Her feet decided for her; she sprang from the tree and darted deeper into the woods. Another trill echoed, and Silla dared to glance behind her. The man was gaining on her, his axe drawn. Panic flared higher.

And then, Silla collided with something hard, her vision exploding red. Something circled around her, pinning her arms to her sides. As the red haze cleared from her vision, she looked up into the face of a man with a bushy black beard and pale blue eyes remarkably like those of the man she'd just kicked. He squeezed her tighter until her face pressed into his chest, and she gagged on the smell of his unwashed body.

"Release me!" she screamed, kicking at him. He twisted her around until her back was pressed to his chest. A heavy hand clamped over her mouth, her arms shackled by the other.

"Mind her feet." The man she'd kicked breathed heavily as he caught up with them. "Kunta," he added with a hate-filled glare.

"What of the blades?" asked the man who held Silla.

"I grew distracted," replied the man. "*She* hid beneath the wagon."

"Focus, Vilmar. The rhodium. What of the rhodium?" repeated the man who held her, sounding exasperated.

"They're better warriors than we were led to believe. There was little chance we'd best them." Vilmar was silent a moment, regarding Silla as if he was appraising livestock.

When he spoke, his words chilled her.

"But fortune favors us, brother. Now we have *her*. She'll get us the blades."

SEVENTEEN

"**W**alk," barked the warrior who held her, and Silla stumbled through the trees toward the Road of Bones. Her thoughts ran wild. She struggled against his grip, but the harder she fought, the tighter he held her. And as they marched back toward the road, the silence of the woods made her stomach coil tighter. The Bloodaxe Crew would never trade their weapons for *her*.

At last, they reached the road, the sounds of battle having faded entirely. They stepped onto the road, the trees opening up to overcast midday light. The smell of death polluted the air. Bodies were strewn everywhere, and Silla forgot how to breathe for a moment. Her gaze landed on the corpse of an Iron Ravens warrior, a bird pecking at his eyeball, then bounced to another, shattered bone and mangled tendons dangling from a severed leg.

The Crew was crowded around the wagon, where a lone Iron Ravens member was held down between Jonas and Rey, pleading for his life.

"Hae!" called out Vilmar. "We found your girl. We'll trade you for her."

Her gaze bounced from Rey's murderous glare to Jonas's seething blue as they looked up from their ministrations.

"Keep her," growled Rey. "You would do us a favor."

Silla's pulse grew erratic, a flash of panic leaving her hot and shaky.

Her captors exchanged a look of confusion. Words of desperation spilled from her mouth, but they were muffled by the warrior's hand. She began to fight his grip once more, but paused as a wet gurgling sound reached her ears.

Vilmar fell to his knees, blood oozing from his neck, where a handaxe was now buried.

It all happened so quickly she hadn't a chance to think, to react. Her hair ruffled lightly. A faint hiss met her ears. Hot, wet liquid splattered her face. The man behind her choked, his grip loosening. He fell forward, into her. Silla's knees hit the rocky ground, jarring her so hard her teeth rattled. Then she was flattened beneath the warrior's unbearable weight.

She lay face down on the ground, pinned between the road and the man's massive body. The scent of earth mingled with the reek of body odor, and she was too stunned to move.

"Help me get this arse off her, Gunnar." Hekla. It was Hekla's voice.

The weight was eased from her, hands looping gently beneath her shoulders, and she was rolled onto her back. Silla blinked up at Gunnar, Hekla, and Sigrún, their faces warping and bending above her.

"You all right, dúlla?" Hekla asked.

Silla slowly sat up, sucking in a harsh breath at the pressure on her wrist. "They—he discovered me beneath the wagon. I had no weapon. I had no choice but to run."

"You're safe now. Iron Ravens...worse than tide scum," Hekla added, spitting on the ground behind her.

"My thanks," Silla murmured, but inside, she was screaming. Wiping her face, the dead warrior's blood smeared across it. She reeked of it, could feel him all over her...and that blade. It had been inches from her face. What if their aim had been off? She could have died! She'd been scarce inches from it.

"Thank Jonas," murmured Hekla, pulling the axe free from Vilmar's neck and wiping the blood and gore on the dead man's breeches. She held the weapon out, pointing to the triangular pattern carved into the haft. "It's his handaxe."

Silla's lips parted a hair's breadth. Jonas.

Gunnar crouched beside her. "They hurt you, Hammer?"

Silla lifted her shaking arm, turning it to examine her wrist. She gritted her teeth as pain sliced from it. "My wrist aches, but I will be fine."

Sigrún took her wrist, prodding it gently and turning it side to side. She made a quick succession of hand signals to Hekla.

"Sigrún has an ointment that works miracles," said Hekla, offering her left hand. Silla accepted with her uninjured hand, rising to her feet, but froze in place.

A low, agonized wail rattled the air, setting the fine hairs on the back of Silla's neck on end.

"What—"

"Rey and Jonas question the last of them," answered Hekla.

Silla's gaze found its way back to the wagon, landing on the two warriors holding a man pinned between them. They were a terrifying sight—faces flecked with dirt and blood; Jonas's golden hair streaked with red; Rey's knuckles torn open. And between them, the beleaguered Iron Ravens survivor cowered, Rey's hevrít pressed to his knuckle.

"Anders," rasped Rey. "If you'd like the blessing of a swift death, you'd best start talking. You'll soon run out of fingers, and I'll have to start on your toes." The man wailed, but Rey cut him off. "Who betrayed us, Anders? Who told you of the wagon's contents?"

"No one!" bleated the man. "We searched you as we would any other wagon on the road."

Rey made a soft tutting sound, hacking through bone and tendon as effortlessly as Silla cut into an onion. As the finger fell to the wagon with a soft *thunk*, Silla felt faint.

The man had only two fingers left.

Anders howled, triggering a shiver so violent it hit every notch on its way down Silla's spine. She slammed her eyes shut.

"I do not think you'll pry answers from him, Axe Eyes," said Ilías wryly from behind him.

"We shall see, No Beard," growled Rey, turning back to Anders. "He'll talk, or I'll bring him to the edge and keep him there until he begs for the mercy of death. Anders, your lies do nothing but delay your fate," continued Rey. He turned to his friend. "Jonas, tell me. Do the Iron Ravens greet travelers with more than twenty warriors armed to the tooth?"

"I've not seen it in my life. And I've walked this road many times."

Rey turned back to Anders. "Jonas has never seen it, Anders. I've never seen it. Which means you are a dishonest man."

Jonas scowled at him. "Who told you of the weapons, Anders?"

"N-no one! There was no tip."

A sickening crunch preceded another shrill screech. Rey yanked the man's arm behind his back, wrenching it to an unnatural angle, then twisting until another nauseating crunch sounded. He placed the man's mangled arm back on the wagon.

"Stop!" pleaded Anders. "Stop!"

Silla spoke up, her voice ringing clear across the road. "They knew of the rhodium. One of the men in the woods asked about it."

While Rey refused to acknowledge her words, Jonas's blue gaze found hers, dropping to the wrist she held cradled to her chest. His eyes seemed to burn into her skin, and Silla released a shaky breath as he turned his attention back to Anders.

"Anders," said Jonas with mock disappointment. "How thick-skulled are you? You *will* die. The manner is your choice, yet you choose only more pain." His grip on the man's arm tightened.

Rey chopped off another finger in a jerky movement which betrayed his calm demeanor. As Anders bucked, Rey and Jonas held the man firmly in place.

"Last chance, Anders," warned Jonas. "You're nearly out of fingers. You do not want Axe Eyes to start with your toes. He'll begin with a hammer."

"I-it was Leif!" Anders howled. "Leif from the Owl's Hollow. H-he tipped us off."

Rey's lips curled into a snarl, then he put his head beside the man's ear and spoke so low Silla barely heard the words. "It took you *nine fingers* to tell the truth. Nine lies you told me, Anders. You are not an honest man, and I should not grant you a quick death. But I've no use for you, and we must be on our way."

His head tipped up, and he pinned Silla with a look so cold her veins frosted over.

It was a message—a warning.

Rey's eyes seemed dispassionate, dead on the surface, but she saw what lurked below. A glimmer of excitement. Of enjoyment. There was something wrong here. Something so very wrong.

She knew what was coming. Knew she should look away. She willed herself to do so, but her body would not cooperate. Rey kept his eyes on Silla as he ran the blade across the man's throat, severing it effortlessly. Finally, her stubborn eyelids slammed shut, but they couldn't block the gurgled chokes which filled the air. Then it was utterly silent.

It was at that moment, Silla realized her mistake.

She should never have crawled into that wagon in Reykfjord.

Rey wasn't just an unpleasant, controlling warrior: he was more dangerous than the monsters in the woods. She'd feel safer sleeping in the wilderness than near this man.

Rey let the body fall to the road and stalked over to her, crowding her with his massive frame. Evidence of death and violence clung to him, making her heart crash against her ribs.

"You afraid of me, *Sunshine?*"

Silla blinked at the name. He wielded it like a weapon, in a mocking way meant to cut. Swallowing the lump in her throat, she did not answer and refused to meet his gaze.

Apparently, her demeanor told him everything he needed to know.

"Good. Next time, do as you're told."

She flinched as he took her injured wrist in his enormous hand, his skin inexplicably warm considering how cold his soul was. Rey turned her wrist over and frowned.

"Get in the wagon."

———

THEY MADE camp earlier than usual that night. After Silla had washed the blood from her face and thrown up her daymeal, the Bloodaxe Crew quickly took off down the road. They stopped only briefly for a mid-day meal, to rest and water the horses.

Silla's wrist was puffy and red, throbbing angrily by the time they pulled into a clearing well off the Road of Bones. Thankfully, Rey had not bound her hands to the wagon. Perhaps having seen firsthand how utterly useless she was in violent situations, he'd finally deemed her harmless.

Though her shaking had subsided, Silla was on edge, jumping at the chirp of birds and the snort of horses. Sigrún dug the ointment out of her saddlesack and helped Silla slather it onto her wrist before wrapping it in strips of linen. It did a remarkable job in reducing the ache and swelling, yet still, as she sat, her mind was hazy and stuck on the events earlier in the day. She retreated early to bed, clutching her father's tunic and the heart-shaped rock.

And yet they brought her no comfort.

The scene on the road replayed in her mind. The handaxe passing inches from her face. The hot splatter of blood dripping down her cheeks. The warrior's keening wails. The look in Rey's eyes as he cut that man's throat. His eyes—they were so cold. So...unaffected.

They haunted her.

She couldn't shake the feeling that she'd made a mistake joining the Bloodaxe Crew. She hadn't realized until far too late they worked for the king, but there was also something *wrong* with Rey. The look on his face as he'd sliced that man's fingers off.

"He *enjoyed* it," said the little blonde girl, lying on her back in the grass beside Silla. "That man is dangerous."

"Thank you," whispered Silla. "You are truly putting my mind at ease."

It was well into the night when she rolled over for the thousandth time. Her stomach knotted tightly; her mouth was dry.

"Remember," said the little girl. "Remember your promise."

Silla pulled herself to a sitting position. The girl was right. She'd promised herself if she felt she was in danger, she'd leave. Mind made up, Silla gathered her things and shoved them into her bag. The fur trim of her hood tickled her cheeks as she tightened it around her face.

And then, she left, the little blonde girl trailing behind her.

The fire cast light upon her back. She wasn't sure how, but she knew *he* sat there, watching her pick her way toward the edge of the woods.

"Don't look back," advised the little girl. "It will only make his head swell larger."

She walked into the trees and made her way toward the Road of Bones. The farther she got from Rey, the more the knot in her stomach loosened, the tightness of her shoulders eased.

"We survived the walk from Skarstad," said the little girl in an irritatingly chipper voice. "We can make it to the next village on foot and seek shelter. There will be other parties to travel with."

But Silla's feet faltered as the realization hit her. "Axe Eyes has our dagger and hammer." She ran a hand down her face. "We're defenseless."

A curious nagging sensation filled her—the kind one has when they've just left home and have forgotten to drown the embers in the hearth. "Have you forgotten something?" asked the little girl. But the idea was dispelled by a quick rummage through her sack.

Alone in the woods in total darkness, Silla's throat burned with tears. She remembered the Twisted Pinewoods with sudden vivid clarity. The suffocating silence, the despairing solitude, the knowledge no one would ever know were she to die. She was as insignificant as a speck of sand on a long stretch of beach.

What was she doing? Walking from uncertainty toward sure death?

She had a moment of lucidity. If Rey had intended to kill her, he'd have done so already without hesitation.

"Rey thinks you're weak," said the little girl. "Perhaps this was a test. What if he was trying to frighten us away?"

Silla clenched her teeth. He was just like the rest of them, those who thought strength was simply a measure of how hard you swung your sword. He underestimated her resilience. He equated her niceness with weakness.

"Then we shall show him just how wrong he is," growled Silla, turning on her heel.

———

SITTING BEFORE THE FIRE, Rey passed the whetstone along the blade of his handaxe.

It was done. She'd left.

He should feel relieved, and yet...he did not. Instead, he felt a strange desire to chase after her. To keep her from walking to her death.

It is inevitable, he thought. *Her death is inevitable. Best for her to meet it head-on.*

When he thought of the ambush, anger kindled within his veins, threatening to overpower him once more. Anger at what? At Leif's betrayal? Not truly. Leif was nothing but an acquaintance—one who'd kiss Rey's axe when next he was in Reykfjord.

Anger at the Iron Ravens who'd tried to trade the woman for the rhodium blades? Yes, in part, though before he could dispatch them himself, Jonas's handaxe had claimed retribution. That *should* settle him.

And yet, he was not settled. He was angry—with *her*. She had not listened to his orders and had been hurt because of it. Because the Bloodaxe Crew hadn't been good enough. Because he hadn't.

And that was the crux of it. How could they do their job while taking care of this woman? She was not meant to travel with them. She was distracting. Could land them in danger. And the woman was not honest, he'd known this from the start. There was something she was not telling him, he could feel it in his very bones. There was the scar at the corner of her eye which had caused him to hesitate the first time he'd tried to kill her. And those words...

It takes a small man to be ruled by fear, and a large one to show mercy.

Rey *knew* those words. His own father had spoken them to him, to his brother Kristjan. The words had been like hearing a ghost. He'd turned them over in his head long into the night and into the next day, his thoughts drifting to places he did not like for them to go.

She needs to leave, he'd decided. A clear mind was more vital than her help in retrieving the book from Kraki. And if he'd taken his frustrations out on Anders, it might have been for her benefit.

She needed to know who it was she rode with.

It seemed Rey's demonstration had the desired effect. She'd left of her own volition.

She's gone now, he thought. *You'll be able to focus on the job at hand.*

But with that thought, he saw movement at the edge of the glade, a red cloak emerging from between the trees. A small figure strode toward him, her steps fierce and determined. The whetstone he'd been passing over the blade stilled, surprise prickling through him at the sound of her approaching footfalls. It was nearly imperceptible, but he saw it—the look of satisfaction on her face as she stared him down.

The woman marched up to him, pulled her hood down, and lowered her face bare inches from Rey's. She was so near, he could count the freckles scattered across the bridge of her nose, could smell her scent—spring, when the mountain blooms were freshly opened.

"I know what you're trying to do, Rey," she said with ferocity. "It won't work. I've already lived through my worst nightmare. You cannot frighten me away."

Rey was struck speechless, nothing but a jagged breath escaping him. Triumph slid across her face, a faint smile curving her lips. And then, she spun on her heel and returned to her abandoned furs amid the other slumbering figures, laying down beneath them.

Fuck, thought Rey, running a hand through his hair.

And at last, he understood: this girl might not be able to swing a blade, but she had the spirit of a warrior.

EIGHTEEN

S kraeda stared dazedly at the endless rows of pine trees lining the Road of Bones. Her copper braids rustled in a light breeze carrying the surprising warmth of summer. Such a thing was short-lived in Íseldur; soon it would carry the kind of chill which lodged splinters beneath one's skin. Her head pounded, her back ached, and Skraeda could not help the images of soft feather beds from forming in her mind's eye. Soon, she'd need to rest.

The girl in the red cloak had clearly vanished. After days of riding along the Road of Bones, of stopping at each village and farmstead she came upon, there had truly been no sign of her. And now Skraeda had ridden farther than the girl could have possibly traveled on foot.

You were too rash in leaving Reykfjord, she scolded herself. The woman was likely still there, laying low until the search for her died down. What a fool Skraeda was, traipsing through the countryside searching for something that could not be found. *Another failure*, she thought. *The queen will be angered.* The very thought made Skraeda squirm in the saddle.

Another thing ruined by Skraeda's impulsive nature. In the delirium of her fatigue, she was helpless against the memory surging forth.

Water dripped nearby, the rhythmic ping filling the silence. The scent of hay and damp rocks hung heavy in the air, and as Skraeda leaned back against the cold stone wall of her cell, dread began to fill her.

She'd been too brash, she knew that now. Just a little too good to be believable—

she should have let the men in the mead hall win a few more games, shouldn't have returned to the same hall for the third night straight. Skraeda knew this now. Knew that she should have listened to Ilka.

"Come and find honest work with me, Skraeda," her twin had begged.

"Honest work?" Skraeda had scoffed. "Why should I work myself to the bone when I can win a week's wages in a night playing dice?"

"It is too dangerous, Skraeda," Ilka had warned, her voice wavering just a bit. "If you keep reading their emotions, they'll soon catch on to you. You'll draw unwanted attention to yourself."

It was a grounding thing, to have this person who cared so deeply about her well-being. When Skraeda's impulses had gotten the best of her, Ilka could always be counted on to calm her, to force logical thought.

"At the very least, be smart, Skraeda," Ilka had said, throwing a long red braid over her shoulder. "Be patient."

She should have listened.

But logic and patience had flown from her mind when she'd seen the portly man seated in the mead hall. This one could never turn down a wager, she knew it of him. Her fingers had itched, as though some part of her pleaded not to engage with him. Instead, she'd strode straight for him. Her greed had been her undoing. Skraeda was so focused on the prospect of bleeding sólas from him for the third night straight, she'd failed to notice the Klaernar waiting in the shadows. They'd swarmed in on her the moment she'd sat on the bench.

And now she was in a cell.

And soon, she would be put to the pillar.

I'm not ready to die, *thought Skraeda, fingers of panic spreading through her. And she certainly did not wish for a Galdra's death—bound to a post for public ridicule. Forced to bleed for their Bear God, then crushed to death by stones.*

She sucked in a desperate breath.

A cough echoed down the hall, and Skraeda's ears strained. Now there were voices, soft and muffled. A man and a woman. Slowly, they grew louder, until at last, she could make sense of their words.

"A Shadow Hound," the man was saying. His voice was brittle and aged. "And a Solacer."

A woman's soft sigh met Skraeda's ears. "Where are the Ashbringers hiding? What use have we for another empath? A Shadow Hound...I suppose Ástvald can make use of them in Svaldrin."

Outrage gathered in Skraeda's gut. Didn't they know what a Solacer could do? The power she could wield beyond simple emotional regulation?

The footsteps grew louder. Though her cell was lined with Hindrium, clearly it had aged, as her gift bled through. She could sense the faintest wisps of their emotions—curiosity and disappointment. Before she could question this unusual combination, Skraeda found herself face-to-face with the queen of Íseldur.

She gasped, scrambling to her feet. Though it was futile, she smoothed her soiled skirts, ran a hand along her matted and tangled hair. Skraeda felt entirely unpresentable to be staring at royalty...and yet, here she was.

Queen Signe was as beautiful as had been reported in the mead halls. Clad in a gown of ivory, the arctic fox fur wrapped over her shoulders shone even in the dim light of the prison. Her famous white-gold hair, coveted by the Norvalanders and Urkans alike, was woven into intricate braids that showcased golden earrings dangling from her ears. The queen's eyes were ice blue, and as they skimmed over Skraeda, her lips turned down, a ribbon of disgust unspooling in her aura.

Skraeda's stomach clenched down. You are worse than nothing to her, she thought. She was vermin. Unnatural. A thing to be despised and disposed of.

"This is the Solacer, Your Highness," said the man.

Skraeda's gaze flitted to him, landing at once on the red scar slashing across the left side of his face. The man's eye had not been spared, leaving a sliver of milky white surrounded by a lumpy mass of flesh where his eyelid should have been. Short and clad in a brown robe with deep sleeves, he was balding.

"Yes," mused the queen and turned to move on.

"Wait," said Skraeda, to her own surprise. What was she doing?

The queen paused, then turned to face her.

"I...I can be useful," Skraeda heard herself say. "I can help you."

Queen Signe pursed her lips. "You are brave to speak so boldly to me," she said. Her voice was rich and honeyed, and Skraeda swallowed at the sound of it. "We have no need for Solacers."

"I am no ordinary Solacer, Your Highness," Skraeda asserted. "You seem to be searching for Warrior Galdra. And my abilities allow me to sense them out."

The queen's gaze grew so sharp Skraeda could feel it scratching at her skin. "How so?"

Skraeda drew a calming breath. "The Galdra have a...signature of emotions. Their angst and fear can make them stand out in a crowd."

The queen glanced at her companion.

"Your Highness, we have no need of more Solacers right now," said the old man. *"They are abundant. Common."* The man's distaste for her was plain to see, even without her ability to sense his emotions. But the queen was looking at Skraeda, threads of curiosity looping brighter.

Show her, *Skraeda told herself.* You must show her how useful you can be. This could be your only chance for survival.

"I guarantee that I am the best Solacer you've ever housed in these cells," said *Skraeda, her voice growing more confident.* "My Queen, I am at your disposal. Let me be your secret advantage." Using only the gentlest of touches, she pulled on the queen's curiosity.

"What is your name, Solacer?" asked Queen Signe.

"Skraeda."

"And I am to believe that you would turn on your own kind, Skraeda?" mused the queen, a smile teasing the corners of her lips.

"What have the Galdra ever done for me?" The lie tasted bitter in her mouth, but her longing to live made it easily palatable.

The queen's smile deepened. *"Is that so? How would you prove yourself to me?"*

"I have access that the Klaernar do not. The Galdra see me as one of their own. Let me bring them to you. Is there a skill you need?"

"Ashbringer," said Queen Signe, folding her arms over the embroidered bodice of her gown. *"We need many of those with fire magic."*

"I know an Ashbringer!" Skraeda said, her voice rising. You can't, she thought, her heart pounding. But she wanted to live, needed to live, and in that moment, nothing else mattered. *"If you free me, I will bring her to you."*

The queen silently observed Skraeda for a long moment.

"It is a risk," mused the man in the brown robe. *"But it has grown difficult to source Warrior Galdra as of late. Perhaps this could work."*

"Yes," said the queen, her dark blue eyes still on Skraeda.

"Let me prove my loyalty, Your Highness," said Skraeda. *"You won't regret it. I swear it to you."*

Queen Signe tapped a perfectly shaped nail on her chin. *"I see fire in you, girl. I see ambition. Perhaps a bit of myself, really."* She was silent for a moment. *"I will give you one chance. If you fail to bring me an Ashbringer in one day's time, I will send the full force of the Klaernar after you. You won't make it to the pillar, Skraeda. And I assure you, your fate will be far worse than a stoning."*

Skraeda swallowed, but she kept her spine straight. *"I will bring you an Ashbringer, Your Highness. I won't let you down."*

A raven swooped low overhead, its loud caw jarring Skraeda from the memory. The pinewoods climbed back around her, the rutted Road of Bones stretching before her. In the distance, she could hear a large number of the birds making a fuss over something.

You must find the girl, she told herself. *You must not disappoint the queen.*

But her mind was muddled, her bones so weary. She'd need to find an inn and sleep the night through. Once her head had cleared, she would decide what to do next.

As she rounded a bend in the road, a gruesome scene unfolded before her. Corpses—two dozen at least—seeping blood onto the earth-packed road. A flock of ravens swarmed over the bodies, fighting to pick at their faces and hands. What had happened here? Skraeda nudged her horse forward, the black birds complaining loudly as they were displaced from the corpse at which they picked. Dismounting, she bent to examine the body, her eyes tracing the sigil on the shield lying nearby—a black raven with a sword held in beak.

"Iron Ravens," she murmured, looking around. She knew of this warband —they prided themselves on picking the weapons from their victims. How poetic that they now lay slain in the road, their own weapons likely to be scavenged by passers by.

Her eyes fell to a blank space within the corpses, as though the battle had avoided this location. A wagon, perhaps, had stood here? Squatting low, Skraeda examined one of the bodies nearby—a blood-stained warrior missing all but one of his fingers. Most interesting—an inquisition of sorts had occurred here. While not her own preferred method, Skraeda respected a warrior who did what they needed to get answers.

She studied the pair of rutted tracks on either side of this space. Yes. It seemed to have been a wagon. And as her gaze settled on the swath of red in the middle of the square, Skraeda's heart quickened.

A square of red woolen fabric, torn perhaps from someone's clothing as they hid beneath the wagon. Stepping nearer, something flashed in the dim light of the morning. Skraeda picked it up and examined it closer. A brown lock of long, curly hair.

A smile curved Skraeda's lips, fatigue draining from her body and hope swelling in its place.

"You are not so far ahead of me, are you, girl?" she said aloud. "And now, I know. You travel by wagon. And you've found yourself some companions."

NINETEEN

Silla found there was a certain power in having made an important decision. The day after the Iron Ravens had attacked the Bloodaxe Crew, she awoke filled with confidence, revitalized and fueled with fresh determination. She *would* find a way to convince the Bloodaxe Crew to take her to Kopa. And the knowing feeling in her stomach told her she'd passed a test of sorts.

Silla made her way toward the stream at the edge of camp, dropping to her knees in the plush carpet of heath moss and splashing her face with frigid water. Rolling up her sleeve, she examined her wrist. Though still red and puffy, the throb had lessened to a dull ache. Experimentally, she closed her hand into a fist, then relaxed the muscles.

Across the bank, a small, quilled, mouse-like creature caught Silla's attention as it scuttled across the moss, vanishing amongst the bracken and into the woods beyond. As she stared after it, it dawned on Silla that she'd ventured farther north than she ever had in her life, that she was seeing new, strange sights and there would only be more to come. Perhaps the quilled mouse was a reminder from the gods that even the smallest creatures are resilient and adaptable.

"Skarpling," came Hekla's voice from her right. "Shy little things common in these parts and even more amongst the heather in the Highlands."

It was the first time the two of them were alone since the revelation of Silla's lies. She swallowed, then spoke from the heart. "Hekla, I know I've said it but must again. I'm sorry for suggesting my husband beat me. I went with your assumption, and I am ashamed. I wish I could take it back."

Hekla's amber eyes regarded her before she dropped to her knees and began to doff her prosthesis.

She tried again. "I'm afraid I've been cursed with a disobedient tongue. It speaks before I form proper thought and locks up when it should not."

Hekla chuckled. "Ilías may suffer from the same malady." She was silent for a moment. "You own your mistake, and for that, I will forgive you. But I caution you not to do it again." She rubbed the water along the exposed skin of her residual limb, her face melting into something like relief as the water came into contact with the patchy, irritated skin surrounding the metal joint. "And we *must* teach you how to defend yourself. It troubles me that you cannot."

Silla settled into the grass beside Hekla, leaning back on her elbows. "My father tried, but I was an awful student. I simply *despise* the violence. The thought of hurting another makes me ill."

"You needn't be a warrior," said Hekla, splashing water onto her cheeks one-handed, "but if you do not learn to defend yourself, you give power to your enemies. And with that power, they'll make decisions on your behalf. You put your fate in the hands of others."

Silla was silent a long while. "You're right. I've been complacent, content to place the burden of my safety on the shoulders of others. If I am to survive without my father, I must learn to do this."

Hekla sank back onto her haunches; her lips pulled into a wide smile. "I can teach you some knifework, and you'll be better prepared when you're on your own once more." Her smile faltered.

"I saw you fight from beneath the wagon," said Silla. "You are remarkable. Truly amazing."

"I thank you, dúlla. It has been a long road to get to this place. I had to relearn how to do almost everything, from dressing myself to mounting a horse. I'll admit, it has been trying. But I was motivated. Revenge does wonders for one's ambition."

"Revenge. Against...your former husband?"

Hekla twisted her prosthesis over the metal anchor until it clicked. "Yes. Each time I drew my blade, I imagined the look of fear in his eyes when I returned for him. When he realized the wife whose arm he had cut off and left for dead would be the one to end him. I wanted him to know—he did not break me, as that was never his choice to make. I wanted to see the moment he realized that everything he had done to me—every slap, every punch, every kick —was kindling. It built me up into a raging wildfire, and now it was time for him to burn."

Silla's mouth fell open. "Ashes. You are truly amazing."

"I alone set my fate. And you will have the same freedom, Silla," said Hekla with a smile. "I live my life by a feeling. That knowing in your stomach. And mine is telling me that you are an ally and friend. So it is decided—I will help you learn to defend yourself. And I shall do what I can to sway Axe Eyes to take you to Kopa. Though, as you well know, he is as stubborn as a rock goat."

Chills ran down Silla's spine. This woman had been in the lowest of low places, was powerful, brave, and didn't care what anyone thought of her. Despite her hard exterior, Hekla was soft and kind and generous. Silla wanted to be like her. And gods' sacred ashes, but she wanted Hekla in her corner.

"My thanks," she replied, but it was insufficient. She wasn't sure there were words that could express her gratitude.

"We will find the warrior within you, Hammer Hand," said Hekla with a smile.

Silla shook her head. "I hope never to feel like that again—helpless and panicked, waiting on others to save me."

"Remember that feeling, dúlla. Take it out when we train. Turn your pain into power." Hekla paused. "All of the Bloodaxe Crew have had times of misfortune. It has made us who we now are. What is it they say? Without rain, there would not be flowers?"

"I've had plenty of rain lately," murmured Silla.

"That means the sun must be on the horizon."

Sun on the horizon. Silla liked the idea. Hope bloomed in her chest, and she didn't push it down. She let it sit there and let herself feel it.

SILLA WENT through the motions of the morning as if nothing had happened the night before, and if Rey's scowl was a little deeper, she didn't let it dull her. In fact, she forced her brightest smile as she passed him a bowl of porridge, even as she heard him muttering something about *too much*.

Jonas approached, and Silla busied herself dishing up a bowl of porridge for him.

Don't play games you cannot win.

Silla cleared her throat, pushing the memory aside. He'd killed the Iron Ravens who'd held her, and she wasn't sure what to make of it. Again, he'd protected her, though by day, he rarely met her eyes and spoke only in one-word answers. As she handed Jonas the bowl of porridge, Silla searched for the right words, but he retreated across the fire before she could find them.

When she climbed into the wagon that morning, Silla paused. Next to the pile of furs, her dagger sat in its sheath, and when she pulled it out, she found it freshly sharpened. She glanced at Rey's broad back as he sat stoically upon Horse.

"Aren't you going to bind me?" she asked.

He answered without glancing over his shoulder. "After seeing you react to the battle yesterday, I've decided you're more risk to yourself than to me with that blade. Careful, Sunshine. The sharp part bites."

A smile spread across her face, and she hoped he'd look back and see it. Rey might think he'd landed a blow just now, but Silla knew who the true victor was. Something had shifted since the night prior. She didn't shiver, didn't feel the knot of tension in her stomach near him. He didn't frighten her as he had before.

She hoped he knew it. She hoped it ate at him.

———

FOR THE EVENING MEAL, Silla prepared rabbit stew once more. It was not amazing by her standards, but as she passed the bowls out, the eagerness on the Bloodaxe Crew's faces told her it would more than do.

"It is a shame you haven't any milled oats," she said between mouthfuls. She knew she could work culinary magic with just a few extra ingredients. She'd been sprinkling these ideas like seeds. They'd soon be stopping in the city of Svarti, and she wondered if they'd pick up more provisions. Skalla Ridge— where they'd take temporary leave of the Road of Bones to make their way to Kraki's village—loomed ever closer. She needed *something* to convince them to take her farther north.

"I could prepare a sauce or panbreads. I've heard you can capture wild yeast from the air to grow bread starters—" Pain knifed through her skull so sudden and intense she flinched and stopped mid-sentence. *Skjöld,* she thought, and her body rejoiced at the thought of the leaves. Somehow, it had slipped through the cracks of her mind to take her daily dose. Silla tugged on the thin leather cord around her neck, freeing the vial. Her lips fell open, a choked noise escaping her.

No no no no no.

The stopper was ajar.

Her mind whirled with half-formed thoughts—when; where; how. How. *How* had this happened? How would she make it to Svarti? How would she survive the wrath of her headaches?

Silla dumped the single remaining leaf into her hand and broke it in half. She blinked back tears as her body screamed and her mind hurtled around. She placed the other half of the leaf back into the vial.

One night after this until Svarti. Half a leaf left.

She could do it. She could make it work. Half was better than none. But her mind was in dangerous waters, pulling her down into dark despair. *More. Not enough. Fool! How could you let this happen?*

The pain in her skull began to dissipate, but her thoughts had only begun their torment. The leaves were a layer of comfort, of security. Without an assured supply, she felt naked and vulnerable. She wanted to sob, wanted to scream, wanted to pull the hair from her head. She wouldn't make it without her father. She couldn't even hold onto her skjöld leaves. How could this have—

Silla felt his cold gaze from across the fire.

"What is that?" asked Rey, nodding toward the vial.

Her eyes met his, and she was grateful to be pulled from the riptide dragging her under. "Skjöld."

The look Rey sent her could have shattered stone. "Why would you take a herb like that? Do you know how dangerous it is?"

Silla forced herself to laugh, but it came out too high. "Dangerous? It's a headache remedy."

Rey jabbed a stick into the fire with unnecessary aggression. "The fanatics in Sunnavík love it. Helps them 'feel closer to the gods'."

Silla stared at him, tasting his words, but failing to digest their meaning. "How would it do such a thing?"

Rey shrugged.

Silla looked down at the vial, a new range of emotions chasing themselves across her mind. Fanatics? Dangerous? No. Her father would never give her something unsafe.

But he left you.

He lied to you.

You never even knew his true name.

"You must be mistaken," Silla forced out. Standing, she made her way around the fire, collecting the dishes. She was grateful when Rey stalked off into the forest, as it made it even easier for her to avoid him that night.

———

"FORWARD GRIP," said Hekla. "Hold the blade upward, in the opposite direction of your smallest finger."

The cloud-covered sun was still high, but the air had grown decidedly cooler, causing their breaths to puff into the air. Silla's mind kept circling back to the vial hanging around her neck, to how hollow and empty it was. Though the sharp bite of the headache had been dulled, an ache still wrapped around her skull, and she could not quiet the voice in her mind.

More. Take the last half. Take it.

Silla threw herself into defensive practice as a diversion. Wrapping her left hand around Silla's right, Hekla showed her the proper placement of her fingers along the dagger's hilt.

"Hold it firmly, dúlla, just like that."

Silla drank in each word, reminding herself of that feeling of helplessness. She never wanted to feel it again.

"This hold works well for slashing and stabbing upward. It will feel most natural to you as it is similar to chopping food."

Hekla adjusted her grip, then stepped back, satisfied. "Most importantly: when you stab someone, make sure that you mean it."

"Stab them like you mean it! Such wisdom, Ribs!" roared Ilías, elbowing Gunnar in the stomach.

"Is this part of training?" asked Silla, rubbing her temples to try to dissipate the ache. Silla glared at the men seated by the fire, passing a flask of brennsa between them. They were deep in their cups, and apparently, *she* was their entertainment. Thankfully, Sigrún had left on one of her prowls through the bush, and Rey was still nowhere to be seen. "Dealing with them?"

Hekla waved them off. "It is good to grow used to distractions. Do not pay them any heed, dúlla. They just want to see what happens when a little cat gets her claws out."

"Little *cat*?" Silla couldn't keep the indignant note from her voice. She forced a breath in through her nose as pain pulsed in her skull.

"Oh, I know you've got a mountain cat in there, and I'm going to bring her out. But these fools are quick to judge." Hekla sent her a pointed look and lowered her voice. "Prove them wrong."

Silla put her hands on her hips. "I will." She cast a look of annoyance toward Ilías. "Why does he call you Ribs?"

"'Cause she makes me laugh so hard my ribs ache," bellowed Ilías. Gunnar chuckled.

"Because he grabbed my tit, and I broke his ribs," replied Hekla smoothly, leveling Ilías with a stern look. "Best to remember I could do it again, kunta!"

Silla looked between the two of them, then burst into laughter.

"Ilías, stop distracting my pupil," yelled Hekla. "Now, back to our lesson. When you are stabbing someone, you cannot hesitate. The Bloodaxe Crew can handle combat, but for you, surprise is necessary, and you get only one chance. And...go!"

Silla ran through the stabbing motions Hekla had demonstrated once, twice, three times...

A dull, smacking noise diverted her attention. Jonas. Chopping wood. He swung the axe down with powerful momentum, splitting the wood effortlessly. *Merciful gods.*

Silla watched from the corner of her eye as Jonas paused to roll the shirt-sleeves of his linen tunic up. Each roll revealed another inch of muscled forearm. The air seemed to have warmed by several degrees, and she forgot all about the ache at her temples.

"Go!" barked Hekla. Silla half-heartedly repeated the motion.

Jonas retrieved the axe, the muscles beneath his exposed skin bunching and shifting as they absorbed its weight. His shoulders strained against his tunic as he rolled them backward. Positioning a piece of wood on its end, the light of the fire played along his golden hair and tanned cheekbones.

"Go!" Silla sliced through the air.

He brought the axe overhead; his lips pressed together in concentration, his intense gaze honed in on his target. She could make out the thick, corded muscles of his neck, could see the shift of abdominal muscles beneath his shirt. And then the axe cut through the air with such aggression, she forgot how to breathe for a moment. The axe connected, wood splintering, severing the log in half.

She tugged at the collar of her dress.

"Go!"

Loosened from his braid, strands of his hair fell onto his forehead, and Jonas brushed them back.

Hekla's voice cut through her thoughts. "Silla? You've stopped? Oh, eternal fires—" Hekla smirked. "Here we go again."

"I'm not distracted," said Silla quickly—too quickly—turning back to Hekla with flushed cheeks.

"Mmm-hmmm."

"Shall I go again?" asked Silla, desperate to change the subject.

Hekla tapped her metallic fingers along her dagger, studying Silla with amusement. "You do not want to go there, dúlla."

"Go...where? I'm not going anywhere." It sounded like her voice had risen an octave and felt like her face was on fire.

"He's...how shall we say this...popular with women. I trust Jonas with my life, but to the women he's involved with—" She stuck her tongue out. "His nickname is the Wolf for a reason. He does not treat them well."

"I wasn't—I did not—" Silla didn't know how to finish her sentence.

"Of course you weren't." Hekla winked. "But you should have this knowledge—in case the thought enters your mind. Now, go through the motions once more."

TWENTY

I t was Jonas's fault she could not sleep. Silla tossed under her furs for most of the night, sweat dotting her brow, though she felt icy cold. The ache in her skull persisted, though she'd grown so used to it, it was like background noise. And no matter how many times she rolled over, she could not seem to get comfortable.

Each time she closed her eyes, she saw him swinging the axe and heard his whispered words in her ear.

Don't play games you cannot win.

Those words echoed in her mind, over and over, a choir of baritone voices rolling over her shoulders and reverberating down her spine. Curse that man and his ridiculous forearms, the distracting way he swung the stupid axe. Who split a log with a single swing? How utterly ludicrous.

Silla forced herself to recall the rest of the horrid things he'd said.

I won't have some mouse coming between me and my sólas.

There, she thought, victoriously. The man cared for nothing but coin. Clearly, he was selfish. *Except that he saved you from the Iron Ravens,* came a meddlesome voice from within. *And he helped you through your panic when you had that nightmare. And he followed you in the woods to keep you from danger...*

Irritated, Silla rolled over for the third time that minute.

Eventually, sleep did find her, and with it, vivid dreams. She dreamt of eyes like a pool catching beams of summer sunlight, sapphires sparkling and shifting as she stared up into them. Fingers skimming along the sensitive spot behind her knees, over the smooth skin of her inner thighs. Lips soft as silk brushing against hers.

The image shattered, then reformed, and she stared at the battered form of her father, rusted red oozing across his chest as he drew shallow, rattling breaths. She could read the emotions in his icy-blue eyes: regret, the need for more time, fear, but not of death, racing for him like an avalanche down a mountain. Fear for *her*.

Who were my parents? she asked him.

His lips moved. She lowered her head, eyes widening as the names reached her ears...

Silla jerked upright, gasping. She quickly assessed her surroundings— buttery, golden sunlight streaming through pine boughs and onto the lumpy, moss-covered clearing. Cold sweat misting her brow. Soft snores from slumbering figures nearby. Silla prodded her neck. No pain.

She wasn't back there, on the road near Skarstad. She was safe now.

She pressed a hand to her stomach to calm her jangling nerves. The names. What were their names? They were there, shimmering just out of reach, a memory she might retrieve if only she stretched far enough...

The echoes of the dream clung to her as she prepared daymeal, as she sank into the furs, as the wagon trundled down the road. Her father died a thousand deaths until she had memorized the look in his eyes, the rattle of his last breaths. Yet no matter how many times it happened, she could not hear the names he'd spoken. He'd died for her, to protect her, and it curdled her stomach. The nauseating twist in her gut spread throughout the day until it infected every corner of her body.

It's your fault he's dead.

"Don't be silly," said the little blonde girl, nestled in the furs beside her. "You couldn't have known that would happen."

But the thought hit Silla in the very core of her being, raw pain shredding through her. He was dead. He was gone. Perhaps she was in denial. Her ears still strained for the sound of his voice; her nose searched for his familiar scent. Silla pulled his tunic from her bag. Pressed it to her nose. Inhaled.

Your fault, your fault, your fault.

Tears filled her eyes, and Silla squeezed them shut. If only she'd paid better attention to his attempts to teach her defense, she could have unsheathed her dagger, could have helped him fight.

"And he could have told you the truth," said the little girl angrily.

If only she'd been a better daughter. If only he'd trusted her to hold these secrets.

"You should think hearthfire thoughts," suggested the girl.

But Silla was powerless as the ache bled through her, those torturous questions cycling through her mind.

Why didn't he trust you?

Who are your blood parents?

Why does Queen Signe want you?

"Hearthfire thoughts," said the girl. "Kittens. Swimming. Poking my fingers into bread dough..."

With an exasperated sound, Silla straightened up, twisting the unruly strands of her hair back into a braid. Ignoring the throb at her temples, she grabbed the leather tie from her wrist and used it to secure her locks in place. Her eyes drifted to the road beyond the wagon. Jonas rode silently on his brown mare, his face calm, but his eyes holding that intense, unreadable look.

A shiver of awareness ran down her spine, and Silla froze. The raw pain of grief had momentarily been dulled; it was the first time she'd felt anything beyond it in hours. And it was the same that night in the woods. The draw of the leaves, the grief and loss...it had all been pushed aside.

Silla lay back in the furs and closed her eyes, letting herself remember the first part of her dream. The graze of fingers along her legs, the caress of his lips against her own. Her blood thrummed and heated, an ache settling between her legs. She let out a shaky exhale. What fresh torture was this? What was it about this irritating man? And why could she not stop thinking of his stupid, handsome face? Silla didn't know what it meant.

"Nothing good," muttered the little blonde girl. And with that, she burrowed under the furs until she disappeared entirely.

"WE'VE RUN out of firewood, Wolf."

Jonas looked down at the bone-carved dice he'd just rolled. A raven and two polar bears were etched into their sides; as poor a roll as he'd had all night. He'd already lost enough sólas to Gunnar that his stomach burned with guilt. Those were sólas that should be going toward his hoard, and now they'd be pissed away by Gunnar in a mead hall. With a breath of irritation, Jonas stood.

"I'm out," he grumbled, grabbing his axe and sauntering into the woods. Dead pine branches were wet and furrowed with moss in these parts, and so he wandered deeper, in search of the dry, stringy lichen.

He was two minutes into the forest when he heard Silla fall into step behind him. What was she doing? His stomach burned. It seemed as though he'd only just managed to push her from his mind. He didn't know how, but the woman had gotten under his skin; it had taken all of his efforts to ignore her throughout the day.

Jonas had followed behind the wagon, his eyes drawn to her whether he liked it or not. Something had been bothering her all day. It was clear enough to see, though none of his business.

And now she had followed him into the woods.

She wants to continue her games, he thought to himself, pure, male satisfaction coursing through him. He recalled the soft heat of her body as he'd pushed her against the tree, the fire in her eyes as she'd provoked him. His anger had excited her.

And her taunting words had heated his blood more than she likely knew. It had taken every ounce of his will to walk away from her, not to have his hands all over her curves, to discover if she tasted as good as she smelled.

Jonas scowled as that same need flared in his body. He reminded himself she was a liar, a stowaway, a burden on the Crew. Jonas forced his thoughts to Ilías's socks. Grimwolves. His father.

Well. That always did the trick.

A twig snapped, and he sighed, turning with a glower. "What do you want, Curls? Why have you followed me?"

Her face flushed, and she bit into her lower lip. "I was told it is dangerous to wander the woods alone. Someone must protect you, Wolf."

Jonas cocked his head to the side. He liked her daring more than he cared to admit. "And who will protect you, mouse?" Fire flared in her eyes, and his blood pumped faster. *Fuck*, thought Jonas. He wanted to see it again.

"I will protect myself," she said fiercely. "I've been practicing with Hekla."

He smirked. "So I've seen. You've nearly achieved the skill level of an eight-year-old."

She huffed, crossing her arms over her chest, diverting his attention to that area. Yet again, he found himself wondering what hid beneath those horrid dresses.

"At least I am trying to better myself," she said harshly. "Not wasting my nights away."

"What are you implying?"

"I'm not implying anything. I'm *saying* that you told me you had better things to do than escort me while I forage, and as it turns out, *better things* is simply losing your sólas in games of dice. And here I thought you were so covetous of your precious coins."

Irritation burned in his chest. He hated that she'd honed in on the thing that irritated him so much. Dropping his axe, he stalked toward her. She drew in a breath but held her ground. Gods, this woman. He wanted to punish her impudence. Taste her skin. Scrape his teeth along her fluttering pulse.

Jonas lowered his face, bare inches from hers. Watched as her pupils dilated. "Are you trying to provoke me, Curls?"

She inhaled sharply. "Perhaps."

His gaze dropped to her lips, then settled back on her eyes. They were dark; depthless; the kind of eyes he could get lost in. "Didn't I warn you not to play such games with me?"

"Maybe I don't want to win," she whispered. "Maybe I just want to play."

Heat spiked down his spine as he stared at her. Placing his hand at the base of her throat, he slid it slowly up until he cupped her jaw. Satisfaction welled inside him as goosebumps spread across her skin. "Are you quite certain about that, Silla?" Her eyelids fluttered, and Jonas could not suppress the satisfied smile curving his lips. "I might be a danger to you."

"Perhaps I...like that." Her cheeks flushed pink, but she continued.

A surprised chuckle rose from the back of his throat. "You've no sense of self-preservation, have you, woman? How is it that you've survived twenty winters in this kingdom?"

"I don't know," she breathed, then closed her eyes. Her brows drew together, shoulders slumping, and she seemed to fold in on herself before his eyes.

All the heat in his blood dampened in an instant. He took a cautious step back, his hand dropping from her jaw. "Why did you really follow me?"

Her lips drew down at the corners, fingers wrapping around the vial hanging from her neck. "I cannot sit there," she said. "I cannot...think. I needed to walk. Need a distraction."

"A distraction?"

Silla looked away, hugging herself. "I won't bother you. I just need to walk."

If he were a better man, Jonas would ask her what weighed on her. What had extinguished the fire in her eyes so abruptly. But no one would call him a good man, and so Jonas simply said, "Very well," before carrying on through the woods.

They walked in silence for several long minutes, Jonas pausing when he spotted the stringy lichen. It didn't take long for him to collect all the wood he required, but he sensed she needed longer, and some foolishly soft spot within him chose to indulge in her needs.

"I should thank you," Silla said at long last, peeling the lichen from a stick she'd picked up. Her eyes lifted to meet his. They were so hollow and lost. Where had those flames gone? What had smothered them? "For freeing me from the Iron Ravens. Thank you for that."

In his mind's eye, Jonas saw her again in the clutches of the raven scum, felt the rage burn through his veins once more. He'd drawn his axes and buried them in their skulls without thinking.

Jonas clenched his teeth. "They are vile," he said at last. "Scavengers. Did you know how they got their name? They deal in weapons, picking them from the corpses of their victims."

Silla's hand reached up and squeezed the vial until her knuckles turned white. She held onto that thing like it would keep her from the pits of despair. "Thank the gods above I crawled into your wagon."

He scowled at her, but the bite of his gaze quickly softened. He was slowly coming to realize how wrong his initial impressions of her had been—she was up before them all to cook the daymeal; did the washing without question or complaint; practiced with Hekla for hours in the evenings. It was clear she was no stranger to hard work.

Jonas did not like that she'd snuck into their wagon. But the more he considered it, the more he could understand the desperation she might have felt. Once, he too had relied on the kindness of others. He searched for the words to tell her that, perhaps, he'd been wrong, but could not seem to find them.

"How is your wrist?" he asked instead. Dropping the firewood, Jonas brushed lichen filaments from his hands as he stepped toward her. Tentatively, he took her forearm in his hand, dragging the woolen sleeve up slowly. Her jagged intake of breath made his heart pump harder.

Jonas scowled. Though the swelling had greatly faded, her pale skin was marred by black and purple bruises, the sight making his anger flare.

"It is much improved. Sigrún's ointment truly works."

He saw the pulse throbbing beneath the delicate skin of her wrist. Saw a spark of something back in her eye.

Unable to stop himself, Jonas pushed her unruly curls over her shoulder. "And your neck?" he asked softly. He dragged a finger along the curve where neck met shoulder. "That has healed as well."

A shiver rolled through her.

Heat was pooling in his stomach. Jonas's eyes met hers. "Are you cold, Silla?"

"No," she managed in a bare whisper.

They stared at one another as the air crackled between them—it was the feeling of anticipation, of charged potential, like before a lightning storm hits.

"Jonas!" called a male voice, cleaving the tension like a freshly sharpened dagger. Ilías. "The fucking fire has died, you arse!"

Cursing softly under his breath, Jonas stepped back. He let out a sharp breath, then collected the firewood he'd discarded. "We should get back."

Hugging herself, Silla nodded tightly.

They walked back to camp in silence.

TWENTY-ONE

The next day was as exciting as watching grass grow. They trundled through dense woods for the majority of the day, stopping in a clearing where Silla prepared the evening meal. And now, after tucking the last of the dishes into the kitchen crate, she waited for Hekla for her nightly lesson. The evening was cool, darker than usual—the clouds had threatened rain all day but had yet to follow through with it. *Good*, she thought, carrying the crate to the wagon. While she was dedicated to learning knife skills from Hekla, she loathed the idea of practicing while drenched.

Silla's eyes darted to the fire where Jonas sat beside Rey, his dagger running along another piece of wood as he carved a fresh figurine. Each night, he carved a new one, tossing it into the fire once completed and starting fresh the next day.

As the light hit his golden beard, his blue eyes lifted, locking with hers. Silla's body heated through, caught somewhere between desire and sheer embarrassment. What had come over her last night?

She'd been seated by the campfire, suffering through the headache squeezing her skull like a serpent's embrace, battling the urge to take her last leaf portion. And then she'd watched him step into the woods, axe hefted over his shoulder. After making certain the rest of the Crew was deeply immersed in their game of dice, Silla had slipped after him.

Maybe I don't want to win. Maybe I just want to play.

Heat flushed her cheeks at the memory. She'd said that. To the Wolf. And she'd wanted him...desperately so. Could read the hunger in his own eyes. For a moment, she'd thought he might kiss her. Might distract her from it all.

Eternal fires. She still wanted him. Yet she did not like him in the slightest. It was maddening. Confusing.

Jonas's lips quirked up at the corners, as though he could read her thoughts, and her stomach grew hot and liquid. With a shaky breath, Silla forced her gaze away.

All day, she'd been thinking of his hand, sliding up her neck. The way Jonas had looked as though he was ravenous for her, as though he wished to devour her. Though the dull ache from her half dose of skjöld lingered, Silla had not wallowed in her grief today; she had not dwelled on her flight from danger, nor the mystery of her blood parents.

"Your fixation on him makes me want to retch," grumbled the little blonde girl, leaning against the side of the wagon.

Silla shot her a murderous look.

"He's a *boy*." The little girl wrinkled her nose. "And aside from that, you know better than to let him get so near to you."

"You're right," Silla whispered. "It cannot happen again."

Her eyes fell on the black-haired man to the left of Jonas, and she let out a long sigh. She was no closer to winning the favor of Axe Eyes than she'd been the day of her discovery. He had scarcely spoken more than a few clipped words to her, stalking away from camp most evenings. Silla hadn't a clue of how to gain his trust. She knew in her heart her cooking was not enough to persuade him to take her to Kopa.

In a few short days, they'd reach Skalla Ridge, and with each step closer, her stomach knotted tighter. How would she convince him to take her all the way to Kopa?

"I must find a way," said Silla.

Hekla strode from the forest, damp clothes strung over her sound arm. "Ready to practice?" she asked, spreading the garments along a drying line with her left hand.

Silla nodded.

The two women positioned themselves away from the fire and began working through movements. Hekla was showing Silla how to block an incoming attack while simultaneously slicing at her opponent. Driving her right arm up, Silla braced her left to block the sheathed blade hurtling toward her neck.

"Good," said Hekla. "Again."

Silla adjusted her hold on the dagger into what she now knew was the reverse grip. She repeated the motion, a little faster, with more force. Hekla's face grew taut, and she doffed her prosthesis, scratching the skin beneath with a sigh of contentment.

Silla's eye fell upon the metallic arm. "Is it heavy?"

Hekla smiled. "My old one was heavier than a boulder. Feel this." Hekla handed the arm to her.

Silla weighed it in her hands. "It's so light! Where did you get such a thing?"

Hekla cocked an eyebrow. "Rey's grandmother provided the name of a talented metalcrafter. He built this for me—had to pay extra for the sharp parts. The metalcrafter's wife also fitted my clothing with magnetic clasps that make it easier to dress. Only grievance I have is that it itches like the plague in the warm months."

Hekla adjusted her slackened grip on the dagger, diverting them back to practice. "Now, this time, I'll come from your left. Aim for my armpit—a guaranteed weak spot in the armor, and if you aim your blade right, they'll bleed out."

They ran through the motions several times, Silla's finesse improving with each trial. *It simply takes practice*, she thought. Practice she could do. She was not afraid of hard work. After another half hour, her brow was misted with sweat, her arm muscles aching.

"Hekla," said Silla, wiping her forehead with the sleeve of her dress, "I've a question for you."

Hekla put her left hand on her hip. "Go ahead."

"Your situation where you do not rely on a man. Do you ever grow lonely?"

"Lonely?" asked Hekla, twirling her dagger in her hand. "No." Hekla leaned in and lowered her voice. "That's what Gunnar is for."

Silla's eyes flared, and she glanced toward the fire, to where Gunnar sat with Sigrún and Ilías amid a raucous game of dice. Thank the merciful gods they hadn't watched her lessons again tonight. "Gunnar? *That* Gunnar?"

Hekla shrugged.

Silla's lips parted. She hadn't had the faintest idea there was anything between them. Questions piled up in her mind. When? Where? How did she guard her secret? But her mouth came up with, "You and Gunnar are *together*?"

Hekla smirked. "If by together you mean worshiping one another's bodies, then yes. We are *together* on occasion."

"You are together, but not...together."

Hekla sighed. "I do not give a name to things. I do what I want, when I want, and with whom I want. And at times it is with Gunnar."

Silla pressed her lips together. "I hadn't the slightest idea you liked him at all."

"Like him?" Hekla snorted, then looked up. "Oh gods, you're serious. Eternal fucking fires, Silla. I *don't* like him most of the time. Perhaps...I like parts of him." She cackled.

Silla nodded. Before Jonas, she'd never have believed it possible to desire and dislike someone all at once. "I believe I understand."

"What is this about, dúlla? Are you feeling lonely?"

That was one way of putting it. Lonely. Guilt-ridden. Sad. In desperate need of a distraction. "Perhaps"

"Well, Svarti is a day's ride. If you wish, we can find you a distraction there."

"Perhaps," repeated Silla, though it did not feel entirely right. But perhaps wrong was precisely what she needed.

———

JONAS STARED LISTLESSLY at the figure in his hand, his blade peeling another curving layer of wood as he shaped the warrior's helm. To his left, Ilías, Sigrún, and Gunnar clustered around a game of dice. To his right, Rey sat quietly, lost in his own thoughts.

Laughter from the edge of the clearing drew his attention—Silla and Hekla, running through a basic attack move that Jonas had learned as a child. Not for the first time, he wondered how this woman had survived as long as she had without even basic knowledge of how to wield a blade. Jonas had asked her the same last night, and she'd wilted like a flower before his eyes. He'd wracked his mind, trying to understand her response. Perhaps she'd thought of her father, had been filled with worries of how she'd survive without him.

Not your problem, he reminded himself. The woman had meddled in things she should not. Her misery was not his concern.

Jonas forced his gaze away from her. They had not spoken since the night before, and when she'd handed him his meals that day, he'd savored the flush creeping up her neck. In the light of day, the boldness he'd seen twice now in the woods had evaporated entirely. Though he tried, he could not forget it; he yearned to see that side of her once more.

To his great dismay, Jonas could not keep his eyes from wandering to her. Watching the emotions play across her face was like a game. The adorable scowls she cast at Rey when he was not looking. The grim determination when she worked with Hekla. The emotions which had swamped her when she sat in the wagon—anger and frustration eventually giving way to sadness.

He had the strangest desire to take her sadness away. To make her smile until the dimple in her cheek showed. To ensure the spark never left her eyes. Perhaps it was why he enjoyed angering her so. Something warm unfolded in his chest, making him uneasy.

Jonas drank deeply from his flask, watching as Silla brushed grass from her dagger. *Soft sentiments bring nothing but weakness,* he reminded himself, reinforcing his inner walls with iron and steel. He would not go there. Would never go there. *You must avoid her before this goes any further.*

A loud sigh from beside him reminded Jonas of Rey's presence. "I need you to take her to the market in Svarti," Rey said, drawing his own flask out and drinking deeply.

Jonas's gaze snapped to Rey. "What?"

"When we're in Svarti, bring her to the market and help her purchase enough provisions for the next stretch of the journey."

"Why me?" groused Jonas.

Rey glared into the flames. "You are the only one I can trust to watch her, Jonas. Already she has No Beard, Fire Fist, and Rib Smasher wrapped around her finger."

Jonas exhaled roughly.

"I enjoy the food," said Rey quietly. "If I'm to suffer her presence for the next several days, I should enjoy my meals at the very least. And she'll have an eye for things that Sigrún does not." Rey turned to Jonas, surveying him in that cold, detached way of his. "I can trust you, can I not?"

Jonas's brow wrinkled. "Of course. Why do you ask?"

"Do not make her one of your conquests, Jonas." Rey's gaze slid to the licking flames. "I have promised to deliver her safely to Hver. But...she is not an honest woman. There is something she hides."

Jonas forced himself to snort. "Hábrók's arse, Rey. You think I've developed a liking for the Aunts of Ursir's House?"

Rey's eyes hardened, but his gaze held steady on the fire. "I suppose she is not your type. But in case the thought enters your mind—I order you not to bed her."

Irritation flared in his chest. Ordered? Jonas did not like the sound of that word on his Bloodaxe brother's lips. It gave him the urge to do the opposite.

Laughter from where Hekla and Silla trained diverted their attention. Rey made a derisive sound as Silla attempted to block Hekla and instead got her feet tangled in her skirts. She fell to hands and knees with a peal of laughter.

"I should not have let her live," Rey muttered. "This Istré job is far too dangerous to have her with us. We should be planning for it, and instead, I find my thoughts troubled by her. There is something she does not tell us, Jonas."

"Perhaps." Jonas watched Silla brush moss from her skirts. She bent to pick up her fallen dagger. As his eyes traced the dip of her lower back, the swell of her backside, he let out a sharp exhale. "Or perhaps you simply scare the piss out of her, and she behaves strangely around you."

Rey glanced at him, unconvinced. "She does not fear me." His contempt was clear. "There is something she hides. And I will discover what it is."

Jonas watched his Bloodaxe brother from the corner of his eye. So Rey was not so happy with his decision after all. "She will not be with us much longer, Rey. And it could be worse."

"How so?"

"She does not try to talk to you, does she?"

"She hums. I'm not sure she even knows she does it. It's quite irritating." Rey drank deeply from his flask, wiping his mouth on his sleeve. "I do not hate the food. Let her get what she needs."

Jonas huffed. "Fine."

He glanced up. Hekla and Silla walked toward them, smiles painted broadly across their faces. As Silla tucked a wayward strand of hair behind her ears, she stumbled over a rock. With a laugh, she turned back toward the rock.

Jonas choked as he heard the word *sorry* leave her lips.

"Malla's tits," muttered Rey, dragging a hand down his face. "Tell me she did *not* just apologize to a rock."

TWENTY-TWO

Skraeda batted the flies away as she stared at the pair of melted faces. Nestled into the dew-adorned grass, she admired the contrast—glistening pearls of liquid adjacent to blackened eye sockets oozing some sort of...eyeball sludge. The corpses had been cut loose from the stockade wall to which they'd been bound and laid on the ground, she'd been told.

Turning to the Klaernar kaptein, Skraeda pursed her lips. A curious crowd had gathered, several King's Claws pushing them back to ensure they kept their distance. She despised the eyes of so many looking upon her, preferring to dwell in the shadows. And the overwhelming swell of emotions from the crowd only drove her irritation higher.

"He's quite dead," Skraeda stated, her voice sharp.

"Quite," said the man—Kaptein...Bolsund? Boskuld? Already, she could recall nothing but that he'd been sent up from the south.

How the Klaernar had found her, Skraeda did not know—they'd pounded on the door at first light, making her regret her choice to spend the night in a lodging house rather than in the wilderness where she would most certainly not have been bothered. But she'd wanted to question residents of this small hamlet to see if anyone had seen the girl and her companions, and it had been far too late to do so when she'd arrived the night before.

How fortunate the Slátrari had struck and spared her the trouble of banging on doors.

Skraeda blew out a long breath. "Kaptein, I'm quite eager to get on the road, so if you please, out with it."

The kaptein looked about as happy as she was to be in this sorry excuse of a hamlet. Frowning, he studied her. "I was informed you were in the area," he said hesitantly. "I've heard whisperings of you."

Inwardly, Skraeda groaned. Whisperings were dangerous. Once she'd apprehended the girl, she'd return to Reykfjord, find the Klaernar who'd been so busily 'whispering' of her, and cut the tongue from his mouth.

"Corpses have been appearing," continued the kaptein. "I'm sure you've heard of this murderer, this Slátrari."

Skraeda looked at the man expectantly.

"They are...burned, as you can see. As of late, they were in the Reykfjord area. But now it seems the killer is on the move."

"And what of it?" she asked, exasperated.

"Magnus Hansson wants it dealt with," blurted the kaptein.

Magnus Hansson, thought Skraeda, goosebumps running up her arms. The Heart Eater—one of few men in Íseldur who truly frightened her.

"It is not my problem," she said curtly. "I will address the crowd and be on my way."

The Klaernar's hand shot out, wrapping around her upper arm. Skraeda looked at his hand. It took every ounce of her will not to cut it from his arm and stuff it down his throat.

"I know you've assisted the Klaernar in Reykfjord, Clever Tongue," the man hissed at her. "I was hoping you could do the same here."

Skraeda could hear the unspoken threat—*I know what you are.* Her chest filled with blistering heat, anger stinging her throat.

The kaptein was still speaking. "All I wish to know is if you can sense any trace of guilt amongst the gathered. Surely, you'd like to see the killer captured. For the safety of our kingdom."

Skraeda took a calming breath. *Lamb, Skraeda,* she reminded herself. *Let him think you a lamb.*

"Very well," she forced out. "I should hate to think of a killer on the loose." Approaching the crowd, Skraeda pushed her braids over her shoulders. She would sense out the crowd while getting answers of her own. "Well met," she called out. "I search for a woman."

The kaptein grunted behind her, but Skraeda pushed on.

"I promise a great reward to any who can provide information." Skraeda allowed her senses to stretch out. Fear and distrust spooled broadly from the crowd's aura, and it required precision to push them aside and look for those finer threads. Amid such chaos, with so many present, truly, only a practiced Solacer like Skraeda could achieve such a thing.

"But what of the Slátrari?" wailed a woman.

"He's killed our Gothi!" shouted a man.

Anger looped and reeled from the crowd, and Skraeda used her touch to lull it, to soothe the sharp edges and ease the tension.

"The Klaernar are here now," continued Skraeda. "And in a moment, they will continue their work. But not until I know if any have seen a girl—red cloak, curly brown hair, wears a vial on a tether around her neck."

"What are you doing?" muttered the Klaernar in her ear.

"I'm sensing for anyone who...looks angry," she lied from the corner of her mouth. "The killer would want attention, would he not? Would want credit for the kill? He would be angry that I'm asking of the girl, angry that he is not getting the attention he feels he deserves. Let me try to root out your culprit, Kaptein."

With a grumble, the warrior backed away.

A smile curved Skraeda's lips, and she continued prodding through the crowd, not for anger, but for surprise. There were heavy ribbons of angst and quivering fear, and she thumbed through them until she found what she was looking for—vibrating brightly in the back of those gathered. Honing in through the crowd, Skraeda focused on an older man.

"You," she said, meeting his gaze. "You know something, I can tell. Step forward, my good man, and tell me what you know." Skraeda unhooked a leather pouch from her belt and held it out. "Your reward awaits you."

The crowd parted as the man stepped through—wiry and wrinkled with age, his woolen cloak was patched in several spots, and he pulled a threadbare cap from his head, clutching it to his chest. "I m-may have seen her," he said quietly, squinting up at her. "I passed a band of warriors on the road, late yesterday. A woman sat in their wagon, wrapped in a red cloak. It was strange, I thought, a woman like that traveling with warriors."

Skraeda's brows furrowed. It made sense that the woman traveled with warriors, given the corpses she'd passed on the road. "And her hair?" she prodded.

The man's eyes darted to the pouch of coins, then back to Skraeda. With a sigh, she withdrew three golden sólas and handed them to the man.

"Her hair was braided, but some had pulled loose. It seemed to be curly."

Skraeda exhaled. "My thanks, old man," she said, tossing him another sóla.

Turning, her eyes settled upon the kaptein, his gaze roaming through the crowds. She placed a hand on the kaptein's shoulder. "Your killer is not here," she said softly. "Better luck at the next corpse, Kaptein." She tried not to smile at the man's audible groan, but his misery only added to her joy—the woman was less than a day ahead of her.

But then Skraeda frowned.

The city of Svarti was near. If she did not catch her soon, the girl could vanish amongst the crowds.

TWENTY-THREE

T he lush greenery of the woods fell away to pastures of golden wheat and rye, bending and whipping as a breeze rushed through them. Silla spotted the first brown timber walls of a steading nestled amongst the gold, then a second and third. As the farmsteads became more frequent, anticipation built.

Leaves, her mind chanted, pleaded. *Leaves*. It grew to a desperate chorus reverberating inside her but did nothing to fill the emptiness—only one thing could fill the void. But Svarti. They neared Svarti. And soon, her supply would be replenished, and Silla would be whole again. Would feel like herself.

But as Svarti neared, a different type of anticipation built as well. Would the queen's mercenaries be waiting for her at the gates? Scouring the streets for her? By the time the wagon approached the stockade walls of the city, her whole body was knotted with strain.

When they passed through the gate, she exhaled the tension in one long breath; there was no blockade checking travelers as they entered the city. But being back in a city, back amongst people, made her nerves skitter. Danger seemed to lurk around each corner. They could be here, lying in the shadows, waiting for their chance to pounce upon her.

Silla tried to distract herself from the worries. The hypnotic clop of hooves slowed as buildings rose alongside the wagon. Sinking lower in the flatbed, Silla surveyed the city. Svarti was a slightly smaller version of Reykfjord, a palette of browns and stoney grays punctuated with mossy green. After so many hours of boredom in the wagon, the city pulsed with life. The ring of hammers, boisterous laughter from a mead hall, the creak of wheels, and the splash of puddles all wove together in discordant harmony. They passed forges and shops, turf-roofed homes and shoddy street stalls.

Silla's spine straightened as they passed the blue sign of an apothecary. The throb in her temples intensified at the sight.

Need. Need.

"Soon," whispered Silla, tracing the outline of the coin purse pressed against her hip in that hidden pocket. It was risky to spend some of her precious sólas, and yet not a question at all.

The fanatics in Sunnavík love it.

She didn't know where Rey's words came from, but they sparked anger in her chest anew. Either Rey was mistaken or he'd *lied.* Because Silla knew her father, who'd done whatever he could to keep her safe—who had *died* to keep her safe—would never give her anything so dangerous as what Rey had described.

At last, they pulled to a halt, and her eyes fell upon a white sign adorned with inky black feathers, *The Boar's Head Inn* scrawled across it.

"Out," said Rey, slapping the side of the wagon. Silla scooted off, pulling her bag over her shoulder.

Rey stretched the woolen tarp over the wagon, securing it to the sides. A boy appeared from the stables, taking Horse's reins, and Silla stroked her forehead affectionately before following Rey.

"How many men guard the stables?" he asked the boy as they made their way to the door of the Boar's Head. "Do they keep a clear head? Are they drunkards?"

The corners of Silla's mouth tugged up.

She dropped onto a sheepskin-draped bench in the entry while Rey arranged the rooms. Her eyes found Jonas. He leaned against the opposite wall, arms crossed over his buckled armor. His gaze lifted, trapping her own for one blazing second. Silla's body responded as though they had touched—her foolish heart doing flips in her chest.

You must keep your distance, she reminded herself, but her body did not seem to get the message.

Finally, Silla managed to look away, forcing in a deep breath. After several long minutes, Rey turned and strode across the room, iron keys clutched in hand. A pair of guests who'd just entered the inn scattered from his path, and Silla couldn't help but notice the relief on the face of the innkeeper. Even they knew he was a nightmare in the flesh.

His eyes were glacial as he loomed over her. "Magnus paid for it. Pick a roommate or sleep in the barn."

Her teeth snapped together, but she was distracted by the cool metal slide on her shoulder, squeezing gently.

"Room with me, dúlla," said Hekla, a smile stretching across her face. Silla finally let her smile free, relieved to have one ally in the bunch.

As she made her way to the door, a large hand encircled her wrist, drawing her to a stop. Jonas looked down at her with irritation. Skin buzzing beneath the warmth of his touch, Silla looked at her hand.

"I've been ordered to bring you to the market," he said with resignation, withdrawing his hand.

"Ordered?" Her brows drew together as she looked up at him.

"I should like to bathe before going. Be ready in thirty minutes."

And with that, Jonas sauntered to the door. Silla sighed. Going out *in public* with Jonas. It would not be a restful afternoon, that much she knew.

———

APPARENTLY, the Bloodaxe Crew had far more sólas in their budget than Silla and her father ever had; rather than a hayloft above the stables, they could afford proper quarters. Though small, the lodgings held wooden beds spread with sheep and deerskins, a hearth with firewood stacked nearby, and a bench on which sat a basin of fresh water for washing.

"You can take the first wash, dúlla," said Hekla, pulling her prosthetic arm off with a sigh and laying it on the bed. She rolled her shoulders, tilting her neck from side to side. "Ashes, I need a break from this cumbersome thing. I'm off to guard the wagon, but tonight, we'll drink our fill at the mead hall." Her eyes shone with the promise of fun. With a small smile, Hekla left the room, her right sleeve hanging empty.

Silla toed off her boots and stockings, then stripped bare. Splashing water on her face, she used the lump of ash soap beside the basin to wash the grime from her skin, working her way down to her toes. She finished off by washing her hair—to the best of her abilities in the small basin—before squeezing out the water and running her comb through the curls.

Pulling on her cleanest dress, Silla braided her hair and sat on the bench. She stared into the empty hearth. For the first time in eleven days, she was not running from something or someone, was not crafting lies to evade Axe Eye's relentless questions.

Silla pulled her father's tunic from her bag. Held it to her nose. Breathed in.

"I miss him," said the little blonde girl, having appeared on the bench beside her.

"As do I," murmured Silla in reply. It had been the two of them against the world, and now...what? Everything had changed, not only the loss of her father but her entire perception of the past and future.

"But he lied to you," said the little girl, swinging her feet. "He's not even your father."

"No," Silla said, her voice hard. "He *was* my father. Kinship goes far beyond blood."

"His name was not even Matthias," said the girl. And this, to Silla was the hardest betrayal of all. He was Tómas. A stranger.

How had he gotten her? Had she been kidnapped? Were her blood parents alive and searching for her? Was Silla even her name? Would she ever find answers to these questions, or would they torment her forever?

I cannot do this. It hurt too much to think of him. And so, Silla shoved her grief back into its cage—locked the door and swallowed the key.

Then she left to meet Jonas.

TWENTY-FOUR
SVARTI

Silla and Jonas walked down the earth-packed central road of Svarti, an awkward silence stretching between them. Goosebumps spread along her arms, and she was unsure if it was because of the Wolf's presence beside her or because she went without a cloak. She'd vowed not to wear the red cloak in Svarti; in case *they* knew she wore red.

Ignoring the dull pounding in her skull, Silla glanced over her shoulder, searching for anything which appeared out of sorts. Any hint someone followed, any strange looks, and she'd slip down a side street and vanish. But gods willing, the queen's men did not realize she'd found a ride so soon and had made it all the way to Svarti.

Glancing to her left, Silla shivered. The silence hanging between Jonas and her was painful, and she searched for something to say—all she could think of was the intoxicating slide of his hand along her throat. She felt Jonas turn to study her and hugged herself tighter.

"Are you cold, Curls?"

A breath gusted from her—he'd spoken those same words a few nights before. "I...forgot my cloak."

Jonas sighed, sliding out of his black cloak and handing it to her.

"My thanks," she said, pulling it over her shoulders and securing the bronzed clasp in place. Drawing the hood up to shield her face, his scent and the lingering heat from his body sank into her.

They passed one of the Bear God's acolytes. In one hand, he clutched the curved canine tooth of a bear, strung on a slender leather cord which wrapped around his wrist. The other held a hide-bound book from which he read. Silla tensed as wisps of his sermon reached her ears.

"...the Bear is the embodiment of the Father, the Husband, the Son, he who shall be worshiped and obeyed..."

Those of Ursir's House had always instilled a sense of deep unease in her. Thankfully, the man's voice soon faded, and with it, the tightness in her shoulders.

Leaves. Need.

Silla's hand moved anxiously to the vial, rubbing the smooth surface. The throbs in her skull grew needier by the hour. She must get to the apothecary—and soon.

The air was decidedly cool, and she dipped her hands into the pockets of Jonas's cloak. Her fingers folded around hammered silver—his talisman. Pulling it out, she examined the three interlocked triangles etched into the surface.

"What are you doing?"

Jonas snatched for it, and Silla spun away. But his large hands latched onto her shoulders, clamping down hard and forcing her toward him. Silla's eyes met pure blue fire, and she hesitated. Jonas's body was as tense as though he was ready for battle, a vein in his temple pulsing. She'd enjoyed goading him in the woods, but this...this was beyond playing.

"This is no joke, Silla. Give it to me."

Swallowing, Silla handed the talisman to him. "The tether is broken."

He did not answer.

"It is significant to you?" she asked softly.

"Yes." Jonas's fist clenched around it so tightly his knuckles turned white. "It is all I have left of my old life. This and Ilías."

"Is there meaning in the symbols?"

Jonas hesitated, then slowly opened his hand to reveal the disk. "The triangles represent the pillars of my line. Family, respect, and duty. The three qualities those of my bloodline must strive to uphold." He tucked the talisman into his pocket.

"It is important to you, then. To carry these attributes of your family?"

Jonas breathed in deeply through his nose.

Silla chewed her lip, watching the blond warrior. Any softness he'd revealed had been replaced by his usual stony look. "Very well, Wolf, we shall not speak of it. I only wished to understand you."

"Why bother? You're leaving in a few days."

Silla's gaze snapped to the dirt-packed road with that rebuke. *Yes. Why would you waste your time trying to understand this insufferable man?* But still, his contradictions confused her. Intrigued her.

Protective, yet combative.

Selfish—covetous—and yet the talisman suggested family was important to him.

And the way he'd looked at her in the woods...

"Very well," Silla said at last. "What shall we speak of, then?"

"Perhaps those dangerous games you so like to play?"

Her cheeks flamed. "It was a moment of weakness." She knew he was baiting her, and she hated herself for biting.

Jonas chuckled. "If you say so."

A jagged sound escaped her. "What does *that* mean?"

"Only that you seem in frequent need of distraction."

"Twice," she huffed. "Don't let it go to your head, Wolf. I thank the gods above Ilías called for you. I was not of sound mind."

"Liar."

Her gaze shot to his. "What?"

"I've seen you watch me, Silla." She shivered as her name rolled off his tongue. "From across the fire. As you ride on the wagon. Did you know that your every thought is displayed clearly on your face? And you have had some very wicked thoughts."

"Ashes," Silla huffed, quickening her pace. But Jonas's strides lengthened, matching hers easily. "You think highly of yourself, Wolf, don't you?"

Jonas only shrugged.

"Your arrogance is astounding." An exasperated sound escaped her. How could she have wanted this impossible man? She'd gone temporarily mad; there was no other explanation. "I was...lonely. Missing my father."

"If you say so, Curls."

"Well...I do! Say so." She tugged her hood down farther over her head, wishing she could burrow away from the man beside her.

"Isn't this just what you want? To argue with me? Does it not excite you? Bring a thrill to your blood?"

"Does it thrill you to anger me?" she snapped.

"Yes." His honesty startled her. "It brings a spark to your eyes."

Hearthfire thoughts, she told herself, massaging her temples. *Clean bed linens. The smell of freshly baked bread. The clucking sound made by chickens.* Her pulse gradually declined, the tightness in her chest loosening.

A horse-drawn cart lumbered toward them, and they stepped to the side to allow it room to pass. Movement from the road thankfully distracted her from Jonas's proximity. A puppy darted into the street, its soft ears flopping as it ran directly into the path of the horse-drawn cart.

"No!" Impulsively, Silla lunged toward the small creature, scooping it up in her arms as she darted across the street. She felt a whisper of touch as she rushed past the horse's hoof, but momentum thankfully delivered her safely to the opposite side of the road.

The cart driver hurled curses at her, but she could not hear his words over the blood roaring in her ears. She leaned against the wall, clutching the puppy to her breast, the eyes of those in the street upon her.

Fool! she thought. *You should not have drawn such attention to yourself.*

But the puppy wriggled happily in her arms, the soft velvet of its tongue on her cheek drawing her from her dismay. A smile cracked across her face, and she scratched behind his ears.

"Naughty little thing," she murmured. "You must be more careful."

A boy of eight or nine ran out, concern lining his face as he looked along the street. Catching sight of the puppy, he sagged with relief. "Klofi!"

"He was nearly trampled," she warned, trying and failing to sound stern as she handed the dog over. The puppy covered the boy's face in kisses, delighted to have found its human. Her heart swelled, and she stored the moment away for future hearthfire thoughts.

The boy thanked her, then scampered down a side street.

Jonas appeared beside her, shaking his head. "Your survival this long is honestly a miracle."

She threw him an incredulous look. "You'd have watched a puppy be trampled?"

"Some beasts are not meant to survive," he mused.

"Merciful gods, Jonas," she muttered. "Just when I think you can get no worse, you go and open your mouth."

"And here I thought you enjoyed the look of my mouth."

She pressed her fingers to her temples, trying to massage the growing tension from her skull. "You are such an arse. If I'm not mistaken, you seemed to like the look of mine as well."

"Oh, I did. I do." He grew silent, his brilliant blue gaze lingering on her mouth. "I've not stopped thinking of those lips for days." For a moment, he looked vexed with himself, but then his expression shifted, the cocky demeanor returning. "I wonder if they're as soft as they look." His voice dropped lower. "I wonder how you'll taste."

"Eternal fires," muttered Silla, her skin growing hot and tingly.

"And I wonder if the dowdy dresses and act of innocence are a trick, because good, sweet girls do not have a tongue as sharp and wicked as yours. And merciful gods, Silla. I am no good man, because all I can think of is drawing you into my furs and discovering what else that tongue is capable of."

His words vibrated under her skin long after he'd stopped talking. She blinked several times, trying to force thoughts back into her hazy mind.

"Dowdy dresses? They have *pockets*. They are practical! We travel the Road of Bones!"

A laugh rumbled through him, a beautiful, genuine sound. She peeked at him and found his face softened; his eyes crinkled slightly at the corners. Ashes. Why must he look like that?

"*That* is what you took from my words?" He ran a hand along his crown, tugging on his braid. "You are...unexpected."

Jonas continued down the road, and with a deep breath, Silla followed. She adjusted the hood of her borrowed cloak as she caught the gleam of shining silver and black shirts of mail—two Klaernar, approaching on their right. The men were impossibly tall, buckles jangling against their boots; tension coiled tighter in her chest with each step closer. She felt the weight of their gazes on her, scraping along her cheeks like a freshly-sharpened dagger.

Do they know? Has word reached them from Reykfjord?

The Klaernar's steps slowed, the hand of the nearest wrapping around his sheathed hevrít. Time seemed to slow. Silla held her breath, keeping her gaze on the rutted road of Svarti.

And then, the Klaernar walked past her, the clank of their iron buckles growing fainter with each step. Her mind was spinning, spots blinking in her vision. Silla forced her muscles to unclench, took a few deep breaths.

You must remember what is at stake, she told herself.

Jonas watched her. "Are you well?"

Forcing a smile on her lips, she nodded slowly. She needed a diversion, something to keep her worries from driving her mad. "Let us start over, Jonas. *Please*. Surely we can speak of something else." She thought for a moment. "Tell me something true about yourself. Something only a friend would know. Nothing lewd," she added.

He shot her a look of surprise. "True?"

"Yes. Tell me something real." She crossed her arms, then uncrossed them, glancing over her shoulder.

Jonas was silent a while, and she wished he would say something—anything—to quell the tension still gripping her.

"What would you do if you were not in the Bloodaxe Crew?"

His thumb ran along the rough edges of his beard as he considered the question. "Ideally, I'd have enough sólas never to work again. I'd live in a palace and be fed meat and ale by beautiful women."

Silla rolled her eyes. "Has anyone ever told you that you are shameless, Jonas?"

"*Many* times." Jonas sighed. "Why should I ever wish to leave all this? Freezing my bollocks and eating Sigrún's shite cooking for months on end. What could be better?"

"Sounds as though you don't love it."

Silla hazarded a glance at him. With his scaled leather armor, weapons secured in his belt, and his hair shorn along the sides of his skull, Jonas looked every bit the fearsome warrior she'd seen battling the Iron Ravens. The thought that this man had just confessed he wanted to take her to bed...it made her head spin.

Jonas was silent for a long time. "I suppose the thrill has worn off."

"Why do you keep at it?"

"I've need of the sólas."

"As you've made me well aware." Her brows knit together. Why had he such need of sólas? "Could you not find some other way to earn them? Is happiness not important?"

"It is...complicated."

"How so?"

Jonas hesitated. "I must keep an eye on Ilías."

"You're a kind-hearted brother."

Jonas huffed but did not elaborate. So he *did* have a strong sense of kinship. She had noted that the brothers often sat together huddled in conversation and games of dice. And it was easy to imagine the brothers might complement one another—Jonas tempering Ilías's reckless edge, Ilías providing the levity Jonas lacked. She examined the cold and selfish man beside her, wondering if perhaps there was more than met the eye.

"If you did not need to watch over Ilías *and* had no need of coin, what then would you do? If you could do anything you desired?"

He let out an exasperated breath. "I do not know."

"I would have my own farmstead," she said, partly to fill the silence, partly because it made her feel like her insides were as soft and fluffy as a freshly baked sweet roll. "With a few animals and a large garden. I would spend all day by the cookfires with my hands in dough, a big pot of skause bubbling, and at the end of the day, I'd sit in a nest of sheepskins with a cup of hot róa by the hearthfire." She paused for a moment. "And I would have chickens."

His brows raised. "You've thought that over."

"Long days working in kitchens lost in dreamy thoughts." She shrugged. "What would you do?"

"Killing is the only talent I've ever had. What is the point of dreaming of something that will never be? This is my life. I am not fated to do anything else."

"But...it *can be*. How many winters has Ilías seen?"

"Twenty-one," said Jonas. There was a cold edge to his voice, a warning she ignored.

"Does he *truly* need your protection? He seems quite capable."

"He needs it."

She sighed. The finality in his words told her he was done with this conversation, and so they walked on in silence for several minutes.

Silla smelled the market well before they reached it; livestock and woodsmoke and the hot steel of a blacksmith's forge. Excitement and apprehension mingled in her gut—the market would be crowded, and she'd need to stay vigilant. As they rounded the corner, it came into view. It was a mix of tables shaded by awnings and open shop fronts. Nervous goats and sheep bleated, the blacksmith's hammer clanged loudly, and crates were unloaded from wagons with wooden *thwacks*, altogether creating an atmosphere of chaos.

Pressing her hand to her stomach, Silla's eyes darted around the square, identifying any Klaernar she could see; a pair at the far end, strolling past a bread-maker's table; another pair leaning against the wall of a shop, selling brightly colored strips of tablet weave.

Four of them, then, she thought to herself.

A strange, shivering sensation in her veins caught her attention, and she turned to find Jonas studying her. Arms crossed over his chest, the light caught on his golden cheekbones and the strands of his beard. Silla found she could not look away.

"Oi!" barked a deep, male voice.

Shoved from behind, Silla went sprawling, landing on hands and knees on the dirt-packed road.

They've found me, she thought, panic rising. *It's done.*

TWENTY-FIVE

T he clamorous sounds of the market grew distant as Jonas's vision darkened at the edges. Anger boiled in his chest, and his gaze honed in on the man who had knocked Silla to the ground—warrior's build, boiled leather armor, mouth in an arrogant twist as he pushed past them. Seizing his collar, Jonas drove his fist into the man's jaw.

Silla let out a sound of distress as she scrambled to her feet. But it did not matter as his task was set, and Jonas would not stop until he was done. The bearded man did not hesitate before swinging his own fist in reply. But the warrior did not know who he faced—did not know that Jonas had years of dodging fists and perfecting his own brand of justice. Ducking, Jonas easily evaded the blow, smashing his fist into the man's stomach. He felt the distant burn of pain, knew his knuckles would ache tomorrow, but right now, there was only bloodlust coursing through him.

"Jonas," pleaded Silla, drawing the hood of her cloak—of his cloak—deeper over her face and glancing around the market. He didn't tell her how much it pleased him to see her in his cloak, but perhaps he would after he taught this warrior a lesson in respect.

"Apologize," spat Jonas, driving his fist into the man's chin.

"Jonas!" Silla pleaded again, more frantic. He ignored her. This was his business, and he meant to finish it.

Fire burned behind the man's eyes, and Jonas knew his message had not yet been received. The man growled, swiping his foot behind Jonas's own, sending him crashing down on his back. A meaty fist cracked across Jonas's cheek, his vision shimmering for the briefest of moments.

As a metallic flavor prickled along his tongue, Jonas smiled. Catching the warrior's next blow with his fist, he smashed his forehead forward, cartilage and bone crunching from the impact. The man blinked, his eyes going glassy as blood gushed from his broken nose. In a move he'd practiced a hundred times, Jonas rolled them swiftly, his knees pinning the man's arms to the ground as he straddled him. Drawing his open palm back, Jonas slapped him across the face. It was a move meant to shame more than anything else, and as the man's ruddy cheeks reddened further, Jonas knew he'd achieved it.

"Apologize to my companion."

The man spat red, struggling beneath him. Jonas slapped him so hard, the crack echoed off a nearby building.

"I can do this all day," he snarled.

The man blinked, the outline of Jonas's hand clear on his cheek. A smile curved his lips, knowing this warrior would wear his badge of shame for all to see.

"S-sorry, miss," the man managed to rasp out.

Jonas lifted him by his collar, his shoulders coming up off the ground. "I want you to remember the feel of my fist on your skull the next time you think of putting your filthy hands on a woman, kunta," hissed Jonas, delivering one last punishing blow to the man's cheek. The man's head snapped to the side, and Jonas let him fall to the ground.

Standing, he looked around. A crowd had gathered and now began to disperse. But Silla...there was no sign of the curly-haired woman.

Jonas scowled, rubbing his knuckles. Where had she gone? As he surveyed the crowd, his gaze landed on her at last. Standing in a shadowed nook between two buildings, she brushed the dirt from her skirts, glancing nervously toward Jonas.

With the battlelust singing in his veins, Jonas had the urge to push her up against the wall and kiss her senseless. He wanted to taste her skin; wanted to hear the breathless sounds she made; wanted to see what hid under those dresses.

All day, the two sides of his mind had been at war—the quiet, sensible voice urging him to keep his distance, reminding him to keep his guard up and focus on the task in Istré. But the impulsive voice was louder and relentless, encouraging him to tease; reminding him of her sweet scent, the way she'd looked at him with bottomless, dark eyes. *Harmless*, it told him. She would be leaving soon. Rey would never find out. Why shouldn't they amuse themselves while she was still here?

Jonas sauntered toward her, a smile curving his lips. Crowding her deeper into the corner, he propped himself against the wall. She'd grown strangely tense, sending furtive glances over his shoulder, and he positioned his body to shield her from the market's view.

"Why did you do that?" she demanded, adorably displeased.

Jonas frowned. "He pushed you. He disrespected you and, thus, me."

She folded her arms across her chest. "It was not necessary."

"I disagree, Curls. I will not stand to be disrespected. And I will not stand to see you disrespected." He'd worked hard to get to this place of honor amongst warriors and would do what it took to retain his standing. Never again would he tolerate disrespect.

"But you hurt him. It was violent, and so..." She chewed on her lip.

"Did I frighten you, Silla?" He fought the urge to slide his palm along her cheek, sensing she would not appreciate it. "Or were you frightened *for* me?" A smile curved his lips at the irritation plain on her face.

"I was not frightened for you," she retorted. Silla leaned against the building, tilting her face to the sky. "It was brutal. I did not like it."

"It is the way of warriors. That was nothing but sport."

"Sport," Silla repeated. Her gaze slid over his shoulder once more before settling back on him. "You drew such attention to yourself."

Jonas's smile deepened. "Yes," he replied, "and now none in this market will lay a hand on you again."

"It is not how we did things, my father and I," she muttered.

"Then your father has done you a disservice by shielding you from the ways of the world."

Her gaze grew distant, and he wondered where she'd gone. "Yes," she murmured. "He has." With a deep sigh, Silla adjusted her cloak. "Well, I suppose we must get on with this task." But she did not move. A strange look crossed her face as she stared over his shoulder, then tried to smother a laugh.

Jonas frowned, then looked behind him, confused when nothing seemed amiss. "What is it?"

Silla's smile deepened, the dimple appearing. "I believe I am beginning to understand you." Amusement danced in her eyes.

Jonas folded his arms over his chest. "What do you 'understand'?"

"It seems you have many admirers, Jonas," said Silla, nodding over his shoulder.

Jonas turned to the crowd in the market. A mother with a baby perched on her hip glanced their way, head snapping back for a second look; an elderly bread-maker across the lane stared unabashedly; a trio of teenagers peering coyly as they sauntered by.

Jonas was so used to such looks, he scarcely noticed them anymore. He looked at her with a casual shrug. "What of it?"

She seemed beside herself with glee. "I understand now why you're so sure of yourself. You get any woman you want, don't you?"

"Eventually." He stared at her, hoping she understood.

She held his gaze for a moment, then shook herself away from the wall. Striding into the crowd, Silla called over her shoulder to him. "Come on, Wolf! I know what we need."

Jonas trailed behind her as Silla loaded their baskets with onions, carrots, cabbage and apples. They purchased bread, butter, honey, hard cheese, dried fruit, and a variety of salt fish and smoked elk. He watched Silla browse a herbalist's stall, carefully picking bundles of herbs which he didn't know the names for. After he'd paid the vendor, they moved on to the next stall. Over the next several minutes, they purchased sacks of flour, barley, and oatmeal, to be collected shortly by Ilías with the wagon. Jonas spotted a spool of leather twine, purchasing it to repair his talisman's tether.

Even from the shadows of her hood, he could make out the dazed smile on Silla's face as they walked down the road toward the Boar's Head Inn. After watching her readjust the basket on her arm for the third time, Jonas sighed and took it from her.

Silla threw him a grateful smile, but her attention was diverted by a blue sign across the road. "Hold here a moment, Jonas. I have a quick errand I must run." Without giving him a chance to reply, she darted across the street and into the apothecary.

After a few irritating minutes, Silla emerged from the building, smiling wide as she held her necklace in one hand. Jonas scowled as she placed a small leaf into her mouth.

"Why do you take those leaves?" he asked, nodding at the vial.

She leaned on the wall beside him, tilting her head back and closing her eyes.

Her body seemed relaxed, more at ease. "They're for my headaches," Silla mumbled.

Jonas narrowed his eyes. "And what Rey said? Does that not worry you?"

Silla's eyes flew open, and she leveled Jonas with a searing look. "I do not know Rey, but I do know my father—he would never give me anything so dangerous."

"Well, I *do* know Rey, and he wouldn't say such things lightly."

She wouldn't look at him, and Jonas understood it well enough—the conversation was over.

They walked back to the inn in silence.

TWENTY-SIX

Seated at a long table in the mead hall, Silla tried her best to look as though she belonged. She wished she'd kept Jonas's black cloak; instead, Silla had worn her own, but sitting in the crowd with her crimson hood drawn up had felt as good as announcing *here I am*, and so she'd removed it, placing it on the bench beside her. Without the shadow of a hood, she felt exposed, and her eyes surveyed the crowd in the hall for the tenth time in just as many minutes. Compared to the pristine stillness of the road, the noise and scent of ale were an assault on her senses.

She and Hekla had found an empty space on the bench next to the hearth-fire, a wolfhound napping nearby. After dining on roasted trout and blistered turnips, they'd failed to chase down the overwhelmed barmaid, and Hekla had stalked off to order ale straight from the barkeep. Silla's hand caressed the vial hanging around her neck. Full. Replenished. The ache in her skull warded off by a full leaf. She felt lighter, filled with warmth. Strong—like she wouldn't splinter apart and fall to ruin. Like she might actually make it to Kopa.

More. Take another.

She breathed in. Held it. Exhaled slowly.

The slam of a door diverted Silla's attention. A group of four Klaernar stepped into the mead hall, and it felt as though the temperature had suddenly dropped by several degrees. She watched the tallest of them with trepidation as his gaze swept the hall, then landed on her. And then he began to make his way toward her, the others trailing behind. Blood chilling, Silla dropped her gaze to her hands. Her hands...what did she usually do with these things?

Silla swallowed. From the corner of her eye, she tracked the movement of the Klaernar as they drew nearer. They were still walking directly toward her. Goosebumps broke out across her skin. Were they coming to apprehend her? Should she get up and run? Where was the nearest door?

Her heart thundered as the tallest Klaernar paused behind her.

You've waited too long to flee, you halfwit, she cursed herself. There was no way out for her now. Silla's heart pounded hard in her ears.

A hand landed on her shoulder, and she jumped in fright.

"Miss," said the Klaernar.

He was speaking to her. It was over. She'd been found.

"Miss," repeated the man, his hand squeezing tighter. "Is this yours?"

A breath shuddering from her, she turned and looked up to meet the man's gaze. He towered over her, stern eyes regarding her from beneath furrowed brows. Her gaze fell upon the tattooed marks running along brown cheekbones, the black beard twisted into twin braids.

"P-pardon me?" she stammered.

"Is this yours? It was on the floor."

Her eyes dropped to his hand, her red cloak clutched in his fist.

"Oh," she managed, taking it from him. "Y-yes. My thanks."

The man nodded, but, to her horror, he climbed onto the bench beside her. Another Klaernar sat beside him, the remaining two rounding the long table and seating themselves across from the others.

Her gaze fell upon a whorl in the table, and Silla clasped her cloak so tightly she lost sensation in her hand. This...was not ideal. Could she get up and leave?

No. That will draw too much attention, she thought. *Stay for a short time, and then take your leave.*

The barmaid found the Klaernar at once and took their order. And as the men leaned on the table they spoke in hushed tones, and Silla strained to hear their conversation.

"How many horns of ale must we feed you, Brak, before you tell us what brings you to Svarti?" asked the one beside Silla.

An enormous man across the table—the pair of blond braids in his beard reaching well below his shoulders—chuckled. "Not much to say, really. All I know is I've been called down to Sunnavík. The details are sparse."

"They have you riding the Road of Bones to reach Sunnavík? Surely a ship would be faster."

The man across the table glanced over his shoulder, before leaning in closer to the group. "I was instructed not to take a ship. 'Tis a bit strange indeed."

The group grew silent as the barmaid returned, passing out horns of ale.

As she left, the blond-bearded man spoke. "And you, Runolf, what tidings have you from Svarti?"

The black-bearded man to Silla's right chortled. "Not much to tell of Svarti either." The man leaned across the table, his voice lowering to a low rasp. "Though we've just had word the Slátrari struck to the south of us. Two more bodies—the village Gothi and a prominent land owner."

Silla blinked at this revelation. Had this murderer been one of the travelers they'd passed on the road? The thought caused a shiver to crawl down her spine.

"Monstrosity," spat one of the other Klaernar. "Dishonorable Galdra scum. I should like to show him my blade."

Silla's brows furrowed.

"Could be a woman," interjected another. "Those Galdra women do not know their place in the world."

The group voiced their agreement.

The black-bearded Klaernar beside Silla leaned further into the group, and she tilted her head to hear better. "Have you heard of the problems in Reykfjord?"

The fine hairs on her arms stood on end. Had word reached them of Signe's hunt for her? But they had not recognized her...

"Berskium mine destroyed," the man continued, in a near whisper. "Kommandor Thord is scrambling to arrange import from abroad."

"Is the mine no longer usable?" murmured the blond-bearded one, his brows furrowed.

"I do not know the details," rasped the man beside Silla. "Only that there was an explosion. And that there might soon be a shortage of berskium."

Silla's attention was diverted, tension loosening within her at the sight of Hekla approaching with horns of ale tucked under her left arm. She took a steadying breath and tried to block out the sound of the Klaernar's voices.

They do not recognize you, she reassured herself. *They do not search for you. Sit for a few more minutes before making excuses to leave.*

"How was the market, dúlla?" asked Hekla, handing her a horn of ale and sliding onto the bench beside her.

Silla ran a finger around the rim, then took a sip. She wrinkled her nose at the bitter taste. "The *market* was great."

"I gather Jonas was an arse?"

Silla's lips pursed. "He goes out of his way to make things difficult."

"You didn't ask him to get out his axe and chop logs for you then?"

Silla glared at Hekla. "Now that I know his temperament, I find myself cured of any...attraction I might once have felt." Gods, she was such a liar.

Hekla's amber eyes twinkled. "I'm pleased to hear that."

Laughter burst from the group of Klaernar to Silla's right, and her hand tightened around her horn of ale. She forced her attention back to Hekla's voice.

"What did he do? Do I need to rearrange his pretty face?"

Silla patted Hekla's hand in amusement. "My hero. I'm afraid it was Jonas rearranging faces. He punched a man...many times."

"Why?"

"He shoved me, and I fell. I...I was in the way, blocking the path—"

"That'll be reason enough." Hekla sipped her ale, then studied Silla. "Jonas has a particular disdain for the rough-handling of women. I used to call him our White Knight, like the ones in those tales from the Southern Continent. Until I realized there's nothing noble about how he treats women."

Silla's brows knit together. Jonas's strange protectiveness. *It is my foolish conscience and nothing more.*

Hekla continued. "Beyond that, there is a...code of sorts amongst us warriors. When you are disrespected, you must answer with strength."

Silla frowned. "I suppose..."

"I might have done the same, dúlla," said Hekla with a grin. "Though I'd have gotten my claws out to play. I love seeing the biggest warriors piss themselves with fear."

"Ashes, whose wagon have I crawled into?" muttered Silla, sipping her ale.

"What else did Jonas do? Was he an arse to you?"

Silla smiled. "Don't worry. He was quarrelsome to start, but we moved past it."

"Are you sure?" Hekla scoffed. "These man-boys. They've been on the road too long; I swear it, Silla. They forget how to use the thing attached to their faces. Think it's only good for drinking brennsa."

Silla wrapped both hands around her horn. "It was fine. I got him talking eventually."

Hekla smirked. "And what did you speak of with the Wolf?"

"Oh...convictions of the mind and the merits of dresses with pockets. The usual, really."

Hekla snorted. "What?"

The barmaid arrived, laying trenchers of skewered fish, roasted chicken legs, and flatbreads with pots of butter and skyr onto the table before the Klaernar.

Silla forgot what they'd been speaking about. "Where is Gunnar tonight?" she asked Hekla.

Hekla let out an exasperated breath. "Rey has him watching the wagon. They have two guards stationed outside the stables, but no. Rey no longer trusts any but his own. He sniffed them! Asked them when their last drink was. The smaller one looked ready to piss himself. Then Rey decided we'd watch the wagon ourselves."

Laughter bubbled up inside her. "Oh, for the love of the stars. That man is the most distrustful person I've ever met."

"You've no idea."

"Well, my apologies. I suppose it's my fault that Gunnar is on watch."

Hekla waved her off. "You and the Iron Ravens. Those rhodium blades are valuable, and it's best not to have them stolen. I suppose it's not the worst idea." A mischievous look crossed her face. "So, dúlla. Still in need of a distraction?"

"Gotta piss," said a male voice from beside her. An elbow jostled into her as the black-bearded Klaernar to her right climbed off the bench and stalked down the aisle.

Silla's pulse pounded loudly in her ears, and she tried to refocus her attention. "I believe the ale shall be distraction enough tonight." She took another sip and grimaced. "Ugh. Do people truly *like* this?"

"Eh. It grows on you."

"What grows on you, Rib Smasher?" Ilías sank onto the bench across from Hekla. "Must be my charming personality." He waggled his eyebrows.

"Yes. *That* grows on you...like a rash. Or a fungus."

Silla threw her head back with laughter, but it died as Jonas dropped onto the bench beside his brother—directly across from her. As he sat, his long legs stretched out so far that the side of his boot came to rest against the edge of her own.

"Good evening, ladies," he drawled. "I hope you are well?"

It was just the touch of boots, yet it felt strangely intimate. Silla slid her foot away.

"Where is your retinue, Wolf?" teased Hekla. "Should you not have a woman hanging off each shoulder by now?"

"The night is young," Jonas replied. He shifted, his foot nudging back against Silla's, their calves now brushing. She was somehow aware of every tingling point of contact, each wisp of warmth that penetrated her clothing.

"Ale, Jonas?" asked Ilías, holding out a hand. Jonas dug into his pockets, procuring several sólas and handing them to his brother.

As Ilías ambled toward the barkeep, Hekla scoffed. "You do know Ilías is a grown man perfectly capable of handling his own sólas, don't you, Jonas?"

Jonas leveled her with a hard look. "I don't ask after your kin, and I expect the same courtesy from you, Smasher." He leaned on the table, his eyes sliding to Silla, lips quirking up in a knowing smile. *I'm wondering how you taste*, it seemed to say. With a jagged breath, Silla looked into her ale.

"Did Silla the Selfless tell you what occurred today?" he asked. "Her valiant act of heroics?"

These people and their gods damned nicknames, she thought, scowling.

"No." Hekla looked at her expectantly.

"Oh yes. She saved a puppy from being trampled. Was nearly flattened by a wagon in the process. Thankfully, fortune shone upon you. Silla the Martyr is not nearly as satisfying a name."

Silla inched her leg away from his once more. "Yes, well, Jonas would have simply watched the creature die."

"This is how the unintelligent are culled, Curls. It is the reason our world is not populated by half-witted fools."

Silla met Jonas's gaze, heavy and dark. There was a challenge in that look, one she returned with her own fierce glare. "That puppy was simply in the wrong place at the wrong time. I believe it a sad reason to die."

Jonas licked his bottom lip. "Perhaps it was in the right place, as Selfless Silla rushed to the rescue."

The black-bearded Klaernar was back, his shoulder brushing hers as he settled down on the bench.

With a shaky exhale, Silla took a sip of ale. "Where is Rey?" she asked, to change the subject.

"Meeting a friend," said Jonas.

"A friend?" laughed Silla. "What, is there a gate to the eternal fires somewhere nearby?"

Hekla snorted. "Just around the corner."

Smiling at her joke, Silla was distracted for a moment. And then the warmth of Jonas's leg grazed against her own as he now pressed his knee against hers. Her body's response was immediate—a jolt ran straight up her leg.

Ilías returned, handing a horn of ale to Jonas. Lifting his own horn, he proclaimed, "To soft beds and cold ale."

Silla lifted her horn, meeting his crooked grin. She brought it to her lips and drank the cool liquid back, hissing as she set it down. "It tastes like tree sap," she moaned, Ilías snickering across the table.

Laughter boomed from the group of Klaernar beside her, and Silla jumped. "Have you been up north before, Silla?" asked Hekla.

She shook her head, trying to calm herself. Soon, she could leave. Soon.

Hekla continued. "It's cold as ice but beautiful. I believe you'll like Kopa. It is not quite so frigid as it's built under a dormant volcano..."

But Silla was not listening. Jonas had shifted, his leg sliding along hers and his boot coming down and resting heavily on top of her foot. Gods, this intolerable, insufferable man. She yanked hers away from him, her knee knocking into the Klaernar sitting to her right.

The tattooed man turned and stared down at her; Silla could feel the collective eyes of the rest of the Klaernar upon her as well.

"My apologies," she murmured, cheeks flaming.

After a few measured heartbeats, the man turned back to his companions, and they continued their conversation.

You must leave soon, Silla told herself. *But you must do so without rousing the suspicions of the Bloodaxe Crew.*

Jonas's foot sank back down on top of Silla's. Her breath hissed out between clenched teeth. Silla could strangle Jonas at this moment and sent him a glare to tell him as much. But then another thought materialized—two could play these games.

Silla pulled her foot from under his, dragging it up the inside of his calf as slowly as possible. As his hand tightened around his horn of ale, her lips twitched in satisfaction.

"...folk in the north are a touch different from those in the south. More superstitious; they believe in the mythical," Hekla chatted on, unaware of what was happening beneath the table.

Silla's foot continued its lazy travel above Jonas's knee, then along his upper thigh. He adjusted himself on the bench, while Silla shifted to the edge of her seat to move her foot closer, closer, closer. When it was inches from its destination, she dropped it back to the floor. Jonas hissed out a breath, and Silla smiled into her ale as she took a casual sip.

"...Shall soon be the Longest Day," continued Hekla. "If fortune favors us, we will make it back from Kraki's to the town of Hver with time to enjoy the celebrations."

"That would be fun," murmured Silla absently. Jonas rolled his shoulders.

"Does anyone care for another?" asked Silla, clambering off the bench.

Hekla shook her head, her horn still half full. "But you've not yet finished yours..."

"I crave a cup of water. I'll be but a moment."

Silla meandered through the crowd until she reached the barkeep's counter. Leaning on it with one elbow, a buzz built in her head as she looked back at the long table. The Klaernar clustered to the right of where she'd sat, Jonas directly across. It was a pit of serpents, one she had no intention of rushing back into.

Two women propped their swaying bodies against the counter to her left, the slur of their words informing Silla they were pleasantly drunk.

"Did you see him?" one of them said. "The warrior over there with the blue eyes and the golden beard. Merciful gods." The woman sighed.

"Where? Show me," asked the other with a hiccup. The first woman pointed in Jonas's direction. "*Oh*. I'd let him roll me in the furs."

"That's a friend of mine," said Silla, a wicked plan taking form. The women blushed, but she leaned in conspiratorially. "He's unmarried."

The women leaned closer. "Is that so?" asked the first one. She was quite beautiful, with blonde hair and full lips, long dark lashes framing her eyes.

"Yes," continued Silla. "Jonas loves nothing more than a woman with confidence."

The first woman raised her eyebrows. "Oh?"

Silla smiled. "Mmm-hmm. Especially one who is brazen enough to walk up to him and tell him the...intimate things she likes."

The first woman bit her lip and looked back toward Jonas. "Truly?"

"Oh yes," said Silla. Perhaps it was a cruel trick to play on the women, but her desire to get even with Jonas was far greater than her guilt. "If I had a liking for him, I would saunter right up, sit down beside him, lean in close, and whisper into his ear..." She whispered the words to the women.

Straightening, the women exchanged curious looks, then laughed nervously.

"Should I?" asked the first one, raising an eyebrow.

"Go on, Dagny," encouraged her friend.

"Yes, go on, Dagny," echoed Silla eagerly.

Dagny took a deep breath and made her way toward the table.

Silla watched with giddy amusement as Dagny slid between Ilías and Jonas on the bench. A startled look crossed Jonas's face as Dagny's arm skimmed around his shoulder, the beautiful woman leaning close to whisper into his ear.

Jonas's head snapped toward the bar, his eyes locking onto Silla's with that dark and dangerous look once more. The giddiness in her blood was swept away by the sudden and desperate need to get herself out of the mead hall and safely behind the locked door of her sleeping quarters. Turning on her heel, she pushed through the crowd and out the door.

Her heart pounded loudly in her ears as she tore down the path leading to the back of the mead hall where the lodgings were located. As she rounded a corner into the square at the rear of the building, she struck something hard and stumbled backward. Large hands curled around her shoulders to steady her, and she looked up in surprise, her gaze colliding with Rey's.

The man was a mountain, apparently a literal wall of stone—she'd have the bruises to prove it.

"Why are you in such a rush?" he asked grumpily, releasing her shoulders as though she carried the plague.

Her mouth did that thing again where it regurgitated scraps of meaningless information, and she was powerless to stop it. "So...excited. Soft bed and had ale and...must relieve myself. And..."

"Your mouth moves faster than your mind, doesn't it?" he interrupted, a hand scrubbing over his black beard. "I suppose it was too much to hope you'd be searching for another wagon."

She forced her brightest smile. "But if I were to find another ride, then I'd miss your sparkling wit, Axe Eyes."

"And I'd miss the incessant humming that makes my skull pound."

She blinked. "I don't hum." Did she?

He stared at her for a beat too long.

Just as Rey opened his mouth to speak, Jonas rounded the corner. One look into his stormy eyes had Silla questioning her life choices. Her gaze dropped to his hands, fisted around her red cloak.

"Eternal fucking fires," muttered Rey, eyeing Jonas. "Everyone's in such a gods damned rush tonight."

Jonas took in Rey for the first time, the tension receding from his eyes. "Did they know anything?"

Rey ran a hand through his hair. "No..." His mouth opened to say more, but his eyes landed on Silla and narrowed. "I'll buy you a horn of ale, and we can discuss it."

Jonas looked past Rey, glaring at Silla. "You left your cloak in the mead hall, Selfless," he said, a warning in his voice. "You should be more mindful."

"Selfless?" muttered Rey. "Do I want to know—no. I do not."

Her fingers tingled as she took the cloak from Jonas. A smile played on her lips. "My thanks, Jonas. That was very kind of you to fetch it for me. I'm sure it was most inconvenient for you to leave your friends in the mead hall."

Silla did not miss the way his hands twitched, nor did she miss the look he shot her—filled with the promise of retribution. And she wasn't sure what it meant that her stomach flipped with anticipation.

"Will you give Hekla my apologies? I'm suddenly overcome with fatigue."

Rey nodded, then he and Jonas turned back to the mead hall.

Silla exhaled. She couldn't help but feel as though she'd dodged a rolling snowball, but the avalanche was still on its way.

TWENTY-SEVEN
THE ROAD OF BONES

Silla had mixed emotions about leaving the city of Svarti. On the one hand, leaving behind the Klaernar and the need to constantly look over her shoulder was wonderful. On the other, they were now just a day and a half's ride from Skalla Ridge, where they'd take a three-day detour to the alpine village of Kiv to visit Kraki. The odds of convincing Axe Eyes to take her to Kopa were next to nothing. And there was still the need to wheedle information from the mysterious Kraki—a task she'd scarcely considered.

His weaknesses are pretty girls and brennsa, Rey had said. Thus far, all Silla had come up with was to try to charm Kraki over a cup of brennsa. She'd just need to make sure her tongue didn't slip and she kept her wits about her while drinking.

It's a terrible idea, she thought. But no matter how long she considered the task, Silla could not come up with anything else. She'd need to talk to the Bloodaxe Crew and learn some more about Kraki.

After the evening meal that night, Silla prepared a compress with the herbs she'd purchased at the market for Hekla's irritated skin—a recipe her mother had once taught her, and one she'd made over the years for her father.

"Leave it on for an hour, then rinse it off in the stream. It should help with the itching," she'd murmured to Hekla after spreading it across her residual limb and securing it with strips of linen.

Hekla had looked at Silla with shining eyes, then squeezed her in a tight, one-armed hug which crushed the breath from her.

"You do not understand; this has been driving me mad, Silla," said Hekla, after releasing her. "I can feel some relief already. Thank you!"

Sitting before the fire, Silla smiled. It felt good to help someone. But now Hekla had slunk off into the woods, Gunnar following not five minutes later. Alone by the fire, her thoughts bounced between the task with Kraki and her father.

She would never see her father's ice-blue eyes again. Would never feel the squeeze of his bear hug. Would never hear his booming laugh nor his calming voice. It had been the two of them together for so long. Who was she without him?

She was alone now. All alone in this world.

Silla tried to shove her grief back into its cage, but it seeped through the bars, filling her with pain.

The leaves will fix this. One more to numb your pain. To forget about your father.

"You could move your feet," said the little blonde girl from across the fire. "Distract your mind from the dark places."

Wiping a tear away, Silla's hand delved into the pocket of her apron dress. Two apples and a pair of flatbreads were wrapped in clean linen, offerings she would leave on the edge of camp.

"One for the gods, one for the spirits," she whispered, pushing to her feet.

"I thought you didn't believe in the gods anymore," said the girl.

I don't know what I believe, thought Silla. While it was true she didn't understand why the gods could have allowed her to suffer the horrors she had, there was solace to be found in believing they had a plan for her. And if there was even a slim chance that making an offering would earn her good fortune, then Silla would do it. Grabbing the Bloodaxe Crew's spare cloak—she'd 'forgotten' her own red cloak back in Svarti—she slipped into the woods.

Perhaps it was a bit reckless, perhaps it was futile, but already the sorrow she'd felt by the fire was displaced by a small shimmer of optimism. Silla walked for several minutes through the forest, eyeing the patchwork of lichen covering the tree stems, searching for the right place to arrange an altar. Skarplings darted across her path, while clamshell mushrooms with scalloped edges sprouted from tree trunks.

Silla's feet paused as she spotted an enormous linden tree with sprawling, moss-covered branches blotting out the sky. At the base, the trunk scooped into a hollow opening, a cluster of white flowers peeking out from within. Stepping closer, Silla's heart squeezed at the delicate curved stems and bell-shaped blooms —blooms she knew would curve up to the moons on cloudless nights.

"Moonflowers," whispered the little blonde girl.

And in that moment, Silla's wavering faith grew a bit more sturdy. Surely this was a sign from the gods, and the perfect place for Silla to leave her offering. Dropping to her knees before the ancient tree, she pulled out the apples and flatbreads, arranging them around the moonflowers. And then, she clasped her hands together and said a silent prayer.

Please. Help me convince them to take me to Kopa. Help me find safety.

A whisper of movement from behind her had Silla leaping to her feet and drawing her dagger. The blade pressed into the hollow of a man's neck, but she stopped before she broke the skin.

"Well done," said Jonas, bringing his hands together in mock applause. "You're getting better. Perhaps you now have the skill of a nine-year-old."

Jonas had shed his leather armor, his warrior's build evident beneath a simple blue tunic. A hevrít, handaxe, and sword were belted at his hips, and she looked up at him, her gaze tracing the curve of his smirking lips, then landing on his blue eyes. Her heart thudded loudly as she fought the urge to pull his lips down to hers, to run her fingers through his beard.

Instead, she pressed the dagger deeper, the blade dimpling his skin but not drawing blood.

"What do you want, Jonas?"

His smirk deepened. "Will you keep that dagger at my throat?"

"Perhaps," she mused, keeping her face stern. "How do I know you are not a danger to me?"

His eyes darkened. "I've already told you, Curls. I *am* a danger to you."

"What?"

Jonas moved fast, catching her wrist in his large hand and knocking the dagger free. Before she knew what had happened, Silla's arm was twisted behind her, her back pressed to the hard warmth of Jonas's chest.

"It's adorable you believed you were in control," he whispered, his breath tickling her ear.

"Why did you follow me?" she demanded.

"I might ask why you are leaving the Crew's provisions in hollowed out trees."

Her pulse pounded furiously as Silla chose her words.

"You worship the old gods," guessed Jonas, peering into the stump. "Ah. Two of each. The spirits as well?"

Silla kept her lips sealed firmly shut.

"I do not care about the offerings, Silla," whispered Jonas. "But you know better than to wander these woods alone." His free hand settled on her hip, drifting slowly across her stomach. "And since I have you here, I must tell you— I've been thinking of all the ways I can repay you for what you did at the mead hall."

She closed her eyes, wondering what exactly he had come up with—if it might involve his lips on hers. The thought triggered a torrent of butterflies in her stomach.

"I thought you'd be more appreciative, Jonas. After all, I sent her straight to you."

"Hmm. And you were not taunting me? That is why the woman whispered into my ear," he leaned in closer, his words a bare whisper, "*Let me show you how selfless I am?*"

The corner of Silla's lip twitched, but he pulled her arm tighter, and she gasped. "Will you hurt me?"

"Hurt is not what I had in mind."

Her breathing grew shallow, and she knew he could read her response. Jonas let out a low laugh, a rumble from deep in his chest. "Selfless Silla. I believe you've gotten in over your head."

He drew the hair back from her neck and leaned down, his nose grazing just below her right ear. As his warm breath feathered along her sensitive skin, a sound rose within her, something between a whimper and a moan.

"Do you still want to play those games?" He dragged his nose along her temple, inhaling slowly.

All she could hear was the drum of her heartbeat, her shaky exhales. She wished she hated the feel of him, the smell of him. But she didn't. Not one bit.

You must not get close to him, she reminded herself.

With the last shred of her willpower, Silla drove her elbow into his ribs, just as she and Hekla had practiced earlier in the night. Jonas grunted, his grip on her arm loosening, and she wrenched herself free.

Silla sent a withering glare at Jonas as he rubbed his stomach. "No. If you wish to keep me company, you can walk with me. Otherwise, leave." She hadn't intended to linger in the woods. But the thought of returning to the fire, to her endless thoughts, had her retrieving her dagger, and, without looking at Jonas, stepping deeper into the forest.

With a growl, Jonas followed. "You cannot be out here alone, Silla. It is no joke."

She knew she shouldn't be, and she was glad he had followed her. But she'd die before admitting it. "I survived the Twisted Pinewoods."

"So well that you wound up in our wagon."

She huffed but continued through the woods, studying the strange mushrooms and wondering if any were edible. But she couldn't bring herself to speak to Jonas, content to let him trail behind her. She could feel his agitation with every dramatic sigh and unnecessarily violent snap of a twig.

Gods, what she would do to go back in time and crawl into a different wagon. Had she known it would lead to this...to this oversized sulking warrior following her around, toying with her, testing the limits of her willpower, she certainly would not have done it.

"I want a steading of my own."

Silla stopped dead in her tracks, turning to face him. "Excuse me?"

"Eventually, I will leave the Bloodaxe Crew. I will have a hearth of my own. Land. And peace."

Her brows lifted. "Truly?"

His gaze slid to the tree beside her, fingers wrapping around the talisman that hung from his neck. So, he'd repaired the tether. "My family had it once. A farmstead of our own. Like you, we were cheated from it." A muscle in his jaw flexed.

"Cheated...from it?"

He was quiet for a moment. "There was a dispute of inheritance. Land that should have been passed to me, to Ilías, was seized from us. Not by kin of ours —it was a ruling by the Law Speaker that did not go in our favor. Our land and possessions were unfairly stripped from us."

Silla put a hand on his arm. As Jonas stood half a head taller than her, she had to crane her neck to look into his eyes. "I am sorry to hear that, Jonas."

His nostrils flared as he looked down at where her hand rested. "I don't like to think of it. But I thought...you of all people would understand the feeling of it. To be cheated of one's land."

Silla's stomach clenched. She *hated* the lies—wished there was some other way. Though her land dispute was imaginary, empathy gathered in her. She could see it was a wound he carried. And perhaps she understood him a little more.

As she withdrew her hand from his arm, she flexed it to shake off the lingering feel of him. "I thought you were selfish and money-hungry. But this is why you care so much about this job."

Jonas nodded. "We are close to having the funds to buy it back. Then, we will leave the Bloodaxe Crew. Have our land rights restored. And remove the black mark from our family's name."

Her eyes fell upon the talisman, watching Jonas's thumb scrape across it. Family, respect, and duty. The talisman around his neck, a constant reminder of what he had lost. Of what he sought to regain. She blinked at Jonas. There was so much more to him than she'd initially thought.

Silla decided to lighten the mood. "Did you have chickens on your farmstead?"

Jonas snorted. "What is your fascination with chickens?"

"My happiest memories include chickens. When things were still balanced, my mother and father and I lived in a home in Hildar with a big garden and a swing that hung from the tree. And chickens. It was the happiest of my life. Chickens remind me of feeling settled."

Her stomach tensed. *You've said too much*, she thought. *Jonas need not know you were ever unsettled. He believes you lived on a farm, you fool.* To conceal the panic rising within, Silla turned and kept walking.

"Did your mother teach you how to cook?" asked Jonas quietly from behind her.

"Yes." She bit down on her lip to distract from the melancholy settling into her bones. Her mother was not a memory so much as a smell...a sound. The scent of sweet rolls baking in the oven, the sizzle of an onion as it hit hot butter, the constant, soft humming as she stirred a steaming pot of skause.

She finally found the courage to speak. "When I'm cooking, it feels as though she is with me. Guiding my hands, whispering in my ear to add salt or more thyme. Calling me a bjáni and smacking my hand with a wooden spoon when I add too much salt."

She needed to redirect the conversation. "But you did not answer my question. Did you or did you not have chickens?"

Jonas chuckled. "We had chickens. And sheep. And goats and horses. Rolling pastures of wheat and rye. A longhouse that had seen better days. A smithy, though, that was long abandoned by the time we left..."

Silla heard the openness in his voice, as though he were young again. Unburdened. Free. But there was more to this story, of that she was certain. And while she was curious, she would not pry, just as she hoped he'd ask no more of her mother. Instead, she redirected the conversation once more.

"How did you join the Bloodaxe Crew?"

Jonas huffed. "It was Rey. We met him in Sunnavík. Ilías and I...left home and could not find any warbands willing to take a chance on two farm boys with no experience. We were there for weeks, going from mead hall to mead hall, searching for work. They laughed us out of them each time—Ilías had seen only sixteen winters and had yet to hit his last growth. Our sólas were dwindling, and we had to find...there was no home for us to go back to."

Silla's chest squeezed.

"One day, we went to a new mead hall, and immediately one of the largest warriors started mocking Ilías. I'd had enough of the disrespect and simply... snapped. Apparently, I beat the man to an inch of death. I do not recall it myself. I'm told Rey pulled me off him, dragged me outdoors. Talked to me until my anger receded. Told me he was raised in the north and stories of his moon-touched grandmother and how he came down to Sunnavík looking for work and someone took a chance on him."

Jonas shook his head. "He said he saw something of himself in me, that he liked my loyalty to my brother. That they had need of honorable warriors in their Crew. He made me wait with Ilías while he spoke with the headman of the Bloodaxe Crew. And Rey convinced Kraki to let us join them. The rest is history."

"Kraki was leader before Rey?"

Jonas huffed a laugh. "Yes. He is a tough one to like."

"Have you any words of advice for me?" Silla asked. "How shall I try to get the information from Kraki?"

Jonas paused, looking at her for a moment. Something seemed to pass behind his eyes—anger? Irritation? She wasn't quite sure. "Kraki's ego has always been his downfall. Pander to it, and you might be able to get what you need from him. But..."

The woods fell to silence, and Silla grew impatient. "But?"

Jonas's hand flexed. "Do not turn your back on him. Do not allow him to get you alone."

Silla swallowed, considering his words. "Do you think..." She sighed, feeling hopeless. "Do you think Rey would ever take me to Kopa?"

"No."

There was no hesitation in his answer, and something about the finality made her feel better. So the Bloodaxe Crew wouldn't take her to Kopa. She felt somewhat freed by this knowledge. Eventually, they turned and began to wander back to camp. To her surprise, Silla found she didn't mind Jonas's presence so much. When he wasn't being an arse, he was somewhat enjoyable to be around.

She wasn't entirely sure why she said her next words, but she found her mouth opening nonetheless. "With all that has happened, I've realized life is short, and you never know how much time you have left. You should not waste it doing things you don't love. If you want a farmstead of your own, you will make it happen with or without the Bloodaxe Crew, Jonas; I know you will."

Jonas was silent beside her, but she didn't detect anger, so she continued.

"My mother would say that you do not wait for fortune to come to you. When you want something, you must *make* it happen."

Jonas had stopped walking, and she paused as well, looking up at him. Something shifted behind his eyes, and she felt encouraged. He seemed to be listening. Perhaps he simply needed to hear heartening words.

She kept going. "You must plan and toil and work for it. She *was* speaking of her garden, but I...wait what—"

Jonas stalked toward her, and she took an apprehensive step backward, then another until her back bumped into the hard trunk of a tree.

"What are you doing? Jonas, I—" the words dissolved on her tongue as he planted his hands on either side of her head, caging her in.

Jonas leaned down, his breathing ragged. "I'm going after what I want."

TWENTY-EIGHT

"That's not what I meant!" Silla sputtered, staring up at Jonas.

His gaze slid along her unruly curls and down her frumpy dress. He shouldn't want her—she wasn't his type, was reckless and irritating to no end. But the lust sizzling through his veins was more potent than anything he could remember.

"How is it different? Will you waste time pretending? Or will you be brave and take what you want?" His words were carefully chosen—tinder to her sparking irritation. *There you are*, he thought with satisfaction as fire flared behind her eyes.

Gone was the mouse, and here was the vixen.

"Let me distract you, Silla."

Heat licked up his spine as he held his unwavering gaze on her. Pushing her hair over her shoulder, Jonas scraped a finger along the elegant curve of her neck. Gods, she was so soft. And as she let out a shaky breath, he knew he had her.

They moved at the same moment—Jonas dipping his head, Silla pushing onto her toes. And then, their lips met. Immediately, he could tell she hadn't done this before. Her movements were stiff and uncertain, yet somehow, her inexperience was endearing. And, if Jonas were honest, alluring.

It took all of his restraint to ease her into the kiss, nudging her lips playfully with his own until she relaxed. She was soft as silk, bending into him as though all her defensive layers were being stripped away. In his arms, she was vulnerable, revealing bits of herself to him she'd never shared with another. Gods, but Jonas wanted her. He wanted to push her against the tree, wanted to take her far more roughly than a woman like her deserved.

Silla drew back, her breath fluttering hot against him. "Just a distraction," she whispered against his lips, like some last attempt at self-protection. He dipped his brow in acknowledgment, hardly caring what she said. *More,* was his only thought as he slid his lips back to hers.

But to his irritation, Silla pulled back once more. "To be clear," she said huskily, "this will never happen again."

Hunger flooded his veins, his restraint quickly fraying. "Good."

"Good." Her gaze dropped back to his mouth. "And if you tell anyone, I'll poison your food."

Jonas felt his lips twitch. "Vicious little—"

She cut him off, pressing her mouth firmly onto his. At first, her assertiveness startled Jonas, but then, snapped his restraint clear through.

Fingers digging into her hips, he yanked her closer to feel the swells of her breasts and the press of her hips against him. Jonas slid a rough palm into her curls, tugging until her head tilted to the right angle. And then, he deepened the kiss. *Like this,* he told her with his mouth, parting her lips and exploring her with gentle strokes. As her tongue began to make its own curious movements, a strange possessive clench tightened his chest.

Silla was apprehensive at first but grew bolder, her tongue dipping into his mouth and earning a groan of appreciation from the back of his throat. She seemed to like this sound, her hand moving to his chest and curling around his tunic. Her tentative touch, her curiosity drove all thoughts from his mind. There was only her. Only want—no, *need*—to have her beneath him, showing her how good he could make it.

Jonas's hands moved mindlessly along the curve of her hip, the dip of her waist, the bumps of her ribcage, and everywhere he touched, she felt so good.

Felt so right.

Delirious, he shook the thought away. His teeth nipped down on her soft lower lip, and he smiled against her as she squealed into his mouth. He lived for that sound, began to scheme of other ways to get her to make it. When she returned the favor, he growled and tugged his weapons belt loose. As it fell to the ground, Jonas lifted Silla, rucking up her skirts.

"Wrap your legs around me," he rasped, scarcely recognizing his own voice.

Silla's legs parted willingly, sliding around his hips, and as he pinned her against the tree, Jonas had the vague notion that he'd never been so aroused in his life. Grinding himself against her, he was lost in the intoxicating friction of her body, the small sounds of pleasure she made. One hand tangled in her hair, tugging her head to the side.

Jonas's mouth moved to her neck, and he hovered, breathing in her scent.

"Is this what you wanted?" he whispered against her skin. "Are you distracted, Silla?"

Her shaky sigh sent blistering heat up his spine. Jonas pressed his lips to her neck, kissing a hot line down the length of it. Eyes honing in where her pulse pounded furiously, he scraped his teeth along it, watching goosebumps rush along her skin.

Jonas was supposed to distract her, but he was the one getting lost. Trembling with restraint, he was on the knife's edge of utterly losing control.

"Why do you feel like this?" he heard himself rasp against her neck, hips rolling against hers. He scarcely recognized his own voice, did not seem to be in control of it.

But his question quickly vanished in the haze of his mind, and he brought his lips back to hers and kissed her with unrestrained passion. It was primal fire —too much; too good. He was hard and aching as he pushed into the apex of her thighs.

It was then that he heard it—a vibration in the air. If Jonas wasn't a seasoned warrior, he'd have thought nothing of it. But his instincts told him otherwise.

Quick as lightning, he broke the kiss, easing Silla to the ground.

"Did you hear that?"

Holding herself perfectly still, she stared at Jonas with wide eyes. If he could take a moment, he might take pride in her swollen lips, the flush of her cheeks. But instead, he grabbed his battle belt and drew his sword, turning away from her. A brittle snap confirmed his fears. There was something out there. Behind him, Jonas heard the soft *shick* of Silla's dagger being drawn.

A whistling growl set the hairs on the back of his neck on edge.

"Fuck," muttered Jonas, placing himself between her and where the sound had come from. "Stay behind me."

———

SILLA BLINKED, her senses swarming back to her.

Jonas had taken a defensive stance, his legs apart, sword gripped in hand. But he had no armor, no shield, and he was away from his Bloodaxe brothers and sisters—because of her.

"If I say run," said Jonas in a low voice, "you must run straight back to camp. Do not stop. You understand?"

"Yes." Silla's heart hammered for a completely different reason than it had moments before.

"It's a skógungar," whispered Jonas, his posture easing a touch. "A forest walker. It shouldn't harm us."

As her eyes searched the layers of shadow, Silla saw movement. Her blood ran cold as she took in the creature. Impossibly tall with skin stretched too tight over its face, the thing's eyes glowed like red embers set into the twisted knots of a tree while its mouth was spread in an unnaturally wide smile. The creature hunched at the neck as it stalked forward, its long gangling arms ending in three sharp claws. The skógungar saw them, its mouth spreading wider, revealing rows of razor-sharp teeth.

"There's something wrong with it," muttered Jonas. "What is wrong with its eyes?"

This is why you need the Bloodaxe Crew to survive the Road of Bones, Silla thought to herself. Creatures she'd never seen, could never have imagined, walked these woods. Silla knew nothing of skógungar...what was this thing? Was it a danger to them, or could they simply retreat to the camp?

Jonas widened his stance as the forest walker approached. With its long limbs and unnatural stealth, it was like an extension of the forest itself; a walking tree. But from the malevolent red eyes and smell of decay filling the clearing, Silla sensed it was something altogether different. Something sinister.

The whistling growl sounded again, sending shivers down Silla's spine. It was unnatural, eerie. A warning. Every instinct in her body told her to run, but she held herself in place, as Jonas had instructed.

With a sudden burst of speed, the skógungar charged at Jonas, slashing out with its lethal claws. Jonas sank low in a quick, smooth movement, swinging his sword in an upward stroke. With a disturbing squelch, it landed in the armpit of the monster, causing the beast to stumble backward.

It recovered quickly, launching at Jonas and striking out powerfully with its uninjured arm. Jonas parried the attack but was driven downward. The creature surged toward him, attacking with a flurry of rapid strikes. Silla stifled a small cry as Jonas barely righted himself in time to dodge a blow. What if it hurt or killed him? It was her fault he'd been distracted, that he hadn't had time to find the others.

The creature moved with such unnatural bursts of speed, it was impossible to predict where it would strike. It growled again, this time with a strange clacking sound straight from her nightmares.

"Come on, kunta." Jonas adjusted his grip on his sword, watching the skógungar closely.

The creature drove forward with sudden aggression, slashing its claws at Jonas's face. He evaded, ducking while hacking at its ribs. The skógungar stumbled back with a screech, and Jonas was on it, landing blow after blow, his sword stabbing into the monster's chest until it fell backward. Jonas did not relent, and Silla had to look away as he hacked at its neck, its screeches growing more desperate, before tapering off.

She made the mistake of opening her eyes to see the skógungar's head severed from its body, black blood seeping from its neck; its ugly mouth stretched wide in a smile which would haunt her. Silla buried her face in her hands, her stomach twisting.

"What in Hábrók's arse was that?" muttered Jonas, grabbing Silla by the shoulder and dragging her through the forest. He smelled of rotten things. Of decay and molder. She gagged. When they reached the edge of camp, Jonas stopped. "Shite. We need a story. You were at the stream, and I was gathering firewood when I heard the skógungar and went to make sure you were all right. Understand?"

She nodded, staring up at him. "Thank you," she managed.

He gathered her face in his hands and pressed a kiss to her lips.

"A shame we were interrupted, Curls. Fuck. I smell foul. I'll need to burn these clothes and scrub myself raw."

Silla followed him on shaky legs toward the fire, toward the curious stares of the Crew, and she wondered.

What would happen when the Bloodaxe Crew left her and she had to find her way alone on the Road of Bones?

TWENTY-NINE

SVARTI

A s the mead hall door slammed shut behind Skraeda, she inhaled sharply, the tang of stale urine and ale invading her senses. Suppressing a scream of rage, she strode down the packed earth road, merchants and warriors alike darting from her path. She had not caught up to the girl and her companions on the Road of Bones, and now she sought them out in the city of Svarti. It was impossible, this task, a search for a single blade of grass in a barn full of straw.

A day now she'd wasted, scouring the markets and mead halls and lodgings with no sign of her. As Svarti was the last of the larger cities on the Road of Bones, it was customary for traveling parties to spend several days collecting provisions and enjoying the amenities of the city before the long stretch north. But the woman might have skipped such a thing.

It depended on her travel companions, she supposed, which brought her back to the present—her mission to discover more about these people with whom the girl traveled. Who were these warriors who'd agreed to take the girl north? Had she paid for their protection? Did they know whom they harbored?

The latest letter from Queen Signe sat burned to ashes in the hearth of Skraeda's lodgings, but she could recall each word scrawled on the parchment.

She knew who the girl was. *What* the girl was. Queen Signe had brought Skraeda into the fold, into her central circle of trust, and now the urgency was only higher. Skraeda knew that if she succeeded in this task, her value would only increase in the eyes of the queen. But if she failed...well, Skraeda could not allow her mind to wander to such things.

You will not waste this opportunity, she thought. She could *not* let her queen down. The girl was central to Queen Signe's plans, and Skraeda had sent a falcon south with a letter, swearing to Signe that she would not rest until their target was apprehended.

Now that she understood the girl, she needed to understand her companions. Who were these warriors? Where were they headed? What were their weaknesses? And so, she trudged down the rutted road until she reached the next mead hall. Her eyes fell upon a white sign. *The Boar's Head.*

Pushing open the heavy door, Skraeda stepped inside. As the day wore on, the mead halls had grown more and more busy, and the Boar's Head bustled with a mid-afternoon crowd. Two rows of long tables sat in the hall, candles in iron chandeliers casting shivering yellow light down upon the patrons. Her eyes narrowed on a lone Klaernar, seated at the end of the table, but jumped quickly to the barmaid handing horns of ale to an already raucous group of traders.

As the barmaid hustled back toward the kitchens, Skraeda grabbed her elbow and drew her to a halt. "I search for a woman who might have been in here in the past two days."

The woman blew out an exasperated breath. "There've been many women in here."

"She'd have warriors as companions. Might have a nervous disposition. Curly hair, though it could have been secured. Red cloak—"

"Red cloak?" asked the Klaernar from the end of the table.

Skraeda's gaze snapped to him—wiry black beard set in twin braids; smooth brown skin; dark eyes with the look of a man who'd been on the job for many long years.

"Yes," she said, curiosity bristling through her. Skraeda would have thought the girl would keep a wide berth around the Klaernar, but perhaps she'd thought wrong.

"I've seen her," he said, eyeing Skraeda curiously. "I shared a bench with her and another woman warrior." The man stroked his beard. "What is it you want with her?"

"It is a private matter," Skraeda replied.

"Might I leave? I've many patrons who are waiting," muttered the barmaid.

"Yes, yes," replied Skraeda, her gaze unmoving from the black-bearded Klaernar. Her senses stretched out, the auras in the boisterous pub rich with bright looping filaments of amusement, soft, fluttering threads of sexual desire, and ah...there it was. A very thin ribbon of curiosity, writhing and wriggling.

"What's it worth to you for this information?" asked the Klaernar, his bushy black brows drawn together.

Skraeda sighed, her fingers moving into her pocket, stroking Ilka's braid as she maintained her mind's grasp on the man's thread of curiosity.

"Three sólas."

The man huffed. "No," he said. "I imagine it's worth far more than that to you."

"How so?"

"The flush of your neck tells me you're irritated. The fist you're clenching in your pocket does the same. And when I said *no*, you flinched. Just for a heart-beat, but I saw it."

Skraeda forced in a deep breath. This man was perceptive enough to rival most Solacers—not herself, of course. Perhaps the information he could glean would be quite useful.

Thumbing along the thread of his curiosity, Skraeda skipped past amuse-ment, settling on the thin golden strand beneath. Skraeda had longed to play with this thread ever since she had first discovered it. Unique to the Klaernar, it was thin and delicate. Though it was best to perform such experiments in private, Skraeda had urgent need—this information was essential if she wished to track the girl.

And so it was decided.

Using the utmost care so as not to tear through it, Skraeda pulled the gilded filament and held it in her mind's grasp. The man's pupils retracted until they were as thin as a strand of hair. Skraeda's heart began to pound—the rest of his already muted emotions had snuffed out completely.

"Scratch your nose," she said softly.

His finger reached up and rubbed the tip of his nose. A smile spread across Skraeda's lips. Oh, this was exactly what she'd suspected—she held the man's free will in her grasp. Was it an unwanted side effect of the berskium powder? Or was this golden thread of free will intentional in design—a way for the Urkans to corral their soldiers when needed?

It did not matter. This was how Skraeda would get what she needed.

"Tell me about the woman with the red cloak," she urged. "Tell me every-thing you recall about her and her companions."

The man's voice was monotone and quiet, and Skraeda leaned in closer to hear his words. "The woman warrior she sat with had black hair braided back, a loud laugh, and a prosthetic arm. Two men joined them—tanned skin, blond hair, one with a beard—but the woman you seek quickly left. The larger blond warrior chased after her with her red cloak and returned with another man. Large. Black hair, brown skin, fearsome glare."

Skraeda frowned. She did not know these warriors...it could be almost anyone. But it seemed the man was not done.

"They drank beside us for several hours. The young one was loud, and I heard him say something about Kiv. He said *I'd rather jump off Skalla Ridge than go to Kiv and face Kraki. Can she not retrieve the book herself?*"

Skraeda's brows drew together. "Was he speaking of the woman with the red cloak?" she asked.

"I cannot say," said the black-bearded Klaernar. "The large one punched the kid's shoulder. Told him if he didn't shut up, he'd throw him off Skalla Ridge himself."

"When was this?" barked Skraeda.

The man's bushy brows furrowed. "'Twas...two nights past?"

Skraeda eased her mind's grip on the man's free will, watching as his pupils spread like ink through water. He blinked several times, then scowled at her.

"Well?" he demanded. "What's the information worth to you?"

Skraeda smiled. "Nothing. Enjoy your ale, warrior."

And with that, she left the mead hall. The summer sun was still high, but the temperature was cooling by the hour. Pulling the furs tighter around her shoulders, Skraeda made her way back to her lodgings, lost in thought.

Two days. Had the group left yesterday morning, they'd have two full days' head start on Skraeda. But if they were making a side trip to Kiv, they'd leave the Road of Bones for several days, at which point they'd need to rejoin it.

"I will wait for them at the junction," Skraeda said, a smile curving her lips.

THIRTY

THE ROAD OF BONES

"She's trying to win my favor through Horse," muttered Rey, dragging his freshly-sharpened dagger along his neck, neatening the edge of his beard. "It will not work."

Jonas stared into the cup Silla had handed him minutes earlier, trying to clear his mind. Steam curled into the cool morning air, infusing it with the rich scent of róa bark. The fire crackled low, voices of Sigrún, Ilías, Gunnar, and Hekla mingling nearby as they readied the horses for the day's journey. As Jonas sipped his róa, he was unable to keep his eyes from wandering to the silhouette near the wagon.

Silla had pulled her hair up today, but a twisted coil had fallen loose, hanging in her face. He watched as she blew it away, only for it to fall back where it had just been. Patting Horse's forehead with one hand, she held a carrot to her mouth with the other. His gaze honed in on the small of her back, where her dress curved in and then rounded out around her perfect backside.

His mind was befuddled, his desire for this woman spearing at the crumbling walls of his self-preservation. *Why do you feel like this?* he'd asked, and he'd dwelled on it long into the night. His armor had melted away under her touch. How had he become so lost...so out of control? She was inexperienced—it wasn't something she'd done.

The realization landed like a blow to his stomach.

It was her sincerity. There was no performance, no false encouragement. She was real, so genuine, and had responded with such unbridled eagerness.

He needed to kiss her again.

He needed to make her wholly his.

Jonas tried to shake the thoughts from his mind. It was absurd. He never thought this way. Was not built for such things. But when he recalled how she had looked at him—with optimism, with belief—a warm feeling spread through his chest. Jonas felt as though he could share things with her if he wished, and she would not judge him. He *wanted* to share things. Which troubled him greatly. Jonas understood nothing except that this was a problem, and so he reminded himself affection was a dangerous thing; it only led to devastation and ruin.

With a deep, clarifying breath, Jonas tried to refocus on his conversation with Rey.

"It's quite clever, really," said Jonas. "She has discovered your weakness."

Rey grumbled. Horse truly was Rey's one sensitive spot. Jonas's lips twitched as he recalled the time Horse had gotten rain rot, and Rey had halted their journey to purchase special soap for her. The Bloodaxe Crew had waited a full week while Rey lathered her coat daily before they could finally return to the road.

"I still do not buy it, Jonas. Her story is horse shite."

"Need I remind you? Land disputes are common, Axe Eyes."

Rey glanced at Jonas, tugging the longer strands of beard on his chin taut, then passing his dagger through them. "Apologies, Jonas. I meant no offense."

"I know," said Jonas. "Just...why not give her a chance?"

Rey exhaled, pinching the bridge of his nose. "This job has my mind spinning. It is too important and too dangerous for added complications. And now the skógungar are attacking humans? They should be neutral! Why in the eternal fires would they attack a human, let alone venture so far from the Western Woods?"

Jonas shook his head. He had no answers; only more questions. He'd seen a skógungar only once before. Docile and peaceful, it had walked by the stream where he filled his waterskin, paying him no attention. Though Jonas had heard tales of forest walkers attacking, there was always provocation involved—a woodsman cutting trees in a sacred part of the forest or an ignorant warrior attacking the creatures first. But as he recalled the feral way the skógungar had attacked, the odd, glowing red of its eyes and that putrid stench, Jonas knew—something malevolent was at play.

The night prior, after returning to camp smelling like a troll's arse, the Bloodaxe Crew had hammered Jonas with questions. Silla had barely spoken a word, though he did not blame her. The sight of the skógungar's head hacked off had not been pretty, and she was unused to such violence.

Rey had immediately demanded to see the corpse, though there wasn't much to see—the glowing eyes had extinguished at death, and apart from that, it looked as a skógungar should. But the scent of decaying things—unnatural for a forest walker to carry—had lingered, causing his headman's brows to furrow in thought. The Crew had scoured the woods for signs of others and thankfully had come up empty. All the same, Rey had ordered Gunnar to join Sigrún on watch duty that night.

Jonas drained the last of his róa. "I've no idea why there are forest walkers this far east."

"Istré borders the Western Woods. Could it be related to our job?"

"Perhaps? Impossible to know."

"Hmm." Rey passed a hand over his beard to check the length, before changing the subject. "I've decided to see Kraki alone. With her." He nodded at Silla.

Jonas's gaze snapped up. "You'll take her alone? Why not bring the whole Crew?"

Rey tilted his head to the side, scraping the dagger along the sides of his skull in quick upward motions tapering out at the top. "We are far more likely to gain entry into his home with just the two of us. If the whole of the Bloodaxe Crew shows up, I'd wager Kraki would barricade himself inside his home without bothering to hear us out."

Jonas's chest tightened. The thought of Kraki's wrinkled hands touching her made a primitive part of him wake up and growl. Someone should look out for her. Keep her safe from the old arse.

"Do not let harm befall her," he found himself saying.

Rey's thick black brows dipped down. "Surprised to hear you give a shite, Jonas."

Jonas scowled. "We spoke while at the market, and she's...kind."

He felt Rey watching him and glared into the flames. What in the eternal fires was the matter with him? Jonas had survived by looking out for himself and his kin—the Bloodaxe Crew, that was. Why was he risking Rey's ire for this girl?

"I will keep an eye on her," Rey said at long last, setting his blade aside and rubbing the back of his neck. "You know I have more honor than to let things go that way. You will take the wagon, we will go to Kraki, and meet in Hver in time for Longest Day."

"Do what you must, Rey," muttered Jonas.

Silla padded over to them, brushing her hands on her skirts. "Would you like more porridge, Rey? Jonas? There's some left in the pot."

Jonas declined with a shake of his head, but Rey grunted and passed his bowl to her. Jonas cast a look to the skies—his leader was determined to be an arse. But Silla seemed to take it all in stride, heaping the bowl full. As she handed it to Rey, her lips curved up into one of those smiles which made her cheeks plump up and her eyes sparkle.

Blood warming, Jonas forced his gaze to the ground with a scowl.

It was best they parted ways like this. Because this was the kind of problem he'd spent a lifetime avoiding.

———

SKALLA RIDGE WAS BEAUTIFUL, but it was difficult for Silla to admire it. With jagged fjords cutting straight down to frothing black seas, there was something raw and wondrous about it. It seemed a reminder that nature was cruel and unforgiving—one small stumble and you'd find yourself in a watery grave.

The Road of Bones meandered along the ridge, the brisk salty air rousing Silla from her daze. Gulls flew overhead, their cries like sharp daggers in her skull, reminding her that her time with the Bloodaxe Crew was coming to a close; she'd soon be alone, forging her way north amongst the killers and warbands and monstrous creatures.

An uneasy sense of comfort existed with the Bloodaxe Crew. Axe Eyes was combative, but they'd reached a silent agreement—she would not bother him, and he kept his distance. It seemed to work; she rarely saw more than the back of his head while riding in the wagon.

Once they reached Skalla Ridge, things went downhill quickly.

First, Axe Eyes had informed her they'd be parting ways with the Bloodaxe Crew and would travel alone up to Kraki's home. Next, Rey had led Gunnar's brown mare over and stared at her expectantly.

"I cannot ride a horse," she said, clutching the vial around her neck and bracing herself for his reply. "Can we not bring the wagon?"

Rey blinked at her as though he could not comprehend the words she'd just spoken. "The wagon slows us. It would add a day's travel onto our plans." His nostrils flared. "You truly cannot ride?"

Silla shook her head.

Rey's jaw clenched as he forced the next words out. "Horse can hold two."

Her heart seemed to stop beating.

Share.

A horse.

With Axe Eyes?

"Trust me when I say I am no happier about this arrangement, Sunshine." The large man glowered at her. "It is only for a couple of days."

Couple of days. Her knees had nearly buckled at that. Couple of days sharing a horse with the walking boulder.

With the man who'd tried to kill her.

Twice.

Silla grabbed her bag and sulked toward Horse, blowing a strand of hair out of her eyes. She pulled a handful of oats from her pocket, flattening her palm beneath Horse's nose. "I suppose we'll be spending some extra time together, girl," she murmured. Horse nuzzled along the front of Silla's dress in search of more oats. "Hey now," she laughed softly. "We must keep something for you to look forward to."

Silla licked her thumb, then rubbed a spot of ash on Horse's forehead until her coat was pristine once more. "Much better, you gorgeous girl," she said brightly. Gods above, if she had her own horse, she'd brush its coat and braid its mane with flowers, would make it the happiest creature in all of Íseldur...

Turning in search of Jonas, a low ache began to burn in her stomach. Where had he gone?

She was not entirely sure what to think of the night before. It had been bewildering to go from one extreme to the other so quickly. She could still smell that...*thing.* Could still hear the strangled whistle. Could still feel the ghost of Jonas's fingers scrape along her collarbone, her hip. Silla shivered.

And now Jonas was nowhere to be seen.

"Continue her training for me, all right, Axe Eyes?" barked Hekla from atop her own horse. Hekla, along with Gunnar and Ilías, had protested Rey's plans vehemently, intensifying the burn in her stomach. "She's beginning to pick it up."

Rey's only reply was a dramatic sigh.

Hekla turned to Silla and muttered, "Do not turn your back to Kraki, all right, dúlla? Keep near Rey. Keep your dagger on you."

Silla forced a smile upon her face. "It will be fine," she said, a little too brightly.

Rey unhooked the wagon from Horse. "Where the fuck is Jonas? Gunnar, you'll need to pull the wagon."

Where *was* Jonas? Was he avoiding her? She told herself it did not matter. The kiss had merely been a distraction and would never happen again. Besides, in a few days, she'd be on her own once more.

After Rey and Gunnar fastened the wagon to Gunnar's horse, Rey shoved Silla's rucksack into his saddlesack along with the food she'd packaged up from the crate of provisions. Silla climbed onto Horse, Rey swinging up behind her. She could feel him looming over her, so large he blocked out the sunlight. When he reached for the reins, his arms caged her in, and it was too much. She could smell him—traces of campfire and pinewoods. It felt like he was everywhere.

Mistake, her mind screamed. *This is a mistake.* Had she forgotten about Anders? Of the look in this man's eyes as he'd slit his throat? She swallowed. Her eyes drifted to his gloved hands. They were *huge*. How many lives had those hands ended? Unease shivered down her back.

"Well, this shall be fun," she mused, desperate to fill the awkward silence.

Horse lurched forward, and her hands found the saddle horn. She gripped it clumsily, unused to this new, much higher vantage point and to the sway of Horse's back.

An exasperated breath gusted from Rey, ruffling her hair. "Have you truly never ridden?"

"No."

Rey made a noise of disbelief.

"I'm pleased you find that so amusing." She clutched the saddle horn so hard her knuckles were white. How would she last an hour of this, let alone days?

After several incredibly awkward minutes, Rey transferred the reins to one hand. His other large hand curled around her shoulder, pressing it back. "Sit tall but relaxed. Find her rhythm. Do not fight it."

Silla tried to relax, but each time her back brushed against his chest, she tensed up all over. It didn't help that each snap of a twig along the track had her swinging her head in search of walking trees hungering for her flesh. And with each step along the trail, the silent tension between Silla and Rey grew until it was so heavy, she could feel it in the marrow of her bones.

At last, she could bear it no longer. "Exactly what information do you need me to draw from Kraki?"

He exhaled loudly. "You lasted an entire five minutes without talking. That must be a new record."

Silla scowled, then tried again. "What kind of book is it?"

"You mean you did not hear those details when you were listening in on a conversation you had no business hearing?"

"No."

"Do not trouble yourself about it," he ground out.

She scoffed. "You truly do not trust me. Even though I've agreed to go with you—alone, I might add—to acquire this book."

"Trust is earned."

She rolled her eyes. "And if the book is not there, how am I to help you retrieve the information?"

"With your *golden tongue*, of course." There was no mistaking the sarcasm in his voice.

Right. That.

Silla pursed her lips. "Perhaps you could provide some more details to work with. Jonas has told me Kraki has an ego. And you've told me he enjoys brennsa."

"And pretty girls."

Her brows furrowed. Was Axe Eyes calling her pretty? Silla opened her mouth, then closed it.

"I am using you as bait, in case that was not clear," said Rey.

"Bait?"

"To lure him into opening his doors to us."

"I can be of more use than bait, you know," she said, indignant.

"Right. The golden tongue. As far as I can tell, yours must be broken." She felt his cold gaze bore into the back of her head.

So Silla was stuck with no company save for Axe Eyes, in woods filled with carnivorous trees, *and* would be used as bait for a creepy old man. This task kept getting better and better.

"If you intend to use me as bait, you should at least tell me about this man, Kraki. I've learned he used to lead the Bloodaxe Crew. Is that true?"

"He was headman for many years until he was forced out." The words were pulled from him with as much enthusiasm as he might hold for the removal of an abscessed tooth.

"By you?"

"It was decided by the group."

"But *you* took over as the leader." She was starting to piece it all together. "Surely, you've made him quite angry, Rey. Perhaps you should have sent Hekla or Ilías."

Rey ignored her. "Kraki is old, quarrelsome, and knows how to hold a grudge. The Bloodaxe Crew put up with him because he was damned good at his job. But then he began to slip, putting the Crew in harm's way, and it was time for him to leave."

Silla was certain this was the most words in a row that Rey had ever spoken to her, and she felt as though she deserved a prize. She wanted to keep him talking. "Did someone get hurt? Was it Sigrún?"

"Sigrún? No." Rey paused. "Her burns...she has never explained them, and we do not press her. But yes, someone was hurt on Kraki's watch. There was more than one occurrence."

He was silent for a while, and Silla clutched the saddle, waiting for him to elaborate. "Who was hurt?" she asked softly. He did not answer. "We've got nothing but time, Rey. You can tell me, or I could tell you of the strange dream I had last night."

He made a noise that was part groan, part growl.

"Ilías nearly died. Kraki was confused about the timing of a guard shift change. Ilías took a stab wound." He paused. "Did not help that the bjáni charged without covering his flank." He muttered something under his breath which sounded an awful lot like *believes himself invincible.*

"And there was a time when he did not call for retreat in a situation where we were badly outnumbered. I can thank him for the arrow I took to my thigh." He swore under his breath. "If I had not been wearing lébrynja armor, I would not be here to tell the tale."

"So Kraki resents you for this." Silla paused in thought. "How shall I draw this information from him when I do not know what you need?"

"I shall push the conversation toward it. You can simply be...yourself." His voice was threaded with contempt. "If that does not work, keep him occupied for a few minutes while I search out his home."

She considered the plan for a moment, then smiled. "Very well."

"Very well, what?"

"Simply...very well. Perhaps this will be fun."

"Fun." The word came out as though it tasted bitter.

"More fun than sitting in a wagon with no one to talk to, nothing to read, nothing to do. And it will bring me a step closer to Kopa, so for that, I'm grateful."

Rey made a sound of disgust. It was a torch dropped on parched grass, the anger within her blazing to life and burning up her throat.

The words tumbled out before she could stop them. "Why are you so disagreeable?"

"This kingdom has made me so."

"It must be tiresome, though. Carrying such anger all the time." Picking a fight while trapped on a horse with this man for two days was not her brightest idea, but she could not stop.

"You seem to draw it from me. One of your many talents. Along with apologizing to rocks and creating new names for yourself." Though his voice was calm, his fists clenched the reins with unnecessary force.

Hearthfire thoughts, Silla, she told herself, closing her eyes.

"Wha—what did you say?"

She blinked. Wait. Had she said it aloud? "Shh. I'm thinking hearthfire thoughts. It is a trick my mother taught me to brighten my mood—"

"Gods above. Please do not tell me. I'm certain I do not want to know."

"Do you enjoy being an arse, or does it come naturally?"

He let out a ragged exhale, sending a shiver of unease down her spine. "A bit of each, really."

She huffed. "What do you have against me? You do not even know me." *Don't let it bother you,* she told herself. But it stung, same as it always had. Silla wanted to be liked, and this man was impossible to crack.

"I know enough."

Silla ground her teeth. "You want to judge without knowing? All right. Why don't I try it?"

"Very well."

She considered him for a moment. "Let me think. You are...a man of ambition, but you are quite controlling. It must be important in your line of work, as mistakes can mean life or death, but I think it is more than that. *You* try to create order around you because you've felt out of control in the past." She grew more confident with each word. "You are mean, as you do not wish anyone to grow close to you. You have built a fortress around yourself and do not let others in as you have something to hide. Or perhaps you fear something."

She thought for a moment. "You've been hurt."

"Sorry to disappoint, Sunshine, but you could not be more wrong."

"Mmm-hmm. I believe I am on to something. You look like the type of man who is haunted by his past. A tragedy. Someone close to you died. I am correct, am I not?"

Rey did not reply, but she felt him tense behind her, his wrath like cold fingers on her skin.

A sound of victory slipped through her lips. "Oh, I've read you right, haven't I, Rey? I assure you—each of us have suffered our own personal wounds. I lost my mother. I watched the life leave my father's eyes. I was nearly assaulted in the Twisted Pinewoods. But still, I manage to be polite and kind and find good things to be happy about in this world. You do not have to let the awful things define you."

Rey leaned forward, his chest pressing against her shoulders, reigniting the burn in her stomach. When he spoke, his voice was right next to her ear. "You think yourself better than me because you smile and pretend the world is filled with good men? Because you believe everything will work out for the best? Your optimism is shallow and false, and one day, *Sunshine*, it will get you killed."

Silla swallowed back her response. She'd heard all she needed to about this impossible, arrogant, rude man.

THIRTY-ONE

WEST OF SKALLA RIDGE

They rode all afternoon, stopping twice to water Horse. As they traveled away from the ocean climate and farther up the foothills of the Sleeping Dragons, the lush forest grew more sparse. They passed through fields of wildflowers and magical glades of woolen grass resembling hundreds of tiny sheep bending in the wind.

Despite their disagreement, Silla couldn't help but point things out along the way—the patch of arctic thyme, a rock formation that looked like a throne, and the snow-capped Sleeping Dragons, which loomed larger and more prominent the farther west they rode. She could not stop herself; it was simply lovely to have someone to speak to, even if he despised her. Even if his replies consisted of grunts and one-word answers. Even if he muttered to himself that he *should have thought this through for longer.*

Merciful gods, she must be desperately lonely if even Rey made a suitable companion.

They rode late into the evening, far longer than usual. By the time they stopped, the alpine forest surrounded them utterly—stunted pine trees covered with crusty alpine lichen, shrubby bushes of heather, exposed bedrock veined with dark streaks of blue. The wind was cool, with little to cut it.

Silla's body ached terribly from the saddle. As she climbed down from Horse, her legs tried to fold underneath her.

"Gods' ashes," she moaned. "How long does it take to grow used to that?"

"A few weeks."

She exhaled a frustrated breath, rubbing her thighs vigorously.

Leaves, her mind whispered, punctuated by a throb in her temples. But she pushed aside her need for them, wishing to wash the road from her skin before relaxing into skjöld's comforting embrace for the night.

"Is that a stream over there?" asked Silla, gesturing to the edge of the clearing near a copse of white-stemmed aspen. "I shall splash some water on my face."

Gingerly, she made her way to the edge of the woods, finding a small creek cutting through moss-covered ground. Silla dropped to her knees, the soft moss sinking like a pillow beneath her. It had been a long day for her, and she doubted sleep would have trouble finding her that night. Plunging her hands into the water, she cupped them together and splashed her face. She gasped with the shock of cold, her senses leaving her for a moment.

Something tugged in her stomach, familiar yet unplaceable. The stream grew jarringly loud, the air stirring around her face, and something about this rang bells in her mind. Warning bells.

Silla lifted her gaze from the stream and found two burning red eyes staring back at her.

They blinked.

Time slowed as she took in the creature before her. Six feet tall. White coat matted with blood, torn and hanging in places. Antlers, ghost-white and sharp as daggers.

Vampírudýr.

Vampire deer. Her mind told her this, though she'd never seen one before. She wasn't entirely sure how it was able to provide her with this information while simultaneously forgetting how to move.

Silla opened her mouth to scream but choked on the smell of rotten flesh.

The creature crouched, then sprang.

This was it. This was how she was going to die.

She braced herself for impact, and it came hard and heavy, the vampire deer flattening her against the moss. The breath squeezed from her lungs under the weight of the deer—the pressure intense, overwhelming. She was dying. These were her last moments; of this, she was certain. Silla squeezed her eyes shut, waiting for the fangs to sink into her, to tear her flesh and end her life.

Nothing happened.

Something warm and sticky dripped onto her face. Silla opened one eye and squinted up into a lifeless red orb. Her other eye opened, spotting the small axe buried in its skull. Blood, she realized. Blood dripped onto her face.

The deer was hauled from her, strong hands hooking under her armpits and yanking her to her feet.

"What in Hábrók's hairy arse was *that*?" demanded Rey.

She blinked at him. Her hands groped along her throat, face, and arms, searching for a puncture wound, for an injury. She was dead, she'd been certain of it.

"Wha-what?" she finally breathed.

"What happened to your dagger, Sunshine? You didn't even try to reach it." Arms crossed over his chest, a look of disappointment displaced his usual bored expression.

"What?"

"You fell apart. Did not even try to draw your dagger. All of that practice with Hekla, I thought you'd do better."

It took a moment for his words to sink in. "You *watched* it?" She stepped toward him, anger licking up her limbs, replacing the numbness with searing heat. "You watched it, and you did not kill that...that thing?"

"I had my handaxe trained on it the whole time."

She was seething. "I thought I was going to *die*! I believed myself dead!"

"The beast had followed us for three hours. I wanted to see what you could do on your own." He shook his head. "Disappointing."

"You *let* it attack me? *On purpose?*" Her eyelid pulsed.

"Oh, calm yourself. It did not truly attack you. I killed it first." The corner of his lip twitched as though he were amused with her. *Amused*. "Speaking of it, you're welcome."

The anger was back, as untamed and blistering hot as wildfire. Silla stepped toward Rey, planting her hands on his chest. "You *kunta*! Do not *ever* try anything like that with me again!"

The rage churned through her so fiercely, her vision darkened and the air seemed to crackle. Energy gathered with a strange, buzzing sensation in her hands. Silla pushed. And Rey *flew* through the air.

He landed with a dull thunk at least six paces away. Silla blinked, trying to understand what had happened. Her gaze fell to her hands, then back at Rey, sitting up in the moss and rubbing his head.

"Rey? Ashes, Rey, are you all right?" She bounded over to him, dropping to her knees beside him. All traces of amusement were gone from Rey's eyes as he blinked at her strangely.

He studied her with a dark, inscrutable look. "How did you do that?"

"I...pushed you," she replied, unsure of it herself. "Hard, I suppose. Are you injured? Did you hit your head? I did not mean to hurt you!"

He continued to stare at her, and Silla took a steadying breath. She readied herself for Rey to release his tightly leashed anger, for the inferno she'd seen burning behind his eyes to erupt.

But the taut lines dissolved from his face. Rey threw his head back and laughed.

Rey was *laughing.*

Eyes crinkled.

White teeth.

Dimples.

Dimples.

The combination was like a punch to her gut. Blood rushing around in her head, lips parted, she stared. Tried to comprehend what she was seeing. It made no sense. But when Rey was not scowling at her—when this man *smiled*—she could not look away.

As his laughter continued, she tried to pull rational thoughts back into her mind. What should she make of his laughter? How hard had he hit his head? Could he have knocked the wits from his skull?

She waved three fingers in the air. "Rey, how many fingers am I holding? What is the capital of Íseldur? What is Hekla's second name? Ashes, I do not know that..."

Finally, Rey's laughter halted, and he gripped her by the shoulders, drawing her gaze to his deep brown eyes. Her heart thudded. She forgot how to breathe.

"Next time, do that to the deer, you fool." He pulled himself up and walked back toward Horse.

Silla exhaled.

———

A FEW MINUTES LATER, Silla sat on Rey's bedroll, avoiding his gaze. He'd wordlessly handed it to her along with her sack after she'd washed the vampire deer's blood off her face and made her way back to Horse.

"Take it. I'll rest easily on the moss," he'd muttered.

Was it possible he felt guilty over what had just happened? *No*, thought Silla. That would imply he had a conscience. She'd considered objecting, wanting to owe no debt to this man. But she'd held her tongue, considering how badly she wanted to rest on something soft, even if for one night.

Next, Rey had handed her several strips of smoked elk before stretching his long limbs out on the mossy ground nearby. The last light of the day caught the tattooed tendrils coiling up his neck.

"No fire tonight, as it could draw uninvited attention," he said quietly. "Have you enough layers?"

As if you care, she thought but bit back on it. "I have this cloak. That should suffice."

His brows drew together as he took in the borrowed cloak. "Where is your red one?"

"I...forgot it in Svarti. Hekla said I could use this spare one."

He scoffed. "Forgot it? Gods above, woman."

Sitting in stilted silence, Silla looked anywhere but at Rey. But as she chewed the dried elk, she could feel him studying her as though he was trying to dismantle her bone by bone.

Well, this was just as awkward as she'd expected.

Leaves! The thought took hold of her mind, infecting her with need. The low, constant throb in her temples intensified to a vice-like grip across the top of her skull. Drawing the stopper from her vial, Silla tipped several leaves into her palm.

She picked one up, then hesitated.

Two to forget. Two to wipe the stain of that deer from your mind.

Silla pinched a second leaf between her fingers. Yes. She'd earned it tonight.

Rey's spine straightened. "Those leaves are poison. If you knew what was good for you, you'd stop taking them."

Her gaze flicked to his steely eyes, then quickly away. Silently, Silla tucked both leaves into her cheek, closing her eyes and waiting for the knots and tangles in her skull to unravel. This day had been too long, and she needed to feel like herself again.

But Rey did not relent. "They will ruin your life."

"Stop it," she murmured, her eyes held shut. "Stop pretending." The tension in her head was liquifying, dripping into a puddle of delicious warmth in her stomach. Silla reclined, hands clasped together.

"Pretending? I am not deceiving you. Those leaves are vile. They *destroy* people."

"Do not pretend you care." Her tongue felt sluggish, the words coming out slow and distended.

Rey's voice was harsh against the stillness of the night. "I will not pretend I care. You can keep traveling this treacherous road of yours. I simply thought you might want to know what lies at the end of it."

She opened her eyes and absorbed the first glimmer of stars in the sky. Was her father up there, settled amongst the ancestors with her mother? Were her birth parents there?

Silla's eyes brimmed with tears at the thought, and though she hadn't left an offering tonight, her lips moved in silent prayer anyway. *Sunnvald, protect my father. Malla, grant him courage. Stjarna, light his path.*

Thoughts floated by her like clouds in the sky. Silla did not care about Rey's words. She fixated on the warmth pulsating through her. It was her father's warm bear hug; the smell greeting her on the threshold of their hut; the crackle of fire while she warmed her feet. It was home...the thing she could always return to, no matter where her feet landed. No matter how bad things got.

It was the culmination of her day, the highest peak. And she would not let Rey ruin it for her.

Silla squinted upward and tried to spot the clusters of ancestors. She spotted Hábrók's hammer; Marra's winged horse; Myrkur's serpent army and the Mother Star. Time grew slippery; she was only aware of its passage by the darkening of the skies, the stars growing more vivid.

"Who tried to assault you?"

She blinked at the intrusion of Rey's deep voice. "What?"

"In the Twisted Pinewoods. Who tried to hurt you?" She was dimly aware of the strain in his voice—as if it pained him to ask her.

"Oh. One of the warbands. The Battle Thorns." She shivered. "Don't worry. They're all dead now."

His gaze burned into her skin, and she could feel the questions piling up. From the corner of her eye, she saw his mouth open, then close.

"It was not *me*, for the love of the stars. It was an enormous grimwolf. Perhaps it was sent by the forest spirits. Or perhaps it was part of their trickery and I escaped by sheer luck. It chased after the warriors, and then I ran too—so far, so quickly that I became lost, and the birds had to help me find my way."

Rey muttered something under his breath that sounded like *doesn't have all her horses in the stables*, but she ignored him. Instead, Silla stared at the stars, pondering how they could remain so constant while everything else had changed. A question of her own bobbed to the surface, and no matter what she did, she could not push it down.

"Rey. Who do you know?" she asked in a brittle voice.

"What?"

"Who do you know that takes the leaves?"

Rey was silent for so long that she thought perhaps she hadn't actually spoken the words aloud. But finally, he replied. "My brother took them."

And then he said the words which changed everything.

"He's dead now. They poisoned him."

Silla heard his words, heard the slight catch in his voice. She should say something, she knew she should, but she found herself too tired to speak. Tired of feeling the endless pull, of being caught in this cycle. Uncertainty sprouted in the corner of her mind, and she didn't quite know what to do with it. Silla rolled onto her side, turning her back to Rey.

She closed her eyes, breathing deeply through her nose, trying to drive away the fear growing inside her.

One. Two. Three. Four. Five.

"You can quit anytime you want," said the girl. She sat cross-legged in the grass in front of Silla, plucking white petals from a mountain aven. "You simply do not wish to."

"I know," whispered Silla, her eyes damp.

And then, she was asleep.

THIRTY-TWO

I f Silla had thought their first day of travel had been awkward, it was nothing compared to the morning after the vampire deer attacked her. Her mouth was so dry she could not seem to drink enough water...which in turn led to frequent breaks along the trail so she could run into the bushes to relieve herself, much to Rey's irritation. But beyond the breaks, Rey's displeasure about the leaves was palpable, gathering in the air like a storm of irritation. Silla would not speak of them with him, could not hear of Rey's brother. Her stomach knotted just thinking of it.

Why would he tell her such a thing? She'd pondered it all morning and had decided even Rey would not have made something like that up. But it made no sense—the leaves were a headache remedy; she'd taken them for ten turns of winter now. *Father would never have given you something so dangerous,* she thought. But each time she repeated this sentiment to herself, its effectiveness lessened a bit more. He'd withheld so many truths from her. What was one more?

The trail began to rise earlier in the day, the trees dwindling in size the higher they ascended before disappearing entirely. At last, they reached an endless, rolling field of fireweed, a snow-capped mountain climbing in the distance. It was so unexpectedly beautiful, Silla forgot her apprehension entirely.

"Is that one of the Sleeping Dragons?" she asked, nodding to the mountain when they stopped to allow Horse to graze. Silla ran her hands through the wildflowers, breathing in the bright, grassy smell.

"Fáfnir," replied Rey, cutting a swath of green through the pink flowers with a lazy arc of his sword.

"I did not know it would be so beautiful up here. And the air is so fresh."

Rey responded with another aggravated swipe of his blade.

Picking one of the flowers, Silla brought it to her nose. *Fireweed for fresh starts*, she heard in her mother's voice. "I can see why Kraki should want to live out here. It feels as though I'm in a skald's tale."

"Kraki lives in the arse end of the mountains because he does not wish to be disturbed," said Rey, in a clipped voice.

Silla hummed. "Unfortunately for Kraki, we are quite eager to see him."

Rey did not reply.

She shielded her eyes from the sun, looking toward Fáfnir. "Is that where we travel?"

"Another hour or so."

Silla's gaze fell upon Rey. His shoulders were high, his jaw held tense. "What worries you, Rey?"

Despite his scowl, the sun caught gold flecks in his eyes. "Nothing. I do not worry. I cannot change my fate, so why fret about it?"

Her brows knit together, and she opened her mouth to call him a liar, but Rey cut her off.

"Kraki has wandering hands." A muscle in his jaw flexed.

"I gathered that," said Silla, wondering why he suddenly cared.

Rey crossed his arms over his chest, drawing her eyes to the stretch of the leather scales across his biceps. "I won't let him do anything unseemly. Understand me?"

She fought the urge to roll her eyes—the man was domineering, even when trying to reassure her.

"Get us into his house. Perhaps you could pretend you do not despise me."

"I do not despise you— "

"You're a terrible liar, Sunshine," he said. "You'll have to do better than that to convince Kraki."

In actual fact, Axe Eyes, I am quite accomplished at lying, she wanted to spit back. Instead, Silla wisely snapped her mouth shut.

"And do not let his words unnerve you, all right?" Though Rey's deep voice held a cutting edge, she blinked at the unexpectedly soft meaning.

Silla smiled, recalling the look on his face when she'd returned to camp the night he'd killed Anders. "I think we both know I'm more resilient than I look, Rey."

He stared at her for a heartbeat too long, making her skin buzz and her stomach grow hot. But Silla forced herself to hold his gaze until it slid away. Only when Rey stalked off to retrieve Horse did she allow herself to release a shaky exhale.

———

HORSE PLODDED through the tiny alpine village of Kiv about an hour later, snaking up the foothills of Fáfnir, to where a lone house perched. With each passing step, Rey's stomach clenched tighter, his grip on the reins along with it.

He blamed it on her constant noise—humming alternating with mindless chatter. Her questions were asinine. Did she expect him to answer? And was there something wrong with silence? The woman seemed to feel the need to fill the quietude with unending noise.

And that was just the start of it. There was her hair, wild and unruly and always in his face, carrying wisps of her scent to him. And then there was the way she shifted in the saddle, her legs sliding against his. It was distracting, impossible to concentrate on the task which lay ahead. Sharing a horse had been a terrible idea—he must have had a moment of temporary madness when suggesting it.

They rounded a bend, and a fur-clad figure came into view, leaning on a stone fence. Kraki.

He looked the same as always—tall and broad, still with a warrior's build, though time had weathered his pale face and streaked his blond hair with silver. As they neared, Rey felt the man's bright blue eyes on him, hawkish and cunning as always.

"Never thought you'd have the bollocks to show your face here, Reynir," drawled Kraki.

Rey's former mentor had not unsheathed the sword at his hip, nor had he demanded they turn and ride back down the hill. A promising start.

With a deep breath, Rey dismounted, strolling toward the older man with one hand extended. Kraki's eyes slid to Rey's hand, but he did not take it—no surprise there. Instead, Kraki's gaze lifted to *her*, still seated atop Horse.

"And who have we here? Are you from the alleyhouse in Hver?"

Rey choked out a laugh as her mouth fell open. He could tell indignant words were gathering on her tongue, and he cut her off.

"Not a hóra, Kraki. This is—"

"Well met, Kraki. I am Silla, cook for the Bloodaxe Crew," she said brightly.

It took all of Rey's willpower not to groan in embarrassment.

"Cook?" asked Kraki, laughing so hard he needed to brace himself on his knees. When his breathing had calmed, his glacial gaze settled on Rey. "Have you fucked up the Bloodaxe Crew so soon, Reynir? Seems you've gone soft."

Kraki approached to help her off Horse, but she slid down from the saddle before he could reach her.

Good, thought Rey. He'd need to let Kraki get close but not too close.

"Oh! My apologies..." As her feet connected with the ground, her knees buckled, and she clutched Kraki's arm to steady herself.

"What's the matter, darling?" asked Kraki, his smile dagger-sharp. "Not used to so much time in the saddle? Should have broken her in a little better, Rey."

Silla's nostrils flared as her gaze slid to Rey.

Do not let him rile you, he thought, but his blood simmered hot.

Silla turned to Kraki, smiling sweetly. "My thanks, Kraki. I fear I'm still getting a feel for the saddle."

"Of course, darling." Kraki frowned, looking past her to Horse. "You ride that old horse still? Time to put her down, if you ask me. She's looking old and slow."

Horse snorted, her ears twisting back, while Rey's stomach clenched. Kraki was baiting him, he knew it, and he must resist, but...

"Old and slow," Rey found himself saying. "Sounds familiar." Internally, he chastised himself—he was giving Kraki exactly what he wanted.

"These are my lands, and you will treat me with the respect I am owed, Reynir," thundered Kraki, so loud the woman jumped.

Rey exhaled, then rifled through Horse's saddlesack for a moment before procuring a small cask. "My apologies, Kraki. Let me gift you this cask of Reykfjord's finest," said Rey, handing it over.

Kraki examined it. "I should prefer the gift of your staying the fuck away."

A low growl escaped the back of Rey's throat before he could stop it. After all these years, his former mentor was still able to get under his skin with a few choice words. Tonight would be the true test of Rey's patience.

"What a beautiful view you have up here, Kraki," she interjected in her brightest voice. "You can see all the way to the coast."

"My thanks, darling." He smiled at her, and there was something behind it which made Rey want to knock the teeth from Kraki's mouth. But then Kraki's gaze turned to Rey, and it hardened. "What do you want, Reynir?"

Rey opened his mouth to reply, but she beat him to it.

"It is my doing, I'm afraid," she said with a small smile. "I told Rey I was dying to get a closer view of the Sleeping Dragons, and he mentioned that his mentor lived up here, and...well...I can be quite convincing when there's something I want."

Rey's brow furrowed, but he forced it to smooth out as Kraki's gaze bounced between the two of them.

"Is that so, darling?" asked Kraki, his voice an octave lower. "And how, exactly, did you convince him?"

"Now where would be the fun in that?" she asked. "A girl cannot reveal *all* her secrets."

Her cheeks bloomed pink, her smile growing more coy. Rey blinked at her. Where was the bumbling fool he'd witnessed on so many occasions?

"On our ride up here, Rey told me what an honorable man you are, Kraki," she continued. "A warrior with much glory, with many great deeds done on the battlefield."

Kraki's gaze flitted to Rey for a brief moment before settling back on her. "He did, did he?"

"Oh yes. I've been quite eager to meet you, to hear the tales directly from the man himself."

Kraki's chest seemed to puff up, and Rey wondered...perhaps she had not lied about the golden tongue after all.

Laying a hand on Kraki's forearm, she continued, "And I should expect a man of such honor would also be a gracious host to a pair of weary travelers, would he not?"

"Of course, darling," murmured Kraki, offering his arm. "Would you like to see the home?"

The tightness in Rey's chest loosened. He'd steeled himself for the worst, but she had come through on her promises.

"That would be lovely." She hesitated a moment, then looped her hand through his arm, glaring at Rey.

Oh, it is only the start, Sunshine, Rey wanted to say. Instead, he ran his tongue along his teeth, then followed behind them.

Rey had not seen Kraki's home in many years, and it was apparent his former mentor had put considerable effort into it. Like most of the homes in Íseldur, it was timber-sided and turf-roofed, the front decorated with antlers and an impressive stack of firewood. He followed Kraki and Silla into the home, his eyes taking a moment to adjust to the darkened interior. It was brighter than most homes, a fire blazing from the rectangular hearth set in the middle of the room, and light filtering through a pair of large glass-paned windows at the rear.

"Glass windows?" she asked, rushing to the back.

"Yes, darling. Now, what do you think of *that* view?" Placing the cask down on the floor, Kraki's eyes were firmly planted on her backside, while she obliviously stared out the window.

"Beautiful," she exclaimed.

"Yes," murmured Kraki.

Rey's chest tightened, his hands curling yet again into fists. *This is precisely why you brought her,* he reminded himself.

With a shake of his head, Rey examined the rest of the home. A table surrounded by wooden benches sat against one wall, low-burnt candles clustered upon it. On the opposite side of the room were cabinets and shelves, and stairs leading to a loft upstairs where, Rey presumed, Kraki's bed would be located.

The book, he reminded himself. *Where would Kraki keep it?*

Near the cabinets and shelves were haphazardly stacked crates and provisions. Rey eyed a corner of the room cluttered with items—a decrepit shield tossed carelessly onto a pile of furs, what appeared to be a pair of skis peeking from beneath. Kraki did not have the same need for organization as Rey, and the state of the room made his eye twitch.

Rey's gaze fell upon a floorboard near the edge of the skis—it sat half an inch above the others. *There,* he thought with satisfaction, *the perfect location to stash the book.* But if Rey was to search the place, Kraki would need to be outdoors or incapacitated. His eyes settled on the cask.

"Cup of brennsa, Kraki?" he asked.

His former mentor turned to him, his blue eyes assessing as always.

Let her do the speaking, Rey thought, cursing himself for not trusting her with the information. She was far better than he'd thought, and the old man was clearly not eager to speak to him. Kraki reached into one of the wall-mounted cabinets, drawing out three clay cups and setting them on the table. Uncasking the whiskey, he poured it into each cup, taking one in each hand.

As Kraki pressed the cup into her hand, Rey watched her frown.

"Oh, no," she said. "I thank you, but I do not much like the taste of brennsa."

"Now, now girl," crooned Kraki. "If I am to be a well-mannered host, then you must too be a gracious guest and accept an offered drink." He pushed the cup back toward her.

Rey's teeth clenched as Kraki's fingers encircled her arm and he drew her to a bench before the hearthfire. As expected, Kraki sat too near to her. She shifted a few inches away from him, drawing the cup to her lips with a smile, followed quickly by a wince as she sipped the fiery liquid.

Rey snatched the remaining cup on the table and took a deep drink. Liquid courage would be necessary to get through this night.

"Gunnar still winning everyone's sólas?" Kraki asked with a casual smirk as Rey settled onto a chair across from them.

"Yes," replied Rey, taking a sip.

"You do know he cheats." Kraki chuckled, shaking his head. "And Hekla's mouth is still yapping?"

Rey pressed his tongue into his cheek for a moment but managed a crisp, "Yes."

"I do not miss her constant noise," muttered Kraki. "Always nagging me. At least I can hear my thoughts up here. Plenty of silence."

Rey watched the girl's hand tighten around her cup and found himself in agreement with her for possibly the first time ever.

"So the Bloodaxe Crew has not changed," said Kraki. "Except for this delightful addition." He turned to her, sliding an arm along the back of the bench.

She tensed as Kraki pulled a coil of her hair, wrapping it around his finger. Rey forced down a large gulp of brennsa.

"She is *not* a member of the Bloodaxe Crew," said Rey, trying not to sound too defensive. "She is simply a travel companion for a short time."

"A travel companion?" scoffed Kraki, turning to her. "You should choose your *companions* more wisely, girl. This man has nothing but enemies."

"Kraki," growled Rey.

Kraki turned to Rey. "And you, Reynir. This sounds quite like charity. Did I not teach you better? When you get soft, people get killed."

"You taught me well," Rey asserted. "She is with us for a short time only."

Kraki turned back to her, his eyes sliding to her lips. "How did you convince him, girl?"

"Not in the way you're thinking, you old lech," muttered Rey.

Kraki raised a brow at her. "Truly? How *did* you persuade them, my dear? I'm dying to hear it."

She swallowed, and Rey could see her scramble for an answer. "I...cooked for them?"

"You cooked for them," Kraki repeated slowly, turning to Rey.

"She is a...talented...cook," said Rey with a scowl.

"All right, Reynir," sighed Kraki. "I am no fool. We both know that you would not drag yourself out to these parts without reason. You were wise to bring this delightful girl along with you—she's the only reason you've not been kicked out on your arse. But I tire of these games. What is it that you want?"

Rey regarded his cup for a moment, twisting it back and forth. He'd feared it would come to this, and knew he must choose his words carefully.

"We have a job up north," Rey said quietly. "A complicated problem in Istré to take care of. I do not wish to go in unprepared. We need the book—you know the one. *Creatures of Íseldur,* by Frans Gilmar."

"So you do not know everything after all," said Kraki. "A shame, Reynir. That book has been destroyed—it is a death sentence to own books with any mention of galdur, after all. But fear not. I've memorized each word in the book. If the right person were to ask, I might freely share the information."

Rey held his gaze. "Surely you do not begrudge your former Crew seeking information. People are dying, and we wish only to stop the bloodshed."

"You think highly of yourself, Reynir, to believe I can simply forgive you. It is the same flaw you've always held."

A heavy silence hung in the air, and Rey knew it would take a miracle to convince Kraki to willingly share information with them at this point. He did not care that people were dying. Kraki cared only for his wounded pride, for this grudge he held so tightly.

"I can cook the evening meal," she interjected, leaping to her feet.

Gratitude swelled in Rey's chest. Thank the merciful gods he had not tried this alone. All was not lost. She could still help with this impossible task.

"Allow me to cook the evening meal," she continued. "Everyone will feel better with food in their bellies. I can prepare a stew with whatever provisions you have. Would that please you, Kraki?"

Kraki's icy eyes found hers. "I'd love to taste your stew, darling."

The innuendo was so blatant Rey itched to wrap his hands around Kraki's neck and squeeze until his eyes popped.

Instead, he took a steadying breath. *Get through this evening,* he told himself. *And then you can be rid of him. Of both of them. And all will be set back to rights.*

THIRTY-THREE

KIV

S illa's leg bounced under the table as Kraki's spoon scraped against his wooden bowl. Firelight danced along the walls, the scent of cooking filling the air. Kraki had built up the fire, and it crackled gently in the middle of the room, giving the home a warm and pleasant feel at odds with the tension squeezing her insides.

Leaning back on the bench, Kraki's hands clasped over his stomach, and he examined Silla in a way that made her skin crawl. "Hmm," he said at last. "Your methods of persuasion are different, yet effective."

As she'd cooked, Silla had pondered how she could get Kraki to share the information with them. She'd considered asking him for a tour of his property but shuddered at the thought of being alone with him. She'd considered crushing up some of her skjöld leaves into his stew to make him dazed and easier to distract, but she could not part with a single one.

A third plan had emerged, and, while it would not be as easy, it was all she had.

Silla cleared the dishes from the table, then returned with the cask of whiskey. She poured another cup for Kraki, herself, and, begrudgingly, Rey. They each raised their cups.

"Skál," she said, her eyes locked on Kraki as she lifted the cup to her lips. Silla rested her chin in her palm, tilting her head. "I should like to hear some of your tales, Kraki. What was Reynir like when he first joined the Bloodaxe Crew?"

She refused to acknowledge Rey's murderous glare but felt it on her skin.

Kraki let out a dark chuckle. "Oh...I have tales. I taught this man everything he knows. When he first joined us, he was weak as a little girl. Could not even lift a longsword. Had to start him on a shortsword." Kraki's empty cup hit the table with a resonant *thump*, and Silla replenished it quickly.

She smiled conspiratorially. "I imagine he made *many* mistakes."

Kraki smirked at Rey. "Mmm. Had to save his neck more times than I can count. Always left his guard open. Was like caring for a small child."

Silla snorted, turning to Rey with a cocked brow. He stared back at her with the look which had earned him his nickname. She saw blood and death, a dozen ways he could dismember her body. That look had once struck fear in her, but now, it only deepened her smile.

"Oh, quit it with the *axe eyes*, Reynir," she said, looking away.

A bark of laughter burst from Kraki. "Oh, you're a handful, darling, aren't you?"

"A pain in my arse is what she is," Rey muttered, then gulped back his whiskey.

Now surely, Rey realized—she would do what it took to get his precious information, even if it meant throwing him to the wolves.

Her gaze landed on Kraki. "He tells me nothing. It would please me to hear more."

"I imagine he did not tell you this," said Kraki, leaning toward her. "When he was eighteen, Axe Eyes here was so hungover that he saddled, mounted, and rode off on the wrong horse."

Silla gaped at Rey. "You did *not!*"

He twisted his drink back and forth. "And that is how I got Horse."

Silla snorted, sipping her whiskey. Kraki's cup was empty again, so she quickly refilled it. "And what of her true owner? What had he to say of it?"

"I do not know. I'm certain Horse prefers me anyway," said Rey.

"You're a bandit," teased Silla. "Nothing more than a common outlaw, Axe Eyes." This fact amused her greatly. A chink in the armor of this great and perfect warrior.

Silla propped her chin on her fist once more. Unlike the rest of the Bloodaxe Crew, Rey was so guarded...so secretive. This was her chance to learn more, and she found herself curious. The whiskey warmed her veins and sharpened her tongue. "And what of his lovers?" Her cheeks flamed, but her mouth kept moving. "Women? Men? I suppose *someone* must have a taste for rude men who love sharpening blades."

A tingle climbed up her spine and settled in the back of her neck. She knew Rey watched her but refused to look his way.

Kraki chuckled, then cast a brief look to the roof. "Mm, none that were all that memorable. Oh. But there was that one...Kaera...no. *Kaeja.*"

Silla's lips curved. "Rey...who is Kaeja?" Topping up Kraki's cup, she added a splash to her own, a half-hearted attempt to make her ploy less obvious.

"The spawn of Myrkur," muttered Rey.

A thousand questions sprouted in Silla's mind, but Kraki started up again.

"Rey always kept them around for a while. Never *too* long, though. He always managed to chase them off sooner or later."

Probably when they discovered his affection for murder, Silla thought to herself.

This is what you get for using me as bait, she told Rey with her eyes.

He was not amused in the slightest.

Kraki leaned back, studying Silla. "I know what you are doing, darling, and as I am a man of honor, I feel as though I should put an end to these games."

Silla's cheeks warmed.

"You cannot get me drunk. I have decades of drinking on you." Kraki brought his cup to his lips, tossing the whole thing back. "In fact, my ability to hold liquor is famed in the mead halls. Even better than this arse." He gestured at Rey.

"I'm not...that is not..." Silla spluttered, feeling foolish. How could she have believed this ploy could work? Already, her head swam, yet Kraki looked as sturdy as a mountain.

"You seek information, and I am not unreasonable." He topped up Silla's cup, then slid it toward her. "Let us play a game. For old time's sake, Rey?"

Silla hazarded a glance at Rey and found his *axe eyes* directed at Kraki.

Kraki smiled a lazy, wolfish grin. "Truth or drink. You ask me a question, and I shall choose—answer truthfully or take a drink." His eyes did a lap around Silla's face. "And we shall take turns, Silla. No repeat questions."

Silla swallowed.

Rey slammed his empty cup on the table so loudly she flinched. "She does not drink, Kraki. I will do it."

"No," said Kraki, his voice sharp and cold. "I have heard your truths, Reynir *Galtung*." Kraki spat the name as though it were poison.

Rey's entire body tensed, his hand curling around his cup so tightly Silla feared it might shatter.

"I wish to learn more of this creature here. I will play with Silla or not at all."

Silla ran her palms together, her gaze bouncing from Rey to Kraki. Her insides were warm and fluffy, like freshly baked bread. Happiness and daring bubbled through her. She could do this. She could get Rey his information.

And then the thought floated through her mind. If she retrieved this information, perhaps Rey would be so grateful, he'd take her to Kopa. After all, this was not nearly so easy as he'd led her to believe.

"I will do it," Silla said. "But Rey must ask the questions."

Rey grabbed her arm, his breath tickling her ear as he whispered, "You needn't do this."

She shivered, then shook him off. "I gave you my word that I would get this information, Axe Eyes, and I mean to see it through."

A smile spread wide across Kraki's face, revealing perfect white teeth. "Since I am a gracious host, I shall allow you the first question." He leaned back on the bench and put an ankle over his knee.

Rey rubbed the back of his neck as he took his seat.

"Thick mist...or fog with the sound of a beating heart. Would a creature be behind such a thing?" asked Rey in a brisk, no-nonsense voice. Silla's eyes slid to him, trying to keep her face neutral. Certain details had been muffled beneath the wagon's covering, and this was new information.

Kraki's brows furrowed as he ran a finger around the rim of his cup. "It could be." He did not elaborate.

Silla glared at Rey. *More specific*, she mouthed. He blinked harder and slower than she'd ever seen.

Kraki smirked. His question came without hesitation. "How is it that you came to travel with the Bloodaxe Crew, Silla?"

A small breath puffed from her. This was easy enough. "I hid in their wagon in Reykfjord and convinced them to take me north."

Kraki regarded her with a cocked brow, and something in his eyes told her that her answer had spawned a thousand new questions. Apprehension tightened her chest.

Rey's gruff voice shouldered through her thoughts. "Which creature might cloak itself in pulsing mist?"

Kraki rotated his drink for a minute before answering. "I have not heard of this...pulsing mist. But draugr are known to pull mist from the ground. Though...not enough to cloak them."

Rey ran a hand over his curls. "Draugr," he repeated, as if it meant something. Silla had never heard of the creatures and decided she'd live a happy life if she never did again.

Kraki pressed his lips together, his fingers tracing the rim of his cup. "Why do you travel north all alone, Silla?"

The tightness in her chest spread to her shoulders. *Keep it brief*, she told herself. "It was my father's wish."

Kraki hummed, studying her face. It felt like he could see through her words to what was left unsaid.

"Would draugr enter a home and kill?" Rey asked quickly, and Silla's stomach twisted. What in the eternal fires was the Bloodaxe Crew getting themselves into?

Something flickered behind Kraki's eyes. "I've never heard of them doing such a thing."

Rey cursed quietly, tipping his head to the roof. Silla felt a wave of concern for the Crew, but—no. This was not her problem.

Silla felt faint as she met Kraki's gaze. Why did he answer his questions so quickly, yet time slowed when it was her turn?

"Why is your father not traveling with you, Silla?"

She closed her eyes as pain squeezed her chest. Why had she not anticipated the game would head in this direction? Her eyes flicked to Rey, then back to Kraki. "He died," she replied with cutting calm.

Rey was already armed with his next question. "Do you know of a creature that *would* enter a home? Kill in a way that produces significant blood loss, then take the body?"

This verbal volley was becoming challenging for Silla to keep up with.

Kraki smirked at Rey. "Tut tut. One question at a time." He tossed his drink back, his empty cup thudding against the table.

Silla glared at Rey. *Smarter questions*, she mouthed to him. The corners of his lips twitched, but she didn't have time to consider it because Kraki had already turned to her.

"How was your father killed?"

The blood drained from her face, memories of that day forcing their way to the front of mind. She battered them back, answering in a remote voice she barely recognized. "He was stabbed."

As Rey asked his question, her gaze fell to her drink, the sounds around her dropping away. This was a mistake. She should never have agreed to this. She knew what Kraki's next question would be, knew that Axe Eyes would be watching her every response.

Kraki's question cut through her thoughts and obliterated her chances of avoidance. "Why was your father killed, Silla?"

Stick to your story, Silla, she thought. *Lie like you have a hundred times before.* But they watched her like hawks, she'd had too much brennsa, and that warrior's words echoed in her skull, delaying her reply.

The queen will not kill you. Not right away, that is.

Silla looked straight at Kraki, trying to project confidence. "A land dispute."

Kraki's eyes narrowed. "You're lying."

"I am not."

"I'm no fool, girl. I can tell when I'm being lied to."

It was a foolish, split-second decision, fueled by the brennsa she'd previously ingested. Silla picked up her drink and tipped it back. The liquid blazed across her tongue and down her throat, and she knew she'd made a grave error. She'd as good as admitted to lying. *Again.*

"All of it, Silla." Kraki motioned upward with two fingers. She glared at him before finishing the last of the whiskey. A moment later, her cup was refilled.

Silla's gaze flitted to Rey, their eyes locking. His eyes burned with such intensity that her skin began to singe. Without a doubt, there would be repercussions from this. And yet, with spirals of pleasant, tingling warmth spreading through her, it was difficult to care too much about that right now. Those were problems for future Silla. She forced herself to look away, gazing into her cup of swirling amber liquid.

Silla was so wrapped up in her thoughts that she nearly missed Rey's words. "Klaernar hung with vines and stabbed through. Sun Cross scrawled nearby. Who do you think would do this?"

Kraki leaned back in quiet thought. "Uppreisna?" he murmured, his eyes bouncing to Silla, then settling back on Rey.

"No," said Rey. "The rebels are not responsible this time." Silla's gaze flitted from one to the other. "And the...vines do not fit."

Their eyes were back on her.

"What?"

A crooked smile spread across Kraki's face. "I am considering which question to ask you."

"How is it my turn already?" whined Silla, pressing her hands to her hot cheeks. "I think you should drink, Kraki. To catch up with me."

The older man threw his head back and laughed. "All right, darling. I will humor you." He tipped his cup back, draining it in moments. The man didn't even flinch.

Silla's gaze got snagged on a whorl in the grain of the table. It swayed slightly, and she gripped the edge, trying to hold on. A snort from beside her diverted her attention to Rey. He blinked at her. She blinked back. His expression was softer, as it had been when he'd laughed at her back in that field, his smooth skin marred by a single, black eyelash sitting on his cheekbone.

She reached to brush it from his cheek, but his hand struck out with serpent-quick speed and snatched her wrist. Silla's breath hitched.

"Eyelash," she whispered, meeting his eyes. Her heart thudded in her chest.

"You're drunk, Sunshine," Rey muttered, slowly releasing her hand.

"Nah-uh." Silla's finger skimmed along his cheek, picking up the eyelash. She held it in front of her lips. "I shall make a wish." *I wish to make it to Kopa,* she thought, then blew the eyelash from the tip of her finger.

When she looked up, she found Rey's eyes on hers. "Wishes are for fools," he muttered, with a soft shake of his head.

"Or perhaps for the hopeful," she found herself saying.

"Your optimism is misplaced." He looked away, drinking deeply. Silla supposed she should be irritated, but she only felt curious. What had happened to make him so cold and hard?

Dazed, Silla focused back on Kraki. The older man looked between them, a smile spreading across his face. He looked like a toad, she decided. An evil toad. "What is your honest opinion of Reynir, Silla?"

Her mouth started moving of its own free will. "Most of the time, he's controlling, with the temperament of a troll. Come to think of it, he has the manners of one too." Her voice lowered to a whisper. "And I do not like that he tried to kill me. Twice."

Kraki roared with laughter, and Silla waited for the noise to subside. "But beyond all that, I believe he is secretly soft. He is kind and loyal to his Crew." She pushed the hair back from her face. "I do not understand him. Perhaps he does not wish for anyone to notice his kindness and mistake it for weakness."

Kraki clapped his hands, the sound echoing off the walls. "Oh, this is too good. Best diversion I've had in months."

The bravery provided by the fire whiskey was not enough for her to look at Rey, but from the corner of her eye, she watched his hands clench, then unclench.

He's trying not to attempt murder for the third time, she thought to herself.

The endless silence was eventually disrupted by the rumble of Rey's voice asking something about claw marks... Silla's mind had wandered yet again. She looked between Rey and Kraki, sensing the buried camaraderie, an echo of what had once been. Student and mentor, minds collaborating.

It only lasted a moment though, as Kraki's gaze moved from his drink to Silla's face. He grinned again, and she shivered with the premonition of something nasty.

"Silla, darling. Have you ever been with a man?"

"Kraki," growled Rey.

She stared at her whiskey, wondering if this was the last cup she could tolerate. With a sharp exhale, she lifted it to her lips and tossed it back. The burn was numbed by previous cups, but she hissed all the same as she brought it back down to the table.

Kraki cocked an eyebrow at her. "Impressive, darling." Her face was warm, whether from the brennsa or the question, she was unsure.

Rey's large hand wrapped around her shoulder, squeezing gently. "No more. This game is over."

"I can do it, Reyneeer," she said. Her tongue was not keeping time with her mind. "You think me useless, but I can do things."

Kraki chuckled from across the table.

Rey pinched the bridge of his nose and muttered something under his breath. "It's abundantly clear that you can do things, Sunshine. You need not do *this*, though."

His face swayed, and Silla grabbed the table once more.

Kraki was talking. Was he talking to *her*? "Who do you fantasize about, Silla?"

"Kraki," growled Rey. He seemed distant, like he was standing in another room. "You do not owe him an answer. This game is over." He drew her from the chair and toward the door. The walls of Kraki's home churned and swirled.

Silla looked down at the hand wrapped around her arm. "Your hands are *enormous!*" she blurted.

Soon they were outside, the stars twisting back and forth above her. The frosty alpine wind bit into her skin, but the brennsa in her veins provided an extra layer of protection.

Her stomach turned over. "I don't feel good, Rey," she said, her voice brittle as fresh ice. Her stomach roiled, and she braced her hands against her thighs. Her hair was gathered from around her face, and then she was vomiting, the brennsa burning just as harshly on the way back up.

She retched over and over, her stomach twisting and emptying itself of any and all contents. Something moved against her back in a gentle, soothing motion. At last, when there was nothing left to expel, she stood back up, turning to look at Rey.

It was a dark, clear night, and the sister moons cast light upon his face. His eyes were softer than she'd ever seen, his brows drawn together. If she weren't so tremendously drunk, she'd think he looked concerned.

"Did I do good, Rey?" She swayed. "Did you get the answers you needed? D'you need more information?"

"Yes, Sunshine. You did well."

It was the last thing she remembered.

·THIRTY-FOUR

HVER

J onas sat in a darkened corner of the mead hall, surrounded by unending noise and the scent of old ale. A rowdy group just down the long table from him spoke with the kind of enthusiasm which lodged slivers of jealousy beneath his skin, and he clutched his cup of ale tighter.

It was the eve of Longest Day, and the air pulsed with anticipation. Tomorrow, the tables would be moved outdoors, laid with moss and garlands of trailing leaves and bouquets of wildflowers. The town would go wild, celebrating the longest day of the year with food, games, dancing, and bonfires. It was one of his favorite holidays, and with the food, drinks, and women, Jonas knew he should be excited.

But gloom clung to him like cobwebs, as it had since Rey and Silla had headed westward. His blood felt heavy, oozing through his veins and fouling his moods.

A raven-haired woman approached, a coy smile curving her full lips. Their eyes met for the briefest of seconds, but Jonas looked down at his ale. He hoped she'd take the hint and leave him alone; speech felt too ambitious at the moment. He blew out a long breath. What was the matter with him? He could have any woman in the room. All it would require was a smile and a crook of his finger, and he'd have a soft body in his lap.

But it did not appeal to him.

He could only think of her. *Her.* He screwed his eyes shut and rubbed his palms against his eyelids. What in the eternal fucking fires was the matter with him? She was parting ways with the Bloodaxe Crew, and there was nothing he could do about it.

But each time Jonas closed his eyes, he saw her brown gaze looking back at him. Not just looking but *seeing.* Seeing through all his carefully erected barriers, straight to his true self. And instead of turning away, she looked at him with optimism, with belief.

And when he'd laid on his bedroll last night, he'd felt the ghost of her touch scraping along his scalp, skimming along his shoulders and down his chest. He remembered how she'd moved at first with caution, then with abandon. Her enthusiasm was catching, and it hadn't taken long for Jonas to be consumed by her touch, by her sound, by her smell. The very memory filled him with reckless thoughts—drawing her into his furs and discovering all the ways he could drive her mad; convincing Axe Eyes to deliver her safely to Kopa; bringing her to his farmstead so she could see it with her own eyes.

That last thought shook him from his stupor. It was utter madness...the woman had infected his mind, there was no other explanation.

Focus, he urged himself. *She leaves the Crew, and you must focus on the task at hand so that you can take back what you are owed. A hearth of your own. Land for you and for Ilías.*

Family. Respect. Duty. Jonas closed his eyes, forcing the image into his mind —the longhouse. Ilías. A wife for his brother. Children's laughter filling the home...a home he and his brother had never had. Free from violence. Free from fear. A chance to reshape the future of their bloodline.

"Whoa!" came a man's voice from behind him.

His shoulder jostled, cold liquid splashed across his neck, each drip down his spine a taunt.

Disrespect.

Disrespect.

Disrespect.

Never again, thought Jonas. Extracting himself from the bench, he turned to the source, ale sloshing from the man's cup with each swerving step he took down the mead hall. Jonas's blood crackled and sparked, the corners of his vision charring with darkness until he was engulfed with the need for vengeance.

Never again.

He charged after the man, hand wrapping around his black braid and yanking him backward. Whirling, the man's eyes flared—surprise, then anger. *Good*, thought Jonas, pulling the cup from the man's hand and pouring it slowly over his head.

The mead hall had stilled, all eyes on the two of them. He waited for the blow, anticipating pain's consuming kiss, needing the vigor it brought to his blood. Already he felt more alive, but his mind craved more, hungered for it.

The man's fist drew back, then smashed into Jonas's jaw, snapping it to the side. His vision bloomed red, and the iron taste of blood trickled into his mouth. Jonas turned to the warrior.

Smiled.

Crashed his knuckles into the man's teeth.

Felt them shatter.

He drew his fist back again. Again. Again. Time grew slippery. The mead hall faded away, as the man fell to the floor and Jonas climbed on top of him. As Jonas taught the warrior what it meant to disrespect the Wolf. *Never again,* he thought to himself. They'd taken his home. His property. His respect. *Never again will you tolerate disrespect. Never again will you allow others to make a fool of you.*

Hands wrapped under his armpits, hauling him off the bloodied warrior, and Jonas fought against them. He was not done. Not yet.

"Stop, Jonas," rasped Ilías in his ear, pushing him toward the bench. "Any more and you'll kill him."

Jonas blinked, looking down at the warrior's face—reddened and already beginning to swell. The man groaned, as his friends surrounded him, dangerous looks cast Jonas's way.

"Sit, Wolf," muttered Gunnar, placing a cup of ale into his hand. "Drink."

Jonas tossed the ale back, drinking it down in several long gulps. He did not wish to sit. Battle lust surged through his veins. He needed a woman.

The thought crystallized in his mind, and the world suddenly made sense to him. Silla had broken something within him, and he needed to set it right. Jonas needed to bed a woman, and then he'd be fine. It had been almost a week since Red.

His eyes wandered the mead hall, falling upon the black-haired woman who'd approached earlier. She leaned on the long table, speaking to someone he could not see. The woman glanced over her shoulder, sending him another flirtatious smile.

Jonas smiled back, holding her gaze this time.

And then, he crooked his finger.

THIRTY-FIVE
WEST OF SKALLA RIDGE

I t was another gray day, the alpine air crisp enough Rey had raised the hood of his cloak. As the trail wound through scraggly pine and wild grasses, he found his gaze snagging on the patches of exposed bedrock, streaked with telltale blue veins of halda mineral deposits.

In front of him, she clutched her stomach with a low moan. Having experienced the unpleasant combination of a hangover with the motion of a horse many times himself, Rey would admit to feeling a slight pang of empathy for her. The sway of Horse's back was wreaking such havoc on her stomach, they'd already had to stop several times for her to hurl into the bushes.

She hardly drank any brennsa at all, he thought with a huff. How could she have gotten so drunk off of three cups of brennsa? It was amusing to him.

But Rey's smile fell as he recalled the slide of her finger along his cheek. Not to mention, her expression—those eyes, large and dark, framed with long lashes. Those lips, curved up in the corners, the shadow of a dimple in her right cheek. She'd looked at him as though she liked what she saw.

She was drunk, he told himself.

But drunk or not, the girl had come through on her promises. Without her, he'd not have gained entry into Kraki's home, nor would he have coaxed answers from the man.

Though she'd irritated Rey in the process, he'd admit it had been amusing to watch her try to get Kraki drunk. Digging into Rey's past, trying to play her dislike for him in a game to win Kraki's favor...she was cunning; he'd give her that much. And it hadn't been long after Silla had passed out on the bench that Kraki had dozed off with his head on the table. "Hold your drink better than me," Rey had scoffed as he'd pried up the floorboards.

This morning, the girl had clambered onto Horse without complaint. Her spirit was admirable to be sure.

But Rey frowned. She *hid* something. She had not only drawn answers from Kraki but had revealed something troubling of herself as well.

Why was your father killed, Silla?

A land dispute.

You're lying.

But then she had drunk the brennsa. Which meant she'd been lying to him all this time.

Rey did not tolerate lies in the Bloodaxe Crew. Trust was imperative when you fought shoulder-to-shoulder with one another. But it went beyond the battlefield. For his own safety, Rey needed to know everything about the men and women who traveled alongside him.

And she'd been lying to him all this time.

You'll be rid of her by the end of the day, he reminded himself. But if she had not been honest with him thus far, how could he trust her with the details of the Istré job once they parted? What would keep her from sharing it with others?

It was a problem that had his stomach burning.

They were nearly back at Skalla Ridge. Once they reached it, it should be no more than a few hours to reach Hver. And then he'd be rid of her. Could shake the distracting sounds of her humming while in the wagon—would no longer find himself watching her pitiful attempts to learn knife-craft from Hekla. All would be set to rights.

No more distractions.

They rode in silence for several more hours, the trees growing taller, the forest more lush as they approached the coast.

"I want to talk, Axe Eyes," she said.

For the past hour, she'd been sipping from her waterskin, nibbling on bread, and, apparently, she'd grown to feel more like herself. Rey nearly groaned. Her silence had been too good to last.

They neared the junction to the Road of Bones, prickles spreading along the back of his neck—the birds had stopped chattering, the air unnaturally still. Glancing over his shoulder, Rey's hand went to his dagger.

"You needed me more than you let on," she said, diverting his attention back to her. "Kraki did not have the book, and I got you the information all the same. I've shown you can trust me."

Rey choked. "Trust you?"

"I made good on my word. I've shown you can trust me, Axe Eyes. And I ask that you take me to Kopa."

His stomach churned. "No."

"But—"

"You did make good on your word, and I thank you for that. But there is no place for you with the Bloodaxe Crew."

"How would you have retrieved the information without me?" she demanded, her voice rising.

"I would have managed, one way or another," Rey gritted out.

"How?" she pushed.

"Kraki lied. He had the book. I knew he would never destroy it. And when he passed out from the drink you fed him, I stole it from beneath his floorboards." Rey reached back into the saddlesack, retrieving the book and waving it in front of her.

"I like to be prepared," he continued. He was feeling talkative. Perhaps he liked flaunting his victory in her face. "And you have made good on your word, but that does not make you an honest woman."

"Honest woman, what do you—"

"You *drank*, Sunshine. You've been lying to me about Skarstad. Was there even a land dispute?"

She huffed and crossed her arms over her chest.

Rey couldn't help himself. "What happened?" he demanded. "Tell me."

Her body grew tense, but she remained silent. As Skalla Ridge stretched out before them, Rey steered Horse onto the Road of Bones. To the left of the road, the pinewoods stretched toward the gloomy sky. To their right, the fjords plunged jaggedly down. Gulls cried overhead, the waves crashing into the base of the inlet well below. That strange, prickling sensation had not relented—he had the strangest feeling he was being watched. But when he cast a look around, there was no one to be seen.

Rey's teeth clenched together at her continued silence. "I told you before— I do not allow liars to ride with the Bloodaxe Cr—"

The dagger came from nowhere with motion so fast Rey scarcely had time to throw himself and the girl from the saddle. They landed on the ground so hard his teeth clacked together.

But his warrior's instincts had Rey up on one knee before he'd drawn breath. He slid his shield from the saddle hook, unsheathing his longsword.

"What—" started the girl, but she thankfully came to her senses, drawing her dagger.

"Take my handaxe," muttered Rey, eyes scanning the road from beneath Horse. "Go to the woods and hide." He felt the girl draw it from the loop on his battle belt and heard her scampering into the pinewoods behind him.

Thank the fucking gods, he thought. *She does know how to listen.*

"What do you want?" he yelled, hefting his shield and smacking Horse on the rump so she'd trot away from danger. "Show some honor and reveal yourself."

The only reply was a blur of red hair and brown furs, the glint of steel as a figure flew through the air and shoved into his shield. With a grunt, Rey pushed back, lifting his sword and jabbing it beneath the shield. But the mysterious warrior danced away from his thrust as though it had been anticipated.

It was a woman, he realized, not overly large but not small either. Her flame-red hair was braided along the sides of her scalp, and she was clad in a shirt of gleaming silver mail which looked to cost a small fortune, a fine wolfskin pelt wrapped around her shoulders. As he took in the blue eyes, fierce with murderous rage, Rey scrambled to place her.

"Who are you?" he demanded.

"I have come to feed the ravens," she replied haughtily, then hacked into his shield with a greataxe, splitting it down the center.

With a curse, Rey slammed the rim of the shield toward her, but the woman rolled on the ground with sinuous movement.

"I will feed them your blood, warrior," she spat, back on her feet.

The shield felt cumbersome against such a lithe opponent, and Rey made the split-second decision to throw it aside and draw his hevrít.

"They will feast on your entrails. They will drink from your skull."

He drove forward with a frenzy of alternating slashes with his sword and hevrít, smiling as his blade met flesh, and she cried out in pain. Blood oozed from a gash in her upper arm just below the cut of her mail shirt, but it seemed to have done little harm to the warrior. The woman dabbed her hand on the wound, smearing the blood across her face.

"You do not know who you face, woman," he growled at her.

"No," she snarled, ducking the arc of his longsword. "You do not know who *you* face, warrior."

As though a mist engulfed him, the woods and jagged fjords of Skalla Ridge faded from view, a familiar sight swarming into vision. His little brother, only eighteen, lying upon a soiled pile of furs. Beads of sweat dotted Kristjan's brow, his dark eyes glazed and staring at nothing. Rey's stomach twisted in agony as this invisible wound was torn open anew.

Kristjan, Rey heard himself say. *You waste away. I cannot lose you too.*

Pain blazed through his leg, and Rey blinked until the woman's blood-smeared face swam back into view. He swung his sword with wild fury, but she feinted back with sure-footed movement. Glancing down at his thigh, Rey realized his breeches had torn, blood gushing from a shallow wound.

"You have so much pain, warrior," said the woman, a cruel smile upon her lips. "So much anger for me to feast upon."

With a cry of rage, Rey lashed out with his sword, the woman easily ducking. He was vaguely aware she retreated toward the edge of the ridge but could think no more of it as another memory coalesced into view.

A burial mound, two piles of rocks before it, the snow-dusted mountains of Nordur climbing impossibly high all around them.

I do not remember them, Rey, said a young Kristjan, squeezing his hand. *But I miss them all the same.*

Rey's chest filled with such torment at the memory he could scarcely breathe.

Another lash of pain—from his other leg—followed by a kick, and Rey was distantly aware of his knees buckling, his body crashing to the ground. He sucked in a harsh breath, the gray skies swirling back into view. Gulls circled above, calling shrilly. His head had fallen back too far, and Rey realized—he lay on the very edge of Skalla Ridge, the red-haired warrior looming over him.

"You make it too easy, warrior," said the woman, approaching with a greataxe held in two hands.

"You are—" rasped Rey, realization crashing over him. "Coward! Dishonorable!"

"What does honor bring?" she asked, stepping on the wrist of his sword hand.

Someone was yelling—*he* was yelling. Pain screamed up his arm, and his hand opened of its own volition.

"A swifter death?" The warrior laughed, kicking his sword away. "No. That is not for me. I will take power. And you, warrior, will die with great honor. Though it is a pity to end you so quickly. You have so much pain for me to play with."

Rey's vision flooded once more—scenes shifting rapidly before his eyes. Kristjan, speaking to the timbered walls of their home. *They are here, Rey! Mother and Father!* Rey, watching Harpa weave at her loom, an icy, hollow feeling spreading in his chest. Kaeja, a blanket wrapped around her naked body, excuses spilling from her lips. He could not draw breath, could not move, could do nothing but bathe in the haze of his worst memories.

He was vaguely aware of the red-haired woman hefting her greataxe over-head. Calm acceptance filled him, and Rey waited—to meet his brother, his parents, to walk amongst the stars.

The woman cried out, and the visions abruptly stopped.

Gasping for breath, Rey clutched his chest. His heart beat as though it tried to break free from his ribs. Torment clung to him like a shadow. As his sight gradually returned, a tangle of dark curls became visible. She clutched the handaxe, axe butt facing out, then gasped and dropped the weapon as though it had burned her.

Sitting, Rey rubbed his head. Death had seemed certain, and now...he stared at the curly-haired woman. She had saved his life. This woman, who thought *hearthfire thoughts* and apologized to rocks and got drunk off three cups of brennsa, had saved his life.

"Is she..." started the woman.

Rey's gaze fell upon the red-haired warrior. He truly did not know her. In the absence of any blood, his gaze shot up.

"You're meant to use the sharp part of the axe, Sunshine," grumbled Rey, staring at her in distaste.

"I could not kill her," she whispered, hugging herself.

Rey stood with a glare. "You must learn to react swiftly and without mercy, or it will be your downfall." He did not know why he bothered—it was clear she was a lost cause.

The warrior's chest rose and fell. There was nothing to be done but to finish her off. With a quick heave, he rolled the woman's body to the edge of Skalla Ridge.

"Wait," said the curly-haired woman. "Must you..."

With one last nudge of his boot, the warrior's body toppled over the ridge. Turning back, he scowled.

She wrinkled her nose. "That was..."

He rolled his eyes. "Easy."

"Cold," she said, watching him. "There is something cold about you."

"Why did that assassin attack you?" Rey demanded. "Has this something to do with what happened at Skarstad? Does someone wish you dead?"

Her mouth dropped open, eyes widening. "Me?" she asked in a high voice. "I thought it quite clear it was you she attacked, Axe Eyes."

"She tried to rid herself of me so she could kill you."

But there was a seed of doubt in the corner of his mind. He had many enemies, and it would not be the first time an assassin had tried to end him. The woman pushed her curls out of her face, glancing at the ridge. Her gaze had hardened when she looked back at Rey, and he knew she schemed at something.

"Why would an assassin attack me, *Reynir Galtung*, when it is you who has so many enemies?"

Reynir Galtung.

The name sliced through the air like a warrior's blade, leaving blood and wreckage behind.

Rey's skull squeezed in on him, his knees threatening to buckle once more. He had convinced himself she did not hear Kraki's slip up. But the sound of his true name on her lips had startled him, and Rey cursed himself—he was better than this.

Crossing her arms over her chest, she watched him carefully. "Is this name a secret, Axe Eyes? Something you've kept guarded?"

He tried to smooth the emotions from his face but felt himself failing. Rey had survived this long by keeping these parts of himself hidden, and right now, he felt cracked open and exposed.

"A powerful thing, a name can be," she murmured. Her voice was soft, unthreatening, but in that moment, Rey saw a serpent, poised and ready to strike.

Silence stretched between them as she wrestled with something, but he knew what she'd say before she spoke the words aloud.

"Take me to Kopa, and I will not tell a soul."

Rey closed his eyes, his teeth grinding together. He cursed himself for not killing this wretched woman when she was discovered. For taking her to Kraki.

For having to trust a bitter man like Kraki to hold his secrets. He would not be surprised if the old man hadn't slipped at all; if it had been on purpose.

Frustration festered in his veins. When he opened his eyes, he sent her his most withering glare. "What if I just kill you instead?"

Fear flickered through her eyes, but she quickly mastered it, confidence settling back in place. "You are more honorable than that," she said. "I saved your life. I know you would not repay such a favor with death."

Jaw clenched hard, Rey cast a look to the skies. She had him. Killing her now would not sit well with him. But keeping her alive meant another person—one he could not trust—knew his true name.

Bringing the woman brought risk to the Bloodaxe Crew as well. Magnus would be out for their blood if he knew she traveled with them—if he knew she had knowledge of the job in Istré. And the assassin—had she indeed been after Rey, or had this woman been her true target? Rey cursed himself. He should have bound the warrior and questioned her as he had Anders.

With a heavy breath, his gaze slid back to the woman, studying her for a moment. Bouncing on the tips of her toes, she seemed to be holding her breath. She was small. Weak. She could not even kill a warrior when she needed to do so. This woman had no business riding with the Bloodaxe Crew. And yet, he was stuck with no other choice.

"Fine," he ground out. "Kopa."

A smile spread across her lips, her face melting into relief. Rey forced his gaze away. No good would come of this. He knew it in his gut.

"How do I know you won't break your word, Sunshine?" he asked.

"How do I know you won't break yours?" she asked.

They stared at one another in distaste for several long moments.

"I won't tell anyone, Rey," she said, her voice soft. "You can trust me."

He scoffed. "Right. Trust the woman who's told more lies than truths."

But she held his gaze in that unnerving way of hers. It was now Rey who struggled to hold hers.

"We both know there is safety in secrets, Rey," she said quietly. "I'm good at keeping the ones that matter."

They stared at one another, a silent understanding passing between them. Perhaps they were more alike than he'd thought. That did not mean he trusted her. "Swear it to me," he growled. "Swear me an oath."

"I swear it, Rey. I swear I will not tell anyone your name. And now you," she said. "You swear it to me, that you will get me safely to Kopa."

He glared at her. This was the last thing he needed, not with this job, not with... "I swear it," he grunted. "I swear I will get you safely to Kopa."

She clapped her hands together, that gods-forsaken smile spreading across her face once more. Rey couldn't stand it—her happiness only heightened his misery.

He whistled sharply and waited for Horse to trot back to him.

"You're bleeding," she said, stepping forward. "I can clean it for you if you'd like."

"Don't bother yourself," he grumbled, turning away.

After pouring water over the wounds, Rey wrapped them in strips of linen from his medical pouch. He made to retrieve his shield but frowned at the crack down the center. They had spare shields in the wagon, so he made the decision to cast it aside.

Rey mounted Horse, settling behind the girl. And then, they rode down the Road of Bones.

THIRTY-SIX

THE ROAD OF BONES

Silla tried not to let her excitement show, but it was nearly impossible as she and Rey rode toward Hver. Though the skies were gray, it felt as though sunshine shone within her, and she was powerless but to let it shine. Axe Eyes was taking her to Kopa. Not only that—he'd *sworn an oath* that he'd deliver her safely. And if she knew one thing about this man, it was that he took oaths and honor very seriously.

At the memory of the warrior's attack, her light dimmed slightly. The red-haired woman—Silla had known her immediately. It was the woman from the bridge in Reykfjord, and the realization chilled her blood. Had the woman simply found them by chance? Or had she hunted her down?

No matter, she tried to reassure herself. *She's dead now.*

The attack at Skalla Ridge had been unexpected and frightening, yet it had played out in Silla's favor.

She'd saved Rey's life, and that thought alone made her squeamish with delight.

Oh, how you must despise that, Axe Eyes, she thought, though the entire scene had been puzzling.

Rey had the upper hand on the woman, and then suddenly...he did not. He seemed in agony, and yet the woman did nothing but stand over him. And Silla had not dared voice her questions to Rey, had not wanted to rub her victory in his face too forcefully. She did have weeks of travel with this man ahead of her, after all.

They reached Hver in the early afternoon. As the houses grew more frequent, Silla had pulled on her borrowed cloak, drawing the hood around her face, despite the warmth of the day. *Stay vigilant,* she reminded herself. The assassin might be dead, but that did not mean she could let her guard down. There could be others searching for her along this road—barricades to the town searching travelers.

Bracing herself for the worst, Silla let out a long breath as they passed through the stockade walls of Hver without trouble. A surprisingly sprawling town, Hver bustled with excitement and preparations for the Longest Day. After days of nothing but the wind and the occasional snuffle from Horse, the sounds of rickety carts and calls of merchants were a welcome relief, perking Silla up.

Horse stopped in front of an aging timber building.

"Get off," said Rey in that sharp tone of his. "I'll take Horse around to the stables."

Wordlessly, Silla slid down and grabbed her things from the saddlesack. "What do I tell them?" she asked, peering up at Rey. "The Bloodaxe Crew."

He rubbed the back of his neck with a deep sigh. "Tell them I was pleased with your efforts and agreed to take you to Kopa."

She felt a twinge of guilt as she stared up at him, knowing how he valued honesty above all else, that he likely hated lying to his Crew. But this secret of his she'd stumbled upon was apparently worth lying for.

The wind blew a tendril of hair into Silla's face, and she pushed it back. "I must thank you, Rey, for as I saved your life today, you also saved mine. I imagine that warrior would not have stopped with your blood. I will not speak a word of it past this, but I...owe you my thanks."

His gaze lingered on her for a moment, then he wordlessly directed Horse around the building.

With a soft shake of her head, she made her way beneath an archway hung with a sign which said *The Wolf's Den.* Silla wondered how she'd find Hekla. She could not wait to tell her friend she'd be traveling all the way to Kopa with the Bloodaxe Crew...and soon after Hekla, perhaps Silla would tell Jonas.

This will never happen again, she'd told him, but now...she was in a celebratory mood. Perhaps she'd changed her mind. The idea filled her with heated thoughts.

After a quick investigation in the mead hall proved fruitless, she wandered into a courtyard at the rear of the building. Tables were aligned end to end, a woman arranging curved branches of greenery and clusters of candles along the length of it. Workers hauled casks of ale and mead and pounded crude iron braziers into the ground. The air carried the scent of roasted boar and freshly baked bread, making Silla's stomach growl.

"Silla?"

Her entire body exhaled, the tension of the past several days melting from her like wax from a candle. The words burst free from Silla's lips as she turned to her friend. "I'm coming with you! Rey has permitted it. I'll ride with you to Kopa."

Hekla's brows rose, a smile spreading wide across her face. "Truly?"

"Truly."

Hekla pulled her into a side hug. "Then tonight we shall celebrate! Come, you can wash up before the festivities."

Silla followed Hekla through a darkened corridor and up a flight of stairs to her room. Similar to the lodgings in Svarti, the room held wood-framed beds topped with blankets and soft furs, a simple hearth with a small table and two chairs set before it, and a private section of the room obscured by a woven partition.

Silla washed herself using a bucket of water she discovered behind the partition, her humanity restored as the grime was wiped away. As she peeked her head around the divider, she found Hekla holding up a garment of soft purple.

"I took your clothing to the washerwoman—shush, I do not wish to hear it, and I pulled your purse from the pocket, it's just there on the table."

Silla exhaled as her eyes fell upon the roughspun bag.

"The laundress had a dress left by another guest," continued Hekla, "and you shall need to wear *something* to the festivities tonight unless you plan to walk around naked."

Silla chewed on her cheek. "How much was—"

"A few sólas, but I do not want to hear it."

Silla's eyes stung with tears. "You needn't have—"

Hekla smiled. "You know that I only do as I wish. And I've been where you are. In time, you will pick yourself up, but right now, you still deserve happiness."

Silla's heart squeezed. "I shall repay you, Hekla. One day I will pay you back for everything and more."

Silla stepped into the lavender dress, tying the lacings down the front. It was a simple design made of fine wool in a herringbone weave; long-sleeved and cinched in at the waist, it fell to her feet, the skirts full but not voluminous. The details were what drew her attention; beautiful off-white embroidery around the cuffs and along the neckline, which plunged well below her collarbones.

Once she'd tied the lacings in place, Silla swallowed. The dress was beautiful...and was sure to draw attention. Precisely what she should *not* be doing right now. "Perhaps I should stay in tonight. It was a long journey, and I'm quite tired."

"No!" exclaimed Hekla with startling fervor, the apples of her cheeks growing red. Was Hekla...embarrassed? She blew out a breath. "Look. Perhaps I was selfishly motivated in getting you this dress." Her amber eyes looked to the roof then back to Silla. "Do not laugh."

Silla stared, curiosity nipping at her. "I swear I will not."

Hekla pressed her lips together. "Sometimes I tire of being surrounded by men all the time. They will sit and drink and throw some axes and tell exaggerated tales of battle and bedding women. It's all the same, each time. I wish to have flowers braided into my hair and release flíta and dance around bonfires, and I finally have someone to do that with." Hekla looked at Silla, her eyes twinkling. "Will you join me?"

A smile played on Silla's lips. "Well, I suppose staying in would be improper when there's a celebration in honor of our lustrous kingdom. Sacrifices must be made in the duty of being a good citizen."

Hekla bumped a shoulder against Silla's. "Exactly. Would be improper to stay in."

Silla chewed her lip. "What about Sigrún? Will she join us?"

Hekla shook her head. "She despises the crowds. She might drink a few cups of ale but will soon disappear into the night." She paused. "Now tell me of the trip. Did Rey continue your training?"

Working a comb through her hair, Silla told Hekla the details of their excursion, starting with Rey's so-called training and moving on to everything that had happened at Kraki's home. She avoided mention of the assassin, of Rey's revelation, of her own slip-up at Kraki's. Twisting the sides of her hair back into neat braids, Silla left the rest in a tangle of curls which fell midway down her spine.

Hekla shook her head. "You've got bollocks, girl. I cannot believe you tried to outdrink Kraki. The man's liver is forged of steel." Hekla disappeared behind the partition for several minutes, emerging in a beautiful blue tunic layered with a shining leather vest, the braided details catching the faint light in the room. Hekla's hair was left unbound, shining and hanging pin-straight down her back.

"You look beautiful, Hekla!" Silla exclaimed.

"As do you, dúlla." Hekla smiled, but laughter from the corridor diverted their attention. "Seems the crowds begin to gather," she said. "Shall we head down?"

By the time the two women arrived, the courtyard was teeming with people garbed in their finest dresses and tunics. Without the shadow of her hood, Silla felt exposed, and her eyes darted around the square to ease her ragged nerves.

Folk sat on benches lining the trestle tables; horns of ale and mead were passed around; braziers held crackling flames warming the space. In one corner of the square, an old shield had been mounted on the wall, and a group of long-bearded warriors took turns throwing handaxes at the wooden boss; in another, younger children played a tugging game with a long rope, others chasing one another in a ball game.

No one paid heed to Silla; no dark-clad warriors surged toward her, and the tension in her chest eased slightly. *The assassin is dead,* she reassured herself. *They did not search you out at the town gate. Let yourself enjoy this night. You have much to celebrate.*

"Gunnar is just there." Hekla pulled Silla toward the end of the long table.

Gunnar, Ilías, Jonas, and Rey hunched over the table in the midst of a game of dice, dressed in fine-looking tunics, their hair and beards combed through. Sigrún had joined them, garbed in a plum-colored top. She'd braided back a section along the shaved edge of her hair, and her exposed ear was adorned with shining silver hoops from top to bottom.

Silla's gaze slid to Jonas, her pulse accelerating at the sight of him after so many long days. The glow of the lanterns caught golden strands in his hair—pulled back in a neat braid tonight—and highlighted his full beard. Her eyes settled on the bruise blooming on his left cheek, and curiosity prickled through her.

"Why look, it is our spirited little friend with the knife-craft skills," drawled Ilías, taking a deep sip from his cup of brennsa.

"Well met, Ilías," beamed Silla.

"I was speaking of Hekla."

"*Spirited little friend?*" replied Hekla. "Seems you ask for another rib smashing."

Silla's lips spread in a conniving smile. "I am pleased to see you do own a comb, after all, Ilías."

"In case it is not clear, I spend hours perfecting my look on the road. Expertly Crafted Mess, I call it."

Silla snorted. "Perhaps you should rename it, *freshly awoken cave bear*."

Her eyes darted back to Jonas. Though he faced her, his gaze was fixed on something across the square, his jaw flexed with such rigidity it was clear he was purposefully avoiding her. Something heavy settled in her stomach.

Sigrún's hands moved in rapid gestures.

"Sigrún is glad to see you, Hammer Hand," interpreted Ilías. "We are all surprised that Axe Eyes did not kill you and leave you on the side of the road."

Her mouth twisted up. "It was quite uncertain for a moment there. Has Rey told you the news?"

Silla's eyes darted to Rey, his hands clenched so tightly around his horn of ale it looked like it might smash. She tried not to get too much satisfaction from his situation, but it proved difficult.

"He was so achingly grateful for my help with Kraki, that I shall be riding with the Bloodaxe Crew all the way to Kopa. What did you say, Axe Eyes? That I was *singularly responsible* for retrieving that information?" She couldn't help herself.

Rey growled, sending her his best *axe eyes*. Thankfully she was now completely unbothered by those.

Gunnar and Ilías made room between them, and Silla climbed onto the bench, Hekla climbing in between Jonas and Rey across from her.

"You look ready to shatter hearts tonight, Hammer," Gunnar said with a wink.

Silla groaned, pinching the bridge of her nose.

"He's been thinking of hammer puns for days now," Hekla said with a roll of her eyes.

"Tell us how you cracked Kraki," Gunnar continued, unperturbed.

Rey drank deeply from his horn of ale.

"Why, my wit and charm, of course," she said, raising her brows with her best mysterious look, which shot down again at a huff from Rey. The Bloodaxe Crew's leader leaned his head back and glared up at the skies, the vein in his temple pulsing.

"We played truth or drink," Silla admitted.

Gunnar choked. "*You* played truth or drink?" He looked toward his head-man, then back at Silla. "How many rounds did you make it through?"

"Three," muttered Rey. "She managed *three cups* before vomiting in the bushes."

Jonas shifted beside Rey, his gaze flitting to his Crew leader.

Gunnar's booming laugh filled the courtyard. "Aye, but from the sounds of it, Hammer Hand pounded the brennsa with vigor!"

Ilías threw his head back and howled with laughter. "Three? Aww Hammer, that's entirely unacceptable. We shall have to remedy this while we travel north."

A laugh fell from her lips. "Ashes, no, Ilías. I am done with brennsa until the end of eternity."

Ilías chuckled. "Sure. We've all said that at one point or another." He raised his cup of brennsa in cheerful salute.

"Tell them of the vampire deer," Hekla cut in with a smile.

Silla leveled a hard look at Rey. "He let a vampire deer attack me."

The Bloodaxe Crew burst into laughter, causing Silla's brows to snap together.

"You tried that with *her*, Axe Eyes?" asked Ilías, wiping tears from his eyes.

Silla noted Jonas's dagger-sharp gaze was still held upon Rey.

"Couldn't even draw her blade," Rey said in a monotone voice. He studied her face, his gaze dropping to her dress. Rey's nostrils flared, as though he was disgusted by what he saw. Silla scowled.

"Perhaps I should not have stepped in," said Rey, his eyes meeting hers in challenge.

"Ah," said Silla, holding his gaze. She pressed a steadying hand to her stomach. "But then you'd have broken your word. And we know you would never do such a dishonorable thing as that."

Rey stood, and Silla felt a pang of regret. Though it was tempting, though it livened her, she should not tease him. But it seemed too late. Without a word, Rey climbed off the bench and stalked away.

"What was that about?" asked Hekla, tapping her metal fingers on the table.

"Perhaps his boots are too small," said Silla. She blinked after his towering form, the crowd scattering before him as he pushed through the courtyard. Was he truly that upset about her teasing words? The man had the emotional range of a thunderstorm. "That would explain *so much* about Axe Eyes."

Hekla chuckled, accepting ale from a passing woman. "Gods, if only it were that simple. I've known him through several pairs of boots, dúlla. It's simply his temperament."

Silla frowned. "Why is it amusing that he let me be attacked?"

A small smile played on Hekla's full lips. "Because he has done it to all of us. Had his hevrít on it the whole time, did he not?"

"Yes, but I believed I would *die*, Hekla. I swear to the gods, I saw every bad decision I've ever made flash before my eyes." Silla's eyes flitted to Jonas as she said it. When she saw that his gaze was still fixed, unwavering, on something across the square, her stomach twisted.

She'd thought she looked nice, that perhaps they'd laugh about how she finally wore an attractive dress after she pulled him into a shadowy corner and whispered dark promises into his ear. But no. Something had shifted in the days they'd been apart. Perhaps Jonas was upset she was not leaving the Bloodaxe Crew after all. Perhaps he'd simply had his fun and was done with her.

Hekla warned you, she chided herself. *She told you he was like this.* Fine. He truly was an arse. And she would not let this arse ruin her fun tonight.

Kitchen workers arrived and laid food upon the table—trenchers of spit-roasted boar, grilled trout, butter-roasted turnips and carrots, whole roasted chickens stuffed with wild herbs, sliced bread served with butter, soft cheeses, skyr and honey, and, to Silla's absolute delight, freshly baked sweet rolls.

As the food was spread out along the table, Silla wandered the length of it to inspect the offerings. Following the crowd, she plucked a wooden plate from a stack at the end and began loading it with a bit of everything. She skipped the chicken in favor of an extra sweet roll.

As she sat back down at the end of the long table, the Crew got up to fill their own plates. Silla welcomed the solitude, her focus honed in on her food. She closed her eyes and tasted each bite, savoring the efforts of the talented cooks and relishing the fact that she would not be doing the washing.

"I see you enjoy a sweet roll or two," came a voice from beside her, startling her from her thoughts. Silla's eyes flew open and took in a tall, broad-shouldered man. He flashed her a bright smile, and Silla took in his tanned skin, warm brown eyes, dark hair and beard. Quite pleasing to look at, really.

Silla smiled mischievously. "You cannot live your best life without sweet rolls, now can you?"

The man's smile deepened. "And why does a beautiful girl like you sit all alone?"

Her cheeks flushed. "My friends are just there, filling their plates."

"Then I shall have a few moments alone with you," his mouth twisted as he extended a hand. "I am Asger."

"Silla." She slid her hand into his large, warm palm and shook it. But as she made to pull her hand back, Asger surprised her by turning it over, his lips brushing the tender skin of her inner wrist. Her cheeks heated even hotter.

"And what matters bring you to Hver, Silla?" asked Asger, settling onto the bench beside her and stretching out his long legs. "If you were local, I am certain I would remember you."

"I am just passing through on my way to Kopa," she replied under the heat of his gaze. She gave herself a mental shake. *Guard your tongue, you fool,* she thought, studying the man. He seemed friendly, but that did not mean he could not have other motives. Could he work for the queen?

"A shame, though fortunate for me that you find yourself here tonight." She noted how Asger's dark eyes held her own, how they did not stray to the courtyard. She did not detect anything malicious, any deeper meaning to his words. He seemed simply *interested* in her. And she'd be a fool not to admit that it felt quite nice. A man whose intentions were clear. Who did not seem to play games. It was quite refreshing.

Silla pushed her plate away, turning her body toward her new companion. She brought her horn of ale to her lips and took another sip. "Do you live in Hver, Asger?"

"Yes. I was born here and have not strayed far. Though my work takes me away, I find myself drawn back."

"And what is it you do for a living?" asked Silla, cradling her chin in her hand as she gazed at him.

"Tribute collection for Jarl Hakon," he replied.

"Jarl Hakon?" she repeated. The name sounded oddly familiar, though she could not place it.

"Yes. He has the broadest reaching lands in the north of Eystri territory, though I collect tribute payments only from lands surrounding Hver."

Gunnar and Jonas approached. Several female heads turned in Jonas's wake, and Silla had to dampen the flare of jealousy. *Troll's arse. He's a troll's arse.*

Asger noted her approaching companions and rose to his feet, a look of surprise flashing across his face. "Is that the Bloodaxe Crew?" he muttered, shaking his head. Taking Silla's wrist in hand, Asger brushed his lips against it once more. His touch was featherlight, and her skin warmed beneath it. "Well met, Silla. I hope to see you again tonight."

She smiled as he sauntered off.

Gunnar wagged his eyebrows at her. "Who was that, Hammer?"

Silla snorted. "Asger." Her eyes flicked to Jonas, then away.

"Is that so?" asked Gunnar. "You looked in the midst of an interesting conversation."

"Yes," she said absently. Irritation smoldered in her stomach, and perhaps that is why she added, "He asked me to find him later."

Gunnar chuckled. "Well, you know what they say...what happens on Longest Day stays there."

A small laugh burst from Silla. "Is that so, Gunnar?"

Gunnar's lips quirked a smile. "Aye."

Hekla arrived with her evening meal, and the Bloodaxe Crew regaled Silla with their own tales of Rey's unusual testing methods. Silla finished off her sweet rolls, her eyes scanning the courtyard, still vigilant for any threat. There seemed only jovial revelers, drunken warriors—and the older child or two—enjoying their meal. She forced herself to relax.

At last, Hekla stood. "We're off to diversions that don't concern you lot. Enjoy your ale and games." She winked at Gunnar.

And then, Silla and Hekla sauntered off arm in arm.

THIRTY-SEVEN
HVER

Hekla began their fun by dragging her to a table of older women and young girls busy threading flowers into one another's hair. Silla set to braiding Hekla's hair back, then worked the stems of wildflowers into the cross-sections.

"So, dúlla, you looking for a distraction tonight?" asked Hekla.

Silla mangled the bloom held in her hand, thinking of Jonas. "Yes. I believe I am."

"So what do you like? Tell me. I can help. I already know of your penchant for blue-eyed, axe-swinging men."

Silla jabbed Hekla's ribs with her finger. "Quiet, you. I told you I've recovered from such irrational thoughts." She paused. "I like...kind. A kind man who says what they mean. One who is not a...what did you say? Man-boy?"

Hekla snorted. "Best of luck with that. As far as I know, they're all man-boys."

"I simply want someone warm and sturdy—a distraction. I've dealt with too many troublesome things lately...I want to have *fun* tonight. I want to feel alive."

Perhaps it was the ale, or being here with Hekla, but the more she spoke it, the more Silla felt it.

"We will find you a strong warrior...not too old, not too drunk." A mischievous smile crossed Hekla's face as Silla threaded the last flower into her braids. "Tell me if you see someone pleasing."

Silla opened her mouth to tell Hekla about Asger, but at that moment, a woman appeared with horns in hand. "Ale?"

Hekla grabbed a horn and passed it to Silla, then took one for herself with a murmur of thanks.

"Skál," she said, and they clinked their horns together.

Hekla took Silla's hand and drew her toward the arched gateway leading to the streets of Hver. Apprehension tightened Silla's stomach—it felt safe in this square, but out on the street, with the unknowns...

"Come, Silla," said Hekla, tugging her hand. "There's a bonfire and music in the square, and I've heard they'll release flíta when darkness falls." Reluctantly, she followed Hekla as they made their way toward the musical notes, into the Hver streets, and toward the town square.

A bonfire had indeed been lit, a lively crowd surrounding it. Silla watched as residents kissed their knuckles and cautiously threw offerings into the fire— bundles of herbs, cups of mead, carved swords and axe heads, shanks of beef and mutton. The sight of it filled her with kinship and a fierce pang of nostalgia.

When making an offering to Sunnvald and his mighty steed of fire, her father had told her, *we give only the finest quality of mead, meat, or weapons, and do so with an open heart.* She and her father had made fires of their own, always in secret. Always in solitude.

Hekla pulled a sóla from her pocket and tossed it into the flames. "It cannot hurt," she said with a shrug.

"What of the Klaernar?" asked Silla, glancing around. "Do they not frown upon such public displays?"

"They do not condemn a bonfire," murmured Hekla. "It's not as though the people prance around with a Sun Cross on their breast, chanting to the old gods. Besides...most of the Klaernar are probably drunk with the rest of them."

"You should have reserved some of your evening meal for an offering," said the little blonde girl, suddenly beside her. Silla ignored her, chewing her cheek in quiet contemplation. "Perhaps some of the flowers," nudged the girl.

With a sigh, Silla pulled some petals from the blooms she'd tucked into her braids and approached the fire. As the heat licked her face, Silla opened her palm and blew the petals with a strong breath. They fluttered toward the flames, then were consumed by the inferno.

She kissed her knuckles and bowed her head.

I thank you for your protection, she thought. *I thank you for your shelter. Please, Sunnvald, I beg of you to get me to Kopa. It is all that I ask.*

"We've made it farther than I imagined we would," said the little blonde girl.

A cry rose up from the crowd, diverting Silla's attention. Horns and cups were raised in unison, then quickly drained. The drums began a rapid beat, the little blonde girl swirling the skirts of her nightdress to the rhythm. Soon the crowd began to dance, and after drinking their ale, Silla and Hekla joined in. For the next hour, Silla forgot where she was, forgot who she was, forgot what had happened near Skarstad, about the assassin earlier that day. She simply lived in the moment, completely free.

It was late when the sun neared the horizon and the sky began to darken. Hekla dragged Silla back down the main road of Hver, the girl trailing after them. A crowd had gathered on a street corner near the inn, and as they edged around it, light flickered from the midst of the group.

"Flíta!" exclaimed the little girl in delight. "Ohh they're beautiful!"

Hekla gripped Silla's arm, pulling her into the crowd. "I've always wanted to do this."

An old woman passed out lidded baskets, Silla and Hekla each accepting one. Making their way to the crowd's edge, Silla peered through the wicker. Though she hadn't seen flíta since her childhood, she recognized them at once. Similar to butterflies, their membranous wings were transparent and thin as silk. And with each flap, orange light flared from the wispy veins.

"Ashes, but this is far more fun than your usual solstice, Silla," said the blonde girl, sticking a finger into the basket.

The girl was right—her past solstice rituals had been limited to backyard offerings to Sunnvald on His day. The feast, the bonfire, the music, and now this practice—she'd never seen anything like it. Was this how everyone else celebrated Longest Day?

Silla frowned. "What is this about?" she asked Hekla.

"Just wait." Hekla gestured to the setting sun, bright orange light spilling across the sky.

The longest day of the year was quickly coming to a close. A hush fell along the street, the flíta flickering serenely as indigo chased the last of the light from the sky. At last, the old woman who'd passed out the baskets gave the signal.

The crowd opened their baskets, and Silla rushed to do the same. The flíta flashed into the night, their transparent wings sparking orange light with each flap upward. She gazed up in raptured silence as thousands of flíta flew into the night, illuminating the sky like living stars. Lips parted in wonder, Silla decided it was the most beautiful sight she'd ever laid eyes upon.

Her eyes stung, and she suddenly felt so small, so sheltered. Anger simmered to life in her veins. Her father had shielded her from so much. What had she been doing all these years? It wasn't living. It had been surviving. The past few weeks had been both terrifying and exhilarating, the highest of highs and the lowest of lows. But it was as if she'd awoken, as if she was truly living for the first time.

"Hope and rebirth," murmured the little blonde girl, staring at the sky in awe.

The echo of her mother's voice rang in Silla's ears. *The flíta are Íseldur's symbol of hope and rebirth, Moonflower. When they reach their old age, they go up in a blaze of light and glory. And when the ashes clear, a caterpillar emerges, and the cycle begins anew.*

Silla smiled at the beautiful winged insects. How fitting to be reminded of them on this, of all nights. Perhaps she was a lot like the flíta. Emerging from the ashes, vulnerable and hungry.

Hekla looped her arm around Silla's waist and rested her head on her shoulder. "My thanks for joining me, dúlla. It is nice to have a friend who is interested in more than simply drinking and fucking."

Silla blinked at her crass words, then laughed. "And I thank you for bringing me, Hekla. That was amazing. Truly."

They made their way back through the arch and into the courtyard of the Wolf's Den. With the darkness, a seductive atmosphere had descended into the square. The children had been ushered to bed, and the courtyard seemed quieter, more intimate. Glancing behind her, Silla was glad to see the little blonde girl had vanished. They walked past a couple entwined in a dark corner, and Silla caught a flash of messy blond hair—Ilías and a brunette she did not recognize.

Hekla snorted and continued toward the corner, where Gunnar and Jonas sat, illuminated by the guttering glow of candles on the long table. Silla's heart lurched. A black-haired woman sat on Jonas's lap, her arm twined around his neck, fingers sliding along his braided hair. Her eyes collided with brilliant blue, and she was trapped...like a fly in honey, pulled deeper into her own misery.

Hekla warned you, she thought, fighting the urge to turn on her foot and run from the humiliation singeing her. Jonas leaned forward, whispering something into the woman's ear. Her raven-black hair was tossed back, full lips parted in laughter.

Silla felt Hekla's gaze on her. "I think I shall get a drink, Hekla," she said quickly. "Would you like one?"

"Nah," said Hekla, her gaze falling on Gunnar. "Shite, we did not find you a man. Are there any—"

Silla silenced her with a finger to her lips. She squeezed Hekla's waist, unhooking their arms. "Do not worry about me. Go have your fun, Hek."

"Are you certain?"

Silla nodded.

"You'll have the quarters to yourself. I will not be back tonight, dúlla."

With a forced smile, Silla wandered to the edge of the courtyard. A table was set out with cups of ale, flames crackling in braziers mounted on either side of the inn's entry. Grabbing a cup of ale, she leaned against the wall of the building. She did not particularly crave a drink, but she needed something to hold onto as she stilled her riotous heart.

Insufferable, she thought. *Arrogant.*

She was a fool and had only herself to blame for it. When they'd kissed, it had been she who'd told him it would never happen again. And yet somewhere deep down, she'd thought he might want more. Thought *she* wanted more. Why was she disappointed? She should be glad to be rid of such an irritating man.

"And here you are," came a familiar voice. Silla turned to see Asger's bright smile as he leaned against the wall beside her. He ran a finger along her braids. "Lovely flowers."

"My thanks." She smiled up at him. Jonas might not want her, but Asger did. And Silla so desperately wanted to live tonight, wanted to keep the high from the flíta and bonfire going. She let her eyes run over his handsome face more boldly than she'd have dared on any other night.

"I was quite certain only the children played with flowers on Longest Day," he winked at her.

"I've never had the chance to," she admitted with a small smile. "I've never celebrated Longest Day like this. I believe I am making up for lost time."

"Is that so?" he asked, gaze dropping to her mouth. "And why have you missed out on such celebrations?"

"Overprotective father," she murmured, turning her body toward him. "Don't worry, I'm all by myself tonight."

Silla felt a pang at her words. Her father would have loved tonight, of that she was sure. Again, came the confusing tumult of emotions—guilt and anger and utter sadness. In an attempt to hide her thoughts, she brought the cup to her lips.

"How fortunate for me." Asger's voice had dropped lower. Reaching for her hand, he turned it over and brushed his lips across the underside of her wrist.

Her stomach warmed. This handsome man wanted her, and she liked that she could tell exactly what he was thinking. He was direct and confident and did not play childish games with her. Tomorrow she'd be back on the road with the Bloodaxe Crew, sitting in that miserable wagon for hours on end, stuck with her anger and endless questions. The thought of it made her desperate to enjoy the time she had left.

Emboldened, Silla grabbed Asger's hand, dragging him between the braziers and into the inn's darkened corridor. As they rounded into the shadows, Asger's hands landed on her waist, and she was pulled back against the warm length of his body. He smelled of ale and traces of sweat.

"Did you bring me here for a reason, Silla?"

She took a shaky breath. Asger turned her around, and she looked up at him in the shadows of the hallway. One hand laced into her hair while the other slid around her back, tracing the bumps of her spine.

"I could not take my eyes off you tonight," said Asger huskily.

Could she do this? He lowered his face toward hers, closer, closer, closer.

Doubt hit her. She did not feel as though her heart would leap from her chest. Her skin did not buzz beneath his attentive gaze, her body did not thrum with the intoxication she craved. Instead, her stomach twisted.

What was she doing?

Before she could consider any further, before his lips could brush against hers, Asger's body was yanked away from her, coolness where warmth had just been.

And then—relief.

Asger growled, whirling. Silla squinted at the silhouette backed by the light from the courtyard.

"Leave," said a cool male voice.

Silla blinked.
Her heart began to drum.
A warm rush of tingles ran up her spine.
It was Jonas.

THIRTY-EIGHT

*J*onas is here. Silla's mind was hazy from the ale, and she backed up until the cool timber wall pressed into her spine. The scene before her felt more like a fever dream than reality.

Asger, stumbling back with a snarl. Jonas, arms crossed over his chest, his gaze harsh and unblinking.

He disrespected you, and thus, me.

Silla's palms began to sweat as Jonas's words flashed back to her. The two men sized each other up—Jonas had several inches on Asger, and his biceps hinted who might come out on top in a fistfight. *He won't hurt him*, she tried to reassure herself. But her mind's eye showed her the warrior at the market, his face swollen and bloodied.

"What do you want?" Asger spat.

"Leave. Now."

Asger's eyes flitted to Silla, then back to Jonas. "Do you know this man, Silla?"

Her initial shock had faded and was replaced by irritation. "Unfortunately," she snapped. What did Jonas think he was doing? Was he bent on ruining her fun, or did he only want what he could not have?

"Leave now," Jonas repeated, shoving Asger's shoulder toward the courtyard.

"I will not leave her alone with you," growled Asger, reaching for his belt—for the hilt of his dagger.

Jonas exhaled sharply. "I'd advise against that."

But Asger was unperturbed, hand wrapping around the handle.

"No!" Silla sprang forward, placing herself between them with a hand on each man's chest. "Stop."

Turning to Asger, she could feel the warmth of Jonas's body sink into her back. A rush of disorienting heat flooded her, but she forced her eyes to Asger, opening her mouth to speak.

Asger beat her to it. "I won't leave unless you wish it. What do you want, Silla?" He looked down at her with silently pleading eyes, and the words dried up on her tongue. She did not wish to humiliate him before Jonas.

Asger placed a hand on her shoulder, but Jonas swatted it away. "Don't touch her."

Silla's mouth dropped open, but she quickly slammed it shut. Whirling on Jonas, she leveled him with a look of fury. "What is this, Jonas? Has your foolish *conscience* burdened itself with my safety once more?"

Their gazes held, and her blood seemed to pump slower, hotter. But as Jonas ran a hand over his hair, she blinked. He looked flustered, a bit unsure. "I need to speak to you. Alone."

"*Now*, Jonas? Now, when you've had all evening?"

Asger cleared his throat, and Silla flinched—she'd forgotten he was there for a moment. But a slow smile crept across Jonas's face, and she knew he could read her reaction. *Do you want me to deal with him?* his gaze seemed to say. Silla hesitated.

Jonas had already locked eyes with Asger over her shoulder. "Silla wants you to leave, kunta."

A sound of exasperation escaped her.

"The only reason I haven't shown you my fist is Silla's dislike for violence," Jonas continued. "Leave now, and you can keep all your teeth. Or we can do it my way." He rolled his neck.

Irritation prickled up Silla's spine. "Stop, Jonas. Give me some space. I cannot breathe." Reluctantly, Jonas retreated a few feet.

Silla turned to Asger.

"This man seems violent. Are you safe with him? What is it you want me to do, Silla?" Guilt burned in her stomach. Why must he be so honorable?

"I'm safe." She forced herself to meet his gaze. "Forgive me, Asger. Please go." He flinched, then turned and strode away, cursing under his breath.

Silla and Jonas were alone in the corridor.

And then, she lunged at him, pushing him squarely in the chest. Startled, this time, Jonas did stumble. "Why did you do that, you overgrown arse?"

He scowled. "I'm simply doing as you wished."

"What—" she spluttered. "I did not ask for that!" She would never tell him she was glad. *Never.* "What is this about, Jonas? What reason had you to ruin my evening?"

Jonas ignored her, prowling back and forth with clenched fists. "You let him kiss you."

"I *did not*, but why should you care? You've made it clear you're not interested."

He stopped, pinning her with a murderous glare. "You must be more cautious. That man might have been dangerous."

"What do you care, Jonas?"

Jonas stalked forward, crowding her against the wall of the corridor. His hands landed on either side of her head and he leaned in, maddeningly near, yet not touching her.

"Who says I care?" he whispered, breath warming her face.

She blinked at him, unsure if she wanted to slap him or pull him closer and slide their mouths together. Jonas moved so quickly she didn't need to decide— his lips pressed against hers, and she sank into him, relieved he'd chosen for her. Hands gliding around his neck, their lips came together and drew apart, his taste and hot gasping breaths emptying her mind of all rational thought.

The frustration and suppressed desire of the past several days were finally freed from them both. Jonas's hands slid around her waist, pulling their hips flush together. An ache building within, Silla arched into him, not nearly close enough. Her hands curved under the hem of his tunic, feeling the smooth, warm skin beneath. It was another hit leaving her head buzzing.

More.

Jonas leaned into her, trapping her hands, and she felt the hardness he'd pushed against her that night in the woods. Heat flared between her legs, and Silla found herself pressing against him, drawing a low groan from Jonas.

"Tsk," came a voice from behind them, a woman scurrying past and down the hallway. They broke apart, and their surroundings swam back into view.

Finally, she remembered—they were in a public corridor. Jonas's chest rose and fell as he fought to catch his breath, and Silla's mind finally caught up with her.

"Why?" she demanded. "Why did you treat me like that, Jonas?"

His pulse throbbed in the hollow of his neck as he stared down at her, but he did not answer. Instead, he leaned in to kiss her once more, but she put both hands on his chest and pushed him away.

"No."

Jonas leaned back, his head thunking against the wall. "I made a mistake."

"Mistake?"

"I've fought it for days, Silla. All night. I cannot stop."

Silla watched his throat bob, unsure of what to say. "Fought what?" she managed at last.

"You've broken me...bewitched me...I know nothing except that I am miserable. All I can think of are your lips; the smell of your hair. How you felt in my arms; the way you made me feel so alive."

Alive, her body chanted. *Alive. Alive.*

Silla Margrét, do not look at him, she thought. She forced her gaze to the wall beside his head. *Do not let him see that he hurt you.*

"A distraction, Jonas," she said. "That's all it was. It was not meant to happen again."

She felt his gaze sliding along her skin, heat prickling in its wake. "And now, Silla? You will be traveling with us for some time now. We have time—plenty of time for distractions."

Her body throbbed, and she closed her eyes for a moment. "You...want that."

"It is all I can think of. Let me distract you, Silla." There was a note of urgency in his voice. He wanted her, and yet—

"You pretended as though I didn't exist tonight!" she blurted.

He opened his mouth, then closed it and swallowed.

"No," she continued. "It was worse than ignoring me. You *taunted* me. With that woman." She crossed her arms.

He palmed the back of his neck. "She means nothing to me. I was...confused."

She wrinkled her nose in distaste.

Jonas threw his head back and looked at the roof of the corridor. "I thought if I bedded her, I could push you from my mind. But I did not go through with it. I could not..." Jonas raked a hand through his beard, then pinned his unwavering gaze on her. "Look. I have Ilías. The Bloodaxe Crew. And I do not get attached to others. It is safer that way. But I...like you. More than I should."

Silla's heart was pounding so loudly she could scarcely hear him.

"Perhaps it...frightened me. Perhaps I thought if I simply left you alone, all would be set to rights. But when I saw you pull that warrior into the corridor, I knew I'd been wrong." He blew out a long breath. "I was wrong to treat you like that. And I'm done fighting it, Silla. You shouldn't be with other men. You belong with me."

Her insides were unfurling with each word spoken, and at last, Silla let her eyes meet his.

Blue, blue, blue.

"What do you mean, *belong*?" she asked softly.

"It means whatever you want it to."

Silla's pulse pounded in her chest, her ears, her fingertips. "Distraction," she whispered. Was she doing this? But she wanted it—she craved the current of energy that seemed to run between them; the way his touch livened her blood and heated her skin. "I want you to take me to your quarters and distract me."

Jonas took a quick breath. They stared at one another for the span of a few heartbeats, before he moved toward her. Hands sliding under her jaw, he tilted her face up, then pressed his forehead to hers. Silla closed her eyes, breathing him in. Leather. Iron. A touch of sweat. It rushed straight to her head and filled her with a swimming sensation—as though she floated on air.

"I'll distract you so well you'll forget your own name."

A laugh choked out of her. "So arrogant, Wolf."

"Confident," he said in a deep voice.

He led her to the end of the corridor, fiddling with iron keys and opening the door. Entering behind Jonas, Silla saw that the room was nearly identical to Hekla's—a wood-framed bed laid with furs and blankets, a table and chairs adjacent to a small fireplace.

Leaning against the wall, she watched as Jonas kindled a fire. After several minutes, flames crackled softly in the hearth, lighting the room and wafting heat toward Silla. Jonas closed the door, shrouding them in privacy, and turned to face her.

Silla's heart was a loud drumbeat in her ears. The room was lit only by guttering firelight which danced along Jonas's golden beard, the curve of his lips, his blue eyes glowing despite the dimness.

She'd thought him handsome, but it was not the right word for him; it was more than his looks, it was the way he carried himself—powerful and self-assured, the kind of man who took what he wanted. And to feel the weight of his attention on her was so overwhelming it made her dizzy. Silla stepped forward, closing the distance between them, her trembling hands reaching out to grasp Jonas's. His large, rough palms slid against hers, sending tingles rushing up her arms. Silla looked up at him and murmured, "I thought of you too, you know."

"What did you think of, Silla?" His thumbs rubbed tender circles on the backs of her hands.

"Your very average lips." She stood on the tips of her toes, brushing her lips against his.

"These tiny things." She pulled his hands around her waist.

"This utterly ordinary body." She ran her arms up his chest, then wrapped them around his shoulders, staring up at him.

Jonas choked out a laugh, his arms tightening around her, and he brushed his nose down her temple. "And see, now you have me wondering if you truly are the selfless woman I believed you to be."

Silla let out a shaky breath, but then they were kissing. He walked her toward the bed and laid her down upon the soft furs. She slid back, and Jonas crawled over her until his elbows were braced on either side of her head. And then he was kissing her again, deeper, rougher, with new urgency. His mouth was hot and wet, his beard rough against her cheeks, and the combination drove her mad.

Silla lost herself so thoroughly, time seemed not to exist. Seconds bled into minutes, but it did not matter. There was only the two of them and the desire sizzling through her, so intense that she could not seem to get close enough to him.

Jonas drew up, but she pulled him back down.

"Don't stop," she said, her words slurring. "I might die if you stop." And she meant it—nothing mattered but more of this, more of this lostness, this heady need that consumed her so completely.

His chuckle was low, sending vibrations through her body and making her gasp. "I couldn't have that," he murmured against her lips. "I've got plans for you tonight." Jonas pulled her hair to the side and kissed the sensitive spot just below her ear. Moaning, Silla pushed herself into his touch, craving more of him.

"I wanted to tell you" —she panted— "there are no pockets in my dress. It is quite impractical. I thought you'd approve."

"I've changed my mind about your dresses," he said, lifting his head.

"What?"

He fingered the embroidery along her neckline. "Keep the dowdy dresses, Silla. I wanted to punch every man that looked upon you tonight." His fingers grappled with the lacings. "Let us take it off now and throw it into the fire."

Her eyes flew open. "You cannot burn it! Hekla bought it for me."

Jonas's fingers worked clumsily on the laces, but he finally succeeded and pushed the dress down, lower, lower, lower, until it was off. He pulled off her undergarments, and then she lay bare with a glorious golden-haired warrior looming over her.

"Beautiful," he murmured, notes of awe and reverence in his voice. His look was possessive as he inspected every swell and dip. As knuckles brushed lightly against her breast, desire spiraled through her. "You're perfect, Silla," he said, staring into her eyes.

Emotion clogged her throat. No one had ever called her beautiful before, and certainly not perfect. But then she reminded herself that this was more than likely what the Wolf said to every woman.

He lowered his face to kiss her, but she placed her fingers to his lips. "You too," she whispered. She wanted to see him, was desperate to feel the slide of his bare skin against hers.

Jonas cocked an eyebrow but didn't need to be told twice. Eyes never leaving hers, he reached behind him, pulling his tunic off in one swift motion. Silla was quite certain she stopped breathing for a minute as she took him in. He was stunning; all lightly tanned skin and chiseled muscles across his broad chest and rippled stomach. And as he toed off his boots and worked his breeches loose, she took in yet another rousing sight. An arrogant gleam settled in his eye as he caught her staring in fascination.

"Proud man," she muttered, with a hint of a smile.

"Confident," he repeated, sauntering toward her.

Then Jonas was settling back over her, the hot drag of his skin against hers as intoxicating as she'd imagined. Their mouths came together in a hot and needy kiss, and as his palm slid along her stomach, her breast, she arched into his touch. His hand skimmed down her stomach, lower, until it reached between her legs, pressing gently and rubbing in small circles. With a gasp, Silla raised herself on elbows, brows knit together.

Jonas lifted his head, his eyes locking onto hers. "You've never known the touch of a man, have you, Curls?"

Silla felt a flush creeping up her neck. Jonas's lips twisted into a satisfied smile as he tucked a tendril of hair behind her ear. "You've no idea how much I like that. My lips, the only to touch yours. My fingers, the only to stroke you." His eyes held a possessive gleam which made the heat in her cheeks rush straight to her core. "Give me your trust, and I will make you feel so good, your toes will curl and you'll see nothing but stars."

"Y-yes," she managed. "Please."

Reclining, Silla shivered as his touch resumed, the fingers on her intimate flesh gently caressing. A long finger dipped inside her, and she clenched as it drew back out. Soon a second finger joined, and it wasn't long before she was dizzy, her toes indeed curling, sounds spilling from her lips—whispers and sighs and ramblings of *yes* and *please* and other more incoherent things. Her insides clenched tighter and tighter, hips lifting off the furs, but he pressed her down with one hand while he thrust his fingers inside her with the other. As he curled and dragged them down within her, Silla cried out.

Jonas made a sound of satisfaction. "Is that for me, Curls? Give me the rest of it."

His carnal words sent her over the edge. The pressure hovered unbearably for one second, two. And then, with a ragged breath, she shattered into a million swirling pieces. Pleasure rippled through her as her muscles shuddered around his fingers. The ecstasy seemed to go on endlessly, Jonas wringing every last drop from her, stopping only once her body had stilled.

She lay there for a small eternity, her breaths shallow, lights bursting behind her eyelids.

This is it, Silla thought. This was the most alive she'd ever felt.

As her vision swirled back into focus, the thundering of her heart fading, she found Jonas staring down at her. Wisps of his golden hair had pulled loose from his braid, falling across his forehead; his soft lips curled into a smile. Gods. He was so primally male at that moment, her stomach flipped and twirled.

"Touch me," he breathed.

Yes, she thought. She wanted to show him how happy he'd made her. Wanted to make him feel just as alive as he'd made her. "Show me," Silla whispered.

His lips curved up as he rolled onto his back, pulling her up so she straddled his thighs, looking down upon him. The firelight caught each ripple on his golden skin, each scar, and the small path of ash-blond hair trailing down his stomach.

Taking her hand in his, Jonas wrapped them around him. As the pressure of his hand withdrew, she kept hers in place. "Is this what you like?" she murmured, moving them slowly down and back up.

"Yes," he said, his voice low.

Emboldened, Silla continued to explore, discovering the places that made him shiver and groan and make his hips buck. Her other hand moved along the rippling muscles of his stomach—he was hard and warm and smooth everywhere she touched. She could hardly believe he desired her. The very thought of it caused a rush, a sweet high to flow through her.

Silla pulled back, looking down at him. "Jonas...I want..."

"What do you want, Silla?"

Looking down at Jonas with wide eyes, she took a deep breath. She'd come this far; she was in this deep. Her entire life had consisted of smart, safe decisions, and tonight, she'd realized how much she'd missed out on. Tonight, she didn't want to think. She simply wanted to feel.

"Make me feel alive, Jonas. Take me. All of me." Her words were quiet and loud all at once.

Jonas stared at her with a wild intensity she could feel in the marrow of her bones. With a low growl, he flipped her onto her back, pinning her into the furs with a kiss of pure, raw need.

"You're certain?" he rasped, exhaling once she nodded. He dragged that hot brand of flesh against her center, up, down, up down, and she clenched on empty air. Silla had a moment of trepidation—Jonas was large, so much larger than her, and she knew from time spent with seasoned women around the cookfires it would hurt. But she wanted it more than anything. Wanted to live big while her heart still beat.

Jonas's words felt distant, muffled. "Sigrún has herbs you can take to prevent a babe. I shall ask her for them. She won't tell."

Silla nodded. Her body tingled with anticipation, with need. Closing his eyes, Jonas muttered curses under his breath as he positioned himself at her entrance. And then he was pressing in slowly, firmly, stretching her. Sweat misted his brow as he worked himself inside her inch by inch. She was full, so unbearably full, and just when she felt certain it was impossible, pain speared through her. Silla cried out, fingers digging into the flesh of his shoulders.

Shuddering, Jonas cursed again, holding himself still while he trailed kisses along her jaw, her neck, all the way to her ear. "Gods, woman. You feel like you were made for me." He rolled his hips with a groan, the burn intensifying as he retreated, then filled her once more.

Is it supposed to feel uncomfortable? she wanted to say, but bit down on her lip and tried to relax.

"You're even more beautiful like this," he murmured, looking down at where their bodies were joined. "Filled with me." He watched in fascination as he thrust back in.

His carnal words lit a flame within her. "Full," was all she could manage, wincing as he drove back into her. So full. So deep.

"I'm trying to go slow, but you feel so..." His eyes fluttering, Jonas pushed into her again. Again. Again.

Goosebumps raced across her skin, and Silla breathed deeply. It was an invasion more brutal than she'd expected, and yet it was exactly what she wanted, what she needed. She was choosing this. Choosing to *live*. Choosing him—Jonas. There was only them, only the pain and the faintest glimmer of pleasure.

"You've given this to *me*," muttered Jonas. His voice sounded raw, scraped. Gaze sliding hungrily along her face and down her breasts, he moved faster, stretching her, filling her. "It's mine."

His words dragged a noise from her—a moan of pure need. *More*, her body chanted, as she scratched her nails down his back, as she lost herself more thoroughly than ever before. With every thrust, the sharp edge of pain dulled a little more until it was nothing but an ache.

Jonas shifted, and she gasped as he went deeper, to a place she didn't even know could be touched. Bliss sparked through her, and, like fire catching, something new began to build. It was pleasure edged with pain, twisting together until they were indistinguishable. Her lips parted, brows furrowing as she explored this new sensation, deeper, more consuming than before.

"Yes. You'll give me one more, Curls." Bracing on one elbow, Jonas moved a hand between them, caressing her most sensitive spot, and she shuddered at his touch.

The world was spinning. "Don't stop."

He increased his pace and pushed her knee up, somehow hitting even deeper inside her. It was kindling tossed onto the fire. Blistering heat built higher, and somehow also deeper, with each surge of his hips, and she was on the verge of something new, something bigger...

His hand slid to her neck, giving it a gentle squeeze. "When you find your pleasure, it's *my* name on your lips."

But his gaze was too intense, too...something, and Silla squeezed her eyes shut as the tension grew unbearable.

"Oh. Oh..."

She came apart with his name on her tongue, a blazing inferno of light and heat and pleasure razing through her and leaving her in smoldering ashes. She was nothing and everything, flying on the highest of highs and drowning in the sweetest of sensations.

She was vaguely aware of Jonas above her. A ravaging groan; tremors running through his arms; his thrusts erratic, then slowing entirely as he spilled inside her. Collapsing onto one arm, Jonas heaved with each breath.

Her mind was utterly quiet.

She breathed in. Breathed out. Opened her eyes to look up at him. She took in the sheen of sweat across his brow, at the broad chest heaving as he struggled to catch his breath, the green flecks in his blue eyes. He was looking down at her with a strange expression—like he'd just discovered something.

When words returned to her, she rushed to say the first thing that came to mind. "Can we do that again?"

He laughed, and her heart spun around. "If you can still form words, I've work left to do."

THIRTY-NINE

The fire had burnt down to coals, an ashy scent lingering in the air. Jonas knew he should really get up to add another log, but couldn't bring himself to leave the furs.

He watched her slender fingers slide along the back of his hand, tracing the mottled skin. "And this scar?" Silla asked. He ought to shut this down. Ought to remember where his focus should lay—the job in Istré; reclaiming his lands. But he couldn't bring himself to regret what they'd done.

Earlier, Jonas had brought the bucket over to clean her thighs, body awakening at the sight of her sprawled out in his furs. He'd been her first. She'd trusted him with that after everything. Warmth filled his chest, but he'd pushed it away.

At some point, he could hold himself back no longer, pressing his lips to hers, and it had all started again. They'd rolled in the furs, limbs and lips dragging together. Jonas found himself worried she'd be sore; but Silla seemed eager, so he'd sunk into her again. The gripping heat of her body was bliss like he'd never known.

Her curiosity, her eagerness, her beautiful, expressive face...it all awakened some primitive thing inside him—like a warrior who needed to conquer. Needed to stake his claim. It had never felt like this, like he could not get enough.

It is only physical, he told himself. *You can bed her without giving away parts of yourself.* But somewhere deep inside him, Jonas questioned it. Already, he'd told her things he rarely spoke of, and the warmth in his chest had only grown throughout the night.

Silla stifled a yawn as a log collapsed in the fire with a burst of embers. Jonas knew they'd have to be up in a matter of hours to commence the next leg of their journey, but at this moment, he was ready to leave the Bloodaxe Crew. To bar himself in this room with her and never let her leave.

"Jonas?" she asked, pulling him back to the present. "This burn?"

"Fire serpent," said Jonas, swallowing. "One of the worst jobs we've taken was to rid Holt of an infestation." His finger went to the corner of her eye, tracing the tiny crescent-shaped scar. "And this one?"

She shrugged. "I've been told I knocked my eye on a table corner when I was two. Not nearly so fun as your stories." But she seemed to retreat within herself for a moment.

"Where did you go?" murmured Jonas, his knuckles brushing along her cheek.

She shook her head, smiling at him. "Nowhere. What about...this one?" Her finger grazed the mark on his cheekbone.

Jonas frowned. "My father."

Her eyes shot to his.

"I got between his fist and my mother. He wore his damn ring."

Silla's eyes searched his face. "Has your father something to do with why you and Ilías were not granted your land rights?"

A muscle in his jaw twitched, and his eyes slid to the furs beside her head. "Yes." He could tell she wanted to ask more and was grateful when she didn't. He did not wish to ruin their time together with thoughts of those days. And yet...if he could tell anyone about it, perhaps it could be her.

Stop, Jonas urged himself. *You must protect yourself. You must keep your focus.* But his arguments were growing more feeble. Silla was a good person. She felt safe. Trustworthy.

"Silla," said Jonas, getting lost in her big, dark eyes. "We must keep this a secret."

"Why?"

"Rey ordered me to stay away from you," said Jonas, tucking a strand of hair behind her ear.

Her hair was in wild disarray, cheeks flushed and lips swollen. It only made her more beautiful. An undone side to her only he got to see. He felt a clench of possessiveness. *Mine.*

"What does Rey care?"

"He believes you'll be a distraction from our job." Jonas let out a long exhale. He knew Rey was right but could not bring himself to care at the moment.

Irritation flared in her eyes. "What Rey does not know won't hurt him." Silla covered her mouth as a large yawn finally broke free.

"Have I worn you out?" Jonas nuzzled into her neck.

"Thoroughly," she said, with a devious smile. "Can you distract me again tomorrow?" She threaded her fingers into his beard, and a shiver of pleasure ran down his spine.

His hands moved from her hip along the smooth skin of her thighs. "Yes. I want to take you under the stars."

She slapped his arm playfully. "So crass. What does it say of me that I like it?"

"It confirms my suspicions. You're no wholesome woman." He squeezed her thigh.

"We need a signal," she continued. "I could twirl my hair around my fingers. Or scratch my nose with my left hand. And then we each make excuses and disappear into the woods."

"I might like that," he murmured, his fingers brushing along her stomach. "Our little secret." He raised himself to press a kiss to her lips.

As he pulled back, she stared up at him, something passing behind her eyes. "If we are to have our fun together, I will not stand for you to treat me as you did tonight," she warned him. "Don't be cruel to me. Can we not be friends around the others?"

Sighing, Jonas stared at the timbered beams of the roof. "We can be friends. I won't ignore you again, Silla, I swear it. But I won't be content to be near you and not have my hands on you."

Silla sat up. "Well, you shall have to restrain yourself. I am a woman of morals after all." A smile teased her lips. "And neither of us wish to face the wrath of Rey."

Silla climbed from the bed, pulling her shift over her head.

"Did something happen on your trip?" asked Jonas. A foreign feeling twisted in his stomach—jealousy, he realized with a start.

A startled look flashed across her face, but she quickly schooled it into a neutral look. "He let a vampire deer attack me. And he was...well...Axe Eyes."

"He did not try anything improper, did he?"

Silla whipped to face Jonas. "No. What? Of course not."

"Good, Silla. I don't want you kissing anyone other than me." Merciful fucking gods. Who was this person saying these things?

Laughter burst from her as she took in the look on his face.

"Why do you laugh?"

"It is...exciting to be the object of your jealousy."

Jonas frowned. "Do not go getting any ideas, woman."

"Such as?" She pulled her dress on.

"Such as trying to make me jealous."

Her eyes sparkled. "Hmm. Suppose I was to set my sleeping furs up next to Ilías, would that make you jealous?"

He let out a low growl. "Do not even consider it."

"And...if I were to sit near to Gunnar at the evening meal so that our legs touched the smallest amount?"

Jonas sighed. "I'd be forced to show him the axe. Don't make me do it, Silla."

She leaned against the door, letting out a long breath. "I wish I could stay."

In seconds, Jonas was across the room, wrapping his arms around her waist, pressing his lips to hers. It was a soft and gentle kiss to end the night, but his teasing tongue promised things to come. Silla sighed as she leaned into him.

"Goodnight, Jonas." She opened the door and walked down the hall.

"Goodnight, Silla," he murmured after her.

———

SILLA MADE her way to the stairs, climbing to the room she shared with Hekla. Fumbling with the key, she was so tired and shaky that her first two attempts failed to slide it into the keyhole. Just as she managed to slip it in, the door was yanked open, a bleary-eyed Hekla staring at her.

Silla stared back, keenly aware of the state of her hair and dress.

Hekla's lips tugged up into a mischievous smile.

"Oh, dúlla. You've a *lot* of explaining to do."

PART II
Ashes

"Great deeds and ill deeds
often fall within each
other's shadow."

-Gisli Sursson's Saga

FORTY

SKALLA RIDGE

H er flame-red hair was out of place in the dank cell. It was too bright, too exuberant in this place of misery and death. Skraeda's chest burned as she stared through the bars at her exact likeness. Hands cuffed with hindrium to neutralize her Ashbringer abilities, Ilka trembled with shock and fear.

"Skraeda, you've made a mistake," Ilka whispered. "You can undo it. You can make things right. Tell them you were wrong."

Skraeda's insides were a maelstrom of emotions—guilt and self-loathing, but strongest of all, irritation. Irritation that after all these years, Ilka hadn't even tried to adapt to this world. She was too soft. Too kind. The galdur flowing in her veins had the potential to give her great power, and yet...she thought it a burden. And Ilka did not seem to understand Skraeda in the least.

"I am doing what I must to survive, Ilka," she said with quiet determination.

She saw it—the look in her twin's eyes that would haunt her forever. The moment Ilka finally understood.

"You are no better than them," spat Ilka, venom finally rising in her words.

Too late for you, thought Skraeda. It saddened her that it had come to this. But in this kingdom, if you were Galdra, it was kill or be killed. And Skraeda wasn't ready to die.

"You should be proud, sister," she said. "Your gift will no longer be wasted on *you. It will be used to shape this kingdom into the queen's vision. It will be your legacy, Ilka."*

Ilka's eyes filled with tears. "You are a traitor to your own kind, Skraeda."

"I am an opportunist—"

"You think only of yourself!" Ilka screamed.

Her voice echoed off the stone walls of her cell. Skraeda could not recall a time when her twin had ever raised her voice, and it stunned her into momentary silence.

Ilka's lip curled into an ugly snarl. "You think yourself brave...think yourself an opportunist...but you are nothing but a selfish coward, Skraeda. You will die miserable and alone, as you've earned."

The words reverberated through her mind, until at last, she woke from her fever dream. Skraeda found herself sprawled on a ledge partway down the fjord. The sun was so bright that for several long moments, Skraeda thought herself immortalized in light amongst the stars.

It was the pecking of a raven which brought her back to this life, plucking at her braids and bringing a sharp flare of pain to her scalp. She swatted at it. With a cry of protest, it took flight, joining the flock circling above, corpse vultures waiting for her to draw her last breath.

And then, it all swarmed back to her—that enormous warrior sprawled on the edge of the ridge, awaiting his death blow. The pain in her skull, engulfing her in blackness.

The girl.

Skraeda had been so lost in the warrior's suffering, she'd forgotten the girl.

How could you be so stupid? she chastised herself. She had not been able to control herself. After days of lying in wait, there they were before her—the girl without her red cloak, but Skraeda recognized her at once. After hundreds of miles and countless nights spent imagining this moment, it was here.

There had been the small matter of the warrior. He was large and skilled, and the moment Skraeda had realized she was outmatched in blades, she'd reached for the thread of his sorrow with her mind's grasp. It had unspooled from the man's aura, and with a few swift yanks upon it, he was on his back, head dangling over the edge of Skalla Ridge.

How foolish of Skraeda to forget the girl.

Her skull throbbed as though in agreement, and Skraeda reached back to rub the swollen lump. Anger kindled within her, and Skraeda felt the need to burn...to destroy.

First, you need to get up the cliff, you halfwit, she told herself.

And then, she began to climb. With bruised ribs and an aching shoulder, it was slow work climbing back up the fjord, and one wrong move would ensure her death.

But she was driven by her need to survive—by her need to correct her mistake and retain the queen's favor. The woman had slipped through her grasp not once, but twice now.

A rare cloudless day, the sun was blinding. Skraeda's tongue felt enormous in her parched mouth, her muscles screaming as she clung to the surface of the fjord. Her hand closed around a root protruding from the craggy cliff face, and she tugged, testing its resilience. The root jerked loose, crumbled rock raining down upon her. Closing her eyes, Skraeda weathered the storm.

After many long hours of climbing, Skraeda surveyed the last stretch of sheer rock separating her from the top of the cliff—six feet of smooth, unblemished stone. There was no footing to be gained here. But an idea struck her.

Sucking in a deep breath, she unsheathed her handaxe and swung it up in a mighty arc. Small bits of stone crumbled down, but her eyes soon fell upon the blade buried deep into the rock's surface.

Success swelled in her chest. With her other hand, she unsheathed her hevrít, slamming the blade into the rock surface several handspans above the axe. Pulling herself upward, blade blow by blade blow, Skraeda did not dare look down—the ceaseless crashing of waves below was reminder enough of her fate should she lose her grip.

The ravens complained loudly from above, and Skraeda's lips curved into a smile.

"You shall not feast on me today," she muttered.

And then, Skraeda pulled herself over the top of Skalla Ridge and lay heaving on the surface. Her muscles screamed, her throat aching for water. The world spun above her for the briefest of moments, but Skraeda forced herself to gather her wits. *You've survived,* she told herself, her hand finding the reassuring contours of Ilka's braid in her pocket. *And now you will finish what you've started.*

Pulling herself to her knees, Skraeda surveyed her surroundings—the Road of Bones driving north along the ridge; pinewoods jutting like green spear tips into the blue skies bordering it; the sheer drop down the cliffs to the ocean below along the other side.

Her eyes fell on a red object nestled into the grass on the edge of the road.

Forcing herself to her feet, Skraeda sucked in a fortifying breath before investigating.

The warrior's shield—severed into two jagged pieces, and held together only by the iron boss—was discarded in the long grass. Skraeda stepped closer. Her eyes traced the axe painted on the shield, crimson coating the blade and dripping into a pool below.

"I do not know this sigil," she said, picking up the broken shield. "But I shall discover whose it is."

The clop of hooves had Skraeda gripping her handaxe tighter, but it was only her mount, cantering toward the sound of her voice. Relief melted through her. Fortune shone upon her at last. She had her horse, her provisions in the saddle sacks, and the sigil of those with whom the girl traveled.

After a long drink from her waterskin, Skraeda mounted her horse and directed her north along the Road of Bones. "I know who you are," she said aloud, "and soon, I will know with whom you travel."

The waves crashed well below the ridge, the ravens cawing above.

"The next time we meet will be the last, girl."

FORTY-ONE

HVER

It was far too early when Silla dragged herself from beneath the furs and crawled onto the wagon. The town of Hver was still sleeping off the celebrations of Longest Day, and the Bloodaxe Crew moved slowly. Ilías swayed in a way which suggested he might still be drunk, his *freshly awoken cave bear* hair mussed in all its glory.

Silla's eyes caught on Jonas's blues. She traced his features, the dark circles beneath his eyes and a long, thorough yawn the only hint of their activities the night before. Her stomach warmed as her gaze fell on his beard, and memories surged forth—the feel of it beneath her fingers, the scratch of it against her neck. As though reading her mind, a small smile curved Jonas's lips—a smile promising more distractions.

As she settled onto the pile of the furs in her corner of the wagon, something hard dug into Silla's back—a book. Three books, to be precise. Pulling them out, she examined the covers. The first she recognized as the book Rey had sought from Kraki: *Creatures of Íseldur*. Her fingers slid over the plain leather cover of the next one, tracing each letter of the words *Herbs of Íseldur- a Complete Guide*. The third book, curiously, was *A Brief History of Íseldur*.

Silla's gaze flicked from the books to Rey. Tall and stoic, he sat upon Horse, sunlight bouncing off his textured curls. "Did you steal this for me, Axe Eyes?"

He tilted his head. "Those books belong to the Bloodaxe Crew. I simply took what belongs to us."

"You *are* a bandit, aren't you, Reynir?"

His low growl made her lips curve up. Evidently, he did not like to be called by his full name.

"And you've entrusted me with them?"

The wolfskin pelt around his shoulders rose and fell as he shrugged. "Books seemed a good way to keep you from talking." He sighed. "Though already I question my judgment."

Her brows furrowed as she studied the broad back of the Bloodaxe Crew's leader. He was bewildering, this man. Rey had threatened to kill her more than once, and now he offered her a simple kindness—a reprieve from her boredom.

Selecting *Herbs of Íseldur*, Silla ran the pages through her fingers. She was positively gleeful, even though it was not filled with tales of romance and adventure.

Silla flipped to the appendix, running her index finger past *redcurrant*, stopping on *skjöld*. Her heart stopped.

She turned to page 233 and read.

Botanical Name- skjöldablóm.

Popular Name(s)- skjöld

Silla scanned past habitat and description until she reached the section she wanted.

Uses- Skjöld has powerful calming properties, historically given in small doses to treat tension in the body and terrors of the mind.

Side effects- blockage of kjarna prevents users from priming. Skjöld is recommended for short-term use only due to the phantom visions and dangerous side effects reported by long-term users.

Warning- Skjöld should be used with extreme caution, as a high dose can lead to pains in the chest, labored breaths, loss of control of one's body, and death. Skjöld is highly addictive. Ending treatment can lead to symptoms including headaches, shaking, fever, nausea, a racing heart, and loss of consciousness.

The words struck her like a slap to the face.

A blow to the gut.

An arrow straight through her heart.

"What does it mean?" asked the little blonde girl, seated beside her in the wagon.

"I don't know," breathed Silla. She re-read the paragraphs. Once. Twice. Over and over until the words penetrated her. Some she did not understand. But the ones she did laid her to ruin.

Ending treatment can lead to symptoms including headaches.

Silla couldn't breathe. Couldn't think. Could only swallow down the words and try to digest their meaning. Skjöld was not used to *treat* headaches.

"Headaches are a symptom of the leaves wearing off," whispered the girl.

Silla wanted to vomit. Wanted to scream. Her mind tripped over itself as she tried to comprehend. All of these years of fear, of anticipation, of being shackled by the skull-splintering headaches. It had all been a *lie*? These chronic headaches were so integrally a part of her, they had shaped her as a person. It was like discovering a piece of her very being had never really been there at all.

She didn't even know herself.

Who was she?

Who in the gods' sacred ashes *was she*?

Silla gripped the side of the wagon amid the churning, writhing anger, trying to hold herself together before she splintered into a thousand shards. She cursed her father, her faith and trust in him shattering once more.

"He lied to you," said the little girl solemnly. "Again and again."

But Silla's mind wouldn't rest at that, because there was more.

Phantom visions were reported by long-term usage...

The girl.

The *girl*.

"Am I a product of the leaves?" asked the girl, examining her hand.

"You must be," murmured Silla. "When did we first meet?" Her mind reached back, trying to recall when she'd started taking them. Everything had happened that one chaotic summer when she was ten years old. It was so long ago...her memories were short, shuffled flashes. Her mother's green eyes. Dill. The eclipse. A flash of white light. Sorrow and misery and running, running, running.

A choked sound escaped her, and she felt herself splitting at the seams. All these years, they'd moved around to escape whispers, to evade the Klaernar's suspicion. All these years of loneliness as an outsider. All these years, spent in hiding and on the run...scarcely living in the process. And for what?

"The leaves," answered the girl. "It all comes back to the leaves."

Skjöld is highly addictive...a high dose can lead to pains in the chest, labored breaths, loss of control of one's body, and death.

The leaves were poison, just as Rey had said. Silla twisted around, her eyes landing on his back, swaying with the movement of Horse. Everything he had told her of the leaves, according to this book, was true. *His brother.* She squeezed her eyes shut.

The vial hung heavy around her neck, suddenly less of a comfort than an anchor pulling her under, drowning her slowly. She had the urge to rip it from her neck and throw it as far away as possible. And yet, she could not. She yearned for them...she *needed* them.

Tears filled her eyes at the sting of this fresh betrayal. Her life was a lie, and the only person with answers was dead. Why? Why would he lie to her about the nature of the leaves? What possible reason could he have to give her highly dangerous, addictive leaves? Leaves that made her see phantom girls. Leaves that forced them to move, to live a miserable existence.

"Was it to control you?" asked the girl. "To keep you dependent on him?"

Silla sank into the furs, numb with shock, as the girl settled beside her, stroking her hair.

"Easy," murmured the girl. "Real or not, Silla, I am here with you."

Silla's mind was stuck on an endless loop, stuck on what she'd read in that book. She relented to the girl's soft touch, tried to put the pieces of her life together. But there were only more questions.

It might have been minutes, perhaps even hours. But eventually, the girl faded into obscurity and Silla's unfocused gaze settled on Jonas. Flanked by Ilías and Sigrún, he rode behind the wagon.

Silla's gaze landed on Jonas, knots of tension slowly melting from her as she watched him. His eyes dragged up her body with a look behind them—intimate and knowing. As though he was charting her, making plans for her. And though her body ached from the night before, she shivered with want.

"You're tired today, Jonas," said Ilías, glancing toward Jonas.

Jonas said nothing, raising an eyebrow at his brother.

"I shall ask for a room far from yours next time," continued Ilías grumpily. "I could not sleep for all the sound coming through my walls." He paused. "It was not the black-haired beauty; I saw her wrapped around another warrior after you left. Who did you take to your bed, brother?"

"I am surprised you noticed anything considering you were halfway to bedding that brunette right in the courtyard."

"Yes," smirked Ilías, then he frowned. "That was promising. Until her sister dragged her away and ruined my fun."

Jonas chuckled. "Perhaps you should pick the less intoxicated ones, little brother."

"But I cannot help myself. The destructive ones simply wish for someone to love them, and I am only happy to oblige."

"You're a villain in the making, aren't you?" said Jonas, though with a note of affection. "Where did I go wrong with you?"

Ilías smiled as though proud. "But you...*your* fun was not ruined, Jonas. Who was it?"

Jonas let out a long exhale.

"Since when are you quiet on the details?" pressed Ilías.

Jonas cast a look at the skies. "I do not wish to discuss it, Ilías."

"You disappoint me, brother. Where is the fun in that?"

"I grow weary of this talk, Ilías. Go ask Fire Fist about his night."

"I think not," said Ilías. "I prefer my bollocks intact, not shredded to ribbons."

As Jonas chuckled, Silla made a note to inform Hekla that her trysts with Gunnar were not as secret as she thought.

Ilías would not relent. "My curiosity grows along with your silence. You set me a challenge, and I will take up the task and discover who this woman is."

"Keep on and I shall have to rearrange your face," said Jonas at last, unable to suppress a yawn. "There is no mystery. It was no one special—just a girl."

Silla frowned, but the sun's warmth and the softness of the furs were a potent combination. Her eyelids drooped, and she was powerless as the voices faded and sleep took hold.

———

"WELL, DON'T YOU LOOK WELL-RESTED?" smirked Hekla, adjusting Silla's stance.

They were thirty paces from the fire, on the edge of the glade in which the Bloodaxe Crew had set up camp. The breeze grew ever cooler, carrying the familiar scent of the woods. As they'd traveled the Road of Bones today, the pastures north of Hver had quickly dwindled, coastal forest climbing back up around them. According to Silla's map, they'd continue along the coast of Íseldur for some time before reaching the Highlands and the town of Skutur.

Rolling her shoulders, Silla prepared for another attempt at escaping a rear chokehold. Her temples throbbed lightly, but Silla had not taken her skjöld dose yet. She'd decided she might skip it tonight.

"I am. I slept all day," admitted Silla with a twinge of guilt.

"I know you did. I hate you just a little."

Silla stifled a smile. "If it makes you feel better, I'll likely suffer from sleeplessness tonight."

"Hmm. It helps, but I think I could make my peace if you told me what happened last night."

All day, Hekla had tried to draw details from Silla about her late-night deeds.

Silla pressed her lips together. "I cannot."

Hekla threw her a look of exaggerated annoyance, then positioned herself behind Silla. Her metal arm wrapped around Silla's neck, bending at the elbow joint. "I could squeeze the answers from you."

"Friends do not suffocate friends for sordid details."

"Fine." Hekla sighed. "Now, remember, you *must* catch them by surprise. Keep your movements swift and powerful."

Hekla's prosthetic arm tightened around Silla's neck, her left hand locking it in place. Silla's body curled backward with the force, and she took a fortifying breath. Just as they'd practiced, Silla twisted sideways, stepped back, wrapped her arms around Hekla's waist, and pulled her to the ground.

"That was passable," said Hekla. "Repeat it like a warrior, as though your life depends on it. And don't fear harming me. I can take it."

She repeated it several more times, and with each pass, Silla performed the action with more speed and intensity.

Releasing Silla and stepping back, Hekla clicked her claws in and out with an air of impatience. "I cannot believe you withhold this from me. I thought us friends."

"You are relentless!"

Hekla smirked. "I prefer *determined*."

Silla sighed. "I met a man earlier in the night, and we became...close."

Hekla arched a black eyebrow at her and rested her metallic hand on her curving hip. "Details, Silla."

"Gunnar told me no questions would be asked about the events of Longest Day," whined Silla.

"Provide me a name at the very least!"

"Asger." Silla winced, the awful look on his face as she'd asked him to leave flashing in memory.

"You frowned. What does that mean? Did he not please you?"

"Oh no. He pleased me...many times." Silla clapped a hand over her mouth in regret.

But Hekla doubled over with laughter, and it was contagious. Silla's own laughter bubbled up, and soon the two of them were shaking. Gaze darting toward the fire, Silla found five sets of eyes looking their way.

"And you, Hekla? Did you not tell me I had the room to myself last night? Why did you return?"

Hekla snorted. "Gunnar snores so loudly the walls shook. I was forced to abandon him to get some sleep. Imagine my surprise returning to empty quarters." Her lips pursed. "I am happy for you, dúlla."

Silla opened her mouth to reply but was interrupted.

"I cannot bear to watch this any longer," barked Rey, storming toward them. The throb in Silla's temples intensified. "Your clumsy attempts at defense make my skull ache. This is why you were nearly drained by a vampire deer, Sunshine. Your training is nothing more than an excuse to gossip."

Silla pursed her lips as his long legs ate the distance between them. She hoped he had not heard their conversation.

"Oh stop, Rey," Hekla bristled. "You cannot begrudge us a little harmless fun. Silla is progressing, considering she could not unsheathe her dagger a few weeks past."

Backlit by the campfire, Rey's size and imposing demeanor made the air feel thin. "Could not unsheathe it *two days* past, is what I recall," he said in his deep, layered voice. "I grow weary of watching your pitiful attempts, Sunshine, and have decided you need some assistance."

Silla narrowed her eyes. "What do you care of my defense skills?"

"We are only as strong as our weakest out here," said Rey. "And Sunshine, you drag the entire Bloodaxe Crew down."

Silla could tell her face had flushed and silently cursed herself for reacting to his words. "Perhaps you should remember who it is that cooks your meals, Rey."

Hekla cackled, clapping her hands. "I would take her words to heart, Rey. Don't be fooled by her sweet smile. I believe this one is secretly vicious."

"I don't believe there is anything 'secret' about it," muttered Rey. A muscle in his jaw flexed, and Silla felt a twinge of guilt.

"Well," mused Hekla. "It would be helpful to have him correct your form. It is difficult for me to notice such things when I am positioned behind you."

Rey's face was unflinching. "Then it is decided. Go through the motion from earlier, and I will correct your *many* missteps."

Silla swallowed. Hekla moved behind her, wrapping an arm around her neck, and Silla ran through the movements under Rey's watchful gaze. Everything she had practiced flew from her mind. Clumsy and uncoordinated, she landed in a heap on the ground. Blowing a wayward strand of hair from her face, she climbed back to her feet.

Rey blinked slowly. Silla clenched her fists, fighting the urge to wrap them around his throat. How this man could draw her fury with the simple movement of his eyelids, she did not know.

She licked her lips, flicking a blade of grass from her sleeve. "You made me nervous. I can do better." They repeated it with marginal improvement.

"You're waiting too long."

She tensed as Rey stepped toward her. The firelight accentuated the curve of his cheekbone, his black curls. His hand wrapped around her elbow, easily encompassing the entirety of it, and with a gentle pull, repositioned her arm an inch to the left.

"Drive this into her ribs, and use her body's motion to pull her around."

He released her, and she widened her feet to steady herself. They repeated the movement, Rey's advice bringing near-instant success. A victorious smile began to climb on Silla's cheeks, but was quickly knocked back down.

"Worse than a child," scoffed Rey, though his eyes were glinting. "Again."

Rey ran them through the defense move at least ten times, adjusting Silla's stance, the angle of her elbow, barking out small tips. By the tenth attempt, her muscles were complaining loudly. However, it had been her most successful attempt at bringing Hekla down.

Rey unclasped the wolfskin pelt from around his shoulders and folded it neatly on the ground. Beneath it, he wore a blue woolen tunic, dark tattoos coiling up his neck.

"Now, you will try your luck against me. Try to bring me to the ground, Sunshine. Again." The corners of his lips twitched. As far as Rey went, it was as good as a smile.

Hekla looked from Rey to Silla and back again. "Is there a story here?"

Rey began rolling up the sleeves of his tunic, and Silla's eyes snagged on the muscled forearms covered in more winding tattoos. On his right forearm, the tattoos swirled much like on his neck, but on his left was a twisting, serpentine tail. She found herself wondering how far the ink stretched, what might be etched across his chest...

"She knocked me onto my arse," Rey was saying. "Most competent thing she's done since joining us."

Silla's fingers twitched. "Wish I could do it again."

"Try it."

The man had discovered her weakness—Silla's inability to back down from a challenge. But she was still unsure how she'd managed to send him sprawling. After running it over in her mind, the only explanation she could draw was that she'd caught him off guard.

"Very well, *Reynir*," said Silla, her smile spreading at his scowl. "I shall try my luck."

"Do not call me Reynir," he said slowly.

"Don't call me Sunshine."

They locked eyes, and it was impossible to look away—dark brown with fiery sparks of gold.

Hekla cleared her throat. "All right, you two. On with it."

Rey stepped behind Silla, and she swallowed hard. The man was at least a head taller than her, and when the muscles of his chest and stomach pressed into her back, there was no doubt a powerful warrior stood behind her. And gods, but he was like a brazier—hot, even through the layers of clothing.

Rey's arm slid around her neck, then squeezed. The size of his arm and the pressure on her neck triggered something within her. Time stumbled, and Silla was back on the road near Skarstad, an arm wrapped around her neck as she gasped for air.

The queen will not kill you. Not right away, that is.

Panic clawed up her throat, her heart careening wildly. An animalistic sound ripped from deep within, and Silla's nails sank into flesh and pulled.

With a vicious curse, Rey released her, and Silla crumpled to her knees.

Not him.

Not there.

You're safe.

Silla repeated these thoughts to herself over and over, sucking in desperate breaths.

"Are you all right, *dúlla*?" came Hekla's soft voice.

Silla nodded, clambering to her feet. The throb in her skull was a loud and deafening drumbeat.

Rey rubbed red gashes that ran along his right forearm. The spark in his eyes had built to an inferno. "Only a coward fights like that."

"I cannot do this," Silla choked. And then, she ran into the woods.

FORTY-TWO

er back resting against the trunk of a rowan tree, Silla stared at the small bird. Its gleaming black wings were speckled with iridescent greens and purples, and it rooted through the moss with admirable determination. With a sigh, she tilted her head up to the forest canopy, grip tightening around her dagger. She had been careful not to run far from camp—laughter from the campfire carried through the trees—yet still, the threat of danger loomed in these woods.

The raw ache permeated her body. She hated her father. Loved her father. Missed him so deeply it physically hurt.

Silla didn't know who she was anymore. A liar. A dreamer. Foolishly trusting. Hopelessly naive.

The crunch of leaves sent the black bird aflight and alerted Silla to Hekla's approach. As her friend pressed through the trees, a strange combination of embarrassment and gratitude mingled in her stomach. Hekla wordlessly sank down beside her, offering her a flask. Accepting, Silla tipped her head back, the brennsa scouring a path down her throat.

"We were meant to do this together," said Silla quietly. "Travel to Kopa."

"Your father?" asked Hekla.

Silla nodded, passing the flask back. *Do not spoil your story*, she reminded herself, a tide of self-loathing rising within her. She tired of her enslavement to these lies, of deceiving others—especially Hekla. But Silla was stuck; she had no choice but to continue this act.

"He wished to travel the Road of Bones with me," said Silla wearily. "He had done it as a young man and wished to see its beauty once more."

Hekla brought the flask to her lips.

Silla sighed. "It is troubling to discover how swiftly a life can shatter."

"It can happen damned quickly," replied Hekla, raising her metal arm.

Silla winced. "My apologies, Hekla. I do not mean to be heartless."

"You are anything but heartless, dúlla. It is normal to feel out of control sometimes. It is human."

Silla was silent a moment, pondering her friend's words. "When the men attacked, I was squeezed so tightly around the neck I could not breathe. And when Rey did that, it felt as though I was back on the road. I thought I had healed from it. My bruises have faded, but it seems I have wounds that cannot be seen."

"Do not let Rey trouble your thoughts," said Hekla softly. "He will be fine, though I warrant he'll be ill-tempered for a time. You clawed him like a wild lynx." She chuckled.

Silla pressed her lips together.

"The wounds inside will take time to heal, dúlla. But I promise you—in time, the ache becomes less sharp. The memories, less provoking. You are strong and brave and will conquer this. I know it."

"Brave? Me?" Silla brushed a tear from her cheek.

"You do not avoid what happened to you. You face it head-on. And look— you are living your father's dream. He would be proud of you."

Gods, Silla wished she could see her father once more, despite the lies, despite the anger, and unanswered questions. What would he say if he could see her traveling to Kopa without him—learning knife-craft, riding a horse, drinking brennsa, and staring down warriors twice her size?

"I needed to hear that, Hekla. Thank you for your words."

They sat in silence for a while, and then Hekla stood. "Will you return to camp?"

Silla shook her head. "I would like some quiet. Do you think it is safe for me?"

Hekla surveyed the woods. "We've seen no sign of creatures for days. Listen closely for any strange sounds, and keep your dagger drawn. If you call out, we will hear you."

Sauntering off, Hekla left Silla in solitude. While normally she embraced a certain amount of silence, the ability to hear her thoughts so clearly now hurt.

Leaves. Feel better. Lose yourself.

Her hand moved absently to the vial, then quickly away. Ever since she'd read the passage in *Herbs of Íseldur*, her emotions had swirled. Her blood cried out for the leaves—to feel buoyant, lightened, unburdened. To feel as though she was not held together by string.

But resistance grew within her. Rey had shown her the truth—the leaves were dangerous, and she was stuck on a shadowy road leading to utter darkness.

Silla wanted off the road.

Her hand rose, unbidden, to the vial once more. Her temples felt squeezed, the drumming loud in her ears, and every part of her body screamed for her to take them.

You can quit anytime you'd like.

One leaf. You will stop at just one.

You do not hurt anyone by taking them.

It was amazing how easily the excuses flowed to her, how effortlessly she could justify them. After an entire evening of holding them off, of steadfast resilience, she was weary. And her strength turned to ash before her eyes.

Unstoppering the vial, she swiftly placed a leaf in her cheek.

Sighing, Silla tilted her head up to the forest canopy. The tension in her body eased at the decision having been made, but the burn of guilt quickly replaced it.

She was stuck.

Foolish.

Weak.

As the leaf dissolved in her cheek, the throbbing in her skull loosened.

"You can try again tomorrow," the little blonde girl said softly. Silla stared at the girl, at her upturned eyes and messy blonde hair. She'd plucked a rowan leaf and began to peel each leaflet off.

"You are a comfort and a curse," Silla murmured. She tried not to think about the girl. About the lies. About her dependence. "And you are not real."

"I'm as real as you choose," said the girl.

"Why you?" whispered Silla. "Why of all the visions I might have, do I see a small girl?"

"Perhaps you are trying to remember something," said the little girl, scrunching the leaf in her hand.

"Remember what?" asked Silla. "Has this to do with the dream?" The dream of the blonde girl, ripped from her arms, over and over and over.

"You left me," said the little blonde girl, her face growing sad. But the sadness soon sharpened to fear. "You must keep vigilant, Silla. Do not let him get too close. You are too trusting."

Silla's brows furrowed at the veiled warning. She opened her mouth to ask of whom the girl spoke, but just then, the leaves rustled once more. Hand tightening around her dagger, Silla exhaled when Jonas emerged from the trees. A fur cloak was draped around his shoulders, his hair damp and freshly braided. Silla's eyes fell to the blanket tucked under his arm as he approached.

"Hi," he said, smirking. The dim light in the clearing could not hide the intensity of his gaze as he strolled toward her.

Silla's eyes darted to where the little girl had stood moments before, exhaling when she found no trace of her. "Hi," she said with a small smile.

Silla's body hummed in anticipation as he settled to the ground beside her, his thigh brushing against hers. Sliding an arm around her shoulder, Jonas drew her closer. With a sigh, she leaned into him, the carefully contrived control she'd sustained around him all day falling away now that they were at last alone.

"Was that the signal?"

She lifted her head and looked at him quizzically. "What?"

Jonas's hand worked the fastenings of her overdress loose, and it fell to her hips. "We did not settle on a signal. I thought perhaps clawing Rey's arm like a wild cat might be the signal to meet in the woods."

A sharp laugh escaped her. "We could make it the signal. Though I don't believe Rey would much like that."

He dragged the underdress off of her shoulders, then urged her to lift her hips so he could pull both her under and overdress free with one strong tug.

"Claw up anyone then," murmured Jonas, his lips finding the curve where her neck met shoulder. "Claw marks on anyone's arms, and I shall retreat to the woods immediately."

Her head tilted back, a sigh of pleasure escaping her. "Hekla caught me sneaking back into the room last night. She's tried to pull details from me all day."

"Ilías as well." Jonas tugged her undergarments off, his rough palms sliding over her breasts before he lowered his head and traced them with his tongue.

She gasped at the scrape of his teeth. "I heard."

Jonas withdrew, and her body protested his absence. But it was only to smooth the blanket along the ground. He stretched out on his back, and Silla admired his beautiful shape—broad chest and shoulders, well-muscled thighs, hands that could bring either pleasure or violence. She shivered. It was a warrior's body, and it was hers to play with.

He pulled his tunic off, reclining on the blanket. A delicious tendril of warmth curved in her belly as she crawled over him. This was what she needed —a distraction, to forget, to lose herself for a few brief moments.

"No howling, Wolf," she murmured. Slanting her mouth against his, Silla's hand slid along his bare chest, slipping into his breeches and encircling his hard shaft. She drew back to watch his face as she stroked him slowly, fascinated as his pupils widened with need. Blood humming languorously, Silla felt herself floating away from it all.

Jonas's hands slid under her jaw, cupping her reverently. As her eyes met his, she was unable to look away.

"You're unexpected," whispered Jonas with surprising tenderness. He frowned, growing silent. "Do you wish to speak of it? Whatever it is that troubles you?"

"No," she said, irritated at the reminder. "I tire of thinking of it. Make me forget."

"That I can do." A smile curved his lips, and he rolled her onto her back. "You will see the stars in the skies above you, Curls. And then, I'll make you see more." As he pressed his lips to the sensitive place just below her ear, a shaky sigh escaped her.

She was struck with a sudden moment of clarity—his mouth on her skin was just like the leaves, easing her grief and dulling her anger. Silla wasn't sure what to think of this discovery.

And then, she could not think at all.

FORTY-THREE

Reclined in the soft furs in her corner of the wagon, Silla breathed deeply, tasting salt on her tongue. After Hver, the Road of Bones had sloped downward, traveling beside an expansive black sand beach. It was nice to have something besides the woods to look at—gulls smashing shells on clusters of black rocks; dragon-prowed ships sailing north in the distance; the hypnotic churn of the ocean.

With a small smile, she turned back to her book. Silla had moved on from *Herbs of Íseldur*—though her mind circled back frequently—and had now begun to read through *A Brief History of Íseldur*. She'd quickly realized this was not the sort of history book she'd been shown in school.

"Quite an odd book indeed," agreed the little blonde girl, peering over her shoulder.

There was no talk of the mighty Urkan Sea Kings; no mention of the liberation of Sunnavík by Ivar Ironheart and his berserker warriors; no mention of his brutal blood eagling of the oppressive King Kjartan Volsik, nor his slaying of Queen Svalla and Princess Eisa. There was also no mention of Saga Volsik, raised in Askaborg Castle with the honor of a betrothal to Prince Bjorn. They were strange, these absences, as they were facts learned by all children in Íseldur.

Instead, this book focused entirely on the history of Íseldur, prior to King Ivar's arrival, and Silla drank up the details voraciously. The Volsiks had ruled Íseldur for hundreds of years, the crown passing down through bloodlines, regardless of if a son or daughter bore the blood. As it happened, it was Queen Svalla who came from the Volsik line, with King Kjartan marrying in.

"I like that far more than the Urkan monarchy," murmured the little blonde girl.

Silla had to agree. The Urkan crown passed solely through their sons—one son to raid abroad and seize new lands for the Urkan line and one son to inherit the throne from his father.

Flipping the pages, she examined the illustrations of the royal families of Íseldur for the last several hundred years. While not exquisitely detailed, the images were astounding to examine.

"You'd look a sight in that," teased the little blonde girl, pointing to a drawing of a woman wearing the unfortunate combination of voluminous sleeves and tight cuffs.

"I suppose this was the look favored a hundred years ago," whispered Silla, brows furrowed.

She sighed, closing the book. Her head felt squeezed, like it could not absorb any more information. Most likely because it was still stuck on page 233 of *Herbs of Íseldur.* She'd read that book from cover to cover and then back again. But page 233 was the one dominating her attention—she'd memorized each word on the page, trying to glean new meaning from them. She spent the most time on the passage that caused the hair on her arms to stand on end:

Ending treatment can lead to symptoms such as headaches, shaking, fever, nausea, a racing heart, and loss of consciousness.

She blew out a long breath. None of it sounded pleasant.

The night prior had proven it would not be so simple to stop taking the leaves. With the flow of excuses and the leaves readily available, Silla would crumble faster than stale barley cakes. She needed someone to help her. Someone who would keep her accountable. Someone who would not let her relent.

But the thought of sharing this part of herself was too much. It felt too raw. Too shameful.

Silla ran her palms together as she stared at the frothing seas. Though surrounded by the Bloodaxe Crew, she felt utterly alone.

"You can do it on your own," said the little blonde girl. "Try harder, and you'll succeed." Silla found herself nodding in agreement.

And so, she tried to quit the leaves that night. She tried the next night and the one after that. But the urges were far louder and more compelling than the voice within her.

And time after time, she gave into their pull.

———

REY CLOSED the book with a ragged exhale. His temples throbbed, tension thick in his body. Earlier, he'd helped Hekla with training. That had expelled some of his energy, but still, he felt the need to move. Staring into the crackling flames, he lost himself in thought. He'd picked through the details in the books like a wolf on a corpse's bones. Nowhere was there mention of pulsing mist, nor was there any description of it cloaking creatures. While it did occasionally accompany the draugur, as Kraki had mentioned, it did not conceal them entirely.

Were the witnesses in Istré unreliable, as Magnus had suspected? Or was this foe altogether new?

Rey had taken control of the Bloodaxe Crew when he was twenty-three—three winters past—and never had he had a feeling like this about a job. The pulsing mist, the claw marks, and the blood—there was something in these details pulling at him, like a memory he couldn't quite reach. It was maddening. They needed to understand this enemy, or else they might walk straight to their doom. Gritting his teeth, Rey rubbed his forehead, trying to clear his head so he could think properly.

Laughter from across the fire drew his attention, and he found his eyes tracing the curls tumbling midway down her spine. "You cheat, Ilías!" she exclaimed. There was no malice in her voice, just pure amusement.

The woman had extorted him. The thought alone was enough to make Rey's hand curl into a fist, the embers of his rage to crackle and spark. She had forced him to take her to Kopa, and for that, he should despise her, should ignore her, should make her so miserable she'd run off for good. And yet, he could not.

He could not seem to leave the woman to her own self-destruction.

Rey's jaw clenched even tighter. Though she hadn't mentioned the book he'd stolen for her, he was certain she'd read the section on skjöld leaves. Her hand moved more frequently to the vial tethered around her neck, as though the leaves weighed heavily on her mind. He should have minded his own business, but he'd been compelled to show her the truth. Though he was no fan of the woman, no one should suffer the same fate as Kristjan. And she seemed not to understand the danger of what she took. At the very least, she should know the truth.

She laughed again, the sound stirring something in Rey's blood. His brows snapped together and he forced his gaze into the fire.

Istré, he urged himself, trying to refocus. He needed to think of Istré. Of seeking another opinion on the mist before they got themselves into the thick of it. *Harpa might know.* The thought made his chest burn. *No more side trips,* he vowed.

"Stop, Ilías!" she burst out once more. "Sigrún and I shall not play again with you unless you show us your commitment to honesty. What do you think, Sigrún? What would prove to us that Ilías the Cunning is serious?" She made some slow, basic hand gestures as she talked, Sigrún correcting her form.

Ilías placed a hand on his chest. "I swear on Hábrók's arse that I will not cheat."

"We'll need more than that from you," she said. "A lock from your beard would certainly show your commitment."

Ilías's face contorted in genuine horror. "Surely not, Hammer! You ask too much." He paused in thought. "I'll tell you what I'll do. I shall run naked through the camp to prove my commitment."

If we wanted to see a shortsword, I have one in my scabbard, signed Sigrún.

Ilías choked.

"I missed that, can you translate, Cunning?" asked the woman.

"No!" exclaimed Ilías. "And I'll have you know, it is most certainly a *longsword*."

At that, she dissolved into a fit of laughter.

Rey tried to gather his wandering thoughts. Mist. Claw marks. Draugur... possibly. And that strange incident with the skógungar. That smell, the glowing eyes. And it had ventured so far from the Western Woods. Something was...

Laughter rang through the air. *Her's.* She'd tossed her head back, the curls bouncing with her full-bodied laugh. She laughed as though she was free, warming something in his chest.

Rey scowled, forcing the warmth away. With a rush of anger, he pushed to his feet.

"Where are you going, Axe Eyes?" asked Ilías. She turned and watched him.

Rey bit down on the inside of his cheek. He had more to accomplish on this trip than mere games of dice, and besides that, had restless energy to expel. "Walk. I need to think. I cannot hear my thoughts with all this noise."

He leveled *her* with a hard look, but she did not so much as flinch. Of course she didn't.

And with a growl of irritation, he stormed off into the forest.

FORTY-FOUR

Silla hummed, the empty bucket in her hand swinging wildly as she passed Hekla and Ilías driving spears into the ground to set up the windbreak for the night. Sigrún sent Silla a knowing smile from where she sat with Gunnar, plucking feathers from the grouse. Returning the woman's smile, a flush crept up her neck. Sigrún was the only one who knew about Silla and Jonas. She'd silently handed Silla a small pouch of crushed leaves after Longest Day, using slow hand gestures she repeated several times.

"One spoon?" Silla had whispered. She was gradually starting to pick up on some of Sigrún's hand language, mostly basic words. Ilías, of course, had ensured that Silla learned all the cursing gestures.

Sigrún had nodded, a sly smile creeping across her face.

"My thanks," Silla had whispered, making the hand gesture as she spoke.

Now that Sigrún did not need to worry about the cooking, she was freed up to prowl the woods with her bow and arrow, and Silla had seen her smiling more often than naught. It seemed Sigrún enjoyed the solitude of her excursions into the woods; it was not uncommon for her to vanish for long hours, reappearing well past dark with the next night's evening meal.

And the night prior, Sigrún had returned with four grouse.

Four. Silla smiled. They'd eat like royalty.

Her eyes fell upon the broad-shouldered warrior who dug out a fire pit, his blond braid swinging behind him as he worked. Jonas paused to wipe the sweat from his brow, sending Silla a dark look.

The night prior, while Jonas had been on watch duty, they'd waited until the Crew had fallen asleep, then had snuck into the woods. Twice, she'd seen stars, twice his name had fallen from her lips in desperate whispers, and each time, she grew more insatiable. Jonas was the perfect distraction. Silla grew to crave him during the day, her body's ache a reminder of what they'd done the night prior. Thoughts of her father, of the leaves, of her guilt and fear and sadness, were all pushed aside by sordid memories of him—the slide of his bare skin against hers, the wicked things he'd muttered in her ear.

Silla Margrét, she scolded herself as she pushed into the pinewoods at the edge of the glade. *Evening meal. Focus, bjáni.* She wound her way between tree trunks, the sound of rushing water intensifying as she crested a hill. A bank cut steeply down to the stream, and Silla grabbed onto branches and roots to ease herself downward.

Her feet skidded from under her, the bucket tumbling down the hill. Hands and feet digging in to stop her slide down the slope, pain sliced through her palm. Thankfully, her body stopped a foot from the water.

She exhaled sharply, relieved she had not ended up drenched, but annoyed she'd skinned her hand. Inching toward the water, she dipped her hand in and rinsed away the dirt. She frowned at the red and raw skin as she lifted it from the water.

"Fortunate it is my left," she mused. She'd still be able to butcher the grouse, chop the vegetables and all the rest of it.

Then she felt it.

The skin on the back of her neck prickled, the rush of the stream growing boisterously loud. The tug in her stomach was a feeling she now recognized— danger was near.

Silla unsheathed her dagger, her gaze dragging from the water to stare up into familiar bone-chilling eyes.

Vampire deer.

Eyes like burning coals blinked at her, the creature baring its dagger-sharp teeth. This one towered—well over six feet tall, its antlers gleaming red at the jagged points.

Faster than lightning and ghostly silent, the deer sprang. Driven by pure instinct, Silla raised her left arm to block, swinging her right up with a choked cry. The thought to aim for its neck materialized from the back of her mind, and her body responded, angling the dagger to the right. It slid home, right into the deer's neck.

Light exploded in her vision, dissolving quickly as teeth snapped inches from her face. Silla grunted under the crushing weight of the deer. She couldn't breathe, but it did not matter. All that mattered was keeping those teeth away from her. Her left hand found purchase beneath the creature's jaw, and she used every ounce of her strength to push it away.

The deer let out a guttural noise, bucking and thrashing. Silla tried to pull the dagger free, but it was stuck, the momentum of the deer having impaled it deep into its neck. Her muscles strained, threatening to give way, but she gritted her teeth and dug deeper, searching for that last kernel of strength.

She was running on pure battle thrill now, sticky warmth oozing down her right hand and dripping onto her face. Yet a quiet confidence filled her as the deer's movements weakened.

She wasn't going to die today.

She had to hold on just a bit longer.

She was not going to die.

After a small eternity, the deer's movements faded to twitches and spasms. Silla squirmed out from beneath it, her exhausted muscles finally unclenching. Collapsing on the bank, her lungs filled with sweet, blessed air. She was numb, her limbs tingling distantly, and she could not look at the enormous form beside her.

Through her exhaustion, a swell of victory expanded in her chest. She'd done it! She had killed a vampire deer.

But then she heard it. A snap from across the stream. Slowly, Silla turned.

Two more burning red orbs blinked at her.

They run in herds, Silla thought, panic gripping her by the throat. Her dagger—it was buried in the corpse beside her. Curling in on herself with a whimper, she braced for impact.

An impact that never arrived.

A soft thud preceded a wet hiss which had Silla sitting up. The deer lay across the stream, the hilt of a hevrít protruding from its eye.

Gravel skidded behind her.

"I'll admit you've surprised me, Sunshine. Perhaps there is hope for you yet."

She could not suppress the grin spreading across her face as she turned to

Rey. Watching her with stern eyes, he rubbed the back of his neck. He nudged the deer with his boot, its head wobbling back.

"It is a large one you've felled."

Though she was not cold, Silla began to shake with full-body tremors. Rey disappeared downstream, returning with the discarded bucket and sinking onto the dry riverbed beside her. It felt like a lifetime had passed since she'd first descended the bank.

"It is the battle thrill," said Rey. His deep voice was unexpectedly soft. "It gives one extra strength, but when it wears off, the body can be left empty and shaking."

She let him take her trembling hand in his, dipping it into the bucket and rubbing the blood clean from it. As his palm slid along her own, the vibrations in her body seemed to calm.

She felt unexpectedly safe.

It made no sense, of course. The man had tried to kill her twice, did not want her near his Crew. But all the same, Silla found herself watching Rey's precise movements as he cleaned the blood from her hands.

Eventually, Rey rose, refreshing the water and then sinking onto his knees. A soft ripping sound filled the air, his face level with hers. She looked into his eyes, trying to count the golden embers as he began to clean her face.

He hates you, she reminded herself.

But with each gentle swipe of cool, damp fabric across her cheeks, her trust in him seemed only to grow. At last, his large body eased to the ground beside her. Dazed, Silla's teeth clattered together, and she stared into the rushing waters of the stream.

"Open your mouth," said Rey, and Silla obliged. A hard, round object was placed onto her tongue, and as she crunched it between her teeth, her eyes widened.

"Hazelnuts?" she asked.

"They can help replenish you," he said. "I'm afraid you'll need fresh clothes. Shall I fetch Hekla?"

"No!" she said, the loudness of her voice startling her. She cleared her throat. "Please. Let us sit, just for a moment."

They sat in silence, and to Silla's surprise, it was neither awkward nor heavy. Instead, it was a restful silence, peaceful and restorative. Gradually, the shaking subsided, and Silla's senses returned to her. The enormity of what had just happened sunk into her. She had killed a vampire deer, had nearly been killed by a second one. Nearly. Which meant...

"You're an arse, you know that?"

Though his face was shadowed, she could sense his amusement. "I knew you had the strength to handle it alone."

His unfounded confidence in her was amusing. "But you were watching."

"I saw the deer nearby when I filled my waterskin a few minutes ago, and decided to see what you could do."

"How long was that—*thing*—there?"

"Five breaths or so," he replied. "You did not hesitate, and that I was glad to see. You wielded your blade with confidence. But there is always a lesson to be learned. What did you learn today?"

Silla bit her lip, staring at the stream. "To watch for other deer?"

"True, but more so than that, you must always retrieve your weapon. And to speak of that..." He grabbed the antlers of the deer, wrenching it over and yanking out the dagger. After running the blade through the stream, Rey dried it on his breeches and handed it back to Silla.

As he sat down, her lips parted a hair's breadth—Rey's sleeve was torn. Had he ripped his tunic to clean the blood from her face?

"How do you feel?" he asked.

Silla considered. "Strong. Like a warrior." Confidence bloomed in her stomach. She felt capable. It was the reminder she needed: she *could* do hard things.

He snorted. "I meant the shaking, but I am pleased to hear your confidence has grown. That is the most competent thing you've done so far. Knocking me on my arse comes second."

Silla smiled, and a thought crossed her mind. "Rey..."

"Yes?"

"Nothing." She shook her head. Her hand moved absently to the vial, but she forced herself to let go.

"Come, Sunshine. Tell me what troubles you."

She shook her head again. "I-I cannot."

"You can. And we shall not leave until you tell me. So get on with it."

She pressed her lips together, her pulse jumping wildly at the very thought of what she was considering. Could she? No.

"Out with it. I'm getting hungry, and there are grouse back at camp that we need to get to. And by we, I mean you."

"Let's go." She swatted him, but he grabbed her elbow, turning her to face him.

His gaze was intense, yet the usual sharpness was absent. "Ask me, Sunshine. I swear to you I won't be an arse."

She heard his unspoken words loud and clear. *You can trust me.*

Looking away, she focused on the swirling stream. Silla tried to remind herself of the heartless way this man had ended Anders and the assassin at Skalla Ridge. That he worked for the king, and she could not trust him.

But the knowing feeling in her stomach told her something else. It told her with this, perhaps Rey could be her ally. Rey, who had told her the truth about the leaves from the very start. Rey, who had lost a brother to them. He had not needed to share that with her. There had been earnestness there; real pain. Rey understood better than anyone else.

Silla was tired of the constant pull, of this deadweight wrapped around her neck, dragging her lower each day. She was tired of feeling tired, of being stuck in this endless loop. And Silla knew Rey was stubborn as the eternal fires and would not let this go.

Taking a deep breath, she pulled the necklace from around her neck and pressed the vial into his hands.

Thick black eyebrows rose as he noted what she'd given him.

"Can you hold this for me?" she asked quietly.

Rey nodded, his face softening the slightest bit. "Very well."

He said it so casually, as though she had not just peeled off a layer of her very being and handed it to him. As if she had not just admitted her most shameful secret.

"Do not—" she cleared her throat, straightening her spine. "I do not want it back."

"Understood." Rey slid it into his pocket, and she regretted it already, longed to snatch it back and tell him it was a joke. But it was too late for that, and she knew he'd never give it back to her, no matter what she said.

Silla had stepped off the cliff, the world whizzing past her, and though she looked for a branch to grab, there were none to be found. There would be no turning back. It was time for her to fly.

Or to fall flat onto her face.

Silla's throat bobbed, dread coiling in her gut. What might she face tonight, tomorrow, for who knew how many days?

One foot in front of the other.

That's how she would take things. That was how she'd always done it.

———

SILLA WAS sure the grouse had been delicious, but she could not recall its taste. Certainly, the Bloodaxe Crew had enjoyed it. They'd nearly licked their plates clean, complimenting her profusely, but Silla had simply nodded absently. She had gone through the motions the entire evening, her mind elsewhere—stuck on the vial in Rey's pocket. Her body screamed for the leaves, each thought in her head twisting back around to them.

What had she been thinking? It had been a moment of madness. She'd just been attacked—had nearly died. It was the shock. Surely Rey would understand —would hand the vial back to her when she asked.

No, she thought. *You gave it to him for that reason. He's a giant, stubborn arse. There is not a force that would compel him to return it to you.* Her hand moved to her chest, where the vial had hung. But there was no comfort to be found there now, only hollowness. A loss which felt as profound as the loss of her father in this moment.

Ten years having never missed a dose. Ten years of daily dread as she anticipated the headaches. Ten years of lies, lies, lies.

The pounding in her head came first. Starting as a dull throb, the intensity built incrementally until it was an exquisite drumbeat forcing her to lay her head in her hands. By the time she crawled under the furs that night, her brow was dotted with tiny beads of sweat, her body somehow simultaneously blistering hot and so cool she shivered.

All night, sleep eluded her. By morning, the sky swirled, and she was falling...falling into a terrifyingly deep, dark abyss, where there was nothing... nothing to grab to slow her plummet, to ease this plunge. It was dark and empty and hollow, like her, because Silla was nothing but a vessel...a vessel for those damned leaves...an empty thing filled with lies.

Sounds blended together. Silla tried to hone in on the murmured words around her, but they were slipping, sliding through her grasp.

Maybe you'll die.

The thought did not fill her with the dread she expected. It felt a lot like peace; like resting her feet.

Or maybe you'll be freed.

What would it feel like to be freed from the shackling headaches? Silla did not know, could not imagine a life without them. Without the leaves...

Leaves. Need.

She tried to push the thoughts aside, but more, more, more crashed into her, burying her beneath them.

This can all be over in a heartbeat.

One leaf would put an end to this misery.

Just one leaf.

Finally, sleep found her, as did the feverish dreams from which she could not wake.

FORTY-FIVE
HVER

S haking the fatigue from her body, Skraeda walked between the tables in the mead hall adjacent to the Wolf's Den Inn. One hand was plunged in her pocket, stroking the smooth contours of Ilka's braid, while the other clutched the broken shield with that mysterious red sigil painted upon it.

Thank the gods that Hver is not such a large place as Svarti, she thought. The towns along this stretch of the Road of Bones were all the same—small, enclosed by circular stockade walls, limited to one or two mead halls. *You won't be able to hide from me, girl.* A dark smile spread across her face.

The large warrior's failed attempt to end her had given Skraeda a gift—the element of surprise would be back on her side. But the end of the Road of Bones neared, and there the Northern Junction forked to Kunafjord in the east and Kopa in the west. If she picked the wrong way, the girl could slide through her fingers once more and vanish into either of those cities.

Though it was late afternoon, the crowd in the mead hall was sparse, giving Skraeda pause. *Longest Day*, she thought. *Has it passed already?* Time had grown shifty out on that ledge as she'd clawed herself away from death's grip.

Her gaze honed in on the barkeep, an older man drying a cup with a scrap of linen. Skraeda strode toward him, the man's hand pausing. Loops of fear writhed brightly from his aura, and she forced herself to soften her expression.

"My good man," she said, adding her soothing touch to dampen the man's fear. "I am in need of a knowing person who can help me identify the sigil on this shield." She hefted the thing up.

"A-Asger," he muttered, nodding down the long table. "You'll want Asger. He is knowledgeable in such things. Travels a lot, meets many people."

Skraeda turned, taking in the man in a green tunic hunched over a cup of ale. She sensed him out—anger and disgust and sadness twisting around him. The man was wallowing about something.

"My thanks," muttered Skraeda, ambling toward Asger. Hand clamped around his cup, he glowered at his ale. As Skraeda approached, he turned his scowl to her. "You are Asger?" she asked.

His brows lifted, gyrating filaments of surprise jostling away the ribbons of anger. He nodded.

"I am told you are the man who can help me identify the owner of this shield." She hefted the thing once more, eager to discard it for good.

"The Bloodaxe Crew," said the man, staring at the broken shield. "That's the Bloodaxe Crew's sigil."

The Bloodaxe Crew? thought Skraeda with surprise. She knew the name immediately—had heard tales of their deeds in her time spent in mead halls. Monster-hunting mercenaries. What would the girl be doing with the gods damned Bloodaxe Crew of all people? And why would they be taking her north? How had she convinced them?

She's cunning, thought Skraeda. *More cunning than you'd thought.*

"They were here," the man continued. Skraeda's gaze snapped to his warm brown eyes. Beneath them hung dark smudges—Asger nursed a hangover, it appeared.

"Tell me," she demanded, seating herself on the bench across from him. She tried to quell her emotions, but the need for vengeance blazed hotly through her. The barkeep set a cup of ale before Skraeda, and she handed the man a coin with a curt nod.

Asger eyed Skraeda warily, angst and surprise twisting from him in warm, wavering tendrils. "Why do you wish to know?" he asked.

Reaching out with her mind's touch, Skraeda soothed the man's angst, discovering a filament of anger writhing hotly nearby. With a twitch of her lips, she tugged gently on it.

"Vengeance," she said simply, watching as his anger only grew.

"Seems we may have something in common," said Asger.

Curiosity bristled through Skraeda, but Ilka's voice pleaded patience.

Wait for your rabbit, Skraeda.

Asger ran a hand through his hair, tousling it. "They were here for Longest Day celebrations. Stayed at The Wolf's Den. I recognized them at once." His hand twitched. "There was a woman with them."

Skraeda tried to keep the eagerness from her voice. "A woman?"

The man looked away, jealousy unspooling in wild loops. "Told me her name was Silla. That she was traveling to Kopa."

Kopa, thought Skraeda, exhilaration running through her. This was an unexpected bit of information that she'd long craved. The woman was headed to Kopa, and now Skraeda's search had narrowed just a bit more.

"This woman was with the Bloodaxe Crew?" she asked.

"Yes," he gritted out. "It was the Bloodaxe Crew. The blond one with the scar on his cheek was violent. I think they are lovers." The bitterness in his voice was plain to hear.

Busy, busy, thought Skraeda. Was this how she'd earned a ride with the Bloodaxe Crew? But Skraeda did not judge a woman without a chaperone for doing what she must to survive in this gods-forsaken kingdom. "And you are certain they are headed for Kopa?" she asked, strumming the man's jealousy.

He eyed her. "The *woman* was heading for Kopa. The Bloodaxe Crew, I do not know." He stared into his cup. "She...she seemed a nice person. I do not wish harm to befall her. But that blond warrior...I would not mind if someone were to make a mess of his pretty face."

Skraeda smiled. "That could be arranged," she said, standing and throwing a few sólas onto the table. "I thank you for your time."

Making her way back onto the streets of Hver, Skraeda breathed deeply. Her muscles ached, her head throbbing with fatigue, but she was elated. She now knew where the girl was headed *and* with whom she traveled. Skraeda vowed she would not rest until the woman was in her custody.

"Skraeda Clever Tongue," came a male voice from behind her.

Skraeda turned, her exhilaration quickly dissolving into irritation as she took in the Klaernar kaptein standing before her.

Smoothing the emotion from her face, Skraeda nodded. "Kaptein?"

The man smiled, the tattoos along his cheek pulling into a curve. "We've had a falcon from Sunnavík telling us you might be in the area." The kaptein reached into his bearskin cloak, retrieving a scroll and handing it to Skraeda. Puzzled, she unrolled it, her irritation blazing higher with each word she read.

Skraeda,

Go to Skutur and find Kommandor Laxa for further instructions. He now heads the search for our target.

Yours,

Queen Signe

Skraeda could feel the queen's displeasure with each letter scrawled onto the page. It was infuriatingly short. Abrupt. As though she had no time for additional words.

Her chest felt squeezed, her temples pounding.

Skraeda forced herself to focus. Skutur was in the direction she was heading, but Kommandor Laxa...who was this man?

You place a Klaernar above me, my queen? she thought, enraged. That was not how it worked. It was never how it worked. Anger stirred within her, heat flooding her palms. Gods, she wanted to set fire to the scroll, wanted to lash out and burn something...

Not here, Skraeda, she urged herself. *Not near the gods damned Klaernar.* She'd manage her anger in her own ways once they'd left her.

Sucking in a fortifying breath, Skraeda looked at the Klaernar kaptein.

"Very well," she said tightly. "My thanks."

Turning on her heel, Skraeda went to find her horse.

FORTY-SIX

THE ROAD OF BONES

J onas cursed under his breath as Silla let out a low moan from the back of the wagon. Another gray day, it felt all the more gloomy without her light shining upon him. For a full day and night, she'd been feverish, and with each hour which passed without her waking, his worry grew stronger.

"Did the deer bite her, Rey?" Hekla had inquired this morning, holding a cold cloth to Silla's burning forehead.

"No," he'd replied while sliding the blade of his hevrít along a whetstone. Most would think Rey unconcerned, but Jonas knew his headman well, had fought alongside him for years—he recognized a hint of worry in the line between his brows.

Rey had been quiet on the details of what had happened with the deer, simply that she'd 'handled herself'. But Silla had been uncharacteristically silent upon her return. Something had happened; Jonas was sure of it. What were the odds she was attacked by a vampire deer, then fell sick shortly after? It was suspicious, and the more he considered it, the more Jonas grew certain Rey knew what had happened.

He keeps things from you.

Jonas's stomach twisted at the thought, and his mood soured even further.

He will take her from you.

Jonas schooled his face into cool indifference as the thought materialized, reminding himself that she was nothing to him. What they had was fun. A distraction. He did not care.

Liar.

"Tell me about it again," Ilías said, startling Jonas from his thoughts. Warmth filled his chest, easing his tension. Ilías always knew the right thing to say to lift his spirits.

"Rolling fields of wheat and barley that glow golden in the setting sun. A longhouse made of sturdy oak. A handsome hearth with plenty of space for kin to gather. We will expand the house so that we can each have our own private quarters." Jonas felt lighter already. "Your quarters will be on the opposite end of the home from mine, brother, so I won't have to suffer your complaints of any loud guests I have." His growing smile faltered, as a new thought emerged.

And for the first time in his life, Jonas allowed himself to imagine a life with a companion—a curly-haired woman sitting beside him at the long table. Silla, humming as she stirred a pot over the hearthfire, the smells of her cooking filling their home. Silla, tossing handfuls of barley for a flock of chickens.

He could give her chickens.

His eyes fell to the tangle of curls peeking out from beneath a mound of furs, and a wave of panic filled him. What if she didn't wake up? Jonas's stomach twisted and knotted itself as he clutched the reins.

"Do you ever..." Ilías's voice dropped off, drawing Jonas from his despair.

"Ever what?" prompted Jonas, his gaze hardening back on the wagon.

"Do you ever think that perhaps our past is not our future?"

Jonas's brows furrowed as he turned over his brother's words in his mind. "No," he said, with absolute certainty. His hand found the talisman around his neck. "Family, respect, duty. Nothing is more important than restoring honor to our bloodline, Ilías. *Nothing.*"

Ilías nodded silently, chewing on his lip as he stared blankly ahead.

"What is this about, Ilías?" asked Jonas sternly.

"I enjoy traveling with the Bloodaxe Crew. After all we've seen, it is hard to imagine a life on a farmstead as fulfilling."

The knots in Jonas's stomach turned to coiling eels. "It won't be for a few years yet, brother," said Jonas. His voice sounded tight, even to himself. "You'll tire of the road soon enough. And when you see the farmstead, you will remember it all. You will love the peace. The stillness."

"Perhaps you're right," said Ilías with a sigh. "The first thing I'll do is build the finest bed. Top it with a mattress stuffed with wool and feathers. Drink myself stupid, then sleep for a week straight."

Jonas chuckled.

"What do you think's wrong with Hammer?" asked Ilías. "Could not be the food as we all ate it. Perhaps a wolfspider youngling's bite?" He was silent a moment. "She'd best wake up soon. Siggie's cooking tastes like rusted nails."

Jonas pinned his brother with a murderous look. "Don't be an arse, Il. The girl burns with fever, and all you can think of is your damned daymeal?"

Ilías sent him a pointed look. "It was a joke, Jonas. Learn how to take one."

"I know how to take a joke. Learn how to tell one."

"Malla's tits, Jonas. What's crawled up your arse today?"

Jonas just scowled.

Ilías exhaled dramatically. "Of course I wish Hammer Hand a swift recovery. I like her. She's amusing. Even Axe Eyes begins to warm to her." He snorted. "Did you see him at the evening meal last night? I swear to the gods, he nearly *smiled*. He was proud of her for killing that beast."

Jonas's spine stiffened.

The sound of hoofbeats thankfully stifled the sharp words gathering on his tongue. Jonas looked over his shoulder to see two riders driving their horses hard along the road.

Curiosity prickled his skin as the riders gained on the Bloodaxe Crew. *What has them in such a rush?* he wondered.

The riders slowed as they brought their horses up beside the Crew, and Jonas took them in—an older man, perhaps in his fourth decade, and a younger one with a paltry beard.

"Hae," said the older man. His face was lined with tension and fatigue. "Best you make haste."

Rey slowed Horse, the wagon bumping to a stop. "What is it?"

"The Slátrari has claimed two more victims on the road."

"When?" asked Rey sharply.

A shudder rolled through the man. "Discovered this morning south of us. Burned so badly they could not be recognized by their own kin."

"Fuck," muttered Ilías, frowning. "Now that's not a way I'd choose to meet my end."

"Aye," said the man, kicking his horse. "We'll be off if you don't mind. Keep safe."

"Same to you," Ilías called out.

The men quickly vanished from sight. Jonas watched Sigrún riding ahead of them, her hand stroking the burn scars along the side of her neck and skull. Never had she explained the origin of her scars, and for the first time in many years, Jonas found himself pondering the agony she must have felt, not just during, but long afterward. Perhaps in a way, the Slátrari did his victims a kindness by ending them.

But as his gaze fell on the curly-haired woman lying sick in the wagon, fear twisted inside him anew, pushing all thoughts of the murderer away.

·FORTY-SEVEN

The dreams had no ending and no beginning, blending into an unending torment from which Silla could not wake.

Her father lay on the road near Skarstad, blood oozing from a dozen stab wounds. Breaths rasping, he beckoned her closer.

I loved you like my own kin.

Who were my blood parents? she asked, lowering her ear near to his lips. Mouth moving, his whispers reached her ears, yet she could never grasp the names, could never know the truth Matthias had withheld from her for all these years.

A thick haze descended upon her, and when it dissolved, the dream had shifted.

Smoke stung her nostrils and ash choked her throat. Exceptionally warm, she looked down to see black tendrils pouring from her palms, embers hissing and snapping brightly within the darkness. Silla held her arms in front of her, tingling with delight as the smoke pulled free from her hands, twisting upward into a column of churning shadows.

A sound diverted her attention—a man, secured to a pillar, pleas spilling from his lips. She was filled with an intense feeling of righteousness. Of justice. The smoke dove down his throat, the scent of burning hair and roasted flesh meeting her nose.

The man screamed.

And Silla smiled.

Dream shifting, the little blonde girl coalesced before her eyes. It was the same as always: footfalls bouncing off the walls, growing louder as the men neared their hiding place.

"Listen to me, sister," said the little blonde girl.

Sister? thought Silla, heart pounding.

The girl ran a hand along her cheek, drawing Silla's attention back to her blue eyes with that familiar, elegant tilt.

"What will happen when I stop taking the leaves?" asked Silla, trepidation filling her.

"This may be the last time you see me," whispered the girl.

A tide of sadness rose within Silla. The girl had become the only constant in her life throughout everything. "I will miss you," Silla said quietly. "Though perhaps that is strange."

"Try to remember me, won't you?" said the little blonde girl.

"How could I forget?" asked Silla as the door burst open, men pouring into the room.

Like always, the girl was pulled from her arms, her hand yanked free from Silla's. An ear-piercing scream of anguish filled the air, making goosebumps prick Silla's flesh.

Silla stared into the girl's blue eyes and tried to memorize them. Hands wrapped around her own waist, yanking her backward. The girl's face was serene as she was pulled away. "Come and find me, sister. I *need* you."

Shock washed over Silla—all her life, the girl had said the same thing: *don't leave me.*

Come and find me.

It was a challenge.

It was a message.

"I will," whispered Silla.

WHEN SHE AWOKE, Silla was certain of two things.

One—the girl *was* her sister. And two—her sister was alive, somewhere in the Kingdom of Íseldur.

She sat up, her head throbbing. It was dark, a faint flicker of light dancing on the walls beside her. Walls? Groping around, Silla felt the soft muss of furs beneath her, the scratch of a woolen wall.

A tent. Silla was in a tent.

Just then, the tent flaps pushed open, a shadowy form entering.

"You've awakened!" shrieked Hekla, making Silla jump. Hekla ducked her head out of the tent and called out, "Hammer's awake!"

"How long was I asleep?" asked Silla, her voice raspy.

In a sudden rush, she remembered—the leaves. She had done it. She'd made it through the sickness that came with ending treatment. A disbelieving smile spread across her face.

"Two days."

Silla's mouth dropped open. "Two days?"

"Yes, dúlla. Eternal fucking fires, you've been ill. Ilías thinks it was a youngling wolfspider's bite, but we could not find any markings. Gunnar believes you reacted to something you ate. Of course, they've placed wagers on it. Kuntas."

Silla blinked. Rey had not told the Bloodaxe Crew of her dependence on the skjöld leaves. She wasn't sure what to make of it.

"Have you any water?" she croaked.

Hekla rummaged around, then pressed a waterskin into her hand. Silla swallowed greedily, water dripping down her chin and onto her dress. She did not care; her body was so parched she felt shriveled.

Hekla watched her. "How do you feel? Would you like some broth? We have soup by the fire. Siggie prepared it." Silla could hear the warning in Hekla's words.

Her body felt weak yet strangely alive. "Yes *please* to broth. But..." her voice trailed off. "The tent? Why am I in a tent?"

"Weather has turned brisk. We've had frost and a cold northern wind the past few days. We near the Highlands now, and Rey ordered the tents dug out. More work, but the warmth is well worth it."

Silla found her cloak lying beside her bed. Her bed? She was lying on *someone's* bed.

"Whose bed am I—" but the familiar scent hit her nostrils.

"Jonas. I suppose the Wolf has a heart after all." Hekla cackled, and Silla was grateful the darkness concealed her blush.

Silla groped until she found her boots. Pulling them on, she then fastened her cloak around her shoulders and followed Hekla through the tent flaps.

Though the sun had set, the campfire lit the clearing in which they'd made camp. Spindly trees and robust bushes provided little cover from the icy wind, which carried a grassy scent. As Silla stood, her vision swam, and Hekla eased an arm around her waist, helping her behind a thicket so she could relieve herself.

As they made their way to the fire, Silla's chest felt full to bursting. They were all there; the whole Bloodaxe Crew reclined lazily around a crackling fire. Her eyes flew to Jonas first—his shoulders wrapped in a black fur cloak, hair freshly shorn on the sides. Sitting with Ilías and Gunnar in the midst of a game of dice, Jonas's head swung around, eyes locking with Silla's. His jaw shifted slightly, his tight posture easing just a bit.

"Hammer!" boomed Gunnar, clapping loudly as Hekla eased Silla onto a log near the fire. "Like a cat with nine lives. What is this...three lives used up on this journey? You'd best start rationing."

Silla threw him a wry smile, but her gaze quickly found Rey. Seated near the fire, Hekla's prosthetic arm was pinned between his knees as he dragged a whetstone along the claws. And as their eyes met, the corners of his lips twitched. It was not a smile, but it was as close as it got with him. Contrary to the irritation she typically felt from Rey, she sensed something else now—pride, perhaps, and the same strange, unsubstantiated confidence in her he'd shown when she'd killed the vampire deer. It filled her with unexpected warmth.

Sigrún passed her a bowl of broth, a spoon, and a knob of bread, and Silla dug in, suddenly ravenous. As she chewed, Hekla told her of the past two days, including that two men had overtaken them, fleeing from the Slátrari. A shudder passed through Silla at that. To think that this murderer shared the road with them...to think they might have passed them, might have looked upon the monster's face without even realizing it.

But looking around the fire, she couldn't help but feel comforted. If she was to share the road with a murderer, she was certain there was no place safer for her to be than amongst the warriors of the Bloodaxe Crew.

———

"ARE you certain you wish to practice tonight, dúlla?"

Silla nodded vehemently. A full day had passed since she'd awoken from her fevers, and though her strength had not fully returned, she was filled with a restless energy. This morning when Silla had awoken, her head was clearer than she could ever recall, her mood so bright and steps so lively, she was like a more vivid version of herself.

When she'd handed Rey his heaping bowl of porridge this morning with a bright smile, he'd grumbled about it being 'too early for one to be so offensively happy.' She'd snorted. There was far less venom in his words these days.

The trees surrounding their camp were clustered in copses, thorny brambles filling the gaps. Tomorrow they'd reach the highlands, which marked the last stretch of the Road of Bones before reaching the Northern Junction. Kopa had never felt more within reach.

Now that the dishes were washed and stowed away and the evening stretched ahead of her, the cravings were gathering momentum. *Focus, Silla Margrét,* she told herself. *There is only one way forward, and that does not include those leaves.*

Words alone were not enough, however. She needed a distraction. Silla wanted to pull Jonas behind the brambles surrounding their camp and have him distract her from these yearnings, but he was nowhere to be found. Instead, she channeled herself into training with Hekla. And Rey, apparently, who sauntered toward them.

Silla could not suppress her groan.

"Do not go thinking highly of yourself, now that you've felled one little vampire deer," he drawled.

Silla put a hand on her hip. "And *you*, Rey. Don't forget I took you down, as well."

Rey scrubbed his black beard. "I'm certain you won't let me forget."

"Someone must ensure you do not think too highly of yourself either, Rey." She smiled, pleased at the way his black brows shot down. Silla decided she'd relish in reminding him often. "For your safety, of course. It is said that a man with excess pride grows blind to death at his door."

Rey's eyes bored into her, and she forced herself to hold his gaze. "Your father said that as well, I suppose?" he asked.

Her brows furrowed. "Yes. As I said—"

"He was a wise man." Rey studied her intently. "I begin to wonder if our fathers held mutual acquaintances."

Silla's lips parted. "Do you think so?"

Rey stared at her a heartbeat longer. "It does not matter. Both are dead."

Hekla cleared her throat. "Shall we get started on the rear chokehold?" She glanced at Rey, then back at Silla. "You'll start with me, and if you feel ready, you can try Rey once more."

Silla shifted onto the balls of her feet, recalling what had happened during their last practice. But since then, she'd felled the vampire deer and had gotten through two terrible days of skjöld sickness. There was something so empowering about facing the things which frightened her. "Yes," she found herself saying.

They ran through the movements with Hekla performing the chokehold, Rey barking feedback.

"You've somehow grown slower, Sunshine."

"Do you expect the enemy will wait for you to choose which foot to trip them with?"

And her personal favorite, "You cause me to weep, woman, and it is not from happiness."

"All right, *Hammer Hand*," said Rey eventually. "Will you try your luck with me?"

Silla took a bolstering breath and nodded.

He rolled up the sleeves of his tunic, her eyes falling on the now healing marks she'd left upon him. "Stay strong," said Rey. "Be ready. You know what I will do. Always think forward—imagine it before it happens."

She nodded, widening her stance while Rey positioned himself behind her. Her heart began to beat faster at the sheer size of him. It was impossible not to think of how easily a warrior like him could end her.

She let out a shaky exhale, grateful for the looser hold of Rey's arm around her neck.

"I've been thinking about this," said Hekla. "Rey is simply too large for you to fell as you would me. Instead, you'll battle him like Hekla Rib Smasher."

"Hekla..." warned Rey.

"Hush, Rey. She cannot bring you down as a man would. We shall get creative." Hekla looked at Silla, a wicked gleam in her eye. "Pull the arm around your neck, then drive your fist into his groin. Once you've distracted him with his pitiful male weakness, smash your elbow into his ribs."

"What?" hissed Silla. "I will *not* punch him in the groin!"

"Not if you value your life," grumbled Rey, shifting behind her.

Hekla smirked. "Axe Eyes grows nervous, Silla. Use his fear as your power. Remember—the bigger the warrior, the harder they fall. Ready, dúlla?"

"No."

Hekla sighed. "Fine. Simply *pretend* to punch him in the groin. Though if your fist happened to snap back, I am certain it would be fine. Accidents happen, do they not, Rey?"

"If you have an 'accident,' Sunshine, I'll make certain another vampire deer finds you without the protection of my watchful eye."

"You can be certain my fist will go nowhere near *that*, Rey," she hissed.

Hekla grinned, looking between Rey and Silla. "On three?"

After Hekla counted down, Silla stumbled through the motions. It was a disastrous training session, though the fact Rey flinched with each pass brought a small measure of glee to her.

And Hekla, apparently.

"You get too much enjoyment from this, Hekla," grumbled Rey.

By the fifteenth—twentieth?— attempt, she'd grown no more adept, despite the sweat misting her brow.

"Let us finish for tonight and try once Hammer has her strength back," said Hekla.

They wandered to the firepit, where Sigrún, Ilías, and Gunnar huddled around a game of dice behind the windbreak. More and more they found themselves behind the strung-up furs to escape the northern wind, and Silla shivered as an icy gust hit her face. Three tents were clustered just beyond the firepit, woolen fabric stretched across crossbars and secured in place with lock wedges. Inside the tents, sleeping furs were piled with blankets. Sigrún and Hekla had welcomed Silla into their tent, the men pairing off to share their own.

Sigrún clapped her hands together, jumping up with glee. Ilías and Gunnar groaned as they dug into their pockets for coins.

"Count me in for the next game," said Hekla, dragging a crate toward them. "Silla? You in?"

"Perhaps later," Silla replied.

She wandered toward the tents to retrieve her cloak, stepping gingerly through the tall grass and trying not to twist an ankle. Behind the tents, the light of the fire was obscured, and she blinked as her eyes adjusted to the dim light of the nearly set sun.

Without warning, a hand clamped over her mouth; her body was yanked back against the hard planes of a chest. A second arm wrapped around her stomach, pinning her arms to her sides like a steel band. Silla's eyes widened, her heart hammering against her chest.

"Don't scream," rasped a voice in her ear.

FORTY-EIGHT

Silla's pulse thudded beneath his fingers, and Jonas breathed in deeply, allowing himself to relax at last. She'd awoken; she'd recovered from her strange affliction. And at the feel of her warm body, Jonas felt his own affliction building.

Hand splayed across her stomach, he slid it up to the swell of her breast. He felt the moment she realized it was him. Driving her elbow back with surprising force, he allowed her to wrench free. Warmth slid through him at the sight of that fire in her eyes. It pooled in his chest, dripping lower in his stomach.

"You frightened me," Silla said, smacking his arm.

Jonas tugged her to him, dipping down to claim her lips. There was no pause, no slow ease into this kiss—it was urgent and hungry, deliciously hot. He needed her—badly. Jonas crowded her until her back brushed against the tent.

She pulled free from him, breathless. "Jonas," she objected, but he bent past her, entering the tent and pulling her down onto the soft bedding within.

It was dark inside the tent, firelight flickering along the walls as Jonas settled over her. "I've waited many days to do this," he murmured. He sank his mouth onto hers, a greedy need for her consuming him as he fumbled with the fastenings of her dress.

It had been two days without her, two long days of worry and misery. He needed the peace and serenity of her touch. As he tugged at her overdress, Silla turned her head to break the kiss.

"Wait," she whispered. "We cannot."

"Why not?" asked Jonas quietly, a wicked smile spreading.

"Because the Crew—" she paused. "They're just there—only ten paces away."

This scenario aroused him more than he cared to admit. "I can be quiet," he murmured, kissing a hot path down her neck. "Can you?"

He focused his kisses and nips at the area just below her ear, each breathy sigh he drew from her driving his maddening need higher. With a ragged exhale, she arched into him, and he knew he had her.

"Is that a *yes*?" he whispered.

"Yes," she panted.

Heat shooting low in his belly, Jonas yanked her dress so hard that she gasped. And then, there was only the frantic need to have her. "You wear entirely too many layers," he muttered, peeling her shift and underdress carelessly. Something ripped, but he gave it no heed because, at last, he looked down upon her bare form.

Silla's hands curled under the hem of his tunic, tugging it over his head while he grappled with his buckle. Finally, Jonas came down upon her, his skin sliding languidly against the warmth of hers. He dragged his teeth down her throat, inhaling long, jagged pulls of her scent. The tent was silent save for the rustle of bedding and their husky sighs. Gunnar laughed from the fire, Hekla's voice a low reply, and Jonas let out a soft sound—knowing they were right there sent heat prickling down his spine.

He dragged his fingers down her center, barely stifling a groan. "Gods. You've missed me, woman, admit it. You're ready to take me so soon."

Silla reached for him with a slow, delicious stroke. "It seems you've missed me as well."

"As much as I enjoy the feel of your hand," he muttered, his hips bucking, "only this will satisfy me right now." He pressed his fingers inside her, smiling as she clenched around him.

"More," she panted. "Need." The slight slur to her words told Jonas her need matched his own.

"I did miss you," he admitted in a low whisper, positioning himself at her entrance. "Your wicked mouth and your warm heat." He hesitated. "I worried for you." *It changed everything*, he could not say, *when I thought you might not wake up. It made me want things I shouldn't.* But the thought alone made him feel flayed open and vulnerable, and he could not speak the words aloud. Instead, he showed her with his body.

———

AFTERWARD, Jonas lay sprawled on the bedding, fighting for breath, Silla tucked into his side, boneless and limp. He knew if he could see her face, she'd have a dazed, surprised expression, the same she always had in the afterglow. Like she could not figure out how they'd gotten here.

He was not quite sure himself.

Silla began to shake, and Jonas slid his hand over her mouth before the laughter could bubble up. She shook uncontrollably against him, and he could not help the smile she coaxed from him. She did that. Made him smile. Made him...happy. She was light and warmth and all things good. All things a man like him did not deserve.

But he was taking them all the same.

Once Silla regained control of herself, she turned and smiled up at him. "I thought for certain they'd hear us," she whispered. The tent was dark, but the light filtering from the fire highlighted the corner of her eye, her slanted cheekbone, the curve of her jaw.

"Perfect," muttered Jonas, twining his fingers with hers. For a moment, he could have sworn a frown crossed her lips, but it was gone so quickly, he couldn't be sure. "You are perfect," he repeated, watching her carefully.

Whatever insecurities Silla might hold, to Jonas, she was perfect, a thing he never knew he needed, a complication he'd never seen coming.

Silla brushed her knuckles along the scar on his cheek, her frown certain this time. And Jonas heard the words she did not speak. *What happened to you?* Exhaling, he felt that strange urge to share—after all, if anyone could understand, it would be her. He took a deep breath and prepared to speak his greatest shame aloud.

"You know how it feels to be denied of lands that are rightfully yours, Curls. I wish to tell you the full story of what happened to me—to us."

Silla gave his hand a gentle squeeze. Of course she did. She was perfect, this woman. His Silla.

"I killed my father." He was hot and cold all at once, but forced himself to continue. "He was a cruel man who beat my mother. When I was younger, I was too small, too weak to help her. She told me to take Ilías to the elm tree on the edge of our property. We'd climb it and hide from our father, watching the clouds and imagining the adventures we'd have when we grew older. It was our safe place. The place where we dreamed of a better life."

Jonas exhaled a long breath.

"As I grew older, I defended my mother, but it seemed only to make things worse. He'd knock the sense out of me, then return to my mother with new vigor. We lived in constant fear of his anger. Dark spells, he called them. Claimed it was not his fault. It was never his fault. The day it happened, he finally went too far. He killed her." Jonas paused, his fists clenching. Silla's hand ran along his arm, her touch reassuring. "I sent Ilías to the elm tree and returned to the house. My father was weeping over her corpse. I snapped. I pulled him off my mother, and made him pay for every punch he'd ever delivered."

Silence stretched between them. Jonas squeezed his eyes shut. Had he blundered in telling her this? He'd never before told anyone, not even Rey. What if she never looked at him the same?

His foolish mouth kept going. "We went to the Assembly, and I placed myself at their mercy. We had witnesses, good friends and neighbors who attested to my father's violent nature. The killing of my father was ruled as just. But his...his killing of my mother was ruled as murder."

Her throat bobbed.

"In doing so, the Law Speaker stripped my father of lands and confiscated all of his money in the Crown's name. Ilías and I were left without an inheritance. With nothing but a black mark on our name, we decided it best to leave our community. Only the kindness of a few friends and neighbors got us enough coin to get to Sunnavík. That is when we found Rey and the Bloodaxe Crew and began to make a name for ourselves in this kingdom."

Eternal fires. He swallowed back a boulder-sized lump in his throat. He was hollow and yet...lighter. It was a relief to tell someone. And if anyone was to understand, it was this woman, who too had been unjustly stripped of what belonged to her.

He watched her pick and choose her words. She opened her mouth, and he braced himself for the worst. But like always, Silla surprised him.

"I killed my mother, in a way."

Jonas's brows shot up, and he blinked quickly. After a moment, he rubbed his thumb against the back of her hand in what he hoped was an encouraging gesture. He was dreadful at this, but for her, he'd try.

"It happened when I was ten. Ten years have passed, and I am still confused."

Jonas sensed she was equally unsure of sharing this with him, so he remained quiet.

"If I had not forgotten the gods-forsaken dill, things might have ended differently." She licked her lips. "I returned to the market to get it. There had been an eclipse, and I forgot to place it into our basket in the excitement. So I returned to retrieve the dill while Mother prepared the bread dough. When I got home, she was gone. Taken. By the Klaernar."

Jonas tensed.

"A neighbor tipped them off about a Galdra in our home. Lies, of course—we have no magic. I had a troubling incident with the neighbor girl. An argument. She claimed I...flared light from my palms. But I did not. It was a ripple in the pond, an errant flash of light off the water's surface. She was a flighty girl. Wildly imaginative. And she told her parents, who told the Klaernar. The most troublesome part of it all is they claimed my mother confessed that it was *she* who flashed the light. She told them she was an" —she searched for the word— "Ashbringer. I do not even know what such a thing is, but I do know my mother was not it. She was no Galdra."

She frowned. "What could she hope to gain by telling them this? I do not understand. To protect me from their scrutiny? I've pondered it so many times. Had I been home, I could have explained about the pond, about the flash of light. I could have defended her." Her voice had grown hollow, her eyes haunted. "The next time I saw her, she was strung on a pillar, shackled and bridled. I cannot forget her eyes. Her beautiful, shining green eyes. I could tell she wished for me to look away, but I refused. I wanted her to see someone in that crowd who loved her. I...I watched the whole thing. I watched her die. I was forced to cast a stone. I helped end her life, Jonas."

She trembled, and he pulled her closer, stomach twisting. He did not know what to say, so he held her tightly as several silent minutes passed.

Silla pulled back and looked up at Jonas with wide, honest eyes. "You are a good person, Jonas."

He choked.

Her mouth was set in a hard line. "You are. I see it in the way you care for your brother." Her brows furrowed. "I know not everyone would do what you've done for him."

He stared at her in silence.

"You *are* a good man, Jonas."

"I'm not a good man, Curls." He drew a lock of hair from her face and pushed it back. "But you make me feel as though I could be one."

Silla blinked at him, and his chest felt too small for his heart.

"What?" she asked. "Why do you look at me like that?"

He brought his lips to hers in a slow, deep kiss. Jonas pulled back, leaning his forehead on hers. "I want to see you after Istré. What if I came to Kopa and paid you a visit?" He ran a hand along the smooth curve of her cheek. "Would you like that?"

She nodded, and Jonas was an eagle, soaring through the air, unburdened and free. Sitting, he rummaged through his discarded breeches until he found it. "I made something for you," he whispered, pressing the disk into her palm.

His stomach burned as he watched her hold it to the flickering light. The layered triangular symbols were shaded against the dark grain of the wood, a leather strap dangling from a small hole cut in the top of it.

"It is like your talisman," she whispered, looking up at him.

"I want you to have it." Jonas studied her carefully. "Something to hold on to while we are apart. Do you like it?" He found himself holding his breath.

"I love it, Jonas," she said, running her thumb along the grooved surface. But there was something buried in her words, something he could not identify. "It's beautiful. You have such a talent for woodcraft."

Taking the talisman from her, he gently drew the leather strap over her head, settling the disk above her heart. Warmth flooded his chest at the sight of her in that talisman.

He leaned down to kiss her but was interrupted by Gunnar's loud bellow.

"Attack! Ready for an attack! Something comes!"

FORTY-NINE

Silla's fingers dug into Jonas's forearm as the words sank into her.
Attack. They were under attack.

A thousand questions flooded her mind. Who? How many? And most importantly, *why*? Was it the queen's men? Had they found her?

"What should I..." Silla asked, blinking rapidly as she watched Jonas yank on his clothing.

"Stay here," he growled, pulling on his tunic. "Do not leave the tent."

Her stomach twisted into knots as she watched him dress. The closeness they'd just shared—she felt connected to him, and dread filled her at the thought of harm befalling him.

"Be safe," she whispered.

His eyes locked onto hers, stern and serious and fearless. He leaned into her, his hand cupping her jaw as he pressed his lips to hers. "And you," he said softly.

Her chest squeezed, but the sound of splintering wood diverted her attention. "Go," she urged him. "You must go."

Firelight on the tent wall darkened as figures rushed by it, yells of the Bloodaxe Crew filling the air.

"Stand strong," growled Rey from beyond the tent wall. "Shields up, spears at the ready!"

The distinctive sound of blades knocking against wooden shields filled the air, and Jonas cursed as he fumbled with the buckles of his armor.

"Jonas!" bellowed Ilías. "Where in the arse end of the wilderness are you? I have your spear, you dumb kunta!"

"Here!" Jonas replied, fastening his battle belt, then rushing from the tent. "Coming!"

A rush of cool wind roused Silla from her numbness, and she pulled on her underdress. A hideous clicking sound made her hands pause mid-motion.

"What is that?" she whispered.

"Aim for the guts!" bellowed Rey. "Avoid the fangs. Do not get separated!"

Fangs?

Fangs?

A shrill sound filled the air, catching each hair on the back of Silla's neck, standing it on end like the fur of a frightened cat. Shaking her head, she found her overdress and yanked it on, then groped for her dagger, unsheathing it shakily.

"Where's Silla?" demanded Hekla, and Silla's stomach turned over.

"I'm here!" she called out. "In the tent."

"Stay there!" barked Rey. "Do not come out. You'll only get in the way."

Another screech—louder now, as though whatever it was had just broken through the clearing. Ilías bellowed, and Hekla screamed; the sounds of battle filled the air—grunts, scratchings and soul-piercing shrieks of whatever it was that attacked the Bloodaxe Crew.

The tension in her body knotted tighter, her heart thundering in her ears.

It was then that she saw it—a flash of white light. At first, Silla thought it to have come from outside of the tent, from the creatures. But with slowly dawning horror, she realized that it did not come from outside the tent at all.

It came from *her.*

Silla felt as though she was outside of her body, looking down at a disheveled girl with pure white light which swirled—*swirled!*—from the under-side of her forearms. "What in the eternal fires..." she murmured, the dagger falling from her grasp. The sounds of battle beyond the tent grew muted, her world focused on this thing, this wondrous yet damning white light.

It was impossible, and yet there it was.

She touched a finger to her skin, gasping at the coolness. What was this magic? Was this galdur swimming in her veins? Her memories flashed back to a conversation held moments before.

She claimed I...flared light from my palms.

"No," Silla murmured. Ice-cold realization dragged down her spine.

The leaves. The leaves had worn off.

Side effects: blockage of kjarna prevents users from priming.

Silla hadn't understood this sentence—had mused over it time and time again. But now, looking down at her arms, understanding shocked through her.

Whatever the words meant, they related to magic. The leaves had *suppressed* her magic.

Silla was Galdra.

And things started sliding into place—her mother's confession; the flash of light; the way Silla and her father had fled from the Klaernar. The leaves. Silla's mind was like a cup filled to the brim, beginning to spill over the sides. As she stared at the light pulsing from her veins, she understood nothing except that this meant trouble.

More trouble.

"Strike!" bellowed Rey, and the firelight winked out.

Reeling, Silla was dragged back to the moment. It was utter chaos out there. Insect-like chittering, a squeal, Hekla's scream of fury, the thunk of shields knocking together, and Rey's continual commands.

She forced in a deep breath, reaching for her dagger.

"Tent!" was her only warning. Silla's muscles tensed, her grip around her dagger tightening.

And then the tent roof was driven down, a massive form knocking her onto her back. The iron cross bars bent like twigs; the cloth shredded as though it was parchment, and cold night air rushed over her. The light from her exposed forearms spilled upward, landing on glinting rows of dagger-sharp fangs, each as long as her foot. The creature shrieked, its rancid breath smelling of dead, rotting things, and the teeth snapped down at her, gnashing together inches from her face.

Move! she thought, rolling onto her stomach and crawling across the tent floor. The walls had collapsed in, the woolen fabric thick and cumbersome to push through. Her neck prickled with the premonition of danger, and Silla rolled onto her back, the creature striking where she'd been moments before.

The beastly thing recoiled, looking down upon her. From this angle, Silla saw eight eyes glowing like the embers of a fire, shaggy gray fur covering an enormous body—a wolfspider, she realized, but it was too late for this knowledge to help, as it lunged at her with unnatural speed. She swung her dagger, but it hit empty air as the creature recoiled with an ear-shattering shriek. The sound was so horrid, so hideous, she yearned to cover her ears, but her training with Hekla had taught her better.

Rising to her feet, Silla caught sight of a spear protruding from the creature's belly, black ichor oozing from the wound. The creature thrashed, its face passing inches from her. Unflinching, Silla saw her chance, and she waited, counting.

One. Two. Three.

She lashed out, her dagger slicing across the row of eyes.

The spider scuttled backward with a screech, and Rey was there, wrenching the spear free and shoving it back into its underbelly. Black liquid gushed from the spider, and with one last shriek, the creature's legs bent, and it crashed to the ground. Rey rolled free and ducked beneath his shield with not a heartbeat's time to spare, wasting no time in charging back into the fray.

Heaving for breath, Silla choked on the putrid scent of decay. Covering her nose, she took stock of her surroundings—two giant spider corpses filled the clearing, one tent collapsed, the wagon tipped on its side, and the Bloodaxe Crew huddled behind a shield wall near a third giant spider at the far end of the glade. The shield wall opened as Rey darted inside.

The spider raised its head, red eyes looked directly at Silla. Swallowing, she glanced at her forearms—the light, the gods damned light was drawing the spiders to her! She yanked her dress sleeves down, but it spilled faintly from beneath the fabric. How did she turn it off, how did she...

The spider stepped toward her—right over the shield wall. With a collective bellow, five spears thrust upward into the spider's underside.

Relief rushed through Silla as the beast crashed to the ground with a bone-shaking thud, but it was short-lived. Her arms were glowing, and the Crew would no longer be distracted. Whirling, she rushed to her tent—thankfully intact—and crawled inside. The light illuminated her surroundings, and she quickly found her cloak and the pair of wolfskin gloves which Hekla had loaned her. Her hands shook as she pulled the gloves on, slipping her arms into the folds of the cloak.

Silla emerged from the tent, coming face to face with the human wall known as Axe Eyes.

"Did you light a gods damned *torch* in the tent?" he seethed. "You foolish woman, the wolfspider is drawn to light! You could have been killed."

"I..." Silla swallowed. "Yes?" She silently prayed her cloak and gloves shielded the light from his view.

He scrubbed a hand over his face. "It's as though you have a death wish."

"I did not hesitate," she reminded him. "I did not cower...much. I slashed its eyes."

Despite the moonless night, Silla could see the subtle flex of Rey's jaw. "So you did," he said slowly. "Well done. It was diversion enough for me to get a killing blow in." As her mouth dropped open, Rey whirled and strode toward the Bloodaxe Crew.

Reluctantly, Silla eased toward the Crew. The wagon had been set upright, but it lurched to the side, part of the undercarriage damaged. They spent the next hour setting the contents of the wagon back in place and salvaging what they could from the damaged tent. After a heated discussion of whether it might draw more wolfspiders, they decided to burn the spider corpses to rid the glade of that horrid scent.

The Bloodaxe Crew washed spider gore from them in shifts; thankfully, Silla had managed to avoid the stinking black sludge and did not need to risk unveiling her arms. Instead, she set to reheating the evening meal's leavings over the fire and prepping hot cups of róa for the battle-weary warriors. One by one, the Bloodaxe Crew settled around the fire. It was late, but residual energy seemed to linger in their blood as they recounted the glory of the fight. Silla dazedly listened on as the Crew discussed the strange smell and red eyes of the wolfspiders, and whether this might be linked to the unusual red-eyed skógungar they'd encountered all those days before. After the meal had been served and dishes washed up, Silla settled onto a log, tugging her hood around her face as she stared into the dancing flames.

It had been a long night, and she'd been weary before the attack. Now she was beyond, running on air. Just as she readied herself to make her excuses, Rey spoke.

"Why were you in Jonas's tent?" he asked in his deep, rumbling voice. The conversation around the campfire stuttered, then died.

Silla's body grew numb, her heart thudding in her ears as all eyes fell upon her. "I..." she stammered. Her eyes met Jonas's across the fire, pinched and tight. The chaos with the spider, with the light in her forearms, she'd forgotten entirely about this.

Fool, she thought. *You should have known Axe Eyes wouldn't miss that detail.*

"Let us ask Jonas," said Rey in a cool voice. "Why were you in the tent with Silla, Jonas? Why did it take you so long to join us for battle?"

Jonas cleared his throat, but did not answer.

Rey produced a flask from his pocket and took a deep swig, wiping his mouth on his sleeve. "I know it couldn't be what we are all thinking, Jonas, as I recall strictly ordering you not to do so."

Silla chewed on her cheek, staring into the flames and wishing they could burn her to ash.

"Someone had best start talking," snapped Rey.

Jonas exhaled. "Silla and I are..." He shrugged.

Unnatural stillness followed this non-confession. Rey frowned.

"What?" prompted Hekla. "You're...what?"

"Fucking!" exclaimed Jonas. "We're fucking, all right? Merciful gods. We are grown adults. Do not make this into some scandalous thing."

"Jonas!" moaned Silla, clapping a hand over her eyes. The incredulous stares of the Crew burnt her skin like fiery pokers. "Could you not say it some other way...*any* other way?"

"Dúlla," groaned Hekla, a hand on her forehead. "I warned you of him."

"I know," said Silla, pressing her lips together as Jonas threw a murderous glare at Hekla. "And I took that into consideration."

Hekla turned her glare on Jonas. "You hurt her, Wolf, and you'll have me to answer to."

"Oh, for the love of the stars," muttered Silla, closing her eyes.

"How long?" asked Rey, his voice cold and hard as iron.

A muscle in Jonas's jaw flexed. "Since before Skalla Ridge."

"You've lied to me," muttered Rey, staring at Jonas. "Why, Jonas? Why do you dishonor me like that? Why do you dishonor your Crew?"

"I meant no dishonor—"

"You lied to me," growled Rey. The vein in his temple pulsed, and Silla swallowed hard. "You went against my orders."

"Your orders were foolish," snapped Jonas, his voice rising.

Rey stood, stepping away from the fire and crossing his arms over his chest. "You dig yourself in deeper, Jonas. You are a fool, to be sure. A fool who cannot master his own desires. You've gone too far this time. We agreed to protect her, and, instead, you've taken advantage when she was alone and mourning her father."

With a sharp inhale, Silla stared at Rey.

Jonas's hand curled into a fist. "It was not like that. I simply offered myself up as a distraction, and she accepted..."

Rey shook his head slowly, rolling up the sleeves of his tunic. "Own your mistake, Jonas. Take back your honor."

Jonas's face transformed, his pupils dilating so wide his eyes looked black. He stood and strode over to Rey, their faces bare inches apart.

"You want me to say it?" snarled Jonas. "I did it. I went against your orders and lied to your face. But I did not force her, and she wants me as I want her. And I...care for her. Punish me as you must, Axe Eyes," said Jonas with a glower, "but I would do it all over again. I would not change a thing."

Jonas and Rey stared at one another, two warriors chest to chest. Rey's jaw flexed, as he appeared to consider his options.

"You know I cannot stand for lies in this Crew. We will settle it the old way. With fists." Rey dropped his battle belt to the ground, his blades landing with a resounding *clank*.

Jonas's gaze flitted to Silla, then back to Rey. "Very well," he said, dropping his own weapons.

"Wait," Silla started, standing, but it was too late—chaos descended as Rey lunged at Jonas and brought him down to the ground. The warriors rolled in a storm of fists and elbows. "I don't want this!" she yelled out, her stomach twisting as Rey's fist collided with Jonas's cheek. "Stop it, you fools!" Silla turned to the Bloodaxe Crew for support, but she was met with an impatient set of amber eyes.

"Dúlla. Tell me Jonas is not Asger. Oh, Gods. *He pleased me...many times.*" Hekla dragged a hand down her face. "It makes sense now."

"In my defense, there *was* a man named Asger," murmured Silla, guilt prickling her stomach. "Jonas threatened to smash his face in."

"Silla!" exclaimed Hekla, her eyes narrowing on Silla. "How could you keep all this from me on this boring road where nothing exciting ever happens? I thought us friends."

"Believe me, Hekla, I wanted to tell you..." Her voice trailed off as Jonas landed a fist to Rey's stomach. "Must they do this?" she asked, gesturing helplessly to the wrestling warriors.

Hekla shrugged. "It is their way."

Silla's eyes met with Sigrún's across the fire, the small blonde woman covering her smile with her hand. She sent Silla a knowing look as she shook her head softly. It seemed to say *I've been waiting for this.*

"*You're* the woman that kept me up on Longest Day," accused Ilías, diverting her attention.

Silla's cheeks warmed. "I..."

"I cannot hear it," he said dramatically, putting up a hand. "This is like discovering your little sister and older brother have been sneaking off to the hayloft."

Silla crossed her arms over her chest. "Ilías, we are *not* related."

"So Jonas has been nailing our Hammer," boomed Gunnar.

Sigrún made a quick succession of hand gestures.

Ilías interpreted. "Sigrún asks how many strokes of his axe did it take?"

"Pawed by the Wolf, and yet you live," Gunnar added. "Did he make you howl?"

The Crew erupted in laughter.

Silla groaned, rubbing her forehead. "You're children. All of you!"

Ilías shook his head, a smile on his face. "I would not pick it," he mused. "You and my brother. But perhaps you will be good for him. Perhaps you'll divert his attention from money and vengeance." His eyes grew distant.

Exhaustion overwhelmed Silla, the night's events taking their toll. "I've seen enough," she said, rising to unsteady feet. "Good night." Silla sent a look of distaste at the men rolling on the ground.

"Man-boys," she muttered, stalking off toward her tent.

———

WHEN SILLA AWOKE the next morning, she was sweltering hot, and the reasons became quickly apparent. One—a large male warrior was wrapped around her, and two—she still wore her gloves and cloak.

Glancing over her shoulder at Jonas, Silla's stomach twisted. A purpling bruise bloomed on his cheekbone, and his knuckles were raw and split. He'd told the whole Bloodaxe Crew that he cared for her—had traded fists with Rey. Silla chewed her lip, the twist of her stomach coiling tighter. She did not wish to create turmoil in the Bloodaxe Crew and hated that she had.

It had been a tight fit with three women in the tent...but add a male warrior, and they were nearly piled atop one another. Peeking around, she saw that the occupants snored softly, and decided she was safe. With a gentle nudge of her sleeve, Silla exhaled. The skin beneath was pale and dull—no shimmer, no churning white light.

Removing Jonas's arm, Silla wiggled out from the cocoon of his body and crawled from the tent.

The cool morning air kissed her skin, and Silla sighed with relief. Biting her lip, she looked down at her arms. What had caused the light to gather in the first place? And why had it stopped?

You will not remove the gloves until you reach Kopa, she vowed to herself. Skeggagrim sheltered those who fled the Klaernar. Perhaps he would know how to help her with this...magic. Frowning, she shook her head slowly. This was nothing but more trouble. She should not have quit the leaves. Should not have listened to Rey.

Looking up at the sky, Silla sighed—another dull day, the sun cloaked by gray clouds. In the light of morning, the aftermath of the spider attack looked even grimmer—the stems of young trees snapped in half, shredded wool and snapped iron bars of the flattened tent, the wagon tilting unnaturally to the side.

A lone figure sat before the fire, wolf pelt wrapped around his shoulders, coarse curls catching what little light came through the clouds. With a sigh, Silla approached. Sinking down across from Rey, she took in the darkened bruise on his swollen cheekbone and frowned.

"I am sorry," she said. "I did not mean to come between you. I meant you no dishonor." Silla hesitated. "I was lonely," she added softly. "He made me forget." She felt she owed him this explanation. Why, she was unsure.

Rey glowered at her a moment, then poked the low-burning fire with a stick. It popped, sparks floating skyward.

"I...thank you for your concern for me," she tried.

"It is not concern for you, Sunshine," Rey bit out. "That is *your* business, and you will be gone soon enough. I must maintain honesty amongst my warriors. A difficult task when such a dishonest person travels with us."

I am not the only one with secrets, she thought with quietly sparking anger, but she did not voice it aloud.

Silence stretched between them for a long moment, before Rey spoke. "We must go to the next town, a place by the name of Skutur, and seek repairs for the wagon. The wheel does move but it catches on the wagon body with each turn."

"Very well," she said. "What can I do to help?"

"You can prepare the daymeal," Rey said in an even voice.

Silla nodded and retreated to fetch water for the porridge.

FIFTY

As the Bloodaxe Crew entered the Highlands, the cover provided by trees and brambles vanished, and they braced against an ice-tinged wind. It frosted the coils of Silla's hair, filling her with trepidation— how cold would it be in Kopa? Would she be able to weather the long, bleak winters of the north? Thankfully, her worries were tempered by the beautiful sight—rolling hills of green grasses streaked with vibrant purple heather.

It was only an hour before they rode into Skutur. A mid-sized town, it bustled with people setting about their morning routines. The scent of freshly baked bread blended with hay and horse and iron, the smells of a town that was just busy enough to set Silla's teeth on edge. Pulling up the hood of her borrowed cloak, Silla sank lower on the horse she shared with Jonas—with the undercarriage of the wagon damaged, she'd ridden with him to lessen the weight for Horse to pull. The poor animal's pristine white coat was already lathered in a sheen of sweat.

Apples and carrots for you tonight, thought Silla.

They rode along the main street of Skutur, passing shops and inns, timber-sided homes, and a mead hall which had seen better days. Three v-shaped pillars stretched toward the sky as they passed through the central town square, ten or so Klaernar clustered before them.

A shiver ran through her, and she held her gaze on the horse's mane. This town had a strange feel to it that Silla did not like. They rode out of the square in silence, stopping before a woodcrafter's shop. The Bloodaxe Crew dismounted, milling about while Rey bartered with the craftsman inside his shop.

Silla, meanwhile, searched her surroundings from beneath the shade of her hood. The central road was busy, shopkeepers sweeping their stoops and rearranging displays. Livestock and people walked about, energy and movement all around her. No one paid heed to her, but still, she could not shake the feeling of being watched.

A large hand slid around her hip, and she was pulled back into Jonas's warmth. "Curls," he whispered in her ear. "What troubles you?

"Nothing," she lied, her eyes unable to stop searching for anything out of place.

Jonas caressed the wooden talisman hanging around her neck. "I like seeing you in this."

"I still find this pairing a little strange," said Ilías, watching them warily.

"Get used to it, brother," said Jonas. There was such...certainty in his voice. Swallowing, Silla looked away.

It was then that she felt it—needle-sharp prickles crawling down her neck. Shaking away from Jonas, Silla looked down the road toward the central square of Skutur.

The woman warrior wore furs over her shirt of chain mail, a shock of copper hair gleaming in the light.

Silla blinked to clear her vision.

It cannot be, she thought. *She is dead. I watched Rey push her off the ridge.*

"Silla?" Jonas's voice was muffled by the pounding of her heart.

The warrior woman's eyes were upon the Bloodaxe Crew, but they meandered down the road, landing on Silla. Their gazes locked. Silla's breaths grew shallow. And then, the woman strode toward her, and something finally snapped into place. This was no vision. However impossible it was, the woman was real. And she was coming for Silla.

Panic rose in her throat. The assassin would out her, would spill her secrets to the Bloodaxe Crew and ruin her chances of getting to safety. Silla needed to draw her away from them, then evade her.

"I require some air...some quiet," she heard herself telling Jonas. Her voice sounded pinched, unnatural. "I shall return in a moment."

"Do you wish for some company?" asked Jonas, concern in his voice.

"No," said Silla. "Just some time alone with my thoughts."

Silla stepped back, then turned on her heel. Hastening down the road, she turned into a laneway so narrow, she could brush her hands along the buildings on each side. A flash of light diverted her attention, her eyes shooting down. The light...it was back, churning from her wrists. Quickly, she drew them into the folds of her cloak. Why of all the times for this light to appear did it do so when danger was present? It would lead the assassin straight to her!

Ducking beneath strung-up linens, Silla zagged between closely constructed homes, the narrow space opening up to yards enclosed by wattle fences. Picking up to a run, Silla leaped over one of the fences, her cloak snagging on the sharp end of a willow branch. "Oh, porridge," she whispered, turning to lift her cloak loose. Movement between the homes caught her eye, and she stilled.

Hair, orange as flames, materialized as the woman stepped onto the lawn. She stopped, a smile curving her lips. "You can run, little Galdra, but you cannot hide from me," said the assassin.

She was waiting, Silla realized. Waiting for her to run, waiting for this sick game of cat and mouse to continue. Panic overwhelmed her, and Silla's feet refused to move. For a heartbeat, the two women stared at one another.

And then, Silla *ran*.

She shook loose from her cumbersome cloak, abandoning it in the garden, and with all the strength she had, she hurtled over a second wattle fence. Tearing between two closely-spaced homes, she spilled into a narrow laneway. Disoriented, Silla let the knowing place in her stomach choose for her, guiding her back out onto the main street of town.

Clutching her glowing forearms against her chest, Silla was thankful to see the light pouring from her was muted. Footfalls beat the dirt-trodden road behind her, and she knew the assassin was close, was gaining on her. For all of her training, Silla was no warrior, she was just a kitchen girl. It was inevitable that the warrior would catch her, and she knew her only chance was to hide.

Hazarding a glance over her shoulder, Silla caught a glint of silver as the assassin unsheathed a blade. Her shoulder rammed hard into a man, who cursed at her as he stumbled back.

"S-sorry!" Silla managed, pushing past him and down the road.

Twenty paces ahead of her, a shepherd ushered a group of sheep destined for market, two dozen or more cloudy fleeces filling the street. Silla saw her opportunity. A fresh wave of energy powered her limbs, and she dug to new depths, darting around them just as the flock spanned the street.

Her breaths sawed in and out as she darted down the road with urgency—this was her chance to find a place to hide.

A building loomed ahead of her, taller than all the others in town. Its spire stretched high to the skies; where once would have been Sunnvald's sunburst, now sat a large raven.

"Temple," gasped Silla. Her feet slowed, and she glanced back—the assassin struggled with the flock of sheep, the shepherd yelling out as he hefted his wooden crook. People had gathered around, watching the red-haired warrior in curiosity.

Turning back to Sunnvald's temple, Silla pulled at the boarded-up door to no avail. Without allowing herself a chance to second guess, she ran along the side of the temple and into a large grassy rear courtyard scattered with several outbuildings. A set of stairs led up to a second boarded-up door at the rear of the temple, wooden planks gaping wide at the base.

Lunging up the stairs, Silla pulled at the board, falling on her backside as it came loose all at once. She threw herself at the door, yanking it open, and closing it as silently as possible behind her.

She was in Sunnvald's temple.

Silla was startlingly aware she'd never stepped foot in such a place. Inside, it was dark, light spilling between the cracks of the boarded-up windows and from beneath the doors, the undulating light from Silla's forearms further illuminating the abandoned space. The temple was dusty and in disrepair, debris and rubble scattered about, lightened patches on the wooden floors suggesting where benches and altars might once have sat. Alcoves, which once might have housed the statues of the gods, were filled with piles of crumbled stone. The walls were gouged with the bite marks of axes, as though furious men had tried—and failed—to bring down Sunnvald's home.

"Sunnvald, protect me," whispered Silla, inspecting the room for a hiding place.

"Malla, grant me courage."

She crept toward a shadowed corner where shards of broken timber were piled.

"Marra, bless me with wisdom."

She lifted her elbow, shining her light upon the heap. Planks with protruding rusted nails were piled with splintered chair arms. But beneath the debris, an angular shape in the floor caught Silla's eye.

"Stjarna, light my path."

With as much speed and stealth as she could muster, she pushed the debris aside, revealing a faint outline which made her heart leap—a trapdoor. Dropping to her knees, Silla dug her fingers into the floorboards, working around until she could grasp on to the square of flooring. With a tug, it lifted and slid aside. Blood rushed in her ears as she stared into the black hole below.

"Come out, little Galdra," called the warrior from beyond the door. "I know you are in the house of the old gods."

With a deep breath, Silla dropped below. Her feet hit the uneven ground, and, thankfully, when pressed onto the tips of her toes, she was able to reach up and slide the trap door into place. Darkness engulfed her, lit only by the light glowing from her forearms. It was cold, and smelled like old things. Musty, long-dead things.

Silla was in the crypt.

Holding her forearms aloft, Silla took in her surroundings: a small, square room, a stone pillar in the center of it, images of the gods carved into it— Sunnvald on his steed of fire, Malla with her sword of frostfire, Marra riding her winged horse, Stjarna pouring a pitcher of stars from above, Hábrók in hawk form, soaring over a battle with his hammer clutched in beak, and Myrkur peering up from his dark cavern, the eternal fires burning from braziers on either side of him.

Move, halfwit! Silla chastened herself, forcing her feet onward. She did not have time to admire artwork long thought dead. If she wished to live, she needed to move. Four stone-hewn doorways led from each wall of the chamber, and she rushed down the central one. Her stomach clenched as she heard the distinctive grating of wood—the trapdoor sliding open.

"I can smell your fear," called out the warrior woman. "I've already said it: you cannot hide from me. I will find you no matter what. It is my gift, little Galdra."

Reaching a fork, Silla pushed down the left-most tunnel, raising her forearms to cast light. Gravel crunched underfoot as she pounded down the passageway. How far did these corridors stretch? Could they lead to an exit? Could she escape before this woman caught her?

Silla's light billowed and swelled, and she cursed herself again. How could she hide in the darkness with this light...with no cloak to shield her from detection?

She was foolish, and her fortune had finally run out. She'd be caught, killed...

Silla stumbled into an open space, a high-ceilinged circular room with no exit. The walls of this room had a strange sort of masonry about them; oddly shaped rocks fitted together precariously, as though they were not mortared in place. As Silla surveyed the room, panic crawled through her limbs. A dead end. There was no exit—her eyes fell upon a venting hole at the base of the wall. Could she squeeze into it? She ran to it, placing a hand on the wall as she ducked her head into the hole and craned her neck upward: daylight distantly above and a trickle of fresh air. Her heart leaped.

The stone she'd braced herself upon crumbled to the ground. Righting herself, Silla looked down—and gagged. She spun in a circle, her heart a loud drum beat in her ears. The walls of this room were not made from stone.

Bones were neatly stacked from floor to ceiling, assembled together like an intricate puzzle. The entire structure looked perilous, as though it could crumble down at any moment. Leg bones filled the majority of the space, with skulls interspersed. *Skulls!*

What was this horrid place?

"I see you've found the Ossuary," said the red-haired warrior, stepping into the room.

Silla whirled, drawing her dagger as her back hit the wall of bones, near the small opening.

The woman was taller and broader than Silla, and she moved with the gait of a confident warrior. Her red hair was again braided in rows along the side of her skull, a predatory glint in her blue eyes. There was an arrogance about her as she leaned against the wall, unbothered by the bones and Silla's obvious distress.

A plan took shape in Silla's mind; it was mad and desperate and her only chance at escape.

As the warrior's eyes fell upon Silla's forearms, her brows lifted. "I see you are finally revealing your true nature."

"Stay back!" snarled Silla, her dagger slashing out. *Easy now, Silla. Let her believe you a cornered cat.*

The warrior held up her hands. "Calm yourself, girl. You and I are more alike than you could ever believe."

"I doubt that," snapped Silla.

The warrior chuckled, crossing her arms over her chest. "We've not been properly introduced. I am Skraeda. And I too have a gift."

"This is no gift," said Silla, nodding to her arms. "This is a curse. It is a death sentence."

"Perhaps so," mused Skraeda. "They *do* make us fight to survive."

Us. The word settled into her, loosening her focus. Silla's brows lifted. "You...are Galdra?"

"Yes," said Skraeda, watching her intently.

She is leading you somewhere. Let her think you follow. Let her believe you are softening.

"Why does it do this?" Silla asked, thrusting her arm forward. "How do I make it stop?"

The woman laughed, the sound bouncing off the bone walls of the crypt. "You cannot control it until you've had your heart and your mind united. You must go through the Cohesion Rite."

"You speak in riddles," said Silla, disappointed. More questions and never answers.

"You poor girl," tutted Skraeda. "You're all alone. You've had no one to guide you with your galdur." She paused. "*I* can tell you things."

"And why would I trust you?" asked Silla.

"Because in this, we are alike," said Skraeda. "Like you, I am Galdra, though my gift works differently. They call me a Solacer." Skraeda smiled a dark, knowing smile. "As a Solacer, I sense emotions, can enhance or dampen them as I desire; it is how I tracked you so easily. But I am more powerful than that. I've honed my skill over years of practice, and have sharpened it into a weapon. I can use it to weaken my foes by pulling on memories attached to these emotions."

Skraeda crossed her arms over her chest. "One tug on anger, and a great injustice is relived. A yank on dread, and their greatest fear comes forth. And desire...pull on that thread, and they'll grow distracted by amorous thoughts." She chuckled softly. "Warriors are more easily undone than you'd ever expect."

"That is how you bested Rey?" asked Silla. Rey, the most powerful warrior Silla had ever seen—on his back, at this woman's mercy. Until Silla had clobbered her with the butt of an axe.

"I thank you for the headaches I now suffer nightly," said Skraeda, her lip curling. "But yes. Your friend. So much anger and pain in that one."

Silla's dagger fell limp to her side. *Let her believe you hopeless. Let her think the fight has drained from you.*

Skraeda's lips curved into a victorious smile. "Let us put an end to this pointless chase. Your fate is set. Come with me, and you'll see your sister once more."

Silla's plans crumbled in an instant. "What do you know of my sister?" she asked hastily. Too hastily. *Do not appear too desperate, Silla.*

Skraeda studied her carefully. "She is in Sunnavík. Don't you..." Brows quirked, the warrior's lips curved up into a fox-like smile. "You truly do not know. Your fool of a father."

Silla clenched her dagger tightly. She might not agree on much with this woman, but on this, she did. Matthias had truly been foolish to leave her ignorant in this world.

"I offer this to you as a treaty," said Skraeda. "Come with me to Sunnavík, and you will see your sister. No more of this" —Skraeda twirled a finger in the air— "rushing about the kingdom. You can stop running. Have some peace."

Silla stared at the woman, an undercurrent of anger running through her veins. There was no peace for her in Sunnavík; of this, she was certain. But her sister...the temptation pulled at her, and she needed to be sure.

"But the queen...she intends for me to die," said Silla, watching Skraeda's face carefully.

There it was—a subtle twitch of her eyebrow was all it took for Silla to have her answer.

"The queen is a just woman," said Skraeda. "She is good to her allies. If you prove to be helpful, she'll be kind in her way. Hand me your weapon, and let us leave this place."

"Very well," said Silla, resigned.

Skraeda pushed off the wall, and Silla made her move—throwing the dagger with all the strength she could in Skraeda's direction. Her aim was horrible, but luckily for her, it did not matter. The knife hit the wall with a *thwack* falling uselessly to the ground.

"You might be brave, but your skills are pitiful," chuckled Skraeda. Before she could lunge at Silla, a skull cracked to the floor in a cloud of dust. A second bone toppled to the ground a heartbeat later, a third one cracking against Skraeda's head. Before the warrior could turn around, the entire wall of precariously arranged bones was tumbling down onto her.

Silla lunged to action, squeezing into the venting shaft and hauling her body along the stones. Thankfully, the narrow tunnel was not lined with bones, though dust and that ancient scent of things long dead loomed heavy in the air as she shimmied up toward the light. Pulling herself along the shaft, she hissed as a fingernail tore, as her dress ripped, but watched vigilantly for loose stones.

The space was narrow, the walls pushing in on all sides. Silla's head spun, but she kept her gaze on the circle of light above her.

"You will regret that, girl," growled Skraeda.

In the shaft. She is in the shaft, Silla realized. As her hope that Skraeda would not fit in the space died, she redoubled her efforts. Her muscles burned, and her fingers bled, but it was this or death. Pulling herself upward, a stone in the roof wobbled. *This one,* she thought, hope filling her. Silla dragged herself up, inch by inch, her progress slowing as the shaft steepened. Her back braced against one side, her feet digging into the other, she shoved herself upward.

A strange probing sensation in her skull made her pause.

The circle of light shining from above flickered, then vanished as black fog rolled in. Her vision shifted, and there *she* was.

Her tilted blue eyes wide with terror, the blonde girl ran her hand across Silla's cheek. "Look at me," her sister whispered. "Just breathe. We're not alone. Malla and Marra watch over us."

The door burst open, boots flooding into the room. The girl was yanked backward. Her hand ripped free from Silla's. A high-pitched scream filled the air.

"Don't leave me!" the girl cried.

Daylight bloomed distantly above her, the dusty crypt scent filling her nostrils. The shaft. She was back in the venting shaft.

She's using her galdur on you, Silla told herself. *Keep a clear mind.*

She had no time to dwell on it, the grunts just below her told her all she needed to know: Skraeda was gaining on her—and quickly.

"I'll pull you from this passage, you insolent kunta," she growled from behind her.

Silla pulled herself up, her muscles screaming in protest.

"I'll tie you to the back of my horse and make you walk all the way to Sunnavík."

That odd sensation was back, nudging and prodding at her mind, and Silla knew it was Skraeda. She willed herself to shut her out, but it was to no avail—the daylight above her rippled with darkness until it was engulfed, and she was back in that room.

Hands wrapped around Silla's waist, and she was pulled away from her sister. She opened her own mouth.

And screamed.

A hand clamped over it, muffling the sound. A door slid shut, and darkness surrounded her. Tears streamed down Silla's face.

Her sister. They had her sister.

"Forgive me, my king," murmured the man who held her. Silla looked up in shock. The voice was unmistakable, the one she'd heard her entire life. Matthias—Tómas—kissed his knuckles and bowed his head.

"Saga," she said to him. "We must get Saga."

He looked down at Silla and smiled sadly.

"Hush now, Eisa," he said in a familiar soothing voice. "We cannot reach her."

She felt hollow, like a piece of herself was missing.

Matthias wiped the tears from her cheeks and picked her up. "Don't cry now, it will be all right. We'll have a little adventure, Eisa, just you and me."

The sound of her father's voice faded away.

She was back in the tunnel, blood coursing frantically through her veins as she lay stunned at what she'd just seen. It could not be. *She* could not be.

Eisa.

Her chest tightened. Squeezed. She could not breathe. Could not think. Did not realize tears flowed down her cheeks until she tasted salt. And then, she was choking on them—on her tears, on the memory, on the weight of what this meant. Eisa.

Saga.

Oh gods.

A stone dug sharply into her back, and it was the reminder she needed to keep moving upward. She did not have the time, the space, the luxury to think of what it meant. There was only upward. Only survival. *The loose stone,* she reminded herself, as she hauled herself up inch by painstaking inch.

"Would that please you to walk behind my horse, little princess?" asked Skraeda.

Silla's hand paused.

"Oh...you know now. I pulled rather hard that time. Was that your worst fear, *Eisa Volsik?*"

A breath puffed from Silla's lips.

Skraeda continued. "Such a *sheltered* life you've lived, princess." The warrior laughed, a dark sound that rattled Silla's bones.

"You wished to see your sister again. I'll make you see her while you walk, *Eisa.* I'll make you see her until your mind is addled and you cannot form a thought. It is easy work for me, to play with the threads of your emotions. Perhaps I can find some of your dear mother and father."

Move! Silla urged herself, forcing her body upward. One foot...two feet, and it was enough.

The narrow tunnel was angled sharply, but Silla was able to lay on her back with her arms braced above her on the walls.

"Stop!" Skraeda shrieked, realizing Silla's plan.

She found the loose stone and kicked at it. Kicked at it once more. The smell of dust grew in intensity. Silla kicked again. Again. Again.

The stone came loose, and Silla allowed herself to smile. Drawing her knees as high as she could, Silla kicked up with both feet. A shower of stones tumbled loose, small and large alike, and it was enough. Enough to block Skraeda's passage.

"Wait!" screamed Skraeda, her voice muffled from beyond the barricade.

Silla shimmied onto her stomach and hauled herself upward. She was ten feet from freedom. Ten feet from fresh air. Ten feet from leaving this horrid place behind and getting back amongst the Bloodaxe Crew and onto the Road of Bones.

One last pull and Silla was climbing from a hole in the yard behind Sunnvald's temple. A stone outbuilding stretched above her, the skies so bright, she was momentarily blinded.

Strong hands grabbed her by the shoulders holding her upright. A large body blotted out some of the light.

She blinked and blinked again.

"What are you doing, Curls?" asked Jonas.

FIFTY-ONE

Stomach clenched tight, Jonas's eyes roamed over Silla. Her face was smeared with dirt, curls wild and astray, and her arms…

Stepping back, he stared at her arms, at the pure white light pulsating from her veins.

"What?" he muttered, taking her hand in his and examining her wrist. The light—it swelled and crested in intensity, and when he pressed a finger to her skin, it was cold as ice. "Silla?" he asked, waiting for an explanation.

But her eyes were fixed on something beyond his shoulder. Tugging him close to her, Silla's hands snaked under his cloak and around his back as she drew his lips down upon hers. Eyes closing, he returned her kiss, hoping her touch would ease his mind, would bring him some answers, because at this moment, nothing made sense. The cold from her forearms penetrated through his armored jacket as she pulled him tighter to her and backed them up against the stone outbuilding.

He parted her lips, but the scent clinging to her was wrong, all wrong—dust and earth, and something he could not quite place.

A noise stirred from behind him, and Jonas pulled up, looking for the source. Silla's hands tightened against his back, the chill sending goosebumps up his spine. Or perhaps it was the three tattooed faces which made him shiver: three Klaernar, rounding into the yard. With each menacing step forward, their long-bladed hevríts clinked against their mail shirts.

Jonas's hand inched toward his own blade, but he forced it away as the three men fanned out amongst the outbuildings. "Can...I help you?" he asked the nearest of the bunch, his brows furrowing. Pressing her face into his chest, Silla's shoulders rose and fell with rapid breaths.

"Don't mind us disrupting your fun," chuckled the man. "Unless you've seen a girl with curly hair run by this way."

"No," said Jonas, his voice coming out lower than he'd intended. "Afraid not. My woman and I have been here for some time and we've not seen anyone come past."

The man nodded, ducking around one of the buildings.

Jonas's gaze turned to Silla, staring up at him with pupils blown wide. Her entire body trembled, and the urge to protect her made his muscles tense.

"Please, Jonas," she asked in a soft voice. "Take me far from here. Please, I beg of you."

Casting a cautious look over his shoulder, he unclasped his thick woolen cloak and wrapped it around her shoulders, glimpsing the shining white light once more.

He had not imagined it.

"I will need answers," he rasped.

"Yes," she whispered, sagging into him.

His arm snaked around her shoulders as he drew her against him, fighting the urge to shake her and demand she explain herself right now.

They hastened down the lane behind the temple, Silla shrinking further into herself with each step. At last, they reached the rear of the woodcrafter's shop, where the horses were secured. Ilías reclined on a bench, an apple in hand. Silla sniffled, recoiling deeper into the hood of her borrowed cloak, and Jonas nodded at his brother.

"Everything all right with Hammer?" Ilías asked, his blond brows snapping together. Her trembles had intensified, and she leaned against Jonas as though she'd crumble without him.

"She's unwell," said Jonas. "We shall ride ahead and settle at Black Rock. That was the plan for tonight's camp, was it not?"

Ilías bit into the apple, nodding. "Believe so. I'll tell the rest. Go on."

Jonas helped Silla mount his mare, taking care to keep the black cloak in place as he climbed up behind her. She sloped back into him, and his arms encircled her shaking body. He was not sure what exactly had happened once Silla had left the Bloodaxe Crew, but something hadn't felt right about it—the tension in her shoulders, her unusually quick strides. After a few minutes of consideration, he'd wandered down the road after her. And when she'd darted from a laneway onto the road without her cloak, the hair on his arms had raised.

When Jonas saw the red-haired warrior chasing after her, saw the woman draw a blade, he'd broken into a run, only to lose them as a flock of sheep had overtaken the road. He'd seen them though, rounding the back of the abandoned temple. A panicked feeling had crawled through him, but the knowing feeling in Jonas's stomach had told him to linger.

He'd been frantically pacing around the outbuildings at the rear of the temple when her curly head had popped out from a hole in the ground, disheveled and panicked, with white light flowing from her arms.

His stomach burned the longer he considered it. Silla was Galdra.

A neighbor tipped them off about a Galdra in our home. Lies, of course—we have no magic.

She'd looked him in the eyes and had told him that just yesterday.

Jonas felt sick. He'd shared things with her...things he had not even entrusted with the Bloodaxe Crew. It was impossible to think she'd lied to his face. Not his Silla.

Jonas's grip on the reins tightened as he steered his horse down a side street to avoid the town square. They passed a pair of Klaernar, banging on a shop door. A chestnut coil of hair spilled out from beneath her hood, and he tucked it back under, just as they passed another pair of Klaernar, their dark eyes scrupulously studying all who passed them.

The town was swarming with Klaernar, all searching for someone.

Jonas's teeth clenched down.

With a nudge of his feet, he urged his mare to quicken her pace. They'd soon have men at the stockade walls, if they did not already, searching those who entered and left Skutur. But perhaps they thought the girl on foot, which would give them a chance.

You are risking your future for a girl who lied to you. The thought materialized from thin air, setting Jonas's teeth on edge.

But he found himself considering it all the same—the consequences of harboring a Galdra were a cell or the pillar. The end of his dreams of reclaiming his lands. Five hard years of work making a name for himself in this world scrapped, just like that. At the sharp yelp of a hound, Silla flinched in his arms. Jonas tucked her closer against his chest and adjusted the cloak over her. She needed him. And his chest squeezed at the thought of harm befalling her.

Your valiant acts bring nothing but trouble, son.

Jonas grunted, shaking his head. They were his father's words. The words of a man beating his child.

The shadows grew tall as they neared the towering stockade wall. The noise of the central part of Skutur had died, and it was silent save for the clop of hooves, a raven complaining from a post in the wall. With a gentle pull of the reins, Jonas slowed his horse. His eyes met those of a guard standing atop the wall, and he returned the man's curt nod.

As they passed through the gate, Jonas released a long breath.

They were out of the city.

"Hold tight," he murmured to Silla, and kicked his horse into a gallop.

———

BY THE TIME he dared stop, Jonas vibrated with tension. After an hour's hard ride in the brutal winds of the Highlands, he'd led his tired horse off the Road of Bones, slipping below a rocky outcrop to shield them from the winds. A river snaked through the rolling hills of grass and heather, fed by snowmelt from the Sleeping Dragons.

Securing his horse, Jonas slid from the saddle and helped Silla down. He turned to her expectantly, his muscles tensing as she rushed to the stream, tearing his cloak from her shoulders and snapping the fastenings of her over-dress loose. As she clawed at her underdress, it snagged in her tangled hair, and she wailed in frustration.

"Let me, " said Jonas softly, stepping toward her.

She sagged. It would have been amusing if not for the desperation pouring from her. With gentle fingers, Jonas freed her hair from the dress and eased it off her. She stripped herself naked except for the wooden talisman hanging around her neck, then ran into the frigid river and scrubbed at her skin.

Jonas watched her, his stomach sinking lower. Something terrible had happened to her. To his Selfless Silla. *Not your Silla,* came his shadowy thoughts. *You do not even know her. She is Galdra!* His chest clenched at that, but it was impossible to hold his anger while watching her madness. The water was bitterly cold, her skin growing pink.

"You should not stay in for long, Silla," he said to her. "You'll catch a chill." She made no motion that she'd heard him. After scouring her face and body clean, Silla dropped to her knees and washed her curls. The girl would be beyond cold by now.

At last, she emerged from the stream as she squeezed water from her hair. Jonas picked up his discarded cloak and held it open for her. She did not meet his eyes as she stepped into the cloak, her skin red and prickled all over. Wrapping the cloak around her, Jonas heard the clink of her chattering teeth.

"All right now?" he asked softly, pulling her into his arms.

She nodded. "I couldn't sit in it. In that filth. I could feel the dead on my skin."

"Did anyone touch you?" he asked in a low voice. "Did anyone lay a hand—"

"No," she said quickly. "No."

Jonas tried for patience, but he'd never been an even-tempered man. "Shall I build a fire? The tinderbox is in the wagon, but—"

"No," she said. "The smoke. We cannot draw attention to our whereabouts."

She turned in his arms, clutching his cloak around her naked body, and looked up at him. Water droplets clung to her lashes, her curls wet and tumbling over her shoulder. She was stunning and tragic and vulnerable all at once, and he felt the need to drive a blade into anyone who had upset her so badly.

"Thank you for taking me away from there, Jonas," she whispered.

A thousand questions crowded his mind and he wanted to scream them all at once. Jonas's teeth ground together as he waited for her to explain.

Her shoulders rose and fell with a heavy breath, and she stared at his chin. "I believe I am Galdra," she said.

It was entirely insufficient. "Believe? You *believe* you are Galdra? I think that was readily apparent when your hands glowed like the auroras, Silla."

She flinched, her hand drifting out from within the folds of his cloak.

Jonas took her hand in his, turning it over to examine her forearms—dull and pale once more. "Where has it gone?"

"It seems to do that," she said softly, her eyes studying him with an apprehension that made his chest squeeze. Jonas did not wish for her to look at him like that. He'd swept her from town, hadn't he? Why did she look at him as though she could not decide if she trusted him or not?

"What do you mean?" Jonas asked, trying to soften the harsh notes in his voice.

"The lights come at the most inopportune times, then vanish without warning," said Silla. "I do not understand it."

"You looked into my eyes and told me you did not have magic, Silla." His hands curled into fists. *She's held the truth from you. It is an act of disrespect.* But he banished the thought with a shake of his head.

"I did not know! The...the leaves, Jonas. I stopped taking the leaves, and my arms started...glowing."

"Leaves?" repeated Jonas. His eyes dropped to her collarbones, his talisman nestled between them. But her other necklace—why had he not realized sooner? "Where is your vial necklace?"

She chewed on her lip. "I gave it to Rey."

"What?" demanded Jonas.

Silla blew out a sharp breath. "I...I gave it to Rey. To hold on to for me."

Her words landed like a blow so fierce he grew dizzy. Rey. She gave the necklace to Rey. She had entrusted *Rey.* The secrets were piling up too quickly for Jonas to keep up. *She has played you for a fool.*

"Why?" he demanded. "Why did you give the necklace to Rey?"

Silla pressed her lips together, as though she did not wish to speak of it. Why did she not want to share this with him? He'd shared his shameful past with her. She *owed* him the truth.

"I-I needed to take a break from the leaves. I was taking too many, Jonas, and they addled my mind. They were not good for me." She paused as if considering her words. "Rey knew things about them, so I thought...I thought he might help me with them."

Another realization took shape in his mind. "When you were sick," said Jonas. "That was from the leaves, was it not?"

Apprehensively, she nodded.

"Why did you not ask for *my* help?"

Because she plays you, he thought. *She makes a fool of you.*

Silla swallowed. "Rey had an understanding of them—"

"You should have come to *me*, Curls." He worked to calm his rapidly rising pulse.

She's still a good person, Jonas tried to reassure himself. *She's still a kind person. She's simply not an honest person.*

"But...I believed you did not wish for anything but a diversion, Jonas," she said in a soft voice. "You did not want to hear of the mess my father left me with. And...this was a shameful thing for me." She paused. "Perhaps I did not want things to change between us. I did not wish for you to look at me differently."

"But you trusted *him*."

"I'm sorry, Jonas, it was not planned..."

Rey had helped her quit taking the leaves. She was Galdra. Hordes of Klaernar hunted for her. A red-haired warrior had chased her through town in broad daylight. He started to question everything he thought he knew about her. Was her name even Silla? Was she even from Skarstad?

A headache pierced his skull, and he pressed his thumbs down firmly on his temples. A new realization crystalized. She fled the Klaernar, which meant...

"There was never a land dispute, was there?"

She bowed her head with a soft exhale. "No."

It was a dagger slid between his ribs. Their shared experience, the one which had led him to trust her—to open up to a woman for the first time in his life—it had all been a lie.

"There are so many lies, Silla, I cannot even count them. All of this time, you've been nothing but deceitful." *You should never have told her your history,* he thought. *This is what you get for letting her near your heart.* "Was anything you told me true?" His voice rose higher, a flock of startled birds taking flight from the grasses beyond the river.

"Yes. I swear it to you, Jonas," pleaded Silla. "I know this looks terrible, but I beg you to believe me—my mother, my stories, they are all true. I did not wish to deceive you. I *hated* every moment of it."

Her skin had a pallid look to it, her teeth chattering, and that familiar feeling in his chest squeezed in. Despite the lies, despite the fact he did not even know this woman, he did not wish to see her suffer.

"Come," he said softly. "Let us get you dressed."

He helped her into the dress, then offered her his flask—a mouthful of brennsa always warmed one from the inside out. Jonas pulled a roll of wool blankets from his saddlesack, laying one out on the ground, and wrapping the other around her shoulders as she sank down beside him. Reluctantly, Jonas drew her close to him. He could not help himself—he wanted to be near to her.

Yet, she had deceived him. He'd told her things he'd never told another, all because of her lie.

He felt like a fool.

His thoughts were a battlefield, warring for control, until all he felt was muddied confusion.

Never again will you allow yourself to be disrespected.
She was only frightened.
She's made a fool of you.
She did not know she could trust you, but now you've shown her she can.

"I did not wish to lie to you," she whispered, looking at him with unease. "I...I had to come up with a story on the spot to convince Axe Eyes not to kill me. If I had known you had a history, I'd have..."

"Come up with a different lie," said Jonas bitterly.

She wrung her hands together. "It was life or death. He'd have killed me, and you wouldn't have lost sleep over it—"

"That was weeks ago, Silla," he interjected. "You've had weeks to speak the truth."

"I'm sorry," she said quietly, putting her hand on his arm. Her touch was warm. Soft. Grounding. A reminder that she was still his Silla. He stared listlessly into the rushing waters.

Jonas felt sick. Everything which had drawn him to her—her honest and genuine nature, their shared experience with land disputes, her kind, gentle heart—it had been false all along.

Her hand squeezed gently, and the bile rising in his throat eased back down. Jonas breathed deeply, trying to imagine what he would have done were he in her place. She'd been all alone. Had nearly perished in the Twisted Pinewoods. Had lost her father and was running for her life. Axe Eyes *would* have handed her over if she'd admitted the Klaernar chased her; she was right in that.

"I cannot fault you for trying to stay alive," he said at last, scrubbing a hand over his beard. "But, fuck. The Klaernar have been chasing you all this time?" He grew lost in thought. "That is why you looked so worried in the market in Svarti. Why you borrowed my cloak?" His eyes darted to her. "Why you left the mead hall that night in such a rush?"

Hesitantly, she nodded. Jonas's chest squeezed. She'd shouldered this burden all alone for so long. She'd made so many mistakes, had gotten herself into such a mess.

"What should I do, Jonas?" Silla asked quietly, as though reading his thoughts. "We are close to Kopa, but I worry. I do not wish to put the Bloodaxe Crew in danger."

An incredulous laugh escaped him. "Danger? Look around, Silla. We travel the Road of Bones. Our camp was attacked by wolfspiders last night. We are surrounded already by danger."

She chewed on her lip. "What if the Klaernar come for me again? What if they find me with you? I cannot implicate you—the penalties for harboring a fugitive are harsh, Jonas."

He laughed, unnaturally deep. "It is too late for that, woman."

"I'm sorry," she whispered. "I did not wish to bring danger to you." She put a hand to her forehead. "I must tell the Bloodaxe Crew about...this." Silla waved her arms around. "I must warn them of the Klaernar. I cannot have anyone hurt because of me."

Jonas's brows drew together as he considered. "Yes," he said slowly. "We must be prepared for the possibility that the Klaernar could attack." He was silent a moment. "Though, Axe Eyes might send you away, Silla." A treachery of ravens flew overhead, and Jonas stared at them as he spoke. "I could not bear for that to happen. Here is what you will do: stay silent for now—do not tell the Bloodaxe Crew about this yet. We will speak to Rey together after I've had time to think. It is five day's ride from Kopa. You must keep gloves on at all times until we arrive." He frowned. "What, exactly, is *in* Kopa?"

She cringed. "I hate that I've lied to you, Jonas," she whispered. "I despised every minute of it." She patted her hip. "I have the address of a man who helps those in need find shield-houses."

His heart was numbed already, this new barb had no bite. Jonas pinched his lips together all the same.

Silla frowned. "My pocket!" She fished a hand up her skirts, feeling around. A look of dismay crossed her face. "My pocket has ripped. Oh...The letter is gone!" She pressed fingers to her lips, blinking quickly. "I-I have the address memorized."

Jonas watched her quietly, weighing what to do. Such a predicament she had gotten herself into. Clearly, she needed his help. A firm hand. Guidance. A decision passed through him, a slow smile curving his lips.

"You can relax, Silla. You are with me now," he said. "I will ensure your safety, but you must do as I say. Do you agree to this?" He tilted her chin to him, staring into her large brown eyes.

Her brows were furrowed, and he ran a finger down the line between them. After a moment, she nodded.

A smile spread across Jonas's face. "Good. You needn't worry, my Selfless Silla. I will get you to Kopa, and we will figure out the rest together."

FIFTY-TWO

SKUTUR

S kraeda's fingers tapped along the scarred ashwood table as she waited for Kommandor Laxa to enter. The small room at the front of the Skutur garrison longhouse was nearly bare—two chairs and a table, torches set into the walls casting light into the space. A thin wall separated Skraeda from the rest of the Klaernar dining in the great hall beyond on what smelled of stew and freshly baked bread. No feast fare tonight—the girl had evaded them. *Again*.

Her stomach growled all the same. She'd been waiting for Laxa for an hour, if not more, had been offered no food, nor the chance to scrub the dirt from beneath her fingernails. The residue of the dead clung to her. A weaker woman would have let it get to her, but not Skraeda—she could not allow these arrogant kuntas the benefit of seeing weakness in her.

And so she waited.

Her eyes settled upon the flickering flames of a reed torch, unable to keep her thoughts from drifting to the events earlier in the day. She'd ridden into town the night prior, after driving her mount hard all the way from Hver. After a blissful night of sleep, she'd made her way toward the Klaernar garrison hall... only to see the Bloodaxe Crew's sigil riding through the town. Warriors—six of them—plus a wagon which had seen better days.

And then, there she was. Eisa, right there, in the midst of Skutur.

Fortune had shone upon Skraeda at last. After days...weeks of pursuit, the girl stood there, just before her, surrounded by warriors of the Bloodaxe Crew. And to Skraeda's delight, she'd rushed from their protection and fled into the streets. It had seemed so perfect.

Too perfect.

Shame filled her chest. Eisa had slipped through her fingers *again*. Skraeda had made a grave error, had let her pride get the best of her. Perhaps she'd been too confident. Perhaps she'd allowed herself too much fun. She could not help herself. How often does one find themselves in the company of fallen royalty? And the girl had not even known. It had only dawned on Skraeda when she'd mentioned Eisa's sister...the girl had had no idea it was Saga Volsik. As she'd tugged on the thread of Eisa's fear, Skraeda should have known she might draw forth a memory of Saga. After that, she had sensed confusion, disbelief, and bewilderment. Until that moment, the girl truly had not known she was Eisa Volsik.

What a fool her adoptive father had been.

And what a fool Skraeda had been to judge Eisa weak. She had, after all, evaded the queen's oathsworn warriors near Skarstad. Had twice evaded Skraeda. And now this. The girl was slippery and deceptively resourceful. And Skraeda had to admit she admired Eisa's spirit, the way she fought for her freedom. It reminded her of herself.

That did not mean she wouldn't find her and make her pay for the shame she'd cast upon Skraeda. Thrice now she'd slipped through her fingers. Kommandor Laxa would certainly unleash a verbal lashing upon her.

But worse, Her Highness would be displeased.

Discomfort slithered in Skraeda's stomach, and her hand dipped into her pocket, the square of parchment bringing her comfort. "There is no room for failure," she told herself, reaffirming her vows—Skraeda *would* find Eisa, would bring her to the queen.

Her survival depended on it.

The doors swung open, a tall Klaernar warrior stepping into the room. Skraeda stood, playing the games of honor the King's Claws so enjoyed.

"Kommandor Laxa," she said, with a nod of deference.

Like all Klaernar, the man was tall and broad, three tattooed slashes running along his cheek. A bearskin hat sat upon his graying head, his beard long— midway down his chest—and twisted into twin braids.

"Skraeda Clever Tongue," said the kommandor, giving her an assessing gaze. Two younger Klaernar warriors stepped in the doorway behind him.

Skraeda loosened her mind, sensing out their auras. Impatience and irritation, but more troubling was the feeling they shielded something from her.

The kommandor sank into a chair across the table from her.

A woman with the ice-blonde hair of a Norvalander bustled into the room. As she placed a basin of water onto the table, a thrall tattoo peeked out from the underside of her wrist.

The kommandor nodded at Skraeda. "So you might wash before dining."

Finally, thought Skraeda. Finally, they show her the respect she was due. Wordlessly, she dipped her hands into the tepid water, scrubbing the dust of the dead from them.

"The girl has gone," said the kommandor, watching her closely. "Each home has been searched. Each outbuilding, sheep shed, and woodpile in the area."

Skraeda let out a long breath, scrubbing at a stubborn patch on her hands. She would let the man say what he would. Would let him think what he needed to.

"You were alone with her, Skraeda," he said roughly. "Did she speak to you?"

Skraeda lifted her hands from the basin, flicking the water off. Did the foolish man think she would simply share such hard-earned details with him? Did he think her a fool? She pulled her lips into a deferential smile. "Yes, kommandor," she said. "She and I spoke, though only briefly."

The thrall returned, laying a trencher of bread and a bowl of stew before Skraeda. Pulling the basin off the table, she retreated from the room.

"Fortune shone upon the girl once more," said Skraeda, watching the kommandor as she dipped the bread into the stew. "She was quite frightened."

"And yet she escaped," said the kommandor, the venom barely veiled in his words. He breathed in sharply through his nose, then leaned back in his carved wooden chair.

Sensing the warrior's wrath, Skraeda allowed her gift to smooth the rough edges of his emotions. They'd get nowhere unless the man was calm.

After a moment, Kommandor Laxa leaned forward on the table, steepling his fingers together. "Did the girl give any indication of where she might be heading?"

Skraeda brought the spoon to her lips, sipping the broth from it. "North, I would assume, kommandor. She has traveled north for weeks."

The man's jaw flexed as he watched her. "Naturally," he said stiffly. "But once at the Northern Junction, east, or west?"

"I can assess once I arrive," said Skraeda, choosing her words wisely. "I should set out at once. I've wasted hours in this room, awaiting orders."

The kommandor ignored her. "It is assumed at this point she has companions who harbor her, who assisted her escape from Skutur today," he said. "Who are they, Skraeda?"

The tone of his voice told her their game was coming to a close, though she'd scarcely eaten any of the stew. With a sigh, Skraeda set her spoon aside and stared into Laxa's dark eyes. A thread of his irritation twined with revulsion and distrust. They were starting to get somewhere now.

She would feed him some details, then discover his game.

"It must not leave this room," Skraeda said carefully, her eyes flitting to his two minions flanking the door. Their gazes were fixed upon the wall behind her, emotions abnormally smooth. Skraeda's gaze settled upon Kommandor Laxa. "She travels with the Bloodaxe Crew."

Kommandor Laxa regarded her with his dark gaze. "The queen grows tired of your failures, Skraeda."

Her stomach clenched down. She could not let the queen down, she would show her, would make her see...

"You've been removed from the job," said the kommandor, nodding at the warriors behind him.

And so the game ends, thought Skraeda, her hands twitching toward her empty scabbard. With her weapons left at the entry of the longhouse, she would have to rely on her galdur. But distressed by the queen's shaken confidence in her, her gift grew veiled. *Center yourself, you fool,* she chided, sucking in a deep breath and holding it.

As the warriors approached her with violent intent, emotions finally poured freely from them. But her eyes fell upon the shining silver cuffs dangling from their hands, and Skraeda's pulse accelerated.

Hindrium cuffs, she realized, her urgency growing. If they cuffed her, if her galdur became neutralized...

Gritting her teeth, Skraeda forced herself to concentrate—she had the span of three heartbeats accomplish what she needed to do.

The younger of the two was the easiest; his thirst for her blood was strong, and his emotions vivid. Skraeda's mind reached out, sifting through the threads until she reached the thin golden one buried deep within. One tug, and she drew it to herself, wielding it like a set of reins.

The man's jaw slackened, his pupils dilating. A small smile curved Skraeda's lips. "Cut his throat."

The younger Klaernar unsheathed his dagger and slashed it across his companion's neck. Kommandor Laxa leaped to his feet with a yell of surprise as blood spurted through the air, splattering onto the table and walls. The man grabbed at his neck with a startled gasp, but it did little to staunch the flow as his life spilled from him and he buckled to the floor.

"Kill yourself."

The younger warrior slashed the reddened blade across his own throat, pupils dilating as Skraeda released the thread of his free will. Looking down, his eyes widened as he took in the sight of blood gushing from his neck. And then, he crumpled to the floor on top of his brother-in-arms, rivulets of crimson streaming over their bodies and pooling on the floor. The kommandor was near the door, reaching for the pull...

"*Sit*, Kommandor," barked Skraeda, "or you'll be next." No longer bothering to shield his emotions from her, loathing and disgust seeped from him, matching the hatred in his eyes. "Good," she said, as the large man complied, perching on his chair. "We can stop this game of pretenses and speak honestly to one another, Laxa." Skraeda wedged her own chair against the door.

Not a moment later, someone knocked from beyond it. "Everything all right, Kommandor?" came a male voice from the other side.

Skraeda glared at the kommandor, nodding at the door.

"Fine!" he called out. "We are fine. Leave us be!"

The sound of retreating footsteps made Skraeda's pulse calm.

Laxa leveled a glare at Skraeda. "What do you expect will come from this, *Galdra*?" he spat. "You will not walk free from this building. You will be put to the pillar like the rest of your unnatural kind."

"I am too valuable for that." Her voice hitched on the last word, and she cleared her throat.

"The queen ordered it, you fool," growled Laxa. "You have failed her too many times. She has deemed you unworthy of her protection."

"You lie," she spat.

"I speak the truth," said the kommandor. "I have the letter to prove it. Do you wish to see it?"

"Show me!" Flames of fury burned in Skraeda's stomach. The queen. Her savior. It could not be true...

Standing, the kommandor pulled a scroll from his cloak, handing it to Skraeda. Snatching it from him, her eyes fell upon the golden wasp sigil, broken. Skraeda unrolled the parchment and drank in the words on the page. Her body grew numb as she read the words *should she fail once more, use her for your pillar quota*. Parchment crumpling in her fist, her eyes settled on Laxa.

He stood, stepping backward until his spine hit the wall.

Not so arrogant now, are we, Laxa? thought Skraeda, but she could glean no joy from his misery. The queen had ordered her executed. The queen thought her no longer useful. Dread began to sprout in her gut, but she yanked it out. *You must change that,* she told herself. *You will show her how useful you are, Skraeda.*

"What is the plan, Laxa?" demanded Skraeda. She scarcely recognized her voice now. "What is the queen's plan without me?"

"M-more oathsworn warriors," stumbled Laxa. "More warriors, and Maester Alfson's adherent with the wasps. They've been sent along the road, stopping all who pass. Their numbers are great. They will find her. It is only a matter of time."

"*I* will find her," Skraeda vowed. "It will be *me* who brings Eisa Volsik to Queen Signe, and none other."

"You're mad," muttered Kommandor Laxa.

"Yes," she said, her lips curving up. A plan took form in her mind—the slate must be wiped clean. "And you're already dead, kommandor. Sadly, not even the ravens will want your corpse when I'm through."

She tugged on his fear to hold him in place, then closed her eyes and reached for the shimmering pool of galdur tucked beneath her ribcage. Ashbringer was not her primary intuition, but Skraeda's anger made it easy to draw it forth and prime herself.

Kommandor Laxa's eyes widened as they settled on the orange light gathering in her veins. "B-but...you're a Solacer!"

"Yes," purred Skraeda, enjoying the heat of her forearms. With an exhale, she relaxed, magic expressing from her palms in a burst of licking flames. "Did you know, kommandor, that I had a twin?"

His fear was wild now, a whimper escaping him.

"Have you heard of Galdra twins, kommandor? All that time in the womb...more than just blood is shared. My sister was an Ashbringer, though she was too frightened to make use of her gift. It was a weakness of hers. A flaw in her character."

You are nothing but a selfish coward, Skraeda! Ilka screamed in memory. *A traitor to your own kind!*

Skraeda's flames guttered, and she blinked back to the present. "I am no coward, though. I am not afraid of vermin like you, Laxa. A pity," she said, yanking on Laxa's fear as she stepped toward him. He'd soiled himself, held paralyzed as his worst fears played before his eyes. "I do not have time to play with you, kommandor. I'd very much enjoy that. But I must be on my way."

She pushed her flames upon his ridiculous bearskin hat, allowing herself a moment to absorb the sweet sounds of his screams, the beautiful sizzle of his flesh. His skin bubbled and popped. Grabbing the bread from the table, Skraeda bit into it as she kicked the chair wedged against the door aside and strolled through it.

A tall Klaernar rushed at her, his sword raised. His anger was palpable, a throbbing bright loop effortless for Skraeda to yank, bringing the warrior to his knees with a sound of anguish. Disarming the man, she swung his sword into the neck of an approaching warrior. She collected her own weapons from the door, turning to see more Klaernar charging at her. The fire had now spread to the timbered walls, devouring the longhouse with unrelenting hunger. With a smile, she closed the doors and slid the dead Klaernar's sword through the handles.

Standing with her arms behind her back, Skraeda watched as the smoke billowed through into the skies; as the flames caught on the turf roof and spread across it; as the screams of the men inside wove together into a beautiful harmony.

She watched as they burned.

Skraeda's hand slid into her pocket and wrapped around the square of parchment. And then, she smiled.

FIFTY-THREE

THE ROAD OF BONES

S illa stared at the blond warrior who slept beside her, watching the rhythmic rise and fall of his chest. In sleep, Jonas looked peaceful— younger, unburdened. But lying in a tent of their own—purchased by the Bloodaxe Crew in Skutur—Silla felt the world's weight on her shoulders.

She'd been withdrawn and shaky once they'd rejoined the Crew at Black Rock—had skipped practice with Hekla and retreated into the tent early. Jonas had soon joined her, awaking her with soft kisses, and she'd been eager to lose herself, even if just for even a few brief moments. Though he'd bedded her more gently than ever before, Silla could see it in his eyes, could feel it in the air. Her lies had put new distance between them. And there were more she held close to her heart.

Silla exhaled, watching him.

You can tell him, she thought. *Just say it: it is Queen Signe who is after me, not merely the Klaernar.*

They were simple words.

How hard were they to say?

You've let him get too close, Silla imagined the little blonde girl—Saga, she corrected—saying.

Jonas was supposed to be nothing but a distraction, but somewhere along the way, the lines had blurred. They'd grown close. He'd told her things, and she'd felt compelled to share her own past. Perhaps he'd put a spell on her, bewitched her mind with his dizzying attentions. When she was with him, she did not think of the things she'd lived through, did not worry for the future. She was simply there, in that moment, lost to herself and the world.

Now, Jonas wished to see more of her, wished to visit her in Kopa. Drunk on his touch, she'd said yes. But worry crept in from all sides. It did not seem a smart decision. Kopa was unknown. Would it be safe to have visitors in the shield-house? Or would it be better to have a clean break, a fresh slate? A new life for her, with no links to the old one. The more trails she left, the easier it would be for Signe to track her.

This stirred the embers of a troubling thought. Her presence brought danger upon the Bloodaxe Crew, and they deserved to know it—the sooner, the better. *We will speak to Rey together after I've had time to think,* Jonas had said. But it was her trouble, and this felt like something she needed to do alone.

Her mind was made up—Silla would warn them and let things fall where they would. If Axe Eyes left her on the side of the road, so be it. Her friends would be safe, and she would find a way. She'd made it this far. She *would* make it to Kopa.

Kopa. She just needed to get to Kopa. And once there, once settled in a shield-house, she could finally rest. Breathe. Consider the truth.

She was Eisa Volsik.

Her pulse grew erratic, palms beginning to sweat. Silla forced in a deep breath as panic clawed up her throat, the same as it did each time she thought of that name. She'd wanted to know who she was...*what* she was. But now that Silla knew the truth, she wanted to push it all back. Crawl back under the rock she'd lived under for so long.

Eisa Volsik was a name with realities Silla was not ready to consider. Heir to King Ivar's most despised enemy—she'd never know peace, would look over her shoulder for the rest of her life. Would she ever know who she could trust— who might sell her out, or who would use her for their own gain?

And the question which frightened her most of all—would any shield-house be safe enough for Eisa?

Her heartbeat grew wild, her breaths shallowing, and she squeezed her eyes shut.

Leaves, her mind pleaded. *One leaf. Just one.*

One leaf to ease the tension in her stomach, to forget that she was Eisa. And another to stitch her up and make her feel whole again. To feel like Silla.

She'd just wanted chickens. How had things gotten so twisted? So messy?

Hearthfire thoughts, she told herself. *Fields of fireweed with snow capped mountains in the distance. Dancing around bonfires with Hekla. Dimples.* Gradually, her pulse slowed, the tension in her chest loosening. Silla could not allow herself to think that name, could not consider the implications which came with it, or she would crumble completely.

You are Silla; you must get to Kopa, and that is the end of it.

It was all she could do to keep her feet moving, one foot in front of the other.

Get to Kopa. Four more days.

———

REY COULD NOT SLEEP. A nagging feeling kept pulling at him from under his skin. It was an irritating feeling, as though he'd forgotten something and could not quite remember it.

After tossing under his furs for an hour, he finally forced himself to crawl out from the tent he shared with Ilías.

Nodding at Sigrún, who sat by the fire after a night on watch duty, Rey wandered about the camp, trying to determine if he'd forgotten to do something. He checked the freshly installed undercarriage of the wagon, the bags and crates neatly arranged in the flatbed. He checked the crate of rhodium weapons, counting them all. He strolled the perimeter of camp. After checking the horses, Rey leaned against a knotted pine trunk, scowling at the camp. Horse approached, nosing into his chest, and he stroked her absently.

Nothing was amiss; everything was in place.

Movement from the farthest of the tents diverted his gaze—*she* crawled from the one she now shared with Jonas. A shock of brown curls bounced around her; she wore gloves and had Jonas's cloak pulled tight over her shoulders. The cloak Hekla had loaned her from the wagon was notably absent, one of a few peculiarities which were piling up.

She'd been unwell the day before; she and Jonas had ridden off from Skutur abruptly.

Probably to rut like animals.

Rey's frown deepened as he was met with the intense desire to slam his fist into Jonas's pretty face once more.

She and Jonas were a terrible match, and he did not know how she couldn't see it. She might be good for him, but he was *all wrong* for her. Rey loved Jonas like a brother, but the man could be selfish and controlling to a great fault. Jonas would stifle her when what she needed was for someone to...lift her. Empower her.

And Jonas had taken advantage of her—a fact which did not sit well with Rey, no matter how much Jonas claimed to care for her. She'd been alone, had just lost her father. It had a slippery feel to Rey.

"I should have been paying more attention," he muttered to Horse. "How could I miss that?"

Horse nosed his chest, blowing softly.

Because you've been doing your best to avoid her yourself, he thought. *And because it is none of your gods damned business.* Had he not been counting down the days until he could be done with this oath he'd sworn to her? Be rid of the girl?

Four days until Kopa.

Four days until things were set to rights.

Four days until he could stop watching her from the corner of his eye as she cooked the evening meal, or learned a new series of hand signs with Sigrún. Could stop worrying for her safety whenever danger struck. Could stop listening for her laugh and searching for her smiles.

Rey did not know how this had happened. He needed to rid himself of this distraction.

As she wandered toward Sigrún, he noted the tension in her shoulders, the way she chewed on her lip. Something troubled her, and the fact he had noticed made Rey's teeth grind together. He lingered with the horses. They wouldn't talk his ear off, nor hum irritatingly under their breaths. Rey far preferred the company of horses over humans on most days.

But the woman caught sight of him, diverting her course straight to him.

Stifling a groan of irritation, Rey crossed his arms over his chest and watched her approach. She turned on her heel and walked abruptly away from him, then seemed to change her mind and come forward once more. Her brown eyes met his, and his gaze fell upon the new necklace she wore—a carved wooden talisman similar to Jonas's family's crest. Rey's scowl deepened.

"You have something to tell me?" he asked, his voice sounding gruffer than he'd intended.

Nervous energy radiated off her, hands opening and closing into fists. "Y-yes," said the woman breathlessly.

"On with it, then," he grunted.

She bounced on the balls of her feet, refusing to meet his eye. "There may be warriors on the road who search for me."

Rey's brows furrowed, and he studied her silently.

"I do not wish harm to come to you...to the Bloodaxe Crew. You have been kind, you have helped me. If you think it best that I leave, then I will."

His mind worked rapidly, piecing things together. "The Klaernar searched for a girl in Skutur yesterday," he murmured. "You would not happen to know about that, would you?"

She swallowed, and Rey had his answer.

How he had not put it together before now, Rey was unsure. But the pieces were sliding into place, and it all made sense—the lie Kraki had caught her in, how she'd pushed him that day in the field. And, of course, those leaves. He felt a fool now, as realization settled.

She is Galdra, then, he thought. Rey studied her quietly, his mind at war. She'd lied to him, and yet he pitied her. Wanted to help her, and yet, her presence brought complications and danger to his Crew.

He pinched the bridge of his nose. "How many?"

"I do not know," said the girl softly. "But the warrior you killed...the red-haired woman at Skalla Ridge? She did not die."

So the warrior *had* been attacking her on Skalla Ridge. A bounty hunter, perhaps? The Klaernar did not often outsource, but it had been done in the past. Rey's eyes bored into her. "How?"

"I do not know. She came after me in Skutur, and I only narrowly escaped."

His chest filled with unexpected pride, but a throb grew in his temple. "What have you dragged us into?" he growled.

"I—"

"Do not tell me," he said, and her eyes widened in surprise. "I do not wish to know the details." When it came to dealing with the Klaernar, it would be best not to know specifics; in the unlikely chance one of the Bloodaxe Crew were taken into custody, they could claim honest innocence.

"You needn't be bonded by the oath, Rey," she said softly. "I will release you from it. And I won't ever tell your secret; I swear it on my life. I do not wish to bring danger upon you."

Now it was Rey's turn to be surprised. She had honor; he would give her that. Had Rey been in her situation, this is precisely what he'd have done. But he was a capable warrior, and she...she was not.

Rey did not need to consider his options to know what he'd do. He'd sworn an oath to get her safely to Kopa, and he would not leave it unfulfilled, even if at her own suggestion. It wasn't simply the oath, though. He'd grown to...respect the woman. He'd watched her work hard with Hekla, had seen the fire in her spirit. There was a kinship between them, more than she could understand; Rey knew what it meant to keep secrets buried for the sake of safety.

And she *had* saved his life.

That was what decided it for him.

Rey scowled at her. "I swore you an oath, and even if it has turned into the worst of decisions, I will see it through. But I must check with my warriors first. We decide as a Crew what should be done."

The woman rubbed her elbow, nodding at him.

"I thank you," said Rey, trying to soften his words. "There is honor in what you have done. In your care for the lives of my Crew."

She blinked at him, those long black lashes framing her expressive eyes. Rey forced his gaze away. Those eyes held their own current, and he knew better than to get pulled into their flow.

"Prepare the daymeal," he barked, turning on his foot and striding toward the wagon. "And I will call a Crew meeting."

———

SPOONING PORRIDGE INTO HIS MOUTH, Jonas scowled at Silla. Her back was turned to him as she dished porridge into a bowl for Ilías; she had been flighty all morning.

And now Rey had called a Crew meeting.

"You know what this is about?" asked Ilías, sinking onto a log near Jonas. "I swear, I don't know anything about pine needles getting into Rey's bedding."

Jonas raised a brow, regarding his brother.

"And if this is about the missing brennsa, my sólas are on Fire Fist."

Jonas took another bite of porridge.

"And between you and me, I saw your girl sneaking one of the good apples to Horse. So, if Axe Eyes is wondering where they all went, that's where."

His girl. Jonas's lips twitched, warmth spreading through his chest. He liked the sound of that. Rey clapped his hands together in three sharp strikes, and his smile fell.

"Crew meeting," Axe Eyes said gruffly.

The porridge in Jonas's stomach turned over.

"Sunshine here has informed me that there might be some warriors on the road looking for her," said Rey. "Klaernar, more specifically." The unspoken words were plain for all to hear. *Silla is Galdra.* And now the whole of the Bloodaxe Crew knew it.

Jonas's teeth clamped down, his eyes landing on Silla. She smoothed her overdress, then clutched her hands together. She'd told Rey, after Jonas had instructed her to wait for him. She had willingly told him her secrets—had *volunteered* them to him.

Jonas gripped his spoon so tightly his knuckles turned white.

Are you Galdra? Sigrún signed, Gunnar interpreting for a confused Silla.

Before she could answer, Rey jumped in. "We are not going to press her for answers," he said gruffly.

A strange sensation prickled up the back of Jonas's neck. *Why does Rey protect her?* he wondered.

Murmured confusion spread amongst the Bloodaxe Crew, but Rey continued speaking. "You know how I feel about lies," said Rey slowly, looking into the eyes of each warrior. "But this is different. She has come to me willingly to warn us of danger. Has volunteered to leave us if we wish it, so that harm will not befall us. And if we decide to help her flee the Klaernar, in this case, it is best we know as little as possible."

"If the Bloodaxe Crew won't help her, I'll do it alone," Jonas jumped in.

Silla's lips parted as her eyes finally met his, and he sent her a dagger-sharp glare. He had things to say to her in private.

"I swore to her that we would take her to Kopa," said Rey, diverting Jonas from his thoughts, "and I'm of a mind to see it through. As we are a group, I want us to all be in agreement. So let us vote. All in favor of keeping her with us?" Rey raised his arm.

There was a moment of silence, of consideration, and then Hekla's arm stretched into the air. Sigrún, Ilías, and Gunnar quickly followed.

They stared at Jonas.

He chuckled, raising his arm. "Of course, I wish it," he muttered.

Tears filled Silla's eyes, and she hugged herself tightly. "Are you certain? You truly wish to risk yourselves for me?"

Hekla strode to her, wrapping an arm around her shoulder. "Of course, dúlla. We take care of our own." She leaned in, and Jonas heard her whisper, "You'll tell me everything later?" Silla hesitated, then nodded.

"Did you know your girl is Galdra?" asked Ilías from beside him.

Jonas just grunted.

"Very well," barked Rey, and the hum of conversation died. "It is decided then." Rey turned to Silla, speaking to her with a softness Jonas did not appreciate. "How many?"

Silla clasped her hands tightly together. "There were six in Skarstad. And one in Skutur, plus perhaps...ten who seemed to search..."

"Skutur?" asked Gunnar. "Why do you tell us only now?"

The eyes of the Bloodaxe Crew fell upon Silla. "It was a surprise to me," she said, refusing to meet Jonas's gaze. "It took me some time to decide what to do."

"Between six and ten," barked Rey, bringing them back to the task at hand.

Why did he deflect the questions? wondered Jonas. *Why did he protect her?* The prickling sensation was back, crawling along Jonas's skin before understanding settled in. Rey wanted Silla for himself. Jonas could think of no other reason the Crew's headman would dismiss her lies so casually, not to mention shelter a fugitive.

"Now that we know what to expect," continued Rey, "it should not be a problem for the six of us. Have your shields at the ready. Blades sharp. Listen for my command. Sigrún, ride ahead and signal back if you meet men on the road."

"Sigrún, have you any extra lébrynja armor for Silla?" asked Hekla. "You seem about the same size?"

The blonde woman nodded.

Rey turned to Silla. "Have your blade ready. Remember your defenses. Think ahead and anticipate what they will do. And, Sunshine, do not hesitate." The corners of his lips twitched, like the words had some silent meaning to him. As Silla's lips curved up in return, Jonas's blood began to simmer.

He could stand it no longer—such blatant disrespect. Jonas shot to his feet and grabbed Silla by the arm, pulling her behind the wagon. A storm was gathering inside him, and he needed to speak his peace.

"Jonas," she protested, her feet stumbling to keep up with him. "What is—"

His hands curved around her shoulders, and he shook her gently. "You told him without me."

She held herself very still, her brown eyes watching him warily. "Yes," she said. "It was a thing I thought I should do on my own and as soon as possible. I should have told him last night, Jonas."

"You trust him." Jonas's insides twisted. He hated this—it was Rey, his brother-in-arms. But he would not have her act this way; did she not realize she made a fool of him?

"I—"

"You told him your secrets," said Jonas, his grip tightening.

"I couldn't let anyone be at risk of danger. What of it, Jonas?" Her eyes flashed in challenge.

Clearly, she did not understand. *Ah, your Silla,* he thought. *She is young and naive. She needs you to explain it to her. Help her understand.*

Jonas cupped her cheek tenderly. "I do not want you speaking to Rey anymore," said Jonas softly.

"What?"

She was adorably displeased. His thumb swiped across her lower lip.

"You will no longer train with him, and if you need to speak to him, you will do so through me."

Her brows drew together, and she pulled his hand from her cheek. "Jonas, you cannot ask that of me."

"You're with me now, Silla. You wear *my* family's sigil." He brushed his lips against hers softly.

"Jonas," she said, her gaze bouncing from one eye to the other and back again. "What has gotten into you? I do not know what troubles you, but let me put your mind at ease: you're the one who knows me best in this world."

Jonas laughed, a brittle sound he did not recognize as his own. Best in this world? Pitiful if that was true. But in time he would know all her truths.

"Come here," he said, gripping her wrist and pulling her toward him. Jonas glanced over his shoulder, his gaze colliding with Rey's. His headman stood by the wagon, arms crossed over his chest, watching Jonas with pure distaste upon his face.

Good, thought Jonas, claiming Silla's mouth with his own in a kiss that left them both breathless. When he drew back, he looked into her troubled brown eyes.

"You agreed to do what I said, Silla. Think twice before going behind my back again."

Jonas stalked off to saddle his horse, leaving the curly-haired girl leaning against the tree.

FIFTY-FOUR

A s the wagon trundled down the road that morning, each small movement in the forest caught Silla's eye. Thankfully, they had passed through the open Highlands and re-entered the forest, protecting them from the wind. If Silla recalled correctly, this meant they had nearly reached the Northern Junction where they'd leave the Road of Bones and head west along the final stretch.

Kopa. She was nearly there. It was so close, she could taste it.

And yet a disquiet had settled in her bones. Silla was relieved she'd told Rey, was glad she'd warned the Bloodaxe Crew that they might be in danger. But Jonas's reaction had been unnerving.

You're with me now, Silla. You wear my family's sigil.

His possessive words, which once had made her blood thrum with need, had now taken on a new, unsettling meaning.

"I belong to myself," Silla whispered. When today was over, they would talk, and she would tell him as much. When he'd cornered her behind the wagon, she'd been too stunned to speak. Yet again, she wasn't sure how they had gotten to this place. He was meant to be a distraction. How had they gotten so off course?

This was precisely why she was meant to keep her distance from others, particularly from *men*. Feelings were complicated. Pride and entitlement and ego were not things to be trifled with. Jonas had been a comfort to her, a balm to her grieving heart. But things had taken a troubling turn, and Silla did not have room for more problems in her life. Her hand found the talisman, hanging around her neck.

Kopa would be a clean slate. A new life. A fresh page.

You will need to end things with him, she thought. *Ease him down gently.* Silla pulled the talisman over her head and laid it down in the wagon.

A shrill whistle pierced the air. Whirling in the wagon, she found Rey's arm lifted, hand curled into a fist. The horses came to a stop. It was quiet on the road for several heartbeats, and then the distant sound of hooves on hard-packed earth met her ears.

Rey was beside her before she could blink, yanking her from the wagon and pushing her to the woods. "You have your blade?" he asked with cutting calm.

Her heart pounded with the force of a war hammer. Silla nodded, patting her hip where she'd replaced her lost dagger with one of the Bloodaxe Crew's spares.

"Go to the woods and do not come out," he said, giving her a gentle push. "And remember, Sunshine—"

"I'll use the sharp part this time, Rey," Silla interjected with a smile. "Be safe!" she said to the Bloodaxe Crew, tears blurring her eyes. They nodded solemnly at her. Her eyes met Jonas's steely blue, lingering for a long moment.

Silla fled into the woods and did not look back. Clad in Sigrún's scaled leather armor, she marveled at how swiftly she could move without her cumbersome skirts. Hopping over a fallen pine, she spotted a hollowed-out trunk covered in moss and climbed inside. And then, she waited. A raven called out from somewhere high above; a wasp buzzed by her ear, and she fanned it away.

Crouching within the stump, her pulse now thundered in her ears. Would Skraeda be there? Would Rey be able to defeat her? Would it be mercenaries like near Skarstad? Klaernar like Skutur?

The pounding of hooves came to an abrupt halt, and Silla peeked out from the stump counting five warriors. The tension in her chest loosened. *Five.* That should not be a challenge for the Bloodaxe Crew. Perhaps they would not even break a sweat.

A voice sliced through the cool air. "Morning!"

The deep timbre of Rey's voice echoed off the trees. "Is there something you need?"

"We search for a young woman. Curly brown hair, about this high. Has a small scar beside her left eye. Might go by Katrin."

Rey was silent a moment. "No one with us goes by that name."

"Very well. We shall take a quick look in your wagon and be on our way." Parchment rustled. "Orders from the queen. She is *quite* eager to bring the girl to Sunnavík."

An ache grew in Silla's stomach. *The queen.* How foolish of her to think the mercenaries might not reveal this to the Crew. Rey had not wished to know, but she should have been more forthcoming and told him all the same. She should have told them the full truth...that she was Eisa...

Her temples squeezed in, her heart thundering. Panic began to claw up her throat. *No,* she thought. *Not now.* Silla took a fortifying breath. *Hearthfire thoughts,* she forced into her mind. *The scent of pinewoods and campfire. Panbreads, pulled fresh and fluffy from the embers of the fire. A little boy hugging his puppy.*

"What does the queen want with her?" Even from within the stump, Rey's voice sounded tight.

"That is between the girl and Her Highness."

"We have private business with the king, and he has forbidden us from sharing the contents of the wagon," said Rey.

"That is disappointing," said the stranger. "Because the queen has promised a handsome reward to those who deliver her the girl. And we shall not leave until we have searched your wagon."

"You understand that we will defend the wagon by blade," replied Rey cooly.

"So be it," said the man.

Silla had held out some faint hope they would resolve this by words, but now that hope twisted into fear.

A horn blew, then steel clashed. Merciful gods. They were fighting. This was happening.

It is only five warriors, Silla reassured herself. The snap of a twig behind her had goosebumps rushing across her skin. Silla grappled for her dagger and unsheathed it. Closing her eyes, she breathed deeply.

It was nothing, she told herself, but then there it was again—another crack.

From the road came the distant clang of swords and muffled shouts. A curious buzzing sound caught her attention, and she craned her ears to determine the source. A yellow wasp flew into the stump, causing her breathing to shallow. Another wasp. Was there a nest nearby? Silla held herself as still as she could. It was so quiet the buzz seemed to echo in the stump, a maddening sound making her stomach tighten.

It happened so quickly—pain seared from her scalp; hands hooked under her armpits, hauling her from the moss-covered stump; her knees buckled as she was dropped roughly onto the moss and needle-strewn ground.

Time seemed to slow as Silla blinked at her surroundings—a brown-bearded warrior stood before her in unmarked black chain mail; countless similarly clad mercenaries prowled from the dark depths of the forest. Off to the side stood a smaller man, the brown hood of his cloak shadowing all save for the long, double-braided beard flowing down his chest. His hand was lifted, palm facing the sky, and as her eyes fell upon it, Silla found the source of the buzzing sound.

What in the eternal fucking flames? Staring at the man's arm, Silla felt faint. It was covered in a writhing, crawling mass of wasps.

"I am not a man easily surprised, Adherent," came the gruff voice of the warrior gripping Silla by the shoulder. He was half a head taller than her and armed to the teeth.

Rey's words rang in her ears. *Always think forward—imagine it before it happens.* She swallowed the fear down, focusing on the things she could control. The fool thought her untrained and had not noticed the dagger she'd drawn up her sleeve.

Reverse grip. Block left. Aim for his neck, swing overhand.

"The creatures did their job, well," the warrior was saying.

A scream built in her throat, and she let it free as she lunged at the mercenary, her arm swinging overhand. As expected, he did not anticipate her speed, nor her training, and the blade sank into his neck.

The motions were familiar—drilled into her muscles. But the hot, sticky blood coating her hand, the metallic smell of it in the air—that was new. And nothing could have prepared her for the look in the warrior's eyes—surprise and rage blended—as his knees buckled and he crumpled to the ground.

Ashes. She'd just taken a life. She'd just...

Her mouth fell open, but her senses surged back to her. Silla pulled her dagger free, and scrambled toward the road, the horde of mercenaries on her tail.

Darting toward the Road of Bones, Silla opened her mouth and screamed, "men in the woods!"

She burst through the trees just as Gunnar cut down the last remaining warrior. As expected, they'd handled the five men easily. But now...now Silla drew more warriors than she could count straight to them, and the Bloodaxe Crew reacted quickly, forming a small shield wall backed against the wagon.

As she ran onto the road, their shields parted, and she was drawn inside the wall.

"Are you hurt?" asked Jonas, turning to her.

"Road, Jonas," barked Rey. "Stand strong. Spears ready."

The darkness was disorienting, and Silla was pushed to the back of the Crew, spear butts knocking into her. Silla pressed her back into the wagon, fear slamming into her.

"Chain mail," she panted. "Swords. Shields. Hevríts. No helms." *No redhaired woman*, she thought. Where was Skraeda?

"Good," said Rey. "Chain mail will slow them. Aim for the neck. Thighs. Armpits—"

The men were upon them then, bodies crashing into the shields, swords hacking down upon them. The sharp crack of wood and resounding clang of steel filled the air. Silla was jostled, knocked by spear handles and elbows.

The Crew were patient, lying in wait for the perfect opportunity to thrust their spears between gaps in the shields, and they then worked in pairs to make their kill. Silla watched as Ilías slammed his spear into the thigh of a warrior taking him down to the ground, Rey finishing him off with a thrust to the neck.

In front of Silla, Sigrún nocked an arrow in her bow.

"Open!" bellowed Hekla. Jonas and Ilías angled their shields back for a bare moment, but it was enough. Sigrún let the arrow loose, landing in the eye of a blond-bearded man. The brothers closed up the wall before the warriors could take advantage.

It was fascinating and invigorating and terrifying all at once.

Sunnvald, protect them, she prayed. Would the gods answer her call when they'd abandoned her so many times before? Silla pushed the thought away and persisted. *Malla grant them courage. Hábrók, guide their blades.*

"Under the wagon, Sunshine," growled Rey, and Silla did not hesitate, crawling on her stomach until she was under the middle of the wagon.

The shield wall broke open, and chaos descended. Six of the Bloodaxe Crew against countless warriors who thirsted for their blood.

Silla watched from under the wagon. With a furious bellow, Rey hacked into a giant of a man's face, yanking his handaxe free while ducking the blow of an opponent who approached him from behind. Shields up, Jonas and Ilías drove the warriors back, using the weight of their opponents' mail against them. Men stumbled, falling prey to the crush of boots as they were trampled. The brothers positioned themselves back to back, blades a blur as they drove into those weak spots Rey had identified—armpits. Thighs. Necks.

It was a bloodbath.

Men fell, screams and sickening squelches and the relentless clash of weapons filled the air. Hekla's scream rose above them all, drawing Silla's attention. A frenzy of alternating slashes of sword and claws, blood coated Hekla's face, and Silla prayed that it was not her own. Gunnar's blade was a blur as he hacked over and over, tirelessly defending Hekla's flank. The wagon rocked as Sigrún climbed atop it, loosing arrow after arrow into her opponents.

"She's under the wagon!" a voice boomed, and Silla's entire body tensed. Hadn't she already lived this?

Horse let out a high-pitched whinny, the wheels of the wagon lurching forward. Silla crawled on her stomach to keep up with the movement, but it was in vain—in a rush of motion, Horse took off down the road, the wagon bouncing after her. And Silla was unearthed like a bug beneath an upturned rock. Rolling onto her back, it was too late—hands clamped down on her arms and yanked her to her feet, her dagger knocked from her hands with the smack of a sword's broadside.

The battle raged around her in a dizzying frenzy: Jonas's blond braid coated in crimson as he traded blows with a long-bearded warrior; Rey's blood-streaked face twisted in fury as he battled two opponents simultaneously; Hekla's claws tearing open a black-haired man's throat.

Silla's wrist was snatched and bent brutally behind her back. A noise gushed from her, but she didn't recognize it as her own. It was guttural, a wounded animal. The man continued to wrench with such force she could feel the bone warping.

"Stop!" she howled.

"Shut up!" he yelled, grabbing a handful of her hair and dragging her toward the woods. Three warriors stood with their backs to Silla, creating a barrier between her and the Bloodaxe Crew. Twisting them around, the warrior shoved her forward. Silla's feet slipped, pain screaming through her arm so intensely all else was blocked out. Seconds, or minutes, or perhaps hours passed. They were in the woods now, pine trees surrounding them.

"Please," she begged. "Please, my arm."

The man's grip on her arm loosened the barest amount, but it was enough for Silla's vision to swarm back into focus—to see that they'd stopped before the brown-cloaked man. Her eyes widened, and she slammed her mouth shut, wasps flying from the mass on the man's hand and landing on her face. They crawled up her cheek and across the bridge of her nose, nausea and revulsion churning within her.

"It is her," confirmed the brown-cloaked man. "Eisa Volsik."

Sounds faded away as the realization formed. *The wasp,* she thought numbly. A wasp had landed on her nose that day in Skarstad, before her father had been killed. Of course she'd thought nothing of it. But now, she wondered...had the queen tracked her with *wasps*?

Steel clashed from behind her, a warrior's scream of fury. The man who held her lurched. His grip loosened. Silla wrenched herself free and whirled on her captor, just in time for the warrior's cough to splatter blood on her face.

As a new assailant grabbed for her, Silla lunged for the axe clutched in the dying warrior's hand. With a vicious swing, she felt axe crunch through bone and cartilage as it sank into the approaching man's face.

Her first kill had left her startled. Her second only fueled her determination.

Always retrieve your weapon, she heard Rey saying, and she yanked the axe free, hefting it over her shoulder as a figure approached her flank. But the flash of a golden beard had relief inundating her—Jonas. Jonas. Jonas. Jonas.

His sword drove into the wasp man's neck, an angry swarm of yellow and black flashing toward them. Pain stung from her arm and her neck, but Jonas grabbed her and hauled her through the woods before flinging his cloak over the pair of them. Under the cloak, he gathered her face in his hands.

"Are you hurt?" he demanded, his hands moving over her body.

"It's not my blood. Jonas, what — "

He peeked out from beneath the cloak, and, satisfied the wasps had lost interest in them, flung it off entirely.

"Stay here!" he growled. "Don't move." Then he was gone.

She sank to the forest floor, leaning against a tree. The wasps had settled on the nearby corpses, and she stared at them numbly. The man had spoken as though the wasps had confirmed her identity, but she did not understand.

Her arm throbbed. Her eyes stung. Panic scratched at her throat as she replayed what she'd seen on the road. There were *so many* of the black-clad men. Could the Bloodaxe Crew fight them all off?

She blinked quickly, staring at the forest canopy. At the sunbeams and gold dust hanging in the air. It smelled of damp grass and the copper tang of blood.

Of life and death. It felt as though hours had passed when dry leaves rustled nearby, and the breath crashed from her. Silla held herself still and surrendered to whatever was to come.

"Get up." It was Rey.

Silla clambered to her feet but staggered backward. His face was so thoroughly coated in blood, it was scarcely recognizable; his specialized armor was torn at the shoulder and thigh. Combined with the tension rolling off him, he looked truly terrifying.

Silla's legs were weak—as though someone had rattled the earth and she could not quite get her footing. "Are you hurt?" she asked in a brittle voice.

"No." He led her back toward the road, though she noted he favored his right leg.

"But your leg. Is the Crew safe? Was anyone injured?"

"Yes," he said through clenched teeth.

Silla's heart dropped like a stone through water. They stepped onto the Road of Bones, and she brought a hand to her mouth. A heavy quietness had fallen—as if even the ravens did not dare to crow. Her eyes swept the road, over the bodies strewn like driftwood on a beach.

A dream she'd already lived, these steps now twice in memory. Time had passed, but the scene was the same: death and annihilation. The blood. On her hands.

Silla counted those she saw standing. Jonas. Hekla. Sigrún. Rey. Gunnar. Where was Ilías? She whirled, her eyes searching. Where was he?

Her eyes landed back on Jonas, shoulders bowed as he knelt on the road. Her mind was numb, but her body chose for her, stepping toward him.

Ilías lay sprawled before him, dark liquid seeping from his armor and pooling on the earthen road.

Jonas placed Ilías's sword into his hand, forcing his little brother's fingers to close around it. Eyelids fluttering, a trickle of blood ran from Ilías's parted lips as he sucked in a labored gasp.

"Gods damn it, Ilías," cursed Jonas, his voice breaking.

Silla could not breathe. Not Ilías. No.

"Ilías. Look at me, brother. I need your attention."

Ilías's eyes flew open, the whites flashing against the taut lines of his face.

"You fought well, brother," said Jonas quietly. "You fought with honor and bravery. And now you're going home. Remember the field at the north end of the farm? Remember it, Il?"

Recognition flashed in Ilías's eyes.

"Good. Go and find the elm tree we used to climb. The one with all the dead branches on the back. Remember that one?"

A garbled sound escaped Ilías.

"Go to the tree. Remember to stay away from the back branches. That is where you fell and cut your arm. Do you recall when I had to pull the twig right out of your arm?" He laughed, but it was thick with emotion. "Don't do that. Climb the front side, all right, brother?"

Silla took a shallow, gasping breath.

"Remember how peaceful it was in that tree? It was so still and restful. Nothing and no one could hurt us when we were up there. Remember, Il?"

Ilías blinked hard as if to say yes.

"Watch the sunsets and the storms rolling in, and imagine all our adventures together. I will join you there when it is time. Promise you'll wait for me there, Il?" He choked out the last of the words.

Ilías stared up at Jonas, his focus intense upon his older brother. The sharp angles of pain and fear had eroded to a softer expression. Silla imagined it looked a lot like love and, perhaps, acceptance.

"Good," said Jonas. "I can tell your mind's eye shows you the tree. Wait for me there, brother. Together we will travel amongst the stars." His voice wavered.

Ilías's hand squeezed tighter around Jonas's. It was intimate, a moment not for her. Silla retreated, bracing her hands on her thighs as her breaths grew violent. Stomach churning, she squeezed her eyes shut. It was a nightmare from which she could not awaken.

This was *not* meant to happen.

Dear, sweet Ilías.

It should have been *her*.

A strangled sob escaped from Jonas, a sound filled with such anguish, it ripped into her soul. Silla fought against the need to crumble—she needed to be strong. For him.

She turned cautiously and stared at Jonas, hunched over his younger brother's motionless body. She longed to take a step closer, to wrap her arms around him, but she sensed he needed space at this moment. Instead, she turned to face the rest of the Crew. Hekla, Gunnar, Sigrún, and Rey watched her. With a deep breath, she tried to bolster herself for the ensuing volley of words. She deserved every barb they sent her way and would take everything they threw at her.

She deserved to be punished.

Sigrún's face was pale as milk, her eyes round and vacant. Rubbing her scarred wrist, she stepped backward once, twice, then turned on her heel and ran to her horse. Within moments, she was galloping down the Road of Bones.

"The queen," gritted Gunnar, drawing Silla's attention. "The *queen* was after you?"

"The land dispute," added Hekla, her voice tight. "Those men in Skarstad. They were after *you* in Skarstad. Not your father. *You.*"

"I...yes," breathed Silla. "I'm sorry." It was insufficient. She grappled for the right words but came up empty. Nothing could convey the depths of her sorrow.

Their Bloodaxe brother was dead. Nothing could right this wrong.

Tears gathered in Silla's eyes. "I did not want to lie to you. I was frightened and desperate, running for my life."

Hekla turned her back on Silla, shaking her head. Gunnar could not meet her gaze. But Rey...Rey's *axe eyes* bored into her skin with the heat of a thousand suns.

"I did not think anyone would get hurt," pleaded Silla. "I...I simply wanted a ride..."

"It was an honorable death," Rey said in a rough voice, looking away at last. "Ilías died with his blade in hand, after fighting with glory. It was no straw death for our brother."

Gunnar and Hekla murmured words of agreement. A flask was passed amongst them, each drinking deeply.

Silla's gaze found Jonas's back. With a deep breath, she stepped toward him. Kneeling beside Jonas, she took his bloodied hands in hers. He leaned on her, and she gathered him in her arms, drawing his head to her chest.

"You can let go with me, Jonas," she whispered.

Hands stroking the blond warrior's hair, smoothing down his shoulders and back, Silla held on as Jonas relinquished control and let himself cry.

FIFTY-FIVE

<p style="text-indent: 0">

His body still swayed with the movement of the horse as Jonas dismounted. Pain thundered from his shoulder where he'd taken a hard blow, and he was relieved for a moment, relieved to discover he was capable of feeling anything.

He'd been numb the entire afternoon. Disbelieving. His mind was an empty cavern, his body having taken over.

Movement in his periphery—a halo of curls bounced as she approached. Her arms wrapped around him, her scent surrounding him. Jonas breathed in.

She whispered things in his ear.

"I'm sorry."

"I never meant for this to happen."

"Will you eat something?"

"Can I set up the tent and help you clean?"

Shaking her off, he stumbled away and lifted his flask, pouring the liquid down his throat. It burned, and he savored it—the pain, the reminder that he was alive. Warmth shimmered in his stomach, but it was only the brennsa.

Rey was at his shoulder, his hand landing heavy. He was speaking. Jonas heard words like *grave* and *body*. He was asking what Jonas wanted to do. Does he want to bury or burn Ilías?

Jonas had no words, so he merely nodded, stumbling into the shadows of the woods. He needed to be alone. He felt the ebony shadows enveloping him.

He needed to be in the dark.

———

SILLA STARED at the lumpy form in the wagon, his life the payment for her safety. Guilt clung to her, like sticky cobwebs she could not pull off. Her insides were torn and shredded, and as she stared at Ilías's body, she couldn't keep the thought from her mind.

It should be you.

She should leave. Slink into the woods in the dead of night and leave them. Unburden them. Death and misery followed her. It would be better this way.

Would they come after her, risk themselves further?

Her arm ached. Her heart ached. Her body was heavy with raw grief and fatigue. Silla's hand moved absently to her chest, to the empty place where the vial used to hang. The cravings slithered through her, whispering.

One leaf to feel better.

One more to forget it all.

Silla closed her eyes. Curled her hands into fists. Counted her heartbeats until the thoughts quieted. When she opened her eyes, something flickered inside her. This was not like last time. She was not the girl she was back in Skarstad. She would be strong for the Bloodaxe Crew as they had been for her.

Silla's eyes darted to Hekla, who had just ridden into camp. She'd kept her distance from the others the whole day, hadn't spoken a word to Silla.

You don't deserve her words, thought Silla. *You don't deserve her friendship.*

As Hekla attempted to dismount, her metal hand seemed caught in the reins. Her horse whinnied, prancing to the side, yanking Hekla along with it. "Eternal *fucking* fires!" cursed Hekla, twisting the arm off and leaving it attached to the reins. With an empty sleeve, she stalked to the stream.

Silla edged toward the horse, pulling oats from her pocket and flattening her hand. Hekla's mare blew out a long breath, ears flattened against her head. "Come now, I know you want this," said Silla softly.

The horse's ears twitched forward. She took one step, and another, then nuzzled into Silla's palm.

Tears blurred Silla's eyes as she stroked the horse's nose. "It'll be all right," she whispered. "It'll be all right." But no matter how many times she repeated the words, she couldn't quite believe them. Ilías was dead. Because of *her*. And the thought made her want to vomit.

Instead, Silla stitched herself up, stood tall, and worked her way around the horse, where Hekla's prosthetic arm dangled from the reins. She found the button on the underside of the wrist and released it. As she caught the arm, Silla gasped—dried blood coated it from fingertip to forearm.

Nausea threatened her once more, and she pressed a hand to her stomach. So much violence. So much death. So much blood on her hands.

Forward, she urged herself. *Be strong for them.*

Blinking back tears, Silla got to work setting up camp for the night. She unloaded the wagon, laid kindling into a pyramid with lichen stuffed beneath it, struck the firestone and breathed life into the fire. She set the tripod and trammel hook above it, fetched water and set it to boiling.

Hekla was there, cradling her sound limb against her chest.

"I put your arm just there," Silla said quietly. Hekla would not meet her eye. Swallowing back a boulder-sized lump, Silla pressed on. "Are you hurt?"

"A small mark," replied Hekla coldly. She twisted her arm to reveal an angry cut snaking up her forearm.

"I'm boiling water to clean wounds. I am no expert, but with directions, I can manage."

Hekla kept her gaze on the fire. "Use Sigrún's medical pouch. There are linen strips to dress wounds."

Sigrún had appeared at camp only to wander off into the woods, bow slung over her shoulder. Just as she'd been on the road where Ilías had fallen, Sigrún had looked as though she'd seen a ghost. Silla silently apologized before rifling through her saddlesack for the medical pouch. Finding a small leather satchel, she returned to the fire. Once the water had boiled, she set it aside to cool while she looked through the provisions.

A curse and a crash came from down the hill, and Silla turned to see Rey hurl an iron tent pole across the clearing. His leg collapsed beneath him as he staggered to the ground—it was the leg he'd been limping on earlier in the day.

"Rey?" She rushed forward. "Ashes." Her steps faltered as his *axe eyes* slashed into her skin. With a deep breath, Silla moved toward him.

Rey grunted, the lines of his face carved with pain. His breeches were torn mid-thigh, blood gushing out as he repositioned his leg.

"It was fine on Horse, but now…"

"You'll need that wound stitched," said Hekla, appearing beside Silla. "Come, let us get you to the fire."

Together, Hekla and Silla helped Rey to the fire, easing him gently onto the grass, his back propped against a crate.

Hekla passed him a flask, crouching to inspect his wound. "You'll have to stitch it," she said, without looking at Silla. "I cannot with my hand."

"Me," repeated Silla, her pulse accelerating. "Yes. I'll do it." She tugged off her wolfskin gloves, thankful to see her skin was its usual dull and pale hue. Hekla handed her the sewing kit, and Silla pulled out a thick needle, some thread, and a pair of small scissors.

"Perhaps we should wait for Sigrún," said Rey, his voice a touch lower than usual.

"No," said Hekla. "She could be gone all night, and we must get you sewn up now." Turning to Silla, she started barking out directions.

Silla knelt in front of Rey, pulling at his breeches to examine the wound. It was a single, straight slash, a handspan above his knee, thankfully not so deep as to threaten his ability to walk. But the edges gaped wide, blood seeping from it, and though Silla was no expert, she agreed with Hekla's assessment that it must be stitched. As she brushed her knuckles around the surrounding flesh, Rey flinched. Pausing, she studied him. The warrior's body was rigid, his *axe eyes* trained on her face.

"If you wish me to stab you worse than you already are, then, by all means, keep looking at me like that."

"We should wait for Sigrún," repeated Rey, making to rise, but Silla pressed her hand to his chest.

"Besides the fact she's wandered into the wilds, Sigrún looked in no state to stitch you up." Silla leveled him with a look. "I'm afraid you're stuck with me, Axe Eyes."

He grumbled something under his breath but did not move. Following Hekla's directions, Silla used the scissors to cut the opening in his breeches larger. Next, she held the needle in the flame until it glowed red, before looping the thread through it.

"Now, pour the brennsa over the wound."

Silla took the bottle and hovered it over his leg, but paused at his sharp intake of breath. Where was the perfectly controlled warrior she'd grown to know? Either his emotional restraint had snapped through, or he was...afraid.

She could not work on him when he was so jumpy. And Silla knew the perfect way to distract him.

"You mean to tell me that the fearsome Axe Eyes is afraid of a small needle, *Reynir*?" Silla huffed. "What would your mother say?"

She poured the liquid onto his leg, and he clenched his fists, growling.

"Why do you hate being called Reynir?" she asked as the tension eased from his body.

"Because Kraki and my grandmother are the only ones who call me that —*unh*!"

Without warning, she plunged the needle in, twisting it through the other side of the wound. Silla tried not to blush at the spew of foul words drawn from Rey.

"Is that so? Have you fond memories of your grandmother, *Reynir*?"

"Fond memories of pain and suffering—*fuck*!"

She plunged the needle back in, then out, pulling it a little more taut.

"She sounds precious, Reynir. Please, tell me more about her," said Silla.

There was a snort from behind her. Rey threw an angry look over her shoulder. "Does my suffering bring you enjoyment, Hekla?" he asked through clenched teeth.

"More than it should right now." Grief swept across Hekla's face, and she looked away.

"Focus," said Silla. Guilt burned in her stomach as she turned back to Rey. "Tell me about your grandmother, Reynir."

"She's the coldest person I've ever met. She—gods damn it!" He unleashed a string of the foulest curse words Silla had ever heard as she looped the needle back in for a third stitch—her straightest one yet.

"How many more stitches, Hekla?"

Hekla peered over her shoulder. "At least one more."

Rey growled, trying to sit up. Silla placed her hand on his chest, pushing him back down. "Lay down, you oversized infant. You are a terrible patient."

He pressed his lips together, glowering up at the sky.

"Now, *Reynir*," Silla cooed, readying herself for the next stitch. "You must tell us more about your grandmother. Does she enjoy baking bread? Embroidery?"

"Bread?" he scoffed. "Not my grandmoth—*unh*!"

Silla pushed the needle back in again, repeating the twisting and pulling motion. She held the stitches taut, tied them off, and trimmed the thread with the scissors.

"I thought you were a brave warrior, and yet you cower in the face of a needle."

Silla sat back, admiring her work. She almost smiled but then remembered how Rey incurred this wound, and the guilt rushed back, shredding her insides. With a sigh, Silla followed Hekla's directions to dress the wound. After packing it with a mixture of honey and moss, strips of linen were secured in place.

"You owe me a pair of breeches," grumbled Rey as she secured the bandage. "My best ones, shredded to ruins."

She sat back on her haunches, looking up at him. Hekla had wandered off to help Gunnar set up Rey's abandoned tent, and it was the two of them, alone at the fire. They'd ridden long to put space between them and the bodies on the road, and the sun was nearing the horizon. The last light of the day played across Rey's cheekbone, weariness etched into his face.

Words crowded her mind, yet she found herself speechless.

It should have been me.

I should have told you everything.

I wish I could go back in time and take Ilías's place.

"I'm sorry, Rey," she said at last, cursing herself for such insufficiency. Ilías was dead because of *her*. "I'm so sorry."

His face was utterly impassive. She frowned. The silence was so much worse than anger. She needed him to tear into her—to punish her.

"Why were you taking those leaves?" he asked.

Her brows rose—she'd not anticipated this question and found herself searching for the right words.

"I thought you were simply Galdra," said Rey quietly.

Frost webbed down her spine, and Silla licked her lips, trying to decide what to say.

He stared into the flames. "The leaves, the secrets, the way you pushed me in the field after the vampire deer attacked...it was all that made any sense. I harbor no ill-will toward the Galdra. I was willing to transport you to a safer place." A muscle in Rey's jaw flexed, and the flames of the fire were reflected in his dark eyes. "I thought the Klaernar chased you. It is why I did not ask for details. The less we knew about you, the better. But I was wrong."

Silla was exhausted. The lies, this false life she'd led for so long, were an unbearable weight on her shoulders. She wanted to come clean. To lay herself bare. She opened her mouth to let the truth flood free, but he beat her to it.

"Not killing you when I discovered you in our wagon will be a thing I regret until my last breath."

Her breath lodged in her throat.

"The only reason you live is that gods damned oath. Because of *you*, Ilías is dead. He was a good man. A brother to us all. His death is heavy on my mind, and Jonas is forever changed."

Rey's hand curled into a fist, and when he shifted his gaze to her, his *axe eyes* cut so deep she could feel the mark on her soul.

"You've brought violence and unrest to my Crew, and I will relish the day you leave us."

Her eyes blurred, but she blinked back the tears. It was what she deserved after all.

Your fault. Your fault. Your fault.

Speech was beyond her. Rising to shaky feet, Silla retreated to help Hekla and Gunnar with the tents.

FIFTY-SIX

Night had descended, and with it, the biting cold climbing down into his bones. Jonas sat, his back against the sturdy trunk of a tree, staring into inky darkness. He rubbed his thumb along the textured surface of his talisman, but it brought him no comfort. Ilías was gone. His little brother. His past and his future—the one person who shared history with him, who shared his goals and had his back no matter what.

The gods played cruel tricks upon him. It simply could not be true. He would walk from the woods and discover he'd lost his mind. Ilías would be sitting with the Bloodaxe Crew, and everything would be normal.

Jonas knew this was not true. He knew because his mind kept showing him the moment of Ilías's death blow—over and over again. The chaos of battle, the blood lust singing through his veins. But then she'd screamed, and all else had failed to matter—only the unyielding need to get to her, to save her.

Jonas had abandoned his brother.

Had left the road to rush through the woods just in time to hear those words.

It is her. Eisa Volsik.

Eisa Volsik.

It was impossible. Because Eisa Volsik had been impaled on a pillar with the king and queen of Íseldur seventeen years ago. But Jonas had shaken the disbelief from his mind in order to bury an axe in the skull of the warrior who held her.

Once she was safe, once he knew she was unharmed, Jonas had raced back to the road, but it was too late.

He arrived just in time to see it happen.

Jonas ground his teeth, his heart fracturing anew. He saw it as though it had happened seconds ago—the moment Ilías jumped into the fray when he should have paused and waited for Jonas or Rey or Hekla to have his flank. Saw Ilías swinging his sword into one man's neck, failing to see the two who came at him from the shadows. He saw his brother turn, his future crashing down onto him.

Jonas saw the exact moment Ilías knew. Saw his brother's eyes widen as he swung one last time, futile though it was. Saw the swords hack into him. Once. Twice. Three times. Lébrynja armor was impressively durable but not invincible, and Ilías was dealt not one but two death blows by the warriors who attacked him. Jonas heard Hekla's scream of fury, Rey's agonized roar. Saw Sigrún aim with her bow, dispatching the men with silent rage.

He felt the bloodlust pumping through his veins all over again. He'd attacked like a berserker—with a frenzy he'd never experienced before, a blur of blood and clashing swords and executions without mercy until his sword was slick and the men had all fallen.

Jonas tried to dig himself out from this pit of despair. He pictured the farmstead—the rolling grassy fields, the carved beams of the longhouse, the chatter of kin. But without Ilías, the home was filled with nothing but shadows and somber silence. It had lost all meaning.

The ache in his heart permeated through him, leaving him raw. He was tired and so angry. Angry at Ilías for thinking himself invincible. Angry at himself for failing to protect him. Angry at *her* for drawing the warriors to them.

Why Ilías? The question nagged at him, over and over again. There would be meaning to be found in Ilías's death—there *had* to be. His mother's death had driven Jonas to kill his father. His father had died to purge evil from the world. But what of Ilías? *Why* had Ilías died? He could not answer the question, and the longer he sat, the more it gnawed at him. Why?

It was senseless. Meaningless.

It was unnecessary.

I'm sorry Jonas, she'd said. *I never meant for this to happen.*

But Ilías was dead.

And *she* was the reason.

The queen was after her. Not just the Klaernar. Not the random red-haired warrior he'd seen in Skutur. The gods damned queen had sent an army of mercenaries after her. She'd made an utter fool of him. Had gotten his brother killed.

Selfless Silla. The name was a mockery. She'd kept the truth from him, even after he'd saved her in Skutur. She was a dishonest woman.

A *selfish* woman.

Jonas's blood simmered. She had made a fool of him. Had shredded his dreams into tattered ribbons.

She was Eisa Volsik.

And Eisa Volsik was not his.

———

IT WAS EITHER INCREDIBLY LATE or incredibly early by the time Jonas emerged from the woods. He needed to return to camp, warm himself by the fire, drink some water. He pushed himself up, brushed the needles from his hair, and moved through the darkness toward camp. Firelight winked between the trees, guiding his way. As he exited the woods, the sky stretched wide above, sprinkled with stars.

Jonas stopped dead in his tracks. A shimmer, a shiver, a sparkle lasting for a heartbeat, maybe a little longer. One star, breaking off from the others, traveling across the sky, burning fast and bright before fading into the emptiness.

His heart squeezed, and he blinked furiously.

A lone figure sat by the flames, and as he approached, Rey rose. Jonas nodded at him, sinking toward the warmth of the flames, trying to bring life back to his body. Rey handed him a skin of water and a bowl of cold stew. They sat in silence. Rey was always good with silence.

After Jonas finished the evening meal, after he drank deeply from the water-skin, his chest relaxed, the haze of grief dissipating. He felt almost human again.

Jonas was the one to break the silence. "Tomorrow morning, we bury him."

Rey nodded, steepling his fingers together. "He was a good man. It was a good death. An honorable one."

But Jonas was silent, staring listlessly at the fire.

"If you wish to take time, Jonas, there is no shame in it. I will grant you all the time you need. We shall have to recruit a new warrior all the same." Rey sighed, closing his eyes.

"I don't need time," gritted Jonas. "I will carve my grief into our foes in Istré. I will see this job through. For him."

"Very well." Rey palmed the back of his neck, blowing out a long breath.

"I think I shall sleep if I can," said Jonas, rising.

"Rest well, brother," said Rey.

The night held a chill, and Jonas paused at the wagon. As he pulled an extra sleeping fur from the flatbed, something fell from the folds with a soft thud. Jonas reached into the wagon, his fingers closing around a small wooden disk, leather strap dangling from it.

He braced himself on the side of the wagon, resting his forehead against the cool wooden plank. He knew what it was just from the feel of it—grooves he'd carved himself into the smooth wooden surface. It was the talisman he'd given to Silla. The strap was not torn. She'd *taken* it off.

The raw ache inside him grew and shifted, burning with cold rage. All along, Jonas had thought their sentiments had been equal, but in this moment, he realized the truth. She'd never felt the same way about him. *I need a distraction*, she'd said. She'd been using him. And he...the fool...had thought she was more. Had he not told himself time and time again? Soft sentiments brought nothing but pain, and here was the proof. Jonas had allowed her near his heart, and now he was weak. Pathetic.

He'd become his mother.

Never again. His hand curled into a fist so tight the talisman split down the middle.

It could not stand.

It *would* not stand.

Jonas would not tolerate being made a fool. Being *disrespected*. He had stood by helplessly when he and Ilías had been cast from their lands. He'd been too young then to understand—respect wasn't a thing which was earned. It had to be taken.

And Jonas would take back his honor.

Forcing a calming breath in, he crawled into the tent. Her scent surrounded him, and he paused, breathing her in. Silla's eyes were heavy with sleep as she blinked at him from beneath the furs.

Not Silla, he thought, looking down at her—at this stranger. His chest burned.

Propping herself up on an elbow, Silla frowned. "Did you eat?" she asked softly.

Jonas forced himself to nod and began to strip his bloodied armor.

"Let me wash you, Jonas," she said softly, helping to pull his tunic and undertunic beneath. Jonas was still as she crawled to the entry of the tent and drew a bowl of water inside. Wetting a scrap of linen, she wiped the blood from his face with slow, tender movements.

"Turn," said Silla "I will do your back." The cold linen made a shiver run down his spine as she worked along his shoulder. "I'm sorry," she whispered, so quietly he'd scarcely heard her. "I did not mean for anyone to be hurt."

"I know." Jonas had to force the words through his teeth.

"You helped me through the grief of losing my father," she said, pressing a kiss to his shoulder. "Let me help you with yours."

She set the cloth aside and drew Jonas into the furs, curving her body against his. She whispered soothing things in his ear, caressed his chest with a soft, relaxing touch. But eventually, her movements stilled and her breaths fell to slow, rhythmic pulls.

Jonas stared at her for a long time in the darkness.

She sleeps without care, while Ilías's corpse rots.

He wanted to wrap his hands around her neck, to squeeze the air from her lungs. He wanted to watch panic flare in her eyes as she realized her fate. As she choked on her lies and deceit. But that would be too easy a fate for her. And that would leave Jonas with nothing. Instead, he would bide his time. Would follow through with the plan that had come to him in the cold darkness of the woods.

Jonas would ensure that Ilías's death was not meaningless. That he was not made a fool.

That this woman got everything she deserved.

———

REY ADJUSTED the wolfskin pelt around his shoulders, his breath clouding the crisp morning air. Dense pinewoods surrounded the backroad they now traveled along, and it felt as though walls were closing in upon them. They could no longer travel the Road of Bones, now that they knew who looked for the woman.

The gods damned queen of Íseldur.

Rey could not think of it, it enraged him so badly.

When you get soft, people get killed. Kraki had been right. Damn him, but he had been right, and that stung even worse. All of these years of caution, of never straying from his plans. One act of kindness, and Rey was repaid in the blood of his brother.

What had he been thinking, not pressing her for answers? He *hadn't* been thinking. He'd been caught up in the discovery that she was Galdra, that she fled the Klaernar. But now he thought of it, she'd never confirmed it was the Klaernar who sought her. Had not actually confirmed she was Galdra either. And when she'd tried to speak, he'd silenced her. *Fool,* Rey chastised himself, and the guilt in his chest burned up his throat. Because he knew the blame lay square on his shoulders.

He had made assumptions about from whom she fled.

He had denied her the chance to explain.

He had led his Crew into battle without understanding their foes.

What was the first thing Kraki had taught him? *Know your adversary. And if you do not know them, learn.* And now Ilías was in the ground because Rey had forgotten his way. He hadn't been good enough, and a worthy soul had left the world because of it.

Letting out a low sound, Rey rolled his shoulders.

He was unsettled.

It is Ilías, he told himself, though it was no reassurance.

They'd dug a grave for their Bloodaxe brother—piling rocks atop his body and saying words of respect. Five years he'd known Ilías. Five years he'd fought shoulder to shoulder, had taught him weapons-craft and how to survive the wilds of Íseldur. He'd watched Ilías grow from a scrawny sixteen-year-old to the man he was when he fell on the Road of Bones. He was as good as Rey's own blood.

Rey blew out a long breath. Three of the Bloodaxe Crew rode alongside Rey today, and it seemed so few. It was quiet, in part because the Crew were silently mourning their lost brother, but also because there was no senseless humming coming from the wagon.

Silla and Jonas had lingered behind, Jonas requesting quiet to mourn. "We'll catch up easily without the wagon to burden us," Jonas had said as Rey and the Bloodaxe Crew saddled up for the day.

Rey fought the urge to turn Horse around and ride back to camp. Something felt off, but he was not sure what.

It is Ilías, he repeated to himself. But he was not sure that was it.

Jonas had seemed off. *Of course, he was off,* he told himself. *His brother just died. Grief does not come in the same form for all.*

A twinge of remorse wriggled in his chest. He'd let his anger get the best of him, had unfairly placed the blame on *her* shoulders. He could have been kinder, could have been softer. Could have told her that death was the risk a warrior takes. That Ilías had died with honor, that it was the best kind of death a warrior could hope for. Could have told her the blame rested on Rey's shoulders more than her own.

Rey could have done a lot of things differently. But it would change nothing. Ilías was still dead.

And so he rode on, and the nagging feeling persisted, and Rey wondered how one girl could have so thoroughly brought ruin to his carefully laid plans.

FIFTY-SEVEN

A s though the weather mourned along with them, it was a gloomy morning, mist rising from the ground and lingering amid the pinewoods. Silla glanced at Jonas, kneeling before his brother's burial mound with his head bowed. He'd been in the same position for hours, and the longer he stayed in place, the more the ache in her chest grew. Jonas was broken by Ilías's death, and Silla could do nothing but respect his request that she stay with him. Her eyes darted to the neatly stacked pile of rocks, the ache deepening.

How had it come to this? She'd just wanted a ride, had simply wanted to get to Kopa. But now it was a mess, a horribly tragic mess, and the burden of guilt and grief weighed heavily on her. Ilías was dead because of her, and the knowledge made her sick. She should have told Jonas what she'd discovered from Skraeda, that she was Eisa Vols...

Nausea roiled in Silla's stomach as her insides shrieked violently. She slammed her eyes shut.

Not her. Not her.

She could not face it—the name, the implications. Not yet, not with everything which had happened. Each time she thought the name, her body's response seemed to grow worse.

You are not her, she thought. *You are Silla. And you just need to get to Kopa.*

To get to safety. Denial wasn't the healthiest way to cope, but at this moment, it was all that was holding her together. As Silla repeated the words in her mind, her nausea gradually eased.

With a sigh, her gaze landed on the burial mound. Everywhere in camp this morning had been the reminder of Ilías—his horse, his bedroll, the extra bowl she'd pulled out while serving the daymeal. Shortly after eating, the Bloodaxe Crew had set to work digging a grave. Ilías had been laid to rest, sword in hand, with his flask and his woolen cloak and the best of the furs—provisions to make the afterlife more comfortable. They'd laid flowers and piled rocks atop him, spoken words to honor his bravery and glory.

There was no mistaking the coldness Silla felt from the Bloodaxe Crew; they did not speak to her, nor spare her a glance—not Hekla and certainly not Axe Eyes.

You've brought violence and unrest to my Crew, and I will relish the day you leave us.

The memory of Rey's words widened the wound in her heart. For a brief moment, she'd had kin, people who'd cared for her. People who'd fought for her. But like everything in her life, it was not meant to last.

Sooner or later, everything you care for gets taken away, Silla thought, but then chastened herself. *You have no one to blame but yourself. You should never have let them get so close to you.*

Her eyes landed once more on Jonas. Though she'd planned to end things a day before, she would not abandon him in his grief. She would help him, as he'd helped her.

And though she would not rush his mourning, they'd been here hours, and her throat was parched. His saddlesack lay nearby, and Silla moved to it as silently as she could, rummaging for a waterskin. She pulled loose the stopper and brought it to her lips. The skin was nearly empty, the water warm with a strange earthy flavor to it. Grabbing the second empty waterskin from the bag, Silla rose to her feet and made her way to the stream.

It took less than a minute to reach the edge of the brook, a vivid blue against the stone beneath. Kneeling next to a cluster of purple-blooming heather, Silla felt a strange rush of happiness. Her brows furrowed. What exactly did she have to feel happy about?

The Bloodaxe Crew hated her.

Ilías was dead.

Jonas was broken.

It was a mess. And yet...she was happy.

Ecstatic, really.

A cool breath of wind caressed her face. As Silla dipped the waterskin into the current, a euphoric shiver ran up her spine.

Stoppering the waterskins, Silla breathed in. The day felt less gloomy, the weather less mournful. Unable to suppress her smile, Silla pushed to her feet, stumbling over a bush of heather. Where had that come from? With a sigh, she climbed back up the slope, tripping on a stone.

She looked at her feet. The ground swelled like an ocean beneath them.

Jonas was at her side, an arm sliding around her waist.

"There you are," she smiled at him. The gray clouds beyond him exploded with small bursts of light.

She seemed to look down upon herself, her mouth speaking freely without her permission. "My heart is heavy, Jonas. I wish I could have died in place of Ilías. Will you forgive me? Can you find it in your heart to ever forgive me?"

The Wolf smiled at her, his eyes nearly black.

"Please, Jonas. Can you fuhgif...mih?" The last words came out garbled. She tried again. "Faf meh?"

Silla shook her head. The urge to lie down was overwhelming, and Jonas eased her onto the soft, mossy ground. His beautiful face looked down at her, upside down. It twisted and churned before her eyes, shattering, then reforming.

The words he spoke, however, were clear as daylight.

"No. I cannot forgive you."

She blinked up at him, realization and a familiar euphoria crashing over her and coursing through her blood. The leaves. He'd drugged her with the gods damned leaves.

"You are a dishonest woman. My brother is dead because of you. But not all shall be lost." His words were cool and sharp. Eyes darker than midnight, his face swam above her. "I will turn you in, *Eisa Volsik.*"

Her lips parted, and she was distantly aware that Jonas should not know that, that she should be afraid. But there was only happiness and joy as the light bent and stretched before her.

Jonas's words went fast, then slow, jumping and skipping around. "I warned you, Curls. I am not a good man. You should have listened."

Jonas moved away for some time, and Silla lay watching the clouds churn and race across the sky. How many leaves had he given her? She'd never felt this out of control before, never so incapacitated.

But then, she was distracted, pressing her fingers into the soft moss beneath her. It bent, then flexed back up. So soft. So pliable.

A hand was under her back, Jonas looming above her. She wished to tell him his eyes were more beautiful than a mountain pond in the sunlight, but her mouth would not open. The ground moved beneath her—no, she was lifted—and then she found herself seated on a horse, leaning into the hard warmth of Jonas.

"This won't be pleasant, but we'll need to make haste," came his voice from behind her. The horse lunged with such force, she slumped forward. But then his arms were around her, and that made her smile.

The trees rushed by in a dizzying blur of greens and browns and ghostly white stems.

What are you going to do? asked a familiar voice. Silla's blood sang in exhilaration—the girl was back! She could not see her, could only hear the familiar child-like voice. *You let him get too close to you,* said the girl sadly.

Saga, Silla breathed. *My sister.* Indescribable joy filled Silla at being able to name her. After all these long years, the girl finally made sense. She smiled despite the bobbing of her head as the horse galloped along the road.

Time ceased to have meaning; it was just swirling trees and blue sky, the constant rise and fall of the horse, light shimmering and twisting before her as bliss flowed through her veins, sparking pleasure in her fingers, her toes, her hair.

At some point, the rhythmic movement ended, and Silla found herself lying on the ground in the darkness. A dark form loomed over her—Jonas, she realized—studying her. Her eyes found his blond beard, her gaze sliding to that beautiful, soft mouth she longed to kiss.

"Silla, Silla, Silla," he said, leaning over her.

But then, a flash of memory. Something was wrong. A question in the back of her throat moved to the tip of her tongue as he drew back. There was coldness in his eyes. Malice.

"How could you?" she asked, her words barely a breath. The stars above swirled, but less violently than the clouds had earlier.

"Silla. *Eisa.*" Jonas spat the name. "I heard those men in the woods speaking. I heard it all. Heard your true name." He frowned. "Why did you not tell me?"

"I could not," whispered Silla. *Not her. Not her.*

Jonas's brows furrowed. "Why did you not trust me, Silla? Why did you lie to me over and over? You could not even tell me your *name?*" His fingers dug into her shoulders, his eyes growing dark. "I told you *everything.* I bared my soul to you. You were mine, and you *owed* me the truth—to tell me everything. But you just lied."

"I did not lie. I *cannot* be her. I do not accept it."

"You *are* her, you fool," hissed Jonas, his face contorting until he looked anything but handsome. "The gods damned queen hunts for you." He forced in a breath, and when he spoke, his voice was disarmingly calm. "I figured it out, Silla. I discovered why Ilías had to die."

Silla felt her brows furrow.

"Ilías died so I would get my lands back," continued Jonas. "His death will not be meaningless, Silla, don't you see? You will bring me a handsome reward, and Ilías's death will *mean* something." There was madness in his voice, sending goosebumps rushing along her arms.

"I cared for you," she whispered. She wiggled her toes. Her wrist twitched. Her senses were returning.

Emotion filled his eyes. "I cared for you too," he said, shaking his head. "I cared for you more than any woman I've ever known, *Eisa.* I thought we could be something, you and I. I thought you could make me into a good man." The softness in his eyes sharpened to cold fury. "But instead, you ripped out my heart! You lied to me. You got my brother killed. How could you think there was a future for us after that?"

She recoiled, gulping down a deep, desperate breath.

He glared at her. It was Jonas, but not the Jonas she thought she knew. This version was so cold, so angry. "Do not be sad, Curls. This was how it was always fated to end. You came into my life so that I could grow rich. I will get my lands back because of you." A smile curved his lips. "And you will get to Kopa in the end, when I hand you over to the Klaernar."

The leaves were wearing off. She was coming down, crashing hard, falling through the skies like a burning star, doomed to smash and burn. Sadness swelled inside her, and she wanted to curl in on herself and cry.

Jonas slid a hand behind her back and pulled her to a sitting position. A waterskin was placed at her lips, cool liquid in her mouth. It might be drugged. But she was so thirsty, and so Silla swallowed. He put bits of bread into her mouth, and she sucked on it, then swallowed. Jonas repeated this a few more times, then something different was placed in her mouth. Something bitter, crumbly, earthy...another leaf, or maybe two. She tried to spit, but he held her jaw in his hand and her muscles would not cooperate.

Tears sprang to her eyes. He forced water into her mouth again and tilted her jaw backward. Silla tried to cough, but it was no use. Instinct took over, and her body betrayed her by swallowing.

"You've done well," Jonas whispered in her ear, running a finger down her neck. His touch made her veins burn with fiery rage.

But the rage dissolved into more bliss, more euphoria. She stared at the stars and moons, dancing and flickering before her eyes. It was the most beautiful sight she'd ever seen.

A single hot tear shimmered down her cheek.

They rested for a few minutes, or perhaps a few hours. Silla fell into a restless sleep, dreaming but never being able to clasp on to the dream, to see the images, the faces. It was all distorted, shuffled into chaos. She stirred awake frequently, and before long, she found herself back on the horse, with the familiar rise and fall and the wind in her ears as they galloped into darkness.

She came in and out of lucidity. Each time when she seemed to regain her senses, her rage smoldering awake, her limbs tingling and twitching back to life, he forced more leaves down her throat. After a while, it was not euphoria anymore; it was an endless billowing dream with the clatter of hooves, the smell of leather, and a blur of black or green.

Silla was stuck in a living nightmare from which she could not awaken.

———

JONAS'S MOODS alternated between gloom and anger.

When he thought of the Bloodaxe Crew's discovery of what he'd done, when he thought of the burial mound he'd left behind, his spirits sank, shrouding him in sorrow.

That was when he forced himself to look at her. At *Eisa*. The sight of her sent wrath burning through his veins, renewing his purpose. Family, respect, duty. Those three words anchored him in his task, and he drove his horse down the road with fresh vigor. They made great time, having quickly passed the Northern Junction and setting off along the Black Road. They were well on their way to Kopa now.

The night Ilías had died, Jonas had not slept. His mind's eye showed his brother's death an infinite number of times. *She'd* drawn the warriors to them. Had lied about who chased her. And because of her, Jonas had not been by his brother's side when he'd needed him the most. Because of *her*, he had failed completely in the only job which mattered.

But that was only the start of it. Because there were also the lies...so many he could not even track them all. Silla had made a fool of him. He'd trusted her, had thought she cared for him. Jonas had thought she was the best thing that had ever happened to him, but he'd never been so wrong.

She was a nightmare in disguise.

All night, thoughts had circled, easing his guilt, but adding kindling to the flames of his anger.

She's made a fool of you.

She was never going to tell you her true name.

She never cared for you.

And the thing that had finally roused Jonas from despair.

Give your brother's death meaning.

It all made sense. There *was* meaning to be found in Ilías's death, though it would not be handed to him. Jonas would have to take it for himself.

While the Bloodaxe Crew dug Ilías's grave, Jonas had slipped away and searched through Rey's saddlesack. Finding the vial of leaves at the bottom, bitterness had freshly coated Jonas's throat as he recalled yet another betrayal of Silla's. Getting rid of the Crew was easily done, though as they rode off down the Road of Bones, a brief wave of shame had hit Jonas. It was the end of an era. The end of his time with the Bloodaxe Crew, and he had not so much as given them a goodbye.

It is the only way, he thought. *They must not grow suspicious.*

Drugging Silla had been easier than he'd expected, and after leaving her writhing like a fool in the grass, Jonas had knelt again before Ilías's grave.

"Forgive me, brother, for not being by your side when you needed me most. Forgive me for cavorting with a vile woman, for sealing your fate in blood. I swear it to you, Ilías, I will avenge your death. She will pay retribution. She will suffer for what she has done." Jonas had kissed his knuckles and bowed his head. And then, he'd mounted the horse with her and ridden along the Road of Bones, avoiding the backroad on which the Bloodaxe Crew traveled.

A smile curved Jonas's lips. He'd promised he'd get Silla to Kopa, and it seemed he'd make good on his word. On horseback, they could make far better time than with the wagon. Jonas estimated they'd be at the Klaernar's garrison hall in Kopa soon.

Family, respect, duty.

In a few short hours, he'd avenge his brother's death. Would be one step closer to restoring his family's honor. And this woman, who'd shattered his life so thoroughly, would pay dearly for the disrespect she'd shown him.

FIFTY-EIGHT

KOPA

D *rip.*
　　Her head pounded.
Drip.
Her mouth tasted like ash.
Drip.
The smell of damp hay surrounded her.
Drip.
Silla grimaced. What in the gods' sacred ashes was that cursed dripping noise? It almost sounded like she were indoors. Which was impossible because...

Silla's eyes flew open, memories flooding her until she brimmed over with disbelief.

You will get to Kopa in the end, when I hand you over to the Klaernar.

Jonas. The leaves.

Drip.

Blinking, she took in her surroundings in the dim light—cold stone floor strewn with hay, black stone walls, iron bars. Silla swallowed hard, bile rising in her throat. She was in a prison cell. He'd done it. He'd gone through with it. Jonas had turned her in.

"No," she whimpered. "No. No no no no." She crossed to the bars, pressing her face between them, and strained to see down the hallway. It was long and dark, disrupted by torches mounted along the corridor wall. Despair climbed into her bones, making itself at home with nausea and the painful headache throbbing against her skull.

Drip.

"Jonas?" she called, desperate to discover she'd dreamed it all. "Jonas?"

"Sorry," came a female voice from down the hall. "It is only us here."

Silla's back hit the cold stone wall, and she closed her eyes. She did not need to dig deep within herself to know—she felt it in the beat of her pulse, in every lungful of dank air she breathed in. But she had to hear the words.

"Where are we?"

The woman hesitated, then replied in a gentle voice. "Klaernar outpost. On the edge of Kopa."

Her knees buckled. She dropped to the ground, letting the truth sink into her.

Kopa. Jonas had taken her to Kopa.

He'd *tricked* her.

Had drugged her with the leaves.

Had taken her against her will and turned her in.

I warned you, Curls. I'm not a good man. You should have listened.

Hekla had warned her. The little girl had warned her. Jonas *himself* had warned her. Why hadn't she listened?

Because you're a naive fool, Silla, she told herself. She buried her face in her hands, the reality of her situation sinking in. It had all been for nothing. Her father's death, her thousand-mile trip. She'd made it to Kopa, but found herself at Queen Signe's mercy all the same.

Drip.

A ragged sob shook her body, and she felt as though she were crumbling into a million pieces.

"How could you do this, Jonas?" she whispered. How could Jonas, of all people, betray her like this?

I told you everything, he'd said. *I bared my soul to you. You were mine, and you owed me the truth—to tell me everything. But you just lied.*

But it wasn't a fair comparison—Jonas's truths were nothing but history, while Silla's...hers were a matter of safety. Of life or death. Should she have told him? Never mind the fact that she had not come to terms with it herself, that she'd been on the verge of ending things with him. She was going to move on. Start over with a clean slate.

Drip.

Perhaps she had gotten what she deserved. She'd lied to protect herself, but Jonas had gotten hurt. And Ilías had died.

And she was in a cell.

Silla folded herself over her knees, surrendering to despair. It overwhelmed her, great sobs shaking her body.

"It's all right, girl," said the woman down the hall. "Let it out."

Silla cried until her eyes ran dry. The last time she'd cried like this had been in the Twisted Pinewoods, back near Skarstad when she was all alone in the forest.

Drip.

"You're different now," said a familiar voice. "You're not the same person."

Silla's head shot up, warmth filling her chest as she took in the little blonde girl—her familiar torn nightdress, dirt-smeared face, and tilted blue eyes.

She had not seen the girl since she'd stopped taking skjöld leaves, and the sight of her filled Silla with remembrance, with a yearning to return to a simpler time when all she'd needed to worry about was whether her father was working himself too hard and what she should cook for the evening meal.

And yet the girl was a tether yanking Silla out of her anguish, because with her messy blonde hair and knowing blue eyes was a reminder of what Silla had forgotten, or had buried for the moment.

"Saga," she whispered. Her sister. She had a sister.

Drip.

Rather than filling her with dread, with nausea, thinking of Saga triggered a wave of questions—what was Saga like? Did she love thunderstorms and sweet rolls and the smell of cooked onions? Did she babble when she was nervous? Did Saga think of her sister? Did she dream of her? Saga lived with Queen Signe. Lived amongst enemy wolves. What would that do to a person? What would it do to your sense of self, to your mind?

Silla was filled with yearning—to meet this girl whose phantom she'd seen for a decade, who she'd dreamed of her whole life. As though a part of her had never been able to let go of Saga.

Come and find me, Saga had said in that last dream. *I need you.*

"I must find you, Saga," Silla whispered to the girl, whose lips curved up.

"Yes," said Saga, sinking down beside Silla and hugging her knees. "But first, you must get yourself out of this mess."

It was old and new blended together—the girl was with her like old times, but knowing she was Saga felt altogether different. And in that moment, renewed purpose brought Silla back to life. This was no longer simply about her own well-being. She needed to be strong, needed to find a way out of this situation.

Because Saga needed her.

Silla wiped her eyes, taking several deep breaths and trying to ease the pounding in her head.

She got to shaky feet and paced her cell, trying to get her bearings. The walls were made of dark stone—volcanic in appearance. Her cell had three solid walls and a window, far too high and too small for her to fit through. What would Hekla do in this situation? Silla's heart squeezed at the thought of Hekla. Another relationship ruined by her lies.

Drip.

Silla froze. A faint sound echoed from down the hall. Footfalls. Someone approached.

Think, thought Silla. *What is the plan?*

The footfalls grew louder, then came to a stop. Two shadowy figures loomed beyond the iron bars; light from the torches glinted on rivets in their mail shirts and the snarling silver bears upon their shoulder plates. She could not suppress her sharp intake of breath as she looked up at the Klaernar.

"Evening meal," grumbled the shorter one, lowering something to the ground and sliding it beneath the bars. "Eat."

Smells of cooked food reached her nose, and Silla closed her eyes, ignoring the urge to drop to her knees and shovel it all into her mouth. "Why am I being held?" she asked, aiming for her best authoritative voice. Unfortunately, it came out hoarse, rusty from disuse. She cleared her throat and tried again. "I demand to know why I'm being held."

The taller one crossed his arms over his chest. "Since you've awoken, the kommandor will wish to speak to you."

"You will tell me why I'm being held, and you will do so immediately," she replied, emboldened perhaps by the bars between them.

"Cannot," said the short one. "And will not."

"Where is Jonas?" she asked, wincing as pain seared through her skull. "The man who brought me. I must speak to him. A grave error has been made and must be sorted."

"You've a sharp tongue," said the taller one, his lips curling into a malicious smile. "That'll be fun. But let me advise you, Galdra—you're best to limit your words to *yes* unless you wish to wear a bridle."

Silla swallowed.

"She'll learn soon enough," said the shorter one.

Silla frowned, trying not to let them rattle her. "I shall refrain from food and drink until you bring me Jonas."

The tall one snorted. "It is *your* problem. What do we care if you eat or not?"

"Your kommandor will care if I fall sick." It was a risk to reveal that she knew this much, but she had to work with what little she had.

"I've scarcely eaten in the last day...or two." She fumbled over her words, trying to determine how much time she'd passed in the haze of the leaves. "Have scarcely drank any water. I've had skjöld leaves forced down my throat and will soon suffer from the sickness as they wear off."

She raised a trembling hand as proof of her deteriorating health. "If I do not soon drink, I shall fall even sicker. I would guess your kommandor might grow angered."

The Klaernar looked at one another, and something flickered across their faces.

"Bring Jonas to me," she said quietly. "Now."

The two Klaernar scoffed and disappeared down the hall.

Silla leaned against the wall, then sank to her knees. She stared at the tray of food, the flask of water. Her body screamed at her to eat, to drink.

"It is best to listen to them," came the woman's voice from down the hall. "If you try to play games with them, they shall play their own vile kind."

Nauseated, Silla crawled to the tray, shoving it under the bars as hard as she could. The tray slammed against the wall with a resounding clang.

She leaned against the wall for what felt like hours, the pounding of her head growing louder, sweat dotting her brow. She was burning hot and icy cold all at once. Silla remembered this from the last time—soon, the dreams would start. Only this time, there was no one to press water through her lips, no one to lay a cool cloth on her brow. She was in it alone this time.

"I'm here with you," whispered Saga, and tears stung Silla's eyes.

Saga was here. Saga was with her.

Silla lay down on the cold stone floor, her body shaking as lucidity faded.

―――

"WHAT IS WRONG WITH HER?"

She dreamt of a dragon made of ash and billowing smoke, embers snapping from within its towering form. It loomed above her, warmth flowing from its body as it drew nearer and nearer. Silla knew she should run, but she was so very tired she could scarcely move. She hadn't even the energy to muster fear.

"She's sick."

Tendrils of shadowy smoke enveloped her, surrounding her completely. The dragon's power pressed against her, steam hissing where it prodded her skin, triggering a faint prickle of pain. There was something familiar about the dragon—frightening, yet protective, and she relaxed into its exploratory touch.

"The kommandor won't be happy."

The dragon's touch warmed her body, shaking the cold from her bones. Awareness trickled back to her. Her eyelids fluttered, then opened. Darkness surrounded her; the cool stone floor pressing into her side; cold sweat slicking her body.

Silla took in the two shadowy forms standing outside her cell, a tray clutched in the hands of the shorter one.

"She's awake," said the taller one, relief in his voice.

"Evening meal," said the shorter one, sliding the tray beneath the bars. "Eat."

Silla pulled herself to hands and knees, pain clawing with fiery talons inside her skull. She crawled toward the tray and used her last reserved energy to push it back.

Collapsing to the floor, she was unable to do anything but breathe in. Breathe out.

"Jonas," she whispered.

"Foolish girl," muttered one of them. "You must eat. You do not want to anger the kommandor."

She did not reply. And eventually, the echo of their footfalls faded.

———

SKRAEDA STARED at the closed gates of Kopa. For the tenth time that hour, she cursed Kommandor Laxa for delaying her departure. Eisa had slipped away like a wolf into the darkness, and Skraeda had spent three frustrating days scouring the Road of Bones, finding nothing but ravens feasting upon a pile of warrior corpses.

"So they aid her willingly," Skraeda had mused, taking in the bloodshed with a smile. The girl could not have done this; it had to have been the Bloodaxe Crew. They'd risked themselves and their reputation for Eisa. *Do they know who you are, little Galdra?* she'd thought as she'd ridden down the road with renewed vigor. But the trail had grown cold soon after. The Bloodaxe Crew were no fools; surely they'd camp well off the road and knew to cover their tracks.

And now she found herself in Kopa, the sealed city gates barring entry. Skraeda was certain she knew why.

They had Eisa, and they weren't taking any chances.

"How?" she growled under her breath. How had the King's Claws gotten their hands on Eisa when Skraeda had spent weeks on the girl's trail?

I must be the one to hand her in, she thought, her chest tightening. The queen had deemed her dispensable, and this was her only chance at redemption. Once Skraeda handed Eisa to the queen, all would be set to rights. Queen Signe would welcome her back into her embrace, would see her value once more.

Elbowing past the merchants gathered below the gate tower, Skraeda relaxed her mind and searched for what she needed. Anger and impatience stirred the air nearby, but that was not what she sought. With a soft exhale, she ignored the strong emotions and searched for something lesser—boredom, with a hum of disdain. Klaernar.

Drawing the threads to her, Skraeda skimmed through them until she found what she needed. Soft and fluttering gently beneath the bulk of the man's emotions, she found the fine golden wisp. The thread of his free will came easily to her. With a gentle twitch, Skraeda watched the Klaernar blink.

"I require entry," she called up to him.

"Best of luck with that," muttered a merchant from behind her. "They say no one enters, and no one leaves the city."

"Come down, and let me through the doorway," called Skraeda, ignoring the looks blistering into her back.

Retrieving her saddlesack from her mount, she abandoned the horse and made her way to the heavy wooden door to the side of the main gates. After a moment, the iron hinges groaned as the door swung open.

"Hey!" called the merchants, anger gathering in their voices.

The Klaernar pushed the door shut behind her, turning a key in the lock.

"My thanks, you useful man," said Skraeda, holding the reins of his free will taut and in her control. She took the sad fool in. His pupils were bare pinpricks in his brown irises, hands slack at his sides. "Now tell me where they hold the girl who's caused such fanfare."

"Eastern garrison hall," he mumbled.

Skraeda's hand curled into a fist. "Show me," she gritted out.

The Klaernar led her through the black stone streets of Kopa for a few short minutes, stopping at a broad and squat building. Like all of the strange buildings in Kopa, this one was hewn from dark volcanic stone, shuttered windows spaced evenly across the base, a single window on the second level set beneath a peaked roof. Beyond the garrison hall, a forest stretched toward the defensive walls.

Surveying the building, she counted the pairs of Klaernar patrolling the perimeter. Two. Four. Six. And that was not counting those within.

Skraeda blew out a frustrated breath. The place was crawling with them. A good warrior was confident in their abilities but also knew their own limitations. And this garrison hall simply held too many Klaernar for Skraeda to deal with at once.

"How am I to get to you, little Galdra?" she murmured.

The idea came to her like a seed on the wind, rooting itself in the forefront of her mind.

Turning, Skraeda smiled, then retreated down the road.

FIFTY-NINE

"Curls."

Her eyes fluttered open to a pair of scuffed boots. In the back of her mind, Silla thought there was something vaguely familiar about them, but could not muster the strength to think any further. Empty. She was so empty.

"You win, Curls. I'm here."

Awareness rushed through her—and she found a small reserve of energy buried deep within her. Pushing herself up, her gaze climbed the form until they reached a pair of brilliant blue eyes. Jonas sat on a stool in the hallway, flickering torchlit making his shadow gutter on the wall. For a moment, Silla could do nothing but stare at him. Was he real? A phantom?

"All right, I'm here," he said softly, and at last, she believed her eyes. "Eat something. You will need your strength."

Her gaze landed on the tray before her, and Silla finally gave in. Jonas was truly here, and he was right; she needed all the strength she could get.

Wordlessly, Silla pulled the tray toward her, devouring the bread before working on the cold bowl of soup. Like a wilted plant coming back, life flowed into her as she worked her way through the food, then washed it down with as much water as she could tolerate.

Setting the waterskin aside, Silla leaned against the stone wall.

"Better?"

She tilted her head. "There are bars between us, Jonas."

"It is for the best, Silla. You are Galdra, after all. You're a danger to yourself and others."

She frowned at him. "You *drugged* me, Jonas. You knew the sickness I suffered the last time I stopped taking those leaves, and you forced them on me all the same!"

His face showed no evidence of remorse. "Difficult choices are made on the path to glory."

"Glory?" she sputtered. "How is this glory, Jonas? You've deceived me. You've drugged me, taken me against my will...it is dishonorable."

"Says the liar. You've no legs on which to stand, Silla, when you're the most dishonorable person I've met."

Her body flushed with heat. "You confuse dishonest with dishonor. They are not one and the same, Jonas. I was dishonest for my own safety. Because look—look what has been done with the truth!"

"You can blame no one but yourself, Curls."

"Jonas. It is *me*. I know I'm more than money to you." She hated the waver in her voice when she needed to stay strong.

Jonas was silent, his face impassive, and she realized—he would do it again in a heartbeat. To him, she was a commodity—a thing to be used for his own personal gain.

She tried a different angle. "Jonas, what would Ilías think—"

"You do not get to speak his name!" Jonas leapt to his feet, his shadow swarming up the wall behind him.

She swallowed, then tried again. "You've made a mistake; your grief has twisted you, Jonas. It is clear you are not of sound mind. Let us talk; let us figure this out."

"Oh no," he said, his voice so cool it could frost the bars of her cell. "My mind is clear. For the first time in my life, I am thinking straight. And I have you to thank for it."

"What?"

He stepped toward the bars. "Oh yes, Curls. I must thank you for teaching me the dangers of protecting others. It has brought me nothing but sorrow. It cost me my brother."

"Jonas, I—"

"I do not care what you have to say," he interrupted. "You cannot alter your fate." Jonas crossed his arms over his chest. "It was not in vain, you and

I. You will get me my lands back, and for that, I suppose, I should thank you."

Silla stared at him, looking for the man she thought she knew. But his eyes were hard and dark. There was no twinkle, no softness there. Gone was the man who'd followed her into the woods so harm would not befall her. Gone was the man who'd given her his family's talisman, who'd whispered soft things into her ear.

Silla shivered because she knew. Knew there was no getting through to him.

She stared at Jonas, memorizing his face and committing it to memory: the sky blue of his eyes, the subtle upturn of his lips, giving him a perpetually amused look, the pale scar on his cheek she'd traced a hundred times with her fingers and lips.

"For a time," she said quietly, "you were a great comfort to me, Jonas. The only good thing I had in this world." She sighed. "I would thank you for that. For helping me forget."

When he said nothing, she let the words flow from the knowing part of her. "One day, you'll wake up, Jonas, and realize the mistake you've made. By then, it will be too late. Shame will stalk you until your last breath."

Jonas stared at her with quiet violence. "I shall wait until the queen's men arrive with my reward," he said in a low voice. "But do not expect me to return to your cell. You can starve yourself all you want, but I won't be back."

He turned and left. And Silla knew this time, it really was for good.

She leaned against the wall, listening to the steady drip. Her stomach was knotted. The darkness in his eyes, the coldness...she could not shake it. How had everything gotten so twisted?

"What a shite-shoveling kunta."

Silla blinked, roused from her despairing thoughts. It was the woman from down the hall. A small smile curved her lips. "Yes."

"Was he your lover?"

"Something like that." Silla frowned. "What is your name?"

"Metta. You?"

"Silla." She bit her lip. "How long have you been here, Metta?"

Silence for a moment; then, "Four weeks, I think."

Four weeks? Silla's mouth fell open. "How...why haven't you been..."

"Do what they say." The woman sounded stoic. Resigned. "If you do what they say, they will keep you alive. The ones that bring difficulty do not last long."

Blood roared in Silla's ears. "Have there been others?"

Metta's harsh laugh echoed down the hall. "Yes. Ten, perhaps twelve women? Two men."

Fourteen souls come and gone from these cells. Silla's stomach folded itself in half. "They were put to the pillar?"

"I assume. They were taken and did not return."

"And the girls...did they fight against the Klaernar?"

"They protested when the Klaernar came for them. Some kicked, screamed, fought against them. Some cried and pleaded." After a moment of silence, the girl continued. "If the kommandor wants to see you, you must tolerate him. He's the worst of them. Do not argue or cry. Pretend...just tolerate him."

A chill settled in her bones. "Tolerate what, Metta?"

When the girl did not reply, Silla shuddered.

Wrong! her mind screamed. Wrong, in every sense. It had always felt wrong. The pillars. The Lettings. The Klaernar and their stones and violence.

"What are the charges against you, Metta?"

The girl huffed. "Charges. Witchcraft. And I've as much magic in me as a rock."

Silla bit her lip and waited for the girl to continue.

"A group of Klaernar came to my parent's food stall at the market. I brought their evening meal to them. They had the gall to suggest they should eat for free. I suggested otherwise."

The girl was silent for a moment. "My mother always said my sharp tongue would land me in trouble, and I suppose she was right. They came to our home that night. Read the charges. Put a sack over my head and threw me into the wagon with a bunch of other girls. I could hear them...crying and pleading. For once in my life, I stayed quiet. We drove through the night, with no blanket, no cover from the snow. When we stopped, the sack was pulled off. I could not feel my fingers. The cold stole one of the girls in her sleep. The rest of us were thrown into cells. Girls have come and gone. Two men as well. And now it is just us."

"But you have no galdur," said Silla, trying to understand.

"Their *quota*, they say," said Metta. "They have a number to reach. It does not matter if the charges are just. They simply need to fulfill their quota."

Bile rose up Silla's throat as Metta's words sank into her. Her adoptive mother had not been Galdra, and part of Silla had always suspected the Klaernar were not so picky as to who ended strung up. But hearing such blatant confirmation that the Klaernar were putting regular people on the pillars...it shook her.

When she spoke, Silla's voice was hard and determined. "They will pay, Metta. I will get out of here, and then I will make them pay for every life they've stolen."

Metta said nothing. Perhaps she did not believe Silla. Perhaps she'd heard similar from the others. Or perhaps it was simply that Metta had spent four weeks in a cell, doing what it took to keep herself from the pillar.

They fell into silence, but somehow, knowing Metta was just down the hall was a small comfort to Silla.

SIXTY

T he waters of the Hvíta river rushed beneath the Basalt Bridge as the frigid wind scraped across Rey's cheeks. Drawing up the hood of his cloak, he directed Horse over the bridge.

Kopa stretched before them, a sprawling city of black held in the stoney embrace of the fire mountain called Brími, thankfully long dormant. Though he was a grown man, Rey still felt the same wonder he had as a child when he took in the stonework of Kopa peeking from beyond the defensive walls; black spires and archways, cobbled streets and buildings sculpted from volcanic stone, marvelous feats of construction accomplished by the class of Galdra known as the Smiths.

The crowning glory of Kopa was Ashfall, a fortress of spires reaching for the skies like tangled black thorns. Carved into the base of Brími, it was the beating heart of the north, housing Jarl Hakon, who ruled over Eystri lands in King Ivar Ironheart's name.

The constriction in Rey's chest tightened, drawing him toward Kopa.

It had been three days since they'd buried Ilías—three days since he'd last seen Jonas and the woman. Rey's stomach had clenched tighter with each hour which passed without their arrival, and though he'd sent Gunnar and Sigrún scouting along both the backroad and the Road of Bones, they'd returned without tidings.

They'd vanished, and Rey knew at once that something was very wrong.

The memory of Jonas pulling on her wrist—he hadn't heard what Jonas had said, but the look in his eyes had told him enough. He should have stepped in. Should have...done something. But the rest of the day had been chaos and violence and death and grief, and all else had faded from his mind.

Rey prayed to all the gods he knew that his hunch was wrong, that his Bloodaxe brother would not hurt her. The very thought gave him the intense urge to drive his axe into someone's skull. But grief could do terrible things to a person, and Jonas was not himself.

The knowing feeling in his stomach would not allow Rey a moment's peace. And so, after sending the Bloodaxe Crew on to Istré, he found himself at Kopa's doorstep, vowing he would not rest until she was safe and Jonas had some sense knocked into him.

For the hundredth time since he'd spoken them, Rey wished his parting words to her had been softer, kinder. That he had admitted his own guilt in Ilías's death. *He* was the leader of the Bloodaxe Crew. *He* was the one who had led them into battle without understanding exactly what they faced.

And the Crew had agreed, together, that they would face these warriors on her behalf. Not to mention, there were always risks heading into battle; it was a part of their life. Traveling this road held dangers, as did each job they took. And Ilías was no fool, he'd have known death a possibility, and still, he'd accepted.

Reaching the far end of the Basalt Bridge, a cluster of wagons and carts came into view near the fortified stone walls of Kopa, people milling about. Drawing up the reins, Rey brought Horse to a stop and climbed down.

The gates to Kopa were shut. They were *never* shut.

Rey approached a merchant wrapped in a red cloak. "Do you know why the gates are closed?" he asked, nodding to the walls.

The man shook his head, blowing out a frustrated breath. "Been waiting here all day, have heard nothing but that no one gets in or out of Kopa." He gestured to his covered wagon. "My provisions from Kunafjord will soon spoil if they do not let us in. Bad enough we've had a short growing season. And now this." The man paused. "The only one who's passed through was a strange woman earlier in the day."

The hairs on the back of Rey's neck stood on end. "Woman?"

"Red-haired. Rude. Left her horse and was let through the side door by the Klaernar."

The warrior, thought Rey. That red-haired warrior he'd pushed off Skalla Ridge. It had to be her. And that only made his urgency grow.

Rey eyed the walls, his gaze honing in on two Klaernar who surveyed the crowd from atop the gate. Leading Horse by the reins, Rey approached.

"Hae!" called Rey, catching the Klaernar's gaze. "I've an important message for Jarl Hakon."

Their faces were unflinching. "No one gets through the gates," said one.

Rey drew an irritated breath. "It is important, and I am well known to him. If you fetch Jarl Hakon, or his son Eyvind, they will vouch for me."

"This comes from above Jarl Hakon," said the Klaernar cooly. "No one enters or leaves the city."

Above Jarl Hakon? thought Rey. That could only mean a handful of people in all of Íseldur—King Ivar, Magnus Heart Eater, or one of Ivar's hirdmen, the band of bodyguards which never strayed far from the king. *Or perhaps Queen Signe,* he thought, his spine prickling.

Rey turned, his mind whirling. He needed to get into Kopa, could sense he was already too late.

What have you done, Jonas? Rey had thought if he could only find Jonas, could only talk some sense into him...if anyone knew the pain of losing a younger brother, it was Rey. But the knowing feeling in his stomach now twisted into alarm.

Mounting Horse, he trotted back across the Basalt Bridge and down the Black Road for several miles. A childhood of summers spent playing with Eyvind amongst the city would come in useful today. Every city had hidden exits, and Rey happened to know precisely where Kopa's were located.

Leading Horse off the road, they meandered through the trees for several long minutes before Rey dismounted and secured her to a tree. Here the Hvíta river was shallow, and with the spring runoff from the mountains long gone, it was easy enough to wade across. Pushing through the forest, the western corner of Kopa's defensive walls loomed ahead. The pinewoods were interspersed with scrubby alder and goat willow along these parts, making it impossible to see the doorway carved into the black basalt walls unless one knew precisely what they searched for.

Rey's fingers scraped along the rough-hewn stone, looking for the one which stuck out just a hair's breadth too far...there it was. He pressed it in, and a door swung open, the creak of iron hinges like nails scraping along his spine.

Though Rey had expected the sound, he did not anticipate the Klaernar standing directly behind it, lunging at him with a glinting blade. Feinting left with scarcely a heartbeat's time to spare, Rey grappled for his sword, drawing it just in time to meet the man's next blow.

"Who are you?" demanded the Klaernar. "How do you know of this entry?"

Rey slashed at him just below the ribs, but his blade glanced off the warrior's shirt of mail.

"My brother in arms has been killed," grunted Rey, parrying the man's attack. "One of my warriors has run off with my...*charge.*" He swung his blade in a strong arc, aiming for the weakened chain mail. "And I'm in no mood to answer your gods damned questions." He smiled grimly as rivets sprung free from the shirt, pinging against the stone wall, and his blade sank deep into the Klaernar's belly.

Kicking the man off his blade, Rey stepped over him and strode into the darkened tunnel.

A groan slipped from his lips as he stepped from the passageway into the forested area beyond. A contingent of Klaernar stood, blades drawn, and he rushed to count them. Ten. Fifteen. *Fuck.* Twenty-three.

"Throw down your weapon," called one—a bearskin cloak wrapped around his shoulders indicated he was at least of kaptein's rank.

"Very well," muttered Rey, throwing his sword to the ground.

"How do you know of this entrance?" demanded the kaptein.

Rey unsheathed his dagger and tossed it onto his sword, the clang absorbed by the forest floor. "Why is the city locked down? Is this about the girl?" he asked. Never in all of his years in Kopa had he seen Klaernar posted here, but never had he seen the gates shut either.

This will complicate things, thought Rey with a grimace.

The kaptein's eyes narrowed. "Whom do you speak of?"

A thin wavering note in his voice betrayed the kaptein. *So this does have something to do with her,* thought Rey. He decided to chance it; they would not live to tell, in any case. "What does the queen want with her?" he asked, unsheathing his hevrít and tossing it to the ground with his other blades.

The Klaernar kaptein blinked quickly, ignoring Rey's question. "All of them," he snarled, nodding at Rey's boot.

Studying the men from the corner of his eye, Rey drew the dagger and tossed it aside. *Twenty-three Klaernar including the kaptein,* he thought. *You do love a challenge.* It had been days, and he was aching to express.

"What interest has the queen with a Galdra girl?" asked Rey, though he had little hope that they'd answer—not yet anyway.

He should have demanded these answers from her, should have insisted upon the truth, but his mind had been clouded with grief and anger. What mess was she in, this curly-haired woman whose smile was like sunlight? How had she gotten herself into such trouble?

Perhaps if she'd felt safe to confide in Rey, he could have prevented this from happening, could have kept her from the Klaernar's clutches. His stomach burned. Rey knew what the Klaernar did to their prisoners and knew that Kommandor Valf was a particularly vile beast. If she was under his watch, if he laid a single finger upon her...Rey could not finish the thought.

"Hands up!" barked the kaptein. Two of the Klaernar edged forward, iron fetters in hand.

A smile curved Rey's lips as he lifted his hands, drawing his galdur and priming himself in seconds. Rolling his neck, he caught sight of the black veins on the back of his hand. It had been days, and his galdur strained so hard to be freed, he scarcely had to think to express it.

"What's the matter with him?" asked one of the King's Claws, eyes wide as he stared at Rey's palms.

Dark, smoky tendrils spilled from them, billowing upward into the sky and gathering in a great cloud of swirling ash. Rey exhaled in relief, filled with the primal power which made him feel more like himself than anything else. The knot in his stomach eased, the grief, the worry, displaced by the need to destroy.

To *burn.*

"What, this?" asked Rey, flicking a wrist. In the blink of an eye, his smoke shattered into twenty-two tangled wisps which pulsed and thickened, embers snapping within. "This is death coming for you."

With Rey's silent command, the smoke bent to his will, tendrils stretching out toward the Klaernar who now charged at him with swords drawn. He'd excluded the kaptein for the time being—someone must provide him the answers he sought. Blackness swarmed at their tattooed faces, and as fear forced their mouths open to cry out, the darkness tunneled down their throats.

The next part went as it always did: men choking on their own screams, grabbing at their throats, flailing as they burned from within.

"It is no use," murmured Rey, honing his focus to a sharpened point. Twenty-one was truly a stretch for him, but he loved a good challenge. But then, he scowled. Twenty-one. There had been twenty-two Klaernar excluding the kaptein.

From the corner of his eye, he tracked the kaptein backing away, his hand on the hilt of his sword, and then...

"Fuck," muttered Rey. A figure crashed through the underbrush, fleeing in panic—one of them had escaped. "This will bring trouble," he muttered to himself. But he could not loosen his grip on the other Klaernar, not until they were dead, and the kaptein had now drawn his sword. Gritting his teeth, Rey drew more galdur, pulling from the external halda stores tattooed upon his chest and expressing a fresh ribbon of ash. This one, he sent to the kaptein, encircling the man's neck, a smoky caress warning him against any foolish ideas.

The faces of the Klaernar were crimson now. Eyes bulging, liquid seeped from their sockets as they finally began to crash to the ground, clawing and crawling to no avail. Next came the blisters, bubbling and popping, before their skin turned molten, sloughing off in sheets. The forest was filled with the acrid scent of singed hair and burnt meat, the sizzle of flesh and whimpers of dying men.

A better man would be sickened at the sight—faces melted, smoke and steam rising from contorted bodies. But Rey felt only exulted. Though not on his list, he relished their deaths.

Once they'd all stilled, he surveyed the forest in hopes of spotting the escaped Klaernar, but there was no sign of him. Through the char came the distinctive odor of urine. "You've pissed yourself," Rey said with distaste, turning to the kaptein.

"Y-you—" stuttered the kaptein. He was shaking now. "You're the Slátrari. The murderer!"

Rey smiled, stepping toward the kaptein. The name was ridiculous, but he had to admit he enjoyed the notoriety. The stories had spread wide, and when he came for his targets, they grew so very frightened when they realized what their fate was.

With a twitch of his finger, the smoke tightened around the kaptein's neck, the man hissing as his skin turned the most beautiful shade of red. With another twitch Rey could have it blistering, but no. Not quite yet.

"Talk," said Rey, leveling the man with a dark look.

"S-she's in custody," said the kaptein, wincing as the smoke singed the tip of his ear. "We're to man the doors. All of them. No one gets in or out until a convoy takes her to Kunafjord."

"And then..." urged Rey, his gaze hardening.

"And then she's to sail to Sunnavík." The man practically panted.

If only the people of Íseldur could see how fearsome these Klaernar really are when death comes for them, thought Rey bitterly.

"Why?" growled Rey.

"I-I know no more than I've told you," said the man. His voice had reached that shrill pitch it always did when they foresaw death. "I w-was only following orders."

"Who?" glowered Rey.

Thankfully the man did not need further direction. "Valf. She's in Kommandor Valf's ward. Eastern garrison."

Rey's hand curved into a fist, his lips lifting into a snarl. Turning his back on the kaptein, he snatched his discarded weapons and strode toward Kopa's eastern quarter.

The kaptein's screams rang in his ears, and then, the woods fell deathly silent.

SIXTY-ONE

Silla's eyes traced the knots and whorls on Kommandor Valf's door as the taller of the Klaernar knocked upon it. Cold iron manacles cut into her wrists, and she shifted uneasily. She looked down at her dress—garishly red and low cut, it was cinched so tight she could scarcely breathe.

The two Klaernar had arrived at her cell with soap, a bucket of water, a pair of slippers, and the red garment. She'd been instructed to bathe and dress, and when they'd returned, the Klaernar had led her through the garrison hall and up a flight of stairs to the kommandor's private quarters.

As she felt herself sagging, Silla remembered Hekla's words.

Everything he had done to me, every slap, every punch, every kick, it was kindling. It built me up into a raging wildfire, and now it was time for him to burn.

This is kindling, thought Silla. *No matter what, they will not see me break. And one day, they will burn.*

Silla straightened her spine as the door swung open, Kommandor Valf's large frame filling it. He was tall and broad with a long black beard set into twin Urkan braids. His lips curled into a smile that did not meet his eyes, and he yanked her into the room by her manacles.

"I expect no disruptions," snapped the kommandor. The door clicked shut behind her, followed by the ominous slide of the lock as Kommandor Valf secured the room.

Standing far too near, Valf drew a key from his pocket and began loosening the manacles. As they clanged to the ground, Silla rubbed her wrists, feeling anything but relief.

She studied her surroundings. Valf had made his way to a heavy wooden table situated in the middle of the room. An iron chandelier hung above, candles casting shivering light down upon two heavy ceramic jugs and a plate loaded with food. Silla's traitorous stomach growled, and she hugged herself tightly—the daymeal had not been brought to her cell that morning.

Eyes sweeping the room, she took in the rest of the details. On the far end sat a fireplace sculpted from the same polished black stone as the rest of the building, a low-burning fire crackling gently within. Hanging above the hearth were several smaller tapestries, glistening threads of gold and browns and reds twisting together in geometric patterns that caught the light in an odd sort of way. Flanking the hearth were shelves crammed with books and sheaves of parchment, and, to Silla's great distaste, several busts of King Ivar in varying sizes. On the opposite end of the room, the shutters were cracked open in a window, dim light filtering through it.

Kommandor Valf gestured to two fur-draped chairs by the fire. "Sit."

It was not an offer, nor was it a suggestion. Swallowing, Silla crossed the room and lowered herself onto one of the chairs. Her gaze settled onto a black basalt bust of King Ivar set on the shelf beside Valf's chair. The king scowled at her even from within polished volcanic rock.

Hideous, she thought, careful to keep her face neutral.

The kommandor appeared at her side, the plate of food held in his hand.

"Your daymeal," he said. Again, this was not a question. Nerves jangling, Silla accepted the plate. Valf sank into the chair beside the bust, sipping from a cup as he regarded her. "Eat," he said.

Her stomach growled again. It had been days of watered-down soup for day and evening meals, never quite enough to sate her hunger. And the plate before her held temptation in the worst possible form—sweet rolls.

After a long moment of consideration, Silla plucked the sweet roll from the plate, taking a tentative bite. Layers of buttery warmth met her, and she practically groaned, going back for a second, much larger mouthful. After finishing the roll, she moved on to the meat and cheeses, eating in silence to the last bite.

"I see you enjoy your food," said the kommandor, the corners of his lips hitching up.

A flush crept up Silla's neck, and she clasped her hands, then unclasped them, unsure of what to do.

"You're nervous," murmured Valf.

Silla's eyes met his. "Do I have reason to be?"

The kommandor's gaze roamed her face. "No harm will come to you if you are cooperative, dear."

Silla tried not to flinch.

The kommandor continued. "From what I've heard, you've a defiant temperament. A bit of a sharp tongue."

Silla forced herself to look at him directly as she spoke. "I've been confined to a cell for days without charges explained. Perhaps you could be so kind as to fill me in, Kommandor?"

That ugly smile crossed his face again. "We are both too clever for such games, dear. Will you not admit to who you are?" He paused. "Shall I call you Eisa, or do you prefer Silla?"

The blood drained from her face, her stomach clenching tight.

Eisa.

The name stalked her, no matter how hard she tried to escape. Her hands trembled, and she forced in a deep breath.

Hearthfire thoughts, she told herself. But she had been brought to Kommandor Valf wearing an obscenely low-cut dress. Had been betrayed by her lover. Had no one and nothing left in this world.

Saga, she thought. *She had Saga.*

Her spirits lifted incrementally, and she forced herself to answer the kommandor.

"Silla," she heard herself say.

"Silla," he repeated. "We've sent a falcon to Queen Signe to inform her you've been apprehended, and already we've heard back that she is quite eager to retrieve you. She arranges for a ship to bring you south to Sunnavík from port at Kunafjord."

Silla tugged at the sleeve of her dress.

"Your friend Jonas has informed us that in addition to learning of your bloodlines, he's discovered your unusual...abilities," continued the kommandor, rubbing his jaw. His gaze fell to her hands.

She clenched her teeth. *Jonas* had discovered?

"Of course, you know our official stance on that...abomination." He wrinkled his nose at her. "But you are here. Your fate is set. There's no reason for you to withhold anything from me. Tell me, dear, what exactly *are* your capabilities?"

Silla wanted to burst into laughter. *Well, kommandor, I glow like the auroras. A most useful skill to have when you are running for your life. Does not draw attention in the slightest.*

"I do not understand my capabilities," she said instead.

"That is most unfortunate." The kommandor brought his cup to his lips, tipping it back. "Though there *are* ways to untangle these truths. And since it will be several days before the queen's ship is arranged, you and I will have some fun discovering them. I've a knack for drawing them out."

Silla clasped her hands together with such force her knuckles turned white. While she did not know his methods, Silla was quite certain she did not wish to learn them.

"I don't suppose the queen would approve of you playing with her new toy," she said, her gaze steady on Kommandor Valf.

"On the contrary, dear. Her Highness has asked me to confirm your galdur. I am a great friend of her advisor, Maester Alfson. Do you know of him?"

Silla shook her head, shifting restlessly in her chair.

"The maester, well, he's got an inquisitive mind and loves to discover how things work. He's quite dedicated to his craft and has a particular interest in the workings of magic. Nothing pleases him more than taking a thing apart and reassembling it."

A chill ran down her spine at this first hint of what truly awaited her in Sunnavík. Ashes, what kind of monsters were in that castle with Saga?

"Fear not, Silla. I am much less a craftsman, though I do have my methods," said the kommandor. "Might I refill your cup?"

Silla shook her head. A chill spread through her blood at this unsettling news, and she shifted once more in her chair.

"Yes, dear. We shall discover the workings of your magic. And do you know, we've already started our first session."

Gripping the arms of her chair, Silla blinked into the man's cold, dark eyes. The chill seemed to have spread to her skin, accompanied by an odd sensation—tension gathering in her veins.

When the Kommandor continued, there was a growing excitement in his voice. "Alfson tells me it is about *energy* and balance. The skjöld leaves create a barrier too great for one's powers to manifest, quelling them. But there is another leaf with the opposite effect. When taken, it lowers the barrier and forces one's powers to surface. A catalyst, he's called it."

Her skin was thrumming now, and Silla looked at her empty plate. Realization slid down her spine like ice-cold water, and she closed her eyes. Fool. She was such a gods damned fool.

"Yes, dear. The catalyst was baked into that sweet roll. And look, your magic is stirring. I see it is true, then—you have a unique gift."

Silla leaped from her chair, turning her palms up and staring in horror at the white light blazing from her veins. The two prior times she'd seen the iridescent light, it had been softer, gentler, a whisper inside her. Now it raged through her like a glacial river over rapids, the cold shoving against her skin as though it demanded release. The pressure seemed to build with each breath, but she did not know how to let it free.

Kommandor Valf appeared beside her without warning. His hand closed around her wrist, gripping it so tightly, she winced. He traced a finger up and down her arm as she tried to wrench herself free.

"You seem to be an Ashbringer, though your skin is cold to touch," he murmured. "What is this? I've never seen it before. You glow!" There was something alarming in his voice, a greedy excitement. "Alfson will be pleased with you. He will want to open you up and see if you glow on the inside too."

Silla sucked in a harsh breath, the room tilting on its axis. She had to get out of here.

"But why should he have all the fun? I am eager to see it too."

He shifted behind her, yanking her firmly to his chest. Her shock and panic overwhelming, Silla thrashed to get free. The kommandor drew a dagger, and before she could think, he sliced it down the palm of her hand.

Silla screamed as hot pain blended disorientingly with the coldness of her galdur.

"Well," said the kommandor.

The room shifted back into focus, and she assessed the situation. Crimson blood oozed from her palm. Her wrist was gripped tightly in his much larger hand, the dagger clutched in his other. The kommandor's chest pressed against her back, trapping her in place.

As he leaned over to look at her wound, she gagged on his sour ale breath. "Naught but red. I'll admit, I am dismayed. But what of your bones—"

Before panic could take hold again, Silla had a moment of clarity. *This* was what she'd trained for all those weeks with Hekla and Rey. Each practiced elbow, each lunge, each punch had led her to this precise moment.

If she wanted freedom, she'd have to remember what they'd taught her.

As the kommandor clutched her middle finger and brought the dagger down, she drove her elbow back into his ribs. Breath hissing from the man, Silla slapped clumsily at his wrist, and the dagger clattered to the floor.

"You kunta!" His arm wrapped around her throat, constricting until she could not breathe. "You've sealed your fate now. If you bring me pain, I will return it to you tenfold."

But his words grew stifled until all Silla could hear was Hekla's voice in her mind.

Pull his arm forward.

Drive your fist into his groin.

Elbow him in the ribs.

Wrench yourself free.

Silla's body performed the movements as though she had done it a thousand times, and at last, she swung herself from his grip.

She scrambled away from the kommandor—bent double as he tried to regain his senses—but he lunged after her with sudden aggressive speed, grabbing the hem of her dress. A loud rip filled the air as a swath tore through the skirts. The fabric ripped loose, and she stumbled forward with the momentum, her hands catching on the edge of the table. The heavy ceramic pitchers clunked together.

Kommandor Valf righted himself, his face tight and flushed. "You disappoint me, dear. I thought we could be friends. But now you shall suffer."

Ignoring the tension beneath her skin, the distracting brightness of her arms, Silla grabbed the ceramic jugs, her hands dipping under their surprising weight. Whirling with one clutched in each hand, she flung them at the kommandor as he lunged at her. In smooth, practiced motion, he feinted left, then right, dodging them easily. Ale and mead splashed to the floor, the jugs clattering loudly. The kommandor charged toward her faster than she could anticipate. Silla turned and tried to throw herself out of reach, but it was too late.

The kommandor grabbed a handful of hair, yanking her head backward roughly. A howl ripped from her throat as pain blazed across her scalp. Her hands grappled blindly, looking for something, for anything, but they came up empty.

"Understand this: I would have shown you kindness."

Her head was jerked backward, and her feet scrambled to keep up. She drove her elbow back toward the kommandor's ribs, trying to remember her defenses, but everything was falling apart—the move was sloppy and ineffective.

Valf's grip on her hair loosened, and he shoved her roughly to the ground. Her hands and knees connected forcefully with the wooden floor, jarring her so hard, she thought her teeth might crack.

"Thankfully, the queen does not need you in pristine condition." His boot collided hard with her ribs, driving the air from her lungs and sending pain shooting across her chest.

Silla tried desperately to draw in breath, but her body seemed paralyzed. Eyes widening, she tried again. Again. Nothing. No air. Panic flared through her, distracting her from the boot swinging for her once more.

Red.

There was nothing but red hot pain blinding and imprisoning her. She curled in on herself with a whimper and waited for the next blow. At last, she managed to suck in a breath, but her relief was short-lived. Heavy hands turned her over and pinned her shoulders to the floor, a weight settling on her chest. Her vision cleared, landing on the tapestries hung above the fireplace. From this angle, she could see them more clearly.

Hair.

They were woven from human hair.

Reds; golds; browns; blacks—a multitude of samples twined together and mounted above the hearth like trophies.

How many women? Silla wondered, panic scratching up her throat. How many women had this monster violated before putting them to the pillar?

The kommandor straddled her, a cruel smile spreading across his lips. "Scream, dear," he rasped, drawing his hand back. "I do so enjoy it."

His open palm slammed across her cheek. Pain lashed sharp and hot across Silla's face. She blinked, then blinked again, until the figure looming over her came into focus. Her blood chilled at the sight of him. Eyes malevolent, the kommandor's lips had curled into a victorious smile.

He drew a dagger from his belt, and Silla braced herself for the end. But instead, he gripped her hair, cutting a swath of it loose and bringing it to his nose. "A memento so that I might remember our time together."

Silla flailed beneath him, hands scratching up his arms, but all it seemed to accomplish was to incite the kommandor's anger. Tossing the dagger and swath of hair aside, he slapped her again, knocking all sense from her. The room spun as the kommandor gripped her throat and squeezed with one hand, the other reaching for the buckle of his belt. Silla could not breathe. Lights popped before her eyes, her hands groped uselessly at her sides. Panic flared in her stomach.

"We shall have fun together, *dear*. Though I'm afraid it will be more fun for me than for you."

Everything was distant. Her ears buzzed. Darkness crept in from the corners of her vision.

But then—the kommandor's hand flinched. His grip loosened. Silla sucked in a lungful of air. Time slowed. Valf's face loomed above her, his expression strangely vacant.

Her hand twitched, fingers grazing against something rounded. Something cold. Her fingers closed around the handle of the heavy jug. She gripped it tightly, then swung it in a mighty arc toward the kommandor's temple with all the strength she could muster.

The impact was a dull thud reverberating down her arm. Silla stopped breathing as she watched the kommandor. He blinked, then fell limp onto his side.

She gasped in desperate breaths, scrambling out from under him and to her feet. What had happened? Why had he stopped choking her? But Silla hadn't the time to ponder these questions. He rasped deeply from behind her, a growl building in his throat. His hand closed around her ankle, fingers digging tightly into her flesh.

Her gaze collided with polished black stone. The beady eyes of King Ivar's basalt bust glowered at her. Silla reached for the solid stone and heaved it off its shelf, grunting with the pressure against her cut palm. Using the momentum from the weight of the bust, she swung it toward the kommandor's prone form and let go.

Silla could swear she heard Hekla's laugh of approval as the bust landed with a sickeningly wet smack right on the kommandor's head. It cracked like an eggshell, blood and brain matter oozing out around the black stone.

A twitch of his legs. A rattling breath. And then, he moved no more.

Silla stared at the broken body of Kommandor Valf, blinking once, then twice. She'd done that. She'd killed him. She'd—

A knock at the door disrupted her thoughts. The struggle. They'd been loud. The Klaernar outside the kommandor's door were knocking, rattling the knob.

"Kommandor?"

Her eyes swept the room, falling upon the window. Silla grabbed the kommandor's woolen cloak from a hook in the wall and threw it around her shoulders in an attempt to dim the light coming from her arms. She rushed to the windows and flung the shutters as wide as they would go, peeking cautiously out.

A group of Klaernar rushed along the pathway below, presumably to the garrison hall entrance. Her breath hitched at the sight beyond that. The city of Kopa sprawled out—layers upon layers of black buildings, roofs, and spires stretching to the toothy mountains beyond where a vast fortress was nestled.

Silla had made it to Kopa, and she yearned to tell her father, to scream it across the rooftops.

"Focus, Silla," she whispered with a shake of her head. Now was not the time to grow sentimental. She was in Kopa, but she was far from safe.

"Skeggagrim," she reminded herself. "House with the blue shutters beside the Dragon's Lair Inn." Climbing onto the window ledge, she dangled a leg out. Somewhere in this city was freedom. It was so near, she could taste it.

A cluster of scrubby bushes sat below the window, but as she was on the second floor of the garrison hall, it was too far to jump down safely. Gripping the window ledge, Silla turned her body to face the exterior wall. Her slippers were lost during the struggle, and her bare feet groped the stone wall for a foothold. Gritting her teeth, she clung desperately to the wall. Her dress whipped in a gust of wind, and she looked down. One step, maybe two more, and she'd jump.

The sound of splintering wood met her ears, a male voice yelling out as the door to Kommandor Valf's quarters was breached. Silla dropped her foot down, desperately searching for yet another foothold. As she put pressure down, the stone underfoot crumbled away, and she fell through empty air, her mouth open in a scream she didn't dare allow escape.

She landed hard on her side in the bushes, the breath knocked from her lungs and the piney smell of juniper in her nose. Silla lay stunned, unable to pull in air.

A stern, tattooed face appeared in the window above, and life rushed back to Silla.

"She's climbed out!" yelled the Klaernar, pulling himself out onto the window ledge.

Silla was distantly aware of branches scratching up her arms and legs but was soon wrenching herself free, racing down the cobbled street.

"Blue shutters," she repeated through gritted teeth. "Dragon's Lair Inn." She had to find it. It was all she had.

But as Silla tore down the road, she failed to see the black hawk soaring overhead.

SIXTY-TWO

printing down the road, Silla plunged her arms into the folds of her stolen cloak. Between the black wool and pinning her arms to her chest, she was able to smother some of the light pouring from her forearms, but the sensation beneath her skin was driving her mad—ice-cold tension screaming to be released. *What kind of impractical power is this?* she thought. A cold human torch that could not be snuffed?

The sounds of Kopa met her ears—the hammering of blacksmiths and clop of hooves, the hum of conversation. She was lost in this city, needed directions. Pushing against the urge to stay hidden, Silla ran toward the sound. The road curved, widening into a busy thoroughfare. People milled, going about their day, oblivious to the girl who ran for her life. A man walked her way, bearskin cap settled low on his head, woolen cloak pulled high on his shoulders.

Is it cold? Silla wondered. Her feet were bare upon the rough flagstones, but the cold did not penetrate her. There was only the need to get to safety and the relentless pressure of her galdur asking for something she could not give.

"Please," begged Silla, looking at the man. "I must find the Dragon's Lair Inn. Is it near?"

The man slowed, the corner of his mouth tugging down as he took in her attire. His breath puffed the air, and Silla glanced over her shoulder. There were shouts behind her—the Klaernar were on her trail.

"Please," she repeated, frantic. "Is it near?"

The man's gaze snapped to hers. "Down this street, cut through the path beside the blacksmith's and you'll see it just there."

She was only a few streets from safety. From her new life.

Silla's spirits lifted, and she pushed on down the road, calling over her shoulder, "My thanks!"

And then, she ran. Stones dug into her feet as they slapped against the volcanic cobbled streets, the northern wind whipping her hair and cloak into a frenzy. She tugged the cloak over the mad glow of her arms, yet still, it permeated the fabric. Heads turned her way, and Silla was aware she made a scene.

But the Klaernar were somewhere behind her and she'd killed their kommandor and her future lay down this road.

House with the blue shutters beside the Dragon's Lair Inn, she told herself, over and over. It was a chant, a prayer, a plea, and with each repeat, her purpose became rooted deeper.

The road grew more congested as she ran. Silla pushed past carts, knocking a woman's shoulder as she plowed along the street. The clang of the blacksmith's hammer ringing in her ears, Silla turned right, pushing down the pathway beside the forge. And soon she was bursting from the pathway onto a narrower street. Her feet slid to a halt as her eyes settled on the large stone building, just a bit to her left. Twin shields were mounted on either side of a heavy wooden door, dragons painted in green upon them. From above the door hung a sign scrawled with the words that made Silla's heart sing. *The Dragon's Lair.*

Her eyes slid to the aging blue shutters on a small, nondescript home to the left of the inn. Her vision blurred as tears crept in. She'd made it. Here it was— the home beside The Dragon's Lair Inn.

A thousand miles she'd traveled to get here. She'd survived vile monsters and warbands, had gone toe-to-toe with terrifyingly large warriors and assassins. She'd gained and lost friends, had taken a lover and felt the sting of his betrayal. Had discovered the truth of her bloodline and that she was Galdra.

Silla stepped toward Skeggagrim's home a different woman than she'd been a month earlier. She was stronger. Wiser. More alive. And hungry.

It was a small, ordinary home sculpted from black stones. Silla stood so near, she could see that the stones were not solid black, but were threaded with deep blue veins that caught the light. An ashwood door hung on iron hinges, windows closed tight with blue shutters. Pushing open the gate in the wattle fence, Silla breathed deeply.

She stepped to the door and knocked.

Her heart pounded in her chest, and her body trembled. Silla breathed in, then out. Once. Twice. Three times.

The door swung open.

"Hello, little Galdra," said Skraeda.

———

REY'S BREATHS sawed in and out of him as he stepped from the pinewoods, the eastern garrison hall looming before him. He bent double to catch his breath, an ache growing in his muscles. So many Klaernar had nearly drained him, but his mind remained fixated on the one that had fled. He should chase the warrior down—silence him for good. But the man was long gone, and Rey decided finding her was the more pressing matter at the moment.

His body complained, and he knew he'd drained his galdur lower than it had been in years. Reaching into a leather pouch secured to his belt, Rey drew out a pinch of dried green needles, the sharp woodsy scent curving up his nostrils. He dropped them on his tongue, chewing briefly before giving up and swallowing with a grimace. The bitter taste of the vakandi leaves lingered, but he felt the stimulant begin to work immediately, loosening his tensed muscles and pushing energy into his blood. He'd pay in sleep later, but right now, there was urgency.

He surveyed the garrison hall. Dozens of windows flanked the heavy entry door, but his eyes fell upon the lone window on the upper floor, beneath the peaked roof. That would be Valf's window. He prayed that was not where she was.

Jogging from the trees, Rey drew his sword.

Fire blazed through his veins at the thought of her in the hands of the Klaernar, days now. What had she endured? A fierce desire filled him—to turn their door into kindling with his axe, then to redden the blade with their blood. To burn and destroy the King's Claws and their garrison as should have been done long ago.

But the knowing feeling in his stomach grounded him. This was madness. He was better than this, better than letting his base urges get the best of him. Bursting into a garrison hall filled with Klaernar was not a sound idea.

His feet stilled as Rey neared the building. Voices, filtering from the opened window above.

"Dead?" demanded someone. "And the girl?"

"Climbed from the window. A contingent is in pursuit—"

"Send another!" barked the voice.

Rey eased back into the woods. *She escaped,* he thought, his heart swelling. Somehow, this did not surprise him. She was clever, his girl. A survivor.

Not your girl, he chastised himself. The fight, the vakandi leaves must be going to his head.

Shaking himself, Rey slid his sword back into its sheath and turned to face the garrison hall. He closed his eyes and listened to the distant shouts of the Klaernar.

Rey strode deeper into the forest and ran.

———

SILLA STUMBLED BACKWARD, but her cloak was seized, metal biting into her throat as Skraeda dragged her into the home. Her mind whirled, trying to understand how it was that the red-haired assassin had come to be in Skeggagrim's home.

Her heart fell as the realization struck her.

"Yes, little Galdra," said Skraeda, pinning her against the door with an arm shoved into her collarbone. "My thanks for leaving me the letter."

Silla's stomach twisted as her gaze slid over Skraeda's shoulder, examining the home for signs of Skeggagrim. It was dark and still, torchlight catching those curious blue minerals in the black stone masonry. A single room, it was long and rectangular, stairs leading to a loft above, a woven room divider at the far end, likely sheltering the sleeping space. It smelled of woodsmoke and the must of damp stones—and something metallic.

The light from Silla's forearms lit Skraeda's face from below, shadows pooling under her eyes and nose. "Did you like my gift?" asked the warrior, the blade scraping along the sensitive skin of Silla's neck.

"W-what?" asked Silla.

Skraeda likes to talk, she thought. *Keep her going. Buy yourself time.*

"My gift, Eisa."

Skraeda smiled, too wide, too toothy, and Silla shuddered at the name. "Don't call me that," she gritted out.

Skraeda ignored her. "I hope it was easy for you to escape the garrison hall. Nasty man, that Kommandor Valf. I waited in the woods. Found the threads of his emotions and bided my time. I knew he'd want to meet you. Knew you'd pique his interest." Skraeda's face was so near, Silla felt warm puffs of breath on her cheeks. "When I sensed fury from him, then lust, I felt it was time to tug on the thread of his free will."

"F-free will?" repeated Silla.

She glanced again around the room. *Where is Skeggagrim? Has she harmed him?*

"A little discovery I've made about the Klaernar that has proven quite useful." Skraeda lowered her voice, a conspiratorial smile upon her face. "Parts of their minds are altered, making the thread of their free will readily accessible. I believe it a side effect of the berskium powder they take."

Silla did not know what Skraeda spoke of but wisely kept her mouth shut. *Look for a weapon,* she thought. *You need an advantage.*

"A simple tug on his free will and the Kommandor was no longer in control," continued Skraeda.

Her words distracted Silla, and it suddenly made sense—Valf's hesitation; the pause which had allowed her to breathe, to grasp the jug. "You. You froze him!"

"Yes," murmured Skraeda, studying Silla. "I lost his thread soon after and quickly returned here. What did you do to him?"

Silla flinched at the memory. "I crushed his skull in."

"Good," drawled Skraeda. Her lips curved down at the look of distaste upon Silla's face. "They make us this way, little Galdra. They make us fight. Mold us into killers. It is the way of this world."

Keep her talking, Silla urged herself. *Find her weakness, and then exploit it. Like you did with Kraki.*

"Is that what happened to you?" asked Silla, unable to keep the note of contempt from her voice.

Emotion flickered behind Skraeda's blue eyes. "If you live in this kingdom as Galdra for long enough, you must grow your own claws to survive. I've seen enough to know that no one truly good is meant to last in this world."

"Who did you lose?" asked Silla.

Find her weakness, she urged herself. *Skraeda is human. She has flaws like us all.*

"I had a sister," Skraeda seemed lost in thought. "A twin. She was too kind for this world. Too weak. Too frightened to use what was gifted to her by the gods."

"What happened to her?" prodded Silla.

Skraeda sighed. "She was not fated to live. Her Highness granted me my freedom, and Ilka was the price that needed to be paid. Did you know that Queen Signe was the first person to look upon me with something other than disgust? Not even my own parents wanted a Galdra daughter. They sent me... sent *us* away. But the queen...she has never seen my galdur as a curse, as an unnatural thing to be snuffed from this world. She is not like her husband, afraid of the Galdra. She sees the potential, the power to be gleaned from us."

"She sounds like a forward-thinking woman," murmured Silla.

"She is a visionary. And she is not afraid to sacrifice for what this country needs. If that means some must die for Queen Signe's vision to be made a reality, then so be it."

A shiver ran down Silla's neck. "Who must die?"

"Some of the Galdra."

"Me," said Silla.

Skraeda nodded, her eyes growing sad. "And Ilka was also fated to die in order for the queen's vision to be made reality. She did not wish to go, but it was necessary. And now...now Ilka's gift lives on. Her legacy will reshape this kingdom."

Silla's eyes narrowed. Skraeda was willing to sacrifice her own twin. "You're mad."

"I'm *devoted*. And you will get me back into the queen's good graces."

"Where is Skeggagrim?" demanded Silla, unable to play these games any longer. Her stomach was knotted with the need to know.

The blade at her throat bit into her skin, but the pressure from the arm on her collarbone lessened. "I'll introduce you. We're old friends now, Grimmy and I."

Silla swallowed as Skraeda pulled her away from the door. The warrior positioned herself behind Silla, twisting an arm back while keeping the blade at her neck. With her arms uncloaked, white light flooded the room, so intense that Skraeda flinched.

"Poor girl," said the warrior, unclasping Silla's stolen cloak and tossing it to the ground. Skraeda squinted, examining Silla's forearms. "Did he give you the catalyst? You must be miserable. Your galdur wishes to be freed. And soon it shall."

Silla bit her lip in puzzlement. She *was* miserable—the unreleased tension was like an itch she could not scratch.

Skraeda shoved her toward the divider at the rear of the room, and Silla's bare feet stepped dubiously forward. The closer they neared the divider, the greater the knowing feeling inside Silla grew—urging her not to look beyond the barrier.

But she had to know.

As she stepped past the partition, her eyes fell on the figure sprawled on a low mattress. The space was still as death, the metallic scent stronger here.

"He takes the long slumber." A dark gash across the bearded man's throat was coated in congealed blood, suggesting he'd long been dead.

Dead. Skeggagrim was dead, and with this knowledge, Silla's hope bled from her. Another person's death on her shoulders. The guilt rose in her throat until she felt like she would choke on it.

"You killed him," Silla whispered. Her dreams of a shield-house shattered into a thousand shards.

Kopa was supposed to be safe, was supposed to mean freedom. But it was just another lie. Just as each fresh start with her father had been, Kopa was nothing but another false hope.

There would be no safety for her.

Nothing would change.

Despair slithered through her. She'd fought and clawed and dragged herself to Kopa, had escaped the Klaernar, Skraeda, Queen Signe's men, and the monsters, all with the hopes that there was an end to her suffering. And yet, here she was once more. No better off than she'd been on the road near Skarstad.

What do you want from me? her mind screamed to the gods. *My unending torment?*

She was tired, so tired that she had to lock her knees to prevent herself from crumbling to the ground.

"You win," Silla said softly. She could play these games no longer.

"Little Galdra," said Skraeda, a hint of sympathy in her voice. "It is a difficult thing to realize you're powerless. I too have been there. It is a cruel world for the Galdra, but fear not, you shall not know it much longer."

Silla's eyes flew wide. "What?"

Skraeda laughed, a sharp sound that landed like pinpricks.

"I lost everything because of you," spat the warrior. "Did you know, the queen tried to have me executed? *Me.* Your escape in Skutur cost me the queen's esteem. I was one of her *favored.* And now, she thinks me worthless."

A harsh breath gusted from Silla.

"Your fear tastes delicious, little Galdra. I'll admit I've craved it for many days now. You've caused me a great deal of trouble, and I hunger to see you suffer."

"B-but the queen wants me alive," stuttered Silla. Hadn't the men said it when they'd tried to apprehend her? Silla's mind felt warped, all wrong. Her galdur tingled, the pressure distracting, and she could not think when she needed to most.

"Yes," drawled Skraeda, turning away from Skeggagrim's corpse. Releasing her arm, the warrior pushed Silla against the black stone wall, the dagger back at her throat as soon as she whirled.

"The queen wants you for your galdur." Skraeda's arm drove against Silla's collarbone, pressing her against the wall. "Whatever it is you have in your blood, she's been told it is of great value. Instead of delivering you to her as I'd originally intended, I will take your galdur for myself. And then, it will be I who is so greatly valued by the queen. I will be her favored once more."

Silla's knees tried to buckle, but Skraeda held her in place. "T-take?" she managed.

Skraeda's arm left the base of Silla's throat as the warrior fumbled for something in her pocket. Holding it between her thumb and middle finger, Skraeda lifted it for Silla to see—a curving crystalline vial with a metal cap on the end, glacial-blue liquid encased within.

"Míkrób," said Skraeda with a soft chuckle. "I am told there are tiny living things in this liquid. You will ingest them and host them while they feast on your galdur, acquire it in their bodies. Once they have gorged themselves and created more tiny spawn, I will take them from you, bring them into my own body, and your magic will become my own. And then, little Galdra, I will grant you the gift of the long slumber."

Silla's mind flailed, trying to understand her words. She could not grasp the details—only that yet another person tried to use her for their own gain.

It angered her, the light from her forearms flaring brighter with her rage.

All this time, Silla had thought safety was a place. That if she worked hard enough and traveled far enough, she'd finally find the refuge she sought. But there wasn't such a place, not in this kingdom. Not with her bloodline. Not with galdur flowing in her veins.

If Silla wanted freedom, she'd have to carve it for herself.

And she'd start with Skraeda.

Her eyes narrowed on the red-haired warrior. "No," said Silla.

The air throbbed as though it had a heartbeat. The galdur in Silla's veins gushed through her like an uncontrolled river, her fury only spurring it faster.

Amusement softened Skraeda's face. "No? Little Galdra—"

Silla's skin buzzed, fizzed, like thousands of popping bubbles in her hands, and with that, she planted them on Skraeda's chest and pushed with all her might.

The warrior's face twisted with surprise as she flew backward through the air, a tangle of flying limbs and copper braids. A loud crack split the air of the tiny home as Skraeda rammed into the woven divider, splintering the willow branches.

Silla did not wait for Skraeda to recover—the warrior was faster, stronger, far more adept with weapons. All Silla had was her mind and the element of surprise.

And Silla knew that if she ran, Skraeda would chase. There was only one way to end this.

Leaping onto the stunned warrior, Silla yanked the crystalline vial from Skraeda's fist and threw it against the wall. It shattered, leaving a wet spot oozing down the black stones, and filling the air with a potent, sulfurous smell.

"No!" screamed Skraeda, her hand closing around Silla's neck. "You foolish girl. Do you know what you've done?"

Silla shoved her forearms at Skraeda, the white light brighter than the sun and near blinding. The warrior's grip loosened, and she reeled back, eyes squeezed shut.

Keeping one arm above Skraeda's head, Silla grabbed the sharpened edge of a willow branch from the woven room divider and slammed it into Skraeda's armpit.

The warrior screamed, her back arching. Her eyes flew open, pinning Silla with a murderous glare.

Silla grabbed another sharpened branch, raising it up.

Something scraped against Silla's mind, and she had just a fraction of a second to prepare herself for the memory. The room spun around her, then faded from view.

"We're not alone. Malla and Marra watch over us." Two girls under the table, their small bodies hugging each other tightly.

Silla shook her head, trying to drive Skraeda from her mind. Fear gripped like a fist around her ribs, squeezing tighter, tighter...

Skraeda grabbed Silla's hair and ripped her to the side, rolling on top of her.

The broken twigs of the divider dug into Silla's back, and she fought like an animal—clawing, kicking, snarling, and bucking—anything to get the warrior off her, but the fear...the fear was overwhelming, siphoning the energy and fight from her.

Skraeda pinned Silla's hands to her sides with her knees as she straddled her. "You didn't tell me you were a Blade Breaker." Skraeda's brows furrowed. "Are you a twin, girl? How do you have Ashbringer *and* Breaker intuition?"

Silla only grunted, fighting against Skraeda's weight.

"Such a waste," continued Skraeda. "I'd have enjoyed your skills. I'd have put them to use, not shunned them like this kingdom would have you do. But now you'll die."

"Coward!" spat Silla. Skraeda's touch invaded her mind, like nails clawing into her skull. She knew what would happen next.

The room twisted, blackness misting her vision.

The girl was yanked backward. Her hand ripped free from Silla's. A high-pitched scream erupted from her throat.

"Don't leave me!" the girl cried

Silla sucked in a disoriented breath as the room blinked back into focus. Fiery red hair, blazing blue eyes, a glinting dagger in the warrior's grip.

"Traitor!" Silla screamed. Skraeda's touch raked into her mind, pulling and shredding without precision.

Silla was expecting it as darkness crept in from the edges of her vision.

Matthias looked up at Silla, breath rattling from his lungs, red oozing from a dozen stab wounds. "I loved you like my own kin."

Black stone walls, a great weight upon her chest. Skraeda's malevolent grin as she looked down upon her victim.

"You betray your own," wheezed Silla. "You're a traitor to your own kind."

Skraeda flinched, then recovered, her anger only growing higher. But Silla had sensed it—the loosening of Skraeda's grip upon her mind. She pounced on this hesitation, hacking at the exposed flaw in the assassin's perfect armor.

"You betrayed your own twin," spat Silla, hope blossoming as Skraeda's hold slackened further.

"I did what I must—"

"You think only of yourself," Silla cut back, her eyes falling upon Skraeda's belt—to the ivory hilt of a blade. "You think yourself brave, but you are selfish and a coward. Your kin are dead because of *you*."

An anguished expression filled Skraeda's face, and Silla wrenched her mind free from her grasp.

Silla jerked her hand loose.

Grabbed for the ivory hilt.

Raised her left arm to block Skraeda's incoming dagger.

Thrust the blade deep just below the warrior's collarbone.

Lips parting, a wet choke escaped from deep within Skraeda. Hot blood seeped from the wound, collecting on the ivory hilt and seeping down Silla's hands. The women stared at one another for a long moment. Silla watched emotions chase one another across Skraeda's face—disbelief, anger, resignation, relief.

Relief.

That was what made Silla's heart squeeze because she understood it entirely. It was freedom from trying to survive in a world thirsting for her blood, from having to do terrible things just to survive. Relief because, at last, she could rest. For this brief moment, she understood Skraeda. Pitied her. Looked at the blade and considered it for a moment. She was so very tired.

Saga, she thought. *Saga.* Silla pushed the red-haired warrior off her chest and clambered to her feet.

Blood leaked from the corner of Skraeda's lips, and she blinked up at Silla. The red-haired warrior's hand lifted and fell weakly. With a shaky breath, Silla turned to leave.

"Don't..." wheezed Skraeda. "Don't let me die alone."

Her feet faltered. She could walk out that door, and it would be what Skraeda deserved. But despite what she'd seen, despite everything she'd lived through, she was not that person.

Turning, Silla knelt beside Skraeda. Unsheathing the dying warrior's hevrít, she pressed the hilt into her hand. "You shall have this protection while you walk amongst the stars," she murmured.

"You see..." said Skraeda softly. "You see what they do to us? You see how they make us live?"

As Silla watched the red-haired warrior draw a last rattling breath, watched her eyes go from seeing to vacant, numbness crept through her. She should feel relief. Elation, perhaps. Instead, she only felt tired.

Silla paced the home, trying to push through the wool shrouding her mind. Skeggagrim was dead, any prospect of a shield-house gone with him. Jonas had betrayed her. The Bloodaxe Crew would not give her a passing thought. Her father was dead.

Alone, she thought with despair. *You're all alone.*

Everything was in shambles. She needed time to collect her thoughts, time to ponder what her future held. Her skull buzzed. She did not know what to do, where to go.

Could she stay in the home? Her eyes fell upon Skraeda's corpse, then darted to the shattered room divider beyond that. Her skin itched with the need to leave, to get herself far from this place.

Mindlessly, Silla went to the front door, pushed it open, and stepped onto the streets of Kopa.

"She's there!" exclaimed a male voice.

Silla turned to face a horde of Klaernar.

· SIXTY-THREE

The Klaernar charged at her before Silla had a chance to think. Turning on her heel, she fled down the road past the Dragon's Lair Inn. Running. Again.

Will it never end? Silla wondered, tears springing to her eyes.

Like hounds on their prey, the shouts of the Klaernar nipped at her heels, driving her panic higher. But they were faster and stronger; their feet were not bare. The impossibility of her situation dawned on her, and she choked on a sob.

A flash of greenery from the end of the road caught her eye—the forest. Perhaps she could lose them in the woods between Kopa and the defensive walls, could find a place to hide until her galdur calmed and she could slip from the city. It was impossible, and yet, her only chance.

She was near, and then, she burst into the forest, twigs and needles digging painfully into her feet. Lifting her red skirts, she tore through the woods, dismayed by the glow of her skin. How could she escape them when she was lit up like a beacon fire?

As Silla cast a look over her shoulder, she failed to see the arms that reached out and wrapped around her waist, pulling her into the bushes. She was smothered against the hard trunk of a tree, a body pinning her in place beneath its bulk. Darkness swallowed her, and she could scarcely breathe beneath the oppressive pressure, but Silla fought, kicking and punching, clawing and scratching, a wild animal desperate for freedom.

Silla's eyes burned with tears as her wrists were gathered against her chest, another hand smothering her mouth.

"Shh. It's me, Sunshine. Calm down."

Silla's mind struggled to comprehend, but her body coursed with the primal need to flee; her limbs held a life of their own, flailing and kicking.

"It's Rey. Be calm."

"Rey?" Silla's whisper was muffled by the hand covering her mouth. It was Rey. Her body calmed a little more with every heartbeat, desperation dissolving into disbelief.

Rey had come for her? Silla was confused and overwhelmed, incapable of thought.

His grip loosening, Rey shifted, and Silla was finally able to fill her lungs.

"Shh," he whispered again, his hot breath feathering along the shell of her ear. The scent of pinewoods and campfire lingered on him. "Hold yourself still, keep under my cloak. They come, but we are disguised in the bushes."

Their shouts heightened, twigs snapped nearby; chain mail clinked as the Klaernar neared.

Panic gripped Silla's chest. She could not be discovered, not after everything she'd been through. She had no fight left in her. If they tried to take her, she'd grab a blade and end herself...no matter what, she would *not* go back to those cells.

"That way!" yelled one of the King's Claws, and Rey's body pressed her tighter against the tree. Silla's fingers curved around the buckles of his armored jacket, clinging to him.

Her senses faded to nothing but sounds—her heart thudding in her ears; the crunch of needles beneath boots; a long breath in then out.

The voices faded, the clang of armor and brush of foliage dwindling into obscurity. Silla didn't dare hope, and yet...it seemed the Klaernar had passed by; Rey and Silla had not been detected.

That bare minute had felt like hours. Rey eased himself away from her, and the thunder in her ears subsided. The stillness of the woods was somehow more eerie than it was comforting.

Accepting a hand out of the bushes, Silla stood, dizzy and disoriented, searching the woods for signs of the Klaernar.

"They truly did not see—"

Her question was cut off as Rey's hands slid around her shoulders, fingers prodding frantically up her neck and across her cheek. "Where is it? Where are you hurt?"

The panic in his voice made her falter. "It's not mine, Rey. Not my blood."

He exhaled, his fingers dropping to her chin, as he gently turned her face first to one side, then the other. The backs of his knuckles traced along her flaming cheekbone with featherlight touch.

She met his gaze, darker than she'd ever seen it—anger in the clench of his fist, the set of his jaw.

"I'll kill them," he muttered.

Silla swallowed, unsure what to make of that statement.

Taking a step back, his familiar mahogany eyes quickly fell upon the bare skin of her arms. They widened at the light that blazed from her veins.

Silence stretched between them.

Shaking his head as though he were dazed, Rey glanced around the woods. "We must leave. They'll return when they do not find you."

His gaze landed back on Silla, a line appearing between his drawn brows. His eyes moved down the red dress and up, then Rey made a sound in his throat and looked away. Silla wrapped her arms around herself.

"Where are your shoes?" Rey unfastened his black cloak, wrapping it around her shoulders. "They did not touch you...elsewhere, did they?"

She closed her eyes, her fingers running along the short patch where the Kommandor had cut off her hair. Slowly, she shook her head. Overwhelm was growing, threatening to swamp her. Thankfully, Rey seemed to sense this. Grabbing her hand, he paused, looking down.

"It's cold," he murmured, his brows drawing together. With another shake of his head, his hand tightened around hers, and he led her deeper into the woods. "There is a hidden exit," he said. "This way."

The woods grew thicker, the underbrush clawing at Rey's borrowed cloak and scratching at Silla's bare legs. Rey turned to her.

"Climb on my back," he said in a low voice.

She opened her mouth to protest, but Rey beat her to it.

"You cannot walk through here barefoot."

Rey squatted down, and Silla clambered onto his back, wrapping her arms around his broad shoulders, her legs around his waist. Her dress cinched up obscenely, and Silla's cheeks heated as Rey hooked his arms around her bare thighs.

Now is not the time to worry about modesty, she thought, clutching Rey as he took off briskly through the woods.

Twice they paused to huddle behind a tree, the Klaernar passing by in their continued hunt for Silla. The shouts of the King's Claws rose up from nearby more times than Silla could count. But, by some miracle, they reached the corner of Kopa's defensive walls undetected.

Climbing down from Rey's back, Silla sucked in a harsh breath.

Bodies—more than she could count, strewn on the ground. Faces melted like wax from a candle, steam rose from the corpses, filling the air with a nauseating combination of roasted meat and singed hair and something sickening yet sweet. Silla clapped a hand over her mouth at the sight of them, eyeless bodies frozen in their last desperate poses—mouths agape in silent screams, one arm reaching up to the skies, others outstretched as though trying in vain to crawl away from death.

She bent double, retching into the bushes.

Her stomach had not quite settled when Rey's hand wrapped around her upper arm, tugging her through a narrow tunnel and out a door into more pinewoods. As the door slid shut behind them, Rey turned to her.

"The Slátrari," she managed weakly. "Those bodies...was that the murderer? He was *here*? So near to us?"

"Must be," muttered Rey, strangely unconcerned.

His eyes fell upon her forearms. Taking her wrist gently in his hand, Rey turned it over to examine the light. She braced herself as his gaze slid up, holding hers for several anguished seconds.

"You truly *are* filled with sunshine, aren't you?" he said at last, an almost-smile twitching his lips.

Silla watched him examine her light, puzzled by his fascination. Rey placed two fingers in the palm of her hand, the warm copper tones of his brown skin enhanced by the glow of her white light.

"So cold," he murmured, his fingers gliding along her inner wrist and down her forearm. Goosebumps spread in the wake of his touch, the light eddying around him.

Rey's throat bobbed, and their gazes locked, the golden embers in his eyes burning hotter. She tried to brace herself for harsh words, but knew if he unleashed them on her, she would crumble completely.

Silla pulled her hand back. "I made it to Kopa," she said. "Your oath is fulfilled."

Those embers in his eyes burned hotter, sparking into her skin.

"What are you waiting for?" Silla snapped, turning away. "You can finally be rid of me." Tears spilled down her cheeks, and she hated herself for them.

"Look at me, Silla."

Silla.

Had he ever said her name before? It felt different in his voice—deep and layered, as though it had texture.

The gentle pressure of his fingers sliding under her jaw, his indomitable heat penetrating her skin. Rey tilted her face up, and Silla was greatly aware of the size difference between them. He could have killed her a thousand times over, and yet here he was—sheltering her from the Klaernar, wiping tears from her cheeks.

"I came to take you from Kopa," said Rey quietly. "I will bring you to safety."

More tears fell. "There is nowhere safe for me. I thought Kopa would be... but it will never end. This is a death sentence." She raised her glowing arms.

"It does not have to be, Silla. I know people." He smoothed her tears away once more. "Go north. Go to Kalasgarde. It is a town in Nordur lands. There are people there who can shelter you."

"Why?" she asked. She did not trust him. Did not know if she could ever trust again. "Why would you help me? Your oath is fulfilled."

Rey swallowed, her attention falling to the knot in his throat, then tracing the swirling tattoos peeking from beneath his collar. Silla had never seen them so close before. She'd thought they were black, but this near she saw that they were the deepest of blues, partly transparent like wisps of smoke.

"This has nothing to do with the oath," he said.

"What is it then?" Silla studied him, wondering what his motives were, why he might risk himself to help her.

"You're Crew now," said Rey. "And we do not leave anyone behind. So let us leave this place and find Horse. I will get you to safety."

She fought back a fresh wave of tears, confused and overwhelmed.

"I *won't* turn you in, Silla," he said. "You needn't ever worry of that with me." There was something buried beneath his words, a meaning she could not understand.

But Silla finally broke. A strangled sob escaped her, and she went boneless. His arms slid around her, pulling her closer and holding her upright. She couldn't explain it—how despite everything, she wanted so badly to trust him. How he felt like a blanket of safety.

"He tricked me," she whispered. "He forced the leaves down my throat and took me and gave me to them like I was nothing."

"I know," he said, his shoulders tensing. "It is dishonorable. He is not the man I thought I knew."

Silla let her tears run free, tears at Jonas's betrayal, at Ilías's death, at what the kommandor had tried to do, at what Skraeda had tried to do. She was cracked, a part of her forever broken.

"You're not alone now," said Rey, his hand smoothing over her hair.

You're not alone. She had not realized how badly she needed to hear those words. When she'd thought she had nothing, had no one, *Rey* had come after her, and though she did not understand it, he wished to help her.

At last, she pulled back from him, wiping her eyes.

His gaze fell to her plunging neckline, a muscle in his cheek tensing. "Did they force you?" he asked. "Tell me what happened."

She stared up at him. "The kommandor cut my palm. He beat me and tried to choke me. He was going to...he would have...but I" —she pulled her bottom lip between her teeth, the broken skull of the kommandor flashing before her eyes— "I killed him—the kommandor. I...crushed his head with a statue. And then I climbed out the window."

Rey's brows shot up. "You killed Kommandor Valf?"

Silla nodded. But there was more to say, and she needed to tell *someone.* "I ran to the house. To Skeggagrim's house—he was meant to help me settle into a shield-home. But when I got there, Skraeda, the red-haired warrior, had killed him. And she tried...tried to make me drink something strange, but I fought her off. And I killed her, too." Silla shuddered. She was a killer.

She'd taken *many* lives. Her soul would be forever tainted.

"I had to kill her. I had to *end this.*"

Rey shook his head, his lips twitching. "Gods, I was wrong about you."

"What?"

"You're a fighter. You have a warrior's spirit." There was a note of respect, of reverence in his voice. "You did not hesitate when you needed to act. They tried to harm you, and you answered in blood. You did not cower. You met them head-on and bested seasoned warriors."

Her mouth fell open a hair's breadth, but she remained silent. Rey examined the wound on her palm from the kommandor's knife.

"We will dress this later. I do not have provisions with me."

"We must go back!" Silla said with a gasp. "There is a girl who needs our help, Rey. Her name is Metta. She's been in the cells for *four weeks*."

"We cannot." Rey dropped her hand and looked back at the defensive wall. "There are too many Klaernar. It is an impossible task. And we *must* go, or they will find us. We must leave here now."

"But..." Her voice wavered. The thought of leaving Metta in a cell made Silla's stomach lurch. But at that moment, the voice of a Klaernar rose somewhere beyond the wall. Silla shifted closer to Rey.

"I know someone," Rey said. "I will see if my contact can help Metta. We shall speak to them together. But we must leave. *Now.*"

Rey offered her his back once more, and Silla's exhausted limbs were only too pleased to accept.

"Rey," she said cautiously, clinging to his back as he ran through the woods.

"Yes?"

"How did you know where I was?"

He was silent for a moment. "When Jonas did not return, I had a...sense that something had occurred. And given that we'd learned that the queen searched for you, and his grief over losing his brother, it did not seem a stretch to imagine Jonas would hand you over for a reward."

"How did you know I was in the woods?"

"I tracked the Klaernar's voices, and remembered your fondness for running into the forest. I'm thankful that I guessed right." Rey was silent a moment. "Why does the queen want you, Silla?"

Silla's stomach clenched tight, her pulse pounding in her temples.

Tell him, she urged herself. *He came back for you. You can trust him. I'm Eisa Volsik. Say it. It's not hard.*

But her muscles tensed, and her fingers dug into Rey's shoulders, nausea churning in her stomach once more.

"Perhaps another day," he said, his voice unexpectedly soft. "You've been through a lot. Tell me when you're ready."

A breath gusted out of her, her body relaxing into him. "Where are the others?" she asked. "Hekla and Gunnar. Sigrún." How had the Bloodaxe Crew gotten so small?

"They've gone to Istré with the wagon and instructions to wait for me. Hekla recruits new warriors..." Rey sighed, and Silla felt the heaviness in that breath.

"I'm sorry, Rey," she whispered. "I never meant—"

"I know," he said. "And I am..." He exhaled. "I regret my harsh words when we last spoke. I wish I could take them back."

Silla was taken aback—something told her that Axe Eyes did not often apologize. "You had every right to be angry with me."

"We all agreed as a Crew to take on the task of your safety. Yes, to know it was the queen who chased you could have been helpful. But we agreed to take on the risk—Ilías included. You do not bear the burden of his death. If anyone, it is me. I am leader of the Bloodaxe Crew, and it was I who brought us into battle without proper preparation."

"It is not your fault, Rey. You're a good leader." She buried her face in his shoulder.

"You and I are a lot alike, Silla," said Rey.

Surprise flickered through her. *Reynir Galtung,* she reminded herself. *He too has his secrets.*

"I understand you better than you might think. And I know your heart—it is too big for this world. I understand that you only wished for safety."

Again, she sensed that Rey held something back. But as she was not ready to share her true name with him, she did not press him on his own mysteries.

After wading through a river, they reached Horse, and Silla slid down Rey's back, landing on the forest floor.

He rinsed her wound with water from his skin, bandaged it in strips of linen, then helped her onto Horse, climbing up behind her.

"Keep your arms hidden in the cloak and your hood up," he instructed, urging Horse forward. "There's a canyon I know of that will shield us from view. Three days in the canyon, then we'll stick to a goat track south of Istré."

Silence stretched as long as the road ahead of them as Horse took off at a gallop. Exhaustion engulfed Silla; her galdur seemed at last to have calmed, but her limbs were heavy. She leaned back into Rey, his hard chest a reassuring presence behind her.

"I suppose it wouldn't kill me if you wanted to hum," Rey said, as they entered the canyon some time later. Layered black walls edged with green moss climbed up on either side, a stream ribboning through the flat base of the canyon.

Examining the volcanic stone, Silla said absently, "I don't hum."

He huffed a laugh. "Hate to break it to you Sunshine, but you hum."

"I think I would know such a thing."

"Apparently not," he muttered.

A small glimmer of warmth flickered deep inside her. "I know you're trying to cheer me, Rey," she said with quiet gratitude. "But if you are serious in this task, you should let me steer."

"Steer?"

"Give me the reins. Let me direct Horse."

"Not a chance." He glowered, grip tightening. "If your sense of direction is anything like your common sense, you'll have us lost in an hour."

"We're in a canyon!" she said, affronted. "There is only one path to take!"

"No," was his stern answer.

"Are you frightened I'll steal your only friend?" she shot back.

Rey scoffed. "With the number of treats you've snuck Horse, I'm certain you've already stolen her loyalty."

"You're such a smart steed, aren't you girl?" she asked, patting Horse's withers. "So smart and so brave. I shall spoil you all the way to Istré."

"You'll ruin her!" Rey groaned behind her.

Silla smiled secretly to herself. And by the end of the day, she did indeed hold the reins, directing Horse between tall canyon walls. It was frightening to trust Rey after what Jonas had done. But he alone had come when she had no one. And surely that counted for something.

And then Silla thought it—all this time, she'd been searching for a place to feel safe, but what if she'd been looking at it all wrong? What if safety was not a place, but was a person? People? Without her father, she needed to find others like her, allies who could teach her how to be safe in this world.

Silla sighed. There was so much she did not understand. Could she truly trust Rey? What awaited her in Nordur? How did she control the unruly glowing lights under her skin? And now that she knew her true name, would she ever find allies—or would she be doomed to a life spent in hiding?

And Saga—Silla had scarcely allowed herself to think of her sister who lived amongst her enemies. *Come and find me*, the little girl had said to her, and Silla had vowed that she would.

Her future was clouded with uncertainty. There was bound to be more danger. And yet, Silla found herself humming.

EPILOGUE

ASKABORG CASTLE, SUNNAVÍK

S aga Volsik believed a lot of things—a daily cup of yarrow tea was good for the constitution; regardless of what her foster mother said, black was a perfectly appropriate color for a high-ranking lady to wear; and dwellers of the Southern Continent had the absolute most splendid of curse words.

But aside from all that, she was a believer in luck. Some might say life was merely a game of odds—the likelihood of ill fortune was equally balanced with the good. But Saga liked to think there was more to it than that. That in some way, your fate was set at birth, and free will and choice only got a person so far.

It was hard not to notice how some people were simply lucky. The sun seemed to shine on them wherever they went, flowers bursting all around their irritating feet. Everything came so *easily* for those people, and infuriatingly, they seemed to think *they* had something to do with it.

No, Saga wanted to lash out. *You haven't earned it. You've simply won when hands of fortune were doled out.*

Some might call her bitter. But Saga knew what it was to draw the foulest, most plague-ridden of luck. Perhaps she clung to this belief for the small measure of comfort it brought her—to think she hadn't done anything to earn the horrid series of events which had landed her in this place; that in the endless variations of how that awful day had played out, Saga's ill fortune would have smashed her life to bits anyway.

She'd been born a Volsik, the most famous of bloodlines in all of Íseldur. This should have put her in company with those of good luck. But it seemed that the more you had, the more you had to lose. And Saga had lost it all.

Her family.

Her freedom.

Her grip on sanity.

That last one, to be fair, would be a challenge for even the luckiest of folk who'd lasted four weeks without leaving their chambers. It had started as a game —how many days could Saga last without leaving her chambers? To Saga's enormous delight, weeks had passed without summons. For a time, she'd wondered if they'd forgotten all about her. She'd allowed herself to imagine never having to set foot in that great hall again, surrounded by people who either pitied her or wished her dead.

But then, her lady's maid Árlaug had arrived with news that Saga's presence was requested by the queen. Which was how she found herself leaving her chambers for the first time in a month, clad not in black, but a gown of lilac to appease her foster mother's tastes.

It was bad enough the remnants of Saga's dream still skittered through her. Her sister, again. All month, it had been the same. As if she needed another reminder of the night the winds of her luck had shifted. That arm snaking around her waist, wrenching her from little Eisa's grip. And gods, but those screams—so anguished, they still echoed in Saga's skull.

She tried to push the sound to the back of her mind as she followed Árlaug through the corridors. Beyond the safety of her chambers, Saga's pulse throbbed, the tension in her chest tightening with each step further from it.

"I'm feeling a touch under the weather," Saga tried as they neared the grand staircase. Open, it was so open, and she gripped the railing to keep her balance.

But Árlaug would not be swayed. "Her Highness says you're to meet with her, even if you've suffered a death wound."

"Not a death wound," said Saga. "Worse. 'Tis an illness. I'm certain it is catching."

Árlaug gave her a hard look.

"Nits?" Saga tried, her desperation growing. "Leprosy?"

Árlaug mercilessly soldiered down the staircase. "Now, mistress, it won't be so bad as you think. Just go on, meet with Her Highness, and that'll be that. 'Tis not such a hard thing to put on a smile for an hour or so."

The word *smile* only made Saga's lips droop.

The pampered girl does not appreciate all that she has, wafted Árlaug's thoughts, with a sharpened edge of irritation.

Saga's feet faltered.

Does she not realize the people of Sunnavík are starving? But of course she does not, she's too busy feeling sorry for herself. I would gladly wear her gowns and drink her róa and—

Swiftly, Saga wove her mental barriers back into place, securing her Sense behind them. Her nerves were so on edge, she hadn't noticed her partitions had frayed through. Gods, but she needed to gather herself before meeting with Signe.

Noting that Saga had paused on the staircase, Árlaug turned. "The queen made it clear if you don't come on your own walking feet, she'll send Thorir to cart you down."

Saga's face soured even further. "I'm coming," she said, resuming her descent.

As they reached the doors to Signe's drawing room, Saga's pulse throbbed, and she found herself fussing with her gloves. Árlaug paused, smoothing Saga's blonde hair back, then pinching her cheeks to draw color into them.

With a sigh, Árlaug managed a tight smile. "'Tis a lovely dress," she said. "Though I do not know why you favor those winterwing earrings when you have such lovely jewels to wear."

Unbidden, Saga's gloved hand reached up to finger the earrings. Immediately, she was filled with a confusing combination of nostalgia and heartache and the smell of her mother's lavender bath oil.

Árlaug dipped her brow before hurrying away. And then Saga was alone.

You could run, she thought. Gods, but if only she could run. If only she could feel grass beneath her fingers, rain in the palms of her hands. But Saga was not so foolish as to allow herself to hope. It was a sentiment wasted on the unlucky. And so, she stepped into the room.

The queen's drawing room was far larger than her bed chambers—so large it felt as though it would swallow Saga whole. Her heart beat riotously, the ground undulating like the ocean's surface. Saga put a stabilizing hand on the wall, her eyes instinctively darting for an escape. But the servant's door was sealed, as was the window. The only way out was to turn and flee.

"How kind of you to grace me with your presence, Saga," came the queen's voice from the largest of the fireplaces, quashing any thoughts of slinking out undetected.

She forced herself toward Signe. One step. Two. More. She sank into the chair opposite Signe's. Exhaled.

Congratulations, you've completed the most basic of tasks, she thought bitterly.

She glanced at Queen Signe. They sat in high-backed chairs set before the gilded fireplace, a table laid with two empty cups and fixings for róa. A lavish gilded chandelier hung above, lit with hundreds of candles, which, combined with the golden hearth, cast a flaxen glow upon everything.

The queen herself wore her signature white. Clad in an elegant ivory dress of Zagádkian silk, her famed Norvalander white-gold hair was braided back, showcasing Signe's pale complexion, smooth and soft as a snow blossom's petal. Signe's eyes were a blue so icy Saga could feel their chill upon her skin.

In actual fact, Signe was barely ten years older than Saga's twenty-two years, an age difference which should make them feel more like sisters than mother and daughter. Though to say Signe was maternal toward Saga would be a stretch. Instead, there was tolerance. Inclusion. But not love, and never affection. There had been a time when Saga had strived for Signe's approval. For...something.

When she thought of it now, it was with shame. Signe showered her sons and daughter with the fierce love of a mother bear. For years, Saga wondered if she'd done something wrong to earn Signe's maddening neutrality. In some ways, blind hatred would have been easier for her to understand.

"Saga," said the queen, an edge to her voice, "look at me, darling."

Her smile was so forced, Saga thought she might crack as she made herself hold the queen's gaze. Queen Signe's blue eyes moved over Saga's face, then down her dress. As the queen let out a long exhale, Saga braced herself.

"Have you had trouble sleeping? You look tired, Saga."

You're welcome to stop looking at me, she thought. "Yes, Your Highness," she replied instead.

Signe waved a hand, and a cupbearer rushed over, filling the cups with steaming róa. After spooning honey into hers, Signe lifted it and blew, watching Saga over the lip of her cup. The queen had a way of saying a thousand things without uttering a word. And right now, it was clear Saga did not live up to her expectations.

What was it? She patted her hair, searching for a lock out of place, then caught herself. She knew better than to think her flaws would be so simple to fix.

Signe spoke at last. "Saga, I have given you time, but my patience has met its end. Your...*problems*" —she waved her hand dismissively— "will not resolve themselves by hiding away in your chambers."

Saga's knee bounced so vigorously, her heel began to tap against the floor.

"It is clear you need a firm hand." The queen's eyes bored into her. "Henceforth, you'll join us for all meals."

Tap. Tap. Tap.

"By now I assume you know of the Zagádkians."

Tap. Tap. Tap.

"Soon, they shall arrive with a shipful of grains, and will be negotiating a trade deal with the king to ensure delivery of more."

Tap. Tap. Tap.

"I expect you looking your best in fine Zagádkian silk," continued Signe. "We must make a good impression on the Zagádkians. It is imperative that we get this grain, Saga, and I expect your help in fostering a relationship with them."

Tap. Tap. Tap.

"Speak, girl!" Signe snapped, eyes flashing.

Fetch. Come. Good girl.

Her tongue felt heavy, the art of conversation so clumsy. "Yes, Your Highness."

"You represent this family, Saga, and too long I've been lenient with you. I expect your best behavior in the upcoming weeks. You will attend feasts and prayers and uphold the traditions of this family, as is expected of my daughter. Your behavior these past weeks casts shame upon Ivar and I. It makes it look as though we mistreat you. Have I not treated you like my own daughter, Saga?"

"Yes, Your Highness," replied Saga, the chasm in her chest opening up. "You've been a good mother to me."

"Then what is it, Saga?" asked Signe, hurt. "Why do you hide away in your rooms?"

Saga searched for the right words while trying to still her bouncing leg. How did one explain an irrational thing in a way others could understand? It was impossible. "My mind prefers quiet and solitude." *Safety*, she was unable to say. *My chambers feel safe.*

Signe huffed a laugh. "It would be nice if we could all enjoy such luxuries. Unfortunately for women like you and I, we cannot heed our every whim. We have duty and honor to uphold, and I will tolerate your disrespect no longer."

Saga was silent.

"And that brings me to the next item. Saga darling, too long have you gone without an offering to Ursir." Signe sipped her róa, her gaze lingering on Saga. "A Letting is clearly in order so that the Bear God might restore you to health."

"Your Majesty," started Saga. Phantom pain pierced her elbow, the tender skin etched with a crosswork of red marks. They wouldn't be satisfied until they'd bled her dry, until they'd snuffed out the last of Saga's will.

"You will beg for Ursir's forgiveness." Queen Signe narrowed her eyes. "And then, you will take your place as Bjorn's betrothed. Next season, he shall be fourteen, a suitable enough age to wed. We shall begin wedding preparations after Yrsa's birthday feast."

Saga nodded numbly. No thoughts. Only drifting. Only doing as she was told. "Yes, Your Highness," she heard herself say.

"That is all, Saga," dismissed Signe. "I shall see you for the daymeal tomorrow. And do not forget—a good relationship with Zagádkia is imperative to secure grain for our kingdom."

"Yes, Your Highness," she repeated, like the good little pet she was.

And without so much as a sip of her róa, Saga was dismissed. She couldn't get out of the room fast enough. Her mind spiraled with such force, everything felt like a dream.

Wedding preparations.

Always marriage had been a far-off thing, something for Future Saga to worry about. But now, it loomed on the horizon. Saga would marry Bjorn, and then, she would be one of *them*. An Urkan.

Her skin grew itchy, too tight. *Leave*, she thought. *Run away.*

It was a simple concept, yet so laughably impossible. Saga had, in some ways, made peace with her condition years ago. Honoring her need for safety was a way she protected herself, whether rational or not. It hadn't seemed so much of a barrier as simply...a part of herself. She'd been content, in a way, to let it be.

Suddenly, it felt like shackles.

She could feel the fit of tension approaching, like a hand wrapping around her ribs, squeezing ever tighter. Trapped, she felt trapped, the walls closing in...

The sound of approaching footfalls were clamorous in her ears. Someone was coming. Someone would witness her falling to pieces. It would only be more fodder for their whispers, gods above, Saga couldn't do it...

Her eyes fell on the taxidermied bear, its mouth frozen in a permanent snarl, and she realized which corridor she'd found herself in. With a last, desperate rush, she pressed a stone three paces down from the bear, dashing through the door that swung inwards. Darkness swallowed her as she shut the door, engulfing Saga in the musty scent of ancient, undisturbed rooms. At once, her pulse eased, her breaths growing more constant. Safe. She was safe where no one could find her.

And in a world where Saga had no one, she was reminded of the one ally she had—Askaborg Castle, with its hidden passages known only to her. Invisibility was her cloak of safety, and the castle allowed her to disappear when she needed. Certainly, the Urkans had discovered many of the passages. But there were so very many they had not. She imagined there were some passages in the castle even *she* did not know of.

Saga made her way down the corridor, her feet recalling each step through utter darkness by memory alone. Soon, she'd reach the hidden exit in the library's hearth, thankfully no longer used.

A loud crash, followed by a shriek, caused Saga's feet to stop dead in the corridor. A man's voice murmured through the aging stone wall, but the woman's voice clearly belonged to Queen Signe.

"How could she slip through their fingers? They had her in custody! In a cell!"

Saga edged forward, pressing her ear to the dank stone.

"Very unfortunate indeed, Your Highness." It was Maester Alfson, she realized with a shudder.

"What kind of incompetent imbecile was your friend, Maester? Kommandor of the Eystri branch of the Klaernar. How could an untrained girl best him?"

The hairs on Saga's arms stood on edge at the anger in Signe's voice. So often, it was confined to the quiet spaces between words, never hostile and in the open like this.

"She had assistance, Your Highness. There were casualties. And the strange thing, my queen, is they appeared to have been burned alive from the inside out."

"From the inside?" Her voice softened, tinged with curiosity.

"Yes, Your Highness. They call him the Slátrari, and he's hunted along the Road of Bones. But now the Klaernar believe he helps *her*."

"But Maester, this Slátrari...he appears to have considerable abilities, does he not?"

"I'm inclined to agree with you, Your Highness."

Silence stretched out for several long moments. When the queen finally spoke, her voice was low. "That could be highly advantageous."

"We have a witness who has provided his likeness. Renderings are being passed out through the north of Íseldur."

"Good," said the queen. "Good, Alfson. And the warband?"

"I await their reply."

"Good, Maester. Very good. We cannot let Eisa Volsik slip through our fingers again."

The world disappeared from beneath Saga's feet, and she was falling endlessly.

She gripped the wall. Sucked in a lungful of air.

Eisa.

Eisa Volsik.

Her sister. But her sister was dead. There had been a body. She'd been impaled on a pillar in the pits with Saga's parents. The bodies had been on display for an entire year.

Could it be? Could Eisa truly be alive?

Her world fractured, then reformed, Signe's words echoing in her mind. At some point, she sank to the ground, hugging her knees. She was numb, disoriented, and yet she knew her life had forever changed.

By the time Saga found the strength to rise and brush the dust from her skirts, two facts had crystallized in her mind.

Eisa *was* alive.

And Saga was going to find her.

———

THANK YOU FOR READING! Did you enjoy? I'd be so honored if you'd leave a review. Nothing helps an author more and encourages readers to take a chance on a book than your feedback!

Don't miss more of the Ashen series with book two, KINGDOM OF CLAW, coming soon!

———

WANT **to read Chapter 63 from Rey's POV?** Sign up for our newsletter to get access: https://demiwinters.com/reys-pov-chapter-63/

Or scan:

ACKNOWLEDGMENTS

This book started as a creative outlet but quickly grew into so much more. It became therapeutic for me, a place for me to escape in a world that was too loud and too sharp and too *much* at times.

I wanted to share a softer female character in a hard fantasy setting to show how many definitions the word 'strength' can have. Strength is putting one foot in front of the other, even when you're tired. It's overcoming your fears, fighting inner battles against grief and addiction, it's holding onto the hope that you'll find yourself again when you're so very lost. Strength is finding compassion and forgiveness for yourself amid self-loathing and sadness.

Sometimes, strength is a thousand-mile journey in a world of warbands and monsters, and sometimes strength is in the little things we do each day.

One foot in front of the other; one step at a time. Sometimes, it's all you can do.

This book would not have been possible without the help and input of so many.

First, thanks to *you* for reading it! Thank you to everyone on TikTok and Instagram who encouraged me when I shared bits of my WIP—knowing I was writing something people wanted to read kept me going even when I felt discouraged.

Several books were incredibly helpful in getting the setting just right. Many long hours were spent reading Children of Ash and Elm, The Sagas of the Icelanders, and Valkyrie: The Women of the Viking World, listening to the History of the Vikings Great Course, and watching the Vikings TV series to try to emulate Ragnar's dialogue.

Thank you to my author friends for all the helpful discussions and making me feel like I wasn't alone in my office day after day working on this manuscript — Jess, Abby, Millee and the discord group.

Thank you to my developmental editor, Chersti Nieveen for seeing the potential in this book and helping me sculpt it into something *so much* better.

Thank you to Abby Mann for helping me figure out Jonas's character rewrites and for always encouraging me to add *more*: more gore, more spice, more puns...

Thank you to my beta readers, some of whom read this manuscript in completely unrecognizable form—think: no Vikings, no Skraeda, and a 'nice' version of Jonas: Ashlyn, Kelli, Georgia, Ashton, Diana, Renee, Jen, Maggie, Nicole, Lisette, Millee, Kamea Bella, Priscilla, Jenn, Sasha, Macy, Rachel, Hayley and Pallavi, your feedback has been so helpful in getting the book (and particularly Jonas's character) just right.

Thank you to Ruthie Bowles for your sensitivity read and for ensuring race in this world was portrayed in a respectful way. Thank you to Gianna Marie for your incredibly insightful comments on the characters of Hekla and Sigrún. It was so important to me to have POC, disability and mental health rep in this book, and I could not have done these characters justice without the support of my sensitivity readers.

Last but not least, thank you to my 'husband' and biggest cheerleader, Ben. Thank you for helping me jump off that cliff and start my path to recovery. Thank you for supporting me in all my hare-brained endeavors! Thanks for bringing me French fries and listening to me rant about imaginary characters and for taking the kids on countless adventures while I wrote. Thank you, thank you, *thank you*.

ABOUT THE AUTHOR

Demi Winters is the author of romantic fantasy books featuring softer female leads, grumpy heroes and immersive worlds. Lover of all things fairy tales, fantasy, and romance, Demi lives in British Columbia, Canada with her husband and two kids. When she's not busy brainstorming fantastical worlds and morally gray love interests, Demi loves reading and cooking.

To keep up with her writing endeavors, join Demi's Crew in the Facebook group or newsletter or follow along on social media.

instagram.com/demiwinterswrites

tiktok.com/@demiwinterswrites